DANGEROUS

"I want you. I want to see you naked."

His voice was hoarse. I heard it only faintly, as if from a long distance. A heaviness seized me. I felt that I couldn't move my limbs, that I couldn't raise my head. He undressed me with the gentlest care, and I uttered not a syllable of protest. I was floating on a buoyant cloud of desire, and I wanted to be lifted higher, still higher. And Seth was like a relentless tide; I didn't have the strength or the wits or the will to resist him.

OBSESSION

I lay naked under him. He ran his hands over my body. His embraces became rougher, his kisses more demanding. I could feel the tension and desire in him and it made me dizzy. The tendons in his neck were like tightly drawn cords. A fine mist of perspiration covered his forehead and upper chest. His lips seared my flesh wherever they touched. They were hot and biting and painful, and my body was glowing, yearning for him...even as two tears slid down my cheeks.

Rhawnie, the gypsy girl who only wanted to sing and dance and enjoy life. Seth, the enigma who tormented her by claiming her body whenever he wished, discarding her whenever his own passion became too fierce. Rhawnie and Seth, their love became a dangerous obsession!

S0-BSF-621

Dangerous Obsession

Natasha Peters

ace books

A Division of Charter Communications Inc.
A GROSSET & DUNLAP COMPANY
360 Park Avenue South
New York, New York 10010

DANGEROUS OBSESSION

An ACE Original

First Ace Printing: September 1978

Published simultaneously in Canada

Printed in U.S.A.

1

Rhawnie

WHEN I WAS born the Gypsies named me Rhawnie. In Romany, the language of the Gypsies, it means "great lady."

Lyubov, the leader of our tribe, said that someday I would be Queen of the Gypsies. He was probably drunk when he said it, because everyone knows that Gypies have no queens, or kings, either. Besides, I was only half Gypsy; my mother was the daughter of a Russian count.

From birth I looked different from the others. Oh, I had my father's black Gypsy eyes and olive skin, but my hair was thick and blond, like my mother's. I was a long baby—Lyubov measured me against his forearm—and the women predicted, correctly, that I would grow to be very tall.

They didn't give me a last name then, although I have accumulated several since then, and a couple of titles as well. Lyubov used to say that a name is like a campsite: you move into it, use it, enjoy it, dirty it up a little, and then move on. If you are unlucky and the police bother you there, you don't use it again. The *gorgio,* those who are not Gypsy, expect a person to have only one name, and therefore the Gypsies find it expedient to adopt several, just to confuse them. Names are not important to Gypsies, who disdain anything that constricts and defines their freedom. Freedom is important. Life is important. Being happy today, not worrying about the past or what is to come, finding enough to eat, fooling the *gorgio*—all that is important.

Even when I was just a few weeks old I helped my family earn a living. My mother would take me with her when she went to beg and I am sure I cried piteously while she asked passers-by for a few kopecks to feed her hungry child. As I grew older, I was encouraged to speak up, and I remember crouching in doorways with my grubby hand outstretched, whimpering and sniffling and saying in a small, starved voice, "Hungry, so hungry. A few kopecks, sir. A few kopecks, madame. I am so hungry." Sometimes my mother would borrow somebody else's babies and we would all huddle together, looking pathetic.

A word about begging: it is not as easy as it looks, particularly when you get older and more sturdy-looking. You can't speak too loudly, because you are supposed to be faint with hunger and almost too weak to stand. And at the same time you have to be heard over the noise of the street. One of the secrets of success is persistence: don't leave the *gorgio* alone until they have given you something, even a dirty look or a cross word. Make them notice you! Even as I grew taller I was skinny and emaciated and I always did well at begging.

My education progressed. When I was only three I stole my first chicken. It was almost bigger than I was and I tried to hide it under my skirts as I had seen the other women do, but it kept scratching and kicking and pecking me. I didn't know you had to wring the bird's neck to keep it quiet. But somehow I got it back to our camp, and even though I was scratched and bleeding in a dozen places, I didn't cry. Gypsies admire courage above any other quality, and children are taught from a very early age never to show signs of weakness. Everyone was very proud of my accomplishment and my bravery, and as I recall there was

4

a big feast that night with lots of noise and song and drinking.

You may think that a child's theft of a chicken is not a very appropriate occasion for feasting, but with Gypsies, any excuse to celebrate is a good one. A child's first theft is a landmark, and I had shown myself to be rather precocious and ambitious in this area. It was a sign of great things to come. I became a proficient enough thief: good at smuggling goods out of stores under my skirts while another girl distracted the storekeeper; not so good at picking pockets, although I never really had a chance to develop expertise in that field. But if I got caught I always lied like a trouper. No one ever had to teach me to lie: that came naturally.

When I was older still, I learned to tell fortunes. Now that's a real skill, requiring lots of practice, a shrewd eye, and a glib tongue. A novice fortune-teller learns to read people the way *gorgio* children learn to read books, and she learns to spin her lies in a mesmerizing whisper, so that the *gorgio* goes away thinking that Gypsies really have the gift of prophecy and divination, when in fact all they have is the gift of extracting money from gullible people. But I will speak more of fortune-telling later.

My dear mother died when I was five or perhaps six. (I have never known exactly when I was born. Age isn't important to Gypsies.) I didn't think much about it then, but now, looking back, I marvel at my mother's courage and daring. It couldn't have been easy for the pampered daughter of a *gorgio* nobleman to leave the warmth and safety of her father's house for the uncertainty and danger of life on the road. Perhaps she was bored with the life of a lady and wanted some fun. Or she might have had some trouble with her brother, my uncle Alexei, of whom you shall hear more later. In any case, she saw my father and fell in love with him and never looked back. Two years after she died, my father remarried, a Gypsy girl named Gemma who gave him three strong sons in three years. Now that's a good wife!

5

I always felt sorry for the children who weren't Gypsy, chained to their schoolrooms and compelled to attend church and to learn how to work for their livings. None of us Gypsy children could read or write, but we were all exceptionally well-educated, and not only in the fine arts of lying and cheating. As we travelled all over eastern Europe and even into Greece and Turkey, we picked up a thorough knowledge of different peoples and their customs, and a smattering of over a dozen languages as well.

I loved the travelling. Through rain and snow, in intense heat or paralyzing cold, or in high winds that almost tore the roofs off our caravans. Somehow, the more difficult and taxing the journey, the better the rest afterwards. I remember campsites on smooth meadows and rocky hillsides, in black forests and on the edges of weird marshlands. When Lyubov gave the signal to stop, the caravans rolled into a circle. The horses were put to pasture at once, fires were built. The children played, the women cooked, the men tended the animals and laughed and talked together. We made forays into the surrounding neighborhood for food. Sometimes there was a scrap with the police, or a quarrel with the townspeople, or a fight with an angry farmer. But all that added to the fun.

Almost as important to me as the members of my own family were the horses our tribe owned. I couldn't stay away from them when we were camped, which annoyed some people because girls weren't supposed to have anything to do with the animals. That was a man's province. But I made such a pest of myself, trailing the men around at home and at horsefairs, asking questions, listening to them bargain, learning from all of them and especially Lyubov, that eventually they just gave up trying to make me wash clothes and sew and cook. I learned from Lyubov how to talk to horses, in guttural grunts and whispers. I learned how to groom and feed and doctor them, how to judge their merits, even how to shoe them. Lyubov said that I had a very special talent, but I knew only that the

6

horses were my friends. I loved them and they knew that they could trust me.

And so the years of my childhood and early education passed. So happy, so free. Then one spring, when I was fourteen (or fifteen), the Count Nicholas Alexandreivitch Oulianov, my dead mother's father, came for me and took me away from the Gypsies. They had to give me up, for to refuse would only bring sorrow and retribution down upon all of them. I was heartsick at first, but I convinced myself that I wouldn't have to stay with him for very long, that I would return. I even made a solemn vow, but I'll tell you about that later because it's tied up with the fortune-telling.

Anyway, the Grandfather was a kind man who had never stopped grieving for his daughter. He indulged me shamefully, much to the disgust of his own children and grandchildren. He loved horses and knew almost as much about them as Lyubov. He never tried to make me into a *gorgio*. He didn't force me to bathe or to eat with a fork, and he let me keep my colorful Gypsy skirts and scarves. And even when I threw my schoolbooks into the fire and told him that they were more useful to me as fuel, he only laughed and said that if I wanted to stay ignorant and illiterate and dirty it was all right with him, just so long as I stayed. I did learn French from him though, for in those days most of the Russian aristocrats spoke French exclusively, and some never even learned Russian.

The summer passed. And in September of that year the Grandfather's heart failed him and he died. His son, my uncle Alexei, swore to his dying father that he would care for me and look after me, and he took me to the great grey house in Moscow with his family for the winter.

Now I hadn't minded too much living with the Grandfather. I was still Gypsy, and he seemed to accept my strange customs and even to take pride in them. But I hated his son. Alexei was a man of gross appetites, a leering, lustful animal who sank his teeth into this father's fortune and devoured it in a few greedy gulps, so that in a

7

few months there was hardly anything left of his inheritance. He gambled and he lost, and when he lost he became nearly insane with anger and he vented his rage on his family and his serfs. And on me. He despised me. He hated the sight and the sound and the smell of me. He hated the attention his father had lavished upon me, the scum daughter of his no-good runaway sister. I reciprocated his feelings. I hated all of them—his stupid wife, his pudgy pig-faced children, his cowed, fearful serfs—but Alexei, by his cruelty and savagery, earned a special place at the top of my list of Hate.

I tried to get away from him before we left for Moscow, but he watched me closely and I had no opportunity to escape. You would have thought that loathing me as he did, he would have been glad to see the heels of my boots. But no. He seemed to take pleasure in trying to inflict his will on me and in beating me when I rebelled.

His wife was just as bad. She thought of me as a heathen and she said that it was her Christian duty to civilize me and to make a good God-fearing girl out of me. I had to endure a bath every week. She gave me old ugly frocks to wear that were dark and drab and ill-fitting. I cut them up with scissors. I really got a beating for that. She tried to make me wear shoes inside the house. I refused and they beat me. They even tried to cut my hair! Every Gypsy knows that it's bad luck for a woman to cut her hair, and I told them so. I fought them like a tiger and I got to keep my long braids, but I still got a beating.

My uncle took a strange delight in beating me, I could tell. His breathing would quicken and he would start to slobber, even before he laid a hand on me. And a few times his gross hands would squeeze my small breasts and grope between my thighs when he was holding me down, preparing to strike me with the birch switch he used. I had seen a lot of things in my fourteen or fifteen years, and I wasn't so naive or stupid that I didn't know what he really wanted to do to me, and I was sickened and revolted by him. I suppose I feared him, but being Gypsy I never showed fear in his presence, and I never admitted it to myself.

I had to get away. But how? His serfs were his spies. I was hardly ever alone, and at night the house was securely locked, every door and window, and the keys given to Alexei. Moscow might have been a million versts from Bryansk, where the Gypsies had been camped in the springtime when the Grandfather had found me. Even if I managed to steal a horse, I knew I stood a slim chance of finding them before the winter weather set in with vengeance—assuming that I knew where Bryansk lay in relation to Moscow, which I did not. My sense of direction has never been that good. I knew that I would have to bide my time until spring. But every day my uncle's behavior became more intolerable and my situation more dangerous. I sensed that I probably wouldn't live until spring.

And that is when the Stranger appeared. In November of that eventful year. His name was Seth Garrett, and he was an adventurer, a gambler, some said a devil. But to me he was my rescuer, and my tormentor.

I knew my uncle was entertaining a guest. Through the keyhole of the door to the servant's kitchen, I overheard Vasilly, the ancient family retainer, telling the housekeeper that the master was playing cards in the study with the foreign gentleman he met at Madame Malianova's soiree, and that the foreigner was winning. This made Vasilly unhappy, and the housekeeper, too. They both knew what happened when the master lost at cards.

And then I heard Vasilly say, "He'll be leaving from here before the sun's up. For Paris, I've heard. I don't see why the master made me go to all the trouble of airing and making up the guest room for him if he's only going to stay in it a few hours. And at the rate they're going, they're likely to play until dawn."

Alexei always played until his luck changed, or until he had nothing more to lose. Before I went upstairs that night I sought out Vasilly and asked him, "Vasilly, where is Paris?"

"Paris?" he squeaked. "What do you want to know that for? How should I know where Paris is? How should I know anything—"

"Is it to the south?" I pressed him. Bryansk was to the south. I knew that much. If I could get to Bryansk I could easily pick up the trail that the Gypsies always left when they travelled.

"South?" The old man's voice quavered. "Yes, yes, I suppose it is. But it's a long, long way from here, that's sure. It's not even in Russia!"

I slept on the attic floor. It was my choice, not my aunt's, who didn't see why I couldn't sleep in a bed, with sheets and pillows, like a normal person. I tried to tell her that *gorgio* beds were too soft and that her sheets looked like shrouds, and to a Gypsy anything that symbolizes death is bad luck. White is the color of death, and Gypsies never wear it if they can help it. My bed in the attic was a red eiderdown quilt. That's all. Very portable. All I had to do was unroll it, wrap myself up inside, and go to sleep. I liked the attic. Up there I was close to the stars, close to freedom, and far removed from the rest of the household.

That night I had a wonderful dream. I dreamed that I was riding a big black horse over broad meadows. The horse ran so fast that his hooves didn't even touch the earth. We were actually flying! Higher and higher we soared, and as I looked down I could see little peasant cottages and patches of garden, roads as narrow as pieces of string, and people, like ants, laboring under the hot sun. They looked up at us and the startled expressions on their faces made me laugh.

"Catch her!" they shouted. "Catch her! Rhawnie, the Gypsy!"

I waved to them and spurred my horse on, and we flew still higher, over the treetops, into the clouds. What a beautiful feeling! I can still remember it, almost, if I close my eyes and concentrate very hard.

Then something jolted me out of that sleep and the wonderful dream vanished.

"Wake up!" Rough hands shook me and an impatient voice said again, "Wake up, lazy one! The master wants to see you at once! Hurry!"

"Go away," I groaned. I jerked my quilt up over my head and tried desperately to recapture my dream and the sweet sensation of flying.

"Wake up!" A slippered foot prodded my side.

I squinted into the light of the candle that hovered over me. Old Vasilly hissed at me through his sparse yellow teeth. I struggled to sit up. The coverlet fell away and I shivered. I wore only a thin shift that left my arms naked, and the air in the attic was freezing cold. I looked out through the fanlight at the rooftops of Moscow. The cloud-laden sky was pink, reflecting the glow of the city lights. It was snowing.

"What do you want, Vasilly?" I demanded grumpily. I scratched my head "Go away. Leave me alone."

He hauled me to my feet. For a little old man he was fairly strong. "Get up! Get up!" he wailed despairingly. "Do you want the master to beat me because of your laziness? Or worse, to sell me?"

"What would be so bad about that?" I rubbed my eyes with my fists and yawned. "You'd probably get a master who was a human being instead of an anim—"

"Hush! Come along, there is no time to waste!" He hustled me along. I mumbled something about at least giving me a chance to put on some clothes. But he said, "No time for that! Oh, lazy one, will you lift your feet? He said he wanted to see you at once! At once!"

We stumbled down the narrow stairs to the second floor, where the family bedrooms were located, then down the broad main staircase. Vasilly led me to the drawing room. He tapped lightly on the double doors and pushed them open. He shoved me inside and closed the doors behind me again.

The room was very bright. The candles in the chandelier were all burning, as well as the ones in the wall sconces and in the candelabra on the piano and on the tables. It

11

took a few minutes for my eyes to become adjusted to the light, and I stood there yawning and shivering and rubbing my eyes with the heels of my hands.

"Come here, girl!" my uncle barked. "Into the light, where Monsieur Garrett can see you."

He came up to me and put a ham-like hand on my shoulder. He reeked of whiskey and cigars. I shook him off and glared at him.

"Well, here she is, Monsieur. Your virgin! And I wish you well of her! Ha! Ha! Ha!"

His laughter echoed hollowly in the big room. He gave me a violent push that propelled me across the room, into the arms of its other occupant. He steadied me. When I regained my balance I pulled away from him and stepped back, glowering at him. This was the foreigner I had heard Vasily talking about.

I wondered where he had come from. He didn't look Russian. He was no giant, although he was big enough and massive, with great broad shoulders that bulged inside his clothes. His face matched his build, square and pugnacious. He wasn't at all handsome. His curly black hair was long and tinted with grey here and there, and more grey threads speckled his beard, though from the smooth skin on his cheeks and around his eyes I would have guessed that he was no more than twenty-five. His nose was large and it had been broken. A small scar gleamed on the bridge. Another purple scar ran down his left cheek into his beard. He looked like he had done some hard living. But his dress was elegant and immaculate. He wore a frock coat of a hard-finished dark brown wool, tight-fitting tan breeches, and gleaming riding boots. An abundance of ruffles spilled over his dove-colored waistcoat.

He ran his eyes over me swiftly but keenly, appraising me as I had seen horse traders inspecting an undesirable animal, with a single glance. He yawned behind his fingers and turned away. I felt a prickle of anger at this dismissal, even though I knew that I looked singularly unattractive in my shapeless shift. I was quite tall and pathetically

12

scrawny, with narrow hips and only the tiniest buds for breasts. My hair was half-braided and quite dishevelled, matted from sleep, and my face was thin and pinched with fury. I am sure that my black eyes glowed at him like hot coals under the absurd haystack of my hair.

"Well, how do you like her?" my uncle demanded. "Isn't she a beauty?"

The stranger said in a cool voice, "She is a trifle young for my tastes." His voice was very deep and rather beautiful, like the lowest notes on the piano. But I could tell from the set of his shoulders that this man was angry. I supposed my uncle had led him to expect a splendid Russian beauty.

"Young?" Alexei shouted. "Of course she is young! Virgins have to be young. That way their integrity is assured." He approached me. I stood fast and clenched my fists. "Isn't that true, little poppet?" he purred drunkenly. He put his fingers under my chin and jerked my head up. He moved his face closer to mine, as if to kiss me.

"What do you want from me?" I demanded angrily, slapping his hand away and moving back a pace. "Why did you bring me here? What do you want?"

"I made a little wager at the faro table tonight," my uncle told me. "And I lost. Thank Heaven I did! Say hello to Monsieur Garrett. You belong to him tonight!"

By God, the bastard had wagered me as if I were an insignificant hunk of property!

"Blackhearted dog!" I cried, and I launched myself at him, claws bared, aiming for his eyes. I didn't care that he was three times my size and had a hundred times my strength. I wanted to kill him.

"Get away from me! Get off, you she-devil!" he squawked. He gave a mighty swing of his arm. It caught my shoulder and sent me spinning, but in a flash I was on my feet, coming from him again. This time he was ready for me. He trapped my wrists in his hands. But I ducked my head and sank my teeth into his thumb. He gave a bellow of fury and pain and flung me away from him again.

I slapped against the wall with the force of a cannonball and slid to the floor. I was momentarily stunned and dazed. He pressed in on me, and I saw that he was completely insane with rage. His eyes seemed to shoot red sparks. He gave me a vicious kick in the ribs with his big booted foot. I sucked in my breath as pain flashed through my whole body, but I did not cry out, I did not beg for mercy. I would have died before I opened my mouth to plead with that monster. I would never show him fear.

"Cursed little witch!" Alexei panted. Kick! "I'll teach you a lesson tonight, by God!" Kick! Kick! "You're going to learn to behave yourself!"

"I curse you, Alexei Nicolayevitch Oulianov," I gasped brokenly. I saw a glimmer of fear in his tiny eyes. Of course, he was ignorant and superstitious, as wary of a Gypsy's curse as any peasant. I went on, "I curse you, and when your father looks down from above and sees how you have betrayed your promise to him, he will curse you, too. May you die a violent death! May your blood redden the earth and may dogs eat your flesh! May your wife and all your children perish horribly, and may rats chew their fingers and—"

"Stop it!" he shrieked. He stood frozen with terror for a moment, then he picked me up and slammed me back against the wall. "Stop it before I kill you!"

Then he released me abruptly and slid to the floor. My brains felt as if they had been pounded to jelly. I heard sounds of a scuffle and I pushed the hair out of my eyes so that I could see what was happening. The scene delighted my eyes: the stranger was standing over Alexei, who was flat on his back on the floor. The shining shaft of a rapier led from my uncle's throat to the stranger's hand.

"You damn interfering scoundrel!" Alexei breathed. "You dare—"

"She is my virgin, remember?" the stranger said smoothly. He reached down and jerked Alexei to his feet by his coat collar," then propelled him towards the doors. The tip of the rapier was never more than half an inch from

Alexei's neck. "I would ask you to remember your manners as well, Count."

Alexei was helpless in his grasp, even though he was a full head taller and easily a hundred pounds heavier than the stranger. I watched with glee as the man Garrett lifted my uncle by the scruff of his neck and tossed him into the hallway. I heard a loud splintering crash as Alexei's body fell against the delicate French inlaid table outside the door, smashing it into sticks.

"I'll see you both in Hell!" he roared.

"Don't make promises, dead man!" I shrilled after him.

The stranger closed the doors and turned the key, then he tucked his weapon under his arm and dusted his hands off against each other. He turned to me.

I got painfully to my feet and leaned heavily against the wall, clutching my side. "Don't come near me, you dog!" I hissed at him through my teeth. "Stay away from me or I will put a curse on you, too!"

He gave me a cool stare, with just a hint of a smirk, and said, "You'll live, I guess." His French was different from Alexei's. It must have been his foreign accent.

He turned his back on me and walked over to a table that held a decanter and some glasses. For the first time I saw that he favored his left leg. And indeed, I saw him pick up a thin black cane and sheath his rapier in it! He poured himself a large measure of liquor, then limped over to the fireplace and eased himself into a chair. He propped the cane against the side of the chair, within easy reach of his right hand.

"What are you going to do with me?" I asked loudly. He did not look around. Instead he sighed and closed his eyes. I moved away from the wall and stood about four feet from his chair, just out of reach of that lethal cane. "I tell you, if you lay one finger on me I will scratch your eyes out with my fingers!" I assured him. "I will rip off your ears! I will bite off your nose! And if you try to harm me I will curse you! Like this: may eagles pluck out your eyes and may rats gnaw your bones. May—"

15

"May wolves pull out in my innards and dine on my brains," he finished for me in a bored tone. I felt deflated. Usually *gorgio* dread a Gypsy's curse. He opened his eyes and stared into the fire. "Go away," he said.

"You are letting me go!" I said in an amazed voice. "I know, this is some trick!"

"No trick. As I told your master, you're a little young. And you're far too dirty."

I inched forward and stuck out my chin. "He is not my master! No man is my master! I am Rom! I am Gypsy! I am free!"

The man kept silent. I studied him closely. His scars marked him as a warrior, and his easy disposal of my uncle had certainly proven his bravery. His eyes were fringed by dark lashes, deep under menacing brows. He looked up at me and I saw that they were a startling shade of light blue. I looked down at his hands. They were a fighter's hand, huge and broad and long-fingered. But sensitive, too. He would be good with horses, I decided.

He reminded me of a Russian bear: dark and hairy and treacherous, even when he was quiet. My instincts told me that he was short-tempered and unpredictable, and I had seen how dangerous he could be. In fact, he was just the sort of ally I needed.

"Of course," I said in a friendlier tone, "you did save me from that brute. Not," I added quickly, "that I couldn't have saved myself! But I owe you thanks. Someday I will repay you. Gypsies are not ungrateful for favors, even from *gorgio*."

Silence. He stretched out his left leg and winced slightly.

"You need help with your boots tonight?" I asked eagerly. "You have no manservant?"

When I knelt down in front of him and began to tug off his right boot, he made no objection. But when I lifted his left leg he stiffened.

"Do not worry," I said, "I know how to be gentle." I removed his boot with utmost care and stood up. I saw that the level of brandy in his glass had dropped, and I brought the decanter over and filled his glass to the brim. Before I set the decanter down again I helped myself to a long pull. After what I had been through, I needed it.

He continued to gaze unblinking into the flames. I might have been made of clear glass, for all he saw of me.

"You are going away tomorrow," I said. "Before dawn."

He took a cigar out of an inner pocket. Leaning forward, he picked up a red coal with the fire tongs and lit it. He exhaled a plume of smoke and studied the end of the filthy burning stick.

I blinked the smoke out of my eyes and fanned the air with my hand. "Do not play games with me," I snapped. "I am not a baby that you can tease. I know that you are going, and where. You are going to Paris!"

He shifted in his seat and gave a bored sigh.

"Listen to me, *gorgio*." I knelt beside his chair and grabbed his arm. A wave of hostile tension surged through his body. He turned annoyed eyes on me. I released him but said urgently, "You must take me with you!"

He fixed his steely gaze on me and said flatly, "No."

"Yes!" I insisted. "You must take me, you must, you must! You have seen how wicked he is. A wicked, wicked man! He wants to kill me. He hates me! Look, look here!"

I pulled my shift off my shoulder to display the angry red welts on my skin.

"He did this today," I said grimly. "With his belt. His stupid son tried to kiss me in the hallway—just like his father, ugly brute—but I struck him with my fists and blackened both his eyes! Ugly little pig. Then the coward went snivelling to his mother—she hates me, too. Everyone hates the Gypsies. And Alexei Nicolayevitch came and beat me. Oh, how he hates me! And for no reason, only because I am different, because I am Gypsy. But I am his own sister's child, and he should not treat me that way!"

Now he favored me with an incredulous look.

17

"You don't believe me? You think I am a serf here? Ha!" I lifted my chin. "He is my uncle, that monster! And some day I will cut his heart out!" Using an invisible knive, I pantomimed a mortal plunge into the stranger's chest. He didn't flinch. "Some uncle, eh?" I sat back on my heels.

"Remarkable," he said dryly, tapping his cigar ash onto the floor.

"Do not think I want to leave because I am afraid of him," I said firmly. "No, you must not think that. I fear nothing! But I do not belong here. I am Gypsy. I must be free. Take me with you, Monsieur. As far as Bryansk, that is all I ask. It is on the way! The caravans will be waiting there for me, I know it! Take me!"

I clutched at him again, digging my thin fingers into his forearm. Again he stiffened, but I did not let go. I lowered my voice and filled it with emotion.

"I cannot stay here, living like some *gorgio*. I am Rom," I said proudly, "like my father and his father and his father before that. The old man, the Grandfather, was kind to me. But when he died and that *gorgio* pig brought me here—uh, can you not understand how it was?" I pleaded desperately with my eyes and even squeezed out a tear or two. "Here it is a prison. No stars at night. No forests. No birds. Only this evil man and his wife and evil children, and *gorgio* priests and *gorgio* churches and doors, so many, many doors! 'Be like us,' they say. But I do not want to be like them! I do not want to read and write and sew all day, and sit as still as a rabbit in front of a gun. Pfui! They say that I am like a little savage, but what do they know! They are savages. They are ignorant. And they are all so weak, all so full of fear. I hate them. When I die," I said in a voice throbbing with sorrow, "it will not be from that man's beatings. It will be because I have been in this prison too long. You will take me, I feel certain of it. You are a good man, brave and strong. You will take me." I dropped my head, overcome by the weight of my plight.

He said, "I won't take you with me. But if you ever get

to London, I suggest you go straight to Drury Lane and ask for a job.''

I didn't know what he was talking about, but I knew mockery when I heard it.

''You joke with me!'' I gasped, enraged. ''You laugh when a little child is in danger! For shame, *gorgio*, for shame! I know, you think this is some kind of Gypsy trick, don't you? Well, it is no trick. I want nothing from you, only to be taken away from here. I will pay you! You do not believe? I can beg. I am a really fine beggar, I swear it! And fortunes! Ah, I tell very, very good fortunes. Wait, I will show you. Give me your hand—.''

I slid my grip down to his hand and tilted his palm towards the firelight. He tried to jerk away but I held him fast, as a drowning man holds a spar.

''Ah!'' I cried, as if I had made an important find. ''You have come far, from across the sea.''

He gave a derisive snort.

''I see many journeys,'' I said with utmost seriousness, ignoring his obvious scepticism. ''Your life will be full of journeys. Ah! Wait!'' I peered closer. ''A man lurks. A friend! Beware, Monsieur. A very close friend will betray you.''

''I have no close friends,'' he said, yanking at his hand.

''Do not pull away!'' I cried. ''I am seeing better now, clearer. Wait! It is much clearer—.''

My voice grew fainter as I stared at his palm. And a strange thing happened. I couldn't see his hand anymore, only vaguely colored shadows that moved in front of my eyes like mist, forming pictures and breaking up again. I shook my head to clear my brains, thinking that the brandy I had swilled had muddled them. Yes, the brandy and the beating had made me dizzy.

I plunged on. ''You will travel far to find love, only to find that love has travelled with you,'' I said glibly. The mists formed a face. I saw dark eyes and dark hair. ''A woman,'' I whispered incredulously. ''I see the woman

19

you loved! She did not betray you. There is another! A man with fair hair. She loves him. Where there is love there can be no betrayal." I heard him suck in his breath slightly. Could what I was seeing be true? "But she is weak, very weak. I think—," I saw the little figure lying on a bed. She was dressed in white. "I think she is dying. You must go to her at once. She wants to forgive you. I see— another face! And I see waves, like ocean waves. Only they are red. Oh, no! It is blood! So close, so near at hand! It is—"

I shrieked and covered my face with my hands. Fear. For the first time in my life I knew what it was to be really afraid. For a door had opened and I had seen—

He stood up abruptly. "You were right about one thing," he said. "You are good at this game. But save your Gypsy lies for *gorgio* who believe in that sort of thing."

He fished in his waistcoat pocket and tossed a coin at me. Instinctively my hand flashed out like the tongue of a frog that has seen a fly and my fingers closed around the gold. I looked at it. It was a ten-ruble piece, more than I had ever earned in my life telling fortunes. But tonight I had really earned it. I had really seen—things.

"Your fortune," I said. My voice came out in a croak and I paused to clear my throat. "The first part I made up, because I couldn't see." I swallowed. "But then I told you the truth! May the Evil One come and live inside my body if I didn't! And I saw—"

"I don't want to hear more," he said. "Go back to bed, Gypsy. I will not take you with me. I travel alone, always."

"You will not take me," I repeated softly. I looked up at him. "What is your name?"

"Seth Garrett," he said.

"Se-the." I tried to pronounce it but my tongue balked at the "th" sound. I could get it with practice, though. "Se-the," I said slowly. "A nice enough name. My name is Rhawnie. That is nice, too, no?" I searched his face for signs of softening. I found none, only stoney hardness. Well, I could be hard, too. And clever. I scrambled to my feet. "Well, may God go with you, Monsieur Se-the," I said politely. "I wish you a good journey."

I waited, giving him one more chance to relent. Silence. I whirled and ran out of the room. I raced up the stairs to my attic and threw myself down on the red eiderdown. I shivered violently, but not from the cold. That business in the drawing room terrified me. Had I really seen his fortune?

I rolled over and buried my head in my arms. I knew as well as any Gypsy that fortune-telling was only a joke, an easy way of getting the *gorgio* to part with his gold. It was important to Gypsies in another way, of course. Because the *gorgio* believed that Gypsies were endowed with special gifts, they feared them and respected their privacy. And the true gift of prophecy was as rare among Gypsies as it was among the *gorgio*.

But it was forbidden to Gypsies to practice fortune-telling among themselves. To believe in such things was considered a real sign of weakness. A person who wants to hear things he already knows, his past, is a fool. And one who is eager to know what the future holds has lost his ability to deal with real life in the present. For Gypsies, life is present. Life is now. Not yesterday, not tomorrow. Forget the past and let tomorrow take care of itself. Live for today.

Yet as I had held Seth Garrett's hand, a curtain had lifted in some compartment of my brain. I had really seen the dark-haired woman and the fair-haired man, and I had seen her on her deathbed. As that picture cleared away another had taken its place: my own face! And then waves of blood had washed over everything. A bad omen, that. Really bad. I had felt the presence of Death in that room. But whose death? My own? The stranger's?

I felt confused and distressed. I pulled my quilt tighter around me and tried to think clearly. Surely, to believe what I had seen was just as bad as having my fortune told by another Gypsy. In the fourteen (or fifteen) years I had lived as a Gypsy, I had had my fortune told only once, and even then I hadn't been quite sure just what was happening.

It was the day that the Grandfather came to take me away. I bid my father and stepmother and little brothers farewell. As the Grandfather and I made ready to leave, I saw Django lurking in the shadows near my father's wagon. Django was my betrothed. We were to have been married in the autumn. I ran over to him.

"I will come back," I promised him. "Before the grain is ripe again, I will return." Then I picked up a small jug of wine and dashed it against a rock. "May my skull be crushed like this jar, and may my blood flow into the ground if I do not come back." Gypsies do not make vows lightly. Django and I both knew that this was a very solemn moment.

Just then the ancient crone Ursula appeared and pulled me into the dappled gloom of the birch grove. I had always been wary of the old woman. I felt that she disliked me because I was different from the rest, because my hair was gold instead of black, because my mother was not Gypsy.

"Yes, you will return," the old woman said in a cackling whisper. She held my hand in a grip of iron and her eyes gleamed in her shrunken face like polished onyx beads. Her skin felt dry and unresilient, like paper. No one knew how old Ursula really was. The grove fell silent. The birds were hushed and the wind was still and not a sound came from the nearby ring of caravans. The whole world seemed to listen to the old woman's words. "You will come back after the ripening of the grain. You will come with a man, a *gorgio*, and you will go away with him again. His journey will be your journey. You will be Gypsy no more."

"No!" I cried. "I will always be Gypsy!"

"Silence!" Ursula barked. "You will find us," she went on, "but you will never see us again. Now be off!"

As I ran away from the birch grove, my head was whirling. What on earth had she meant? I would be Gypsy until I died, I was sure of it! And that nonsense about not seeing them when I found them! The old woman was very near death, I thought, and her brains must be halfway into her next life already.

Now I wasn't so sure. Did the old woman have the gift of prophecy, too? She had said that I would return with a *gorgio*. That could mean Seth Garrett. I would trick him into taking me to Bryansk, that would be no problem. Of course the Gypsies would be long gone, but he couldn't abandon me there and he would have to help me find them. So, I would travel with him to Bryansk, and I would go away from there with him. Just as Ursula had foreseen. The vision of my face in his hand confirmed it. And perhaps the attempts of my uncle and aunt to turn me into a *gorgio* would explain the words, "Gypsy no more." I was tainted from living with them, but all that would surely disappear when I got back to the tribe.

Ursula had spoken the truth, and what I had seen was also true. But what about the horror of death that had come over me? I hoped fervently that that part had been a mistake, a false vision.

I knew what I had to do. My course was settled, my plans laid. I threw off my quilt and got dressed. I put on a red paisley blouse with full sleeves, and five voluminous skirts of brightly-colored cotton, one right on top of the other. I wrapped two fringed shawls around my shoulders and tied a small scarf around my head and another around my neck. I brought out my Gypsy bangles from their hiding place under a floor board and slid them over my wrists. Their metallic jangle sounded beautiful to my ears, like Gypsy music. Finally I pulled on the soft red leather boots that had been a gift from the Grandfather. I gathered my few possessions up inside my quilt: my small round crystal for fortune-telling, the richly-tooled bridle that the Grandfather had given me when I cured his horse Blaze, and the small icon that had been my mother's.

Everything was ready. I now had no doubt at all that the *gorgio* stranger was destined to take me back to the Gypsies. I would leave this house at dawn, with or without his knowledge and consent. I went downstairs to see what I could steal.

I had heard that my uncle kept a money box in his study, just off the dining room. The box would be locked, of course, but I wasn't worried. I had a pin or two in my hair and several hours until dawn. The door to the study was locked, but it took me only a minute or two to open it. I parted the curtains at the windows so that the glow of the city would help me in my work. I didn't dare light a candle. Alexei's big desk dominated the room. All the drawers were open, except one. A few twists of my hairpin gave me access to its contents—a large deal box, banded with metal. A padlock as big as my fist clanked against the front of the box.

I shook my head disapprovingly. "So many worries, so many locks," I clucked softly. "This man doesn't trust anybody."

The padlock was stubborn, but I was patient and deft. I worked carefully with my primitive burglar's tools, with one ear cocked for sounds of danger. *Click*. At last the lock yielded to my efforts. Hurriedly I pulled it off the big brass hasp and opened the lid. My heart sank. The box was empty. But wait, there was a small brown-paper parcel in one corner. I should have known that anyone who gambled as recklessly as Alexei wouldn't have any spare cash lying around the house. But the parcel contained a single bracelet, one which I had never seen my aunt wearing. As

I held it up for inspection it winked at me, even in the soft, dim light. I had heard that there were such things as diamonds but I had never seen them before. They were hard and cold, but beautiful. I slipped the bracelet into my pocket, closed the lid of the box and snapped the lock back in place.

"Gypsy thief."

My blood froze in my veins. Alexei stood glowering at me from the doorway.

"You are mistaken, Alexei Nicolayevitch, in what you see here," I said rapidly. "I found this box in the hallway—a thief must have dropped it. But see, it hasn't been opened! He must have heard me moving around and frightened—"

"Liar," he growled. He came closer. I sidled around the desk, hoping to make a break for the door. "Little Gypsy scum. I've got you now! I would be justified in killing you, wouldn't I? And now there's no one around to interfere."

I faked a lunge in one direction, and when he moved to follow, I whipped around the other side of the desk and tore out the door. He pounded after me, breathing hard. I got confused in the darkness and made a fatal wrong turn out of the dining room, away from the stairs. When I discovered my mistake and changed direction, I saw that Alexei had the stairs blocked. I had no choice but to dart into the drawing room and hope I could get the key turned in the lock before he caught up with me.

But Alexei was swifter than I anticipated, and just as I closed the doors he threw himself at them. They burst open and I sprawled backwards, catching the heel of my boot in the rug. I fell and Alexei threw himself down on top of me. Cursing and reviling me, he grabbed my ears and pounded my head against the floor. He was so vast, so heavy that I couldn't move. I could only twitch my arms and legs like a frog crushed under a stone. Any blows I struck made no impression on him at all.

I noticed that the candles in the room were still burning. Vasilly, that poor old devil, had probably fallen asleep somewhere and forgotten to come and put them out. A few of them had extinguished themselves in pools of their own wax. Other small flames jumped and flickered, casting crazy shadows on the walls. I could see Alexei's shadow, heaving and jerking like a mountain in an earthquake.

He lowered his face to mine and kissed me wetly. A tide of loathing rose in my throat. I felt suffocated, over-whelmed. Then he shoved his meaty hand under my skirts and grasped my buttock. I squealed far back in my throat like a rabbit caught in a trap.

He chuckled. "Ah, so now you're afraid of me, eh, Gypsy?" he rasped. "What's the matter, don't you like to be kissed? Little Gypsy slut!"

I was breathless and I couldn't cry out. He jammed himself between my thighs, deep into me. I felt a searing pain, and then a numbness which persisted while he came crashing into me with his loins, groaning and gasping like a man in mortal pain. I closed my eyes and waited for the siege to end. I tried to think of other things, of horses and flying and Django.

Finally he gave a thunderous wheeze and collapsed with his full weight on top of me, his energy spent. I nearly passed out when that mountain came to rest on my frail body, and I was reminded of a flattened rosebud I had found once in a book in the Grandfather's library. Dry, lifeless, squashed into paper thinness. A bad omen, that flower. Gypsies don't believe in picking flowers, because it kills them, and that's bad luck.

Then through the haze of pain and shame and hatred that enveloped my brain, I heard a familiar voice.

"I thought I told you before, Count. She is my virgin."

The weight lifted. I moaned and rolled onto my side, pulling my knees up to my chest.

26

"You had better learn to mind your own business, Monsieur," my uncle growled. "Take your hands off me!"

"I would think that even in this backward land, rape and incest would be regarded as crimes," Seth Garrett said. "The girl is your niece, is she not?"

"That is my affair," Alexei snarled. "Get away from me!"

He threw the stranger away from him. Seth Garrett fell back into a small table. Instead of attacking the man, Alexei dashed to the fireplace. Over the mantle hung crossed sabers, souvenirs of an earlier bellicose generation of Oulianovs. Snatching one down, Alexei brandished it at the intruder.

"And now I'm going to spit you on this steel, Monsieur," he said with grim satisfaction. "I am master here, no one else! What I do with this Gypsy baggage is my own affair. She deserved what she got. She is a liar and a thief!"

Seth Garrett dove behind a chair as Alexei sliced the air with the saber. I saw that the stranger was wearing his boots again, but not his coat or waistcoat. His ruffled shirt was open to the waist, revealing a brown, brawny chest covered with a mat of soft, dark fur. Alexei pressed the attack. Seth snatched up a small table and held it in front of him, using the top as a shield. He was fresh for the fight while Alexei, his vigor somewhat sapped by his attack on me, soon showed signs of flagging. But Alexei held the weapon, and it was only a matter of time before he broke through the stranger's defense and had him backed into a corner. Seth grabbed a candlestick and used it to deflect those blows that evaded his shield. I don't know how he managed to avoid the curved blade, which seemed to me to cut in a thousand directions at the same time.

I staggered to the fireplace, and reaching up I grabbed the hilt of the remaining saber and pulled it off the wall. I planned to attack Alexei from the rear, but the weapon was fearfully heavy and it dragged at my arm. I couldn't possibly use if effectively.

"Over here!" Seth Garrett shouted.

In a flash I sent the saber skittering across the floor to his corner. He held the little table over his head with one hand while he crouched down and took hold of the saber with the other. Alexei's blade crashed down on the wood, slicing off a piece from the edge. Then Seth straightened up and tossed the table aside.

"And now we are equal, Count," he said softly. "Man to man. Blade to blade."

"I will cut you into pieces and feed you to the wolves," my uncle hissed. With a wild cry that was calculated to frighten, but which only succeeded in provoking a grin from Seth Garrett, he launched himself at the stranger, his saber poised to lop off his opponent's head. Seth parried the cut neatly, but the clash of steel on steel sent shivers up and down my spine. There was a flurry of swordplay. I am sure that the only reason the din of battle didn't rouse everyone in the house was that the stranger had remembered to close the doors when he came in. Of course the family's sleeping quarters were at the other end of the house from the guest rooms, which were directly above us. And the serfs knew better than to interfere in anything.

Alexei didn't seem to be planning his moves at all. He slashed in all directions, hoping at some point to make contact with Seth's body. But the stranger never let him get close. He was cool and deft, and once he had sized up his opponent as a lumbering bear who had no idea at all of the rudiments of saber-play, only a mad desire to draw blood, he relaxed and waited for the Count himself to present the moment for the finishing blow.

My uncle was sweating profusely and breathing heavily. He lowered the sphere of his attack and slashed at Seth Garrett's weak leg. But in doing that he left his upper chest exposed, and Seth's saber cut into his upper arm as easily as a razor into a cooked potato. My uncle reeled back and fell heavily at my feet.

I recoiled, as if a serpent had come too close to me.

Seth Garrett looked grim. He stood panting, then he threw down his saber and turned his back on the fallen man.

Alexei reached inside his coat and pulled out a tiny pistol. There was no time to cry out a warning. Without even thinking, I picked up the nearest heavy object, a dazzling malachite vase, brilliant and green as a tiger's eyes, and I brought it down heavily on my uncle's head. I poured every ounce of my hatred for him into that blow, and as soon as the stone met his skull, I knew I had killed him.

I wasn't sorry then, and I'm not sorry now. He was evil. He had done me a great wrong. He would have killed Seth Garrett and he wanted to kill me. He was deserving of death as any poisonous snake.

He gave a horrible gurgling gasp and fell back. His eyes were open but blind. A sea of blood flowed onto the carpet.

"May God forgive you the evil you have done," I whispered. "For surely I cannot."

I wasn't even aware that I was trembling until Seth put his hands on me to move me away from the body.

"Go upstairs, quickly," he said. "They'll think I did it, but by the time they discover him I'll be long gone. Go now!"

"No!" I said. "I'm going with you. I must!"

"You're crazy!" he hissed. "Haven't you done enough for one night? If it hadn't been for you—"

"If it hadn't been for me you would be dead and not he," I informed him. We were both whispering. If we were found now and the alarm raised, we would never get away. "But if that's the thanks I get for saving you—"

"I saved you first!" he snapped. "Damn. I won't take you. Get out of here before it's too late."

I dipped down, snatched up my uncle's pistol, and pointed it at the man's chest.

"If you do not take me, you will not leave here your-

29

self," I promised. "I have killed once tonight. It doesn't matter to me—"

His blue eyes glinted like the steel of the discarded saber. The pistol bobbled in my shaking hand, but I gritted my teeth and steadied it with my free hand. I was fully determined to kill this man if he thwarted my escape.

"Don't be a little fool," he growled. He reached out and plucked the gun out of my fingers, as easily as if he were picking an apple off a low-hanging bough. Only then did the horrors of the evening overwhelm me. I felt weak and dizzy and I pitched forward into his arms. Tears rained down my cheeks and my teeth rattled in my head like the seeds inside a dried gourd.

"I had to k-k-kill him!" I said. "He d-d-dishonored me! I had t-to!"

"Listen to me, girl." His fingers dug into my flesh and he stood me on my feet again. "There will be time enough for hysterics later. We've got to get out of here. Wait here while I get my things—"

"No!" I cast a sideways glance at my uncle's bloody corpse. I shook myself free of Seth Garrett and sucked in great lungfuls of air to clear my head. "No," I said calmly, "it is better if I go. I can move as silently as a cat and as quickly as a fox. You stay with him and I will bring your things, then if anyone comes you can kill them, too."

He thought a moment, then nodded curtly. I slipped out of the drawing room into the icy hallway. I was one with the darkness and I was as stealthy as a hungry Gypsy stalking a wary chicken. I ran up to the attic first and scooped up my eiderdown bundle, then I went down to the stranger's room. His large valise was packed. I gathered it up with his coat, his stock and waistcoat, and his stick. Then I went out into the hallway and back down the stairs to the drawing room.

He turned the pistol on me as I entered, and shoved it into his belt with a wry grimace when he recognized me. I couldn't have been gone longer than three minutes. He finished dressing and looked around.

"What's the matter?" I asked. "Have I forgotten something?"

"I had a cloak. Black fur."

"Yes," I nodded, "I know where they are. I will get it." I found his cloak in the small room near the front doors. I also took a wrap for myself, a rich cape of black ermine that belonged to my aunt, and a couple of deep fur hats.

"We will need a key to get out," I told my co-conspirator. "He locks everything up at night so that I won't get away. You search him." I didn't want to touch Alexei.

Seth Garrett found a bundle of keys in my uncle's coat pocket. We gathered up our things and left the house together, two fugitives, partners in crime.

2

The Troika

WE TRAMPED THROUGH the snow without stopping until we were well away from my uncle's house. A light wind filled our tracks with snow as soon as we made them, and although Seth Garrett was wary and watchful, no one followed us. After a couple of hours we took shelter in a doorway for a moment while he got his bearings. The city was just coming to life. A few sleds scraped past and harness bells jingled in the crisp pre-dawn air.

"Let's see," he said, "there should be a drovers' inn just around the next corner."

"How do you know that?" I wondered. "I thought you were a foreigner."

"It would be a stupid fox that didn't know where to hide when the dogs were after him," he grunted. I nodded approvingly. It was a good Gypsy type sentiment. "You speak Russian?" he asked.

"Of course," I said. "Don't you?"

He gave me an impatient look. "No. I don't. You'll have to translate."

The floor of the public room of the drovers' inn was littered with sleeping bodies. The air was heavy with the drone of snores, and pungent with the stink of unwashed bodies, urine, and liquor. We found a space in a dark corner and sank down on the floor, grateful for a chance to rest until the men awoke. My companion opened his valise and took out a small flask, which he uncorked and tilted to his mouth. He put it away without offering me any. After a while the bodies began to stir. The men coughed and snorted. It was the start of another work day for them.

Finally Seth Garrett stood up and said to me, "Ask if there is anyone who has a troika for hire, to go a long distance. I'll pay well."

I translated for him. My girlish voice sounded strange and incongruous in that roomful of men, and they turned baleful eyes upon me.

"Bah, Gypsy," one growled. "I have never heard of a Gypsy paying for anything. You want to lose your troika and your horses, then take a Gypsy with you and you'll get where you're going with nothing but your boots, if you're lucky."

"Don't be silly," I said tartly. "The man with me is no Gypsy. He is a great gentleman from a foreign land, and he is very wealthy. I have seen his purse, bulging with gold pieces! Well, come on, who will take us?"

Sullen stares and suspicious muttering.

"What's the matter?" Seth demanded impatiently. "What's the problem?"

I wasn't about to tell him that I was the problem, so I said, "They want to know just how far you want to go. I will tell them."

I spoke rapid Russian, hoping Seth wouldn't catch the word "Bryansk." But he did catch it.

"We're not going to Bryansk," he said in a tight voice. "Get that through your head."

"Well, I don't want to go to Paris," I said reasonably. "And Bryansk is on the way. You wouldn't have to lose one day on my account!"

A burly giant swathed in furs came over. "You say you want to go to Bryansk?" he asked in French. Bah, I thought. Just my luck that this devil speaks French.

"No," said Seth. "I want to go to Paris, by way of Warsaw is the quickest route, I think. But if you could take me even as far as Brest—"

"So what's all this about Bryansk?" the man growled. "Bryansk is a hundred and sixty versts to the south, about a week's journey."

I grabbed at Seth's arm. He flinched at my touch but I ignored that. "You must take me there!" I pleaded. "Please, please, Monsieur! Remember your promise, back at the house." I saw his eyebrows go up a quarter of an inch. I thought it wouldn't hurt to remind him that we were the joint sharers of a very guilty secret. "It wouldn't be much out of your way," I went on. "And I will pay you, I swear it! What is a week in the face of a lifetime? Nothing!" I snapped my fingers. "Less than nothing! Now I know that you do not want to be delayed in Moscow, Monsieur," I said meaningfully. "That wouldn't be a very good idea, would it? But if you don't take me—"

He picked me up by the collar of the ermine cape. My feet barely brushed the hard-packed dirt floor. I gagged and plucked futilely at his hands.

"If you want to be a red stain on the ground, like your uncle," he said in a low menacing voice, "you'll keep running your mouth. I suppose if I leave you behind you'll raise the hue and cry, eh? I doubt that, little Gypsy miss. I doubt it very much."

"There is trouble, eh?" the driver rumbled.

"Big trouble," Seth said. He released me abruptly. I regained my balance and pulled myself up with haughty disdain.

"I should have known that no Gypsy would come by a fur like that honestly," the man said glumly. "It is only a matter of hours before the Czar's police get after you. We'd better hurry. My horses are fresh and we can do twenty versts today, at least. This snow is nothing. But you must decide quickly. To Brest directly, or by way of Bryansk?"

I held my tongue but pleaded with my eyes. A full minute passed before he answered. I held my breath.

Indeed, the room seemed to fall silent as we awaited his pronouncement. Finally he spoke one word.

"Bryansk."

Everyone relaxed. I wanted to hug him, to dance with joy, to shout out my happiness for the whole world to hear. I wanted to say, "You see, Alexei Nicolayevitch, you dead bastard, you see! I am going back to the Gypsies after all!" But I contented myself with a broad appreciative grin.

"Three hundred rubles," the driver said brusquely.

"Fine," said Garrett. "Half now, half when we arrive in Brest."

Three hundred!" I yipped. "The man is robbing you! Don't give him any more than—"

"Shut up," the stranger snapped. He picked up his bag and stalked out of the room.

"Blast you, Gypsy," the driver growled in Russian. "What are you trying to do, ruin me?"

"Gypsies aren't the only thieves in the world," I sniffed. "Peasants are just as bad." I picked up my bundle and followed Seth Garrett into the cold morning.

In less than an hour we were ready to go. The driver lashed our luggage securely to the back of the sled and covered it with heavy canvas. The three horses, a tall gelding in the middle flanked by two smaller mares, pawed the ground impatiently and snorted. Their breath hung in the snowy air like frosty puffs of smoke. The snow was a foot and a half deep already and it showed no signs of stopping. The world swam through a thick haze into the color the hours between darkness and morning. And the bells in the tower above Spassky Gate tolled seven.

Our driver climbed up on the seat in front of us and flapped the reins. Seth Garrett and I tucked our fur lap robes more snugly around our legs. The sled glided rapidly over cobbled streets and rutted lanes, past snow-shrouded houses and exotic gold-topped churches, through the already bustling markets in Red Square, in which buyers and sellers seemed to take no notice of the snow and the cold. We drove past St. Basil's Cathedral and the lively inns and mean wooden hovels that seemed to cling to the walls of the Kremlin like barnacles to the sides of a great wooden ship.

I saw the contingent of the Czar's special police before either of the others. They were wearing long grey coats and they were mounted on tall horses. They seemed to be checking every vehicle that was crossing the wooden bridge over the Moskva River.

"You, driver," I called. "You are travelling with me alone, understand? And let me do the talking."

"Wait a minute," Seth said. "What—"

"Shut up and get down, here, under these robes. Hurry, before they see you!" I pushed him under the furs. He crouched on the floor, under my legs, and I arranged the robes to hide him. I pulled the diamond bracelet out of my shirt pocket and slipped it over my wrist.

We drew to a halt at a signal from one of the policemen. "Everyone out, please," he said. "Come on, hurry."

"Just a minute," I said imperiously in what sounded to me like good French. "What is the meaning of this? How dare you stop this troika! I am in a hurry. Drive on, man!"

"Pardon me, Madame," the man said patiently, "but I have my orders—"

"And I have mine. Do you know who I am?" I lifted my chin and hoped my neck was clean enough for royalty. "I am the Princess Tatiana Katerina Petrushka Razin! Goddaughter of the Czar himself! And I am on my way to school. Do you have any idea what will happen to me if I am late?" I rattled my diamonds under his nose and moved my shoulders haughtily inside my ermine. "Why have you stopped us? What are you looking for?"

"Well, your excellency, we have heard that a certain Frenchman—"

I didn't let him go any further. "Frenchman! You dare to tell me that you have delayed me this morning because you are looking for a Frenchman? What is your name? Come on, tell me quickly." The man actually looked shamefaced. "You can see that there is no Frenchman

39

here, can't you? You have eyes, don't you? Then get out of our way, Igor, drive on!" I shouted.

Our driver touched his hat to the uniformed men and we jerked forward. They didn't try to stop me. When I looked back I saw that they were quizzing another traveler.

"Stay where you are until we're well out of the city," I said to the pile of furs at my feet. "And remember, this is the second time I have saved your life."

Soon a gently rolling white landscape lay in front of us. I looked back once again and watched as the towers of the ancient city grew smaller and gradually disappeared in the snowy mist.

I lifted the fur robes. "All right, you can come up for air." Seth Garrett emerged, looking red and furious. "No, don't thank me," I said airily. "Just consider it part of my payment to you." He maintained a steadfast silence. "I don't know why you're angry with me," I said. "Unless you still resent bringing me along. But you had no choice. Do you know what I saw in your hand last night, right before the death omen? My own face! After such a sign not even the Czar of all the Russian could have refused me. And you, you're still acting as if I had tricked you. It was fate, I tell you. I must tell old Ursula about this when I see her. She knows about these things. She will be able to tell me if I truly have the gift of fortunes or if it was just some miracle."

He continued to ignore me. I shrugged at his stubbornness and curled up to sleep. What did I care about his moods? I was free and I was on my way back to the Gypsies. Life was good, very good.

After a few hours we stopped at a way station to rest and water the horses. I was wide awake and I told the men about my little stepbrothers, Sasha and Vanya and Alyosha. I told them about the time I had taken them begging with me in Istanbul and we had brought back a pile of money.

"These *gorgio* will believe anything," I said. "Even that a girl of twelve—me!—could be mother of a baby of four years! Stupid, no? And then another time a man asked me if the Gypsies had stolen me. A lot of *gorgio* think that Gypsies steal children, but why should they when they have plenty of their own? Anyway, my hair is yellow and that's what he thought. So I told him yes, thinking he would feel sorry for me and give me the money to go back to the home that I had lost. But God is my witness, the foolish one was the chief of police and he took me to prison and also my father and Lyubov, our leader. But I was very small then and my mother was still alive, and she came and showed herself to the police and showed them her long yellow hair. The Grandfather once asked me why I thought his daughter ran away with the Rom. What a question! Because my father was handsomer than any *gorgio*, I told him, and because she wanted to be free! What other answer could there be?''

"Gypsies," our driver snorted. "They could talk the legs off a horse if you let them."

"Ha," I sniffed. "These nags of yours couldn't go any slower if they had no legs at all."

"What do you mean?" The man's face grew red. "This is the finest troika team in all Russia!"

"Bah. I have seen better horses carting the dead. Why don't you do them a favor and shoot them?"

The man started to bluster. "Why, you little witch, I'll give you some more bruises to match those you've already got, just see if I don't." He waved his fist threateningly over my head.

"I am not afraid of you, you big peasant," I said tartly. "If you're not careful I'll put a spell on you. All your hair will fall out and your fingers will drop off."

"Mother of God!" The big man crossed himself. "If I were you, sir," he said to Seth, "I would leave her here, in the middle of nowhere. She is the daughter of Satan himself!"

"You are a liar and a scoundrel," I jeered.

"If you were my child I would have drowned you at birth!" the driver shouted.

41

"If you were my father I would not have been born!" I retorted. "I would have shrivelled up in the womb, may my tongue drop out of my head if—"

"Quiet!" Seth Garrett's deep voice split the freezing air. We stared at him. "Both of you get back in the sled," he said softly. "We're ready to go."

But the driver drew himself up. He was taller than Seth, well over six feet, and just as broad. The furs he wore made him seem immense. He had black hair and a bristling black mustache, and he wore a patch over one eye. His skin was seamed and leathery and his age was indeterminable. He could have been forty-five or seventy-five.

"I am Ivor Andreivitch Krasskey," he said stiffly. "And I am a Cossack! I lost my eye fighting at the side of the great General Kutozov, against the bastard French. I am no man's serf, no man's slave. I may be too old to go to war, but I am not too old to whip the pants off some young whelp who thinks that with gold he can buy a man's pride as well as his troika! I will drive this Gypsy no further! You must decide, sir. If you want to travel with this devil's child, you must find another driver."

It took Seth Garrett an hour of cajoling and arguing and another one hundred rubles on the spot to persuade Ivor to continue the journey. By then we had lost valuable daylight and Ivor said we would be lucky to make only fifteen versts that day.

Seth climbed into the troika beside me and said in a low voice, "If you delay us just once more, I swear I'll throw you into the nearest snowdrift and leave you. I don't care where we are."

"What do you mean?" I asked in an injured voice. "I only spoke to him as one would speak to a stupid peasant."

"And I'm speaking to you as one would speak to a dirty Gypsy," he replied. "Hold your tongue!"

Now I knew very well that I was dirty, and I was certainly a Gypsy. But the sound of those two words linked, as he had said them, was an insult.

42

"I am not a dirty Gypsy," I pouted. "And I am free! I say what I please."

We continued our journey in hostile silence. The snow had stopped and the skies were clear when we halted at a mean-looking inn ten miles north of the town of Kaluga. We all climbed out to stretch. Ivor Andreivitch went around to the back of the troika to unload the baggage. I wandered towards the front to make friends with the horses.

"Hey, you Gypsy!" Ivor looked up. "Get away from my horses!"

"I was mistaken earlier, Ivor Andreivitch," I said loudly. "These are very fine horses indeed. Very intelligent, and they work so well together! Worth a lot of money at a horse fair. But I must tell you, this one on the end is looking a little bloated. Not much, just a little. You must give her a light purge tonight and follow up with some molasses in her feeding. I guarantee, she will be better, go faster."

"Oh, so now you're a horse doctor!" Ivor sneered. "You're a little liar, Gypsy. There is nothing wrong with that horse."

"She is slowing the other two down," I told him. "She is easily winded because you let her eat too much."

"I never—"

"Oh, she tricks you!" I laughed. "When you leave them at night, she eats for the other two and then finishes her own food. She is greedy, no?"

"She's always had a big appetite," Ivor admitted. "But I have never seen her—"

"Because she is too smart to misbehave in front of you. Listen, Ivor Andreivitch, tonight when you put them in the stable, separate this little one. In the morning you will see, the other two will have food left and this greedy mare will be asking for more."

Ivor grunted and thought this over. Seth Garrett leaned against the troika with his arms folded over his chest. He looked bemused. I left the horses and stood in front of Ivor.

"Ivor Andreivitch," I said humbly, "I did not know that you were a Cossack or I would not have spoken as I did. You are a brave man, and Gypsies admire bravery above all else. I am only a miserable girl child and I have a loose tongue. I have been without my mother for many years and there is much I have not learned. I have no right to expect one so worthy as yourself to carry a poor creature like me to far off places. The way is long and hard , and the days are getting shorter and colder. I will find my people by myself, before the really heavy snows come. I am half-Russian, and you are Russian. Surely we can speak to each other with respect. I ask your forgiveness for my rudeness. I have no wish to be your enemy." I sighed plaintively. "It would be a very great honor to drive with one who lost his eye fighting for Russia with the great Kutuzov. I have been very stupid."

Ivor stamped in the snow and scratched his head under his hat of red fox fur. "Hmmm. So you think she gets winded only because she is too fat?"

"And because she has air from eating too fast. Why else? You can see from her eyes and teeth that she is healthy. One of the finest horses I have ever seen! But do as I say? give her something to clean her out—castor oil is good enough—and then put a little molasses in her oats to curb her appetite. And keep her away from the other two."

"You Gypsies always did have a way with horses," Ivor admitted grudgingly. "But how did you learn their tricks? I thought they didn't allow women to bother with their horses."

"Ah, but I am only half-Gypsy," I reminded him. "I have always been different. When Lyubov, our leader, saw that I had the gift with horses, he said that I could leave woman's work alone and learn to be their horse doctor. He taught me a great many things. He was a very wise man. And the rest I found out for myself."

Ivor blew out his breath. "And how old were you when your mother died?" he asked.

I sighed mournfully. "Only three. I barely remember

her. I grieved like a puppy, they say. For a whole month I cried and wailed and would not eat. But I have no recollection of that time. It was long ago. You have a mother, Ivor Andreivitch?''

He nodded. ''She was ninety-nine this year, Lord bless and preserve her. Brrh, it's damned cold out here. Only fools would stand outside when there is fire and food within.''

He picked up our things and carried them into the inn. As I swept past Seth Garrett I heard him say, ''Nice work, Gypsy. But you forget one thing: I'm paying him. If he had to choose between money and sentiment, he'd choose money every time.''

''I don't know what you're talking about,'' I said coldly. I had still not forgiven him for insulting me.

''Yes, you do,'' he said. He walked into the inn while I glared at his back. What a schemer. I thought. A girl can't even carry on a polite conversation without some people thinking she's playing tricks.

We sat together at small rough-hewn table near the fire. At one of the other three tables two men were slurping beet soup. Across from them three others drank vodka.

''You know, Ivor Andreivitch, my Grandfather the Count Nicholas Oulianov was in the army that fought Napoleon. Did you know him?''

''I never met him,'' Ivor confessed. ''But I have heard of his bravery.''

''Yes, and I am sure that is why I am so brave myself, because his blood flows in my veins,'' I declared. ''Russians are the strongest fighters in the world, everyone knows that. All the Gypsies say so.''

''Do they?'' Ivor seemed to forget that he didn't want to associate with Gypsies. ''You have travelled a lot, eh, little one?''

''To the sun and back again,'' I said cheerfully. ''Listen, Ivor Andreivitch, I'll tell your fortune if you like. For a good price, too.'' Seth Garrett laughed aloud. ''For free!'' I amended.

The men called for vodka and Ivor ordered milk for me. "I do not drink milk," I informed them. "Milk is for babies. Bring me strong tea with lots of sugar," I told the surly innkeeper. "And some black bread and caviar and good cheese. The rich kind, with cream in it!" The man hesitated and looked inquiringly at my companions. I lifted my chin and said grandly, "Do not ask their permission. I will pay for this myself!" I dug into one of the secret pockets in my skirts and brought out the ten-ruble gold piece that Seth Garrett had given me the night before. "Today I am rich, and a good Gypsy never hoards his gold!" I said. "I will pay for myself and for my friend, Ivor Andreivitch Krasskey, the brave Cossack hero!"

Seth watched me with ill-concealed amusement. I didn't care what he thought. I just needed to insure that if and when Seth Garrett actually abandoned me in a snowdrift, Ivor would come to my aid. Garrett may have had the money, but it was Ivor's troika.

Food came. I dove in, cheerfully stuffing my mouth with bread and cheese and washing it all down with tea, which I sucked noisily through a lump of sugar that I held in the pouch of my cheek. I did notice that both men looked slightly green as they watched me eat, but I supposed that was because they were amazed at the quantity of food that I could pack into my narrow body, I never dreamed they found my manners objectionable. Only after I left the table and curled up in front of the stove to sleep did they apply themselves to the food. Then Seth went to a private room at the back of the inn and Ivor to the stables where he could keep an eye on the horses.

Very early the next morning, before the sun had risen, the owner of the inn attacked me. He pulled me to my feet and started to choke me while he shouted, "Thieving little Gypsy! Thief! I should have known better than to let a Gypsy spend the night under my roof! God give me the strength to wring your thieving neck!"

"Let me go!" I wriggled in his grasp. "Let me go! I have done nothing." I looked around and saw Seth Garrett watching us from the doorway. He was wearing only his breeches and his shirt, and he looked rumpled and angry, as though he had been roused from a sound sleep. "Oh, please, Monsieur Seth," I gasped, "help me! This man is lying! I tell you I have done nothing!"

The innkeeper dragged me over to him and held me by the ear while he said, "Take this little thief out of my inn! I will kill her with my bare hands! I will wrench her lying head right off her dirty neck! Gypsies! Thieves! If you ever bring her in here again—"

"I wouldn't come into this hovel again!" I shouted. "See, I am scratching!" I moved my wiggling fingers all over my body, under my skirts, under my arms, into my hair. "Fleas!" I said. "This place is alive with fleas!"

"Liar! Liar!" The innkeeper hopped up and down. "If there are fleas here this filthy little wretch brought them! Take her away and get out of here! Both of you, get out!"

Seth gave me a dark stare and his mouth twitched, but not with laughter. "Take your things off," he said in a thick morning voice.

"What?" I gasped. "I will not!"

"Take everything off, right now, or I'll do it for you," he said.

"No!" I cried. "If you lay one finger on me your whole arm will fall off, and your legs and your eyes—!" I broke away from the innkeeper and tried to run away, but Seth dragged me back. Before I knew what was happening he was stripping off my scarves and my shawls. I kicked and bawled, "Stop! Stop! Let me go! I will do it myself, I swear it! Just take your hands off me!"

He released me and I jumped back. I gave him a sullen look and started to unbutton my blouse.

"Hurry up," he growled.

"I'm moving as fast as I can," I told him. I took off my blouse and one skirt, the bright orange one I wore on top. "There, you see?" I held my arms away from my skinny body. "Nothing! I am hiding nothing! I tell you I am innocent!"

"Your skirts. Off." His voice was hard and cold; I confess he made me feel a little nervous.

I gave a disgusted snort and peeled off another colorful layer, a skirt of violent purple and orange stripes. I kicked it into a corner. A green skirt followed, then a red one with turquoise dots, and finally a vivid pink skirt with yellow suns and moons and stars tumbling around the hem in a border two feet wide. Wearing only my bright blue shift and my red boots and my jewels, including my diamond bracelet, I stood shivering in the center of the room, glaring at Seth Garrett. He stepped over to the pile of clothing and began sorting through it.

"You will catch fleas, I tell you," I warned him quickly. "This dog house is alive with fleas!" I scratched vigorously to demonstrate.

By this time the innkeeper's wife appeared, rubbing her eyes sleepily, and a couple of the men who had been eating and drinking the night before. Seth Garrett pulled a whole cheese out of my pink skirt.

"Ah!" I gave an astonished cry and put my hands up to my cheeks. "How did that get there? This villain must have put it there while I slept! You *gorgio* devil!" I spat at the innkeeper. "No wonder Gypsies have a bad name!"

"Shut up," Seth growled. Further searching in my secret pockets produced a bottle of vodka and a small sausage. Successive skirts yielded another sausage, a shining butcher's knife, a round loaf of black bread as big as my head, and a whole plucked and trussed chicken.

The innkeeper's wife screamed hysterically. "Robbed! We've been robbed!"

Her husband shouted, "You see! What did I tell you! Filthy Gypsy tramps! Murderous thieves and liars, the whole damned lot of them!"

Just then the outside door opened and Ivor came in, stomping the snow off his boots. "What's going on here?" he asked. Seth Garrett arranged the loot on a table. He shook out my eiderdown and brought over my crystal, my icon, and my bridle.

"Your filthy little Gypsy is stealing everything I own!" the innkeeper told Ivor. "You get out of here! Out! All of you, get out!"

"He is lying, Ivor Andreivitch!" I said hotly. "He—"

Seth said loudly, "Well, is this everything or do I have to turn you upside down and shake you?"

"No!" I protested. "My crystal! My icon! Those things are mine! And—and I paid for the food!"

He said, "Get dressed. We're leaving in five minutes."

"This Gypsy paid for nothing!" the innkeeper bawled. "Did you ever hear of a Gypsy paying for anything?" he implored the onlookers, whose number had swollen to four.

"This man is a liar, I tell you!" I wailed. "You heard him, he hates Gypsies! Everybody hates Gypsies! Oh, oh, why was I so cursed? To be taken away from my family and the people I loved when I was so young and helpless! I am just a child, only twelve years of age! Oh, oh, it is terrible, terrible!"

Seth said to Ivor, "Tell this man to take back whatever belongs to him." Then he left the room. The whole scene had been bilingual, with the innkeeper shouting in Russian, Seth speaking French, and me yelling in both languages.

Ivor translated and the innkeeper squawked, "Take it back? You think I would take back anything that she has worn next to her body? Look at her!" Everyone in the room turned their hate-filled eyes on me. I scratched ostentatiously. "She is infested, louse-ridden! I don't want anything!"

Ivor persuaded him to accept five rubles for the stolen food and to keep his butcher's knife. Then with a final sorrowing glance at me, he went out to hitch up the horses.

The crowd dispersed and I stopped scratching. "*Gorgio* pigs," I muttered scornfully. I dressed in a flash and hurriedly restored my booty to my skirt pockets. When I picked up my cheese and my vodka I admired them for a moment and I kissed each one before I put it away.

"Fleas!" I laughed exultantly. "Ah ha! Stupid fools!"

Seth passed by me without a word and went out to the troika. When I got outside I saw that both he and Ivor were standing in the snow, waiting for me. Their expressions were grim.

"No more stealing," Seth said sharply. He slapped the gloved palm of his hand with the gold knob of his deadly cane. "One more incident like this—if you steal so much as a nail or a hairpin—I'll beat the stuffing out of you and leave you to the wolves."

I turned to my friend Ivor and said beseechingly, "Ivor, I am innocent!"

But his face was cold and his voice hard as he said, "No more stealing. Or I will personally break the fingers of both your hands."

I pushed my lips into a pout. "You *gorgio* don't know how to have any fun. But what can I do?" I threw up my hands. "You take the word of a low innkeeper over that of the granddaughter of Count Nicholas Oulianov! You are both peasants," I sniffed. I climbed into the troika and pulled the fur robes over my lap. The two men were still standing alongside the sled. "Well, what are you waiting for?" I demanded. "You think the road to Bryansk will grow shorter if we sit here all day?"

They sighed and exchanged weary looks, then took their places in the troika. When we had gone about three versts I stuck a garlicky sausage under Seth's nose.

"Here, *gorgio*," I said cheerfully. "Have some breakfast. You will see that Gypsies don't hold grudges."

He gave me a look that would have withered the leaves on a birch tree, then he moved as far away from me as the space in the troika would permit. He looked like he had smelled something really unpleasnt. I shrugged and munched away happily, leaving my companion to stew in his own silence. After a while the purloined goods in my pockets made my seat rather lumpy, and I moved everything into my eiderdown bundle while Seth Garrett watched.

That second day on the road was uneventful. I decided that anyone chasing us would be more likely to go west than south. They had heard that the murderous foreigner was going to Paris, but how could they know that the murderous Gypsy at this side had persuaded him to make a detour to Bryansk?

When we reached an inn where we could spend the night, Seth called for a private room and a hot bath.

"Ah, these *gorgio*" I said to Ivor, shaking my head. "They think if they don't take a bath every three days their skin will rot off." And I laughed at the foreigner's passion for cleanliness.

I helped Ivor to groom and feed the horses and to settle them down for the night, and we went inside together.

"Your master wants you to help him with his boots," the buxom proprietress told me in a sour voice.

"He's no master of mine!" I informed her tartly. But I followed the direction of her cocked thumb to Seth's room. It wouldn't hurt to be nice to him, I decided. And I had seen that his leg was giving him trouble.

I rapped at his door and pushed it open. The first thing I saw was the steaming tub sitting in the middle of the floor. Seth was sitting on a low stool in front of the fireplace. He was fully dressed. I squatted in front of him and pulled off his right boot, and then, very gently, his left.

"Thank you, Rhawnie," he said.

I should have known from his politeness and his use of my name that he was up to something. But I was stupid and unsuspecting and I said, "It's all right. I don't mind doing favors for you."

I got up to leave. He moved up behind me and put one arm around my waist. He slid his other arm under my thighs and lifted me off the floor. The speed of his actions left me no time to struggle, or even to cry out. And the next thing I knew I was floundering on my back in the tub, kicking my feet in the air. He pulled my red boots off my feet and tossed them aside.

"Villain!" I gasped and bubbled. "Traitorous cur! My

51

clothes! My clothes! My jewels! How dare you!''

I scrambled around and tried to climb out of the tub. He put a heavy hand on my shoulder and shoved me down, then he tossed a bar of soap into the water.

"Do you know what this is?" he barked. "Use it. On your body and on your clothes."

"Why do you hate me?" I cried. "What have I done to offend you?"

"We won't go into that," he said curtly. "At the moment, it's not what you've done but how you smell. In a word, Gypsy, you stink. I will not spend one more day with you in that troika unless you clean yourself up. You are to wash your hair, your face, your ears, your hands and feet, and every place in between. Take off your clothes and get started."

"I won't!" I splashed angrily. "You have no right to do this to me! How can I bathe with you standing over me like that? A man! It is not proper, I tell you! I will do nothing until you go away."

He crossed his arms. "You will do nothing if I go away."

"I will!" I looked down. The red of my paisley blouse was starting to bleed into the water. "Oh, oh, everything is melting!" I cried despairingly. "Please, please go away so that I can take these things off! I beg you, Monsieur. I would be ashamed—I will do as you say, I swear it."

He made a wry face and turned his back. I hurriedly pulled off all of my clothes and dropped them over the side of the tub. I cocked an eye at my tormenter. He was sitting on the stool in front of the fire, smoking a cigar. I sank under the water until just my head was exposed. The heat started to work into my chilled limbs, making me realize how cold I had gotten riding in that open sled. I felt warm, really warm for the first time in months. What a wonderful feeling!

I found the soap on the bottom of the tub. I played with it, squeezing it in my hands so that it popped up in the air and came down again in the water with a satisfying splash. On the third squeeze it came down on the edge of the tub, bounced onto the floor, and skittered across the room.

Seth Garrett retrieved it and stood over me. A deep frown creased his forehead. I felt a prickle of nervousness. "I was playing," I said weakly. My trepidation mounted as I saw him take off his coat and waistcoat and roll up his sleeves. "Oh, oh, please, Monsieur," I grasped, "I will wash! I will—"

He ducked my head under water. When I came up, choking and coughing and gasping for air, he applied the soap to my hair. He rubbed and scrubbed and I howled with rage, but what could I do? He unlaced my wet braids and washed and washed until my brains hurt. I thought I had never seen an uglier sight than that monster bending over me, a wet cigar clenched between his teeth. He worked on me like a man possessed, caring nothing for my cries and pleas and tears. He dunked me to rinse my head, then he pulled me up by the elbow and stood me on my feet. And he started to soap my entire body.

I had never known such deep shame, such humiliation. I fought him like a demon, but he pushed me under the water again and held me until my lungs were bursting. He dragged me up again, more dead than alive, and said, "I don't like this any better than you do. For God's sake, stop your squalling. You didn't even bawl like this when your uncle was raping you."

That remark left me speechless because it was true. I covered my face with my hands while his soapy paws moved over me—not too roughly, it was true. What difference did this make, when I had been dishonored already? When I returned to the Gypsies and married Django, I would not be a virgin, sweet and pure. Perhaps he wouldn't want me at all.

I would have to tell my father, who would put the case before Lyubov, and together they would take it up with Django's parents, who would be well within their rights if they called off the marriage. And supposing, when they saw this man Seth and learned that I had been travelling with him, they thought—. But no, not even they would believe that I would willingly lie with a *gorgio*.

"It wasn't my fault," I whimpered. "I swear to you, it wasn't my fault! And I avenged his crime!"

I was really saying the words that I would use with Django, but Seth Garrett said, "I know it wasn't your fault. Nobody's blaming you. He got no more than he deserved. Rinse off now." He pushed me down in the water again and walked away from the tub.

"Django will not want me now," I said sadly. "I am not pure."

"Who's Django?" He brought over a heavy wool robe. "Stand up."

I was too unhappy and dejected to care anymore if he saw me, and I stood. He wrapped the robe around me and lifted me out of the tub and carried me to the fire.

"Django is my betrothed," I told him. "We were to have been married last fall."

"Married? You're only a child." He set me down and before he let me go he sniffed my hair. "Now that's the way a girl should smell. Dry yourself off. I'll send your supper in here. The landlady will hang your things behind the big stove to dry. They should be all right by morning."

He left me alone. I wriggled around inside the robe, pushing my arms through the sleeves, tying the belt around my middle. There was a lot of robe and not too much of me, and it nearly went around me twice. It smelled good, like the man himself. I remembered that I wanted to be angry with him, and I tried half-heartedly to work up a good rage, but too many other things were spinning around inside my head, distracting me. I remembered how his arms had felt around me. I blushed and wrinkled my nose. He had been rough, but he had not been brutal and vicious like my uncle. I began to perceive that all men were not the same, and that a woman may hate it when one man puts his hands on her, and not mind so much when another does it.

A woman. That's what I was now, even though I didn't look much like a woman yet. And for the first time I understood that growing up brings its own special problems and concerns, things that children aren't even aware of—like love and dishonor and coming together with a man in the darkness. But there was so much I didn't know yet, so much I had to learn. I thought about what my uncle had done to me, and I thought about the stranger. And I felt a little afraid.

As the days passed Seth's moods grew worse. I guessed that long hours of riding in the troika in the cold were hard on his leg. His limp was more pronounced, and if anyone so much as bumped his bad knee, he let loose with a string of curses in Russian that would have done credit to a whole platoon of Cossacks. On the fifth night of our journey we stayed in the little town of Pinsk. The posting station there had no private rooms, and Seth Garrett had to sleep on the floor like everyone else.

As I settled myself down for sleep I looked over and saw him sitting on a crude log bench, rubbing his left leg. I debated, should I help him or should I let him suffer? My pride was still smarting from that bath business. But I would show him that Gypsies were good-hearted people who could rise above petty disagreements.

I went over to him and crouched in front of him. "Let me help you," I said. As usual his right boot came off without difficulty, but when I touched his left leg he sucked in his breath. "Hurts bad tonight, eh?" I said. "Do not worry. I will help you. I know how to fix the pain." I eased the boot off and removed his sock as well. I pushed the leg of his breeches as high as it would go over his knee.

"What do you think you're doing?" he demanded angrily. He jerked his breeches down but a stab of pain in his leg made him stop and bite his lip.

"No, no," I said soothingly. I pushed his hands away and uncovered his knee again. "I will not hurt you. I want to see, that is all. Ah, it is as I thought." A jagged purple scar started midway up his thigh, zigged over his kneecap, and ran down the outside of his leg. "This," I said, reaching up to touch his cheek, "is from the sword. But this," I traced the scar on his leg very lightly, "is from a horse."

He jumped when I touched him. "How did you know that?" he asked through clenched teeth.

I shrugged. "Simple. Django has one like it. He limps, too. He was in a race once with a *gorgio* peasant boy. Django won, of course. The peasant was very angry because his friends had lost a lot of money on the race and he was humiliated. When the race was over, Django led his horse around the field to calm him. He was walking, you see. Then suddenly the peasant's horse reared up. And the peasant boy rode towards Django and trapped him against a board fence. He said later that it wasn't his fault, that the wind had blown a Gypsy girl's skirts and spooked his horse, but everyone knew it was a lie. Anyway, Django couldn't get away. The horse knocked him down, and reared up and came down on him again. Not on his head, thank God! But his leg was broken and very bloody, torn in lots of places. He fainted. The pain must have been very great to make him do that, because Django is a brave boy. But he did not cry out, not even once. I was very proud of him."

Seth was silent during this recital. I sensed that he was thinking about his own accident, and how he became lame. After a minute I stood up and searched through my eiderdown. I found what I was looking for, a small brown pottery jar not much bigger than my closed fist. I carried it back and crouched down once more.

"I held his hand and gave him strength while the doctor was fixing his leg," I went on. "But his mother came after a while and made me leave him. She does not like me very much. She says I am bewitched because I like to sing in the rain and dance under the moon. What's wrong with that? But we will learn to live together after Django and I are married. If we marry."

I uncorked the jar and held it under his nose. He started.

"Not bad, eh?" I said with satisfaction. "I made it

56

myself, at the Grandfather's. I threw in some perfume that belonged to Olga Ivanovna, my uncle's wife."

"What is it?" Seth asked doubtfully.

"Some beeswax, some lard. A few herbs and other things. It is not important. You trust me? I will try not to hurt you." I dipped my fingertips into the jar and applied a little ointment to the scar tissue. "Your leg did not break, is that right?" I looked up at him. He gave an infinitesimal nod. "So. The muscles and the flesh were cut apart, and where they have healed they are stiff and hard. And when they are tired and cold, they do not bend easily. And that makes you as cross as a black Russian bear." I rubbed the ointment into his skin, using the gentlest pressure.

"I am not cross," the bear growled.

"No? Then why do you act like a snarling dog all the time? Because you are cold? No, for you have rich furs to keep you warm. And you have plenty of food and drink to fill your belly. Or maybe you are cross because you do not like me and you cannot wait to be rid of me." I looked up slyly while I worked. "You think I cannot tell? You have called me dirty Gypsy and even though I have had a bath you do not like me to be close to you. I think you would rather eat in the stable with the horses than sit at the table with me. I am no fool. You are a *gorgio* and I am Gypsy. We can never understand each other's ways. So?" I shrugged and tossed my braids. "We are together now. And I can see that you have pain. The pain makes you angry. I understand. And even though I do not like you and you do not like me, I know that I can help you. And because I am Gypsy and have a good heart, I will do this for you."

"You talk too much," he said in his rumbling voice.

I grinned at him and spread more ointment on his wound. I rubbed and rubbed, covering an increasingly wider area. I could see that his pain was subsiding. I could feel his relaxing, and the white, pinched look on his face disappeared. I continued to massage and knead the bunched muscles, occasionally rubbing in some more ointment to lubricate and to soothe.

I looked up. "Feels better?"

He nodded grudgingly. "Did you do this for Django?"

"Oh, no! That would be most improper and dangerous. His mother would not allow it."

"And you don't consider me dangerous?" A smile lurked behind his eyes.

I felt a quick blush come to my cheeks and my hands faltered in their rhythm. "You?" I said incredulously. "Bah. You are only a *gorgio*, and an ugly one at that. Besides, I would do as much for any animal."

"Is this what they call Gypsy magic?" he asked facetiously.

"No magic," I said. "You will see." I sat back on my heels and corked the jar. "Now try to walk," I commanded him. "The pain will be gone."

He stood up and put all his weight on his left leg. An amazed look came over his face. He walked gingerly across the floor. His limp was barely noticeable.

He came back to me and flexed his knee. "Incredible," he said, shaking his head. "I would never have believed it. Remarkable. Thank you, Rhawnie." He reached into his waistcoat pocket for a coin.

"No," I said firmly, standing up and shaking out my skirts. "I said that I would pay you, did I not? But I have no money left and you will not let me beg or steal or tell fortunes. So you must let me do this for you. When I leave you at Bryansk, I will give you the rest of the ointment in this jar as a gift." I slid the jar into my pocket. "And I will teach you to do this magic for yourself. But you must do it every night without fail. The muscles in your leg will never be perfect again, but if you keep them soft and loose they will not hurt you. A good bargain? You agree?"

"Good. Fair payment." He gave me a strange look that made the blood rush to my face again. "Good-night, Rhawnie."

58

"Good-night," I whispered.

I went back to my quilt and wrapped myself up. The room was cold but I felt hot all over. I tried to sleep but I could not. I was aware of him, wrapped up in his furs on the other side of the room, breathing deeply. What was the matter with me?

3

Gypsy No More

THE NEXT NIGHT we arrived in the town of Klimjukovici. The inn was already packed to the rafters because the local wheat festival had begun the day before. Seth Garrett bribed the old, half-blind innkeeper, however, and the old man gave up his own room and said that he and his pretty young wife would sleep in the loft.

After supper I spread my eiderdown out behind the stove in the main room. A couple of other fat peasants were already snoring a few feet away from me. No sooner had I fallen asleep than I felt a nudge. I opened my eyes to see a bearded merchant in a long kaftan standing over me. He poked me with his toe again.

"Hello, Gypsy," he grinned. "Want some company in there?"

He sat heavily on the floor beside me and put his hands on my chest. His breath reeked of cheap vodka. I cursed him soundly but he was too drunk to hear. I scrambled up and gave him a stiff kick in the stomach, and he gave a loud snore and fell into a drunken sleep.

I managed to yank my eiderdown out from under him and I went to look for another place to sleep. But a few more guests had arrived and all the good places around the warm stove were taken. I decided that I would creep into Seth's room. I could roll out my eiderdown in front of his fire without disturbing him.

The room was just on the other side of the kitchen. The door had no lock and I pushed it open noiselessly. I stopped, startled, and clutched my eiderdown to my chest. My mouth dropped open.

A single candle flickered on the floor beside the low bed. Seth Garrett was not alone. A woman—the landord's plump, dark haired young wife—knelt on the edge of the bed, her face buried in the sheets and her knees tucked up under her body. She was fully dressed, but her skirts were thrown up over her back and her naked buttocks rose out of the garments like twin moons.

Garrett was stark naked. The orange glow from the small fire in the grate shone on his broad back and on his muscular thighs and arms and tight buttocks. He stood on the floor directly behind the woman, grasping her hips in his powerful hands. He was thrusting, pounding at her. And he was breathing hard.

The woman made whimpering noises and I wondered if she was in pain. But every so often she would giggle softly like an idiot girl I had once seen in a marketplace. As I watched, unable to tear my eyes away, Seth gave a final, convulsive jerk. The woman sighed ecstatically and stretched forward on the bed, and the man collapsed on top of her.

I backed swiftly out of the room and closed the door. Neither of them had seen me, I was sure. I thought that if the floor had opened up and the Devil himself had come into the room, they wouldn't have noticed him. I sat down on the kitchen floor and wrapped the quilt around my shoulders. My heart was pounding so strongly that I could feel the vibrations in every part of my body, even in the soles of my feet. I felt nauseous, I felt frightened, I felt excited and repulsed and angry.

I thought it was disgusting. I could still hear the echoes of pounding and breathing and whimpering in my ears, and the sounds brought back vivid recollections of that horrible night when my uncle—and yet there the resemblance between that occasion and the frantic scene I had just witnessed ended. I had hated it, every ugly moment. And yet the innkeeper's wife seemed to enjoy it. Seth Garrett was certainly every bit as brutal and violent as Alexei had been, and yet this woman had laughed and made sounds of pain that were really sounds of pleasure. I tried to remember if I had ever felt a sensation that was so pleasurable that it made me want to whimper, like a baby at the breast. I couldn't think of one. Yes, she certainly seemed to enjoy what was happening to her. And Seth was a stranger to her. Not even a relative, like an uncle or a husband. But a stranger! It really was disgusting.

I had never seen a man naked before. Gypsies are very modest and they guard their privacy closely: only little children are permitted to run around without any clothes on. I shivered as I remembered his massive muscles bunching and twisting and—

I closed my eyes and told myself sternly that I must sleep. But I felt confused and frustrated, and annoyed because there was still so much I did not know about life. Would I like it when Django and I came together in the dark? We had hardly ever touched. Our marriage had been arranged when we were small, still babies. I wondered if he would be gentle, not like that animal, Seth Garrett. I tried to picture Django in my mind: dark and slender and so quiet. Oh, Django. But the image of Seth Garrett as I had seen him just a few minutes ago kept crowding out all other thoughts. That man was as broad as a bull, as strong as a stallion, and possessed by a devil. I was thankful that I would be rid of him soon.

We reached Bryansk on the evening of the seventh day of travel, as Ivor Andreivitch had predicted in Moscow. We rode out of town to the field where the Gypsies had been camped in the springtime. The field was empty and the smooth snow was marred only by tracks of deer and wolves.

"Well?" Seth said. "Where are they?"

I shrugged. "They have gone. Moved to a new place. It was the springtime when I saw them last, and now it is winter. They would not stay in one place for such a long time. They are Gypsies, remember?"

"You're sure this is the right field?" Ivor asked.

"Of course I am sure! I remember that birch grove very well. And that stream over there is where the horses drank. Only farther down, past those trees. We used the part up here for drinking and—"

"Ivor," Seth growled, "take us back to town. To Bryansk."

"What are you going to do with her?" Ivor asked.

"Leave her there. This is as far as we can take her."

"But—" Ivor started to protest.

"No." I threw off my lap robes and climbed down from the troika. "He is right, Ivor Andreivitch. I said as far as Bryansk and here we are. You do not have to take me further. I can find the signs they always leave along the road and I will follow them myself. Do not worry about me."

"Don't be a little fool," Ivor said gruffly. "You will freeze the first night, if wolves don't get you first. Can't you see those tracks?"

"Any wolf would crack his teeth on her," Seth remarked.

Ivor ignored him. "Where are these Gypsies of yours? How far?"

I lifted my shoulders. "How should I know? April is a long time ago. They might be in Paris now!" I gave Seth a sly look. "But I can find them. I will travel no further with this man. He hates me. Everyone hates the Gypsies! He is in a hurry, like all *gorgio* who think if they hurry they can find happiness before it runs away. And you, Ivor Andreivitch, you are interested only in the gold he will pay you when you get to Brest. Good-bye, Ivor Andreivitch. Good-bye, Monsieur Seth. Do not forget to use the ointment, the way I told you. Every night without fail." I lifted my chin and said solemnly and courteously, "May God go with you. Both of you." Then I turned and trudged away through the deep snow, towards the road that led away from Bryansk. Darkness was beginning to fall. Somewhere an owl hooted. A wolf howled mournfully. He was hungry and he wanted his dinner. Me.

After a few minutes—the time it took for them to agree that they couldn't abandon me—I heard the scrape of sled runners on the snow. The troika pulled up alongside me and I jumped in.

"Ah, my friends!" I greeted them joyously.

"Shut up," Seth growled.

"Do not worry," I said cheerfully. "They have left signs for me to follow and their caravans will not be hard to find. And then, Monsieur Seth, you can go west, to Paris!"

Another week's journeying through heavy snows and deep cold brought us to Novgorod Severskij, about eighty-four versts north of Kiev. We had little difficulty following the Gypsies' trail. Every so often I would spot a strip of brightly-colored cloth tied to a tree limb, at eye-level to one who would be driving a caravan. Gypsies always mark a trail so that other Gypsies may follow them. Sometimes I saw branches twisted in a certain unnatural fashion, or a loose fence rail pointing the way. And we stopped frequently to inquire of villagers and farmers when the Gypsies had passed their way. The tribe had been delayed for almost six weeks in one good-sized town because of some trouble with the police. I rejoiced, because I knew that such a long delay meant that they were not so far away.

At Novgorod Severskij the trail grew warmer. The Gypsies had camped outside of the town only three weeks earlier. And because they were travelling at a much slower pace than our troika and taking longer rests, we would almost certainly find them before another week had passed. My excitement mounted. When we arrived in Kiev we learned that my Gypsies had passed through the city only three days ago.

"You see, you see!" I exclaimed, bouncing in my seat. "It will not be long until I see them all again."

We stopped at an inn in the tiny village of Obuchov near the Desna River, knowing that the next day we would find the Gypsies. I could not eat that night, and long after I should have been asleep I sat staring into the flames of the big fireplace, watching and waiting for something, I knew not what. After a while I couldn't bear it anymore. I took out my crystal ball and held it in front of my eyes. I stared into its depths, feeling guilty because I knew I shouldn't do this for myself, only for a paying *gorgio* customer. But I had to know that they were all right, my Gypsies. I wanted to see them, if only briefly.

And then I had the vision. Horrible. I screamed and threw my crystal down. The men who had been playing cards in another corner of the room gathered around, and Seth crouched down next to me.

"What's the matter?" he asked. "What happened?"

"The crystal," I said hoarsely. "The crystal. I was looking—I wanted to see them. I felt I could not wait. And I saw horses and fire! I heard children crying! And I saw blood, blood everywhere!"

"You dreamed it," he said tersely. "Now put this thing away and go to sleep."

"Bad, bad omen," I said in a terrified whisper. "This is the second time! The first time—you were there! I saw blood, and that very night my uncle died! Now I looked into the depths of the crystal and there was fire!"

"Of course there was fire," he said impatiently. He picked up the heavy glass ball. "What do you expect to see if you look at glowing embers through glass? Look!"

"No, no," I moaned and sank down on the floor, covering my head with my arms, "I cannot look. I shall never use it again, ever. It is cursed! Oh, oh, what is happening! I am dying inside, I can feel it! Fire and blood! I have seen the fire and the blood!"

In the morning we drove the remaining ten versts to the Gypsy camp. I felt sick and terrified, and I was so still and quiet that Ivor asked solicitously if I was ill. I shook my head. I could not speak. The day was grey and low-hanging clouds promised more snow.

We followed a narrow path along the Desna. The snow on the path was well-trodden and recently disturbed.

"Many horses have ridden this way," Ivor yelled back to us over the the din of the harness brass and horses. "Maybe your Gypsies were having a race, eh?"

A shudder passed through me. I said nothing.

The river bent around a rocky cliff. The villagers had told us that the Gypsy camp was on the other side, and that the quickest way to reach it was to fork off from the river road and to drive straight up the lower side of the cliff and down again into the bowl. Ivor stopped the troika at the place where the paths diverged and stepped down from the driver's seat. He motioned with his head for Seth to follow him. They moved off a few paces and stood talking.

I followed quietly and heard Ivor say, "We are only a hundred yards away from a Gypsy camp and there isn't a sound. Mother of God." And he crossed himself. "We must not let her see—"

But I was away, up the path and over the rise. He shouted after me. They knew what they would find. The wind carried to all our nostrils the acrid, sickening smell of charred wood and flesh. Only I had to see for myself. I had to see the fire and the blood.

The camp had been decimated, the inhabitants destroyed. I went down the slope. It had been a good campsite, I noted. Near water, sheltered from the prevailing winds by the cliff on the north and by tall pines on the south and west. When the attackers had ridden in, the Gypsies had been trapped. The camp now looked like a black, running sore on the white landscape.

I picked my way through the smoldering rubble. My eyes streamed from smoke and sorrow. I saw a small bare foot sticking out from under a blackened wagon tongue. I pushed the timber aside and found the body of my little stepbrother, Sasha. Waves of dizziness broke over me I clutched my middle and wretched horribly.

I heard disconnected voices in the background. Meaningless words, empty of feeling:

"What happened?"

"Soldier." It was a quavering old woman's voice. I had noticed a few peasants poking around like scavengers. "Cossacks."

"Why?"

"They said the Gypsies had stolen their horses and tried to sell them back after they painted them! Foolish cheats, the Gypsies. They deserved to die!"

"Silence!"

"They ought to be buried."

"Go to the village and round up the head man and as many strong men with shovels as you can find. They'll be paid."

Bodies were scattered all around. The Cossacks had rounded up all the Gypsies in the middle of the camp and shot into the mob until not one was left standing. Then they had fired the wagons. The horses were all gone. I looked into their faces. I knew them all, every one. Father. Lyubov. Django.

I held him in my arms. His black eyes were open to the sky but they could not see anything. In the several months since I had seen him last a mustache had started to sprout on his upper lip. He would have been very proud of that, because it meant that he would soon be a man. The other men and boys would have made gentle fun of him. I wondered if he had thought of me at all, and if he remembered my promise to return.

A mangy-looking yellow dog came into the middle of the camp from the trees and sniffed at one of the corpses. A shot rang out and the animal gave a convulsive movement and fell, dead. I saw Seth Garrett put away a gun. I stared at him and through him. He came over to me.

"Leave him," he said. "Come away."

I remembered the body in my arms. "It is Django," I whispered. "He is dead. Django."

"I know. Come on. The villagers are coming to bury them."

"He will never know that I came back, that I fulfilled my vow," I said.

He prised my arms loose and lifted me to my feet. I felt as though I had no bones in my body, that I was composed of sorrow and jelly. He led me to a high part of the cliff. I saw the villagers coming, riding in Ivor's troika and in their own carts.

"You don't need to watch," Seth said as the men started to hack out a large pit at the edge of the forest. The ground was hard and the task took most of the day. I did watch, though. I watched as they dragged the bodies over and pushed them into the pit. I watched as old women picked through the smoking ruins. And as a black-robed *gorgio* priest and his acolytes waved censors over the huge grave. Incense mingled with the other inhuman smells around the camp.

When the villagers were about to cover the bodies with clods of earth I stepped forward.

"Wait!"

They stared at me. The priest, who had started to walk away, turned around again and peered at me over his long beard.

I walked to the edge and spoke in a firm, clear voice. "You have left me to go to the Nation of the Dead. You have gone without obtaining forgiveness of the ones you have injured, and without forgiving those who have injured you. In the name of all the Gypsies, I, Rhawnie, forgive you. Gregor, my father. Lyubov, our leader. My brothers, Sasha and Vanya and Alyosha." I named every one of them. And finally, "Django, who was my betrothed. I forgive you all, and I ask you to forgive me." I searched in my hidden pockets for some coins and threw them over the bodies. Then I slipped off my bracelets, including the diamond bracelet that I had stolen from my uncle's box, and I threw them into the pit as well.

Everyone was silent, watching. I took a long breath.

71

"May the curse of God be upon those who did this thing!"

My voice rang out over the charred campsite and echoed back from the face of the cliff. The villagers crossed themselves, and Ivor Andreivitch did the same.

"I know that you were brave in the face of death," I said. Tears streamed down my cheeks as I bid them a final farewell. "I only hope—that I can be as brave when the time comes." I wiped my face hastily. "And now I leave you to God."

I turned away from the grave and the still-smoking wagons and walked up the rise, back to the troika. The horses looked sad and I told them what had happened, even though they already knew. They always know. Their velvety noses were soft and warm. The wind flapped my colorful skirts. They seemed incongruously bright against the bleak landscape, like a parrot in Hell. Then I heard Seth Garrett's footsteps on the hard-packed snow. His limp was worse today, I could tell.

"Before I left," I said without looking around, "the old woman Ursula told my fortune. I did not believe her then, but everything she said has come true. I only tell you because our fortunes are linked, yours and mine. She said that I would find the Gypsies, but that I would not see them. I did not understand her then, but she was right, wasn't she?"

He said nothing.

"And the last thing she said was that I, Rhawnie, who had been born Gypsy, would be Gypsy no more. She was right about that, too. A Gypsy without a tribe is like a piece of a wrecked ship floating in the sea. It is nothing. She was right. I am Gypsy no more."

Seth Garrett said, "I'll take you as far as Odessa." Odessa was the big port city on the Black Sea.

I made no reply. I felt disoriented and bereft. I didn't care where I went or what happened to me. Russia had never been my home. Only the Gypsy caravans had been my home, and they were gone forever.

I went into mourning. For three days I did not eat or sleep. At night when we stopped I would sit in front of the fire or near the stove at our inn and rock back and forth, sighing and keening. Dogs howled and the peasants regarded me with hostile suspicion. I spoke to no one. I did not comb my hair or bathe my face and hands.

"How long is this going to go on?" I heard Seth ask Ivor.

"I do not know," Ivor said. "She told me once that the nearest relatives of a dead person starve themselves for three days after a death. Perhaps she is mourning for a longer time—so many deaths, you know."

But I collapsed after three days, totally exhausted and empty of grief. I slept for a day and a night. When I awoke I astonished Seth by demanding bath water and privacy. That night I sat wrapped in my quilt in front of the fire, struggling to pull a comb through my long hair as it dried, while my clothes dripped on an improvised clothesline. The next day at our evening meal I picked up a fork and used it clumsily. Seth and Ivor stared at me, then laughed heartily.

I was furious with them and with myself. Using a fork was harder than it looked. But I persevered.

"I am not Gypsy now," I announced. "And if I am not Gypsy, I must be *gorgio*. So I must learn your ways."

"Why don't you find another tribe of Gypsies?" Ivor asked me. "They would take you in, wouldn't they?"

I shook my head. "I would not wish them to. I am cursed, or I would have died with the rest. I would only bring them bad luck, I know it."

"Very shrewd," Seth remarked. "You're thinking just like a *gorgio* now."

"You are laughing at me because you think I cannot learn!"

"I think you don't want to learn." He sat back against the wall and lit a cigar. "I think this is all part of a little

Gypsy scheme. You're trying to persuade me to take you to Paris.''

"Ah!" I looked hurt and reproachful. "How can you think such a thing, Monsieur Seth? I know that you did not wish to bring me even this far, and I know that I owe the burial of my people to you. I have much to thank you for. But I know also that you do not wish to take me to Paris. I would not ask it of you. You are taking me to Odessa, no? I am grateful for that, believe me.''

"And what will you do in Odessa, child?" Ivor asked worriedly. "Do you know people there?''

"No," I said, shaking my head. "I do not know anyone else in the world now, except for you two gentlemen.''

"Why don't you take her back to Moscow, Ivor?" Seth suggested. "I'm sure her aunt and her cousins will be glad to see her.''

I glared at him. . . .

Odessa was a filthy, teeming port city. The narrow streets were clogged with beggars, prostitutes, roving sailors and merchants, thieves and pickpockets. Seth and I climbed out of the troika and bid farewell to Ivor. He drove off, waving, and Seth turned to me.

"I'll say good-bye to you, too. I can't say it's been a pleasure, but it's been interesting." He dug in his waistcoat and tossed me a coin. "So long, Gypsy.''

"Don't call me that!" I snatched the coin deftly out of the air. "I am *gorgio* now, just like you!''

We faced each other. He ran his eyes over my particolored skirts and scarves, my fringed shawls and red boots and gaily printed blouse. And then he threw back his head and laughed loud and long. The blood rushed to my cheeks and I clenched my fists.

"You dirty *gorgio* dog," I said, "you dare to laugh at me? You think that being a *gorgio* like you is so hard to do, eh?''

"Anyone can be a *gorgio*," he said. "The world is full of *gorgio*. But being civilized and educated is something else again. And you, my little friend, couldn't learn to be civilized in a hundred years. For the rest of your life you'll be nothing but a dirty little Gypsy. I don't care what you call yourself.''

"You are a liar," I said, narrowing my eyes dangerously. "May the sun fall out of the sky and burn you to a cinder!"

He picked up his bag and walked away, still laughing to himself. I followed at a distance. He thought he could get rid of me so easily, did he? The fool. I had told him what old Ursula had said, and he didn't believe. But he would see that she had spoken the truth. He went into an inn for some food and vodka. I was waiting for him when he came out. He ignored me and walked along briskly. My boots made tapping noises on the cobbled street as I trotted along, trying to keep up with him.

"What is the most civilized city in the world?" I asked as we moved along. "It is Paris, is it not? If I wanted to learn to be a real *gorgio*, to be civilized, that is where I should go, no?"

"No," he said.

"If you took me there I would repay you," I said. "I have no one to care for me now. You cannot leave me in this evil place! I will be dead before the dawn comes, I know it!"

"Good." He strode swiftly down a narrow alley. He limped only slightly. I regretted giving him the ointment. The man had no warmth, no gratitude.

"I think I should go to Paris, Monsieur Seth," I panted. "I think you should take me."

He went into a low building near the waterfront. I asked someone what the place was, and they told me a steamship office. I sidled in and crept up behind him.

"—leaves tonight with the tide," the man behind the counter was saying. "Should arrive in Marseilles in two months, weather permitting."

Seth turned around swiftly, almost knocking me down.

"Did you buy a place for me, too?" I asked eagerly. "I will thank you all my days!" I attempted to kiss his hands but he shook me off violently and walked out of the office. I ran after him. "Do not leave me here, Monsieur Seth!" I bawled loudly. I caught up to him and grabbed his arm. He tried to shake me off but I hung on tenaciously. A crowd started to gather. "You cannot do this to me!" I shouted. "Oh, oh," I looked at the people who were watching us, "this man is my husband and now he says he is leaving me! I am only a child, only fourteen, and I am with child! He gave me no money, nothing, and now he is leaving! I should have known better than to believe a Frenchman's lies. Oh, oh, was ever a girl so unfortunate as I?"

Seth managed to escape before the crowd caught on to what I was saying. I let him go. I knew he was probably going to the ship, and that they would never let me board without a special ticket. But what could I do? I suddenly wanted to be on that ship more than anything else in the world. But I didn't have nearly enough money. I looked at the coin he had thrown me: ten rubles. I hurried back to the steamship office.

"What do you want, Gypsy?" the man at the counter growled. "Get out of here. No beggars allowed."

"I want to get on that ship. The one that's going to France tonight. How much?"

"The cheapest cabins are thirty rubles. A place in steerage is twenty-two."

"No bunk, no bed," I said impatiently. "I will sleep under the stars, in a small corner. How much?"

"Twenty rubles," he said coldly.

"You are a thief and a bandit," I informed him. "To charge a poor orphan child twenty rubles for a few feet of space, without even a blanket! Bah. I would rather walk to Paris. How about ten?"

"Fifteen," the man said. "No lower."

"Ten," I said stubbornly. "I still have to buy food for myself, enough for two months! I will give you ten rubles right now. In cash."

We bartered back and forth and settled on thirteen rubles. That meant I still needed three, plus extra for food. I told him I would return in one hour with his thirteen rubles, and that if he sold my place to someone else I would cut his heart out with the dagger I carried under my skirts. He looked impressed and a little scared, as though he believed that I carried a weapon on my person.

I went back to the wharf and looked up at the ship. My ship. I saw Seth standing at the rail and I waved cheerfully. He managed a weak grin. The fool really thought that he would leave me behind as soon as the tide turned. I would show him.

I chose a place within earshot of the ship. A good location, sheltered from the chill winds yet right at the heart of a busy intersection. People ran to and fro, back and forth. I sat in a doorway and arranged myself: I twisted one leg around so that it would look lame, and I rubbed my hands on the ground and then wiped them on my face. I was ready. But no, the red boots were too shiny, too rich-looking. I took them off and hid them in my quilt. Then I saw a really filthy rag lying in the gutter not two feet away. I retrieved it and bound it around my crippled foot.

"Please, please, give me a few kopecks, sir. Please, madame, a few kopecks. I have had nothing to eat in days. Help me, help me."

The response was good. but not good enough. I made fifteen kopecks in ten minutes, but at one hundred kopecks to a ruble—and I needed three more rubles—I had a long way to go.

Quickly and expertly I shaped my eiderdown bundle into a baby-sized lump. A real baby would have been better, but if this one looked still and dead that would be all right, too. I took up my plaintive crying again, and immediately I noticed a difference. A crippled girl is a pitiful sight, but a crippled girl with a starving baby at her breast, one that is too weak even to cry, that is something really pathetic. I hid the kopecks as soon as they fell on my skirts. It's not a good idea to look too prosperous when you're playing the begging game. And as each coin dropped I tallied it up in my mind: sixty kopecks, eighty, one hundred! Only two rubles to go. Ah, a man with a bad conscience—only one ruble to go!

Then a shadow fell across my doorway. I looked up, into Seth's cool blue eyes. There was no laughter there, only fury.

"Please, sir," I said feebly, extending a filthy, shaking hand. "Just a few kopecks, to help a poor cripple. I have not eaten for such a long time. Please, sir. please help me."

Even as he stood there watching me, a passing sailor tossed me a coin. I snatched it quickly, secreted it on my person, and continued my refrain.

"Business is good, eh, Gypsy?" he asked dryly. "You wouldn't be saving up for a trip to Paris, would you?"

"Go away," I hissed. "I'm crippled."

"I know you're not a cripple," he said loudly. "And I also know that you packed away an enormous meal just this morning."

"Go away! Go away!"

"In fact," he went on in a barbarous mixture of French and Russian that the gathering crowd could barely understand, "you are a thief and a fraud! Thief, thief!" he shouted, pointing at me. "This girl stole my purse! Thief! Help, police!"

I was on my feet. "Are you crazy?" I said. "What are you trying to do to me, get me arrested? Stop that!"

The crowd was making dangerous noises. I picked up my bundle and ran, nearly tripping myself up on the rag that bound my foot. I could hear Seth laughing as though his ribs would burst. I hoped he would laugh himself to death.

But I had no time to think of him. I needed just one more ruble to secure passage on that ship, and I needed it quickly. I found a good place to resume my begging, but when I had accumulated only thirty kopecks I heard the steamship whistle blow. I took all the money I had to the steamship office and said to the clerk.

"Twelve rubles thirty. Take it or leave it. If you don't take it, I will curse you so that you will never have any sons, only daughters."

He took my money and wrote out a ticket for me. I couldn't read it, but I asked another customer in the office to verify that I really did have a place on that ship. Then I ran to catch the ship and I hurled myself at the gangplank just as they were hauling it in. I shouted and waved my ticket at everyone I saw, just so they wouldn't try to throw me off, and they took one look at me and shunted me down to the lowest part of the ship, into steerage. As I moved down, I looked up and saw Seth watching me from the rich man's deck high above.

"Hey, *gorgio*!" I yelled. "I am going to Paris, too!"

When we arrived in Marseilles two months later, in March, I was weak and feverish. I had never been on a ship before, and it had not occurred to me that I would be seasick. But that is what happened. I hardly saw the sky that whole voyage, and I ate next to nothing. A few crumbs of food cadged from the other passengers, and water. But that was all.

We steerage passengers piled off the ship. Immediately I found a place to sit on the wharf. I wanted to lift my face to the warm spring sunshine and reassure myself that there was, after all, such a thing as dry land that did not move. Seth Garrett strolled past, looking fit and well-fed.

"I thought you were going to Paris," he said jauntily.

I shrugged. "How can I go to Paris when I am dying? Good-bye, *gorgio*. You have had your way after all. May God go with you."

"Now, now," he said gleefully, "surely it's not that bad."

A surly dock official came along and prodded me none too gently with the toe of his boot. "No beggars allowed here. Go on, Gypsy, get away. Is she bothering you, sir?"

he asked Seth. "I'll take care of her. Go on, you baggage, get away from here before I have you arrested."

"May the sea reach up and swallow you," I muttered weakly.

"Why, you little—"

"It's all right," said Seth smoothly and imperiously. "She's with me. Let's go, Gypsy."

I felt my tired eyes grow brighter. "You are taking me with you? To Paris?"

"That's right. And I've even thought of a place for you to stay."

As we rode together on the train to Paris—my first time on a train—I tried without success to elicit information from him. Where were we going in Paris? Was I staying with his mother? An aunt? Did he have family there? Why wouldn't he tell me anything?

"It's not important," was all he would say.

We rode from the Gare du Lyon in a closed carriage. As we drew alongside another carriage at an intersection, a fashionably dressed lady leaned forward in her seat and smiled at Seth. He nodded and smiled back, and touched his hat to her. Then we drove on.

"Do you know that woman?" I asked.

"No."

"Then why do you greet her like a friend?"

"Because I would like to know her."

I considered this. "This is very strange. What if she would not like to know you? She does not know your father or your family. What if you were a truly wicked man? Is this a civilized way to behave?"

"Of course."

"Ah. Will I learn to be civilized, Monsieur Seth? Will you teach me?"

"No, but someone else will. Be quiet. We're almost there."

Finally our carriage drew to a halt in front of a tall white house on the Rue de Vaugirard, not far from the Luxembourg Gardens. Seth scribbled a note and handed it to me.

"Give this to the mistress of the house. No one else. Madame Mornay. You can get out now, Gypsy. Farewell!"

The carriage drove away, and I could hear him laughing.

4

Becoming Civilized

"SO THIS IS Seth's little Gypsy!" The tinkle of the woman's laughter filled the room. "Come closer, girl. I want to look at you."

I hesitated.

"Go on, Rhawnie," said Madame Odette, waving her hand. "Do as Simone asks."

I approached the ivory sofa in Madame Odette Mornay's gold and white drawing room. Simone Gallier was an archetypal Parisian beauty of the 1840s: petite, slender, and as cold as a china doll. Her light brown hair was drawn smoothly away from her forehead and swept over her ears into a bunch of perfect curls at the nape of her neck. The style seemed simple enough, but it had probably taken her hairdresser three hours to achieve. Simone had languid green eyes, pale silky skin, and a spoiled mouth that looked like a ripe berry when she pouted, which was often. Her long-sleeved peach-colored morning dress was a masterpiece of her dressmaker's art. Dainty white lace ruffles at her throat and wrists, and tiny black velvet bows, cunningly placed at her waist and bosom, accented her perfectly corseted figure.

I was painfully conscious of how ludicrous I must have looked next to this exquisite creature. In the four months I had been in Paris I had grown two inches taller but no fatter, and I looked decidedly lanky and ungainly. The simple black dress I wore was too small for me, and my wrists and ankles stuck out. Two heavy braids hung down my back to my waist. My white apron and starched collar and cuffs were already smudged and limp, although they had been clean and crisp when I had put them on only a few hours earlier.

I stood awkwardly in front of the dainty perfumed doll on the sofa, hating the way she inspected me as though I were a horse at auction, yet unable to take my eyes off her. I wanted to know more about this woman who spoke of Seth with such possessive familiarity.

"But my dear Odette!" Simone gasped at length. She put a tiny hand to her cheek in an attitude of horror. "She's enormous! These Russian Gypsies must be a race of giants. And she probably eats like a horse."

I narrowed my eyes at her and clenched my fists.

"But she is still a child," Madame Odette said. "A healthy appetite is to be expected in one her age. As for her looks, why, surely you were no great beauty when you were fourteen, Simone." Madame Odette patted her unnaturally red hair as she looked at the younger woman. I could see her gazing at Simone's waist, which, though corseted to an unbelievable smallness, was a shade thicker than her own.

"I have always been beautiful," Simone declared. "And men have always adored me, even as a child. You don't know how many proposals of marriage I have refused this year alone. It's so tedious."

"Including Seth Garrett's?" Madame Odette inquired slyly.

I pricked up my ears. The women had ceased to pay attention to me.

Simone turned pink. "Of course," she said with hollow firmness. "Especially Seth's."

"Ah, he is a most persistent lover," Madame Odette agreed. "So persistent that he stayed in Paris exactly one week in March before taking off for God knows where. He

86

didn't propose then, did he?"

Simone sniffed. "You know what a dreary bore he can be. So obstinate. Anyway, we did have a slight falling out when he returned from Russia."

"Yes, I did hear something about that." Madame Odette fanned herself. "He came home to find you living in his house. He threw you out and piled all your things in the gutter, didn't he?"

"That's a lie!" Simone said hotly. "Really, I don't know who can be spreading such slanderous tales about me!"

"Perhaps someone in the crowd that gathered to watch the scene," Madame Odette suggested.

"Bah! You know how many enemies I have." Simone unfurled her fan with an angry snap and wagged it vigorously under her chin. "It is only natural for these other women to be jealous of me. They all want him for themselves. I am surprised at you, Odette. When did you start paying attention to such dreadful rumors?"

"Since I retired from the stage I have taken a more active interest in human nature," Madame Odette purred. "You must forgive an old woman's amusements, my dear. Remember, I am nearly twice your age."

I looked at Simone, who was gritting her teeth. Surely that statement could not be right. I had overheard Marie-Claire, Madame Odette's maid, telling Cook that the "Old Bat" was seventy-five if she was a day.

"You will see for yourself, Simone," Madame Odette went on, "in just a few short years, how the aging process changes one's outlook on life. Rhawnie, stop that fidgeting and bring us some tea."

I jumped. "What? Tea! Oh, yes. Tea."

"Yes—what?" Madame waited expectantly.

I thought. "Oh. Yes—Madame." I dropped an awkward curtsy and walked sedately out of the room, as I had been taught. Except I tripped over a low table as I looked over my shoulder at Simone, who giggled. I flushed and hated her.

I closed the doors behind me and then listened at the

crack. I heard Madame Odette sigh deeply and say, "Really, Simone, you don't know the time I've had with that child. You should have seen her when Seth sent her to me. Shocking. Simply shocking. A ragged, filthy creature with hollow cheeks and enormous eyes and the most dreadful mats in her hair. You should have heard her scream when Cook threw her rags into the fire! As if she were being murdered. She wouldn't let us cut her hair. She wouldn't sleep on sheets like the rest of us. She refused to eat milk and eggs. All sorts of queer habits she had. And she couldn't even speak decent French. But she's coming along nicely. Even though she was a disaster in the scullery. But then that stupid cow Paulette went and got herself pregnant and had to go home to the country and so I started training Rhawnie as a lady's maid. She's trying very hard to improve, I think."

"Are you sure Seth would approve of this?" Simone asked. "Perhaps he sent the child to you to be educated, Odette. After all, you did run a finishing school for a short time, didn't you?"

I had heard all about that school, from eavesdropping on conversations between Cook and Marie-Claire. After she retired from the stage, Madame Odette attempted to establish a "seminary for young ladies" in her home. Everything had gone along splendidly until the mothers of her charges learned about Odette Mornay's less recent past: not only had she been a great actress in her day but a notorious courtesan as well! I wasn't sure what a courtesan was, but from the way Marie-Claire talked I was sure it was something dreadful. According to Marie-Claire, the scandal had rocked the best families in Paris (whose grandfathers had been intimate with Odette) and the school closed abruptly. It had been a humiliating time for Madame, and she hated being reminded of it.

I was sure that Seth knew all about the finishing school and its failure, and that was why he sent me to Madame Odette. There couldn't have been a girl in Paris less ready for "finishing" than I, or a woman less tolerant of a dirty urchin who didn't even speak decent French. And Seth had decided to play a little joke on both of us.

That had been a dreadful day. Madame Odette had been terrible in her anger, shouting about mortal insults and despicable actions. She was on the verge of throwing me out into the street when Marie-Claire came in to announce that the scullery maid had just run off with the butcher's boy. So I was sent to the kitchens, to wash pots.

"I am sure it was never Seth's intention that the girl be educated," Madame Odette said stiffly. Simone's remark had struck home. "But after all, he could hardly look after her himself, and he knew that I would be kind and charitable enough to take her in. Poor homeless waif."

"Yes, you are the very soul of generosity, dear Odette," Simone said. "Oh, that Seth! Utterly unpredictable! I wonder he didn't bring you a hottentot!"

"My dear, this one was bad enough," Madame Odette sighed.

"But it is good of you to undertake such a thankless task as civilizing a little savage," said Simone. "And of course Seth is paying you to look after her?"

"What?" Odette sniffed. "He couldn't pay me enough!" I suspected that his mocking gesture wouldn't have rankled so if he had paid her something. "I am helping the child out of the goodness of my heart," the old woman simpered. "And of course because I know his family."

"His family?" Simone said eagerly. "You know his family? You mean the man of mystery—"

"Oh, yes," said Madame Odette smugly. "I knew his father very well. That was a long time ago, before he married that little spitfire who had been a pirate."

"What?" I could tell that Simone wanted to hear more. So did I. I applied my ear more diligently to the crack between the doors.

"Forgive me, Simone, but I cannot say more," said Madame Odette regretfully. "Not because of Seth, that wretched boy! But his father did me a great kindness once, and out of respect for him I shall keep his scapegrace son's true identity a secret. Really, the only thoughtful thing that boy has done in his life has been to adopt another name. The way he misbehaves: drinking and gambling and carrying on with the most disreputable women in Paris!" She paused and I heard Simone make a choking noise. "His conduct would humiliate even the humblest family."

"Ah, but you can tell me, Odette," said Simone with great warmth. I heard the rustle of satin as she moved over to sit next to the older woman. "You know that I am your dearest and most loyal friend! Who else would come out and visit you on such an atrociously hot day as this? Paris in July is uninhabitable!"

"Obviously you wanted to satisfy your curiosity about something," Madame Odette said crisply. "You heard about the Gypsy child and you wanted to see your rival."

"Are you mad?" Simone's voice was shrill. "My dear Odette, how can you possibly suggest that I would even consider that dirty little ragamuffin a rival? She is nothing but a grotesque, uncouth piece of trash who attached herself to Seth because she wanted him to take her away from the squalid, horrid life she was living."

With an outraged bellow I burst into the room and confronted Simone.

"I am not dirty," I said in a low, dangerous voice. My fists were clenched and I was quivering with rage. "I am not uncouth. And I am no piece of trash! It is you who are trash!" Simone gave a shocked little cry and put her hand to her throat. I advanced. She leaped off the loveseat where she had been sitting with Madame Odette and retreated behind the sofa. "And if you ever speak of me again in such a way," I said, waving my fists in her face, "I will blacken both your eyes, pull out your tongue, and rip your hair out!"

"Oh! Well!" Simone's eyebrows were somewhere up in her hairline. Her jaw was flapping loosely. "How—how dare you!" she breathed when she found her voice.

"I dare because I am Gypsy!" I shouted. "And a Gypsy never forgets an insult, lady. So beware!"

I left the two women gaping after me and I ran up to my little room on the third floor, under the roof. I was furious with them, furious with Seth, and furious with myself. How dare they laugh at me and insult me and mock me? I would show them. I would show them all. I would be beautiful, more beautiful than any woman in Paris, and all the men would fall in love with me and propose marriage to me five times a day. I would wear peach-colored silk with black velvet bows, and I would carry a parasol and wear dainty kid gloves. And I would break their hearts. All their hearts. But especially one heart. And his I would not only break, I would tear it into tiny pieces and throw it on a dung heap. And he would see what he had lost, and he would be sorry.

I went down to the second floor, to Madame Odette's room. I looked at my face in her vast dressing table mirror. I had to make it beautiful, like Simone's. Let's see, she had worn a little paint on her lips. And I was sure that the pink patches on her cheeks were paint, too. I opened a little pot that had red gook inside and smeared some on my lips. Then I rubbed some more into my cheeks. I wrapped my braids around my head and studied the effect. Not very pleasing. Even a little ridiculous. But it was her clothes that had made Simone really beautiful. I pulled down one of the hat boxes from the top of Madame Odette's armoire and opened it. Ah, a beautiful bonnet would be just the thing. I put it on, jamming it down so hard that it would fit comfortably over my masses of hair. I found a parasol. I opened it and rested it on my shoulder, as I observed Simone had done when she left her carriage and walked up the path to the house. Then I paraded up and down in front of the full-length mirror on the front of the armoire.

Madame Odette came into the room. "What on earth!" she gasped. "This is the last straw! Just what do you think you're doing in here? Put those things down at once, do you hear me? Take off that bonnet! Get out of this room before I take a stick to you!"

I stood in front of the mirror and shook my head dolefully. "It is ugly. It's not right!"

"I should say it's not right!" Madame Odette stormed. She wrenched the parasol out of my hands and tore the bonnet off my head. "I come up here to scold you for insulting my guest, and if that wasn't bad enough—!" She waved her arms at the open hatbox and the few garments I had taken out of the armoire, and at the litter of open pots and jars on her dressing table. Her wrinkled face was bright red under her paint and her old eyes snapped. "Who gave you permission to play with these things? Well, answer me! No one! This is monstrous. I shall call the police. You must get out of this house at once, do you hear? I don't care what you do or where you go. Only get out, this minute!"

The corners of my mouth drooped. "I just wanted to see what I would look like."

"I can tell you what you look like: a clown! A large, clumsy, horrid clown! Oh, was ever a woman so unfortunate as I?" Madame Odette paced the floor angrily, moaning and twisting her hands. "I took you into this house out of the goodness of my heart. And this is how you repay me!" I didn't remind her that I had worked for her for four months and that she hadn't paid me a *sou*. "I will not put up with it any longer. Get out!"

I sat heavily on the edge of her bed and hung my head. "Oh, oh," I wailed despondently, "why did I want to come to Paris? Why did I not die with my family? Why did I let that *gorgio* bring me here? I never wanted to live here. Why—"

"For Heaven's sake, stop that wailing," the lady barked. "I cannot bear it another minute. You are just too maddening for words! Look at you! Red paint all over your cheeks and that horrid mess around your mouth!"

"I will never be a woman," I said sadly. I ran the palm of my hands over my flat chest. "I will always be ugly and big and clumsy. And I will never grow up to be beautiful. You

92

could teach me." I turned great sad eyes on her. "But you hate me. I understand that. Everybody hates Gypsies. You would teach me to be beautiful if I weren't a Gypsy, wouldn't you?"

"I—you—what on earth are you talking about?" she sputtered.

"You are a great lady," I said warmly. "And you are still very beautiful, even though you are old. From the back you look even younger than that Simone!"

"I do!" She lifted her chin and stole a look at herself in the mirror. "Indeed!"

"Oh, yes," I said in a voice that dripped with envy. "I think you must have been the most beautiful woman in Paris when you were young."

Madame Odette drew herself up and said proudly, "I was the most beautiful woman in Europe! Men adored me! I was the most glorious creature they had ever seen, onstage or off. They showered me with gifts, jewels and furs and carriages. And some of them still call upon me!"

"I know," I said excitedly. "I have seen them! You are so fortunate. So blessed with all good things." I stood up and waved my hand at the disorder I had created. "I am sorry about this. I only wanted to see if I could be as beautiful as you someday. But I am ugly, and I know now that it will never happen. I do not know what to do, where to begin. And I shall never know."

I fell into a dejected posture and crept towards the door, hardly able to move because of the great load of sorrow and self-pity that weighed on my heart.

"Oh. Well! Really, this is too—come back here, child."

I obeyed, trying not to look too elated. She had taken my bait, but I would have to play her in carefully. I couldn't lose her now.

"You've just gone about it all wrong, that's all," she said. "You have to use these tools sparingly, you know. Just a soupçon, the merest suggestion. You don't want to look like a painted harlot, do you?"

"What is that?" I asked.

"Oh, you know," Madame Odette said, looking a little flustered. "A woman who—a lady that—"

"Like a courtesan?" I suggested brightly.

"Ah, yes, something like a courtesan. But never mind that. I am telling you that none of this will help you if you don't know how to use it properly."

"But how can I learn?" I asked. "I am so unlucky. I have no one in the world to care for me. No one to teach me how to be a lady. My mother died when I was just a wee baby, and I never had a woman to talk to, to tell me the things I should know when I became a woman myself. My Grandfather the Count Nicholas Oulianov," I paused slightly to give the words emphasis, "was very fond of me. He would have taught me many things, I know. But he died and I am alone, all alone."

"What's this?" Madame Odette looked up sharply. "A count? Your grandfather? You're making this up!"

"No, no, I swear I am not!" I told her how my mother, Galina, had run away with a handsome Gypsy, Gregor, and how she died and her father, Count Nicholas Oulianov, had searched for me and taken me to his estates. "He had much land and many, many serfs. He treated me like a great lady. And he had a big house in Moscow. But he died and his son hated me and he would have killed me if I had not run away with Monsieur Seth. We went to find my Gypsy family but the Cossacks had killed them all." I turned my face away and wiped my eyes with my cuffs. "It was horrible. I saw them all, dead and burned. And my little brothers. And that is why I am alone now." I covered my face with my apron and jerked my shoulders a little.

"Well!" Madame Odette blew her nose loudly. "Here, take this handkerchief and wipe your eyes, child. And rub some of that stuff off your face. A count, you say! You are a Russian noblewoman!"

"In exile," I amended sadly. "I can never go back to Russia. They want to kill me, too. I must live among strangers and depend on their kindness for my livelihood.

And you have been so kind, Madame! To take in a poor orphan child—it was not an easy thing for you, I know. God will bless you. I have been a great trial to you. You are old and your last years should be easy ones. I will go now." I curtsied slowly and turned away.

"Wait a moment, child," said Madame Odette. "Come here and let me look at you." She put her hands on my shoulders and looked up into my face. She was very tiny. The top of her head came only to my chin. "Why, there's nothing whatever the matter with your face, Rhawnie. You have fine bones. Exquisite bones! Ah, if I had had such cheekbones I would still be the darling of the Paris stage! And your eyes! Ah, they are marvelous, so large and warm and dark. Your nose is good, and there's nothing the matter with your chin. Your mouth is much too wide, of course. But that won't be so noticeable when you've put on a little weight. Yes, I would say that in a few years you will be very nice-looking indeed, child. Just give yourself a little time."

"But I do not want to be—nice looking!" I cried. "I want to be beautiful! As beautiful as you were! As beautiful as that—Simone!" I hissed the name.

Madame Odette gave a sharp bark of laughter. "So that's it! You're jealous of Simone! Well, I must tell you if you want to come anywhere near Simone's success with men and her looks, you'll have to worry about a lot more than just your face and your figure!"

"I do not understand."

"You have no manners, child!" Madame Odette threw up her hands. "Look at your disgraceful performance today. Really, you'll have to learn to insult your enemies with more finesse! Ladies never, ever descend to name-calling. They do not talk loudly or scream or drop things or run up the steps like a herd of cattle. Ladies do not trip over furniture, they do not break things. If a lady hears something that upsets or distresses her, she must give no sign of it. She must pretend that everything is fine, and if her mind is busy with some plan, her face must give no

95

indication of it. But you! You have no self-control, no social grace, no—education!"

"I know," I said. "But I do not understand, Madame. You sat with that woman and pretended to be her friend, but you do not like her and she does not like you. It makes no sense!"

"It makes a great deal of sense," Madame Odette said. "If I refused to see everyone I did not like, I would speak to no one for days on end. But Simone and I are ladies, and we have learned how to pretend for form's sake."

"You know so much," I said admiringly. "I have heard that the daughters of the best families in this city came to you to learn deportment."

She stiffened and said, "Yes, that is true. But I am no longer in the business of instructing young ladies. My, ah, health would not permit it."

"Oh." I looked crestfallen. "That is a great misfortune. I would have cut off my hair for a chance to learn from you. I would have found a way to pay you, too. I would have begged in the streets for money. But I have come too late. I am unlucky. I am cursed! I shall never have a home. I will always wander alone and unloved and ignorant over the face of the earth, and no one will care what becomes of me. My Grandfather the Count," I sighed deeply, "would be very unhappy if he could see what has become of the little one he loved."

I looked sharply at the old woman from under my lashes, measuring the effect of my words.

Madame Odette paced the floor slowly. "It is true," she said thoughtfully, "that, ah, circumstances forced my retirement from teaching. I must confess that I have found this state of inaction to be very dull. I have missed the company of young girls." She stopped in front of me and studied me long and hard. I kept silent, waiting. "What a coup it would be," Madame Odette murmured, "to turn a Gypsy scullery maid into the most beautiful woman in Paris! What a pleasure it would be to put Simone's nose out of joint—permanently. And to show Seth Garrett—! Yes, it's possible. It is definitely possible." She walked around me as I stood motionless. "Stand up straight!" she snapped. I obeyed. "Beauty is not enough, Rhawnie. You need breeding! Without breeding you would be as a beautiful weed standing in a patch of exquisite cultivated roses. Do you understand what I am saying?"

"No. Madame."

"The rose," Madame Odette explained, "even the flawed rose, has that unmistakable quality, that something special, that a weed can never have. You do have some breeding. I can see that now. Good blood tells, it always tells. Nobility is written all over you. I don't know why I didn't see it before! But because you were raised by a band of horrid Gypsies, your upbringing has been sadly botched and this nobility has been forgotten."

"They weren't horrid," I said staunchly. "They were wonderful!"

"Yes, yes. But they were wild flowers, child. Weeds! Don't you see what I'm saying? Among Gypsies your life would have been secure. You know their customs, their ways. I am sure that any Gypsy man would have been quite satisfied with you for a wife."

"That is true," I said eagerly. "I was even betrothed! I would be married now if Django hadn't been killed."

"But fortune," mused Madame Odette, "has delivered you into my hands."

"It is my good fortune and your burden," I said humbly. "I have already learned so much, just by watching you and the elegant people who come to see you."

"Have you, indeed? Then you have seen that the men who come to this house are not like Gypsies. A gypsy man might find your wild, uncivilized ways and your lack of manners charming. But any civilized man would be repulsed by them."

"That is true," I nodded. I thought of Seth Garrett's ill-concealed disgust. "I will never find a man to marry me. I am Gypsy no more, and no *gorgio*—no civilized man— would take me as I am. Oh, I need to learn how to be a lady! And you are the only woman in the world who could have taught me what I need to know! But I have come too late."

"Perhaps not." Odette Mornay smiled for the first time. "It may be the best thing in the world that you came here just when I had the, ah, leisure to devote my full attention to your education."

"I cannot believe what you are saying," I breathed excitedly. "You will really teach me? That is so? Oh, Madame!" I fell on my knees and kissed Madame Odette's hands gratefully. "I will never be able to thank you enough! I will pay you," I vowed. "I will beg in the streets for the money to pay you!"

"No, no!" Madame Odette urged me to my feet. "That would be most improper! Unthinkable! Listen to me, child. If you do as I say, if you obey me in everything, you will be able to marry a gentleman. Don't you believe all that nonsense of Simone's about her marriage proposals. Do you think for one minute that she wouldn't be married now if any one of those men had proposed to her?" She rubbed her hands. "We will show them, you and I. We'll show them all that Odette Mornay could have done wonders with their stupid daughters. I shall marry you to a nobleman! To a prince! And that will be payment enough for me!"

"I cannot believe my good fortune!" I exclaimed. "I will do as you say, Madame. I will obey your every command! Oh, Madame, my Grandfather the Count," I sighed rapturously, "would be so proud if he could know about this!"

"You will be the granddaughter of an old friend of mine," Madame Odette decided. "We met while he was visiting Paris—oh, so long ago! He has never forgotten me. He has entrusted you to my care. I shall teach you table manners and dancing and singing. You will learn how to walk, how to speak beautiful French, how to stay awake at the opera, how to dance the waltz—! Ah, there is so much to do! And when I feel you are ready, you will make your debut at the most elegant ball in Paris. I still have the power to make sure you are seen in all the best places.

"We must begin at once! I will see about having some proper clothes made for you. I have some old dresses that might be altered to fit—I hope the allowance at the seams is generous enough. It would be foolish to buy new things until you have finished growing. And until you are ready to be seen in public. I must keep you hidden until at least two months before the Delacroix ball. And no more working as a maid—it's death on the hands. Now stand up straight, straight! Don't be ashamed of your height, my girl. Glory in it! How I wish I had been as regal-looking as you! Be glad you're not a runt like us French women. When you appear in a crowd, no man will be able to look at any other woman! You will be magnificent, glorious, the toast of Paris. I, Odette Mornay, promise you this!"

Late that night I sat in my window and looked up at the stars, and I thought about the journeys I had made: from Bryansk to the Rue de Vaugirard in Paris; from Gypsy beggar to *gorgio* lady. And I thought about Seth, who had said that I would never be anything but a dirty Gypsy. He was wrong. I was willing to endure any discomfort, any torture, just to prove to him that he was wrong. He would never laugh at me again, I vowed. Never. I would learn the *gorgio* customs and habits, and I would know these people better than they knew themselves. I would sleep in a bed and I would wear shoes in the summertime and drab dresses that had only one skirt and no pockets. I would be a better *gorgio* than any of them. I would be civilized.

And when Seth Garrett saw me again—and I was sure he would, for were not our futures linked?—he would see how foolish he had been. He might even fall in love with me. And I would turn the tables on him, and laugh at him, and break his heart.

I worked hard and progressed rapidly. For the next ten months the litany of beauty sounded in my ears: "Don't slouch! Don't eat so fast! Don't eat so much! Don't run!

Don't giggle like that! Here, read this book, it will be all the rage this spring."

"I can't read."

"What do you mean, you can't read? You mean you can't read French?"

"I can't read anything. I never learned."

"Well!"

But Madame Odette did not teach me to read. There was no time. Instead she gave me voice lessons and dancing lessons and speech lessons. She taught me how to twirl a parasol and how to look at a man from under my hat, and how to smile coyly and sweetly when he kissed my fingertips. She taught me how to pour tea from a silver pot, how to eat snails, how to use a finger bowl, how to laugh like a lady and not like a wild Gypsy girl. I mastered the intricacies of corset lacings, bonnet strings, petticoats, and fans. I learned how to dance the polka and the waltz, the mazurka and the reel. And I never again sucked my tea through a sugar lump, at least not when anyone was watching.

Wonderful things happened. I finally stopped growing, much to everyone's relief because I was five feet eleven inches tall. And then I started to fill out. My little breasts blossomed and became as firm and as round as small oranges. I was ecstatic, delirious. Now when I looked at myself in the mirror I saw a woman, a real woman, and not a gaunt scarecrow. My hips were shapely and my legs were very long and slender. I had a tiny waist and a straight back and nice shoulders, not too bony and not too plump, as Madame Odette said. She pronounced my smile radiant, and my carriage graceful. Too graceful.

"Don't swing your hips when you walk!" my mentor cried at least five times a day.

"I cannot help it!" I replied. "That is the way I walk!"

"You are a hussy!" Madame Odette sniffed.

"I am a woman," I laughed impudently. "Why should I not move like one?"

To Madame's annoyance I still refused to cut my hair so

that I could wear it in the style of the day. Finally she decreed that it would be permissible for me, as a visiting Russian countess, to keep my long, thick braids and to wear them wound around my head in a shining, golden coronet.

"And for your debut," she decided, "we will lace them with strings of pearls!"

Even though I hated the idea, I slept on white sheets as a concession to civilization. But I could not bring myself to wear white, even white undergarments. Madame Odette and her dressmaker begged, cajoled, and threatened. They said that for a young lady of my breeding and presumed social standing not to wear white was most improper! And they considered my liking for bright greens, dark blues, sunny yellows and oranges and crimsons deplorable, if not downright tasteless. Ultimately we reached a compromise, and my new wardrobe was made of fabrics in pastel shades that were near enough to white to satisfy society, yet colorful enough to meet with my approval.

The Delacroix Ball, given in May of each year, was to provide the setting for my debut. The Delacroix family was ancient and awesomely respectable. According to Marie-Claire and Cook, Madame Odette had once been "very friendly" with old Grandpère Delacroix, and that was how she managed to procure invitations for us to the ball.

With the arrival of Spring, excitement began to build in the house on the Rue de Vaugirard. Our harried dressmaker rushed to and fro, paying countless calls on me because Madame refused to permit me to be seen in public before the ball. She said she wanted me to burst upon the Parisian social scene with all the dazzle and brilliance of a firecracker. I was heartily sick of my cloistered existence and tired of all the restrictions that had been placed on my freedom, but I took comfort in the knowledge that my seclusion would soon end.

I was like a butterfly ready to break out of my chrysalis.

My training period had been exacting and thorough, and Madame Odette was convinced that I would be able to snare a husband without any difficulty. She was even so rash as to predict that I would be engaged within one month after the ball. Nothing could go wrong, she declared. Nothing could spoil her plans for me.

5

Paris: May, 1843

"YOU ARE A vision! An absolute vision!"

Madame Odette stood back and pronounced judgement on her handiwork. The night of the Delacroix Ball had arrived. In just a few minutes we would step into our hired carriage. But first Madame had to make a final inspection.

My gown was a rich ivory satin, almost a pale gold. Madame Odette had tried to persuade me to wear white for just this one night, as a debutante should, but as usual her pleas went unheard and we compromised on an off-white shade. The bodice of the gown came to a point in front, emphasizing the smallness of my tightly corseted waist. A panel of fine Belgian lace, lined with the same pale gold satin, covered my bosom, rising modestly halfway to my throat. Little puffed sleeves were trimmed with a lace ruffle that dropped to the elbows. Twelve yards of satin flared away from the waist, and a ruffle of fifty yards of lace a foot wide brushed the floor. I carried an ivory fan with lace inserts, and I wore short gloves of ivory silk. The evening was mild, and I had need of no more than an embroidered silk shawl for a wrap. My shoes were delicate kid slippers that matched my gown. My two heavy braids were entwined with ropes of tiny seed pearls, and they were pinned into a massive glowing crown that seemed to add inches to my already breathtaking height. A dainty necklace of similar pearls encircled my throat, and pearls set in gold dangled from my earlobes.

"Now if you can just remember everything I've taught you," Madame Odette said breathlessly. "I am exhausted already and the most difficult part is still ahead of us. I am certain that if anything goes wrong I shall collapse and die on the spot. I beg you, Rhawnie, go slowly and think before you speak!"

I bent over and kissed her withered cheek. "Do not worry, dearest friend! Have I not been taught by the greatest and most beautiful lady in Paris? Oh, I am so excited! Surely it is time to go?"

I could hardly contain myself. Those long weeks of confinement in the house on the Rue de Vaugirard were finally over. I could enjoy music and dancing and laughter, things which I hadn't had since the Grandfather took me away from the Gypsies, over two years ago. I felt absolutely no fear or nervousness about facing the Parisian lions for the first time, only an overpowering desire to have fun.

We donned our wraps, bid farewell to the servants who had gathered to watch our departure, and left the house. Then we entered our carriage and were borne off to the ball.

The Delacroix mansion looked like an illuminated birthday cake, vast and white with tiers of columns and balconies. Strings of colored lanterns supplemented the glow cast by a hundred gas lamps, indoors and out. A long line of carriages crept up the looping driveway, discharging passengers at the entrance. A swarm of exquisitely dressed Parisians of all ages made their way into the house.

"Oh, oh, we should have waited," Madame Odette fretted. "Why did you rush me? You could have made a grand entrance—a really special moment!—and now to arrive with all the rest—! Where were my wits?"

I bounced at her side, craning my neck to see out of the closed windows.

"Stop gawking!" Madame instructed me. "Do you want these people to think you have never been to a ball before?"

"But I haven't."

"That's not the point! When you get inside that house you must act as though you have seen it all before, a hundred times. You are a Russian countess, remember that."

"But why?" I wondered absently. "Why do we have to pretend that I am nobility?"

"We are not pretending anything! You are nobility! And besides, do you think that any of these people would have anything to do with you if they knew that for the first thirteen years of your life you lived like a beggar?"

"I lived like a Gypsy," I corrected her. "We only begged because—"

"Enough!" Madame Odette shivered and fanned herself. "If you dare breathe one word of that to anyone, I will—disown you! Now remember, come back to me after each dance so that I can read your card to you. I don't want you running off by yourself where I can't keep an eye on you. And don't accept an invitation to supper without asking me first! And don't touch the champagne!"

She went on and on, issuing last-minute instructions. I patted her hand distractedly and promised mechanically to behave myself. But in my mind I was already at the ball, whirling around the dance floor in the arms of a man I was going to marry. I wanted marriage as much as Madame Odette wanted it for me. A home and babies and a husband to love me. The Gypsies believed that marriage was the sole purpose of a woman's life, and that nothing but marriage could make a man of a boy. What would this husband of mine look like, I wondered? I decided that he would be very tall, and fair, and very handsome. And of course he would be rich!

Madame Odette's worries about our arrival going unnoticed were unnecessary. As soon as our carriage drew up to the door and I stepped out, assisted by a liveried Delacroix footman, a hush fell over the crowd at the door. Madame Odette and I walked up the broad marble stairs, and the cluster of people waiting to get inside actually parted to let us pass! I saw Madame lift her head a little higher, and I guessed that this was one of the great moments of her life. Every third person we passed knew of the scandal of her failed finishing school, and she hoped that they would witness the triumph of one they had scorned.

Relieved of our wraps, we went into the ballroom to greet our hosts. Heads swivelled as I passed—and most of them tilted up to gasp at my size. I felt regal and beautiful and so excited and happy that I wanted to shout out loud.

Monsieur and Madame Delacroix received us coldly. I suppose they were still smarting from having to endure Madame Odette's presence at their grand affair.

"This is the Countess Rhawnie Nicolaevna Oulianova, the granddaughter of a very old friend of mine," Madame Odette said, presenting me. I curtsied deeply and offered Monsieur Delacroix my hand to kiss. He smiled appreciatively, while his wife, a small woman with dark hair and a mean mouth, nearly broke her face trying to look disapproving. But our grand lie was launched, and I didn't care a whit whether or not those people believed that I was of noble Russian blood and had been gently raised in Moscow. They couldn't prove that I wasn't, could they?

I turned a dazzling smile on Monsieur Delacroix. "I am so happy to have been invited here tonight! Thank you so much. Your home is very beautiful, Madame," I said to the unsmiling hostess. "Much grander than anything I have seen in Moscow."

"Perhaps you will honor me with a dance later in the evening, Countess?" Monsieur Delacroix said with a little bow. I handed him my card and he put his name down near the top. I saw his wife give him a sharp look, which he ignored.

A group of new arrivals came into the room and we moved on. Madame Odette squeezed my hand and whispered, "Nicely done. And here come the young men you are to meet. I know most of them because of their sisters."

A crowd of young men swarmed around us, presenting themselves and asking for the honor of dancing with me in the course of the evening.

"Could I not dance with you all, at the same time?" I asked gaily. "In a large circle, as we did in the Gyp—in Russia!"

I felt Madame Odette stiffen apprehensively, but they all laughed and the oldest in the group, a slim, brown-haired man of twenty, said warmly, "We are fortunate that customs in France are different from Russia, Countess. You will have to endure us one at a time."

I smiled around the circle and said, "I think I shall find your customs most delightful, gentlemen. After all, a man who buys a horse does not watch to see how it runs in a team, does he? Yes, I think I would like to see your paces alone."

Madame Odette winced, but the men were all utterly captivated and laughed heartily. My dance card was filled in a matter of minutes. Then my admirers begged to show me the delights of Paris.

"I would love that!" I exclaimed truthfully. "Perhaps we could go riding sometime? It must be possible to hire a horse—"

They hastened to assure me that it was certainly possible, and slim young man with the brown hair and nice smile offered his own prize-winning mount for my inspection and enjoyment.

"A fine thing," Madame Odette muttered to me when they had drifted away to seek out other less desirable partners for the evening. "Now I will have to pay for an equestrienne outfit! And what was all that nonsense about dancing in circles and buying horses in teams? I never told you—"

"I am supposed to be Russian, no?" I smiled. "They

would not believe it if my manners were too perfect like their own. I think they like me better with just a little straw in my shoes, so they can show me how cultured and civilized the French people are compared to the Russians.''

Madame Odette gave me an astonished look, then she nodded approvingly. ''Very shrewd, girl. You will go far. Did you see the first name of your card? No, how could you? It's young de Vernay. He's a duke, Rhawnie! And a favorite nephew of King Louis Philippe himself!''

She led me away to introduce me to some of her old friends. I had met some of the old gentlemen at the house when they came to call on her. They might have been arthritic and hard of hearing, but they were still ardent connoisseurs of female beauty.

''Charming! Exquisite! Delightful!'' they breathed.

''Yes, the Count was such a dear, dear friend,'' Madame Odette said with a meaningful wink which I did not understand but which made the men chuckle. ''Of course I was delighted to take his dear granddaughter into my home. Her manners are still rather provincial—Russia is such a backward country!—but she is a very quick learner.''

''I should say she is,'' said a voice that I recognized. I looked around and saw Simone Gallier smirking at me. ''Your protégé seems to have made remarkable progress since I saw her last, Odette.''

Madame Odette seemed unruffled by the threat in Simone's tone. She said. ''Yes, Rhawnie's noble origins have stood her in such good stead. But then breeding always tells, doesn't it, Simone?''

Simone's smile became glacial. She favored me with a sneering stare, and then moved away.

''What if she tells everyone that I was your scullery maid?'' I asked Madame Odette in a conspiratorial whisper.

''She won't,'' Madame Odette said confidently. ''For one thing, she wouldn't want the story of your last meeting to come out. So humiliating. And for another, I know all about Simone Gallier and her antecedents. And she knows I know. Tit for tat, dear Rhawnie. Silence for silence.''

The orchestra finished tuning up and launched into the first dance of the evening, a polka. Monsieur and Madame Delacroix led the ball and the young Duke de Vernay claimed me.

"You dance very well," he said at the end of the dance.

"They do the polka in Russia, too," I said. "And the waltz. And all the other dances you do here."

"I wish I could experience them all with you, Countess," he said gallantly. "But I was quite sincere in my invitation to ride. Will you come? Tomorrow? My horses are very fine—"

"I would love to ride with you," I said. "But I must ask Madame Odette. I didn't bring anything to wear you know!''

He looked crestfallen, then hopeful. "Then perhaps we could ride in my barouche? I have a splendid team of blacks. You must see them. Will you?"

I gave him my consent and we drifted over to Madame Odette, who was seated in a small chair under an enormous gilt-framed mirror. As we stood chatting, a sudden movement at my elbow caught my eye. I heard Madame Odette gasp, and as I looked up a familiar face joined mine in the mirror. Our eyes met. I saw myself turn pale, then rosy.

I suppose the young duke made his excuses and went away. I really don't remember. The noise of the crowd faded away and a little shiver of delight and anticipation went through me. I faced the newcomer squarely.

Madame Odette stood up quickly and grasped my elbow.

"Ah, Monsieur Garrett!" she said a little too loudly. "May I present the Countess Oulianova, from Russia. Child, this is Monsieur Garrett, a very well-known, ah, traveller. You have never met him before." Her bony fingers dug into my arm.

I extended my hand. He took it and raised my fingers to

111

his lips. As he bowed over my hand he raised his eyes to mine and said, "I am honored, Countess."

I wondered how I could have forgotten the beauty of his voice. It was rich and deep, with a cutting edge that commanded attention. I studied him. He had changed, but only slightly. His hair was longer and swept straight back from his forehead in a wavy mane. His beard was gone. The knife scar that the beard had partially concealed now shone vividly against his skin, giving him a devilish and more dangerous look. The cut had scored his cheek from the corner of his left eye down to his jawbone. He wore evening dress as unselfconsciously and gracefully as he had worn heavy furs and stout boots. His shirt front was dazzling white and punctuated with little diamond studs, and his black cutaway coat fit him perfectly, emphasizing the broadness of his shoulders and the trimness of his waist.

He leaned indolently on a shining black ebony cane with a gold lion's head at the top, and his eyes flickered appreciatively over my figure. When we were face to face I noticed that our eyes were exactly on a level. At least he couldn't look down on me now. His look paralyzed me and my mouth went dry. I collected ny wits and cleared my throat.

"You have been away from Paris a long time, Monsieur," I said pleasantly. "Do you find the city changed?" A silly question, but just the sort of thing civilized people said to one another when they met.

Seth looked puzzled. "Somewhat, Countess. I am pleased and surprised that my absence has come to the attention of such a charming visitor."

"My dear, we must go," Madame Odette said, dragging at my arm.

I ignored her. "But of course I know that you have been away," I said to him.

And then I realized that he didn't recognize me.

"Ah," I said, savoring the moment, "you do not remember me!"

112

He smiled apologetically and said, "You must think me very rude, Countess. I am certain that—"

Madame Odette tugged at me but I stood fast. My feet might have been nailed to the floor.

"You are certain that if we had met before you would remember me?" I finished for him. "Why? Because I am so beautiful? Ah, but Monsieur Seth, I was not so beautiful then. Do you not recall the little Gypsy who travelled with you from Russia?"

Madame Odette released my arm and fell back, bracing herself.

He stared at me, and blinked, and stared some more. "Rhawnie?" he said incredulously. I gave a happy little nod.

Then to my amazement and horror, he started to laugh. The sound was awful, terrible, deafening. It boomed to the four corners of the room and a hundred and fifty heads swung in our direction. But I didn't see them then. I didn't notice that we had suddenly become the center of attention. Hatred and loathing and fury boiled up inside of me. How dare he. How dare he laugh at me when I had endured the most incredible torments for the past year, learning to be a better *gorgio* than if I had been born *gorgio*!

I pressed my mouth into a grim line and my eyes flashed. I heard Madame Odette murmur, "No, no, Rhawnie, come away, I beg—"

"Filthy swine," I said through my teeth. I stepped right up close to him and struck him viciously on the cheek with my open hand. "Uncivilized boor!" I shouted.

The thunder of his laughter died away but a mischievous light still danced in his eyes. "Forgive me, Countess," he said, stressing my title mockingly, "but I seem to have forgotten the correct way of paying one's addresses to Russian nobility."

He put his arms around me and pulled me into a bone-crushing embrace. Then he kissed me full on the mouth. I squirmed in his arms.

"Villain!" I gasped when he released me. I swung at him

113

again with my closed fist, but he laughingly intercepted the
blow and held both hands under his chin.

The orchestra struck up a mazurka and Monsieur Del-
acroix came over to dance with me. "Oh, good evening,
Monsieur Garrett. I would like, ah, to claim the
Countess—"

Seth let me go. I rubbed my wrists and glared at him.
"Oh, hello, Pierre," he said. "I was just greeting the
Countess. We met in Russia a while ago and she was
justifiably annoyed because I didn't recognize her."

"Yes. Yes, of course." Pierre Delacroix crooked his arm
at me, and I slid my hand under his elbow. As he led me
away to the dance floor I saw Madame Odette slump down
in her chair and cover her face with her gloved hands: I
could still hear Seth Garrett chuckling.

I could feel his eyes on me as Delacroix and I skipped
around the floor together. Watching, grinning, winking at
me. I was careful, whenever my head was turned in his
direction, to let my eyes sweep over him as if he weren't
even there. When the mazurka ended, Monsieur Delacroix led me to the punch table. Martin de Vernay, the
young duke, joined us. But even as I talked and laughed
with them, I could feel Seth Garrett lurking and looking,
just a few feet away.

A new partner came to claim me for the cotillion. Seth
did not dance. He just stood on the sidelines, talking and
laughing and drinking champagne while women swarmed
around him like flies crowding in on a piece of dead meat.
For some reason the sight annoyed me.

After the cotillion, I led my partner to the side of the
room where Madame Odette had been sitting. Her chair
was empty. I looked around but could not see her anywhere.

"She told me to tell you that she was feeling ill." Seth
Garrett materialized at my elbow. "She said you weren't
to worry about her and that you must have a good time.
She's upstairs, resting, I think."

I started to speak but I bit my lip. "Jean," I said to my

partner, ''I am very thirsty. Would you bring me a glass of punch, please?''

Obediently the young man ran off to fetch some punch.

''Will you please stop following me?'' I hissed at Seth when we were alone. ''Stop watching me!''

''I can't help myself,'' he said, blue eyes flashing. ''I can't seem to take my eyes off you.''

''Liar. Go away. Leave me alone!''

''No. Will you forgive me for being an uncivilized boor, Countess? I couldn't help it. You quite took my breath away.''

''I will not forgive you,'' I said coldly. ''And stop calling me Countess. You know very well that I am no Countess.''

''I won't spoil your little game, if that's what you're worried about,'' he assured me. ''You can call yourself the Czarina for all I care. Forgive me?''

''No. Never. You were very rude. You insulted me! You—you didn't even recognize me!''

''Of course not!'' he laughed. Then he said warmly, ''You are the most beautiful woman in Paris tonight, Rhawnie. Not a bit like the scrawny little urchin I brought back from Russia. Your own Gypsies wouldn't know you now.''

I gave a little start. ''That is true,'' I said slowly. ''They wouldn't.''

''Countess Rhawnie.'' Seth took a formal stance in front of me and lowered his eyes penitently. ''I have been a brute and a lout. I beg you to forgive my bad manners. I assure you, it was only shock and amazement that made me act as I did. Will you forgive me? I could not live, knowing that by a momentary slip I had earned your enmity forever.''

I felt a smile lurking at the corners of my mouth and I tried vainly to suppress it. ''Oh, don't be an ass,'' I said brusquely. ''I forgive you.''

''You'll note I didn't apologize for kissing you,'' he said. ''And I don't intend to.''

I shrugged. ''Then you will have that on your conscience forever," I said. "I wouldn't forgive you anyway, for kissing me like that."

"And how would you like to be kissed?" he inquired politely.

"Stop teasing me," I said impatiently, lowering my eyes.

"Of course." He bowed and said in a different voice, "Forgive me again for what must have seemed the grossest insult, Countess. I hope what happened will in no way blight your enjoyment of the ball." Then he walked away, tapping his cane lightly on the floor.

"Well!" I stared after him, nonplussed. The change in his attitude had been so sudden, as though he had tired of the game we were playing and wanted to do something else. I swallowed my disappointment.

Jean returned with my punch, and a few minutes later a pallid, beardless youth appeared to claim my hand for the first waltz of the evening. I whirled away in his arms, feeling that the fun had gone out of the evening for me. I searched for Seth in the crowd but I did not see him. He certainly wasn't watching me anymore. Then I saw him, standing in a quiet, palm-shaded corner away from the orchestra, talking and laughing with Simone Gallier. I stopped dancing abruptly.

"What is the matter, Countess?" my partner asked anxiously. "Is something wrong?"

"I think I have hurt my foot," I said. "I would like to sit down for a moment, if you don't mind."

His eyes filled with concern. He led me to a chair and ran off to get me something to drink. As soon as he was out of sight, I jumped up and made my way across the room to Seth's corner. Simone saw me approaching, and she glared at me and rested her hand possessively on Seth's forearm.

"Good evening, Monsieur Seth," I said brightly. "It appears that my partner for this waltz has hurt his foot and cannot continue. Will you finish this dance with me?"

Simone laughed and said, "You will be disappointed, Madamoiselle Gypsy. Monsieur Garrett does not dance.

He has never even danced with me!''

"I can understand that, Madamoiselle," I said seriously. "I have watched you dance."

Simone's eyes narrowed and she fanned herself. "You can't fool me, Gypsy. Odette thinks she can pull the wool over the eyes of every man in Paris, but just wait until I've told what I know!"

"And what do you know, Madamoiselle? We have said nothing that is not true. I really am the granddaughter of a Russian count, as Madame says. Monsieur Seth here can attest to that. Besides, I do not think that all the men in Paris are interested in what you have to say."

"My dear Countess," Seth said before Simone could respond, "I would be delighted to dance with you. Will you excuse us, Simone? And would you mind holding this for me?" He handed her his gold-headed can and bowed to me. "Countess?"

We whirled away together. "If this is painful for you, you must stop," I said.

"It's no more painful than standing," he said. "And if my leg bothers me, I know someone in Paris who can fix it." His smile would have melted ice. He lowered his voice and said, "Did you miss me, Rhawnie?"

I cocked my head. "No," I said bluntly, "I did not even think of you. And you did not think about me, either, or you would have come to Madame Odette's house to see me when you returned. But what does it matter?" I shrugged. "We can still dance together, no?"

"You're delightful when you lift your shoulders like that," he said. "It gives you a very careless and worldly air, you know. The gesture didn't suit you when you were younger, but you've grown into it." He smiled at me. I found that I couldn't meet his eyes and I turned my head away.

He guided me easily around the floor, and if his leg hurt him he gave no indication of it. I was keenly aware of his strength and grace. I could feel the heat of his body and the power in his hands. I was suddenly conscious of myself as a woman, because I was so conscious of Seth Garrett as a man. He wasn't like the others I had danced with. They were boys, as young and as weak as women.

"I have the feeling, Rhawnie," he said, "that in spite of your vigorous training at Madame Odette's hands, you are still very much a Gypsy at heart."

I tilted my chin. "I am really no different. I have just learned to curse inside my head instead of with my mouth. Except," I amended, "when I am angry."

"And then you flavor your cursing with violence," he said with a grin.

"No. I am violent only when I am very angry." He laughed and pressed me close to him. I gasped and said, "You are holding me too tightly, Monsieur!"

"That's the proper way to waltz with someone you like, didn't Odette teach you that?" He dipped his head and kissed the top of my shoulder. He murmured, "You really are delightful, Rhawnie. And to think I almost didn't come tonight."

"Why not?" I asked in a voice that trembled slightly. "You do not like balls?"

"No. Quite the opposite."

"Well, I am glad that you came," I said. "You are a much better dancer than those other boys, or Monsieur Delacroix."

The waltz ended and we strolled arm in arm back to where Simone was standing, gripping Seth's cane in both hands. Her eyes were smoldering and she said in a tight voice. "It's just like you, Seth Garrett, to let someone else do the dirty work while you reap the benefits. You had it in mind all along to take back your beggar child after poor Odette had cleaned her up and made her into a 'lady.' You make me sick!"

She hurled the cane at Seth and turned sharply on her heel. I took a step. There was a tearing sound and Simone looked back.

"You—you have torn my gown! You little vixen!"

"Oh, forgive me, Madamoiselle," I said abjectly. "I am

so clumsy. What a pity! Now you will have to leave the ball."

With an outraged cry Simone lunged at me. Seth intercepted her, and bending her over his arm gave her rump a single, sound blow with his cane. She couldn't have felt it through all her petticoats, but she bawled like a cat whose tail has been caught in a door.

Seth set her on her feet and said, "You never did have any manners, Simone. No one ever cared enough to beat them into you." Then he took my hand and threaded it under his arm. "You can also learn in life by reverse example, Rhawnie," he said instructively. "Simone, for instance, is a perfect example of how not to be a lady."

He walked away from her. "Bastard!" she shouted after us. "Bitch!" A few onlookers murmured disapprovingly.

"Will you take supper with me, Rhawnie?" Seth asked. "After all, I did dance with you when you invited me."

"I promised Madame Odette that I would ask her permission before I accepted an invitation to supper," I told him.

"I am sure that Odette is feeling too exhausted to want to be bothered," he said with a naughty wink. "Please say you will." He led me into the salon where a sumptuous buffet supper had been laid out. "Aren't you hungry?"

"I could eat a bull," I said with a deep sigh. "But this thing is holding me in so tightly that I cannot even breathe. Madame said that I was to have a little aspic, nothing more."

"What nonsense," Seth scoffed. "How can a girl dance until dawn with only a little aspic to fuel her efforts? Stay here and I'll bring you something more substantial." He foraged at the table and returned with a breast of pheasant, a small camembert, a pear, and two bottles of champagne. "We'll share the loot," he said conspiratorially. "Grab a couple of glasses and follow me."

Laughing, I obeyed. He went out through long French doors to a broad stone veranda that overlooked the Seine.

"Oh, look!" I cried, running to the balustrade. "All the

lights of Paris are swimming in the river tonight! Like thousands of stars. It is so beautiful.''

I heard a small explosion and I looked over my shoulder. Seth poured foaming champagne into our glasses. He handed a brimming glass to me and then lifted his own.

"What shall we drink to?"

I thought for a moment. "If I were still Gypsy I would drink to long life and good travel, to fine weather and many children and no police. But tonight it is different, no! And I am not Gypsy now, I am civilized. Perhaps we should just drink to old friends?"

He gave a little laugh and said, "I would rather drink to beauty." He gazed at me over the rim of his glass while he drank.

I sipped the champagne, the first I had ever tasted. "Oh, it is very good! The bubbles are wonderful! They tickle my nose.''

"You must drink every drop," Seth told me. "It's bad luck to leave a glass of champagne half drunk.''

"Madame Odette said that I wasn't to have any," I said. "She said that it would make my tongue loose and my brains fuzzy.''

"What a dull evening you would have had if I hadn't come along to send Odette upstairs with the vapors," Seth remarked, refilling our glasses. "No food, no champagne, no stimulating conversation. Just dancing and flirting with a lot of boys barely out of short pants.''

"I do not flirt!" I informed him tartly. "Modest young ladies of good breeding do not flirt.''

"Who told you that? You haven't known nearly as many modest young ladies of good breeding as I have, Rhawnie. They're born flirts, every one of them.''

"Not Gypsy women," I said seriously. "If a Gypsy girl is too bold her father will beat her. Why would any man want to marry a girl who looks at all other men? It makes no sense.''

The music started again. A wan youth with pale hair and large hands and feet appeared. "Ah, Countess, perhaps you have forgotten that you promised me this dance?''

"Ah, but of course I have not forgotten you!" I exclaimed warmly, rushing forward and pressing his hand in both of mind. "And I was just going to look for you to tell you that I cannot dance with you now because my dear uncle," I nodded at Seth, "has just returned from a long journey. I have not seen him for so many years—!" I hope you will forgive me, Monsieur.'' I had no idea what his name was; even though it was written on my card I couldn't read it. But I gave him my best smile and said, "Perhaps you will call upon me sometime, Monsieur?"

The young man smiled and expressed his understanding and said that he would certainly call upon me at my earliest convenience. Seth refilled our glasses for the third time. I drank and he filled my glass again. My head buzzed pleasantly and my limbs felt very relaxed, almost liquid.

"I congratulate you, Rhawnie," he said. "For a girl who doesn't know how to flirt, you have displayed a most remarkable natural aptitude."

"I wasn't flirting!" I said hotly. "I just told a little lie."

"Then you were flirting. It's the same thing. What made you say I was your uncle?"

I laughed and threw up my hands. "Who knows? You are not quite old enough to be my father! Ah, I think this champagne of yours inspires mischief."

"I think you're right," he agreed. We touched glasses and drank. "I love mischief."

I held out my empty glass. "Is there more?"

I hoisted myself up on the balustrade and swung my feet. "It is a truly beautiful night. Have you seen the moon?" I dropped my head all the way back. "It is a full moon! A dancing moon!"

"Oh?" He stood in front of me. "Do Gypsies dance in the full of the moon?"

"I do. Gypsies dance whenever they feel happy, whenever life is good! And life is good right now. How I wish I didn't have to go back to Madame Odette. How dull life with her is! But this, this is wonderful!"

I spread my arms to the sky and leaned back. I would have fallen if Seth hadn't put his hands on my waist and lifted me down. I looked at him. Our faces were only inches apart.

"You don't want to drown in the full of the moon," he said softly. "Bad luck."

I put my fingers on his lips. "Bad luck any time to speak of death," I warned. I moved my hand and brushed the scar on his cheek. My heart began to pound. I twisted around in his arms then and looked over the edge of the balustrade. "Ah, there is water below us. Is it the river?"

"No." he touched the back of my neck with his fingertip. I shivered. "Only a fish pond. But you'd still get very wet if you fell in. Will you have more champagne, Countess? It has made your cheeks pinker, and your eyes brighter. You are lovelier than ever."

"Flattering the horse does not make him run faster," I said, regarding him solemnly over the edge of my glass. He smiled. I laughed, too, throatily and heartily. I set down my glass very close to the edge of the balustrade and it toppled into the fish pond. "I feel so happy tonight!" I said passionately. "I want to sing! I want to dance! Tonight I am Gypsy!"

I ran to the middle of the veranda and stretched out my arms. I began to turn, slowly at first, then faster, rotating my head on my shoulders and humming a weird Gypsy tune. I moved my arms sinuously. My skirts rose and fell around me, and as I gained momentum they flew out from my body with my petticoats, displaying a pair of long legs encased in ivory stockings and long pink drawers tied at the knee with satin ribbons.

But I didn't think about my drawers then. I felt marvelously happy, and at one with the night and the stars and the beautiful scene. And I felt that love was near, very near. My dreams would come true.

Finally I stopped turning and reeled drunkenly. Seth stepped forward and caught me in his arms before I fell.

"Ah, thank you," I puffed. "Did you like my dance, Monsieur Seth?"

"I thought it delightful," he said in a voice like dark honey. "And you are a most delightful and delicious young lady."

"I really like this country," I decided with a dazed smile. "I like this civilization of yours. The Gypsies did not dance with each other, you know. I mean, the men and women did not dance together as they do here. The men danced with the men and the women with the women, or else everyone danced alone, without touching. This is much better, I think. You are a very good dancer, as I said before. You are not afraid to move your body."

"That's true," Seth admitted, moving his body closer to mine.

"This dancing has given me a terrible thirst," I said, wriggling out of his arms. We went back to the balustrade and I leaned against the cool stone while Seth filled our remaining glass.

"I hope you don't mind sharing," he said.

"To share is to know one of the great joys of living," I said wisely. "You must always share good fortune so that it doesn't turn bad." I drank first and then handed the glass to him. "You must finish so that we don't have bad luck," I told him. "I am feeling better now. Not so dizzy. And I am very hungry!"

I applied myself to our plate of food, making sure that I left Seth half of everything.

"I think I must still be growing," I said, pulling at the pheasant with my teeth because we had neglected to provide ourselves with knives and forks. "I am always hungry! Madame Odette says that I have hollow legs, but Cook thinks that because I am so tall I will never be satisfied because everything I eat is used up as soon as I eat it. You have seen how tall I am; nearly as big as you!"

"You're magnificent!" he said, toasting me. "I like big girls."

"Do you? I am glad. I daresay that I am the biggest girl you will find in Paris, or anywhere. But I don't mind. Madame Odette says that it makes the men notice me."

"I noticed you the minute I came into the ballroom," he said. "I saw your blond head bobbing out on the dance floor, and I wanted to meet you."

"And then you discovered that we had already met," I laughed. "You were surprised, weren't you? You cannot call me dirty little Gypsy now, can you?" He grinned and shook his head. "Ah," I sighed, taking a bite of pheasant, "it is too bad to have to eat tonight without a fork. I cannot show you what a really fine lady I have become. You know, I can take the meat from an entire chicken without once touching the bones with my fingers!"

"Very impressive!" Seth nodded. "I doubt that I could do that myself."

"Really?" I felt pleased. "Then I can teach you!" I heard voices and looked up. "Ah, it is Monsieur Delacroix and Mademoiselle Simone! Come, come, Mademoiselle, and share our pheasant and champagne!" I hoisted our remaining bottle by the neck. "Do not be afraid. I have forgiven you for your bad manners in the ballroom."

"Have you, indeed!" Simone said. She and Delacroix were followed by a small knot of guests. "I thought that Monsieur Delacroix should be informed that there is an imposter in our midst. This girl isn't nobility! She's a little beggar that Seth Garrett picked up in God knows where, and Odette Mornay is trying to pass her off as a little Russian countess. But in fact, she's been in Paris for over a year, serving as Odette's scullery maid!"

"Did you really?" Seth asked me, with a laugh.

"Oh, yes," I said nonchalantly. "Not a bad job, although I was not very good at it. Warm kitchen. Plenty of food. I was never hungry when I was a scullery maid. It is honest work."

"Take note, Simone," Seth grinned.

"One moment, Monsieur Garrett," Monsieur Delacroix said. "I do not recall that you were invited to this ball. I must kindly request that you leave at once."

Seth reached inside his coat and pulled out a heavy buff envelope. "But of course I was invited, my dear Pierre," he said smoothly. "In fact this invitation was delivered to me in person, last night, by your lovely wife. Would you care to verify her signature?"

A woman in the crowd shrieked; another gasped. Delacroix flushed and said, "Why, no, of course not. All the same—"

"And we know why Simone was invited," Seth went on. "You will see, Rhawnie, how helpful social contacts can be among civilized people. Simone Gallier would never be encouraged to attend such grand affairs as this if she weren't carrying on some grand affairs of her own."

"That's a lie!" Simone squawked.

"My dear Monsieur Garrett!" our host sputtered.

"Oh, you mean that Monsieur Delacroix tolerates Mademoiselle's bad manners because he is fond of her?" I chirped. "What strange customs the French have!"

"You little bitch," Simone seethed. She lunged at Seth, who stepped neatly aside. I crouched down near the balustrade and as Simone approached me I grabbed her ankles and lifted. She disappeared over the railing and we heard a loud splash.

Seth and I leaned over and looked down at the fish pond.

"White water," Seth remarked, pointing at the foaming and splashing below us. "It means there are sharks present."

"Do you think I have killed her?" I asked, concerned. In answer we heard angry bellows.

"Pierre! Pierre!"

Monsieur Delacroix leaned far out over the balustrade, calling out Simone's name. Other guests jostled for room at the railing, too. Suddenly Seth bent over, seized Monsieur Delacroix's ankles, and tipped him neatly into the fish pond, too. Soon his water-logged shouts joined Simone's.

"And now it's time to go," Seth declared. He grabbed my hand and his cane and led me back through the salon. As we passed a serving table he helped himself to another bottle of champagne.

"But the ball isn't over!" I cried.

"It is for us. Come on, I'll take you home."

He called for our wraps and asked a footman to order our carriage. In a few minutes we were darting down the marble steps at the front of the house. Angry echoes from the area of the fish pond reached our ears. A carriage pulled up and Seth opened the door and helped me in. We sat back against the cushions, gasping and laughing, and Seth popped the cork on the champagne and offered me the first swallow.

"They will be very angry with you," I said. "You will never be invited back."

"Doesn't matter. I got what I came for." Seth lifted the bottle to his lips, then passed it back to me.

"And what is that?"

"Diversion. Amusement. Mischief." He tweaked my cheek playfully. "And you. You are the loveliest little mischief-maker of all!"

"Ah, you have been a very bad influence on me," I said sadly. "Madame Odette will not speak to me for a week when she hears what we've done. Perhaps two weeks! And those boys will not come to see me. They were going to take me riding."

"Don't be sad," said Seth. "I'll take you riding."

"You will? You are so kind! Can we go tomorrow?"

"We'll see. Would you like more to drink? It's almost gone."

I looked out. "Are we going to the Rue de Vaugirard? I do not remember riding this way when we came."

"I thought we'd stop at my house first for more champagne. Wouldn't you like to see where I live?"

"Oh, yes! Is it very grand? Are you very rich?"

"You'll see." We rode for a while longer. My eyes felt very tired and I must have dozed off, for my head came down on his shoulder with a bump. "You are very kind," I said sleepily. "You are much nicer to me now that I am beautiful than you were when I was skinny and ugly, no? But I can understand that. Be careful when you choose a wife, though. The Gypsies have a saying: 'You cannot eat beauty with a spoon.' That means you must look for more than beauty when you marry. You're not married, are you?"

"Lord, no!"

After a few minutes I began to hum softly. "This is a Russian song, about a soldier who goes away and the beautiful girl who loves him. She waits many years for his return, until her hair is white. And then one day she is hoeing in the garden and she sees a white-haired man coming down the road, and he comes closer and closer and she knows that it is her lover! Very nice song, very happy." I sang the verses for him, very softly. The tune was slow and dirge-like.

"It doesn't sound particularly happy," Seth observed.

"Oh, but it is! That's just the way the Russians are. Even their happy songs sound sad because they think that happiness will not last. But Gypsy songs are much better. Gypsies know that life is good, and they think that if they are happy today, they will always be happy. Why not? Why worry about tomorrow? Why think about yesterday? Life is so good! Now listen to this song."

I sat up straight, feeling wide awake again, and I began to sing a fast, bright tune. I bobbed my head and clapped my hands. The carriage came to a halt.

"We're here." Seth threw open the door and stepped down. He held out his hands to assist me. I climbed out and suddenly my knees refused to support me. Seth steadied me.

I threw back my head and laughed. "This is so strange!" My words danced on little waves of laughter. "I cannot feel the earth under my feet! And my head is floating away, like a balloon!"

"Let's go inside," Seth urged gently, leading me up the path to the front door and into the house.

"You live here all alone?" I asked wonderingly. "It is so big!"

The round foyer was tiled with black and white marble squares. The walls and arched ceiling were painted white, and between the windows, fluted Grecian-style pilasters supported beautifully molded cornices. A huge crystal chandelier hung from the center of the ceiling, its hundreds of prisms catching the light from the low gas flames that burned in sconces on the walls. Matching inlaid cabinets flanked the front door, each bearing a white vase holding crimson roses. Two white marble busts on pedestals guarded the bottom of the staircase that curved upwards into the shadows.

"My man has gone to bed," Seth told me. "Would you like to see the drawing room?"

"No," I said. "No. I want to dance. Will you dance with me again, Monsieur Seth? Just once more! I shall not ask it again, I promise. But I must dance—!"

Seth propped his cane against the wall and put his arms around my waist. I put my hands on his shoulders and we started to waltz, very slowly, while I sang softly. I closed my eyes and felt his arms tighten around me. Around and around we turned, faster and faster. My song turned to laughter. Then Seth's lame leg gave way and we sprawled on the floor, still clutching each other. One of the ropes of pearls in my hair broke and beads rolled in a thousand directions.

"Oh, wonderful, wonderful, wonderful!" I laughed. We lay panting for a few minutes, recovering. "But I am sorry, my friend!" I exclaimed. "Did you hurt your leg?" I focused on his face with a little difficulty.

"No." He lay half on top of me. I could feel the pounding of his heart under his ribs. He smoothed straying tendrils away from my face and I caught my breath. Our eyes met and I saw no laughter in his, only something— something that I had seen a long time ago, in my uncle's eyes, when—

He framed my face with the palms of his hands and kissed me gently, once, twice. Then he rolled off and helped me to sit up. I leaned against him and gazed into his face. He smiled. "What's the matter, Rhawnie? Haven't you ever been kissed like that before?"

"No," I whispered. "No, never."

"Did you like it?"

"Yes, I think so." I lifted my face to be kissed again. He complied. Then I sighed deeply and grasped the lapel of his coat and rested my cheek on his shoulder. His arms were like a fortress around me, and I felt warm and safe inside. "When I said that I did not think of you when you were away—I lied."

"I know," he said gently, stroking my head.

"I thought of you often. Every day. And every time I learned something new, I said to myself, 'I hope I see that Seth Garrett sometime so that he can see that I am not a dirty Gypsy anymore.' I am glad you came to the ball. I hoped you would come. I knew you would come."

He toyed with the pins that anchored my braids. "I thought about you, too, Rhawnie," he said, starting to remove the pins. He was so deft that I wasn't aware of what he was doing until a fat braid fell to my shoulder. I jumped slightly and he said, "It's all right. I just wanted to see what it looks like loose. Do you mind?" He lowered his head and kissed my neck. A tremor, like a little earthquake, rippled through my entire body. One braid was undone. The second strand of pearls slid to the floor, rattling on the marble. Seth undid the second braid and ran his fingers through the strands. A shower of golden hair enveloped us both. It fell in shining ripples below my waist, covering my shoulders and back and arms like a bridal veil. He buried his face in its softness. "Magnificent," he breathed reverently. "I've never seen anything like it. You're like a Renaissance Venus."

"What is that?" I wondered happily.

"The most beautiful woman man has ever envisioned. The goddess of love, and beauty."

He began to plant soft, light kisses on my face and neck and shoulders. Every time his lips touched my flesh I gasped and shivered. I could feel myself growing heavier and more languid in his arms. He kissed the corners of my mouth and just brushed my lips with his. His breathing was shallow and labored, and I could sense his great excitement. It excited me, too.

"It's getting late," he said in a voice like heavy velvet. "I should take you home."

"Oh, I do not want to leave," I said dreamily. "But I suppose I must. Madame Odette would be very angry with me."

"Oh, she wouldn't mind," Seth assured me. "She and I are old friends, remember? You can sleep in my bed."

"But where will you sleep?" I asked.

"Don't worry about me." He helped me to my feet. "Come on, I'll show you my room."

A small oil lamp was burning on a low bureau near his bed, casting long, wavering shadows. The furnishings in the room were heavy and massive. The windows were draped in dark green velvet that looked black in the dim light.

He left me alone for a few minutes and came back with a bottle of champagne in a bucket and two exquisite tulip-shaped glasses.

"We have a lot to celebrate," he said. He sat on the edge of the bed and motioned for me to join him. I did so without hesitation. You will think I was very foolish, and so I was, but I was also rather tipsy from all that champagne he had made me drink. He popped the cork and filled the glasses. "I drink to you, Mademoiselle Countess Rhawnie," he said warmly, handing me a glass. "You have grown up. You are the most beautiful woman in Paris, and I am delighted that I have found you again."

"And I drink to you, Monsieur Seth Garrett," I said, raising my glass. "You helped me long ago, even though you didn't like me. And I, too, am happy that we have met now that I am grown."

We emptied our glasses. "Now let me help you with your gown," he said, taking my glass. "I can't promise to be as quick and expert as a lady's maid in unhooking your bodice, but I can try."

I turned my back to him and swept all my hair to the

front of my shoulders. He blew playfully on the back of my neck. I shivered and giggled. When my bodice was loose he told me to get out of my dress so that he could unlace my corset.

"I could not let you do that!" I said in a shocked voice.

"Why not?" He tugged at my hair and laughed. "It's not as though you didn't have anything underneath to cover your modesty. Besides, do you think I've never seen a lady in a corset before?"

"I am sure you have seen ladies in much less," I said slowly, suddenly remembering the scene with the land-lord's wife.

"And I have seen you in much less, too," he laughed. "Come on, off with your gown."

I stood up and climbed out of my gown, then after some hesitation, I undid the strings that held up my petticoats and let them fall to the floor, too. He stood behind me and worked to release me from the whalebone cage that had imprisoned me all evening.

"Whoof!" It fell away and I rubbed my aching middle. I still wore a thin chemise that came just below my waist and my silly pink drawers. "Oh, it feels good to be free of that thing! I think that the people who make clothes for women do not like them very much. So foolish, to pinch and squeeze the body like that! Now I really feel like a Gypsy again."

"And," said Seth, handing me a brimming glass, "you have room for more champagne."

"Ah, life is good!" I emptied my glass and plumped myself down in the middle of Seth's bed. I kicked off my dancing slippers and wriggled my toes. Seth took the glass out of my hand and removed it to safety. "Don't you think so, Monsieur Seth?" I asked, looking at him over my shoulder. "Don't you agree that life is good?"

Seth was making himself more comfortable, too. He shed his coat, his waistcoat, and his white silk tie. He lounged across the bed, propping himself up on his elbow. "I think that life has been very good to me tonight, little

Gypsy," he said. He reached over and touched my hair. "You are beautiful. And amusing. And you haven't called me *gorgio* once all evening!"

I laughed merrily. "How can I call you that, when I am one, too?" I threw up my arms and fell back on the bed. "Ah, we are both *gorgio* now! We are both very civilized! You do think I am civilized, don't you?" I asked anxiously, turning my head.

He slithered closer. His shirt was open and I could see the soft hairs on his chest, mostly black but sprinkled with gray.

"In my opinion you are ultimately civilized, Countess," he said. He put his fingers under my chin and kissed me once, lightly and tenderly.

"Why do you do that?" I asked in a small voice. I did not try to move away. I didn't want to.

"Because you said you like it, remember?" He kissed me again, moving still closer until I could feel his weight pressing against my left shoulder and hip and thigh. The kiss was longer, warmer, and I wanted it never to end. On the third kiss he parted my lips and teeth with the insistent pressure of his tongue. I sucked in my breath and turned my head away. "I caught you by surprise," he said, laughing softly. "But you'll get used to it. It's the best way to kiss." He kissed me again, deeply and languorously. Yes, it was good, almost magical the way he made his tongue feel like it was licking at my heart. Hesitantly, I lifted my hands and stroked the back of his neck very lightly. He shivered and lifted his head. "You're supposed to close your eyes when you're being kissed, Gypsy," he said, stroking my cheek with his thumb.

"Why?"

"Makes it better," he promised me. "Try." He kissed my eyelids. "Now keep them closed."

His kisses grew rougher and more demanding. He murmured my name and kissed my throat and neck and shoulders, and he rubbed his hand lightly over my right breast, coaxing it out of my flimsy chemise. He lowered his head to kiss the small pink nipple. I stiffened and cried out, and he kissed me reassuringly on the lips again. Then he untied the ribbon around the waist of my drawers.

I squirmed under him and said breathlessly, "Oh, Monsieur—do not!—what are you?—oh!" He stopped my mouth with persistent kisses and caresses until he felt me relax again.

"I want you. I want to see you."

His voice was hoarse. I heard it only faintly, as if from a long distance. A heaviness seized me. I felt that I couldn't move my limbs, that I couldn't raise my head. He undressed me with the gentlest care, and I uttered not a syllable of protest. I was floating on a buoyant cloud of champagne and desire, and I wanted to be lifted higher, still higher. And Seth was like a relentless tide; I didn't have the strength or the wits or the will to resist him.

I lay naked under him. He was naked, too, looking massive and bronzed in the lamplight. He ran his great hands over my body. I lifted my eyes to his face and touched his cheek very lightly with my fingertips. I was too embarrassed to look lower. One glimpse of the heavy swollen member jutting out from between his legs had confused and shamed me.

"Are you afraid, Gypsy?" he whispered.

"Will you hurt me, like my uncle?" I asked.

"What if I did?" He buried his fingers in my hair and moved his lips over my throat. "Would you cry?"

"You know I would not. I am Gypsy."

His embraces became rougher, his kisses more demanding. I could feel the tension and desire in him and it made me dizzy. The tendons in his neck were like tightly drawn cords. A fine mist of perspiration covered his forehead and upper chest. His lips seared my flesh wherever they touched. They were hot and biting and painful, and I was reminded of a hungry wolf attacking a fallen reindeer.

My body was glowing, yearning for him. Gently I urged him upwards and held him close and kissed him as he wanted to be kissed. He parted my thighs and slid that terrible swollen appendage into my deepest darkness, and I felt no pain, only wonder that I could bear the whole weight of his body on mine and feel no discomfort.

Ah, I wanted to make him happy, to make him love me. Although I felt a bit overwhelmed by his size and power and hunger, I wasn't frightened. This wasn't like that time in Moscow, with Alexei. Then I had wanted to break free, to escape, but now I wanted never to break free. I could feel his passion building and building, and I wanted nothing more in the world than to satisfy him and to please him. He taught me his rhythm and we moved together, surging and rising and falling as though we were being borne along on the same waves in the same sea of pleasure.

Our motion grew more violent. Finally, with a great shuddering sigh, he gripped my hips and released his power. Then he lay still, breathing hard, while his heart pounded like a horse at gallop.

I gazed at him, lying so close to me with his eyes closed. Two tears slid down my cheeks. I wasn't crying, really. He hadn't hurt me and I was not sorry for what I had done. We were not married but I was certain that we would be, very soon. But I was so awed by the enormous power that had possessed him, that had possessed us both, that I could not hold those tears back. I held him close and smoothed the hair away from his forehead and kissed him softly. I even felt a little proud of myself, as though I had single-handedly managed to tame a ferocious beast. In a sense, that is exactly what I had done.

He stirred and opened his eyes. "Well?" he said. "Did you like it?"

"Oh, yes," I said reverently. "Yes. It wasn't like— when my uncle Alexei—you know. It was wonderful. You are wonderful. My Seth." I sighed regretfully. "I am sorry that I wasn't a virgin for you, Seth."

"I'm not," he grunted. "Virginity is more of a nuisance than anything else."

I felt a little shocked by this attitude but I said nothing. Perhaps civilized people felt differently about this than

Gypsies. No Gypsy would marry a girl who had belonged to another man. On the morning after the wedding night, the Gypsy bridegroom carries the stained sheets from the marriage bed to his family, to show them that his wife was truly an honorable girl. But apparently Seth didn't demand that his wife be a virgin. I was glad.

"And this, this is what married people do?" I asked.

"It's not all they do," he said with a short laugh. "There are infinite permutations and combinations."

Those big words meant nothing to me and I didn't ask him to explain. There would be time later, I reasoned. Lots of time. I felt sleepy and happy. And loved.

6

Wisdom Gained

I STOPPED IN the middle of the curving staircase. A bald-headed man was on his knees on the black and white marble, picking up scattered pearls. He looked up.

"Oh? Ah." He got to his feet. He was wearing a long black apron over black trousers and a white shirt. A butler. "Good morning, Mademoiselle."

I came down the stairs slowly, holding the banister tightly. Bright sunlight streamed in through the long windows near the front doors. I shaded my eyes and blinked rapidly.

"Good morning," I said. My voice sounded faint and far away in my ears. "Can you—can you tell me where I am, Monsieur?"

"Where? But you are in the house of Monsieur Seth Garrett, Mademoiselle," said the man politely. His tone implied that I should have known that much.

"Yes, yes," I said a trifle impatiently. "But I don't know where it is, where the house is located. I must go back—"

"Ah." His face showed comprehension. "I will call Boucher, the coachman. He will take you home, Mademoiselle. If you will wait just a few minutes?" He nodded at a straight-backed chair that stood against the curving wall, then he went out.

I sighed and sat down heavily on the bottom step. My head was aching horribly and I felt slightly nauseous. A quiver of apprehension travelled through me, making me feel even worse. I thought about the naked man I had left sleeping upstairs. I remembered my shamelessness the night before and I closed my eyes to the picture. We had made love twice more: once before we slept and again at dawn. Then Seth had slept again and I had lain awake and thought and thought. I felt some elation, a little regret, and a great deal of surprise at the speed with which it had all happened. I needed to go to Madame Odette at once, to explain. Of course I would live with her until the wedding—to do otherwise would be most improper. Ah, there was so much to think about and my head throbbed so painfully—.

After a while I heard the rumble of wheels on cobblestones. The butler reappeared. "The carriage is ready, Mademoiselle. This way, if you please?"

He opened the front doors and followed me out of the house. The carriage was waiting at the end of the path. I remembered the coachman from the night before, but barely. I saw him and the butler exchange glances. I thought they were staring at my loose hair. I would have braided it and pinned it up, but I seemed to have lost all my hairpins, and I didn't really want to think about where they had gone.

Boucher opened the door for me and assisted me into the carriage, and I gave him Madame Odette's address on the Rue de Vaugirard. When I looked back at the house, I saw the butler standing on the path, shaking his head sadly.

Marie-Claire opened the door to me. She gave me a sour look and said, "She's still in bed. She doesn't want to see you."

"Oh. I knew she would be angry—. I must see her, Marie-Claire. I want to explain."

The maid sniffed. "It's going to take a lot of explaining.

I've never seen her like this before. Just don't be surprised if she throws something at you."

I picked up my skirts and walked slowly up the stairs to Madame Odette's room. I found her propped up in bed, and her face looked drawn and pasty under her vivid red hair. I had never known her to look so old, and so weary.

Before I could open my mouth she snapped, "Get out! I never want to see you again!"

"Oh, Madame," I said softly, approaching the bed. "I know you are angry, but I have such good news! I am to be married, just as we planned!"

"I don't care what you do!" Tears of anger and sorrow coursed down her wrinkled cheeks. She didn't bother to wipe them away. "I don't want to hear what you did or where you went or what new shame you have brought upon me. I just don't want to know! You abandoned me last night. After your disgraceful performance I went upstairs to lie down, and you never once came to inquire about me. You are selfish! All you cared about was having a good time and creating—scandal! I heard about what you and that miserable scamp Seth Garrett did to Simone and Pierre Delacroix. Are you mad? Didn't I tell you over and over again until I was hoarse that you had to watch your behavior every minute? And what happened? You made a scene, disgraced yourself, and if that wasn't bad enough, you ran off with that scoundrel, that vagabond, that immoral—cad!"

My mouth felt dry. "But I thought—he was your friend."

"Friend? That man? Do you think he inflicted you upon me because he was fond of me? He doesn't care about anyone, that man. He is as cruel and cold and vicious as anyone I've ever known."

"Oh, no!" I cried. "He was very kind to me, very kind! He—we are going to be married!"

Madame Odette looked at my happy, hopeful face. "Oh, you little fool," she said. "Did he tell you that? Did he ask you to marry him?" I opened my mouth but no sound came out. "I thought not! He ruined you, and you're stupid enough to think that being used and disgraced is tantamount to a marriage proposal! You are worse than a fool! You have managed to wreck whatever chance you might have had to make a good match. Do you think that anyone will want you now, after you have been soiled and discarded by the most notorious womanizer in Paris?"

"But—you never told me," I said weakly. "You—he said—I thought he was your friend! You are wrong about him, Madame! He is not—what you say!"

But as I said those words a picture flashed into my mind: Seth Garrett, naked, pounding at the wriggling, squealing landlord's wife. I felt sick.

"He is everything I say and more!" the woman said with heat. Her old fingers plucked at the coverlet on her lap. "And if you think that all of Paris isn't talking about what you did last night—! Well, you are his whore now. I want nothing more to do with you. I never want to see you again! Leave my house at once! Your lover will take you in. He'll have to. And do you know what will happen to you then? He will use you. He will spend your youth and beauty freely, until they are gone. And then he'll throw you out. Into the gutter, back where you came from. He did it to Simone, and to I don't know how many others, and he'll do it to you. You think you're any different? You think he loves you? He's laughing at you this very minute, because you were simple-minded enough and stupid enough to fall into his snare. No decent man will want you now that he's ruined you! Little Gypsy fool. And I'm—I'm not sorry!"

"Madame," I said sorrowfully. I sat on the edge of the bed and touched her hand. "You are wrong, I know it. He is not like that! He will do the honorable thing, I know he will."

Madame Odette snorted and jerked her hand away. She turned her head on her lace-edged pillow and said in a dull, dead voice, "Oh, get out. Take your things and leave this house. I wash my hands of you. You will never be anything but a dirty little Gypsy. I should have known it. Seth Garrett knew it, or he would not have used you as he did. Go!"

I stood and said, "I will take nothing from you. I came with nothing and I leave with nothing but the dress I am wearing. If I had my Gypsy rags, I would wear them."

"Such pride!" sniffed Madame Odette without looking at me. "Hang on to it as long as you can, girl. When he's through with you, you won't even have pride to fall back on."

"Good-bye, Madame," I said softly. "May God stay with you."

She gave no sign that she heard me. She lay on her bed, defeated, a stalwart little galleon whose final voyage had ended in shipwreck.

I left the house without taking anything from my room and without saying a word to anyone. Marie-Claire watched with satisfaction as I came down the stairs and left the house. She closed the doors firmly behind me, and I heard her say tartly, "Good riddance!"

I walked up the Rue de Vaugirard to the Boulevard Saint-Michel, and I stood at the busy intersection for several minutes while the passers-by jostled and stared at me. To be sure, I was an odd sight that morning, in my sweeping ball gown that was already collecting grime from the streets, with my hair rippling around me like a mad-woman's. I had no money for a carriage. I would have to walk. Having only the vaguest notion of where I wanted to go, I followed the Seine, crossed the Pont Alexandre to the Right Bank, and headed west towards the Bois de Boulogne.

Many hours later, weary and dishevelled, I reached a street named the Rue de Montmorency and I recognized Seth's house. I hadn't seen anything of the neighborhood the night before, and that morning I had paid only scant attention to landmarks when Boucher drove me away. But after wandering aimlessly for half the morning, I finally found the place.

The house stood well back from the cobbled street. The lawns were spacious and well-manicured, and ancient trees lent generous shade. The structure was built of the same greyish stone as the Louvre, and like the Louvre it had a square mansard roof that was covered by scalloped grey slate shingles. The center portion of the house was three stories high, and it was flanked by two lower wings. Low black iron railings guarded all the windows except those on the first floor, which opened onto a brick terrace that ran around the entire building.

I lifted the brass knocker, a graceful thing in the shape of a woman's hand. The highly polished oak doors flew open and I was confronted by the butler, now wearing a black coat and a black stock at his neck.

"Mademoiselle!" His eyes widened. He hesitated only a moment, then stepped back to allow me to enter.

"Where is Monsieur Garrett?" I asked.

"He—ah—if you would care to wait I will announce you, Mademoiselle, ah—?" He waited for me to supply my name.

"I will announce myself," I said steadily. "Please tell me where I can find him. Is he in his room?"

I started towards the stairs. The man hurried after me. "No, wait, Mademoiselle. He is in the study, down here. If you will follow me?"

He passed through an elegant drawing room just off the foyer into a small, square, book-lined room. Seth sat in a leather chair with his feet propped up on a highly polished Louis XIV desk. He was smoking a cigar and reading a newspaper. A glass of whiskey stood at his elbow.

He looked up when I entered. "Oh." He lifted one black eyebrow. "You're still here? I thought you'd gone home." He gazed at me briefly, taking in my less-than-elegant appearance, then gave his attention once more to the newspaper.

I looked around at the butler, who was standing silently

behind me. He gave me a sympathetic look and backed out of the room, pulling the double doors closed as he went.

"I have been home. To the Rue de Vaugirard, I mean."

"Oh?" He turned the page and puffed his cigar.

I swallowed. "Madame Odette was very angry about last night. She told me to leave her house. I did not know where else to go, so I came here. She said that you—that you were not really her friend."

"That's too bad." He didn't look up.

"I must know, Seth," I cried, stepping closer and resting the palms of my hands on the desk. "You are going—you will marry me, won't you? Madame Odette said that you would not, but she was very upset, very angry. You will marry me, I know it!"

"Marry you?" He looked up. His expression was one of vague surprise. "Marry you?" he repeated. "Why on earth would I do that? Go back to Odette, Rhawnie. She'll forgive and forget."

"I do not understand," I whispered through a tight throat. "After last night—"

"What about last night?" He sounded bored.

"You made love to me! We did—" I paused to moisten my lips, which felt numb and dry, "we did as married people do! Now we must marry! It is the honorable thing!"

Seth Garrett twisted his mouth into a pitying smile. "My dear little Gypsy, I never do the honorable thing. Run along now, back to Odette." He lifted the newspaper in front of his face, shutting himself away from me behind a wall of print that I could not, in my illiterate ignorance, penetrate.

Somewhere in the room a clock was ticking softly. Each stroke seemed to reverberate in my ears, louder and louder: dishonor, betrayal, disgrace. Dishonor. Betrayal. Disgrace. I couldn't breathe. The room felt uncomfortably close and warm. My hands were heavy, leaden.

A brass paper knife lay on the desk, within my reach. I snatched it up, and holding it blade down, like a dagger, I threw myself at him over the top of the desk.

He was unprepared for my attack. The knife slashed through the newsprint. He moved his body out of the way, but not before the blade tore a hole in the soft black velvet jacket he was wearing. Then he grabbed my wrist and twisted until I dropped the knife. The chair fell over and we rolled on the floor. He pinned me under his body and rested the tip of the knife under my chin.

"Kill me now," I told him. "Kill me or I swear I will try this again, and the next time I will not fail."

He glowered at me. Our postures were very like the ones we had assumed the night before, in love. But there was no love or desire between us now. Only fury and hatred.

"I am not afraid of your knife, *gorgio*," I said, drawing my lips back from my teeth. "I am no coward. You are the coward. You! If I had a father or brothers to defend me, you would pay for what you have done!"

"Get up." He tossed the knife aside and jerked me to my feet, keeping a tight hold on my arm.

The doors burst open and the butler said breathlessly, "Monsieur, are you all right? I heard—"

"Everything's fine, Jules," Seth said curtly. The anger left his eyes and a slow smile spread over his face. "Prepare a room for Mademoiselle. And send Boucher to the Rue de Vaugirard for her things. The old bitch won't have any use for them."

"Yes, Monsieur." With a bow and a curious look at me, the butler left the room.

I pulled away from Seth and rubbed my arm. "I will not stay here!" I said. "I would rather beg for my bread in the street than spend one more minute under your roof!"

He laughed harshly and righted his chair. "You'd get a lot more than bread, my fine lady." He sat back and crossed his arms. "It's a big bad world out there. They'd make mincemeat out of you."

"I am not afraid! I can look after myself!"

"What are you getting so excited about? I'm offering you a place under my roof. That's what you wanted, isn't it? Run along. Jules will show you your room." He picked up his newspaper again, made a face when he saw its condition, and threw it down.

"You don't want me," I said in a low voice. "You don't love me! I won't stay here, I tell you! I won't!"

"Yes, you will." He slid down in his chair and closed his eyes. "You have nowhere else to go, remember?"

I picked up my skirts and ran out of that room. Through the drawing room. Across the black and white marble floor of the foyer. Away. I had to get away from him!

The butler, Jules, suddenly appeared in front of me, out of nowhere, like a forest spirit in Russian folk tales. "Your room is ready, Mademoiselle. If you—"

I brushed past him without a word and threw open the front doors. Down the path, up the street, racing until my heart was bursting inside my chest, until I felt limp and weak and exhausted. I stopped to catch my breath and looked around. I didn't know where I was, how far I had come. It was afternoon already. The sky was leaden and a light rain started to fall. A chilly wind swept through the streets. I had no wrap, not even my light shawl—which I think I had left in Boucher's carriage—and I shivered.

I started to walk east. The steady drizzle soon soaked the lace on my sleeves, pasting it to my arms. My gown was becoming sodden, too, and heavy, and my hair was plastered to my face. Carriages rolled past, splashing me with dirty water from the cobbles. I felt very hungry and light-headed. I remembered that I had had nothing to eat since the cold pheasant the night before, and nothing to drink but champagne—

I had been such a fool, such a gullible idiot! Living like a *gorgio* had made me soft and stupid. To have believed his lies, to have let him seduce me—. It had been so easy for him, so easy. I was like a ripe fruit, ready for picking.

Enough. A Gypsy has no regrets, no sorrow about the past, only joy and acceptance of what life has given him today, now. Don't think about him anymore, I told myself sternly. Forget him. Forget.

I walked for hours, aimlessly, hardly seeing where I was going. Occasionally men would speak to me. They would stop me and inquire in leering voices if I needed help. I shook them off and pushed on. I went into a bakery to ask for a scrap of bread. The proprietress took one look at me and my soiled gown and began to rant.

"Get out of here before I call the police! What kind of business do you think I'm running? This isn't a charity kitchen for whores!"

I swirled away into the rain. True, if I had looked like a Gypsy, or even a normal *gorgio*, I would have had better luck. Darkness was closing in. I still had no money, no place to sleep. I took shelter from the rain and wind in a doorway. A man coming out of the building stared at me, and then he said.

"Would you like to come up and get warm, little lady? I have some very nice wine—"

I shook my head and left my shelter. Perhaps I could find some Gypsies, I thought. Every city has Gypsies. I would go to them and say, I am Rom, I am one of you. They would take me in because I spoke their language. But what then? I was tainted, defiled, shamed. No self-respecting Gypsy would marry me. Being raped by a man when you're a child is one thing, but giving yourself to a man who is not your husband—oh, what a fool I had been! I would never have a husband, Gypsy or *gorgio*. No husband. No babies. What kind of life was that?

An old woman approached me. She was dressed in black, from head to two. A bad omen, I thought. But then I had noticed that many older women in France wore black all the time.

"What's the matter, dearie?" she said kindly. "You'll freeze if you don't come out of this rain." She looked kind and her tone was solicitous. "I have a little place, very near here. We'll soon get some hot soup into you. Come along."

I permitted myself to be led. The inducement of warmth and food was very powerful. And the old woman looked

148

sincere and honest, if I was any judge. We went up three flights of stairs in a grey, gloomy building that stank of too many people living too close together. She pushed open a door and motioned me inside. A man was warming his hands at a small, black pot-bellied stove. He turned around and scowled at us.

"This is my son, Gaston," the woman said. "Look, Gaston, I found this poor creature out in the street. What happened, dearie? Running away from home? They don't understand you, is that it?" She cackled.

I was too tired to explain. "Something like that," I said. Gaston heaved himself out of his chair near the stove and beckoned to me to take it. I sat down gratefully and stretched my hands out in front of me. The woman pressed a cup into my stiff fingers. I sipped. It was tea, scalding and strong, the way I liked it.

"Why don't you take off those wet things?" the woman suggested. "I have something you can wear, I think."

"What?" I looked up. "Oh, no, thank you. I'm just fine, the way I am."

Gaston spoke for the first time. "You take this coat, then." He draped something heavy around my shoulders. "Better than nothing."

I gave him a weak smile. He was large and coarse and stupid-looking with small brown eyes and a protruding lower lip and a heavy jaw. His hair was thick and dirty and a greasy forelock hung over his eyes. His coat smelled of sweat and rancid oil and sour wine.

The tea warmed my insides, and the fire dried my hair and clothes. I think I must have fallen asleep, for the next thing I knew Gaston was on his knees in front of me. He was clawing at my bosom and kissing me wetly.

I tried to push him away, but he gave a peculiar gurgling laugh and put his arms around my waist. I wriggled and squirmed.

"Let me go! Take your dirty hands off me, *gorgio* pig! Let me go!"

He lurched to his feet, pulling me up with him. I saw that

his trousers were unbuttoned and starting to slide down around his hips.

The old woman screeched, "Oh, isn't my Gaston a fine lover! Such a good lad! Don't forget, Gaston, you owe me five francs for this one. It's not easy to get them to come up."

Gaston made moaning noises and dragged at my skirts with one hand while he held on to my waist with the other. I jerked my knee up suddenly. He gave an agonized yelp and doubled over. I darted for the door, but the old woman got there first.

"And just where do you think you're going?" she demanded fiercely. "You'll pay for hurting my boy! I didn't bring you up here so that you could cripple my son!"

"If you are his mother then he is the Devil himself!" I said angrily. "Get out of my way!"

"You ungrateful little slut!" The hag raised her hand. "I'll teach you to abuse a stranger's hospitality! Gaston, get over here! Hurry up!"

Gaston groaned. "Oh, she killed me! I'm dying!"

The old woman gripped my arms and yelled, "Hurry up! I'm holding her! You can punish her! Hurry!"

The man snarled and came towards us. I took a deep breath and shouted, "Police! Police!" At once the woman released me and skipped out of my way. I raced down the stairs and out of the house, straight into the arms of a man who was passing. We rocked together and almost fell, but he put his arms around me to steady me.

"Whoa, hold on there! Where are you going in such a hurry, young lady?"

"Let me go!" I puffed. "Take your hands off me!"

"Wait, wait, I won't hurt you," he laughed pleasantly. "Just calm yourself, child. What's the matter? Are you in trouble? Perhaps I can help."

I looked at him. He was elderly, about fifty-five or sixty, with white hair and a white mustache. He wore evening dress and an opera cape with a red lining. His smile was kind and solicitous.

"You look all in, you poor child," he said sympathetically. "Are you hungry?"

"Yes, yes, very hungry. If you could just let me have a few francs, Monsieur, I would be so grateful." My brain worked fast. "I am running away from my father. He is a terrible man, terrible. He beats me every day! I couldn't take it anymore and I just ran and ran and now I'm lost and cold and hungry. Please, Monsieur, just a few francs? I won't trouble you—"

"No trouble, no trouble," he said heartily. "Of course you shall have your francs. But where are you going? You have a place to sleep tonight?"

I shook my head. "No, Monsieur. I am going—to my fiancé. He will care for me until we are married. My father hates him and won't let him come to the house, but we meet sometimes, in church."

He smiled. "In church? Your father must think you very devout."

"Oh, yes, very," I said quickly. "But he doesn't suspect anything because I always go with my grandmother who is very old and deaf. She sits with her eyes down, so she doesn't even know that Gaston and I meet there."

"Gaston, eh? And what does he do, your Gaston?"

I cast a furtive glance upwards, in the direction of the room from which I had fled. "He—he is a saddle-maker," I said. "Please, Monsieur, just a few francs! I wouldn't want any friends of my father's to see me. He has very many friends. He would kill me if he caught me. Please?"

He clicked his tongue and shook his head. "It's a terrible thing to quarrel with one's family. I have a daughter myself, no older than you. I would be most upset if she ran away—not that she would have any reason to want to leave me! I am very good to her. I'm afraid I even spoil her. But if such a thing should ever happen, it would please me to think that she had turned to a gentleman in her time of need. I am not from Paris myself. I live in Lyon. I own a bank there. Listen, child, why don't you come back to my hotel and have dinner with me? Then we can see about finding you a place to stay until this business is settled."

I regarded him with suspicion. "And what would I have to do for my dinner, Monsieur?"

The white-haired gentleman looked momentarily confused, then shocked. "My dear child! I would never take advantage of one so young and so innocent! And in this time of distress! It would be like—well, like taking advantage of my own child. What an appalling, disgusting thought! I am sad that you should mistrust me, my dear. It is a commentary on the times we live in that an offer of charity immediately provokes suspicion."

He looked very kind and grandfatherly. I felt a little sorry for what I had said.

"You must be chilled through," he said worriedly. "Here, take my cloak." He threw his cape around my shoulders. It felt slick and cold rather than warm. "It really was very silly of you to run off without making better preparations. Ah, the young are so impulsive, so headstrong! Listen to me," he laughed, "I'm scolding you just like a father. Only I hope I am a better father than yours! Imagine, beating a young woman of your age. It's a disgrace! The man should be jailed."

He hailed a passing carriage.

"Thank you, Monsieur," I said when we were seated and he had given the driver the address of his hotel. "I met some very evil people—I just barely escaped! Thank you for helping me."

"There, there," he patted my hand in fatherly fashion. "I am just glad that I happened to come along at the right time, Mademoiselle. You are fortunate that some less honorable person didn't find you first!"

His hotel was on a quiet street. It was small and less elegant than one might have expected from his dress and manners. He nodded familiarly to the clerk at the desk and escorted me up the stairs to the second floor. His room was large and comfortable with a large bed in the corner, a dresser and another low table that held a tray with a bottle and some glasses, and a couple of soft chairs in front of a gas fire. He went at once to the liquor tray.

"You must have a little brandy," he said. I sat in one of the chairs and he brought me a glass.

"I don't think I want anything to drink," I told him.

"No? It's only a small glass. And you need something to take the chill off. Go on, take just a sip or two. You don't have to finish it. Now tell me, where does this Gaston of yours live?"

"What? Oh, Gaston! He lives—in another part of the country. In—in Lyon!"

"Lyon!" The old man smiled. "That's quite a coincidence. Perhaps I have even used one of his saddles."

I felt lost for a second before I remembered that Gaston was supposed to be a saddle-maker. "Oh, yes, saddles! They are very fine saddles, very beautiful!"

"I'm sure they are. Now where does he live in Lyon?"

"I do not know," I confessed, taking a sip of the brandy. It tasted terrible and it burned like fire, but it warmed my insides nicely. "I have never visited him there."

"And yet he comes all the way to Paris to meet you in church," the old gentleman marvelled. "What remarkable devotion! And I don't mean devotion to God!" He laughed heartily at his little joke. I smiled weakly. "Are you warmer, my dear? Here, drink some more of your brandy, just a little. Does wonders for a chill. My own daughter takes some every night before she goes to bed. For her constitution. Well, I suppose you want to go to Lyon as soon as possible? I would take you, but I cannot leave Paris just yet. Business, you know. Perhaps there is a room in this hotel you can have. You can stay here, away from everyone, including your father. You'd be quite safe, and when I was ready to go we could travel to Lyon together."

"Yes," I said distractedly, "that sounds like a wonderful plan." My stomach complained noisily. "Oh, I am so hungry. You said we could have dinner here?"

"Yes, indeed! How inconsiderate of me! I'll go down and order. We'll dine here, shall we? So much cozier than downstairs. They serve very nicely here, very nicely.

What would you like? How about a nice filet and some Bordeaux?''

"No wine, just tea, if you please," I said, forcing myself to smile sweetly. I felt very tired and hungry and I wished he'd get on with it. "It sounds wonderful."

"Splendid. I'll be right back."

He went out. I wandered around the room. It had a bare, unlived-in look. I peaked in the top drawer of the dresser. It was empty. So were all the other drawers. I looked under the bed. No suitcase or valise.

"Looking for something, Mademoiselle?"

I stood up quickly. My host came into the room and closed the door. He turned the key and dropped it into his pocket.

"Yes, Monsieur," I said. "I wanted a pair of dry socks. I thought you might have something I could borrow. But all your drawers are empty. I find that very strange. Are we in the wrong room?"

I inched slowly around the perimeter of the room, towards the door. He grinned and came towards me.

"What's the matter, child? Don't you trust me? After all, I have a daughter—"

"I think the only daughter you have is in your head," I said sharply. "Please get out of my way or I'll call the police." He came closer. "Police! Police!" I shouted.

But the ploy that had frightened the old woman only made this man chuckle. "You don't think anyone is going to pay attention to that nonsense, do you? We're not in Pigalle now, my dear."

"The hotel—the guests! They'll hear me!"

"Not they! I'm a very good customer of theirs. Very well known to the management. I come, I go, I pay my bills on time, I tip well. Now be a good girl and come sit on my lap."

I dodged past him but he grabbed my loose hair and dragged me towards the bed. I flailed at him and tried to pry his fingers loose, but even though he was old he was strong. Or else he had had experience in handling angry women.

"Let me go!" I scratched at his wrists and plucked at his fingers. He was tearing my hair out by the roots and it hurt.

"Now, now, calm yourself, child! I'm not going to hurt you. I want to talk to you. Business. You could make yourself a lot of money, you know. And I can help you."

"What do you mean?" I demanded angrily. "You mean you would pay me if I slept with you?"

"Something like that," he chuckled. "You're obviously new at this game. But I can teach you a lot, my dear. Everything you need to know." He pulled me into an embrace and tickled my chin. "Now why don't you get out of that silly wet dress and we'll get started." He leaned forward to kiss me.

I boxed his ears and sprang away from him. I reached the door in a single bound and rattled the knob, then beat on it with my fists.

"It's locked, remember?" he laughed. His good humor was as horrible as Gaston's idiotic slobbering. "I have the key in my pocket. Why don't you come and get it?"

"You evil son of a louse-infested dog!" I said furiously. "You can't keep me here against my will! Unlock this door and let me go!"

"When I'm ready. I think you ought to listen to me, my dear. I have a proposition to make."

"I know what kind of proposition you are making and I'm not interested," I snapped. "When my father hears about this—and Gaston!—"

"You don't even know who your father is," he said with a broad grin. "And as for Gaston—he's about as real as that daughter of mine. Everything you told me was a lie. That doesn't matter. Everything I told you was a lie, too. We're even. You're not running away from home; as I said, you would have made better preparations. I think you're just a poor, green little whore who's running away from her procurer or an angry customer. You really shouldn't try to work for yourself, my dear. A woman is such a soft, weak creature. So defenseless. You need a man to stand up for you, to protect you."

He came towards me again. I darted and dodged, but the room was small and I could not escape him. He backed me up against the door and put his arms around me. I tried the knee trick that had worked so well on Gaston, but he anticipated it and chopped viciously at my upraised thigh with his fist.

"Save that for someone you really want to hurt," he advised me. "I'm your friend."

"You are dirt!" I scratched at his face with my fingernails.

He caught my hands and pressed hard on the undersides of my wrists with his thumbs. The pain was sudden and intense. "Naughty, naughty," he clucked.

I screamed and I struggled, and when he got tired of it he gave me a stunning blow to the side of the head that made my brain buzz. I went reeling across the floor.

"You whores never learn," he said sadly. "Now let's go back to bed."

I scrambled to my feet and backed around the two chairs in front of the fire. He followed, slowly and steadily, and the smile never left his face. I skirted quickly around the bed and slithered past the dresser, and finally I stopped in front of the liquor table. He smiled kindly and stretched out his arms to me. I groped behind me. I found the bottle and grasped it by the neck. When I judged that he was close enough I hoisted the bottle and brought it down on his head, in one long, swift movement.

A trickle of blood oozed down his cheek. He looked dead. Then his eyes rolled around and he slumped to the floor. Still smiling.

Quickly, I fell on my knees beside him and searched through his pockets. I found the key, as well as a billfold full of money and a shining gold watch. I stuffed the last two items into my bodice and clutched the key in my hand.

I tiptoed to the door, unlocked it, and slipped into the hallway.

Just as I emerged from the room, a woman with vivid red hair and a brightly painted face stepped out of the room next door. She looked at me curiously.

"Hello, sweetie," she said companionably. "How's business tonight?"

I gulped and gurgled, then I bolted down the stairs. The man at the desk looked up when he heard me.

"Ha," he leered knowingly, "that didn't take long. Old Louis is more of a man than I thought."

"Help, murder!" came an ear-splitting scream from above. "Murder!"

"What have you done?" the clerk shrilled. "Come back here, you little slut!"

But I was out the door and pelting as hard as I could down the sidewalk. I could still hear their shouts. A whistle screamed after me, too, and then I heard pounding footsteps. I looked over my shoulder. Two policemen were chasing me, shouting at me. I dodged down an alley. At the end a solid wall rose up to meet me. A dead end. Several doors opened onto the alley. I chose one and found myself in a tailor's shop. An old man was sitting cross-legged on a table with a length of dark fabric on his lap. He looked up, startled.

"Good evening, Mademoiselle," he greeted me politely, as though I were an customer instead of a rain-soaked fugitive.

"Good evening!" I panted. "Which way—the street?"

He pointed to the other end of the room. I ran through the shop and emerged on a street again. I looked to my left and saw someone running towards me. So I ran to the right.

Rain was falling heavily, blinding me and soaking me. The sharp wind felt like it was turning the moisture on my skin to ice. I was nearly dropping with fatigue. Footsteps beat the cobbles in pursuit. They came closer and closer. I ran up one dark street and down another while visions of bloodthirsty Cossacks flashed across my mind. They would kill me when they caught me, I was sure of it. They would slaughter me as they had slaughtered my family, my tribe. Everyone hated Gypsies.

My lungs were bursting and I couldn't breathe. I took shelter in a doorway and crouched down with my satin skirts pulled up around my shoulders for warmth. I was sure that I had killed the man. As I had killed my uncle. I tried to remember if I had felt any pulse while I was searching through his pockets. He had felt stiff. He had certainly looked dead, except for that smile. I had killed a smiling man. If the police caught me they would hang me, or else they would lock me away in some jail for a hundred years. Every Gypsy knew that to kill a *gorgio* was a very stupid thing to do. Very stupid.

"Hey, you. What are you doing here?"

I looked up. A black-clad policeman was standing over me, his right hand resting on a lethal-looking club. My mouth went dry. I was aware of how I must have looked to him, with my hair lank and sodden and my gown filthy and shredded. I looked like a murderess.

"Long live the Gypsies!" I screamed, leaping to my feet. He fell back, surprised, and I darted past him to the street. I had gone about a hundred yards when I heard the piercing shriek of his whistle.

I ran for all I was worth. I could feel every stone, every crack between the cobbles through the thin soles of my dancing slippers. My legs felt tight and sore and a stitch in my side pained me so severely that I could hardly keep going. But the picture of that policeman behind me spurred me on: I could see him gaining steadily, perhaps even drawing his gun so that he could shoot me in the back.

Then I tripped over a curbstone and went sprawling in a vast puddle. When I got halfway to my feet I saw a carriage bearing down on me. It was drawn by four enormous horses—sixteen flashing hooves—and travelling at breakneck speed.

I tried to stand but my feet became entangled in my wretched petticoats. I threw up my arms. Then I closed my eyes and murmured, "Sweet Mother of Mercy!"

Men shouted. A woman screamed. The rumble of the wheels on the wet cobblestones sounded like thunder on the Day of Judgement.

Strong arms closed around me and lifted me as the carriage swept by. For a moment all was silence. Then I opened my eyes and saw Seth's face hovering over mine.

"Oh, no," I moaned. My head dropped, onto his chest. "Not you."

"Yes, me. Are you all right?"

I gave an infinitesimal nod. His arms felt so strong, so secure. Like a bulwark against danger and horror.

"Hold on there!" The policeman ran up. "In the name of the King I arrest you—"

Seth swung his arm. The man staggered and fell flat on his back in the puddle.

We raced along on foot, down a dank, narrow alley where the running rainwater came up higher than my ankles. We reached a small square. Seth's horse was tethered to a hitching post outside a wineshop. He lifted me up on the horse's back and climbed up behind me. We wound through a maze of twisting streets and alleys before we reached the Seine. I slumped against him, thankful for the warmth of his body and the timeliness of his rescue. Yet I felt dejected and defeated because my efforts to escape him had landed me right back in his arms, where I had no wish to be.

We arrived at the house on the Rue de Montmorency. Seth pulled the horse up at a side door and shouted for Jules. The butler appeared instantly, as if he had been awaiting the summons, and held the horse's head while Seth lifted me down and carried me inside.

"There is a fire in the rose bedroom, Monsieur," Jules said. "And some brandy."

"Good. Tell Boucher to look after the horse. And prepare a bath."

"Yes, Monsieur."

He carried me across the foyer and up the curving staircase. I could feel the unevenness of his gait and I was certain that his leg was hurting him dreadfully. He pushed open a door on the second floor, not far from his own room, and dumped me on a large, soft bed.

"Suppose you tell me why the police want to arrest you," he said, standing over me with his hands on his hips.

I couldn't look at him. I rolled on my side and said, "I killed a man. In some hotel. He pretended to be nice to me but he wouldn't let me go. So I hit him with a bottle. He deserved it! He was trying to—to dishonor me!"

He made a derisive noise. I heard the clink of glass and the pouring of liquid. He pulled me into a sitting position and shoved a tumbler into my hands.

"Drink."

I sniffed. "No! I don't want any! That man tried to make me drunk on his brandy and—"

"Shut up and drink or I'll pour it down your throat."

I pouted and shrugged, but I obeyed him. This brandy didn't burn and it had a nice taste. I emptied my glass.

He took the tumbler away from me and said, "On your feet." I hesitated. He put his hands on my arms and lifted me. I might have been a child, he did it so easily. I stood in front of him, glaring at him resentfully. He looked angry, too.

"How did you find me?" I asked.

"Just happened to be passing," he said gruffly. "Take those things off."

"I won't!" I flashed.

He gripped the edge of my bodice and wrenched it roughly away from my body. My victim's billfold and watch dropped to the floor. He said, "Jesus. You never learn, do you, Gypsy?"

He stripped off my gown, my sodden petticoats, my corset, my drawers. Everything. I was naked and shivering. Then he wrapped a rough scratchy blanket around me and pulled it tight around my shoulders. Our faces were inches apart and I was trembling. The corner of his mouth twitched and his eyes grew large and dark. He grabbed a fistful of hair and jerked my head back. His lips burned my throat. I felt as though I were dissolving, melting like a block of salt in a rainstorm that grows smaller and smaller as the water pares it away and the earth absorbs it.

The blanket fell away. He moved his hands over my body, not lovingly as he had the night before, but possessively, greedily, like a miser handling his gold. Sudden stabbing sensations in my middle made me catch my breath. They were painful and thrilling at the same time. I tried once to push him away, but my arms had no strength.

I could feel his manhood swelling and straining under his breeches. He unleashed it and led my hand to it. I recoiled, but he held my hand closed around it. It was velvety smooth, as hard and as hot as a poker yet throbbing with life and longing. I moaned and parted my lips. He filled my mouth with his tongue. We sagged together and sank to the floor. I pressed my body close to him and guided that terrible, wonderful thing into me. His thrusts went ever deeper as he pounded me mercilessly and ravaged my flesh with his mouth and hands. A growing sense of urgency and desperation possessed me. I clutched him tightly. I think if he had taken himself away from me at that moment, I would have died of sorrow and despair.

My frenzy grew. I was as lustful and animal and wanton that night as any harlot, and I didn't care. Once I felt that I couldn't bear any more and I begged him to stop. He paid no attention, and even quickened his movements. Somewhere deep inside me a chasm opened. I shuddered and quivered. My passion mounted and crested and exploded, and then it began to ebb away. Seth gave a few more convulsive jerks and lay still.

I could not look at him. He had asserted his mastery over me, and not only had I allowed it, I had begged for it. In my mind and soul I was still free, still Gypsy. But my body belonged to this man. And he knew it.

He took himself away. I felt bereft and cold. I could feel

him standing over me, exulting in his power. I lay with my eyes closed and my arms thrown over my face until he had left the room. And then I curled up on the blanket and sobbed like a civilized woman. It was the first time in my life that I had ever given way to tears. Even when I had mourned for my Gypsy tribe I had not cried like that. I hated him for reducing me to such a state.

I should have known better than to try and escape him. I had forgotten Ursula's prophecy. I had forgotten that our journeys and our futures were linked. As Lyubov used to say, "You can't hide from God in a rabbit hole." You can't escape your fate.

There was a soft knock on the door. I pulled myself together, mopped my face, wrapped the blanket securely around my naked body, and stood up.

"Come in."

It was Jules. "Your bath is ready, Mademoiselle. Madame Mornay sent a trunk with your things this afternoon. I unpacked. You will find everything either in the armoire or in your chest of drawers."

"Thank you. Where is Monsieur Garrett?"

"He has gone out again. I don't expect him until very late. There is a card party at Monsieur Dumas'."

Yes, cards. I had fogotten that he played cards. Hadn't I come into his life in the first place because of cards?

I followed Jules to a small wood-panelled room near Seth's bedroom. A large tub full of steaming water stood in the center of the floor. A pile of soft towels lay within reach on a chair. My own robe hung from a peg on the wall, next to a large robe of maroon silk. On a small shelf over the washstand stood an assortment of articles for shaving and grooming. A soap cup and shaving brush, hairbrush, comb, and scissors. A leather case held his razors. My eyes flashed back to the scissors.

"If there is anything else you need, Mademoiselle," Jules said, "please do not hesitate to ring. Here is the bell pull, and there is one in your room, near the door. Perhaps I can fix you some supper?"

"No, thank you, Monsieur Jules," I said quietly. "I could not eat." I looked around. "It is a very fine house. Did he win it at cards, too?"

Jules looked startled. "Yes, Mademoiselle, I believe so. The house is very old, and it belonged to the same family for over two hundred years. The young man who lost the house was the last of the line, I believe."

"Ah. He must have been very upset, to lose his house," I said. "Where did he go? Did he have another house somewhere?"

Jules looked distressed. He frowned and the frown seemed to work itself halfway across his shining bald head. "I believe the young man shot himself, Mademoiselle," he said. "A great tragedy."

He left me alone. A great tragedy, I thought. To lose everything, and your pride along with it. To be shamed by a man like Seth Garrett. I went to the washstand and picked up the scissors.

I looked at my pale face in the mirror, and I remembered the wide-eyed *gorgio* debutante in the pearls and the ivory gown who had looked forward to her first ball with such excitement. Was I really that girl? Only one day later, and I felt so much older. I felt as old as Eve.

I could never marry. I would live in this house until Seth Garrett tired of me. He would use me for his pleasure and I would let him, because I could not help myself. I would be his whore. I smiled grimly. I was shedding my innocence as quickly as a snake sheds his skin.

When I was still very young, the women in our tribe had cut off all the hair of a young woman named Irina. Irina had kept to herself for months because she was unable to face the rest of us while she wore that badge of shame. I didn't know then what she had done to deserve such an awful punishment, only that her husband had been in a *gorgio* jail for many months and that Irina had been living alone. They had not been married long enough to have children. But now I remembered that around that same time a young Gypsy named Pinkus had gone off to live with another tribe, far away. That was remarkable enough in itself, but I heard Lyubov say that he was lucky to get away with his skin intact.

I had learned some hard lessons in the past twenty-four hours. I had learned that every deed has its price. And that a foolish woman pays dearly for her mistakes.

I heard a carriage stop in front of the house, and I heard the tap of his cane on the bricks as he came up the path. The taps stopped as he entered the house, then resumed as he climbed the stairs and came down the hall. His gait was very slow and heavy and uneven, as though his leg hurt very badly. I didn't care. I was glad.

He stopped outside my door. He opened it and came in.

I lay with my eyes closed, pretending to sleep. He undressed in the darkness and climbed into bed beside me. I didn't move a muscle. He rested on his elbow, looking down at me. He put his hand on my cheek and threaded his fingertips through the fine hair at my temples. When he slid his hand down the shafts it met nothing but air.

He bounced out of bed and lit a lamp. He held it over me and said, "Christ." He grabbed my shoulder and made me sit up, and he moved the lamp over me as though he couldn't believe what he saw. "Christ."

I had left four inches all around. I felt as naked as a new duck.

"I could not bear my shame," I told him. "You have made me your whore. But you cannot make me happy about it, and you cannot give me back the respect for myself that I have lost."

He set the lamp down on the low table by the bed and said disgustedly, "I haven't made you anything. Listen, Rhawnie, all women are whores. Every damned one of them. And all men are rogues. The smart rogues and whores make their fortunes. The stupid ones, the weak ones lose everything."

"Like that boy who killed himself because you took his family's house?"

164

"I didn't take it. He wagered it, foolishly, and he lost."

"I made a foolish wager, too. Last night. I was sure that I would win, that you would marry me. But I lost. I have learned my lesson well. I know that I have made a bad bargain, Seth. But I will stick to it. I will live with you and eat your food and make love to you. I will not try to run away again. Where would I run? And I will not try to kill you. What would that earn me except death on a *gorgio* gallows or many years in a stinking jail? But I will not forget how you have hurt me. And I swear to you that I will find a way to hurt you back."

He stared at me for a long moment, saying nothing. Then he got up and walked out of my room.

7

Playing Cards

JULES CAME IN late the next morning with a breakfast tray. He set it down near the bed and went to the windows to open the curtains.

I rubbed my eyes and sat up. "Bonjour, Monsieur Jules."

He smiled. "Bonjour, Mademoiselle. Just plain 'Jules' will do, I think. I am not used to more." If he was surprised to see me with no hair he gave no sign of it. The model manservant.

"Are there no maids here, Jules?" I asked.

"No, Mademoiselle. I am the only live-in help. Except for Boucher, of course. But he lives over the stables. Two women come in every day to clean and launder when the Master is home."

"Ah. Is your Master such a miser, then, that he makes you do all the work by yourself?"

"The Master dislikes having too many people about the place. Especially women," he added.

I grunted. "I don't know if I should feel flattered or frightened."

"Flattered, of course, Mademoiselle," he said. "There has never been a woman living in this house before, not since I've been here."

"Really? What about Mademoiselle Simone? She lived here, didn't she?"

"Ah!" He gave a short laugh. "But not for long! And only while Monsieur Seth was away. He soon put a stop to that nonsense!"

"Yes, so I've heard," I said glumly. "Thank you for unpacking for me. I didn't expect to return, you know. Your efforts might have been wasted, Jules."

"Oh, no, Mademoiselle. Monsieur Seth assured me that you would come back. He said that he would bring you back if he had to—". He stopped himself but I had heard enough.

"Indeed?" I said softly. "He told me he found me accidentally. What time did he leave the house yesterday?"

Jules' eyes twinkled. "About an hour after you, Mademoiselle. He was very angry. I don't think he expected you to—run away."

He bowed slightly and left me alone. I didn't even look at the breakfast tray. I wasn't hungry. A bad sign, that. I am always hungry. I got out of bed and slipped my robe over my nightgown. I examined my new home in the light of day.

The room was very large and it faced the street. The furnishings were low and gracefully modelled and beautifully inlaid with floral patterns in different woods. Seth told me later they were from the First Empire, whenever that was. The walls were covered with rose-colored silk, and the curtains at the windows, the upholstery, and the bedspread were the same color. In addition to the bed there was a chaise longue, a couple of padded chairs and a couple of straight-backed ones, a small dressing table, a tall armoire, a chest of drawers, and a washstand. A thick rug, ivory with a border of small pink wreaths and green garlands, covered the floor. A nice-enough prison, I thought.

Seth came in without knocking. I knew it was he and I didn't bother to turn around.

"Not dressed yet?" He came around the end of the bed and stretched out on the chaise longue, which was only a few feet away. "You haven't touched your breakfast, either. You'd better eat something. We have a lot to do today."

"I will do nothing," I said disconsolately, putting my hand to my shorn head. "I cannot go out—like this."

"What are you going to do? Sit here until it grows back?" He tossed a newspaper over onto the bed. "You might be interested in the little item on page four. It appears you didn't kill your friend Louis after all. Just gave him a bad headache."

I didn't even glance at the newspaper. "I can't read," I said.

"Oh? Well, the good stuff isn't in the paper anyway. The old gent was one of the most notorious whoremasters in Paris. He told the police he was attacked by a young man, a common thief who escaped with his billfold and his watch. The whore who saw the thief and the desk clerk both backed him up."

"Then the police aren't looking for me anymore! That is strange." I saw that Seth was looking a little smug. "You had something to do with that, didn't you?"

He shrugged and folded his arms across his chest. "I had a word with a high official in the Ministry of Justice last night, that's all. He owes me a favor."

"And now I owe you a favor," I said bitterly. "I am in your debt for saving me. But I don't care! I almost wish the police were after me!"

He laughed. "You wouldn't say that if you saw the Saint Lazare Prison for Women." He got up and threw open the doors of the armoire. "God, Odette's a cheap old bitch. I wouldn't let my scullery maid be seen in these rags." I caught the reference but held my tongue. He pulled out a blue walking dress and tossed it over a chair. "This will have to do for now. I'll take your over to Irma's today and buy you some decent things."

I had heard of Madame Irma on the Rue de la Paix from

Madame Odette: her clothes were exclusive, expensive, and it was said that she had only five customers in all of Paris, although she could have had a hundred times that many if she wanted to.

Seth approached the bed. "I'll give you half an hour to get ready," he said. "Then I'll toss you into the carriage the way you are."

I stared at the tips of his shoes. "Why did you bring me here?" I asked dully. "Why didn't you just let me go?"

He gave a short laugh and lifted my chin. "Because, my long-legged Gypsy Countess," he said, grinning, "I don't want any other man pissing in my fountain until I've drunk my fill."

I flinched at the coarseness of his remark and jerked my head away.

He went on, "You will find that I like life on my own terms. I like to have my own way whenever possible. No man or woman tells me what to do. And no woman comes into this house or goes out of it without my knowledge and consent. You will stay here until I tell you you can go, and not before. Enjoy yourself, Rhawnie. You're the envy of half the Parisian demi-monde today. I'm easy to live with and not ungenerous. You can have anything you want, within reason: clothes, carriages, baubles."

"Anything except my freedom," I mumbled.

"I'm not a jailer," he said. "Treat it as a learning experience, if you like. I'm the teacher and you're the pupil. And I must say, thus far you've shown a most remarkable natural aptitude—for love."

I pushed my ten fingers through my hair. Shame. "I should have plunged those scissors into my heart," I said.

He laughed. He left the room and he was still laughing long after he closed the door behind him.

I hated him. I hated him for showing me what a wanton I was. I hated him for taking over my life. But that was what old Ursula had said, wasn't it: that my life would be his life?

We dined out that night. After we got home I went

straight to my room and undressed. I waited for him to come to me. Two hours passed. Finally I heard him come up the stairs. His tread was heavy and slow, and I suspected he had been drinking. I braced myself for the onslaught. But it never came. He went to his room and closed the door and never even poked his head in to say good-night. I told myself that I felt relieved and thankful, but I suppose I would be a liar if I didn't admit that I was a little disappointed.

A week passed. Seth Garrett might have been my uncle—no, not my uncle!—but an older brother. He never touched me except to help me in and out of carriages or to drape a wrap over my shoulders. He never came to my room, not even to chat. He never gave the slightest indication that I was living under his roof for any purpose other than to take shelter from the elements. You might have thought that I was an honored guest, and not the girl he had made his mistress.

I began to feel apprehensive. Perhaps he didn't find me beautiful anymore? I never should have cut my hair. Although when it was brushed and curled it looked quite attractive. I told myself not to be silly, that I was glad that he left me alone. It occurred to me that he had another woman someplace, and I experienced a pang of jealousy and anger. How dare he!

The first garment that came from Madame Irma was a riding habit, a beautiful costume of green velvet trimmed with black. The jacket was tightly molded to my figure, and the skirt was long and flowing but split up the middle so that I could ride like a Gypsy. Seth brought it to my room early one morning—one week to the day after I had come to his house—and tossed it on the bed.

"Put it on," he ordered. He sat in a chair and smoked a cigar and watched thoughtfully while I shed my nightgown and donned the habit. Then Jules brought in two more boxes, one containing a black top hat with a little veil and the other a pair of fine riding boots, black and shiny and of a soft kid.

When I was fully costumed he said, "Now come with me."

We went out to the stables. Boucher led out a huge black stallion with a white streak on his forehead. It was the most beautiful horse I had ever seen in my life. I stood stock still, lost in admiration.

"How do you like him?" Seth asked. Boucher grinned broadly.

"He is wonderful," I breathed. I walked around the animal, stroking his flanks, feeling his legs, patting his nose and talking to him in Romany, the only human language that horses really understand. That horse and I became friends immediately.

"He's yours," Seth said. I looked at him sharply, to see if he was joking. "Don't you want to try him?" He gave me a leg up on the horse's bare back.

I laughed and cantered him around the stable yard. The horse was tempermental and nervous and he danced sideways and reared several times. I hugged him tightly with my knees and let him show off.

"I like him!" I shouted. "He is still a little wild!"

"Like you," said Seth, grinning. And like you, I thought.

I named the big horse Blaze, after the horse of my Grandfather's that I had loved so well. Seth and I rode together in the Bois de Boulogne that day. Three new gowns came that afternoon, and in the evening he took me to see a revival of *The Three Musketeers*. What a story! I fell in love with D'Artagnan and decided then and there that I would be an actress. Afterwards we went to the Cafe Champlaine for a champagne supper. We had a private room all to ourselves. But Seth was still on his good avuncular behavior and he didn't try to take advantage of the situation.

His mood was gay. He was witty and warm and attentive, and he made little jokes about my stealing the silver and snitching the crystal.

"We should have had Irma put pockets in your gowns to

make it easier for you," he said.

"I don't do that anymore," I informed him. "Why should I steal when you will give me everything I want?"

"Because stealing is more fun," he said. "And because you're a bandit at heart. I wonder if old Louis has bought himself a new watch?"

I sniffed and said, "I thought those things would come in handy. How did I know that you would find me? Besides, it is good for Gypsies to steal. Your Bible says so."

"I thought you couldn't read?"

"I have heard about it," I explained coolly. "Have you never heard that at the crucifixion of your Jesus there were supposed to be four nails and the Roman soldiers could only find three because some Gypsy had stolen the one that was meant for His heart? Jesus said after that that it was all right for Gypsies to steal."

"You're making this up."

"I am not! When was the last time you have read the Bible?"

He laughed and said, "You know, Rhawnie, for a girl who was an accomplished thief at the age of four, you're remarkably prudish about love."

I blushed a little and said, "That is different. Gypsies are very strict about such things. Men and women do not sleep together until they are married—to each other. Young girls guard their honor very carefully. But you know all this."

"Yes, I do. But why should married people have all the fun?"

When we got home he said, "You run up to bed now, Rhawnie. It's been a long day. Good-night."

"And what will you do?" I asked.

"Some heavy drinking. I've gotten behind in my daily quota. I need to catch up."

I went to my room and sat on the edge of the bed. I felt annoyed. And irritated. And frustrated. What kind of game was he playing? I was still attractive to men; I had seen the way the men at the theater and the restaurant had looked at me. And that same light still shone in Seth's eyes from time to time. So what was he waiting for?

He came up the stairs. I held my breath. He passed his own door and paused outside mine. My heart pounded. I waited. Then he turned around and went back to his room and closed the door.

I waited a few minutes, and then I crept out into the hallway and tapped on his door and pushed it open. He had taken off his coat and waistcoat and his shirt was open.

"I cannot get out of this dress by myself," I told him. "I think I need a maid to help me."

He smiled a little and shook his head. "No. One full-time woman in this house is enough. Come over here. I'll help you."

"This has been a very nice day." I turned my back to him and he busied himself with the hundred and one hooks and eyes on the back of my bodice. "First a beautiful suit to ride in, then a wonderful horse. And more gowns and the theater and dinner."

"I'm glad you enjoyed it." He was deft and quick. "There, all done."

I turned around, holding the front of the bodice up over my breasts. "I would have thought you would want me to show how grateful I am."

He lifted his eyebrows and smiled. "I wouldn't want to force you to do anything that is distasteful to you," he said with just a hint of sarcasm.

"Oh, I don't mind," I said graciously. "It is inevitable, no? There is no reason to put it off. But perhaps it is rude of me to talk about it. You would prefer to have me in your own way, in your own good time. And you may not even want me at all—." I gave him a small smile and a shrug and turned away, as if I were leaving.

He laughed and pulled me swiftly into his arms. "I'm glad you're being sensible about this."

"Why not? A Gypsy knows how to enjoy life. I would like it better if I were married. But I shall never marry. It is not in my future. So I can learn to enjoy love without being married. I have done my penance." I pulled at a golden curl over my ear. "Every time I look in the mirror I am reminded of my weakness and foolishness. But that is past. It is over. I cannot fight my fate. You are my fate, Seth. You."

His kisses were very warm and knowing. It wasn't like being kissed by that idiot Gaston or by the old man with the white hair and mustache. It was like being bathed in pleasure and delight, like lying on a riverbank after a swim and baking your naked body in the sun, like riding a horse bareback and laughing into the wind because you knew that nothing on earth could catch you. This was like sitting next to a blazing fire on a cold night, like lying on soft pillows inside a caravan while rain pounded on the roof and eroded the earth under the wheels. It was better than sucking hot tea through a sugar lump, and almost as good as forking food into an empty belly. It was simple and necessary and right.

Whenever we lay together, that night and any time after that, all the bad feelings I harbored against him, the hatred and the anger and resentment, seemed to disappear. For as long as it lasted I felt whole and complete and happy. Seth taught me a few of his "permutations and combinations." I overcame my instinctive shame and prudery and learned my lessons well. I discovered that a man insane with pleasure is virtually helpless. I liked to work my woman's magic on him. The only time I had any power over him at all was when we loved.

I began to see how I could avenge myself on him, how I could punish him for what he had done to me. I would make him love me. I would become as necessary to him as his drink. And then, somehow, I would use that power to destroy him.

We rode together every morning when the weather was fine. In the evenings we dined out or went to the theater or a concert. Three or four times a week Seth sent me home alone and went off to play cards somewhere. I wasn't much interested in his card-playing; in fact I had an ingrained aversion to it. I'm not sure why. Because my uncle had wagered me and Seth had won me? Or because gambling symbolized everything about him that I hated: his coldness, his callousness, his cavalier attitude towards all his possessions, including me.

I had been with him one month when his light-hearted mood changed abruptly. One night he was unusually silent and tense, the way he had been when we were travelling in Russia together. I asked him what he was thinking.

"I'm thinking about someone who is dead," he said softly.

"Who?"

He gave me an angry look. "None of your damned business. Leave me alone."

I cocked my head and looked at him. "The dead don't like to be remembered like that, with anger and sorrow," I told him.

"Shut up and leave me alone," he snarled. That was the afternoon. We went to the opera that night, to see Bellini's *Norma*. I fell in love with Pollione, the Roman soldier, and decided that I had to be an opera singer.

"I can sing much better than that fat sow," I told Seth as we rode home after the performance. "Any Gypsy can sing better than that." I had a good ear for tunes and I sang the first lines of the first-act aria, full of trills and swoops and glides. I really did sound better than the soprano who had sung Norma. But Seth didn't think so.

"Shut up," he said. "Stop that noise."

"It's not noise," I said defensively. "It is singing! When I feel happy I—"

"Shut up. Or you can walk home."

I subsided, resentfully. We made love that night, in spite of his mood. Or because of it. I had been with him long enough to know that he used love as he did brandy and whiskey, as an aid to forgetfulness. He was quick and cold and passionless. When he was finished he left me without a word.

The next morning Jules was in the middle of cooking something and he asked me to take Seth's breakfast up. I tapped on his door and went in. His bed looked like a battlefield, rumpled with the covers and pillows every which way. He lay on his back, stark naked, snoring heavily. The room reeked of whiskey and stale cigar smoke.

I set the tray down next to the bed and went over to the windows. I opened the curtains, flooding the room with light. Seth moaned and threw his arm over his face. It was raining heavily, I remember. I stood for several minutes watching the water slide down the window panes and drop from the eaves and rustle the leaves of the chestnut trees outside. We would not ride that day.

I turned back to the room. "Good morning," I said brightly. I sat on the edge of the bed. "It's a wretched day. Are you going to sleep forever?"

"Go away," he muttered, turning on his side away from me.

"You're just feeling bad because you drank too much last night," I said briskly. "Come, drink your coffee before it gets cold. You'll feel better—"

"Don't want any coffee," he growled. "Take it away and get out."

"You're like a nasty bear today," I remarked.

"Leave me alone, God damn it!" He sat up quickly and swung his arm at me. I leaped out of range. He picked up the coffee pot and hurled it at my head. I ducked and skittered out of the room.

I made my way back to the kitchen. I was hot with anger. Jules took one look at my face and said, "So he's like that today, is he?"

"If you mean he's like a mad dog when somebody steps on his tail, yes, he's like that," I said bitterly. "I hate him. I hate him!"

Jules shook his head. "I hope this one doesn't last too long. Last time it went on for three weeks."

"What went on? I don't understand."

"He gets black moods once in a while," Jules explained.

"Oh, I've seen his black moods before," I said. "Sometimes he won't talk to me for hours on end."

"I bet you've never seen him like this," Jules said.

Jules was right. That day was the start of a mood that I hadn't seen before. Seth stayed in his room until late afternoon. He appeared in the kitchen, where I was helping Jules chop onions for a stew. Seth hadn't shaved and he had dressed haphazardly, with none of his usual careful attention to his costume. His eyes were glazed with drink—I could smell it from across the room—and he was limping badly, one reason for his bad humor, I thought.

He drank for three days, taking no food at all. And all that time I was trapped in the house by heavy rains. He didn't speak to anyone, not to Jules, not to me, not to his friend, a jovial man named François Nerval, who called on the second day. Jules and I tiptoed around, speaking to each other in whispers. I didn't dare sing. Not that I felt like singing.

Then on the fourth day the weather cleared. I rejoiced that my period of enforced inaction was at an end. I put on my habit and took Blaze out to the Bois.

I hated trotting sedately up and down bridle paths, and there were open areas beyond the western edge of the park that Seth and I used for racing. When Blaze and I were clear of the trees, I whipped him up and we galloped across the plain. When I finally pulled him up I laughed aloud because it felt so good to be outdoors again, on a warm, fine day in early June.

I heard the thud of hooves on turf and I looked around. A rider came towards me from the trees, a man mounted on a fine chestnut horse. When he was very close I saw that it was Martin de Vernay, the young duke who had been so attentive at the Delacroix Ball.

"Countess!" he said happily, reining in his horse. "I saw your wild ride and I wondered if your horse was out of control. I'm glad I was wrong."

I felt suddenly shy of him. "Yes. He likes to run. We both do."

"Magnificent animal," he said, running an appreciative eye over the black stallion. He looked into my eyes. "I've been hoping that I would see you again, Countess."

"I am no Countess," I said brusquely. "Please excuse me, Monsieur. I am late—." I wheeled Blaze around and galloped away from him. I could feel the hurt expression in his eyes, the bafflement in his face. What do I care, I thought angrily. He is nothing to me. Nothing.

When I got back to the house Jules was arranging masses of lilacs in the twin vases in the foyer.

"Would you like some in your room, Mademoiselle?" he asked.

"Oh, Jules, I have told you again and again that it is bad luck to bring dying things into the house!" I shook my head. "But they are so beautiful—. Perhaps, just a small bouquet?"

He smiled warmly and I laughed and tripped up the stairs. I halted abruptly. Seth was waiting at the top. He looked awful, rumpled and with three days growth of beard on his cheeks and chin. His eyes were red-rimmed and bleary. He leaned heavily on his cane.

"Where have you been?" he demanded in a whiskey-soaked voice.

"Why do you ask?" I said coldly. "Did you run out of liquor and need someone to run to the wineshop for you?"

"I asked you where you've been!" he barked. I tried to pass him but he blocked me.

"I have been riding in the Bois," I said, waving my short riding crop at my costume. "I should think that would be obvious, even to one in your condition."

He moistened his lips. "You're not to go without me, do you hear? You are not to go out alone."

I regarded him with a mixture of pity and loathing. "I do not take orders from a drunk," I said.

He grabbed my arm. "I'm master here!" he snarled. "And you'll damn well do as I tell you! Go to your room."

"Take your hand off me. You're hurting my arm."

"I'll hurt more than that, Miss Impudence," he said, shaking me roughly.

"I am not your slave," I told him. "Let me go—ahhh!"

He twisted my arm behind my back and dragged me close to him. The stink of whiskey on his breath made my eyes water. I thought my arm would break if he didn't release me soon. I lifted my riding crop and struck him a light but cutting blow on the neck. The next thing I knew I was staring up at him from the floor. My ears were ringing. I put my hand to my nose. It came away bloody.

"Do you feel better now?" I asked softly. "Now that you have shown me who is master here?"

He swayed. "Get up," he said hoarsely. "You're not hurt."

"And neither were you," I said, getting to my feet. "You just like to club young women for fun. You remind me a little of the Grandfather when he was dying. He had good days, and then he had days when he could barely lift his head, he was so weak. But even on the days when he was feeling well, the disease still lived in him. It grew stronger and stronger while he grew weaker and weaker. Until it finally killed him."

"Shut up," he snapped. "I'm not interested in your curses, you damned Gypsy."

"It's no curse." I dabbed at my nose with my handkerchief. "Only the sickness in you isn't in your body. It is in your soul, in your heart. Drinking whiskey won't make it go away."

He seemed to grow large with anger. He loomed over me, cane uplifted, wavering. I gazed back at him steadily and reproachfully. He made a quick movement, as if to strike me. But I didn't flinch.

"I am not afraid of you, sick man," I said huskily. Then I brushed past him and went to my room.

Jules appeared in a few minutes with a bowl of ice water and a cloth.

"Did he hurt you badly, Mademoiselle?" he asked solicitously.

I shrugged. "Not too badly. But my head aches like there was a devil inside it." I lay back on the chaise longue and he dipped the cloth in the water and pressed it lightly over the bruised area.

"This will make it feel better," Jules assured me. "I know. I used to be a barber."

"Better than being a barbarian," I grunted under the cloth.

"I agree, Mademoiselle." His voice was apologetic and sorrowful. "Will you leave him?"

"How can I leave? Where would I go? I have no one in the world to love me. Ah, I have suffered worse beatings. This was nothing. I think he must have a very big devil inside him to make him like this. A very great sorrow. Do you know what it is, Jules?"

"No. Mademoiselle, I don't." He picked up his bowl and went away.

I closed my eyes. I thought not of Seth but of Martin de Vernay, gentle and handsome and eager. He didn't know what I was, what sort of woman. He had treated me like a lady, and I had been rude to him. Because I was ashamed. By now I had seen enough of life and heard enough gossip finally to have a clear understanding of my own position. I was Seth Garrett's mistress, his property. Any time he tired of me he could throw me out. Or beat me. Or rape me. Resentment flooded through me. Why couldn't he have stayed away a little longer? I could have been married by now, to Martin or someone like him, someone who would really care about my feelings, who would love and protect me.

But it was not to be. In the eyes of the world I was a low creature. A whore. But whores gave themselves to many men, and I had had only Seth. So in a sense I was married to him. If I stayed faithful to him I couldn't be called a—no, I couldn't say the word again, even inside my head.

Two more days passed. I didn't go out. There was no point in stirring him up again. It's a wise Gypsy who looks after her own skin. But then he appeared in my room one morning, freshly bathed and shaved and dressed for riding.

"Let's go," he said curtly. "I've been cooped up in this house long enough."

I was brushing my hair and I paused in mid-stroke. "Are you sure you're steady enough to sit on a horse?" I asked.

"There's nothing the matter with me. I wasn't sick."

I looked at him. His face was drawn and pale. His riding jacket fit rather loosely around the chest. I wasn't surprised that he had lost weight; he had eaten nothing for a week or more. Without another word I stripped off my morning dress and put on my riding clothes. He sat on the bed with his hands on his knees, saying nothing, watching me through tired eyes.

"I'm ready," I stood in front of him and drew on my gloves.

"I meant it when I said I didn't want you to go out alone," he said in a watered-down voice.

"Did you?" I couldn't help the hardness in my tone. "I thought you were joking."

His lips tightened. He rose and we went out. We cantered through the trees until we got to the open plain, then I challenged him to race.

He shook his head. "I think Hugo has a loose shoe." Hugo was his big roan. "You go ahead. Ride out and come back, and then we'll head for home."

I nodded and urged Blaze forward, towards a fallen oak tree. Blaze cleared it easily, soaring over it as though he had wings. I patted his neck fondly, and when I looked up I saw a rider come out of the trees at the end of the field. It was Martin de Vernay again.

I pulled Blaze up short. He reared high and danced.

"I've been haunting these woods," the young man said. "Hoping you'd come again. Please, can we talk?"

I looked back over my shoulder. I could see Seth waiting for me. "No. I can't stay," I said. "Please, try to understand." I turned Blaze and rode away, hoping that he wouldn't follow.

"Who was that?" Seth asked when I reached him.

"Nobody," I said with a little shrug. "One of the silly boys I met at the ball. I can't even remember his name. He thought my horse was out of control and he wanted to see if he could help."

We went to the Opéra Favart that night. The program was *Lucia di Lammermoor*. As usual my entrance provoked a turning of heads and appreciative murmuring, at least among the masculine segment of the audience. Their female counterparts whispered and fanned themselves when they saw me, as though they smelled something dreadful. They hoped that I would look in their direction, just so they could snub me. But I knew better than to greet anyone who was not a friend of Seth's. Even the women I met at the Delacroix Ball made a point of not speaking to me, since I had become one of *those women*.

At intermission several of Seth's friends came to our box to pay their respects. Among them was Martin de Vernay. He clung to my hand a second longer than necessary and complimented me on my fine horsemanship.

"Ah, so it was you in the Bois this morning," Seth remarked. "Did you hope to keep Rhawnie from breaking her neck? I have warned her about taking chances but she pays no attention to me."

"I think we need have no fear for Mademoiselle Rhawnie," Martin smiled. "She rides like a hussar!"

Martin stayed for the whole intermission. His presence made me feel nervous and breathless. Seth and his friend François Neval chatted and laughed together while Martin gazed soulfully at me and I stared out over the audience. Then Seth said, "Listen, Rhawnie, I'll send you home without me tonight. François and I have business."

The business, I knew, was cards. I nodded. Martin spoke up, "Perhaps you would permit me to take you home, Mademoiselle? It would be a pleasure and an honor."

"No, please don't trouble yourself," I said quickly. "I would like to come with you, if you don't mind?" I said to Seth. He looked annoyed, then gave a curt nod of consent.

Martin looked crestfallen and left the box with a cool nod and a shallow bow.

"You weren't very nice to him," Seth said. "You shouldn't discourage rich titled men: they make excellent lovers."

"For God's sake leave me alone," I hissed. "I don't like him! He's a baby. A bore! And I'm not looking for—anyone."

Seth chuckled. "Remember, social contacts can be useful."

I gave my attention to the action on the stage and to the glorious music of Donizetti. How I wished I could be down there, singing beautifully and reaping applause and love.

The card party was at François' home, an elegant mansion not far from the Louvre. All the players seemed to know each other. The men greeted me warmly, remarked to Seth that they hadn't seen him for a while, then settled down to play. The few women at the house avoided me like poison, so I watched the action at the card table from behind Seth's chair.

The game was faro, still popular all over Europe. It didn't look terribly complicated: the men bet that certain cards would win, and then the dealer—they took turns dealing—would deal two piles, one card at a time, face up. If the card turned up on the first pile it was the dealer's win; if it appeared on the second it was the better's win. The men also bet that certain cards would be "high" or "low" on a particular deal.

Seth lost on deal after deal. Every time he bet a card would win, it lost. I could sense that his mood was growing blacker.

"Your luck has deserted you, Seth," François laughed. "Rhawnie, you're not trying hard enough to inspire him!"

"Perhaps I am distracting you," I said to Seth. "I shall leave you." I leaned over his shoulder as he was about to place his bets and said softly, "Play the six of hearts and the king of clubs; and the ten of spades and the queen of diamonds."

"Why in hell should I?" he growled.

"Why shouldn't you?" I wandered into the drawing room at the other end of the house. A group of women in one corner looked up, saw who it was, and retired behind their fans. I smiled at them and sat down at the piano. I picked out tunes I knew and loved and sang softly to myself. Seth didn't have a piano. He said he didn't like music at close quarters, but he really didn't like me to sing.

"Good evening, Mademoiselle. Have you tired of cards already?"

I looked up. A tall, slim man with a very prominent nose and a mane of light brown hair leaned gracefully against the piano.

"I do not play cards," I said with a smile. "It seems rather a silly pastime. You win money one night only to lose it the next. You do not play either?"

"I'm afraid not." His smile was very warm. "But please, go on with what you were doing." His French was very good, but slightly accented. I knew that he was a foreigner, as I was.

"It was nothing special," I said with a shrug. "I just sing to pass the time."

"What's that you were playing when I came in?"

"A song I learned as a child. A Gypsy song."

"Sing it for me, will you?" he asked. He gave me a dazzling smile. "And I will try to play it for you."

He sat on the stool in front of the keyboard and ran his incredibly long fingers over the keys. Music cascaded out of that piano. I looked at him, astonished.

"You play so well, Monsieur! Much better than Madame Odette."

"Thank you. Now for your song."

I sang a sad Gypsy song about unrequited love, and the man was miraculously able to follow me and to play the exact chords that were needed to evoke the proper mood of pathos and longing.

"That is wonderful," I breathed when we were finished. "Are you sure you haven't heard that song before?"

"Quite sure. How about another? Do you know any Hungarian Gypsy songs? I learned some of them as a child."

I knew several because we—our Gypsy tribe—had travelled through Hungary several times while I was growing up. I lost my shyness and let my voice float free.

My accompanist applauded me. "What a wonderful instrument! Such a rich, bright sound! Who is your teacher?"

"I have no teacher. I just sing," I told him.

"A marvelous natural talent!" he said warmly. "You are very fortunate. But you would sound even better with a little teaching. I will give you the name of good man at the conservatory here in Paris."

I laughed. "I could not go to a conservatory! It wouldn't be possible. Besides, the man—the person I live with doesn't like me to sing. He says it gives him headaches."

"He is a fool," my new friend declared. "Do you know any opera arias? How about 'Casta Diva' from *Norma*?"

He played the song I loved. I sang it with him, wordlessly. I had heard it only once but I could remember every trill, even though I didn't know the words.

"Excuse me!" A plumpish woman with blond hair bustled over to us. My friend stood up and she threaded her hand under his arm. "Dear Franz, you're always running off! Such a naughty boy! But I always know where to find you—at the piano." She gave me a cold glance. "Come with me and have some supper. If you will excuse us, Mademoiselle?" I was obviously excluded from her invitation to dine.

The tall gentleman very gently removed the woman's hand from his arm and said, "But I have already had my supper, Louise. This beautiful young lady and I have dined on music, and I think we would like still another course. Will you excuse us?"

The woman blanched and sniffed and left the room, and her skirts swished angrily.

"Come, nightingale," said my friend Franz, resuming

his seat at the piano. "Do you know any Shubert? This one is very simple. I can write the words for you—"

"Please don't bother," I said quickly, feeling slightly embarrassed. "I cannot read very well. Just teach them to me and I will try to remember."

He laughed and taught me the words and the music to "The Nightingale," a very short, sweet song. He was not much of a singer, but he played the piano wonderfully well. We passed the next two hours together. I sat next to him at the piano and sang while he played. I taught him Gypsy and Russian songs and he taught me songs in German and Italian. People drifted into the room to listen. Franz told them they would be permitted to remain only if they stayed absolutely quiet. Astonishingly, they obeyed. When I was tired of singing he played alone, a thrilling, chord-filled composition which he said he had written himself. I was very impressed and I told him he sounded like he had six hands instead of two.

Then the evening was over. The card game broke up and the players came into the drawing room. I heard Seth's unmistakable tread and the tap of his cane. He came over to the piano and told me that it was time to go. Franz stood up and greeted him.

"Is this your friend?" he asked me. I blushed slightly and nodded. "You are a very lucky man, Monsieur," he told Seth. "Your ward has a great musical ability. I would teach her myself if I were going to stay in Paris for any length of time."

"That's very kind of you, Monsieur Liszt," Seth said. "Fortunately Rhawnie has other abilities as well."

I hurried out of the room to get my wrap. I could hear the men laughing. Damn him, I thought, why does he have to be so crude? I said as much to him as we drove back to the Rue de Montmorency.

He gave a dry little laugh and said, "There isn't a man in Europe who appreciates the finer things in life more than Franz Liszt. He's the biggest womanizer on the continent. You may be sure that whatever lessons he wants to give you wouldn't be musical."

"You're making this up," I said angrily. "I don't believe you!"

"No?" He laughed. "If you could read I'd show you stories in the newspapers. As it is you'll have to depend on gossip for your information. Ask anyone. François. He's known Liszt for years. And procured for him."

"Oh, brute!" I turned my back on him. "Someday I shall learn to read, just you wait and see. If you cared about me, you would teach me!"

"No, I wouldn't," Seth laughed. "I like you better ignorant. Beautiful and ignorant." He leaned over and kissed my shoulder. A shudder of delight ran through me. "Don't be angry, Rhawnie. Doesn't it give you a good feeling to know that you've conquered the most famous pianist in Europe?"

"Have I really?" I cocked my head. "Think of that. And he said I had a beautiful voice! Do you think he meant it?"

"No, I think he was just trying to seduce you." He grinned as I flounced angrily and then he said in a slightly different tone, "Tell me, Rhawnie, how did you know which cards I should play?"

I shrugged. "I just knew, that's all. I had a feeling. Did you win?"

"Yes. On all of them. Not only once but twice. How did you do it? Gypsy magic again? Did you have a vision?"

"No, no vision. I think I must have been lucky, that's all. Such a silly game. The card has to win or lose, isn't that right? That means that half the deck is a winning half and the other other half loses. I had—how do you call it?—good odds."

"You catch on quickly," Seth said. The carriage was slowing. When we got inside the house I started up the stairs to bed. But Seth called me back.

"Come in here a minute." I followed him into the small salon near the dining room that he used as a card room when his friends came. The evening had turned chilly, and he lit a fire and poured us each a little brandy. I remembered that he hadn't drunk very much that night. He'd had his fill the week before. "Now sit down," he said. I obeyed. He brought out two decks of cards. "We're going to try a little experiment. Choose four cards. One from each suit will do. Put them face up on the table in front of you."

I did as he said. He started to deal two piles. All four of my cards turned up on my pile.

We repeated the procedure twice more. Both times my cards won. Seth tried cutting the deck before he dealt. And once he used a fresh deck at the last minute, trying to defeat my intuition, I suppose. But still I won.

"Amazing." He blew out his breath and sat back in his chair. "How do you do it?"

"I'm not doing anything," I said sleepily. "Can't we go to bed now?"

"Not yet. I want to try something else." He chose four cards from his deck and placed them on the table, face down. "What are they? Tell me."

I gaped at him. "How am I supposed to know what they are? I don't read minds!"

"Shut up and concentrate. What are they? I'll tell you this much: there's one card from each suit."

I sighed deeply and closed my eyes. He waited silently. Then I said, "The eight of clubs. The two of diamonds— no, hearts. The ten of spades." I frowned and rubbed my temples. "And the ten of diamonds."

He flipped the cards over. They were all there, the ones I had named.

"Damn." He finished his drink and stood up to pour himself another. "Do you think you could do that again?"

He chose four more cards. I identified half of them and then gave up. "Too many pictures," I said wearily, resting my head in my hands. "They are all the same."

"That's close enough." He revealed the cards, all picture cards. "Damn," he said again. "What else do you know, Gypsy? What else do you—see?"

"Do you want me to tell your fortune, *gorgio*?" I grinned. I stretched out my hand. "Cross my palm and I will tell all."

He laughed and reached across the table to take my hand. "I don't want to know all. I just want to win at cards. You're a genius, Rhawnie! I adore you!" He kissed my fingertips. My heart gave a queer little lurch. "What would you like as a reward for being such a good girl tonight? A diamond necklace? A sack of golden florins?"

"I just want to go to bed," I said wearily. "With you."

"You shall have your wish." He came around the table and lifted me out of my chair and held me close. He caressed my face and ran his thumbs gently under my cheekbones. "You're full of surprises, aren't you, Gypsy? What else have you got in store for me, I wonder?" He kissed me sweetly, and then he hugged me tightly and threw back his head and laughed. "Ah, talk about luck! We're going to win a fortune, you and I, Gypsy! And now to bed."

He helped me out of my gown and corset and tucked me in. Just before I closed my eyes I saw him smiling down at me warmly. Quite a change from the brute who had hit me just a few days ago. Then he turned down the lamps and lay beside me, holding me close, as if to protect his suddenly valuable Gypsy from the terrors of the night.

The next day he taught me how to bet.

"Your ability will be wasted if you don't know how to handle your money," he told me. "If you put everything on your first four cards you'll scare the competition off. You're going to have to learn to play with them, to coax their money out of them easily without letting them know that they're going to lose repeatedly, understand? Now. In faro you can bet on whether a given card is going to win or lose, and you can also bet on whether the winning card will be higher or lower than the loser. Ace is low, king high."

I chose four cards and he dealt a sample hand.

"Why do you play cards for your living?" I asked him. "Have you always done this?"

"No. What's the difference how I earn my money, as long as I have enough to buy what I want."

"Your beautiful home and your clothes and your women," I said softly. He gave me a sharp look. "Don't be angry with me," I smiled. "It's so early in the day; too early to quarrel. I just like to know things."

"You don't have to know anything," he said brusquely. "Just be happy with what you get out of it. You see, your king is a winner—of course. And so is your jack of clubs. Now what are the odds on the jack being higher than any other card?"

I screwed up my eyes. "What do you mean?"

"There are fifty-two cards in the deck, thirteen in a suit. If the king is high that means that only two cards are higher than the jack, the queen and the king. Ten cards are lower, ace through ten. It's a safe bet that the jack will be high, but you won't find too many takers. So you copper your bet—you put a six-sided chip on it to indicate no bet—which means you want it to lose. Now look at your eight of hearts. Odds are that it will lose to the other card, right?"

I thought hard. "No. More cards are lower. It has a good chance of winning."

"Three francs says it loses. Will you take my bet?"

"How do I do that?"

"Put three francs on the eight to win, not the turn but as high card. The odds are in your favor, aren't they?"

"But I do not have three francs."

"Here." He gave an exasperated sigh and tossed me a handful of coins. Then he dealt the hand. The eight lost on the turn—it appeared on his, the dealer's pile. But it was higher than the six, which turned up on my pile.

"Very confusing," I remarked. "Have I lost my three francs?"

"No, you've won three francs from me."

"But the eight lost!"

"Yes, but it was still higher than the six, right? You can bet on that eight two different ways."

I gathered in my winnings, three francs, and said, "You

know, I think I like this betting. It is as easy as stealing. What else can you bet on?"

"Anything. Bet that it will rain tomorrow if you meet someone who says it won't. Bet that the king will make a speech, or that Jules will serve mutton for lunch."

"But that's no bet," I protested. "I know that Jules is making *boeuf à la bourguignonne.*"

"Ah, you have inside information that I don't have. I might be stupid enough to take your bet and you would win. Not strictly honest. But most people who gamble aren't honest."

"Huh. So gamblers are like Gypsies. And I can bet on horses!"

"Certainly. Horses, cocks, oxen. You can bet on men: wrestling, boxing, foot racing, hurling rocks or spears or logs. Don't Gypsies bet?"

"Why should they? For a Gypsy all of life is a gamble!"

He was crazy. He made me play with him all that day, until midnight. Jules had to serve our lunch in the card room, and we played as we ate. Late in the afternoon I became so tired and dizzy from looking at cards that I threw a deck in his face and ran out of the room. Seth dragged me back. I protested loudly, but he kissed me until I was limp.

"But I don't want to play anymore," I said in a small voice.

"You want to learn how to make your fortune, don't you? You have a gift, Rhawnie. If you use it properly you can have anything you want in the world. Anything."

"But I don't want anything," I said despairingly. Except you, said a small voice inside me. I was startled. I didn't want him! But I leaned hard against him and said beseechingly, "Couldn't we stop for a little while? Please?" I put my arms around his neck and kissed him softly. I could feel his determination to continue ebbing away. "Please?"

"You're very hard to resist," he said.

"It is intentional."

"I know." He laughed and swatted my rump. "Get back to the card table, wench."

I glared at him. "I don't want to! I hate cards! I hate you! I will never play, ever! You want me to cheat these people to make you rich, but why should I? What will I get out of it, eh? Tell me that much!"

"Exactly half," he said. "From now on, everything I win will be split two ways. Half for you and half for me. We're partners, Rhawnie."

"Partners?" I sat down heavily. "You mean I will be rich? You will give me money? When? When will you play again?"

"On the night of your debut. Maybe. But not before."

"You are evil," I said sullenly. "You think you can make me do anything. You think I am your puppet!"

He gave me a bemused look. "You're right, Rhawnie. That's exactly what you are. My puppet."

He taught me how to deal from the bottom of the deck, how to stack the deck, how to palm a card and hide it up my sleeve.

"You won't need these tricks if you play in good company," he said. "But you have to know them so you can spot them."

I learned those tricks quickly, with a speed that astounded him. "Simple, like Gypsy tricks," I told him. "When I was four I could slip a dozen eggs into my blouse in ten seconds. I was even learning how to pick pockets—but the Grandfather took me away." I sighed regretfully.

"And you learned how to palm whole chickens and loaves of bread," Seth grinned.

"So?" I lifted my chin. "A girl has to live, doesn't she?"

He worked very hard for the next week, taking one day off to go to the races at Longchamps. I won a packet on the very first race. "But not because of any special feelings," I told Seth. "Only because I could see that of all the horses on the track this one was the fastest and the best. Could not everyone see that?''

S̓eth, who had backed a loser, did not answer.

He coached me carefully, creating imaginary situations, describing partners and dealers, teaching me how to read a card player's face even if I couldn't read his mind. He told me that a losing man will often bet more heavily—and more foolishly—than a winner. He described the faro game with my uncle Alexei in Moscow.

"He wanted to bet his house. I told him I wasn't interested. I said that I never bet on anything that was too big to take to bed. And so he bet me one virgin.'' He grinned at me. "I would have saved myself a lot of trouble if I'd refused his bet.''

I shook my head. "I would have met you anyway. It was fate.''

He cheated shamelessly and scolded me when I failed to catch him. I cheated and crowed happily when he failed to catch me. Finally he declared that I was ready. We would go to Albert de Blazon's gambling hall on the Rue des Fleurs near the site of the old Bastille. The place was currently fashionable and scores of rich Parisians and visitors from all parts of the world went nightly to indulge their passion for gaming. Seth said that there I could match wits with the best players in Paris. And I would win.

I wore a gown of pearl-gray satin with short puffed sleeves, black gloves and black ornaments, including an enormous black bow in my hair. I wore my hair loose, in masses of golden ringlets that framed my face.

Seth looked wonderful in evening dress. Diamond studs glittered on his shirt front. And his cufflinks were real gold coins from ancient Rome. He said that they were a gift from an Italian marquesa whom he had bested at cards.

"And at love?'' I wondered.

"Of course,'' he said smiling. We arrived at the Chez Albert. "Are you nervous?'' he asked.

"Oh, no. I am excited. I suppose you will be very angry if I lose?''

"You won't lose. And if you bet foolishly, it won't

matter. It's your first time out. You're here to learn, and you can learn fastest by matching your skills against the best.''

"But you are the best. Or so you tell me."

"See that you believe it, always," he said. "A kiss for luck." He kissed me tenderly before we went inside. A sweet wave of happiness rippled through me.

Monsieur Albert de Blazon was a Spaniard or Portuguese who had started his career in Paris as a waiter and run dice games on the side. His elegant salon was strictly illegal, but a flow of payments into the right bureaucratic pockets assured its continued existence, and the flow of rich patrons to his tables assured his continued success and wealth. The games at Chez Albert were faro, roulette, dice, baccarat, and twenty-one. Seth promised me that he would teach me all of them, but first I had to show him that I had mastered faro.

There were few woman present other than the beautifully dressed courtesans who plied their trade among the wealthy patrons. Seth told me that Albert took half of whatever they made. Partners, I thought ruefully. A suite of lushly appointed rooms upstairs was reserved for their use, to insure that a client would return to play after a relaxing interlude in the arms of one of those lovelies. The highly-born ladies in the place were mostly old dames whose passion for cards had long ago supplanted their passion for anything else. Odette Mornay was there. When she saw Seth and me enter the main salon, her pencilled brows went up and she turned away quickly.

"Spiteful old bitch," Seth said. "Just don't play with her. She cheats like the devil and she's good at it."

He led me past the roulette wheels and dice tables to a quieter room at the back where the faro tables were located. He found an empty chair at a table where three bankers and a cabinet minister were enjoying play. I smiled brightly at the players and the dealer, and took my place behind Seth's chair. Our plan was to let Seth start play and then to relinquish his place to me when we felt that I was relaxed enough to handle it.

I watched the men make their bets. Seth was a different man when he gambled, alert, involved, excited—the way he had been at the Delacroix Ball, when he was in pursuit of a quarry. Winning was the only thing that mattered to him. I guessed that he would play for pebbles or buttons or matchsticks—it wouldn't matter what the stakes were, as long as he won.

The top of the faro table bore printed representations of all the cards in the deck, one picture for each card. There were two of these set-ups, one in front of the dealer. Bets were made by placing chips on the cards of one's choice. The dealer dealt his cards from a small wooden box that insured against stacking or peeling a card off the bottom of the deck.

"Any suggestions?" Seth asked in a whisper after he had lost on his first bets.

"Queens of clubs. Ten of spades. Five of hearts. King of diamonds."

He nodded and made his bets. His cards won. He reached up and pressed my hand and I squeezed his shoulder. After a few more deals he excused himself and asked me if I would like to sit in for him. I said I would, if he didn't mind my losing. He gave me a quick kiss and left me a large stack of chips.

As I took my chair I smiled at the dealer, a handsome young man in his twenties.

"Mademoiselle's first time at the faro table?" he asked with a grin.

"Yes, Monsieur. Do you have any advice for a beginner?"

"Yes," growled one of the other players, "don't start."

"It's all right," said another, "Seth Garrett is buying her chips. Doesn't matter to me if she loses everything."

"My advice is don't shed tears if the cards don't fall right," the dealer said. "Very well, Mademoiselle, make your bets."

I put twenty francs each on the king of hearts, the jack of

diamonds, the ten of clubs and the five of spades. I knew the ten would lose. The others won, easily offsetting my twenty-franc loss. I raked in my winnings as my opponents cried beginner's luck. They all bet against me on the next round. I won on all four cards that time, and I doubled my winnings because of their bets.

"Would you care to bet against me again?" I asked sweetly. "I will try not to win."

They decided that my luck wouldn't hold, but it did and they lost their money. I always knew which cards to bet on but I was careful not to win every time. A small crowd gathered to watch me play. Seth stayed away.

More players started to bet with me against the house. Then the dealer announced that he was unable to cover all our bets and that he would have to suspend play while he replenished his supply of chips.

"I think I have won enough for one evening," I said decisively. I swept my pile of chips into a handkerchief. "Any more and I won't be able to carry them all!"

The men offered to lend top hats. A few of them made suggestions for ways in which I could spend my small fortune. I bid them all a merry farewell and went to find Seth. He was playing roulette.

"How did it go?" he asked casually. The wheel spun, whirling the small lead ball around its circumference.

"As we planned," I shrugged, trying to match his coolness although I was feeling excited and elated. "I broke the faro bank. And you?"

"Losing." He smiled at me. "Any suggestions?"

"Play five on the black," I said. The wheel turned. Five black lost. We laughed companionably and moved away from the roulette wheel. Seth put his arm around my waist.

"So you're not infallible after all! I'm glad. Otherwise I wouldn't be able to get along without you."

It was a strange thing to say, I thought. I handed him my makeshift sack of chips. "Take care of these, will you? I need to check my hair."

I went to the ladies' powder room and came face to face

with Odette Mornay. "Good evening, Madame," I said courteously. "I trust you are having good luck tonight?"

"I've heard about your luck," the old woman sniffed. "Don't let him take your money. It's yours. You won it."

"I'll be careful," I promised.

"At least you'll have something to fall back on when he leaves you." Madame Odette said, walking away.

"I won't let him leave me," I vowed silently. "He'll never want to leave me!"

Seth wasn't in the main salon when I went to look for him. I peeked in on the faro games, then decided he had gone to the bar. I went back to the corridor that separated the gambling rooms from the bar and came face to face with Martin de Vernay.

"I congratulate you on your good fortune," he said with a polite nod.

"Oh." I felt myself redden slightly. "I didn't expect to see you in a place like this, Monsieur."

"And I did not expect to see you here, either," he said. His blue eyes probed mine. I thought he looked older, and very handsome.

I said stiffly, "If you will excuse me, I am looking for Monsieur Garrett." I added bluntly, "I live with him."

"Yes, I know." He was utterly serious and unsmiling. "Rhawnie, why—"

"Please, Martin," I said softly, "I don't want to talk about it."

"I do. I must! I want to talk to you, alone. Ride in the Bois tomorrow. Please!"

"I can't. He won't let me go out alone. Please, Martin, don't ask me. It's impossible."

"I love you."

My knees felt weak. It was the first time in my life a man had ever said those words to me. "No," I whispered. "No!"

"Yes. With all my heart." His voice was intense and his eyes burned. "Tomorrow, in the Bois, near the horse fountain at noon. Please, Rhawnie. I'll be there tomorrow and every day after that until you come!''

I heard Seth's laughter in the bar. I left Martin abruptly and went in. Seth and his friend François Nerval were toasting each other with whiskey. They saw me and lifted their glasses.

"To Mademoiselle Rhawnie, the most beautiful and accomplished mistress a man could ever hope to have!" François said loudly. I cringed. I was sure that Martin, lurking just outside the door, could hear every word. "Listen, Seth, when you're tired of her, give her to me! I'll treat you like a queen, Rhawnie," François promised. "By God, with your faro winnings I could buy you Versailles!"

The two men roared. I smiled feebly. "If you don't mind," I said to Seth, "I would like to go home. I have a slight headache."

"Of course, darling."

I was surprised. He was not in the habit of using endearments when he spoke to me. We left Monsieur de Blazon's gambling hall together. Seth was euphoric, happier than I had ever seen him. He laughed a lot, and he was lavish with his praise and affectionate gestures. He was so delighted with "our" success at the faro table that he didn't notice my thoughtful silence and my lack of triumph at winning. I had earned more money that night than I had ever seen in my life, and I didn't care. My encounter with Martin de Vernay spoiled the evening for me. It blighted all the delight I would ordinarily have taken in fleecing the *gorgio*.

Seth was exceptionally tender in his lovemaking that night. He was gentle and attentive to my pleasure. But I was distracted and reserved, because my thoughts were full of Martin.

"You're just tired," he said, holding me close. "It's the let-down after all that intensive preparation and the strain of actual play. I'll leave you alone, if you like—"

He started to go but I held him back. "Please Seth, stay with me," I implored him. "I don't want to be alone tonight. Hold me!"

Two days later Seth mentioned that he intended to visit his tailor at eleven o'clock. He left the house half an hour early, and I slipped away at eleven. Neither Jules nor Boucher saw me leave. I went to the Bois on foot. Martin was already waiting.

"I knew you'd come!" He slid off his horse and came forward with hands outstretched. I did not offer my hands, but kept my arms down at my sides. I said calmly, "I only came because it would be unfair to you to let you go on thinking about me, Martin. Please, don't make this harder for me—. I can't stay long. He'll be back—"

"Why do you stay with him at all?" The young duke's voice was bitter. "Everyone knows what he is like. He doesn't love you, and I do!"

"No, you don't understand, Martin. Where would I go if I left him? It's all the same now. And—he needs me." That part was a lie, of course. Seth didn't need anyone, least of all me. But it made my situation sound a little better.

"He needs you to warm his bed and to bring home money from cards," Martin said angrily, with penetrating truth. I bit my lip and turned away. "No, wait, Rhawnie!" he cried. "Forgive me for hurting you. I know it wasn't your fault. Everyone at the ball that night knew what was going to happen. I heard them joking about it. And I did nothing! Why didn't I stop him?"

"I can't bear this," I said in a thick whisper. "I must go—"

"Oh, God, I'm sorry, Rhawnie." He caught my hand. "I wouldn't have hurt you for the world, you know that. I love you so much, so much!"

"No!" I cried, facing him squarely. "You love me the way boys love an ideal, a dream. You don't even know me, Martin. You don't know what I am. Did you know that I cheat and lie and steal—for fun? I was born and raised Gypsy, and I am still Gypsy! Seth understands that, and it doesn't matter to him. But it would matter to you. You hate my cardplaying, don't you? But I love it! I love gambling and taking chances and betting and winning and easy money. I'm as bad as Seth that way. And in other ways, too. We're the same, he and I. Please, Martin, don't torment yourself. You are not in love with me. It wouldn't be right. It's not possible!''

Martin shook his head and said, ''I know you, Rhawnie. I know that you're kind and good and loving. And I know that he's just using you and exploiting you. He'll get tired of you and—''

''No! He is very good to me! He would do anything for me, I know it!''

Why, why was I lying to him? I was telling him exactly what I myself wanted to believe.

''Would he marry you?'' Martin demanded. I looked away. Not even I could tell a lie that big. ''Because I would.''

8

The End of a Dream

IN THE WEEKS that followed Seth was unusually attentive and warm. He presented me with gifts—jewels, gowns, a fine new saddle for Blaze—and escorted me to parties, concerts and balls. We played cards at least three times a week, and I always won.

I tried to be honest with myself. "He is not being so nice because he cares about me," I thought. "When I first came here I was a sex machine. But now in addition to that, I am a card-playing machine, a money machine. Seth Garrett can't love anyone. He is not like Martin."

Seth became increasingly possessive of me. He was reluctant to let me out of his sight at gatherings and even at home. I felt suffocated by his constant vigilance, but when I complained about it he told me laughingly that I was too valuable a property to take chances with. He said he "couldn't afford" to lose me.

He thought of me as property, I thought of myself as a machine. It was the same thing, I thought bitterly.

Martin continued to haunt me. Instead of achieving its desired effect of discouraging his attentions, my meeting with him in the Bois seemed only to fire him with new purpose. We hardly ever had a chance to speak privately after that, but wherever Seth and I went, to the opera or the theater or the ballet, or to gamble at Albert de Blazon's salon, Martin was there, too. He glowered at Seth, gazed at me worshipfully and meaningfully, and often waited an entire evening to speak to me, even for half a minute. If Seth was aware of these attentions to his mistress, he gave no sign. He probably considered Martin beneath his concern.

At the end of June Seth told me we would be spending the summer in England, first in London, to take advantage of the wonderful opportunties to gamble, and then at a country estate he had rented. I was grateful for the chance to get away from Paris and Martin for a while. I told myself that I hoped when we returned to Paris in the Fall, Martin would have found himself a new diversion.

I did not like London. It reminded me of Moscow, dull and gray and dirty, not white and beautiful, like Paris. I wasn't too surprised to find that Seth's command of the language was as good as any native's. I learned to speak fair English, and he laughed at my Russian-Gypsy-French accent. The estate was truly wonderful, with miles of hills and fields for riding, a rambling house with servants, country parties and dances. And cards. Seth and I prospered. He did not try to cheat me, as Odette had warned. He shared with me and I shared with him, equally. I locked my money away in my jewel box. Being a Gypsy, I distrusted banks—I had won a fair amount of money from bankers—and not even Seth could persuade me to put my money where I couldn't see it.

His gray moods were few and far between that summer. He did not suffer another black period at all. I am sure he felt that things were going well for him. Life was full of distractions and his Gypsy mistress had proved to be an amusing and profitable acquisition. If anyone had suggested to Seth that he was becoming attached to me, he might have admitted that it was so: he continued to find me interesting and diverting, and I hadn't yet begun to pall. If anyone had suggested to him that he was falling in love with me, he would have denied it in no uncertain terms. But if any man had suggested that he was becoming obsessed with me, he would have knocked him down.

Yet I was an obsession, I must have been. Why else didn't he leave me alone? He would have told anyone—as he told me—that I was free to come and go as I pleased. But it wasn't true. He controlled every aspect of my life: dress, hair styles, my choice of card partners, my public behavior, my hours of sleeping and waking, the times we made love. I was as much his prisoner as if he had kept me chained and behind bars. I had no real desire to escape, not at first. But the seeds of hatred had been planted in my heart long ago. And there, in England, they started to grow and blossom.

I resented his constant watchfulness. It seemed to me that I couldn't even bathe or use the chamber pot without his spying on me. Perhaps it wasn't that bad, but at the time I thought it was. I thought longingly of Paris and of the house on the Rue de Montmorency that was the home I never had. I thought of Jules and Boucher, and of my horse, Blaze. And I thought of Martin de Vernay, and I began to hope that he hadn't found another love in my absence. I wanted desperately to talk to someone about my situation, and I felt that only one person in the world would understand: Martin. I was becoming as obsessed with Martin as Seth was with me.

We spent a few more weeks in London at the end of the summer, playing for high stakes at the gambling halls in Soho. I lost heavily once or twice, and when Seth wanted to know what had happened to my remarkable, infallible gift, I answered truthfully that I did not know. Most of the time I knew which cards to play, but occasionally I had to gamble, like everyone else. This was the first indication I had that my talent was linked to my emotional state: when I was desperately unhappy, I lost.

Then Seth decided that it was time to go back to Paris. He wrote to Jules, instructing him to prepare the house and giving him the date of our arrival. We took a train to Dover, crossed the channel by steamer, then travelled to Paris by coach. A few days after our return we attended a ball at François Nerval's house.

Martin was there. We were able to dance together only once.

"I missed you terribly," he said when our waltz finally came. "I thought about you every minute. I couldn't bear Paris and so I went south. I couldn't bear that, either. I love you, Rhawnie. I adore you! And I hate—him."

I wanted to ease the torment in his eyes, and I confessed that I had thought about him, too. Martin was ecstatic; this was the first encouraging sign I had given him.

"When can I see you again?" he asked. "Tomorrow, in the Bois—"

"No, Martin. It's harder than ever to get away. I don't want him to suspect. I'm not afraid for myself, but for you—"

"I'm not afraid of Seth Garrett," Martin said grimly. "If I were any kind of man I'd go to him and tell him that I was taking you away from him. You don't want to stay with him, do you? Do you?"

I shook my head. "No, I don't. I'm like a prisoner now. Oh, Martin, it's impossible. Can't we just go on—"

"No. Either you tell him you're leaving or I will. I'm serious, Rhawnie. I want to marry you."

It was the second time he had mentioned marriage. My heart thumped. "If only it were true!" I sighed.

"It is true! I know what you're going to say, that it's out of the question. I know there are a hundred reasons against it—the way you've lived and the way I've been brought up, my title, my family. But that's all nothing, compared to the one reason in favor of it: our love for each other."

Our dance ended. François came over to claim me for a mazurka, and Martin bowed politely, thanked me for our dance, and moved away. I saw him as my hero, my rescuer, my salvation. And I told myself that I loved him.

Seth and I left the ball early to go to a new gambling place François had told us about. I caught sight of Martin when we were on our way out, and I gave him a slight nod, to tell him that he had reason to hope and that I was willing to leave Seth for him.

I played badly that night. I won but bet foolishly. We rode home in silence.

"I must talk to you," I said when we were inside the house. "It's very important."

"Of course, my dear." Seth led the way to the drawing room. He lit the sconces on the walls, poured himself a drink—there were decanters of brandy and glasses all over the house, so he wouldn't have to ring for Jules whenever he wanted to drink—and then he settled back in a soft chair. "Now, what's preying on your mind? Do you want a new dress? Are you bored with Paris already? Where would you like to go? I'm open to suggestions."

A new dress. Leave Paris. He thought me so frivolous. I stood in front of him with my hands at my sides. I didn't want him to see that I was nervous or apprehensive.

"I want to leave you," I said steadily. "Martin de Vernay and I are in love. We want to get married."

I thought he would laugh, loudly and mockingly, but he didn't. He merely lit a cigar—taking an agonizingly long time over it—and drawled, "Indeed?"

I waited. He smoked thoughtfully. Then he said, "So you want to get married. That's very interesting."

"You think so?" I bridled. "Why? Don't you believe that a man would want to marry me?"

"Oh, I believe it all right. I know that fools come in a variety of sizes and shapes and that they show their foolishness in different ways. It is not inconceivable that a man would want to marry, or even that he would want to marry you. But de Vernay? And you?" He permitted himself a chuckle. "It's ridiculous."

"I will leave here tomorrow," I said firmly. "I will take a room in a hotel and—"

"You're not going anywhere, Rhawnie," he said patiently. "Don't get yourself all worked up ahead of time over something that will never come to pass."

"You are saying that you won't let me go."

"I'm saying that if you believe that Martin de Vernay is really going to marry you, you're living in a fool's paradise. Do you really think his family would stand for it? In France a man has to obtain parental permission to marry, whether he's fifteen or fifty. Martin would never get it, never. Besides that, you'd both come to regret it in a very short time. You're thinking of yourself right now. But think of Martin for a minute. He'd be a laughing stock, an outcast."

"We would be able to live with all that! We have talked about it! We are both strong and—"

"You're both full of foolish dreams," Seth said harshly. "I'm sure the whole idea seems very beautiful and romantic to you now, but it would turn sour in just a few days, I can tell you that with assurance." He tapped his cigar over an ashtray. "I don't want to hear any more about this. Go to bed. I'll come up in a few minutes."

"You can't stop me!" I cried passionately. I caught a glimpse of myself in the mirror over his chair. My cheeks were flushed and my eyes looked dark and angry. "You have no right to keep me here against my wishes! You can't!"

"Why not?" he said softly. "I brought you into this house and here you will stay until I give you leave to go."

"Yes, in your own time and on your own terms," I quoted bitterly. "No, Seth. I won't let you ruin my life this way! This is my chance to be happy! But you're so selfish, so greedy that you don't want me to take it! You think that just because you hate life and have no heart, that everybody has to be that way, but it's not true! I want to be married, Seth! I want a husband and a home and a family!" Tears of despair ran down my cheeks and I brushed them away angrily. He watched impassively. "Oh, how I hate you! Why won't you let me go? I mean nothing to you, I know that. I sleep with you and I play cards for you and I hate it, every minute of it! I won't stay! I won't live here a moment longer, do you hear me?"

I ran up to my room and started to throw my things back into the big trunk I had just emptied. I heard him come in. I hated the sound of his tread, that uneven, limping rhythm. Sometimes I heard it in my dreams.

"Can't you leave me alone for one minute?" I said without looking at him. "Every time I turn around, you're there. Watching me, watching me. You tell me what to eat, what to wear, how to talk, when to breathe. As if I had no mind of my own!"

"I know your mind all too well," he informed me. "Just remember, Rhawnie, if it wasn't for me you'd be begging for bread on the streets of Odessa right now, or you'd be dead and buried in Moscow. You're still a dirty little Gypsy in fancy dress—"

With an infuriated cry, I hurled myself at him. I wanted to strangle him, to stop his mouth. I wanted to kill him.

We struggled. He hooked his leg behind mine and fell heavily on top of me when I went down. I squirmed and scratched and bit. He pinned my wrists to the floor and kissed me and kissed me until I was limp and speechless. He eased off me and I rolled on my side and buried my face in my arms.

"Somebody has to keep you in your place, Gypsy," he said. He started to undress me. He had no trouble with the fasteners on my bodice that night: he tore them off. Then he picked me up and carried me to bed. "You're getting ideas above your station."

"I hate you," I murmured. "I won't stay."

He ran his hands lightly over my body, and he kissed me in a hundred and one places. I gave an involuntary groan and I thrashed convulsively. I was in his power.

"You'll stay," he said softly. "You know that, don't you? We belong together, Rhawnie. We have a lot in common, more than you know."

"I know," I said. "My father was Gypsy, but your mother was a pirate."

He paused in his attentions. "Where did you hear that?"

"Madame Odette. She said that you were so ashamed of the way you lived that you used a different name. You're as bad as a Gypsy!"

"There," he laughed. "You see how alike we are! And if our situations were reversed, if I wanted to marry a duchess, you wouldn't let me go, would you?"

"Yes!" I cried. "Gladly!"

"No, you wouldn't." His voice was low, hypnotic. "That boy could never make you happy. You need a man. You need me. I know what you are, and what you want."

He proceeded to demonstrate—as though I needed a demonstration of his skills. He caressed and stroked me gently, stimulating me until I was frantic with desire. The rising tension in my body was more than flesh and blood could bear; it encompassed my mind and spirit as well. I wanted him, I hungered for him. But when I groped for him he eluded me and withheld his prize until I begged him for it. Then he plunged that searing iron into me with a force and ferocity that made me scream.

His anger with me was evident now. He wanted to subdue and punish and enslave me—once and for all. I resisted him. I fought him. I sank my teeth into his chest and tore at his back and shoulders with my fingernails. But the pain only inflamed him further. He retaliated in kind, biting my breasts and belly and thighs. Soon we were soaked with sweat and tears and passion's nectar. It was more like war than love. We were two combatants, each trying to overpower and destroy the other.

I had never experienced a night like that. Neither, I think, had Seth. When it was over and we lay spent and limp in each other's arms, he threw his arm over his eyes and sighed, "Jesus." Nothing was settled, nothing resolved. I was more determined than ever to escape him before he devoured me.

But he redoubled his vigilance. I was never alone. The next time I saw Martin, at Chez Albert, Seth stayed closed by me and I was unable to do anything but give him a little shake of the head and a despairing look, to let him know that I had failed to obtain my freedom.

Then Madame Odette sat down at the table where Seth and I were playing faro. I said that I was thirsty, and he decided that he wanted a drink, too, and went off to fetch champagne for me and whiskey for himself. I leaned over and put my hand on Odette's scrawny arm.

"I must talk to you!" I whispered. "I know how you feel about me—I am sorry I hurt you—but it's very important!"

"In spite of herself the old woman was interested. "What's the matter? Is he tiring of you?"

"Martin de Vernay and I want to go away together," I told her, casting a furtive eye around for Seth. "He wants to marry me. But Seth won't let me out of his sight and I can't even speak to him. Would you take a message for me?

"Are you making this up?" Odette demanded. She leaned over the table and threw some chips down on a face card. "If you're lying—"

"I swear that I'm not! Please, Madame, this is what you wanted for me, what we both wanted!"

I knew that nothing would give Madame Odette more pleasure than to have her one-time protégé desert that rogue Seth Garrett to marry a titled nobleman. She took my message to Martin and returned to the table in ten minutes. Half an hour later she excused herself, muttering something about going to the powder room. And five minutes after that I gave Seth the same reason for leaving the table.

"You may escort me and stand guard outside the door, if you like," I said coolly.

"Not necessary." He tossed back his whiskey. "Your lover decided the situation was hopeless and left, about twenty minutes ago."

Madame Odette was waiting for me in the powder room. "You were right! He is going to take you away tonight! He'll have two horses waiting under the big chestnut tree

215

at the far end of the Rue de Montmorency, at three o'clock this morning. Martin is taking you to England! You'll be married there, by a priest, of course. And you'll live with some cousins of his until Martin smooths things over with his parents. They dote on him and they'll come around in time, I'm sure of it. It's a wonderful plan! But it must be tonight, Rhawnie. The longer you wait, the more impatient Martin will become. And the more chance there will be of Seth discovering something. I will leave you now. Good luck, my dear. I am very happy for you!''

I played well that night and won a lot of money. I was glad. I would need it to replace all the things I couldn't take with me when I made my escape with Martin. I hoped Seth would think that my high spirits came from the excitement of winning.

"I hope you've come to your senses," he said as we left the table. "You don't want to waste your time on that pipsqueak."

I gazed at him from under my lashes. "Perhaps you're right," I said in a silky coquettish voice. "You were very persuasive the other night, you know." I held his hand lightly and swirled my fingers around his palm.

"I intended to be." He looked at me searchingly. I prayed that I wouldn't inadvertently betray myself. But he said, "You're looking remarkably pretty tonight. Even for you."

"It must be my gown," I said, smiling. I was wearing a rich moss green satin with silk overskirts and sleeves, very low cut in front. "The man I live with chose it for me. He has very good taste."

"Good taste in clothes and in women," he grinned.

As we walked to our carriage I noticed that his limp was more pronounced than usual. When we got home I didn't go upstairs at once, but followed him into the drawing room. He poured himself a generous measure of brandy, drank it down, and poured another. Then he sat down in his favorite chair and sighed heavily.

"Your leg hurts you tonight, doesn't it?" I said.

"Like the devil," he admitted. "You haven't been a very conscientious nurse lately."

"You can't blame me," I said. "I told you long ago what you had to do to make it better and you didn't listen."

"No fun in solitary," he said. "Like a lot of things, easing pain is nicer when you have someone around to help."

"Well, let me look at it." I knelt in front of him and pushed up the leg of his trousers. Now that I was about to leave him I felt no hatred towards him, only regret. "Ah, so stiff! You are too stubborn to live, Seth Garrett." I kneaded and massaged the bunched muscles.

He sat back in his chair and submitted to my ministrations. "God, that feels good." He closed his eyes. "I just can't understand what you see in a pimple-faced boy like Martin de Vernay."

"He does not have pimples." I snapped, digging my thumbs into his scar. He sucked in his breath and sat bolt upright. I glared up at him. "How could you understand? You, who have never loved anybody? Martin is as unlike you as—as an angel! He is sweet and gallant and kind."

"Sounds dull," Seth remarked.

"And he cares about me!" I stood up and brushed out my skirts.

"I care about you," he protested lazily.

"You? Bah. You care about the money I can win for you. And about how I bring you pleasure when we lie together. You like to have a beautiful woman to live in your house and sleep in your bed, someone you can show off at the theater and the opera and Albert's gambling den, so all the other men will envy you and think what a fine fellow you are. You don't love me, as Martin does. If I told him that I—that I loved you and wanted to stay with you—and I don't!—he would listen and he would let me go. If you cared about me, if you loved me, you would let me go."

"That's a queer kind of logic," he observed. "If I loved you, Rhawnie, I would do exactly as I am doing now. I'd never let you out of my sight." He reached out and took my hand and pulled me down on his lap. "I'd tell you that you were beautiful and wonderful, and you would know that meant I couldn't live without you. I would please you in a thousand and one ways." He kissed my fingertips and reached up to stroke my cheek. His voice was low-pitched and as smooth as honey and butter. But I knew him too well to believe him. "I do please you, don't I?" he asked. He put his arms around my waist and gathered me close. I hid my face in his neck. "I don't have to remind you, Gypsy, that you've lived in this house longer than any other woman—a lot longer. You hold the record. It's a dubious honor, I admit, but it means something, surely."

I said softly, "You don't love me. Everything you say is a lie. You wouldn't have to say anything at all, you wouldn't have to prove that you loved me because I would know it. The touch of your hands would be different somehow. You wouldn't make fun of me, you wouldn't scold me all the time. You would be kind and warm and caring."

"Oh, my dear child," he said with a rueful laugh, "you're so young. You think that love is generous and good and kind, but it's not. It's selfish. Perhaps the most selfish emotion there is."

"Next you're going to tell me that you've been keeping watch over me and treating me like a prisoner because you love me and you don't want to lose me to someone like Martin." I sat up and looked into his eyes. "Is that true? Are you really insanely jealous of me because you love me, Seth? Do you love me?" I slid off his lap and stood up. "If you did, everything would be different." I waited. He didn't speak. The clock in the hall struck one. I put my hands to my temples. I felt tired and sad and not one bit sorry that I was leaving him. "I'm going to bed," I said. "Will you come, too?"

He looked at me yet through me. "I don't think so," he said slowly. "I have some drinking to do."

"Then good-night, Seth." And good-bye.

"Good-night, Rhawnie."

I could feel his eyes on my back as I walked out of the room. When I reached the stairs I broke into a run and dashed to my room to pack. There was a lot to do before three o'clock. And if Seth was still awake—and drinking—then, Martin would have to wait.

I wouldn't be able to take very much in the way of clothing. I packed a small bag with some underthings, shoes, nightgowns and robe. And of course my cache of money and jewels. I wouldn't leave those for Seth to spend on a new woman. I hid the satchel behind a chair, and got ready for bed. He might come in, there was no telling for sure until I heard him go to his room and close the door.

An hour and a half passed with excruciating slowness. Finally I heard him come up the stairs. He stopped, about halfway between our rooms. I waited, certain that he would come in. But he didn't. He went back to sleep alone. I was safe.

I threw off my night things and put on my riding habit, and I tried to compose myself. But I was as nervous as a new bride, as they say. Not because I was anxious about my husband but because I distrusted and feared—yes, feared—my lover. A strange situation.

An hour struck. Three o'clock, time for my rendezvous. I picked up my satchel and crept out of my room. I paused outside Seth's room. He was snoring, as he always did when he was very drunk. I knew then that he would sleep soundly until mid-morning. Jules wouldn't disturb him, even if he discovered that I was gone. Does a man prod a sleeping wolf to tell him his sheep has run off? Martin and I would have about eight hours head start, perhaps more.

I left the house through one of the French windows at the front and ran swiftly down the Rue de Montmorency. The month was October. The night was clear and the moon full.

"Rhawnie!"

"Oh, Martin!" We embraced and kissed for the first time. "I'm free!" I breathed happily. "Free!"

"Oh, my dearest! I could hardly believe it when

219

Madame Mornay spoke to me! The horses are waiting. Let's go!''

We rode without stopping for about four hours, until dawn. I wished that I could have taken Blaze, but it would have been too risky. The mount Martin had brought me was a swift chestnut mare. We stopped a few times to rest the horses, and early in the afternoon we stopped to rest ourselves. We were about fifty miles north of Paris, on the road to Dieppe, where we could catch a boat for England. The name of the town was Beauvais, I think. Martin asked the innkeeper for two rooms, one for himself and one for his "sister."

Before he left me he knelt in front of me and held both my hands tightly.

"Madame Mornay told you my plan? It will work, Rhawnie. No one will be able to say we're not married legally, when we've been married by a priest and have lived as man and wife for a while. No one, no one will be able to separate us!"

He was so ardent, so young and fine and pure. He reminded me a little of Django. Django would have been just as passionate, just as sincere in his adoration.

"I promise that I will be a good wife, Martin," I said. And I meant it. "I will never shame you or disgrace you. And promise me, we will never speak of the past, of what I have been. We must forget it, or it will hurt our love for each other. Will you promise?"

He promised, kissing my hands and permitting himself one kiss on my mouth. And then he left me alone. So noble, that Martin. I couldn't imagine Seth Garrett behaving so honorably in a similar situation.

I undressed and crawled into my small bed. I was exhausted from riding, yet elated. I really was free, and about to start a new life. I would be married in just a few days. Married! I have never been particularly religious—no Gypsy is unless it suits him to be—but that day I hugged myself and thanked God for helping me to get what I really wanted from life.

In a dream I heard Seth's footsteps and the tap of his cane: tap, STEP, step; tap, STEP, step. I moaned and covered my ears and tried to banish the nightmare.

"Get up. We're leaving."

I sat up and rubbed my eyes. It was Seth, in the flesh. He was dusty and tired looking, as though he had ridden hard and far. And he looked angry.

"How—? What—?" I mumbled sleepily. "What time is it? Where is Martin?"

"Get dressed." He tossed my clothes onto the bed. "We'll talk later."

Just then Martin burst into the room. "What are you doing here?" he demanded. "Leave here at once! Rhawnie is going to be my wife!"

"Rhawnie is my mistress and she's not going to be your anything," Seth growled. "Hurry up, Rhawnie."

"I will not allow this!" Martin threw himself at Seth, who gave him a strong shove. The boy reeled and fell backwards against the bed. He jumped up immediately and charged Seth again. Seth grabbed his arms and pinned them behind his back.

"Don't be a fool, boy," he said angrily. He released Martin and pushed him away. "I don't want to hurt you."

"You can't hurt me, Martin shouted, "and you can't hurt Rhawnie anymore! You're a brute, an animal! A man like you shouldn't be allowed to live!"

He attacked Seth again. Seth repulsed him with one sweep of his mighty fist. The young duke slumped against the wall and blood oozed out of the corner of his mouth.

"Martin!" I started towards him, my arms outstretched, but Seth intercepted me.

"Get dressed, damn you!" he snarled. "Or you'll get some of the same!"

Five minutes later I was sitting beside him in a hired coach, heading for Paris. The horse Blaze was tied on behind. I couldn't bring myself to say one word to Seth. I was outraged and ashamed and saddened at the way he had treated Martin. It had been horrible. And humiliating.

When we reached the house late that night I went straight to my room without speaking to anyone. I unpacked my valise, put my money and jewels back in their box, and threw myself face down on my bed. Jules came after a while and offered food or tea, but I didn't want anything. Hours passed and I lay motionless, like one dead. I thought of my life with Seth Garrett, who didn't love me, and of the future I would never have with Martin, who did. Why had Seth stopped us? Why didn't he just wash his hands of me, let me go?

He didn't come to my room that night. I had breakfast in my room the next morning, and when I went downstairs for lunch he was already seated at his place in the dining room. I didn't speak. I couldn't eat. And neither could he.

At two o'clock that afternoon a man called to see Seth. Jules showed him into the study and when he came back I grabbed his arm.

"Who is that man, Jules? I have never seen him before."

"The Duke de Terné," Jules said. "I believe he is a cousin of the de Vernay family."

My mouth felt dry. "Why do you think he's here?" I didn't really have to ask, but I needed to hear the words spoken.

"I would assume that he has come to offer a challenge to Monsieur Seth, Mademoiselle," Jules said with imperturbable calm. "But don't worry, there have been duels before. Monsieur Seth always wins."

When the visitor had left I went to Seth. I stood in the doorway of the study. He looked up and I saw pain in his face.

"He is going to fight you?" I whispered.

"Damned young fool," Seth growled.

"Don't hurt him," I begged. "Please, Seth. I'll stay with you for as long as you'll have me. I'll gamble for you and—and do anything for you. Only don't hurt him! Please!"

"I'm not a complete villain," he said. "I don't slaughter children."

François Neval came that evening. He and Seth closeted themselves in the study and I listened, my ear pressed against the door.

"It's to be tomorrow morning," François said. "You'll meet on the southwest field in the Bois before dawn. I am to supply the weapons. The usual—twenty paces, turn and— dear God, Seth, isn't there something we can do?" François cried suddenly. "Martin de Vernay is the King's favorite nephew! If anything should happen to him—! You've got to get out of this. Send an apology or something. For the love of God!"

"Don't you think I tried?" Seth rumbled. "That damned snot de Terné tried to insinuate that I was a coward. Pistols at dawn. Of all the damned nuisances." I heard the clink of glass as he poured himself a drink. "Damned Gypsy bitch. She isn't worth it."

"Then send her away!" François said. "Let her go to him if that's what he wants, if it will put an end to this madness! It's what she wants, isn't it?"

"But it's not what I want," Seth snapped. "She belongs to me."

"No woman is worth this!" François yelped. "Even if you don't get killed, you could be exiled from Paris, from France! You know how strict they are about duelling. The King's nephew!" he said again. "I think you've gone mad, Seth. And you know what else I think? I think you've fallen in love with the girl! You have, haven't you? Why didn't I see it before? You've lost your head over that yellow-haired Gypsy!"

"You'll lose your head if you don't shut up and get out of here!" Seth barked. "This is none of your damned business, François."

"None of my business? I'm your second in this mess! I'm your friend! Well, I'll see you tomorrow in the Bois. For God's sake don't drink so much! You know what drink does to a man's aim. Someone could get hurt."

I slipped away, back to my room. Was it true, what François had said? Was Seth in love with me? He hadn't admitted it, but he hadn't denied the charge. Seth, in love with me. It wasn't possible. I tried to remember the conversation we had had—was it just the night before?—when I suggested to him that his behavior was that of a jealous man afraid of losing the woman he loved. He hadn't denied that, either. He had grown thoughtful and he had gotten drunk.

Yes, he loved me. I was sure of it. Buy why did the knowledge disturb me? Why did it make me want to cry? I had wanted something like this to happen. I had always known that the only way I could hurt him was if he loved me. But now hurting him didn't seem so important.

If he were killed, it would end my torment and my imprisonment. It was so crazy! I hated him, didn't I? And yet nothing in the world could compare with the feel of his arms around me in the darkness. I loved to lie against his deep chest and listen to the soft thunder of his heart. Even with my limited experience of men, I knew that what we shared was unusual, unique. I understood his needs so well, as he understood mine. Our bodies fit so perfectly together. If he died—that pleasure would die with him.

And what about Martin? Poor, dear Martin, who cared about me. This duel would cause a scandal, whatever the outcome. Martin was strong and determined, but could he withstand the pressures that would mount from all sides when the story came out? Opposition to our marriage would be stronger then ever. Even the King might intervene.

I couldn't sleep that night. I stood at the window and looked at the moon. And then all of a sudden I had a vision of death. I saw blood pouring out of the moon, dripping on the earth, falling on the trees and the houses like rain. A man dressed in black would die tomorrow.

I ran to Seth's room and burst in without knocking. He was still fully dressed, standing in front of the fireplace with a half-empty glass in his hand.

"What do you want? Go back to bed." He drank deeply. I was amazed that a man could drink so much and still be able to stand.

"I had a dream," I said breathlessly. "I saw a man die! Please, Seth, you mustn't fight tomorrow! I felt it, Death, very close! You remember, I had the same feeling, the same premonition when my uncle—and when the Gypsies were dying. Please, Seth—"

"I've already told you that I wouldn't hurt your precious Martin," he said. "Go away, Rhawnie. I'm not interested in your dreams. Cheer up, maybe I'll be the one to die. You'd like that, wouldn't you."

"No." I whispered. "No, I don't want you— promise me, Seth." I grabbed his arm. He was as solid and unyielding as stone. "Promise me, you won't wear black tomorrow. Please!"

He gave an incredulous sneer and shook me off roughly. "Still up to your dirty little Gypsy tricks, aren't you?" he said. Then he turned his back on me.

A frost fell that night, covering the city and the parks with a white haze, turning the leaves of the chestnut and maple trees of gold. I didn't sleep, and I don't think Seth did, either. Just before dawn I stood at my window and watched him ride out of the stable yard on Hugo, his roan. I couldn't bear the waiting. I dressed quickly and went out to the stables. Boucher tried to prevent me from going, but I took Blaze out without a saddle and rode off towards the Bois. I knew the way, I knew exactly where Martin and Seth were meeting. On that same field where Seth and I used to race, and where I had met Martin for the first time after the ball.

The mist of morning hung low over the frosty plain. I could see a small knot of men standing under the trees near the duelling site. I tethered Blaze to a tree and moved closer, keeping well back and out of sight. I didn't want to distract them but I had to see, I had to know. Seth was wearing a flowing black cloak over black trousers and a white shirt. The fool, I thought. Why couldn't he listen?

And Martin, too, was dressed in black—black coat, black trousers, black waistcoat, and a black stock at his throat. I recognized François and the Duke de Terné. There was another man present, smaller than the rest with a telltale black bag at his feet. The doctor.

François and the Duke de Terné came together, the two seconds. François spoke earnestly, the Duke nodded, then walked back to Martin. He and Martin spoke briefly and Martin shook his head. He didn't want to settle the dispute except by killing. Nothing less than Seth's death would satisfy him.

Seth shed his cloak and Martin his coat. Seth hefted the pistol in his hand and pointed it at the trees, right at me. I ducked down, but I was sure he hadn't seen me. The two men took their places, back to back in the center of the field. I moved closer, so that I was directly in line with them.

The Duke de Terné began to count loudly. Martin walked towards me and Seth away from me. The pounding of my heart kept pace with their steps. The birds in the trees around me awoke to the dawn and twittered as they foraged for breakfast. On the other side of the forest the city came slowly to life. A train whistle shrieked, wagons rumbled over cobblestones. Shopkeepers came out of their homes, breathed the crisp morning air deeply, and headed for their businesses. Mothers dragged their sleepy children out of their beds and made them ready for school.

"—Eighteen. Nineteen. Twenty. You may turn and fire at will."

Martin spun around and fired immediately. I couldn't see past him, I couldn't see if Seth was hit. There was no answering shot.

"Fire, damn you!" Martin shouted.

I broke out of the trees and raced towards them. I had to know if Seth was hurt. He was still standing, but even from far away I could see the red stain on his white shirt front. His pistol was raised and pointed at me. He intended to fire at Martin and to miss. But at the last second he saw me. He twitched the pistol aside just as he fired. I was only about three feet behind Martin when the shot came. I heard him give a surprised gasp. Then he staggered and fell.

I fell on my knees beside him and supported his shoulders. Tears poured down my cheeks. "Martin," I said. "It's me, Rhawnie. Oh, Martin!"

He seemed to recognize me. He smiled and his lips shaped my name. Blood poured from a wound just under his collarbone.

Rough hands seized me and pulled me away from him.

"Stay away from him, you Gypsy whore!" the Duke de Terné hissed. "Stay away or I'll have you arrested and sent to the guillotine!"

"Martin!" I whispered in farewell. "Martin."

I looked around for Seth. He was limping slowly away from the field, away from me. His pistol lay smoking in the grass, its deadly purpose fulfilled.

9

Gypsies in Exile

MARTIN DIED AND we fled to London to escape arrest. Damp weather and chilling cold drove us back to the continent, to Italy. Seth rented a villa in Fiesole, high in the hills near Florence. We stayed only a couple of months before going to Venice for the carnival season and gambling, then we travelled to Rome. That was the spring of 1844. We spent the summer in Switzerland, the autumn in Dalmatia, in a villa on the Adriatic, the winter in Spain and Portugal, and in the spring of 1845 we were back in London again. We had been together nearly two years.

Very soon the places we visited lost their differentiating characteristics in my mind. Life was one long faro game in a steamy salon, surrounded by shrill-voiced people with painted faces and empty hearts who were looking for love and fortune and would find neither. We stayed in a succession of hotels that blurred into one hotel, one suite of rooms where Seth and I quarelled and made love, where I endured his moods and his coldness. Things had gotten very bad between us since the duel. If he loved me at all, as I once suspected, he never showed it. He resented me and blamed me for our exile from Paris—not that he would have stayed there for long anyway, but he hated being moved by forces not of his own making. As he said, he wanted to deal with life on his own terms, in his own way, in his own time.

I resented his controls of my life, but not as much as before, when Martin was alive, and not as much as I resented his brooding. I knew that he was exploiting me for gain, but I sensed that he had come to depend on me as much as I had come to depend on him, for human closeness, if not for love. Of course he wouldn't have admitted that he needed me, not in a hundred years. He liked the money and he liked the sex, certainly. But I am sure that he would have told anyone that he valued me for no other reason.

London that spring was less dreary than usual, and the gambling was profitable and fun. One night in May I played faro with an American shipbuilder in a gambling hall in Soho. The man wouldn't quit until he had lost all the money he had with him, which was almost two thousand pounds. It was the largest win of my life. I was delighted, and even Seth managed to drop the sour expression that had become part of his mask since the duel. But no sooner had we cashed in our chips than we heard a woman shriek and a man shout.

"Police! This is a raid!"

"The cue for our exit," said Seth, holding my elbow and steering me away from the doors through which the law had entered.

"I don't understand," I said. "We have done nothing wrong."

"We've gambled in an unlicensed establishment, darling. Highly illegal."

I clutched at his arm. "They will put us in prison?" I feared nothing else in the world. The thought of being shut away in a grey cell, behind bars—

"They might," he said with a careless shrug. "But not if we get out of here before they catch up with us. Ah, I see they've got the stairs covered." Indeed, a herd of uniformed men in hard, flat hats had surged into the salon, blocking all exits, shouting that everyone was under arrest. The place was a madhouse. "I saw a door, flush with the wall—" Seth said thoughtfully. Then he led me right to a small door, covered with the same brocade as the walls and almost invisible unless you knew where to look. We ducked through and found ourselves on a flight of narrow wooden stairs that led down. They took us to the small coal cellar under the house.

"You are a wonderful fox," I complimented him. "I didn't see that door."

"I'm as slick as any Gypsy," he said modestly. "I wonder if there's a way out of here."

The place was pitch dark. The only light we had was Seth's matches, and they were running low.

"Last one," he said, striking a match. "I can't see—"

I blew it out. Poof.

"Now why in hell did you—" he started to protest.

I slipped my arms around his neck and kissed him tenderly. "Perhaps we will see a glimmer of light from the street," I suggested. "There is surely a window." A long kiss followed. Then a very long kiss.

"You're corrupt," he murmured, kissing me back. "A corrosive influence. I wouldn't let you teach in my Seminary for Young Ladies."

"Then I'll be your pupil," I said. "Your only pupil."

"Tuition is very steep," he warned, holding me close and nuzzling my neck.

"I'll work it off," I promised. We spent the next ten minutes at that foolishness.

Then Seth said, "Let's get back to the hotel." We opened our eyes and sure enough, there was a faint glimmer from high up on the wall. We could still hear muffled screams and shouts from the salon. I was glad, because when we scrambled up the coal heap under the window we made a lot of noise. I even had a fit of giggles, and no matter how sternly Seth spoke to me, I couldn't stop.

We emerged from the bowels of the building onto a darkened side street. A carriage was passing and the driver saw us and stopped.

"For hire?"

"For hire," Seth affirmed, helping me in. He gave the

233

man the address of our fashionable hotel in Belgravia and we rode off. We said not one word on that ride. We were too busy kissing.

Only when we stepped into the light of the small lobby did we see that we were both black from coal dust. We looked at each other and laughed until we were weak. Seth ordered baths. We were still laughing as we washed each other and splashed around like a couple of children in a wading pool.

Seth dried my hair vigorously and I shouted that he was too rough. "Not rough enough," he growled, wrestling me to the floor. He covered me with his body, but I tickled and fought until he rolled off. I fell on top of him and pinned him down with my weight. My wet hair slapped his cheeks. Then like a wet mermaid, I slithered down between his legs and loved him with my lips and my mouth and throat. He groaned, but not from pain, and he writhed with pleasure. All the anger and tension between us was gone. Later we lay together, exhausted but not yet ready to sleep.

"I think you must be Gypsy," I decided. "If your mother was a pirate she must have been Gypsy, too." I rubbed my cheek on his chest. "Everything about you is Gypsy: the dangerous way you like to live, your love of freedom and money. Everything except—" I stopped myself.

"Except what?" he wondered drowsily.

"If you were really Gypsy you would be married now," I said. "And you would have lots of children. Why else does a man live, if not for that?"

"He lives for pleasure," Seth told me. "And to provide for his mistress, who is very demanding and expensive. I can't afford to marry."

"There is an obvious solution," I told him. "Marry your mistress."

He gave a derisive snort. "I haven't been keeping you

234

busy enough, Rhawnie," he remarked. "You have too much time to think."

I awoke before dawn. Seth's place beside me was empty. When I went into the sitting room that adjoined the bedroom I found him slumped in a chair near a window. There was a half-empty glass of scotch in his hand. He looked like he hadn't slept.

He didn't look up when I approached him. I shivered a little in the cold room and pulled my peignoir tighter around me. It was blue, the same color as the Grecian-style nightgown I wore underneath.

"I want to talk to you, Seth." He didn't move, so I pulled up a short stool and sat at his right hand. "I was sick this morning. Yesterday, too. You remember, I almost fainted the other night at the theater. I think I'm going to have a baby."

He raised his head. His eyes were dull, almost grey, like the early morning sky. They bored through my garments, scanning my still-slim figure.

"You're sure?" he asked.

I nodded. "It's been two months."

"Damn." He stood up and drained his glass. He crossed the room to the sideboard and poured himself another.

"You always drink when you're upset," I said quietly.

"My drinking is none of your bloody business," he snapped.

"And you always get angry when I talk about it."

"I get angry when anyone tries to interfere in my business!" Defiantly, somewhat childishly, he emptied his glass.

"Everything you do is my business now," I told him. "You are the father of my baby."

"Are you sure of that?" he demanded.

"Please don't talk like that," I said sorrowfully. "You know I have never been with anybody but you."

"I don't know anything." he carried his glass to the window and watched a rag and bone man making his way

235

down the elegant street. "Of all the damned nuisances. Why in hell didn't you do something to prevent it?" I gave him a blank, puzzled look. "Damn it," he said loudly, "you lived with that old harlot Odette Mornay for nearly a year. Didn't she teach you anything? How do you think women like her avoid conception? Do you think they're just lucky?"

"I don't understand." I felt queasy and I folded my arms around my middle. "I am not to blame, surely. It is a good and natural thing to have a baby, no?"

"You'll just have to get rid of it," he said.

I felt cold. My stomach knotted. "What do you mean?"

"Get rid of it!" He strode over to me and loomed over me like an angry god. "There must be a dozen doctors in this part of the city alone who do this sort of thing. Five or six times a week, if not more. Damn it, Rhawnie, don't you know anything?" How could I know? No one had ever told me anything. "They cut it out, like a tumor!"

My hands flew to my breasts and I jumped up. "No! No, I won't let them do it!"

"You have no choice," he informed me coldly. "Do you think I want to be saddled with both you and a brat? This is one of your tricks, isn't it? You're trying to get me to marry you. Well, you're out of luck, lady. I'm not interested in marrying you, or in playing daddy to your bastard. Our relationship is business, nothing more."

"Yes," I said, "last night was a business meeting, I suppose. What a fool you are sometimes. You have persuaded yourself that you hate me, haven't you? Why? I've done nothing to hurt you. You have had your way with me, in everything. You've made plenty of money with my help. I just don't understand you. I think you must hate all women, not only me. And most of all you hate yourself. That's why you soak your brains in whiskey and why you need things like gambling and travelling. Because you think you can get away from yourself. But you can't."

"Shut up," he said. "I won't have you preaching—"

"I'm sorry for you," I said softly. "Your spirit is as crippled as your leg!"

He slapped me, hard. Tears of surprise and pain flooded my eyes.

"I wish we'd reached that Gypsy camp one day sooner," he said tightly.

I stared at him. He wished me dead. As well as my baby. I turned slowly and walked regally out of the room. I closed the bedroom door gently and turned the key in the lock. I needed to get away from him.

I felt sick and sad and so full of pain that I could hardly endure it. My life was over, finished. He wanted to cut the baby out of my body and I couldn't stop him, I knew that. I couldn't escape him. Or perhaps I could.

I searched through my things for a white nightgown that a dressmaker had delivered by mistake. I had wanted to return it but Seth had told me not to bother. It was very beautiful, soft and silky and dazzling white, like death. I took off my blue things and put it on. It was the first time in my life that I had worn white. It felt cold, like snow.

I opened Seth's shaving kit. On the velvet lining inside lay two straight-edged razors, beautifully sharp. I ran my thumb lightly over one of the blades and I shivered.

No further preparations were necessary. I went to the window, where the light was good, and I made a deep, firm cut on my left wrist. It didn't hurt at first, so sharp was the razor. But immediately crimson blood welled up and gushed out of the wound. It dripped on the floor, like red rain. Awkwardly, with my left hand, I cut into my right wrist. I thought absurdly that I should have done it the other way around. Blood flowed onto my hands and I dropped the razor. The blood came in uneven waves, driven by the pumping of my heart.

I wasn't afraid to die. I felt free of the sorrow that had burdened me since I had been living with him. And free of shame.

The ribbons of blood were beautiful. I felt weak and

lowered myself to the floor. I clutched the windowsill for support while blood ran down my arms and soaked my white gown, my shroud. A sweet heaviness possessed me, not unlike the feeling I got when Seth made love to me.

I heard a voice. It was Lyubov, and he was laughing. "The Gypsy who runs from danger is no coward; the one who stays to be eaten by wolves is a fool!"

"You are Gypsy!" My father, teaching me. "Be brave!"

"Rhawnie!" A younger voice. A boy's voice. "Rhawnie!"

"Django," I whispered. "Ah! I thought I'd never see you again!"

Then I saw broad green fields rimmed by wooded slopes. Daisies, violets, and buttercups were everywhere. The sun warmed the earth. Gypsies, delighted that the winter was over, danced in circles over the fields, their garments more colorful than any flowers. I saw myself, wearing a wreath of daisies in my hair. I ran up a steep slope to meet Django, but he kept receding as I approached him. I feared that I would never reach him.

The sun went behind a cloud. The world was suddenly dark and I felt cold.

A black horse was running up a charred hillside in the pitch darkness. I couldn't see him, but I could hear the pounding of his hooves on the ground. Pounding. And Django, calling my name.

"Rhawnie! Rhawnie, open the door!"

I heard voices, one familiar and one strange. But my lids felt heavy and I didn't open my eyes.

"Those cuts are deep. She wasn't joking. Good thing you had the wits to apply tourniquets. A few minutes more and it would have been too late to save her. Your wife? No. I've seen so many of these. She'll be an old woman by the time she's twenty-five, if she lives that long. A taxing profession, hers. Disease and violence take their toll."

"Shut up. You don't know what she's like."

"They're all the same, son. High-class courtesan or street whore. All the same. We'll keep this quiet. Bad for business, this sort of thing."

After a while there was quiet and I opened my eyes. Seth was standing at the end of the bed.

"Hellow, *gorgio*," I said faintly.

"Hello, Gypsy."

"You look terrible," I said. "So pale. And you need a shave. Are you sick?"

"No, I'm not sick." But his eyes were big and haunted-looking.

I looked down and saw my hands, bandaged in white. I remembered then. "Ah." I felt slightly embarrassed. "So I—failed." I looked up at him again. Two red patches burned on his cheeks and there was a look in his eyes that I knew all too well. "You are angry with me."

"You're damned right I'm angry," he said in a low voice. "If you ever try a stunt like that again I'll break both your arms." We were silent for a while. I found I couldn't meet his gaze and I turned my face to the wall. "You really hate me," he said.

"Oh, no!" I said quickly. "No, Seth. I don't think I ever hated you. I just resisted—my fate. I love you. And I know that you love me. I suppose we couldn't help falling in love, we were together so much, and we are so much alike. Two Gypsies. You know what I would do sometimes? I would pretend that we were married. In my heart I promised to be faithful to you always, and then nobody could call me a—" I found I couldn't say the word. "It didn't seem to be so bad, what I was doing, when I pretended that. But then, with this baby, I knew I couldn't pretend anymore. He will have no father. You called him a bastard, and so will the world. It's not fair to him. A child should grow up with a father and a family, and he will have no one. I have no one, and nowhere to go when you leave me. And I knew in my soul that I could not live with my shame anymore. And that's why I did it. But not out of hate. Only sadness—and love."

He didn't say anything, just glared, and his eyes grew brighter.

"You saved me, didn't you?" I whispered. "You shouldn't have done it, Seth. If you had waited just a few more minutes—I heard the man say so. Why didn't you wait? You wished me dead and I wanted to be dead. Why?"

"Get some sleep," he said sharply. "We'll talk later."

But we didn't talk. I was young and strong and I healed quickly. Or my wrists healed. My spirits remained very low. I had no laughter and little inclination to talk. I felt impatient and fretful and anxious, as though I were waiting for something. For death? No, not just yet. I was waiting for the inevitable, for Seth to leave me. Waiting for the morning when I would wake up and find that he had gone.

He was very careful to keep his razors locked up. The little scissors in my sewing kit disappeared, and he watched me like a hawk when we dined together, fearing that I would slide a table knife up my sleeve, I guess.

The first time I gambled after that, I lost heavily, nearly three hundred pounds before Seth persuaded me to quit.

"You see," I told him later, when we were back in our rooms. "It is hopeless. I'm not good for anything anymore. It's crazy." I rubbed the scar on my left wrist with my right thumb. I did it unconsciously, and habitually. "Yes, I think I am mad. I have always been mad. Those visions of blood and death, they are not normal. And you have said that you've never known anybody who could see cards before they were played. That's not normal! You see, I am crazy. You can have me locked away in one of those places—asylums? Oh, I wish I knew what will happen to me. If I knew—"

He watched stolidly from his chair as I paced the floor.

"I must know," I said to myself, "I cannot live like this much longer. If I could see the future, just a glimpse—!" I knelt in front of the gas fire in the sitting room. "Nothing. I see nothing! Where is my crystal? I need to look at something—'' I went to Seth and grabbed his hand. ''I'll read your hand—'' He tried to pull it away but I clung to it tightly. ''So dark, so dark.'' I rubbed my eyes feverishly. ''Why can't I see?'' I wailed.

''Stop it,'' he said gruffly, shaking me by the shoulders. ''You're hysterical, getting yourself all worked up over nothing. What's the matter with you, Rhawnie?''

I fell forward into his lap and cried, ''I am frightened, so frightened! Just like a little *gorgio* child!''

''Shh, it's all right,'' he said soothingly in his rich voice. He smoothed my hair gently. ''There's nothing to be frightened of, Rhawnie. You can have your baby. And you'll get your skill at cards back. Everything will be fine.''

I gazed up at him. ''And what then?'' I asked in a harsh whisper. I broke away from him and ran to the bedroom.

I undressed myself with difficulty. My wrists were still very stiff and I had trouble manipulating the strings and buttons on my costume. My hands were trembling. What a fool I had made of myself, I thought disgustedly. To fuss about the future like that! It was getting harder and harder to be strong, to be Gypsy. But I couldn't tell him that the thing I feared most was his leaving me. I had already told him once that I loved him, and he hadn't listened. He was my life. All that time I was trying to escape him, I was falling deeper and deeper in love with him.

I put on my nightgown and brushed my hair. It was long, below my shoulders, but I would never forget that I had cut it off once. Perhaps that had been the start of my bad luck.

Seth came into the room. He stubbed out his cigar on an enamel tray on the dresser and looked at me. Our eyes met in the mirror over my dressing table. I looked down.

''I'm sorry I made such a fool of myself in front of you,'' I said. ''It won't happen again. I know how men hate it when women get like that.'' I threw down my brush and went to the open window. The soft breeze from the river billowed my silky skirts out behind me. "Forgive me, Seth. This business has made me weak-minded and stupid, I guess."

He came up behind me and draped a robe around my shoulders. "You ought to find yourself a husband," he suggested brightly.

"Oh, that's a brilliant idea," I said with heavy sarcasm. "Who would marry me now?"

"I'll marry you," he said. He turned me around and cupped my chin in his hand. I gaped at him. "Didn't you hear what I said, Rhawnie?"

"I don't think that's a very funny joke," I said quietly, pushing his hand away.

"It's not a joke. I mean it. I want to marry you."

"No, you don't. You can't. Marry me? A Gypsy girl with only one name, who doesn't even know how old she is?"

"You're old enough," he grinned. "I'll vouch for that."

"But it's wrong, Seth!" I cried. "You just feel sorry for me and you're afraid that I'll try to kill myself again and you don't really love me—"

"I do love you," he said firmly. "You know it. I know it. We belong together. Two Gypsies, remember? Now come away from the window before you catch a chill—"

I couldn't move. Feelings boiled up inside me and tears streamed down my face. He held me close and kissed them away and said my name over and over again.

"I love you! I love you!" I whispered ecstatically. "You will never leave me now and our baby will have a father and a name! Oh, I am so happy!"

We were married in Scotland, where there was no waiting time, no bans. Seth had to translate everything that was said into French for me because my feeble command of English deserted me. I think Seth was nervous, too. When we joined hands, his felt icy and bloodless.

When it was over the minister's wife beamed at us and

said something in garbled English that I *just* couldn't understand.

"What did she say?" I asked Seth when we were outside again.

"She said she'd never seen a bonnier couple."

"Bonny? What does that mean?"

He kissed the tip of my nose. "It means beautiful, and she was speaking of you, not me."

"No," I said, "you are beautiful, too, today. I shall always love you."

"Yes." He mopped his forehead even though the day was cool and misty. "Well, now I know why I've never done that before. Let's go. I need a drink."

He presented me with a matching pair of filigreed bracelets for my wrists. They were exquisite, like little cuffs made of gold lace. He had had them specially made in Bond Street, before we left London. We celebrated by dining out in a stuffy Edinburgh restaurant, and I disgraced myself by drinking too much champagne and laughing loudly. We went back to our hotel and Seth picked me up and carried me over the threshold.

"Do you think we'll be invited to the Delacroix Ball when we go back to Paris?" I wondered. "I am a married lady now, very respectable. I must try to be sedate. Do you think I can ever learn to be sedate. Oh, I love you so!"

His lovemaking that night was very gentle and sweet, but lifeless.

"What's the matter?" I asked jokingly. "Don't you like making love to a married woman?"

"I'm sorry you weren't satisfied," he said a little stiffly. "I've never been married before. It's a new experience, making love to my own wife and not somebody else's."

"You'll get used to it," I promised. "I am. Nothing has changed, not really. We are still the same Seth and Rhawnie as before. What are a few words, a gold ring?"

"You weren't so cavalier in your attitude towards marriage before you got it," he observed. "You were even willing to die if—"

"Ah, hush," I warned him. "We must not speak of that. It was very wrong of me, very foolish. But it is past."

"It's past and you got what you wanted," he grumbled. "Go to sleep, Gypsy. We're going back to London tomorrow."

Seth refused to let me gamble in London. He said he didn't want me to play until after the baby was born, in December. Maybe he was afraid our child would look like a face card, like a knave of hearts. But whenever he gambled, he lost. He said it was the dealers in London, that they were all crooks, and he decided we should go to Switzerland for the summer. But Switzerland proved unsatisfactory for one reason or another and we went to Austria, then Hungary, then Romania.

In Bucharest we hired a maid for me, a mute girl named Anna. I suppose Seth felt a little guilty about leaving me alone so much when he went out to play cards. I chattered to her in a mixture of Russian, Romany, and French, and she always seemed to understand. She was very small, with a pitted complexion and warm brown eyes, and her hair was unbelievably coarse and frizzy. But she was quick and obedient and loving, and of course, quiet. She seemed wary and frightened of Seth. I think he reminded her of someone who had been cruel to her. I never found out.

I knew that Seth wasn't happy about being married. It wasn't so much being married to me, but he felt that he wasn't free anymore, that his life wasn't his own, that I was controlling him somehow, even though I rarely opened my mouth to argue with him and willingly went with him wherever he wanted to go. Travelling was hard for me, for the first time in my life, and I was often sick. But I never complained, never suggested that we stay in one place until after the birth.

I closed my eyes to his unhappiness for a long time, until I couldn't ignore it anymore. I tried to humor him, to lighten his spirits, but he was cold and unresponsive.

We were in Budapest, staying in a lovely little hotel. It was November. Seth gambled every night. I always waited up for him. He came in one night, looking grim.

"You're back!" I threw my arms around his neck and kissed him. "Did you win?"

He detached my arms and poured himself a drink. His clothes reeked of cigar smoke and liquor and cheap perfume.

"Did you win?" I asked again. I already knew the answer. He never won anymore.

"I'm cursed," he said with a humorless laugh. "My luck has run out. I think some Gypsy has put a curse on me."

I hated it when he talked that way. He meant it, that I was to blame for his bad luck.

"We're down to our last thousand pounds," he said. "I'm thinking of selling the house in Paris."

"Oh, oh!" I protested. "Don't do that. We will go back there someday. Please don't sell it."

"Don't nag me," he said. "We need the money."

"No, we don't! We haven't touched my money yet. Take all you want, Seth. I have thousands in my jewels box, you know that. Please, it's yours."

I half expected him to refuse, but he didn't. The next night he lost again. He fussed at me because we couldn't go to Paris. He implied that if he was free he could try his luck in distant places: Russia again, or even China. He spoke sneeringly of the entire continent of Europe as a dead bore and he told me that there was no lack of adventure in America.

I tried to soothe him. "You're tired and losing is hard for you, I know."

"You don't know anything," he snarled. "How did I get myself into this mess."

"Come to bed." I sat on the arm of his chair and combed the dark curls away from his forehead with my fingers. "I'll make you forget your troubles," I whispered meaningfully. "Come."

I took off his white tie and began to work the diamond studs out of his shirtfront.

He stood up swiftly, almost knocking me on the floor. "Damn it, stop pestering me," he snarled. "A man can't have any peace. Leave me alone."

"Why don't you let yourself be happy?" I wondered sadly. "You're fighting so hard."

"Shut up," he said. "I'm going to bed."

The next morning when he was splashing water on his face and chest I saw small red bruises on his shoulders and chest. And there were long red scratches on his back. He didn't even try to hide them from me. He had been with another woman and he didn't care if I knew about it. I felt sick, and I asked him right then if it was true.

"What do you want me to do?" He dragged his razor across his cheek. "Lie to you? You've been around. You know how I am. You can't expect marriage to change a man's character."

"But you were faithful to me for two whole years," I said. "I know you were! I was all you needed then!"

He looked pointedly at my distorted figure. "Things have changed since then, haven't they?"

I put my hands on the little mound of my belly. "Who was she?" I asked him.

"Just a tart," he said off-handedly. "Does that make you feel better?"

"You do hate me!" I cried. "You must, or you would not hurt me like this! Oh, why didn't you let me die in London?"

He paused in his shaving for a moment. "I wish to God I knew," he said.

He continued to gamble. Three nights he didn't come home at all. I cried until I was sick and Anna tried to comfort me. I was careful never to cry in front of him. I didn't want him to see how much I cared.

We went to Vienna in mid-December. The days were very short, and snow covered the ground. The days of waiting for the child to be born dragged by. Vienna was very gay, full of diversion, an elegant city with a rich tradition of fun and amusement and culture, like Paris. I hoped that Seth would feel at home there. But he behaved badly and acted as if I were keeping him prisoner in our hotel, the Grand Hotel de Paris on the Karlsplatz. I could hardly speak to him at all. Usually he disdained to answer me, and when he did it was to offer a cutting remark or a sneer about how I was acting like a nagging wife.

I had never felt so lonely, so desperate, so afraid. I was certain that I would lose him. I took long walks every day, just to escape from the room at the hotel. And one afternoon, on impulse, I went to a Gypsy fortune-teller. I didn't tell her that I was Rom, too. And the old woman confirmed my worst fears.

"Your baby will be a fine boy, a son," she droned. We were sitting over a cup of murky tea in a tavern at the edge of the student quarter. "But watch out for a man. A dark-haired man. He will bring you much sorrow. He is like a crow that wants to burst into flight. If you cut his tether—"

"Be quiet, you hag," I hissed in Romany. "You tell lies! All Gypsies tell lies! He won't go, I tell you. He won't!"

The woman scolded me. "You are Rom and you come to me for your fortune! For shame, girl. You should know better than that. Go home to your husband and think about the baby soon to be born. Think of the many brothers and sisters he will have. Think of your mother and father and—"

"I have no one," I wailed. "Dead. They are all dead!"

The fortune-teller shook her head. "Foolish one. Has he married you?" I nodded. "Then what are you worried about? All men get edgy about this time. He is afraid for you, that's all."

"He is seeing other women," I whispered brokenly.

The woman shrugged. "So? He is still a man, even though you are almost a mother and too big with child to want him. It happens a lot. Don't worry. After the birth he'll be as proud as a prince, and he'll come back to you. Don't worry."

I paid her and left. I needed to hear consoling words from a Gypsy, even though I knew in my heart that they were lies. I wandered into the Prater, the huge park located on the island formed by the Danube River and the Danube Canal. I found an iron chair in a quiet corner, under a statue of a half-draped female. My cheeks were wet with tears and I sniffed loudly.

A man sitting on a chair nearby spoke to me, first in German, then when he saw my incomprehension, in English.

"Such a pretty lady as yourself shouldn't have any reason to sigh," he said kindly. "May I offer my handkerchief, Madame?"

In spite of the pain in my heart, I smiled at him. He was ridiculous looking. His hair stuck out at odd angles from under his hat. It was light brown, like his big mustache, and threaded with grey. His eyes were blue and smiling, with lots of little wrinkles at the corners.

"No, thank you, sir," I said, searching through my reticule. "I have a handkerchief here someplace." I found a fine linen square with a broad lace border; a handkerchief more useful for flirting than for blowing.

"It hurts me deeply to see such beauty unhappy," the man sighed. "Is there anything I can do to help?"

"No, no," I shook my head and smiled at him again. "I am just being silly, I know. The baby and the snow and the cold—" I bit my lip and looked down at my hands.

"Yes, of course," the man said. "My wife was the same way. She cried all the time, as I recall. I felt quite rejected."

"You did?" I looked up. "You're right. I'm not being fair to him, my husband. Am I? He is feeling just as frightened as I, don't you think?"

"Oh, yes," my new friend nodded. "I would say most definitely that that was the case. Definitely."

"Of course," I said decisively, stuffing my damp hand-kerchief into my muff. "We are both nervous. I shouldn't think only of myself. It is very selfish."

"Now you're being a sensible young lady," he said approvingly. "Gracious, snowing again!" He looked up at the sky. It had been snowing for half an hour, his hat and hair were white with snow, but he just now noticed it. "Perhaps I can offer you a cup of tea, Madame." He stood up and gave me a courtly little bow. "Beauty should never feel sad—or cold."

"No, thank you. Some other time, perhaps." I rose and extended my hand. He kissed my fingertips gallantly. "You have been very kind, sir. Thank you. Good-bye."

"Good-bye, Madame. I hope all goes well for you."

I walked out of the park. He was very nice, I thought. Kind. And well-dressed, too. He might have been a businessman, although from what I understood, at that hour of the afternoon businessmen were hunched over their desks. He had an abstracted, dreamy air, like a professor I had met once in Paris. That man thought he had a winning system for faro, and he had been crushed when he lost. Yes, this man reminded me of a professor.

Seth and I dined in the hotel dining room. Neither of us had much of an appetite, but we drank two bottles of wine between us. I didn't tell him about the Gypsy, but I described my encounter with the man in the park.

"You should have taken tea with him," Seth said. "It might have led—to other things." His meaning was clear.

I kept a smile pasted on my lips and said, "Oh, you can't think that he was interested in me in that way!"

"Why not? Some men have very peculiar tastes. Cows. Sheep. Dogs. Gypsies. Even pregnant women." He chuckled into his wine glass. I flushed.

"If my pregnancy disgusts you so deeply, you should leave me," I said sharply. "You feel no loyalty to me. Why should you feel loyalty to a baby you haven't even seen yet?"

"You have a point there," he replied. He raised his glass

to me and winked. "Very logical."

"You are going out tonight?" I asked.

"Of course. Any reason why I shouldn't?"

"Yes," I said. "I think the baby will come tonight. I know it will."

"Nonsense. By my calculations it won't be here for another week yet. Have some more wine, my dear little wife, and don't worry about it."

"No, thank you, Seth. I'll go upstairs, if you don't mind."

"Why should I mind?" he asked lightly. "You're free to come and go."

"Good luck tonight," I said. "In whatever you do."

When I was back in our room, sudden stabbing pain in my middle made me sit down. Anna ran to help me.

"I have felt queer little flutterings all day," I gasped. "I knew it would come tonight. He didn't believe me."

Anna jerked her head at the door.

"Should you get Seth? No, no. These things go on for hours, you know that. I wouldn't want to spoil his fun."

I undressed and went to bed. The pains were far apart at first, every forty-five minutes, then every half-hour. I was happy that it would soon be over. At two in the morning I sent Anna for the midwife, who lived about a mile away. It was snowing heavily, and I hoped she would be all right. But as soon as she left the pains became much worse. The little one seemed to be waiting until we were alone.

"So you think you want to be born in private, eh?" I asked him. "You're up to your Gypsy tricks already."

An hour went by and Anna did not return. I was more worried about her than I was about myself. I struggled out of bed to look out the window. I went out to the sitting room and a terrible siege of pain drove me to my knees. Just then Seth came in.

"What is it? What's the matter?" He knelt beside me and put his arms around me. The stink of whiskey was strong on his breath and he was very unsteady. He had drunk a lot.

"The baby is coming, very soon," I said. I gripped his hand and pressed my face against his shoulder until the spasm passed. "I sent Anna for the midwife—she hasn't come back. I think she is lost, or hurt. You must—"

I couldn't speak. He helped me back to bed held my hands until the moment passed.

"You must fetch Anna," I told him. "Find the midwife, somebody."

"There's no time," he said. "I can't leave you."

"I'm—sorry."

"There's no reason to be sorry. You said it would be tonight and I didn't believe you."

"Did you win tonight?" I asked him.

"Yes, I did. I made a packet. Everything will be fine, Rhawnie."

"I believe you. I love you. Have you ever seen a baby being born?" He nodded. "So have I. When I was twelve—or thirteen, I was allowed to see my father's cousin's baby, little Pyotyr. He was killed, along with the rest. You remember? How that woman screamed! She wasn't very brave, that one. What's a little pain?" I gasped and clutched his hands. He wiped my forehead with his immaculate handkerchief. "It was the most wonderful thing, Seth. So beautiful. Better than watching a horse foal. Horses don't cry. People are so weak. At least babies don't have such long—legs!"

"Easy, take it easy, Rhawnie," he soothed me. "Relax. That's right."

"He is coming, isn't he?"

"Pretty soon."

"What if—the midwife doesn't come?"

"Then we'll just have to bring him into the world without her," he said soothingly. "Don't worry. Don't be afraid."

"I'm not afraid," I said truthfully. "You are here, and you love me, that's all that matters. I want to tell you something. I did a wicked thing. I went to a Gypsy, to have my fortune told. So foolish. Just like a *gorgio* woman." I clamped my teeth down on my lips and closed my eyes. Sweat poured off me. "I was so afraid that you would leave me. I had to know. I have been very selfish. Thinking only of myself. Forgive me. It will be better after this is over. I will be a better wife to you, I promise." I writhed and sucked in my breath. "You are a man," I said. "You need the company of women. I understand. I will be better—"

"You're a fine wife, a wonderful wife," he said softly. "I love you very much. Don't talk anymore. Just be quiet, relax. I won't leave you, I promise."

The baby started to come. I reached for Seth's hand but he wasn't there. He was helping, pulling, telling me to bear down. I chewed my lips until they were bloody so that I wouldn't scream. I didn't want to upset him. He talked to me all the while. I don't remember his words, but his voice was smooth and calming, like velvet. He kept praising me and reassuring me, and I felt safe and confident that everything would be all right.

Then he held the baby up for me to see. A red, wriggling thing no bigger than Seth's two hands. Seth gave it a whack to start it breathing.

"A boy?" I asked weakly. "He is all right? He is healthy?"

"He's fine. Listen to that." Our son displayed the power of his lungs. I rested while Seth washed the baby and wrapped him in clean cloths. Then he rested the wee thing in the crook of my arm near my breast.

I looked at the baby and then at Seth, who knelt at the side of the bed. "Thank you," I whispered. "Thank you for him."

He lowered his head on his arms and gave a long, shuddering sigh. "That's a hell of a thing to do to a drunken man, Rhawnie," he said with an odd, shaking laugh.

"Why did you get drunk?" I asked softly.

"I wish to hell I knew myself. I don't know. But I never sobered up quicker in my life. Jesus."

I stroked his dark head. "You were wonderful tonight. Were you afraid?"

"Scared to death," he admitted. He lifted his head. He looked so drawn and haggard that my heart turned over. His cheeks were wet, but not with prespiration. He touched my face lightly and I kissed his hand. "You are the wonderful one, Rhawnie. Determined not to let on that it hurt, weren't you? You're brave. I hope he takes after you."

"What shall we call him?" I wondered drowsily. "We have never talked about it. How about Stefan, for a cousin of mine—"

"No," Seth said sharply. "We'll call him Nicholas, for your grandfather. Is that all right?"

I smiled and closed my eyes. It was all right.

The midwife bustled in, her voice grating on the stillness in the room. "What a night!" she exclaimed. "All the babies in Vienna wanted to be born tonight. The second one was in labor for twenty hours! What's all this?"

"My wife and I have done very well without you," Seth told her wearily. "We won't be needing you after all."

"What do you mean, you won't be needing me? Did you tie the cord? Where's the afterbirth? Men don't know anything about delivering babies!"

"The cord is tied, the afterbirth is in that basin, if you want to look. It's all there. Here's some money for your trouble. Good-night."

"Well! What are you, young man, a doctor?"

"No," Seth sounded exhausted and irritated. "I am not a doctor. In fact, I'm not this lady's husband at all. I just happened to be passing. Good-bye, Madame."

I heard Seth talking to Anna in a low voice, assuring her that it wasn't her fault that she didn't get back in time, giving her instructions about this and that. Then he stood over me and said my name. I opened my eyes and reached for his hand. He held mine lightly.

"What are you going to do now?" I asked.

"Take a few stiff drinks and go to sleep. I prescribe the same for you, only without the drinks. Rhawnie—" He stopped.

"Yes, Seth, what is it?" An ancient fear tugged at my heart.

He wanted to speak, he wanted to tell me, but he couldn't. He wet his lips and dragged his free hand through his hair and said, "I love you." Then he went out to the sitting room. The baby and I slept, both of us exhausted from our ordeal. Anna finished her ministrations and curled up in a chair, alert for any whisper, any sign of want.

When we awoke a few hours later, Seth was gone. He left some money in my jewel box, enough to live on for a few weeks. And he left a note. I stared at the letters, the dots, the lines. They meant nothing to me. I sent Anna downstairs for the desk clerk, and when he appeared I asked him to read it to me.

He was red-haired, bespectacled, and pompous. "It's in French," he informed me.

"I don't care if it's in twenty languages," I said. "Can you read it or can't you?"

"Yes, Madame." He cleared his throat. You might have thought he was about to address the National Assembly or the Emperor's court. " 'Going to Paris to sell the house and replenish funds,' " he read. " 'Will send for you all soon.' And it's signed, 'S'," he finished with a sniff.

"That's all? Not even a *dear* at the top and a *love* at the bottom?" I demanded.

"That's all? he said. "You can see for yourself—"

Anna ushered him out. A lie. I knew it was a lie. He didn't want to see me again. He waited until after the baby was born to desert me, because he knew I wouldn't kill myself then. But that wasn't really why he left.

Anna came back into the room and held my hands. "I knew it would happen," I said, fighting back tears. "He never wanted to get married. He didn't want the baby. Why, why wouldn't he let me make him happy? I tried so hard, Anna. I love him so much. He is a coward, a coward."

We left the hotel as soon as I was able to get up, and we moved to a cheaper place, really a rooming house, on a crooked street near the opera house. There wasn't much money left after I paid our bill at the Grand Hotel, but at least I still had my jewels, and I knew we could live for a long time if I pawned them. And after they were gone—I didn't know what would happen.

Weeks passed. Winter deepened. My stock of jewels shrank. I decided that I should get a job. But I couldn't read newspapers—I could hardly speak the language in Vienna—and I had no idea where to begin. One day I walked to the Prater, the park. I sat in the same chair, near the statue of the half-naked lady.

"Hello, Beauty," said a voice in English.

I looked up. It was my friend, the little professor. He twinkled at me.

"Ah, it is you!" I greeted him warmly. "I am so happy to see you again, sir. You have been well?"

"Quite well. And you? You have had your baby! How is it? Everything all right?"

"Yes, fine, thank you. It is a fine boy. His name is Nicholas."

"Nicholas." The man nodded. "A good name, that. I have ancestors by that name, I think. And your husband?"

"He had to go away," I swallowed. "Family business. But I'm afraid he didn't leave me with very much money. I think I shall have to find work."

"Work?" The man frowned and rubbed his nose with the knob of his cane. "Let me see. If I were a beautiful young woman living in Vienna in January, and had no particular wish to stay in the city, I think I would go to Bavaria, to Munich. Very nice place, Munich. Friendly. Less mad than here, if you know what I mean. Yes, I would go right to Munich, and I would go to the Royal Residence and ask to see the king. I hear he has an eye for beautiful ladies. He'll help you, I'm sure of it."

"Oh." I tried to look interested, but I thought, poor fellow, he's mad. "That is a very good suggestion," I said. "Thank you."

"I just happen to have a couple of railway tickets that I'm not using," he said. "They're for a train that goes in a couple of weeks and I have decided to go there tomorrow. Yes. Tomorrow. Why don't you take them?"

"Thank you." I said politely. "That is so very kind of you."

"Well, I am sorry I cannot offer you tea today," my friend said. He beamed at me and rocked on his heels. Every now and then his eyes darted up to the statue. "But I am sure we will meet again. In München, as they say in German."

"Yes," I said. "In München."

He bowed and bid me farewell, then strolled away, swinging his cane and humming to himself. I looked at the tickets, and I tried to picture myself in the presence of royalty. But I had nothing to wear! And no jewels! No matter. This man surely knew someone, or he wouldn't have suggested that I go. It was miraculous, wonderful! I ran back to our room to tell Anna. How pleased she would be! And how glad we would both be to leave Vienna. Like London, the city now had bad associations in my mind.

But when I got back and saw Anna's stricken face, my heart dropped to my shoes.

"What is it? What's happened? Is he all right?" I looked at the baby. He seemed to be sleeping well enough, but when I touched his forehead I knew he was feverish. I left the house immediately and returned with a doctor.

"Influenza," he diagnosed. "I've had a lot of cases lately. I hope it doesn't turn into an epidemic. You're looking a little pink yourself, Madame. You'd better lie down. He may get over it. Of course he's still very young. Let's just hope the fever doesn't go up too high. Keep him warm, don't force food into him. I'll stop in again tomorrow."

Three days later, my baby died in my arms. I prepared the body myself for burial, even though I was very sick with influenza. I pawned my last pair of earrings to pay for the funeral, at which Anna and I were the only mourners. Afterwards I grieved Gypsy-fashion. I touched no food for three days. I did not sleep. I did not eat. I did not touch a comb to my hair or wash my face or hands. I sat on the floor of our room, holding myself and rocking and weeping. Then when it was over, I slept soundly for a day and a night.

When I awoke I told Anna to pack our things.

"It is over. I cannot go back. My child is dead and he will not return, Anna. I cannot mourn him for the rest of my life. It would only make him unhappy to see his mother sad, torn apart. We will go to Munich to see the King of Bavaria. I will make my fortune there, I am sure of it, Anna. But I tell you this: no man will ever treat me like that again. I gave my heart to a man who had no heart, who did not know how to love in return.

"I curse him," I said hoarsely, clenching my fists. "He will wander the earth until he dies, and he will never know happiness or love. He will never find peace."

Anna looked wide-eyed and scared. I smiled at her ruefully and hugged her tightly.

"Don't worry, Anna, I don't usually curse people! But he is a special case, that one. Now hurry. We have a train to catch!"

10

The Sport of Kings

"THERE SHE IS. The King's new mistress! A Russian, no less. Don't they look ludicrous together? Humph. She's half a head taller than he is!"

I stiffened. I wanted to snap out a nasty retort to the two taffeta-clad harpies who were murmuring behind their fans; but the man at my side said calmly, "Don't pay any attention to them, my dear. They are silly and mindless and their only joy in life is gossip."

"I would like to thrash them," I muttered. "Spiteful old bitches."

"So would I," King Ludwig sighed. "In fact, I would like to have them broken on the wheel and stuck up at the crossroads with a sign underneath their shattered bodies: 'Punishment for gossiping about the King.' But alas," he sighed, "these are enlightened times. A hundred years ago one could use one's monarchical powers to frighten and intimidate, but no more. A king is just a puppet these days, a symbolic representation of— but there I go again, prattling on like an old woman! At least I've made you smile again, dear Rhawnie."

"I don't care for myself," I said kindly. "But for you. They don't know you as I do. I am so fortunate to have you for a friend."

"And I thank all the gods of fortune that led you to me," the King said. He kissed my hand. "Dear Aphrodite."

We entered the royal box opposite the stage of the exquisite little theater inside the Munich Royal Residence. The audience was on its feet and when the King and I sat, they followed suit. A man wearing a white wig and the livery of the royal family of Wittelsback appeared in front of the curtain and pounded the floor three times with a long stick to announce the beginning of a tragedy. The curtain went up on Goethe's *Faust*.

My command of German was still weak, but I fixed my eyes on the action on stage and ignored the curious stares of the other members of the audience. My attitude seemed to say, "I am here to enjoy the play; if you wish to gossip all night that is none of my affair."

Wherever I went I attracted attention and prompted whispering. And why not? Six months ago, I was a bereaved mother, the abandoned wife of a heartless soldier of fortune. And now I was the intimate friend—some said his mistress—of Ludwig, the King of Bavaria. I had become a power to be reckoned with in Munich. The King, it was said, was a weak man. I dominated him. My enemies said that in a few years I would rule the country through him. It was all nonsense, but that is what they said.

When Anna and I arrived in Munich, I sent her with our luggage to a hotel and I went straight to the Royal Residence and demanded to see the King. I refused to give my name and would say only that we had a mutual friend. I was admitted to an anteroom and asked to wait. An hour passed and I grew impatient.

"I want only a few minutes of his time," I told a secretary in my stumbling German. "But I must see him. It is very important!"

"The King is a very busy man, Madame," the young man said apologetically. "Perhaps you could return in a few weeks—"

"I will not return," I said positively, "because I am not leaving. I will wait until he consents to see me." I hadn't the slightest idea of what I would say to the King when I did see him, but that was beside the point.

The secretary scuttled away. In a few minutes another man came into the room. This one, I saw, was no flunky. He wore a black uniform, and the jacket was richly adorned with medals over the left breast and a red sash that swept from his right shoulder to his left hip. He was quite tall and strapping, with closely cropped black hair and a long, curling mustache. His nose was unusually long and thin and it dominated his face. His eyes were steel grey, without a trace of humor or kindness.

He said stiffly, "I am the Baron Wolfgang Karl von Zander, Madame." He spoke flawless French. Apparently the secretary had told him about my bad German. "I am a friend and adviser of King Ludwig, and of his majesty the Crown Prince Maximillian. If you would tell me your business with the King, perhaps I could assist you."

"I wish to see the King at once," I informed him. "I will tell him my business myself. Please tell him that I am here."

"He is aware that there is a strange woman here, who refuses to give her name."

"He wouldn't know my name if I did give it," I said.

Annoyance flickered across the Baron's dark face. "The monarch of a powerful country like Bavaria is not available to see every visitor who has a favor to ask. Just tell me—"

"I don't believe that the King even knows I am here," I said. "I shall tell him myself!"

I walked briskly to the doors through which the Baron had emerged.

"Come back here!" the Baron snapped. "Stop or I'll shoot you!"

I quickened my pace. I burst through the double doors and said breathlessly, "Please forgive me, your Majesty, but I must talk to you before this man kills me!"

"Excuse me, your Majesty," said the Baron, right behind me. "But this woman forced her way in here without my permission!"

The King was standing in front of a tall window with his

back to us. He was wearing a bathrobe and pushing a piece of bread through the bars of a birdcage. He turned and said calmly, "Put that thing away, Wolfgang. Since when do we brandish weapons at visiting goddesses. How are you, my dear?" He advanced towards me with both hands outstretched. "I am very happy to see you again."

I just stared, open-mouthed. It was the funny man from the Prater in Vienna! I dropped a deep curtsy. "I beg your pardon, your Majesty! I had no idea—"

"Come, come, my dear." The King held my hands and urged me to my feet. He chuckled. "You must forgive an aging monarch his little games. Oh, Wolfgang, are you still here? Please leave us."

The Baron restored his pistol to a holster on his hip and clicked his heels together. "As you wish, your Majesty," he said icily, with a shallow little bow. He gave me a sharp look that made me shiver. Then he turned on his heel and marched out of the room.

"I have made him angry," I said apologetically. "And I have interrupted you. He said you didn't want to receive me—"

"Don't worry about Wolfgang," said the King. He led me to a long couch in front of a blazing fire. "He is always angry with someone. He's really rather a nuisance, but I can't get rid of him. He and my eldest son are close friends. You are looking more beautiful than I remember, my dear! I am so happy you decided to accept my invitation. And how is your dear little one?"

I said quietly, "He is dead. There was an outbreak of influenza in Vienna." I looked away, into the flames.

The King pressed my hand. "I am so very sorry," he said with what I believed to be genuine sympathy. "How dreadful for you. But you're here now! You will live here, in the Residence, and I'll appoint you—let's see. I shall appoint you Official Inspiration to the Royal Poet. That's me. Do you know, when I saw you sitting in the park, I was struck by the resemblance between you and the statue. Do you remember it? Aphrodite. A copy of the Roman copy that I own, and not a bad one. Such an exquisite face, fair and noble and as cold as stone can be. But there you were, right there, the statue come alive. You were crying and I thought my own heart would break on the spot. You were warm and vital and the most breathtakingly beautiful creature I had ever seen. I was very sorry when you didn't accept my invitation to tea. But then we met again. Fate! You told me your troubles and I knew that I had to have you with me, always. Can you understand any of this? I am somewhat of a connoisseur of beauty. But let me show you!''

He took my hand and led me through a maze of corridors into a vast hall. His excitement reminded me of a little boy's, and I knew he was going to show me something of which he was very proud. Busts and statues lined the walls: Roman generals, senators, matrons. There were Grecian boys and men and a pantheon of gods and goddesses. I didn't know anything about these objects, except that they were very old and that I had seen similar pieces in the gardens around Florence and Rome.

''My collection,'' the King said proudly. ''Or part of it, anyway. I have worked for years to amass these items. Some of them aren't even good, but here and there, a gem! This is my real prize. Do you recognize her? Praxiteles' Aphrodite, but not like that pitted marble specimen in the Prater. See how the marble shines, how smooth it is. Isn't she beautiful? And look at her face! She is you, my dear. You!''

The statue was very beautiful, but the only resemblances between us that I could see were anatomical rather than facial: she had nice hips and long legs and big, round breasts.

''You have the same classic beauty,'' said the King enthusiastically. ''Your faces are divided into perfect thirds. Forehead to nose, length of nose, and nose to chin, all equal. Perfectly proportioned! You can see it for yourself." He dragged me to a mirror. "Straight nose. Classic! Wonderful cheekbones. Fine chin. Ah!" He sighed rhapsodically and clasped his hands in front of his chest. "All my life I have been a lover of beauty. I live for beauty, and I surround myself with beautiful things and beautiful women."

"So you want to add me to your collection," I smiled.

"Yes. Quite right." The King nodded approvingly. "You will think that is a fairly selfish reason for asking you to come here, but all men are selfish, are they not? Why should a king be any different? I will take good care of you, I promise you. And anything I can do for you—anything at all!—just ask."

"I would like to learn how to read and write," I said firmly. "I am half-Gypsy, and I never learned."

"Wonderful! Splendid!" The King beamed and rubbed his hands together. "I shall teach you myself. German and English both. Can't read, eh? My word, this will be a new experience for me. A challenge! How can I write verses for you if you can't read them? Now we will have some lunch. I'll have an apartment prepared for you. The one next to mine, I think. I'll ask Wolfgang to move out at once." We made our way back to his chambers. He chattered and skipped and laughed, just like a pleased little boy with a new toy, and right before we went into his room he paused with his hand on my arm. "There is one more thing, my dear." He grew a little red in the face. "I won't ask, ah, anything of you, ah, other than, ah. Other than what I have already, ah, outlined. You are to be my sweet inspiration, nothing more. With perfect beauty one does not need to, ah, meddle. Do you understand what I'm saying?"

"Perfectly," I said. "You do not wish to sleep with me." He blushed and stared at his shoes. I held his hands and said gently, "I am very grateful for that, your Majesty.

Grateful that you wish to be my friend. We will be good friends, I know it.''

"Dear friends," the King agreed happily. "As well as teacher and pupil, goddess and humble admirer. Come, dear Venus, let us celebrate your arrival with champagne. This has turned into a beautiful, glorious day!''

My little suite of rooms was elegantly furnished, bright, and comfortable. Anna couldn't get over our luck at being there, in the royal Residence, just steps away from the King's own rooms. The King came every morning to have breakfast with me, and he visited me in the evening before he went to bed. He always brought something: a piece of jewelry, a vase, a delicate figurine, works of art from his vast collection of statues and paintings. He frequently referred to me as "Venus" or his "glorious Aphrodite," and sometimes I thought that he really believed that I was the goddess of love and beauty, incarnate.

Almost immediately he ordered the court painter, Herr Stieler, to do a portrait of me for his Gallery of Beauties, that notorious collection of portraits of the most beautiful women in Europe, including a Munich shoemaker's daughter and assorted ladies of noble birth from all countries. The King was so pleased with the small portrait that he commissioned Stieler to paint me as Aphrodite, dressed in a Grecian chiton that displayed my shoulders and one breast, as well as one long shapely leg and sandal-shod foot. He attended each sitting of this masterwork, and when it was finished he ordered it to be hung in his own bedroom. Needless to say, that picture created a scandal. But the King didn't care.

"You are always with me now," he sighed rapturously. "Sleeping and waking.''

But not in between. I was puzzled. It wasn't that he didn't like women—in fact, he adored them. Why would he not go to bed with me?

We spent hours together. I applied myself to my lessons

and studied as hard as I had when Seth was teaching me to cheat at cards. By learning to read I would eliminate the last advantage a *gorgio* man could have over me: I would be as accomplished and learned as any of them, and never again could a man leave me a note that I couldn't understand.

King Ludwig was not a conventional monarch. He felt truly uncomfortable with the trappings and ceremonies of royalty, and he loved to walk among his people, stopping to chat with shopkeepers and students and washerwomen. He was a familiar sight in the streets of Munich, walking alone, preoccupied, shoulders hunched against the cold, looking not like a king but like a university professor—exactly my first impression of him.

He was an accomplished historian and antiquarian. Few men in the world could match his knowledge of ancient art. He showed me around the Glyptothek, the first museum in Europe built expressly for the purpose of displaying artifacts to the general public. He was also building a Pinakothek, or museum of painting, which would house his impressive collection of canvases. His love of beauty and his great knowledge of art inspired me, and I learned a lot from him. He was father and teacher to me, and I was very fond of him.

But I soon learned that his command of his position was shaky. When it came to politics, the King of Bavaria was as naive as the bakers and brewmasters with whom he liked to converse occasionally, perhaps even more naive.

By listening closely to palace gossip, I learned that the most powerful man in Bavaria was not the King, nor Crown Prince Maximillian, but the Baron Wolfgang Karl von Zander. His was a name that evoked fear and respect whenever it was uttered. The man had control of the country almost in his grasp. The guards at the Residence were his men, hand-picked and loyal to him. Prince Maximillian, who promised to be as weak a ruler as his father but without Ludwig's saving compassion and generosity, was completely in von Zander's power. Everyone agreed that when the Crown Prince attained the throne, the Baron would rule from behind the scenes.

After I had been in the Residence for one month, the Baron paid a call. Anna came into the sitting room where I was studying a simple German reader.

"Yes, Anna, who is it?"

Anna puffed out her chest and patted her left breast, then stroked a long, invisible mustache.

"Ah, the Baron," I murmured, closing my book. "Please show him in."

I smoothed out my dressing gown and arranged myself on a couch. I was ready to receive him.

The Baron strutted arrogantly into my room. He looked splendid in a white dress uniform with a blue sash across his chest and a gold-hilted broadsword in a filigreed scabbard hanging at his side.

"Good evening, Frau Garrett." He bowed low.

I had been calling myself Madame Oulianova and had been telling anyone who asked that I was newly arrived from Russia. I stiffened slightly and said, "Where did you hear that name?"

He sat next to me on the couch without waiting for an invitation. "Oh, I have friends in Paris and London," he said with a little shrug. "You and your husband cut quite a swath across our continent in the last two years. What a career you have had! Raised by itinerant Gypsies, taken to Paris by an adventurer, educated by a notorious old harlot, and then mistress of one of the greatest rogues in Europe. And you're still so young!" he marvelled. "And now here you are, happily ensconced in the Residence, with a King as your next door neighbor. I envy you your youth and stamina, Frau Garrett. And I envy Seth Garrett." He looked hungrily at my bosom. "He was a fool to leave you."

"I tired of him," I said airily. "I tire easily of boors, Baron."

He grinned. "So do I. Do you mind if I smoke?" He reached inside his tunic and took out a long cigar.

"I'd rather you wouldn't," I said.

He ignored me. He trimmed the pointed end of the thing with a pair of tiny gold scissors that he carried on his watch chain, then he lit it and exhaled a plume of smoke. I fanned the air ostentatiously with my hand.

"I wonder, what do you hope to find in Munich?" he said. "Love? Money? An intimate relationship with the ruling monarch? I wish you luck in that. None of his Majesty's little flirtations last very long, you know. Do you know why? Perhaps you've guessed."

"I don't listen to gossip," I said sharply.

"Of course you do," the Baron said smoothly. "Let me say this: if you're waiting for dear Ludwig to creep into your bed at night and perform like a man, you'll wait forever. He won't. He can't. And that's why his little diversions never last longer than a month or two. Either he gets bored with them or they get frustrated and refuse to stay longer. Terrible thing, frustration. Nothing is more annoying to a beautiful woman than to be looked at and admired and worshipped, but not loved."

"I suppose you are volunteering to compensate for the King's deficiencies?" I asked coolly. "I trust I am reading your meaning correctly. Your phrasing was a little— oblique."

"You are becoming educated, aren't you?" the Baron chuckled. "Using fine words like 'deficiencies' and 'oblique.' Your teacher would be proud of you." He picked up the reader I had been studying and laughed scornfully. "I read this when I was only five years old."

I shrugged. "When I was five I learned how to steal and how to tell believable fortunes to gullible people. Our educations were different: you learned treachery and larceny after you could read and write and I learned them before.''

The Baron flushed slightly. "I was right. You're not a fool. In fact, you could be a nuisance if you're not stopped. What if I were to tell the King that his precious Aphrodite is not a goddess after all, but a whore and an adventuress?"

"He knows all about my past. And he won't appreciate your slandering me, either.''

Von Zander laughed unexpectedly. "You are a rare little bitch, aren't you?" He inched closer to me on the couch and stroked my forearm. "It's refreshing to meet a woman like you in this place. Usually the fool dotes on stupid women who have nothing but their looks to recommend them. But you, you have brains and craft. Perhaps you will succeed where the others have failed, Frau Garrett. And don't worry about that little problem of frustration—"

"Don't call me Frau Garrett," I said sharply. "I am not his wife anymore.''

"What? Not until death do ye part, Frau Garrett?" He laughed unpleasantly and came still closer. I could feel his breath on my neck. "You are ambitious, aren't you? If you were really intelligent you could see the advantage of forming an alliance with the one who wields the real power in Bavaria."

The man's touch revolted me. His hands were clammy and cold, like a reptile. He bent his head to kiss my shoulder and I stood up abruptly.

"Excuse me," I said, "but the thought of any kind of alliance with you is abhorrent to me. I have no doubt that your body is as diseased as your soul, Baron."

He jumped to his feet and gripped my arms. "You would be well advised not to insult me, Frau Garrett. I have killed men for less."

"Let me go! I am not afraid of you, Baron. You are a bully and a pig!"

He grinned, showing twin rows of perfect teeth. "You are a rare treat," he breathed. "You make me feel like a man who— ah, I shall have you yet, I promise you. And you will come to me willingly. You can't go on very much longer, living like a nun in a cloister while the King writes verses to you and talks your ear off about things you don't even care about. You are young, you are passionate. There is only one man in the kingdom who is man enough for you." He crushed his mouth to mine. I twisted my face away, then freed my arm and slapped his face. I left the white imprint of my hand on his flesh.

"Get out of my room!" I said. "And don't you dare come in here again! I don't want any part of you, Not your tricks, not your treachery, and certainly not your body."

The Baron's eyes glittered dangerously. "You will regret this, lady. I promise you. I might have helped you, but now—" He rested his hand on the hilt of his sword.

"I regret nothing," I retorted. "Only that I did not throw you out sooner."

The Baron turned and stalked out of the room. I sighed deeply and sank onto the sofa. Anna came in with a tea tray. She looked anxious.

"No, I'm all right, Anna," I assured her hastily. "But he is a devil, that one. There is something very strange about him. I wish I could place it. He spoke very roughly—he looks quite manly—but there is something hollow about it. It's like an act, a posture. Ah, well. Suffice it to say that I have made a dangerous enemy, Anna. But don't worry. I can take care of myself. Let's have tea! I need something to wash away the bad taste in my mouth."

Anna shook her head dolefully and rubbed her arms as though she were cold.

"You're frightened of him?" I said sympathetically. "Don't be. If he becomes a nuisance I will spread it around the Residence that he tried to make love to me and that I threw him out with a flea in his ear!"

The next day King Ludwig and I were poring over a book of human anatomy when a visitor was announced. "Herr Franz Liszt!"

Ludwig went to meet his guest with hands outstretched. "Franz! What a pleasure! I thought you were in Italy!"

"Now and again." Liszt smiled warmly and shook the King's hand. He saw me. He frowned and then his face broke into a smile. The King started to introduce us, but Liszt said, "Mademoiselle and I have met. Long ago, in Paris. Tell me, Mademoiselle Rhawnie, did you follow my advice and pursue your study of the voice?"

"Alas, no," I shook my head. "I have had no time."

"What's this?" Ludwig asked quickly. "Voice? My Venus can sing?"

"Your lovely Venus would shame a nightingale," Liszt said, bowing over my hand. "Forgive me, both of you, but I cannot stay. Perhaps next time I come, you will sing for me?" he said. "I understand that Signor Loccatelli from Rome is in Munich. He looks senile, acts spastic, and can coax music out of the walls. An excellent teacher."

"Won't you stay for lunch?" the King asked.

"I cannot. Farewell, your Majesty. And Mademoiselle. Au revoir."

The King sent for Signor Loccatelli immediately and I began my formal study of the voice. I learned to read music, and I worked the upper and lower registers of my voice to increase my range, which Signor Loccatelli pronounced phenomenal. He taught me control, and assured me that I did not have to sing loudly all the time. Ludwig attended every lesson, even though both Signor Loccatelli and I protested that he would find the hours of scales and exercises dull and uninspiring.

"No, dear Venus," the King said, his eyes shining, "nothing you do could ever bore me. I close my eyes and pretend that I am walking in a magic forest, listening to the songs of an exotic bird. What do you think, Signor Loccatelli? I would like to build a new opera house in Munich. It will take about two years to finish. Will my Venus be ready to perform at the opening?"

"She is making truly remarkable progress," the old man admitted. "Rarely have I encountered in such a young pupil this feeling for the music and the understanding of the drama of song. In two years your beautiful Venus will be ready to sing in the finest houses in Europe, I can promise you. Yes, your Majesty, I say begin your opera house without delay!"

Six months after my arrival in Munich, after the performance of *Faust,* the King and I were strolling together in the gardens behind the Residence.

"I saw that young Captain von Bulow gazing at you during the play tonight," the King said. "He seems quite smitten."

I puckered my brow. "Von Bulow? Captain? Oh, yes, I remember him. He sends me notes every day, and flowers."

"How charming!"

"But his handwriting is terrible and I have never read one of the notes," I confessed. "So I have no idea what's on his mind. And I hate the flowers! Such bad luck!"

"You are still a young woman, my dear. Ah, if only Liszt would come back to Munich."

"What on earth are you talking about, Ludwig? Surely you're not trying your hand at matchmaking! I have no intention of becoming one of Liszt's legion of conquests. Why should I give the monkeys in your court more to chatter about? Are you really suggesting that I should take a lover?" The King looked abashed. "Don't I have enough to do right now, with my music and my education? I don't want a man underfoot all the time. I am not interested in men and their fatuous attentions or their demands."

"Such a pity," the King murmured. "Such a waste! Did you know they're calling you the Ice Princess around the palace?"

"No! Really?" I sniffed. "Our friend Wolfgang spreading more lies, I see."

"Very likely. You know, a reputation for coldness doesn't discourage attentions. It only makes men want you more. Just one lover would put an end to gossip and the rest would leave you in peace."

"Your logic is full of flaws, your Majesty," I said brightly.

"You must not let a bad experience with one man lead you to condemn the entire sex," the King argued. "Right now you think that love is an illusion, that men are not to be trusted. You are going to devote yourself to Art and Music and Beauty. That's all very well for an old codger like me. I have nothing else in my life. But you are young, full of life, full of passion. You mustn't shut yourself away behind an icy façade. The years pass quickly and you will find yourself alone. You'll have plenty of admirers, of course. But no one to love you."

I stopped on the path and held both his hands. "Of all the men I have met since coming to Munich," I said softly, "there is only one who has earned my respect and affection. I can give myself to no other." I kissed him lightly, just a brush on the lips. "I am not a marble statue; I am not canvas and paint," I told him. "I am a woman. And a woman needs signs of affection when she is loved, not gifts and verses. I am delighted with everything you have given me—please don't misundersand!—but it's very hard being an idol and having someone you like worship you from afar. A woman needs closeness, touching."

Even in the semi-darkness I could see the color in his face deepen. "Ah, oh, well, my dear Venus!" he started to bluster. "It's not that I don't—but I can't really—I am very fond of you!—but—but what you ask is impossible!"

"I have asked for nothing more than closeness and touching. As innocent as two children, that's all. Holding each other in the darkness. Such a lovely feeling! That's all, nothing more. Will you not come to me tonight? In two

hours, say? It would make me so very happy. Please."
The poor man was stiff with fear, I could tell. Now I knew
why he admired beauty from a distance and put me on a
pedestal; when I was close to him he wanted to run to the
hills. "We shall have some champagne," I said, "and I will
sing for you, just you. Gypsy songs. And you shall read
your verses to me. Please say you'll come."

"Of course, my dear," he said. "It would be a pleasure.
Two hours, then?"

I kissed my fingertips and touched his face, then I
slipped away. I had a lot to do.

"Quick, Anna," I said when I got back to my rooms, "I
have to work a spell tonight and I need a few things. Run
down to the kitchen and fetch me some olive oil and lard. I
have plenty of scents up here. And help me change. I need
to find Doctor Teller."

I put on a modest dress and marched down to the apart-
ments of the royal physician. I had to rouse the man out of
bed, and he looked grumpy and disapproving when he saw
who it was.

"Now suppose you tell me just what is wrong with the
King?" I said. "Hurry up, there is no time to lose. I want
to help him."

"Now see here, young woman," the doctor sniffed, "I
won't have you—"

"He is your patient, isn't he? Don't be a fool. You'll get
some of the credit, don't worry. Come on, tell me. What's
the matter with him?"

The doctor squinted and frowned at me. I told him once
again that if he helped me and I succeeded, he would be
amply rewarded. That tipped the balance. He coughed
delicately and said, "The King is impotent."

"What does that mean?"

"It means that he is unable to function normally," and
so on and so forth.

"Why can't he?" I wanted to know. "Was he hurt?

Some kind of accident or injury?"

"Oh, no, nothing like that! His—ah, problem is not physical, but emotional. Quite simply, he adores women but he is terrified of them."

"Yes, I can see that," I said. "Well, as long as it's nothing physical, he can be cured. What have you done for him?"

"He is on a special diet," the doctor said. "Alcohol in moderation and plenty of red meat."

"Diet," I scoffed. "What rubbish."

I went back to my rooms and mixed up a little pot of special "Gypsy" ointment. Then I put on a lacy coffee-colored negligee, chilled some champagne, and sent Anna to bed. The King arrived half an hour later, at one-thirty in the morning. He left at eight and I sped him on his way with a kiss. In his pocket was a small jar of fragrant ointment, and I had instructed him to apply it twice a day to the afflicted area, more often if he had the time. We had done nothing more than lie close together, as innocent as two babies. But I wasn't worried or impatient. It was early stages yet, and I knew my cure would take time. As soon as he lost his fear of me, we would succeed.

It took three weeks. It wouldn't have taken so long if his wife hadn't turned up unexpectedly. Most of the time they lived apart, Ludwig in Munich and the Queen at one of their numerous country estates. I met her, and I knew at once why my friend was terrified of women. This one was a dragon, a she-wolf. She had little tolerance for her husband's interests and activities—she called them his "eccentricities"—and she nagged and scolded him constantly. He in turn behaved like a whipped dog. She didn't regard me as a threat because she thought she knew better.

"Really, Ludwig," she said when she saw me, "each is better-looking than the last. And this one's a giantess!"

As I said, that visit took its toll. He couldn't bear the touch of my hands for three days. I tried to get him to talk about her, but all I could get out of him was a mumbled sentence that I'm not even sure I understood correctly. It sounded like, "She used to spank me." Poor Ludwig.

But the cure progressed. He lost his fear of me and I gained his love and trust. And he was so grateful, the dear man.

"You have given me a gift beyond price!" he told me.

I was happy for him. He had been very kind to me and I wanted to repay him. His self-confidence soared. As a lover he couldn't compare to Seth, of course. But what he lacked in expertise he made up for in enthusiasm.

One afternoon he took me to a site just a few blocks from the Residence on Prinzregenstrasse, and he told me that he was building me a little palace of my very own. He referred to it as our Little Olympus, and he was intensely proud of his plan. He had worked closely with his architects on the design, and he told me that in one year it would be complete.

"But my dear," I protested fondly, "I have been so happy at the Residence, close to you. I don't need a house of my own."

"Of course you do. Nobility must keep up appearances, my dear."

"But I'm not nobility, Ludwig," I laughed.

"Yes, you are. I have given you baronial title to the estate and lands around Ravensfeld. You are a Baroness, dear Venus!"

I stared at him. "You're joking, of course."

He looked hurt. "You know me better than that. It is within our power to confer titles as a reward for services rendered to the crown. You have done us an incalculable service, and we wish to show our appreciation. And we will not brook refusal."

"I certainly shan't refuse, then," I smiled. I had never before heard him use the royal "we." I kissed him fondly. "Thank you, your Majesty." And that is how I became Rhawnie, Baroness von Ravensfeld.

Of course the Baron von Zander was livid when he heard the news. He mounted a real campaign against me. One afternoon when Ludwig and I were riding in my special carriage—it bore a small picture of Venus on the side, surmounted by the royal crest—we were pelted by ripe fruit and stones. An angry mob of students swirled around the carriage, and instead of whipping up the horses, our coachman stopped to berate them. They climbed on the steps outside the doors and hammered at the windows with their fists.

"How dare they! Ludwig, can't you do something? This is outrageous, insulting!" I cried.

"Would you like to get out and walk?" the King suggested mildly.

"And be trampled to death? No, thank you." I shouted up to the driver, "For Heaven's sake, ride through them! Come on, hurry up!"

Finally the frightened horses bolted and we swept forward, scattering the shouting mob. It was the first of many such incidents. The King seemed saddened but resigned.

"My only regret is that they have upset you," he said.

"But you, they might have hurt you!" I cried.

"Oh, no," he shook his head. "They wouldn't do that."

My only confidante was Anna. "I know who is responsible for this," I told her. "The Baron. He sees that my influence over the King is growing and he is frightened because he thinks I have Ludwig under my thumb, the way he has Maximillian under his. The fool! I don't want to rule this stupid country! I only want to live here and enjoy the good fortune that has come our way. And the lies he is spreading! That I have put some kind of Gypsy spell on the King! That I am robbing the country and sending money to confederates aboard! Confederates! I don't know anybody! Such nonsense. I have a good mind to confront him publicly and deny everything!"

Anna put her arms around my shoulders and shook her head violently. Her frizzy curls waved and her homely face was filled with concern.

"You're right," I said more calmly, "it would be a mistake to goad him into doing anything nastier. As long as he draws the line at scandal—I'm used to that—a few angry students don't frighten me."

What did bother me was Ludwig's refusal to believe in the gravity of the situation, and in the Baron's treachery. Every so often he would startle me with a remark like, "I am tired of being King. I have done all I can for them." And, "Maximillian is ambitious; he should rule before he loses the hunger to rule, before he gets too old."

"But the Baron!" I reminded him. "Your son is in his power!"

"Oh, I'm not worried about Wolfgang," the King said. "And you shouldn't worry, either. Beauty was never meant to to strain her brains over politics."

Sweet as he was, he could be rather infuriating, this King of mine.

We spent the summer at Nymphenburg, the estate west of Munich which had been built by Ludwig's grandfather or great-grandfather on the model of the French palace at Versailles. In addition to the main house, which was built in the seventeenth century, there were several smaller houses on the grounds, elegant cottages or pavillions, as Ludwig called them.

Prince Maximillian and the Baron came to spend a week in early September, just before the King and I planned to return to the city. They wanted to enjoy the first hunt of the season. The Baron called on me at the Amalianburg, the hunting lodge where I was staying. I preferred it to the big house, because it was small and private. I invited the Baron to take tea with me on the small terrace that overlooked a sleepy stream. Swans drifted past, gathering at the riverbank to fight for crumbs of cake that I tossed them.

"Will you hunt with us tomorrow?" the Baron asked me.

"And what do you hunt around here, Baron. Yellow-haired Russian singers?"

The Baron laughed. "No, that species is too rare, Baroness, to risk extinction. You are much more valuable to me alive. We hunt wild boar. It's a very thrilling sport, but it can be dangerous. A cornered boar is not like an English fox. He does not stand still and let the dogs tear him to pieces. Boars have been known to charge horses—and men. But perhaps you would prefer a tamer sport, Baroness." Every time he used the title, he stressed it mockingly. "We can fish in the river, for example."

"I am not afraid of Bavarian pigs," I said meaningfully. "I would like to see this hunt of yours."

"I am delighted that you feel you can trust me," the Baron smiled.

"Oh, I don't trust you. Not a bit." Automatically I studied the pattern of the leaves in the bottom of my tea cup. I saw travel, money, love. But no sign of danger or death. "I have heard that some of the most dreadful rumors are flying around Munich," I said thoughtfully. "Even as we sit here, people listening to and believing the most ridiculous stories about me. You and I both know that these tales have no basis in fact. Their source is the imagination of one man: you."

"Dear Baroness!" The Baron's long face widened as he grinned at me. He tried to assume an air of injured innocence, but he was too pleased that his scandal had reached my ears. "I am as fond of you as the King himself, believe me! What possible reason could I have for wishing you ill?"

"None. But a man like you doesn't need a reason. A whim will suffice. You know very well that I'm no threat to your power, Baron. Power doesn't interest me—to keep it is too much like hard work. What you are doing hurts the King more than it hurts me. Why don't you stop?"

"You excite me, Baroness," he said softly, hitching his chair closer. "Ordinarily I have no patience with women. I admit your grasp of politics is a little shaky, but that's not important. You're still not like the rest—stupid, boring bitches. You have known deep passion, strong hatred, and pain." He touched one of the gold filigreed bracelets that Seth had given me. They were the only items of jewelry that remained from those days. It didn't matter. I had plenty of things to remind me of him. The Baron sighed, "These fascinate me. They are so delicate, so exquisite. And unusual. I understand you are rarely seen without them. It's intriguing."

He covered my wrists with his hands, pinning them to the table. His fingers were long and strong, and my attempts to pull away were futile.

"But you wear bracelets underneath as well, don't you?" he asked. He released the catch on the left bracelet and it fell open, exposing the thin purple scar underneath. "London, wasn't it? You see how well I know you. You were in the depths of despair over that absurd gambler. And you persuaded him to marry you. Ah, these are the loveliest bracelets of all. Bracelets of pain."

His face was only inches from mine. His pupils were so small they were almost non-existent, and his eyes looked like metal coins, cold and hard and flashing. I felt simultaneously attracted and repulsed by him. He embraced me, coiling around me like a serpent, caressing and choking me.

"What did it feel like?" he whispered. He was trembling all over. "Did you bleed much? Were you naked when you did it? I would have been. Oh, to feel the warm blood flowing over my naked body! Death must have been very near. So near, so beautiful. Is Death warm, or cold? Tell me about the pain. Show me."

I showed him. I overturned a teacup and smashed it down on the table, then I grasped a sharp-edged shard and slashed at his face. He gave an ecstatic sob, like a man in the heights of ecstasy, and put his fingers to his cheek. Blood oozed through them and splashed on the tablecloth. I leaped up, panting. He didn't move for a whole minute. He just sat there, breathing deeply, eyes closed, mouth slightly open. I was horrified, but I couldn't tear myself away.

"You—you are sick," I whispered. "You are disgusting!"

He opened his eyes and focused on me with difficulty. "I must have you," he said hoarsely. "An alliance—we must join together in love and pain. For the King. And the country—"

"You're crazy," I said bluntly. "I'd sooner bed with a wild boar." And I picked up my skirts and ran into the little house.

The next day, I set off with the hunters. Even though I was on my guard, the Baron managed to maneuver me away from the rest of the party. We urged our horses up a low cliff and stood listening for the sounds of the pursuit. Villagers beat drums and pans and shouted loudly, trying to drive the beasts out from their lairs in the thickest part of the forest into the range of the hunters, who were armed not with guns but with spears. I could hear the baying of dogs and the occasional whinny of a nervous horse.

"They're over there," I said to the Baron. "On the other side of that thicket."

"You're afraid to be alone with me?" the Baron asked, chuckling. "Then we should join the others without delay. Oh, how annoying." He dismounted.

"What's the matter?"

"This one has a habit of sucking in air before he is saddled and letting it out later." He pounded his horse's side with the flat of his hand and jerked the girth tighter.

"He thinks it's a great joke to do it when we're rocking along full tilt. He threw me badly once. You wouldn't mind holding his head, would you, Baroness? Of course, if you are afraid—" He let the taunt stand in the air.

"Of course not." I climbed off my horse and walked around to the front of the Baron's mount. "Why didn't you do this before you left the stable?"

"I did," puffed the Baron, giving the strap a final jerk before fastening it, "but he always manages to hold some in reserve for half an hour later. There, that should do it. Shall we go?"

We walked to my horse and he bent over to give me a leg up. As I was swinging my other leg into the saddle he put his arms around my waist and dragged me down to the ground. He took me by surprise and had me pinned under him before I could begin to repulse him.

"Stop it!" I breathed angrily. "Stop it at once!"

He endured my struggling for only a few minutes before he struck me a vicious blow on the face with his fist. Then he shoved my legs apart and tried to ram something hard into me. It kept bumping into my thighs, and it was certainly not human flesh and muscle. I twisted and squirmed, and when he sat back to reconsider his approach, I kicked him in the face.

He sprawled on the ground. I leaped up. Glancing down, I saw something silvery shining in the grass. It was a riding crop, with an ornate handle topped with a boar's head. Our Baron had an odd sense of sexuality.

I snatched up the crop and began to lash him with it, on his face and neck and shoulders. At first he put his hands up to ward off the blows, but then something strange happened. He let down his defense, opened his arms and lay spreadeagled under me.

"Harder!" he moaned. "Hit me harder, I beg you!"

I stared at him. I felt utterly sickened and revolted. What kind of man was this? I dropped the riding crop.

"You are a depraved animal!" I breathed. And I mounted my horse and rode away from him. That was the end of my day of boar-hunting. I knew there would be no point in telling Ludwig about the incident; he simply could not or would not believe the Baron capable of such behaviour.

When King Ludwig and I got back to Munich, I found that in our absence work on my little house on the Prinzregenstrasse had been accelerated. The Little Olympus was almost finished.

"I wanted it to be ready before winter came," the King told me. "I put two hundred extra men to work on it."

The finished product was truly exquisite, a miniature palace with jewel-box rooms decorated with gilded cornices and mirrors. King Ludwig donated some of his finest works of art to adorn the walls and to fill the empty spaces. I had a fine Rubens in my bedroom, the Praxiteles Aphrodite in my drawing room, and two gorgeous panels by Dürer in my dining room, a naked Adam and his Eve. My music room had a vaulted ceiling covered with paintings of the nine muses, beautiful Teutonic-looking girls, each wearing a scanty diaphanous tunic of a different color from the rest. Enthroned among clouds in the center of the ceiling was Aphrodite herself, who bore, not surprisingly, a remarkable resemblance to myself.

"The Queen and Source of all inspiration," said the King rhapsodically. "You, dear Venus. You!"

My drawing room attracted the usual number of gallants and sycophants. Admirers paid court, dukes and princes vied for the honor of my company at dinner, poets came seeking inspiration and musicians begged me to sing their songs. One night the King brought Franz Liszt to a dinner party I was giving.

Liszt greeted me warmly and kissed my hand. "Ah, the beautiful Golden Gypsy!" he said, giving birth to a title that would follow me for the rest of my stay in Bavaria, and even after that. "You are even more beautiful than I remember, Baroness. Tell me, did you follow my advice and begin the study of voice?"

"I did indeed, Monsieur Liszt," I said. "My King insisted and I had to obey."

"The world is fortunate," Liszt smiled.

"Signor Loccatelli has nothing but praise for her," said the King enthusiastically. "You should hear her, Franz! She really would shame a nightingale now!"

"I would love to hear you sing, Baroness," said Liszt. "Perhaps we can have an impromptu recital?"

The guests crowded around the piano in the music room. I sang Italian songs, Schubert *lieder*, opera arias, and finally some Gypsy songs that Liszt and I both loved. When we were finished our little audience roared its approval. I flushed with pleasure—it was the first time I had sung in public—and I thanked Liszt warmly.

"It was a pleasure for me, too," he assured me. "I want to compose for you. You inspire me!"

"She inspires all of us," King Ludwig said. "Ah, Franz, in one more year my new opera house will be finished. Loccatelli says Rhawnie will be ready to appear in public. If you would consent—it would be such an exciting experience—!"

Liszt said, "I cannot refuse, your Majesty. I would be delighted to accompany the Baroness in her first solo recital. I shall begin at once to compose for the occasion."

Suddenly a window shattered. A woman screamed, and the occupants of the music room, which was on the second floor of the house, surged towards the doors. I grabbed the King's hand and ran to the windows. The street below was clotted with students, all shouting things like. "The King pays for a whore while the people starve!" "The Russian harlot is a spy!" "Must our taxes finance a King's lust?"

We learned later that the leader of the demonstration, which the police soon broke up, was not a student at all but a professional radical. He was doubtless in the pay of the Baron von Zander.

"This is outrageous," I muttered. "They must be stopped." I went out on the balcony that overlooked the street. When they saw me their fury intensified. A stone whizzed past my ear.

"Rhawnie, for the love of Heaven, come back!" the King pleaded.

"My God, will music lose you just when she has found you?" Liszt fretted.

I ignored them. "Why don't you tell the man who is paying you to show himself and accuse me to my face!" I said to the crowd. "Or is the Baron von Zander too much of a coward to denounce me publicly?"

My remaining guests gasped at my foolhardiness. To insult the Baron was tantamount to idiocy. I didn't care. I wished I could tell the world what kind of degenerate reptile he really was. But no one would believe me.

I was determined to show the people of Munich that I would not be intimidated by the Baron's tactics. I rode daily in the parks, accompanied King Ludwig on his strolls around the city, and went out every night to parties, balls and the theater. Once or twice I even went to a gambling salon to try my luck, and I won. Sheer accident, I told myself. But I knew that the old magic was there; yet every moment I spent at the faro table reminded me of Seth Garrett, and it was painful. I didn't stay long.

I wore elegant furs and velvets. My finery, particularly my jewels, became the subject of cartoons and critical articles in the press. One evening at the opera I wore a magnificent ruby necklace that had belonged to the King's grandmother. He presented it to me on his birthday and told me that it was the only piece in his collection that could do me justice. At other times he gave me tiaras, diamond chokers, bracelets, rings. The press had a field day, accusing me of sacking the public treasury. Of course the pressmen were in von Zander's employ. I found that I could not defend myself against the lies they printed. Editorial writers began to suggest that if the King didn't send his tart away, his government would fall.

"Can't we do something to stop him?" I asked the King. "I don't care for myself—but you! Oh, my friend, why should you endure such insults? Every day the crowds get bigger and more hostile and the articles in the papers are more vicious. Where will it end?"

"Aren't you sorry you learned to read?" the King asked. "If you were still illiterate you wouldn't even know that newspapers existed."

"Oh, how can you joke!" I said impatiently. "The Baron hates me and he wants to destroy me. I can understand that. But why must he drag you down, too? Everything evil he says about me reflects on you: I am your whore, therefore you are my whoremaster. I accept precious gifts, but you are foolish enough to give them to me. I am exploiting you and ruining the economy, but you are the king who permits a woman to wreck his life. You see how awful it is, how insidious? He is turning your own people against you. Does he hate you, too?"

"Oh, no," the King sighed. He tossed the newspapers away from him with an impatient snort. "Don't you see, my dear, he wants to force me to abdicate to Maximillian. Then he'll have what he wants: the power to rule. Maximillian is not really weak, but he is certainly in Wolfgang's power. He'll be a puppet while Wolfgang pulls the strings. Quite simple. If you were a real threat to him, he would have killed you long ago."

"Yes," I said. "He said I was more valuable to him alive than dead."

"Yes, because he can use you to discredit me in the eyes of the populace. Don't feel bad. If you hadn't been here he would have found someone or something else to use against me. The winds of revolution and change are blowing across Europe this year, Rhawnie. What Wolfgang wants is inevitable. But I will not keep you here if you don't want to stay. There may be some danger, after all. When these ruffians get excited they sometimes lose their senses and become violent. Perhaps I should send you away—"

"I won't go!" I knelt by the side of his chair and hugged his arm. "I will stay with you always, until they send us both away. Is there really nothing we can do to stop the Baron? Nothing? Do we have to sit and wait until he forces you to abdicate and takes the power for himself? It's so unfair! So—wrong!"

"It's been happening in royal circles for thousands of years," the King shrugged. "Treachery, assassination, scandal. The whole continent is in an upheaval—France, Greece, Italy—why should Bavaria be spared? We are only pawns in the greater game of history, my dear Venus. And I have never been one to stand in the way of history. Now," he shifted in his chair and put the subject out of his mind. "Sing to me, Rhawnie," he said wearily. "Sing something soothing."

He closed his eyes and leaned back. I sang softly to him, Gypsy songs about love and life and longing death. Out in the street in front of my house, the forces of change gathered for yet another demonstration.

11

Revolutionary Gypsy

"ARE YOU FRIGHTENED, Baroness?" Franz Liszt asked me. We stood backstage at King Ludwig's new opera house, a magnificent neoclassical structure located on the Max Joseph Platz, right near the Royal Residence.

"Is it possible to die of nervousness, Monsieur Liszt?"

He laughed. "I have never heard of it happening, but I suppose it's possible."

"Aren't you nervous?" I demanded.

"Not at all. I am merely an accompanist tonight. You are the main attraction."

"But the world will be hearing your 'Five Gypsy Songs' for the first time, as well as your settings of Petrarch's sonnets," I reminded him. "We're in this together. I wish the floor would open up and swallow me."

We waited for the audience to settle down. The air in the hall was electric with excitement and a kind of expectant nervousness. Through a peep-hole in the curtain, I had seen the usual assortment of buxom matrons and uniformed gallants, stout bankers and bejeweled duchesses. But here and there, sprinkled throughout the house, I saw a different type, men who took no interest in the new building or in their printed programs. They looked aloof, isolated by their purpose: to create a disturbance and ruin the performance.

The newspapers that morning had a field day: "We need new railway lines, and the King gives us an Opera House! We need improved Sewage, and the King gives us Art. We need strong Leadership, a sturdy Ship of State to weather the storm of Change that is buffeting the entire continent, and the King gives us his 'dear friend' in yet another vulgar, tasteless display of Immorality!" As a final fillip that writer had trilled: "Let us not forget the lesson of the Bastille!"

It was enough to make even a brave Gypsy nervous.

At exactly eight o'clock the enormous gas chandeliers were dimmed and cranked up towards the ceiling, so that the view of the stage from the uppermost tiers would not be obstructed. Ludwig loved gadgets, and his new opera house was full of them. The audience rose as the King entered his box alone, then everyone was seated. They shifted and jabbered. The din sounded terrible, even behind the heavy curtains.

Liszt held my hands and kissed me on both cheeks. "I will not wish you luck tonight," he said kindly. "You will have that. Instead I wish you peace of mind and of heart. Sing beautifully, and show them what you really are."

The curtains rose on a stage empty except for an enormous grand piano. I took a breath, threw back my shoulders, and walked out. Liszt followed a few steps behind. We were greeted by polite applause—Liszt's star in Munich had been dimmed by his association with me. I gave them a few minutes to exclaim to each other over my height and shape, and to take in the diamonds that glittered on my wrists and throat. I wore a simple gown of pale blue velvet with wide skirts and a fairly modest neckline. My hair was braided and wrapped around my head. Liszt said it looked elegant.

The noise subsided just a little. Then in the lull came loud boos and catcalls from all parts of the auditorium.

I stepped down to the footlights. "I will not sing unless these people are removed," I said firmly. "And I will not sing unless there is absolute silence. I am prepared to wait until midnight.''

"Whore!" shouted one of the troublemakers. Taking his cue the others joined in the cry.

"The King's doxie should not be allowed on our stages! Get off the stage, harlot! Get out of our country, Russian spy!"

A squad of uniformed policemen swept into the hall and descended upon the rabble-rousers. A few of the elegantly-dressed fat women in the audience screamed as the Baron's men were wrenched from their seats and dragged out of the hall. I stood composed and quiet, waiting for it to be over. The police seemed to know exactly who the troublemakers were and where they were sitting. I suspected that King Ludwig had insured that the performance would go on.

In five minutes they were gone, police and prisoners both. The disconcerted members of the audience, who had been jostled by the intrusion, pulled themselves together and resumed their seats. Not one of them left the house. They were all too eager to see the King's mistress make a fool of herself.

I waited until I could not hear a cough or a shuffle. Then I counted one hundred to myself, waiting until the tension in that place was nearly unbearable. Finally I gave Liszt a nod and he played the introduction to "Casta Diva," that glorious aria from Bellini's *Norma*.

My voice floated over the hall, entwining them in the threads of its Gypsy magic, holding them in thrall. I know I sang well for them. Each note was perfectly sweet and clear, and my high trills and runs were flawless.

When it was over the audience burst into tumultous applause. There was even some loud cheering and foot-stamping from that staid crowd. I looked at Liszt, who beamed at me. And I smiled and bowed modestly to my public. I had not made a fool of myself at all, but of all of them. And strangely enough, they loved me for it.

The rest of the performance went beautifully. They seemed to like Liszt's settings of Petrarch, but they were especially thrilled by the "Five Gypsy Songs" he had written for me. Those songs evoked a special feeling, a certain joy and pathos, that could not fail to touch them. At the end of one of the sadder ones, I saw some women dabbing their eyes. I love those songs, and I always included them in my concerts after that. They were mine, and they spoke my soul.

When Liszt and I were taking bows about halfway through the program, I happened to look to my left, at the lowest box nearest the stage. A man was seated there, alone. Our eyes met ever so briefly, and I got a strange feeling, as though a spark had been struck between us. I didn't notice more, except that he was fair-haired. When Liszt and I came back onstage after a brief rest, he was gone. But when I looked up at the royal box I saw a fair head next to King Ludwig's greying one, and I thought it was he. He came back to his box for the last songs and the encore numbers, one of which was a Liszt solo, "Variations on Five Gypsy Songs." That piece became part of his standard repertory, too, until he retired from the stage.

I stood on that stage, listening to the audience's applause, feeling their love, and I had to remind myself who I was: Rhawnie, a Gypsy. Beggar. Thief. Deserted wife of a rogue and a gambler. I knew the people in that opera house didn't really love me, but it was nice while it lasted. And, I told myself as I smiled and bowed to them, it is better than begging for bread in the streets of Odessa.

Liszt was such a showman. He bowed to me and kissed my hand a dozen times, and murmured to me about how wonderful and beautiful I was. The audience called us back a dozen times, and Liszt told me he doubted that he could have gotten such an ovation on his own.

I saw the fair-haired man once more that evening, as I was leaving the opera house on Franz Liszt's arm. He was standing at the edge of the crowd that clogged the square in front of the house, waiting for us to emerge. He towered over most of the stubby Bavarians. Our eyes met, and once again I felt that flutter, that spark.

We went to the Residence for a late supper with the King. Then Liszt, seeing that the King wanted to be alone with me, pleaded fatigue and said he would go to his rooms.

"You know how brilliant you were," Ludwig said to me. "You handled yourself so well when troubles came. And then to sing that punishing aria! And so perfectly! I shall never forget that moment. I was very proud of you."

"Perhaps we could win your people over!" I said excitedly. "I could sing for them in the parks and in the beer halls! What do you think?"

The King shook his head. "No, I think the Baron's plans are too far advanced at this point. He would never allow you to redeem yourself in their eyes, particularly if he thought you had any chance of succeeding."

We were silent. Neither of us had much to say, although there was so much that needed to be said.

"Who was the man I saw in your box this evening?" I asked off-handedly.

"Who?" The King looked puzzled. "Oh, him. No one in particular. The son of an old friend who just dropped in to say hello. An American. Good-looking fellow, isn't he?"

"Yes, very." I saw that he didn't want to discuss it further.

"And now," said the King, rising, "I want to give you something."

"You know I don't want anything more from you," I protested. "I am so grateful for the chance you gave me to sing tonight. That is all I needed to make me happy."

"Ah, but I want to give you something special. A token." He went to a cupboard and brought out a small gilded casket. He set it down on an inlaid table in front of me and flipped back the lid. Fistfuls of jewels winked up at me, necklaces heavy with rubies and diamonds, emerald earrings, diamond pendants. Pieces of jewelry, not one or two but a dozen.

I wondered for a moment if he had lost his senses. He said they were mine, all of them. "I can't take them!" I said.

"They are not so valuable as they look," the King said. "I have given you other things, much nicer. But these are not to be worn, really. Rather they are to be sold when you need money. They are mine, some Wittelsbach heirlooms that don't belong to the state but to me, personally. I have a right to dispose of them as I please, and I want you to take them."

"Oh, Ludwig," I said sadly.

"It's been fun, hasn't it?" he said. "I have enjoyed it tremendously, having you here. You've been good for me in so many ways. Anyway, you have a career now, and I like to think that I have given it to you. And you have something to fall back on when times get hard—and I hope they don't. Soon you might even have a man to love you and to care for you."

I felt a lump riding in my throat. "You're talking as if we'll never see each other again."

"That may be true," the King said softly. "The situation here is getting worse by the hour, and the outcome is inevitable, I'm afraid. We're not blind fools, to think we can go on as we have. It's dangerous for you here, and soon it will be dangerous for me. I'm not a particularly brave man. I won't go down with my ship and fight to the death to keep my crown. I have already made plans to go to England when the revolution comes."

"But I will go with you! I will stay with you! I owe you so much—"

I thought of the little man in the park in Vienna, who had appeared when I was sad and lonely and desperate. He had taken over my life, taught me, guided me. I stared at the floor and brushed away a tear.

He patted my shoulder. "There, there. I'm not sending you away because I don't love you anymore. I do love you, Rhawnie. You are young, and I am getting old. My life is plodding towards its finish, and yours is just beginning. I have taught you all I can. Up to now your whole life has been an education, hasn't it? The Gypsies taught you what they knew, then you went to your grandfather. Then to the Parisian woman, Madame Odette. And your husband. Finally you came to me. All of us taught you and formed you and made you what you are now. But the period of your education is over, Rhawnie. You are a woman with beauty and brains and a skill you can use to make a good living. It would be a grave mistake for you to tie yourself to me out of gratitude. You want a younger, more vigorous man."

"That's not true!" I cried, putting my arms around his neck. "You are wonderful, just wonderful!"

"You are very kind," he smiled, "but it's a wise man who knows his limitations. You gave me back something which I had lost forever. And you restored my self-esteem, which is even more important. But I don't want to hold you back. I couldn't marry you, and you need to be married, to have children. I'm throwing you out of the nest, my dear. And when you go, you can take with you the knowledge that there is in the world one man who loves you and respects and believes in you."

We held each other close. "I shall miss you!" I said. "And I'll make you proud of me, I promise!"

"You're a good, brave girl," the King said approvingly. "I'll come and hear you sing in London, when you get there. But don't hurry. There's a world waiting for you. Go forth and conquer it." He held me away from him and smiled kindly. His eyes were brimming, like mine. We had been good friends. "One more thing," he said in a business-like voice. "You will be receiving a message, very soon. You are to obey any instructions you are given if they are signed with the initial 'S.'" He sighed. "I wish I

could send Pegasus to bear you away to safety. Nowadays
methods of escape have to be rather prosaic, I'm afraid.
Farewell, my dearest.''

''Goodbye, your Majesty.'' I hugged him tightly, and
kissed his cheeks. Then I picked up my weighty casket
and left the room.

I stood in the corridor outside his chambers for a minute
or two. A chapter of my life was finished. The King was
right, it had been fun. Everyone had gained, except,
perhaps, the people of Bavaria. And they were about to
lose their ruler. I walked slowly down the hall, past the
doors to my old rooms, which had been reassigned to the
Baron, I understood.

There was no one in the darkened hallway, not a footman, not a guard. I couldn't help myself. I tried the door to
the sitting room. It was locked, but a quick turn of a hairpin
gained me admittance.

Gaslights were burning but turned very low. My colorful
clutter of pillows and music and *objets d'art* was gone and
the room looked bare and spartan. An enormous desk took
up a third of the floor space. Not a scrap of paper littered
its polished surface. The Baron was certainly a neat, precise fellow. As neat and precise in his life as he was in
executing his evil deeds.

That desk looked very tempting. The repository of a
thousand secrets, and perhaps a hoard of money. I tried
the drawers; they were locked. Baron von Zander was
even more distrusting than my uncle Alexei had been.
Because he had more to hide, no doubt.

The locks on the drawers were rather complicated, and
it took five minutes of twisting and picking with my hairpin
before even one yielded. The only thing inside was a large
leather case, square and flattish, like an envelope. I felt the
contents through the case. Papers, I thought disgustedly.
How boring. I decided to have a look anyway. After all,
money is paper, too.

I found a wad of photographs, acid-stained, quaintly lit,
and stiffly posed in the old style. But the subject matter

was anything but quaint, and the poses, while stiff, were positively mind-boggling.

The Baron von Zander was the featured artist in a dazzling display of fashion and gymnastics. In a few of the pictures he was joined by a young boy, who couldn't have been more than fifteen years old. They were naked, although in one or two the Baron wore boots and an ingenious harness-like affair that combined the features of suspenders and belt. In one he was wearing an executioner's mask and nothing else, and impaling the boy on—but never mind the details. Needless to say, those pictures were a revelation to me. I remembered Ludwig's little speech about my education, and I perceived that one's education is never finished. That Baron was certainly ingenious, I thought. The permutations and combinations of love really were infinite.

I heard a step and some low voices in the hall outside the door. I swept everything back into the leather case, grabbed my casket, which I had placed on the desk before I burgled it, and dove into the kneehole of the desk just as the Baron and his guest came in.

"—delighted you could come tonight," the Baron whispered. "You're sure you weren't seen? Our Max is such a prude, I'm afraid."

"Oh, no," his guest replied in a bored voice. "I wasn't seen. I know how to be careful, Wolfgang."

"Splendid. Let's go into the bedroom, shall we?"

I knew that if the Baron caught me with those pictures it would be the end of Rhawnie, thieving Gypsy beauty.

"Just a second," the Baron said. "I have some fine cigars in my desk. I'll get them."

My heart died, right inside my chest. I decided that I would scream, create a disturbance, and try to get away before he killed me. He walked over to the desk but didn't come around to the front. A good thing: I saw to my horror that a foot-wide expanse of blue skirt was lying on the carpet, in plain sight.

"Oh, here they are. I filled the canister this morning."

Good Baron, I thought approvingly. Such a neat, precise man.

He walked away again, towards the bedroom. I could still hear their voices and when I peeked out I saw that he had left the door open a foot. I couldn't possibly get away without being seen. And I certainly didn't want to stay while he and his friend practiced for their next picture-taking session.

A breeze struck my face. The window was open, I saw. As quietly as I could I crept out of my hiding place, crossed the few feet to the window, and leaned out. It was a sheer thirty-foot drop to the rose bushes below. Not worth it. But I could dispose of my casket and the leather case, and brazen it out afterwards. The objects fell and crashed into the bushes, and I walked to the center of the floor and called,

"Hello, Baron, are you home?"

He came to the bedroom door. He was still dressed, only he was wearing a green silk smoking jacket over his trousers.

"Where did you come from?" he demanded, pulling the bedroom door closed. "How did you get in here?"

"Don't be so inhospitable," I scolded him. "I was passing and decided to drop in and say good-bye. I'll be leaving Munich soon. Sad, isn't it, after all we've meant to each other? How did you enjoy my concert tonight? It was a triumph, wasn't it?"

"Unfortunately I could not attend, Baroness," he said. "I had more important matters to occupy my time. I consider music a frivolous waste."

"Do you? A shame. The rest of the show was very amusing, too. Some men tried to disrupt the performance. But the King had drawn up a seating chart and he knew the names of everyone who bought a ticket and he knew where they would be sitting. You very nicely bought tickets, didn't you? Ten or a dozen, singles, in all parts of the house. You made it very easy for the King to quell your riot."

He flushed. "Don't look so smug, Baroness," he said dangerously.

"Oh, let's part on good terms, shall we?" I offered generously. "I'll have some very fond memories to take with me when I go. I'll bid you farewell too, Wolfgang, dear." I walked to the door and paused with my hand on the latch. I pulled. The door was locked. I turned the key and grinned at him. "Silly of me, to lock myself in when I came. Force of habit. Good-bye, then."

"Not good-bye, Baroness," he said, smiling at me glacially. "Au revoir."

I exited as gracefully as I could and then raced down the hall as fast as a rabbit. I went outside, found my treasures in the rose bushes and extricated them from the thorns with difficulty. I knew what I would do with the jewels: I would have Anna sew them into the hem of one of my petticoats. And I knew, too, what I would do with those remarkable photographs.

Two days later there was a riot in front of the opera house. The newspapers didn't even mention my triumph, but emphasized the enormous cost of the new building and its proximity to the Residence. As if, I thought caustically, I would run over to the King's bedchamber for a quick rendezvous without disrupting rehearsals for too long.

The crowd swelled to five hundred, then a thousand; mounted soldiers were unable to disband the mob. They marched to the Prinzregenstrasse, to my house. They shattered all the windows at the front of the house, and only the presence of twenty royal guards, Ludwig's men, prevented them from breaking down the doors and hauling me into the street.

That night Anna brought me a note that had been slipped under the front door in the confusion.

"A coach will be waiting outside your door tomorrow morning at eleven. Take only what you need for three days' journey and send the rest of your things ahead to Paris. S."

"Secret messages, orders from on high," I muttered. Anna and I bustled to and fro, throwing things into trunks and valises.

We hardly slept at all that night. There were still shouts in the street, and occasionally a weighted missile would come flying in through one of the broken windows. The captain of the guards informed me that their number had been increased to fifty. I gave him instructions about my trunks, and pressed some money into his hand, "for beer when this is all over."

All the servants had left the house, the cowards. In the morning Anna made us a light breakfast of toast and tea and I instructed her to pack a hamper of food for the trip.

"Lots of champagne and paté, and there should be a few jars of cavier lying around. Put them in. And some fruit and cheese. We don't know what this Monsieur S. has in store for us."

I put on a travelling costume of rose-pink satin trimmed with black ribbons. I wore a small-brimmed black hat with a high crown and a wisp of a veil. At eleven o'clock Anna and I stood on the steps of the Little Olympus for the last time. It had never felt like home, but I had enjoyed living there, among so many beautiful things, and I would miss it, a little.

A small crowd had already gathered in front of the house. Someone shouted, "There she is!"

I lifted my chin and started across the street. A carriage was waiting. The driver hopped down and opened the doors with a flourish.

"Whore! Jezebel!" a woman shrieked.

I did not turn my head. I swept through them as though they were so many sheep. They fell back to let me pass, removed by one stroke of an invisible scythe. Anna toddled along at my side, trembling with every step. The guards helped the driver load the luggage, and Anna and I stepped inside. The driver took his place over us, cracked his whip, and the carriage jerked into motion. Something large and red splatted against the window: a fine, ripe tomato.

"Peasants," I sniffed. "What an outrage, Anna. To be driven from my home in ignominy, to be slandered and reviled—well, it's over now. Let us enjoy the ride. It's a beautiful day."

The carriage took us to Augsburg, about fifty miles west of Munich. We met the Munich-Stuttgart train, which was waiting in the station when we got there. The coachman unloaded our things and handed me two tickets for a first-class compartment. As soon as Anna and I had made ourselves comfortable the whistle blew and the wheels of the train started to turn.

"So far our mysterious Monsieur S. has proved himself to be very efficient," I remarked to Anna, who nodded happily. Poor Anna didn't care for danger.

Just then a tall man came into the compartment without knocking. He pulled down the blinds on the door and windows to the corridor and said, "Take off your clothes. There's no time to lose."

I gave him an incredulous stare. It took me only a few seconds to place him: the stranger at the concert, Ludwig's visitor, the man who had observed Liszt and me from the fringes of the crowd after the performance.

"You are too impetuous, Monsieur S.," I said mildly. "I like to be a little better acquainted with a man before—"

"Time for wit later, Baroness," he said briskly. He had a valise with him. He opened it and drew out a black dress, black cloak, and a hat with yards and yards of heavy black veiling. A full mourning costume. "Please put these things on—"

"Black!" I exclaimed, horrified. "How ridiculous. I never wear black. Or white. It's bad luck."

"You'll have worse luck if you don't do as I ask," he said without cracking a smile. He peered under the blind. "You have about four minutes before they get here."

I listened and heard sounds of disturbance farther along

the coach. Doors opened and closed. Official-sounding voices barked orders.

"A search!" I breathed angrily. "They wouldn't dare!"

"They wouldn't dare," my stranger said. "If you want to get out of Bavaria today, you'll do as I say."

Anna and I sprang into action. We stripped off my pink dress and jacket and I put on the black gown. The stranger put the discarded items into his valise. His eyes flashed over me while I was still in a state of semi-undress. My underthings were a vivid, prussian blue. I winked at him and said, "You see? I told you I never wear white."

As soon as I had put on the cloak and the concealing hat, he shoved his valise into Anna's arms and said, "Take this to compartment three, just down the corridor, and wait there until they've gone. Do you understand?"

Anna gave me an inquiring look and I nodded under my veils. When she left the compartment the man sat next to me and tucked my hand under his arm. With his free hand he pushed my head down so that my cheek rested on shoulder. At that very moment two men in uniform, followed by a frightened train conductor, barged into the compartment.

"Papers, please," said one of the soldiers.

"I beg your pardon," said my companion. He had spoken to me in fluent German, without trace of an accent. Now his German was awkward and stilted. "What is the meaning of this intrusion?"

"There is a spy and a traitor aboard this train, sir," said the conductor in a shaking voice. "These men have orders to make a search."

"In the name of King Maximillian of Bavaria!" one of the uniformed men barked. "May I see your papers!"

"Of course," shrugged Monsieur S. He reached into a breast pocket and brought out of a sheaf of documents. "My wife and I are British citizens," he said. "We are returning from Vienna. We took our son there to see a well-known physician, a specialist. It was no use. We—we lost him."

I gave a strangled cry and started to weep softly. The stranger put his arm around my shoulders. The men shifted uncomfortably.

"There, there, my darling," said the handsome stranger in English. "I know it's difficult to speak of it. But we must."

"Please forgive me," I said in English. "I didn't mean to give way like that. He was so young, so young!" I lowered my head. My shoulders trembled.

The senior officer returned the papers and said in English, "We are sorry for your loss, Herr Martin and Frau Martin. But you will understand that a search like this was necessary or we would not have done it. Good day."

They left the compartment. My "husband" took his arm away and let out a sigh.

"I congratulate you," he said, still in English. "Your performance was most convincing, Baroness."

I threw back my veils and faced him angrily. "It is very easy to be convincing when your heart is broken, when an old wound is reopened and a knife twisted in it!" I flared at him. "You are a very clever fellow, Monsieur S. To use a painful memory to elicit believable play-acting from me—!"

He looked quite taken aback and said, "I am really very sorry, Baroness. I had no idea that—you did suffer a loss, then?"

I nodded vigorously. "My infant son. In Vienna. A year and a half ago. You didn't know?"

"No, I didn't. It was an unfortunate coincidence, Baroness, nothing more. Please forgive me." He looked genuinely abashed and penitent.

"Of course, I forgive you," I said. "I shouldn't have scolded you like that. After all, you are my deliverer. So they have had their revolution at last, have they? What a lot of nonsense, revolutions. Bloodless and noisy, just what I would expect from those people. I hope the King is all right. Do you know? Did he get away in time? Is he hurt?''

"So far as I know he is well and on his way to England, Baroness."

I sat back. "That is good, very good. Those sheep have a new king now, and a new royal favorite to worry about."

"Baron von Zander?"

"Yes, Baron von Zander. So he's looking for me! A spy and a traitor! Those were his men, you know. His personal guards. Their uniforms bore his own coat of arms."

"So they did," the man frowned. "He's eager to find you. I didn't anticipate having to use those weeds," he nodded at my costume.

There were footsteps in the corridor. Quickly I pulled down my veils and slid closer to Monsieur S. I let my head fall to his shoulder again, and I wondered if he could smell my rose scent. The steps passed without pausing and we relaxed again. He stood and stretched and I lifted my veils and smoothed my skirts. He took a seat opposite me and regarded me thoughtfully, without smiling.

He was tall, lean and handsome. His hair was dark blond and very straight. He wore it combed to the side, but every so often it would fall over his eyes, giving him an unexpectedly boyish look. His brows were dark and he was clean shaven. Ludwig might have called his nose a little too large for perfect beauty, but his strong chin and large dark-fringed eyes certainly balanced it. His fingers were long, thin and strong. As I studied him I felt something that I hadn't felt for a long time: desire, like a little imp waking from a long sleep, stirred and stretched and came alive inside me. A slight flush mounted to my cheeks.

"I don't really look like the wickedest woman in the western hemisphere, do I?" I asked softly.

He jumped, startled. I knew I had read his mind correctly.

"You were wondering if all those terrible stories you have heard about me could possibly be true," I went on.

"Can one woman really have corrupted a monarch, sacked the treasury, brought down a government, caused outbreaks of hives and plague, and prompted crops to dry up and cattle to die?" I laughed lightly.

He smiled for the first time. "You are a beautiful and talented lady, Baroness. I enjoyed your concert with Liszt very much. You put him in the shade. I suspect there are few women in Europe capable of doing that."

"Only because he permitted it," I said generously. "He was very kind to me."

"I hope I'll be able to hear you sing again soon?"

"Who knows?" I shrugged. "This revolution nonsense has disrupted everything. And if I am to be harassed by ruffians wherever I go—. Where are we going, by the way? I hope you don't think it impertinent of me to ask."

"Not at all. Stuttgart first, and tonight we'll travel to Strasbourg. The sooner we get out of Bavaria, the happier I'll be. This sort of thing really isn't in my line at all."

"But you do it so well!" I said. "What is your line?"

"Very prosaic," he grinned. "I'm a lawyer."

How did you become involved in Bavarian politics?"

"I had business in France. King Ludwig is an old friend of my father's. He sent for me, said it was urgent. I confess I was intrigued, and I had a few weeks to spare while some papers were being readied, and so I came." He gave me a penetrating look that made my little imp swoon, and he said, "I'm not sorry I did."

"I suppose you read the lies about me in the newspapers?"

He nodded.

"The Baron's doing. Don't believe any of them. What did Ludwig tell you about me?"

"He said that you were his dear friend and that he didn't want anything to happen to you." He paused, as if there were something else, but just then Anna came into the compartment and I decided it was time to open the food hamper.

"You didn't think to bring food, did you, Monsieur?" I

asked him gaily. "Men never do think of food in times of crisis. But that is when you need it most."

We had a pleasant little party in our shuttered compartment. I saw Anna giving the stranger assessing looks, and when she bent over me to fill my champagne glass, she gave me an approving wink. I made a little move with my mouth that said I was willing, but was he? Anna and I rarely had need of words.

"Did you bring your wife to France, Monsieur—?" I asked.

"The name is McClelland," he told me. "Steven McClelland. I didn't want to disgrace my country—or implicate her politically—if there was any trouble." I nodded. Very wise. "I have no wife, Baroness. She died some time ago."

"Ah, how sad for you. But you have children?"

"We had five. Two died soon after my wife. It was— typhoid." He looked down, but not before I saw the pain of remembering in his eyes.

"That's very sad," I said. And I meant it. "But fortunate in a way."

He looked up. "What do you mean?"

I tilted my head to the side. "You dear wife died without knowing that her babies were dying, too. That was good, for her. She could feel peace and contentment at the end, knowing that you had all those wonderful children to comfort you when she was gone. She did not know then how great your sorrow would be."

He was silent for a while, then he said, "That's true. She did seem—at peace."

"Please tell me more about your other children," I asked. "How lucky you are to have three! How old are they?"

"The oldest, John, is thirteen. Philippe is ten. And Marie is eight. My wife died seven years ago."

"So small when their mother left them!" I exclaimed. "And who cares for them?"

"They had a governess for a while. And my mother was

wonderful. They all adore her. The boys are in school now and only Marie is left at home.''

"And she is beautiful, your daughter," I said gently. "Like your wife." He gave a little smile and a nod. "You should marry again," I said firmly. "You are too young to be without a wife! She would have wanted it that way, you know. She wouldn't like you to be lonely."

"And how do you know that I'm lonely?" Steven McClelland asked. A smile lurked behind his eyes.

I spread my hands and said, "Gypsies know everything! But you have the look of a man who works too hard. A happily married man wouldn't need to work hard. And he wouldn't want to."

"You're very wise," he laughed. "And very observant."

I shrugged and spread some caviar on a piece of dark bread. "My Gypsy upbringing, my friend. I knew before I asked that you were not married now. You are too thin and you look a little worried. Your wife would have replaced the missing button on your coat and when I cried you would have offered me a handkerchief but you couldn't because you didn't have one. A wife would have made sure that you had one at all times. But I knew you had been married, because only a married man with children could have thought up that very convincing lie about the little son who died in Vienna."

"Tell me about him," he said.

"Another time," I promised, sipping champagne. "We have had too much talk of death and sadness. Anna, our friend's glass is empty."

We talked and laughed about this and that. I liked him very much. He was good and kind. He loved his wife and his children and his family. I thought, I wouldn't put it past Ludwig to try and matchmake, even as his kingdom was crumbling around him. I laughed out loud and my companion looked curious.

"Forgive me, Monsieur McClelland," I said. "But my friend King Ludwig is such a transparent schemer. Of course he had to send for an Adonis to rescue his dear Venus!'' We laughed together. He liked that reference to Adonis. He might have been a lawyer, but he was not above flattery.

We left the train at Stuttgart and immediately entered a waiting coach for the drive to Strasbourg, just over the French border. In Strasbourg, an ancient city with winding medieval streets and a soaring cathedral spire, we checked into a clean middle-class hotel on the Rue de Marengo. After a very pleasant meal in the hotel dining room, my new friend bid me good-night and told me we would travel to Paris by easy stages.

''Forgive me,'' I said, ''but I disobeyed your instructions and had my trunks forwarded to Le Havre. From there I will go to England, perhaps. But I will not go to Paris. I can't.''

''I understand,'' he said kindly.

''No, you don't. You can't. Perhaps someday I will tell you. But you must not let us distract you from your business. Anna and I will take another coach to Le Havre. I am sure there will be no further trouble and I wouldn't like you to inconvenience yourself any more than you already have.''

''We'll see,'' he said noncommittally. And I knew that he wouldn't leave us. He kissed my hand. ''I can't remember when I've had a more delightful travelling companion, Baroness,'' he said with more sincerity than gallantry. ''Or a more pleasant evening. Thank you.''

''And thank you for your help, Monsieur McClelland. Good-night.''

Anna and I were both very tired, and we slept deeply. I was awakened by sounds of a struggle. Rough hands dragged me out of bed and covered my mouth.

A man growled in German, ''Tell me where they are, bitch, or we'll cut your maid's ears off.''

I twisted around in his arms and saw that another man was holding a knife to Anna's throat. Anna's eyes bulged.

She was terrified and trembling.

"You see that?" my captor said. "Now tell me, or—"

I bit his hand. He snatched it away and I squalled, "I don't know what you're talking about! Leave her alone! Get out of here!"

He grabbed my wrist and twisted it behind my back. I thought my shoulder would pop out of its socket. "Tell me or I'll break your arm!"

The only light in the room came from a lantern set on top of the armoire. Just then Steven McClelland came in through the window. There was a narrow balcony running across the face of the building and his room was next to ours. He pulled the man off me, slamming his fist into the brute's jaw and sending him crashing to the floor. The man who was tormenting Anna shoved her aside and ran past us to the window. Steven followed him, but the man leapt agilely over the edge of the balcony and shinned down the drainpipe.

I held Anna close and comforted her. Steven came over to us and I looked up at him. "Wicked fiends!" I said angrily. "To frighten a poor helpless girl like Anna, who can't shout for help! Thank you. Thank you for helping us."

Steven crouched over the unconscious man and searched his pockets.

"He is German," I said. "Of course he is working for the Baron."

"But how did he find us?" Steven wondered. "Damn. I thought I had been so careful."

I shrugged. "Perhaps the Baron had agents stationed all along the border. Strasbourg might have seemed the obvious place for us to go. I fear that I am not inconspicuous, even in a black dress and a veil."

"We're getting out of here right now," Steven said. He gagged the intruder with a handkerchief, then tied his hands with a silk stocking I gave him. "I'll alert our coachman and meet you downstairs. We'll get away from here and then consider another plan. Can Anna ride?"

Anna shook her head violently and sent me despairing looks.

"It's all right, Anna," Steven said soothingly.

We went as far as Phalsburg that night, thirty miles from Strasbourg, and stopped at an inn on the western edge of town.

Steven followed me into my room. I saw he wanted to talk alone and I sent Anna for hot water.

"What were those men after, Baroness?" he asked me. "I think I have a right to know."

"I have no idea," I said, avoiding his eyes.

"I see," he said dryly. "Perhaps they were just garden-variety thieves, not agents of the Baron at all"

"The King did give me some very valuable jewelry before I left. Perhaps the Baron regards them as public property and he regards public property as his own."

"Where are the jewels?" Steven asked.

"Right here." I lifted my skirts and the hem of my petticoat. "See? Anyone would think they were weights, to keep my skirts from blowing up."

"Maybe that is what they're after," he said grudgingly. "You have other jewels as well, in your jewel case?"

"A few."

"It was lying on your dresser in Strasbourg, in full sight. I wonder why they didn't just snatch it and run?" He gave me a sharp look. I smiled, all innocence. Then he sighed and said, "Well, get some sleep if you can. We'll travel together to Nancy. Anna will go ahead to Le Harve, alone, and we'll travel on horseback, by night if we have to. If they're looking for a Baroness who's travelling in style, they'll be disappointed."

"It sounds rather complicated and drastic," I said. "If, as you suggested, those men were common thieves—"

"You don't believe that and neither do I." He sounded tired and he spoke rather gruffly. "If you'd rather go by coach and train, exposing yourself to danger, it's up to you."

I smiled. "Of course I will do as you say. I have riding clothes with me. And I was instructed to obey you in everything. Well, it has been a very long day and night. Once again, I thank you, Monsieur McClelland."

Steven yawned and stretched. "We'll be travelling together for a week or more. Perhaps you could call me Steven."

"I will," I agreed. "And you must call me Rhawnie."

"Rhawnie," he repeated. "It's beautiful. Is it Romany?"

I nodded. "It means 'great lady.' "

"Very appropriate." He smiled wearily. I hoped he would kiss my hand again, but he didn't. He wished me good-night and left the room as Anna was coming in with a steaming basin.

"He is very good-looking, isn't he, Anna?" I sighed. "I feel as though I have known him for years. He's still a little reserved, but we have only known each other a day. He makes me feel quite fluttery and young and silly. Why, I might be fifteen instead of twenty-one. Or is it twenty-two? Good-night, Anna."

12

Gypsy Prima Donna

"IF YOU LOOK south you can see the lights of Paris."

I reined in my horse at the top of a knoll when he spoke. It was dusk, the end of the fifth day of our journey from Le Havre. When I saw the golden glow in the sky I thought of Madame Odette and Jules, of the Delacroix Ball and the house on the Rue de Montmorency, of gambling and horses and Martin de Vernay. So many memories. And woven around them all, like a silken web that colors everything it covers, was the memory of Seth.

I had thought about him a lot since meeting Steven McClelland. They were so different. Seth was greedy, self-centered, moody, careless of other people's feelings. He could no more have spent an hour in the company of a woman like the Baroness of Ravensfeld without seducing her than he could sprout wings and fly to the moon.

Steven, on the other hand, was the perfect gentleman. Maddeningly perfect. In the four days that had passed since we left Strasbourg his attitude hadn't altered: he was still friendly, polite, and warm. If anything, he had grown a little distant, cooler. We were still able to talk together and laugh together without strain or tension, in a way I had never been able to talk with Seth. And he thought I was beautiful—I had seen the admiration in his eyes a dozen times. He couldn't hide that. But he never uttered a suggestive word or made an impolite gesture.

Oh, well. I shrugged inwardly. He was probably a snob. A respected, respectable member of American society with an exalted position to maintain; a valuable servant to his government. I was a lot of things, but not even remotely respectable. This American lawyer probably thought himself much too good for intimate association with a notorious Baroness.

We sat quietly, watching the pink in the sky dissolve into deeper shades of violet and blue. Our horses grazed contentedly under us, grateful for a brief respite from hard riding.

"Why don't you want to go back?" Steven asked suddenly.

I was startled. He had never before questioned me about my past. I had told him a few things, stories from my Gypsy childhood, a vague account of how I got away from Russia and came to live with Madame Odette. But not much else. I didn't think he would be interested.

"Because of the man who took me there in the first place. I can't think of Paris without thinking of him, and I don't want to think about him."

"Why?"

I sighed. "It hurts too much." I told him about Seth—never using his name, though, because I couldn't bear to say it aloud. I related how Seth had left me with Madame Odette, how he had claimed me as his mistress after disgracing me at the ball; how he had discovered my talent for faro, and how he had used and exploited me and never let me out of his sight.

"I tried to run away with a boy, Martin de Vernay. But he killed Martin in a duel and we had to escape to London. I discovered I was pregnant and I tried to kill myself because he wanted me to have an abortion. You've seen the bracelets I wear. They hide the scars. But I couldn't even get away from him that way. He didn't want to let me go. He saved my life then married me. He married me. I still can't believe it sometimes. He hated being married. I didn't want to change him, to domesticate him, to curb his freedom. But he thought I did, and perhaps he was right. In any case, he decided that he didn't want to be saddled with a wife and child. I saw his face after our son was born and I knew—I knew he wouldn't stay. He deserted us, in Vienna. The baby got sick and died, and I went to Munich to be mistress to the King." We were silent for a while. "Quite a sordid story, isn't it?" I said softly. "I can't imagine what possessed me to tell you. Now you'll think even less of me than you did before."

"What do you mean?" Steven's voice came out of the deepening gloom.

"Men like you disapprove of women like me," I said lightly. "It's one of the facts of life. I'm sorry King Ludwig involved you in my problems. You've been very good about it, but I know I've been a nuisance to you."

Before he could reply a shot rang out and a bullet whistled past my ear. My horse reared twice, nearly throwing me, but I hung on.

"It came from those trees," Steven shouted. "Let's go!"

We raced away from the source of the shot, toward a small woods at the edge of the field. We pulled our horses up and I panted, "A gamekeeper, perhaps, thinking we were poachers?"

"No," Steven said grimly. "Gamekeepers don't usually travel on horseback. Listen." We could hear pounding hooves. Several horses. "They know who they're looking for now. A man and a woman, riding. Let's get out of these woods and into open country. We don't know how many are after us and we need to get away before moonrise."

We rode swiftly for an hour or more and finally Steven signalled a halt.

"I think we've lost them. I'm not sure, though. Can you go a little farther?"

"Oh, yes," I answered cheerfully. "I'm not tired."

"You're made of sterner stuff than I am," he confessed, laughing. "I'm exhausted. I suppose Gypsies thrive on danger?"

"It's meat and drink to us," I told him.

"I think we'll disappear. That should throw them off. I know just the place."

Late that night we passed between twin stone pillars that marked the entrance to a country estate. We rode through acres of wooded park land. The bright full moon cast long shadows among the trees. Everything looked water, silvery.

The chateau was a sprawling, low structure faced with acres of windows that caught the brightness of the moon. Pools and fountains were still and quiet, their stone figures looking like persons petrified by a magic hand in the midst of riotous revelry.

"It looks deserted," I said.

"It is." We dismounted and walked up a flight of marble stairs. "There are caretakers living in the cottage we passed a while back. I'll tell them we're here in the morning." Steven pulled a bunch of keys out of his pocket and unlocked the double doors. We went inside. The pieces of furniture in the main hall were all draped with white dust sheets. "I'll start a fire for you in one of the bedrooms," Steven told me. "Then I'll come back and look after the horses."

"I know how to build a fire," I told him. "Such a beautiful house! Is it yours?"

"My family's. My Uncle Philippe owns it now—it came to him when his uncle died a few years ago. But he's married and living in America. He talks of selling it—the taxes are ruinous and the upkeep is terrific, even when there's no one living here—but my mother won't hear of it. So we hang on to it for sentimental reasons, and I look in whenever I'm in the country. I was born here."

"Show me where!" I asked delightedly. Impulsively, I slipped my hand into his.

He led me up a curving staircase and along a corridor. Tall candelabra stood like spidery sentinels in the dark hallway, flanking each doorway. The house was cold and silent, dimly lighted by the moon, full of ghosts and memories. Steven opened the door to a room that overlooked the fountains and the driveway.

He struck a match and lit candles on the mantelpiece over the fireplace. "My mother's room," he announced with great pride. "The scene of her lying-in. My birthplace."

"How proud your father must have been!" I exclaimed.

Steven laughed. "He wasn't here. They weren't married at the time." He saw the startled look on my face and laughed heartily. I laughed, too.

"May I stay here tonight?" I asked. "Do you think your mother would mind?"

"She would be delighted. Make yourself comfortable. I'll look after the horses."

I peeked inside the fuel box. "Ah, there's plenty of coal in the bin. I'll have a nice fire for you when you come in. It's rather cold tonight."

I crouched down in front of the grate. I could feel him behind me, watching. Was he admiring the round line of my haunch and the way my riding skirt pulled around my thigh? Not him, I thought. He's probably thinking about ruinous taxes or business matters or about how he's desecrating his family home by bringing someone like me into it. As if to confirm these thoughts he turned and went out without saying another word.

I sighed. "He is too much of a gentleman," I muttered. "I don't care if he was born before his parents were married."

I got a nice blaze going and shoveled a few coals into a warming pan for the bed. I'd need something to keep me warm. I wasn't going to have Steven McClelland that night, or any other night. I took off my dusty riding clothes and shook them out, then dug around in my valise for a

323

wrapper of lime green silk. I sat cross-legged on a rug in front of the fire and took my braids down.

Steven tapped at the door and came in. He watched silently as I brushed my hair.

"I've brought a pitcher of water for washing," he said. "I'm sorry it's cold."

"How thoughtful you are, Monsieur S," I said, smiling at him through a veil of hair. It was very long and it rippled almost to the floor. I finished brushing and threw it back behind my shoulders. "Come closer to the fire, Steven," I said. "You must be very tired." As he approached me, reluctantly, like a schoolboy in a no hurry to get a beating, I saw two red spots burning on his cheeks. "Are you ill?" I asked. "You look feverish."

He lowered himself into a chintz-covered chair and scowled at me. "I'm fine," he said brusquely.

I switched myself around in front of him. "Let me help you with your boots," I said. "It's a special talent of mine." I worked the boots off and stood them up at the side of the chair. Steven was gripping the chair arms so tightly that his knuckles were white and the tendons on the back of his hands stood out. His face was suffused with anger.

"What's the matter, Steven?" I asked wonderingly. "Have I done something to offend you?"

He stood up so quickly that he almost knocked me down.

"Christ."

He stamped across the room. Quick as a flash I was on my feet, after him. I threw myself in front of him and blocked the door.

"Please tell me what's bothering you," I said. "I won't let you go until—"

He grabbed my hand and pressed my palm against the front of his breeches. His bulging member felt as big as a wine bottle. I gave an astonished little cry, and then I smiled and said pityingly, "Oh, you are so foolish."

I undid the sash of my robe and let it slip to the floor.

Underneath I was naked. I put my hands on his chest and the scent of roses and of warm womanly flesh assaulted his nostrils. He hurled himself on top of me and we sank to the carpeted floor.

I unfastened the buttons of his breeches and slid them over his buttocks. He kicked them away. With something like a sob he brought his mouth down on mine and parted my legs with his hand. The desire that burned in us both flared up like the flame of a match and our bodies ignited like dry timber. The sweet pain of his thrust made me cry out. The flames devoured us and spent themselves quickly, and we lay together panting and trembling.

Then he started to pull away. "I'm sorry—"

I held him tight and said firmly, "Don't you dare apologize or act like a gentleman!"

He grinned and relaxed. "You're right," he said, kissing me. "I'm a damned fool. I've been undressing you in my mind for five days, telling myself to control my baser appetites, and cursing myself every night before I went to sleep for answering the King's summons and going to Munich."

"I understand," I said. "I don't blame you. You think I'm a whore and a wanton and—"

"Be quiet and listen to me for a minute," he said, covering my mouth with his fingertips. "I do not, repeat, do not believe anything I heard about you in Munich other than what the King told me. I know you're no Gypsy witch; and you're not the Ice Maiden of the Rhineland, either. You're a warm, wonderful woman who was badly used by a man who had no more soul than a—coal scuttle. I hate him, because he hurt you and caused you pain. But I could never think less of you because of it. You are yourself, Rhawnie. Wonderfully, beautifully yourself. I don't blame Ludwig for giving up his throne for you."

"Thank you for that," I said, kissing him. "Did the King tell you about how things were between us?"

"Yes." Steven looked serious. "He told me about

his—problem. And about what a comfort you were to him. And about how virtuous you were."

Good old Ludwig. I sighed and said, "Let's go to bed."

We crawled between the warmed sheets and slept, entwined in each other's arms. We were both quite weary, having ridden hard for the past four days. But now we were safe and warm and happy. The urgency had gone out of our flight, for we had found something beautiful, and unexpected.

It must have been midmorning before I awoke. Steven was gone. I felt a stab of fear and sat up quickly. He was standing at the window.

"Ah! Good morning, Monsieur S!" I said in my husky morning voice. I lifted my arms to stretch. Steven grinned at me. He was naked, hard and lean and smooth. "You look like the Apollo Belvedere," I sighed. "You are beautiful."

"So are you," he laughed. "I've never seen a lovelier sight: Venus rising from the bedsheets."

I stretched out my arms to him. "Come to me," I said. "I want you."

Steven looked down at himself and said ruefully, "It's rather obvious that I want you. I've been waiting for you to wake up. I didn't want to bother you, but I couldn't stand being so close—you'd think I hadn't had a woman in seven years."

I welcomed him with a long kiss. Our desperation had gone, and our love that morning was leisured and languorous. We explored each other's bodies with our mouths and hands.

"The King is an old Pandarus," I said. "He knew this would happen."

"He should have told me," Steven grumbled. "I wouldn't have wasted the past four days. In fact, I would have gotten you away from Munich much sooner."

"He was so wise," I reflected. "He knew what the Baron was plotting. He always knew what would happen, but he didn't try to stop it."

"I think he was tired of being King," Steven said. "Ah, my mother would be delighted to know that her bed was being put to such good use."

"Tell me about your wife, Steven."

He put his arms behind his head and smiled reminiscently. "She was small and dark and exquisite, like a doll. But she was kind and selfless, and she devoted herself to me and my children. We were the center of her life. She was always there when someone was hurt, when I was angry or upset. I still miss her. I'd come to her with some absurd problem, raving like a bull because this man was an idiot or that one was a moron, and she'd look thoughtful and say, 'Well, Steven, they can't all be as smart as you. You'll just have to accept that.'"

"How happy you must have been with her," I said. "I'm glad."

"You're very different, you know. Julie was quiet and a little shy. Like a doe. You're a lioness. You devour life and you revel in the things life has to give, happiness and sorrow and even danger. You would have overshadowed her in public. But she would have liked you. She was a very shrewd judge of people."

"You are very good," I said admiringly. "Kiss me again. Maybe some of your goodness will rub off on me."

"If I were as good as you think," he said, "I wouldn't have acted like such a boor and a prig."

"You didn't," I said generously. "You were just afraid of your feelings, that's all. But to be honest, from the very first minute I saw you, I wanted you. I tried and tried to seduce you, but you were a hard case, Steven. I really thought I was doomed to failure."

The only people we saw that day were the old caretaker and his wife. They brought plates of hot food and bottles of wine from the cellars. In the afternoon the skies clouded over and it started to rain heavily.

"Good," said Steven. The roads around here are impassible in the rain. We could be trapped here for weeks."

"Anna would become distraught," I said sensibly. "And what about your business in Paris? Surely you have things to do besides rescuing me."

"Boring nonsense about trade agreements," he said casually. "And I don't have to be back in Paris until next week."

I was silent for a moment, then I sighed. "I'm such a fool to think of him now, when I feel happy. If only I could forget him! But he haunts me, Steven. I was his puppet, his toy. He thought I was imperfect, and he kept trying to hammer the dents out. I hated him! No, I didn't hate him. I loved him, and it broke my heart when he left me."

Steven held me close and said my name, and I hid my face in his neck.

"You are different, Steven," I said. "I don't get stiff and silent when you come into the room. I don't flinch when you touch me or hate myself for wanting you. Desire is a fine and beautiful thing, and with you it is never degrading. I can talk to you, like a friend, and you never sneer at me or mock me or hurt my feelings. You don't want to break my spirit. You don't want to rule me."

He said, "Come to Paris with me."

I lifted my face. His eyes were tender. "I can't," I said. "Can you understand? I can't."

"If you're afraid of the King's men and that duelling business, don't be. King Louis Philippe has been deposed. Another revolution. France has a new king now."

"The world has gone mad," I smiled. "But it's not the duelling. Oh, this time with you has been perfect, like a jewel. I shall remember these hours always. You are very good. But I am still married to him. Let's not talk about it anymore. Please, Steven."

The rain stopped in the middle of the night. Both of us were disappointed.

"Our time together is almost over," I said. "Tomorrow

I will ride to Le Havre alone. It will be quite safe. And you will return to Paris."

"No. At least let me ride with you as far as Honfleur. To be sure you're all right and that they're not watching the ports. Don't give me an argument: I promised the King to take care of you."

We rode in silence all the way to Honfleur. I would take the little ferry across the harbor to Le Havre to meet Anna, who was staying in a hotel that Steven knew.

We stood on the dock. We had ten minutes before the ferry left.

"Take care of yourself, Steven," I said lamely. "And when you get home to America, thank your wonderful mother for me and kiss all your dear children. Ah, it's starting to rain. I'm glad." I made a swipe at my eyes with my sleeve.

"Won't you change your mind? About Paris?"

"No, no," I said quickly. "I feel that it would be wrong for me to go back there with you. I am not the woman I was then. I want to make a whole new life for myself. But we might meet again someday."

"I hope so. I truly hope so." He held my hands.

"I'll give you a reading," I said, turning over his palm. "For free! Ah, I see travel and good fortune," I said glibly. "You will make a lot of money soon. But beware! There is a dark-haired woman in your future!"

"My daughter," he laughed.

"You will marry again," I said slowly, "but not very soon. You will have a long life and you will be happy with your children. Your friends will be true, and your enemies will drown in the sea of their own evil." A warning whistle blew and I looked up. "That is what I see for you," I whispered, "and what I wish for you. Good-bye, Steven! Think of your Gypsy Baroness from time to time. She will be thinking of you."

The boat slid away from the dock and Honfleur was quickly absorbed in a rising mist.

Six weeks later the U.S.S. *Thomas Jefferson* docked in New York. Decked out in my brightest finery, I strode down the gangplank. Anna followed at a slower pace. We were both still pea-green from the experience, but I had assured her that a few minutes on dry land would dispel the sickness.

I hired a porter to look after my trunks, which had arrived in Le Havre a few days before I sailed. They showed evidences of having been searched. Then I got a cab and told the driver to take us to the best hotel in the city. Half an hour later Anna and I stepped into the Plymouth Hotel on lower Broadway. I informed the management—not merely the clerk at the desk—that I was the Baroness of Ravensfield (perhaps he had heard of me?) and that I had had to flee for my life from Bavarian soldiers. All I wanted now was peace and quiet.

"I require absolute privacy," I said. "And please make sure that my room has a piano."

Within the hour a half-dozen reporters were clustered around me in the sitting room of my suite. I wore a lavender dressing gown with trailing ribbons and matching slippers. Diamond pendants hung from my ears, and I wore diamond bracelets over the scars on my wrists.

"It was a perfectly dreadful experience!" I told them in my strongly accented English. "The screaming mob surrounded my house! They were shouting and throwing things, and there I was, alone inside, with only my faithful Anna here."

In the background Anna busied herself with tea. Baskets of flowers were starting to arrive from various impresarios and producers of Public Spectacles, and she was trying her best to indicate to the delivery boys that they were to be taken away and given to sick people in hospitals. Such bad luck, cut flowers. I had permitted Jules to put them in my room at the Rue de Montmorency, and look what happened.

I knew those skeptics wouldn't believe my story, but I didn't mind. I could see the doubt written all over their faces when I simpered and said that King Ludwig and I were "just good friends." Whatever they wrote for their newspapers would be good for business: more people would attend a concert to see the ex-mistress of a deposed monarch than would come to hear just another immigrant soprano.

"They say the King built you an opera house," one of the reporters said.

"He built a new opera house when I was there, and I had the good fortune to sing in it," I corrected him. "The city needed a new opera house anyway."

"But it might not have gotten one if the King hadn't had special reasons for wanting to build one," said the man from the *Daily Letter* with a trace of a sneer in his voice. I said nothing and smiled enigmatically. The reporters moistened their pencils with their tongues and scribbled madly.

"They say that you rode a white horse through the streets of Munich and that you whipped anyone who got in your way," said another man eagerly.

"My horse was black, not white," I purred, "and I permit no man to stand in my way—at any time."

When I felt that I had doled out just enough tantalizing tidbits, I declared that I had a terrible headache and I dismissed them. When Anna had ushered the last one out the door I jumped up and clapped my hands.

"I am a genius!" I crowed. "That interview should sell at least a thousand tickets! Now tomorrow I will hire a pianist—the best I can find. What a shame Liszt isn't touring the country: what a show that would be!"

There was another knock at the door. Anna brought me an engraved business card.

"Mister Ralph Edgar Flood, Esquire," I read with difficulty. Thanks to Ludwig I could read German fairly well, but my command of written English was still poor.

" 'Theatrical Consultant.' Hmm. Show him in, Anna."

Ralph Edgar Flood, I learned later, considered himself a "showman." He modelled himself on P. T. Barnum, but he had none of Barnum's wit or imagination.

"How are ya, Baroness!" he boomed, coming into the room with hands outstretched. "I sure am glad to see you in this country at last. We poor folks here in America have been eagerly awaiting the opportunity to hear your glorious voice."

"Then why don't you buy a ticket to my concert, Mr. Esquire?" I suggested, ignoring his hand. "I know you will enjoy it."

"Ha, ha. The name is Flood, ma'am. The Esquire is just an honorary title, like Baroness." He plopped himself into a chair uninvited while I remained standing. "I wanted to talk to you about a concert, Baroness. It wouldn't be right for a little lady like yourself—"

I laughed. "Come, come, Mr. Flood. A lady I may be, but little—! Never. State your business."

Mr. Flood did so. He wanted to arrange my first concert appearance at the Lyceum Theater, the biggest in New York. I nodded, absorbing this information. He promised me fifty percent of the profits over the gross receipts.

"And what kind of receipts are those, the gross ones?" I asked.

He chuckled indulgently. "Everything that's left after the expenses are taken care of," he explained. "There's the hall to hire—that's about two thousand dollars right there. The program to print, a piana-player to hire, costumes. The folks here like to see lots of fancy dress."

"Is that so? I have seen the great Franz Liszt play, and as I recall, he doesn't even change his clothes in the middle of the performance."

Flood laughed and blustered.

"But tell me more about what you can do for me, Mr. Flood," I urged him. "For example, where will you find my accompanist?"

"I'd go straight to Taylor's Theatricals, ma'am," he said. "The agency on Fourth Street. They have the best musicians in town, for all the best spectacles. Jenny Lind. The circus."

"Excellent. Thank you very much for coming, Mr. Flood. I will consider your offer and let you know. Good day."

Feeling somewhat thwarted and confused, Mr. Flood permitted Anna to show him to the door.

"Tomorrow, after I have told the Taylor Agency what I want," I told Anna when she came back, "I shall go to the Lyceum Theather, I think. I like this country, Anna. They say that in America a man can start with nothing and become rich overnight. Now I can't say that I have nothing—I have my petticoat!—but I should confess that the prospect of great wealth appeals to me. I'm afraid I have developed a taste for riches, Anna. It would be a shame not to indulge this taste, don't you agree?" Anna grinned and nodded. I took a long breath and sang a dazzling coloratura obligato. "Ah, the voice is very rusty! It will take me at least a month to get it into shape. There is so much to do, Anna! Push that button and when the boy comes tell him I want some champagne. We have a lot to celebrate!"

Anna successfully mimed "champagne" for the startled bellboy: she popped an imaginary cork and watched it hit the ceiling, then caught the spilling foam in a glass, twitched her nose at the bubbles, and toasted the boy. Soon we were both sipping sparkling wine.

I looked around. "Drab. Much too tasteful for a Russian Gypsy singer. Some day I shall have my own house, Anna. And I shall decorate it like the inside of a Gypsy caravan! Lots of colors, lots of cushions, and a steaming samovar, always ready with hot tea. But I shall buy a samovar tomorrow, as my first purchase in the new world. Ah, aren't you excited, Anna? Do you miss Europe?"

Anna shrugged.

"Neither do I. I don't miss it at all. This is a new life, Anna. I am free! For the first time in my life, I don't have to answer to anybody! Free, free, freer than a Gypsy! I have a new career, a new future, a new land to conquer, just as Ludwig said! Let us drink—to America!"

Of all the applicants I interviewed for accompanist, the only one who showed exceptional promise was a consumptive-looking young man named David Thatcher. His clothes bagged on his thin frame, his complexion was sallow, he had no small talk. But he played the piano like a fiend. I soon discovered that the object of our interview was not to determine if I wanted him to play for me, but if David wanted to.

I handed him a copy of "Five Gypsy Songs." "See what you can do with these," I said. "Franz Liszt wrote them for me."

He was unimpressed. "Yes, I studied with Liszt in Berlin." He carried them to the piano and sight-read them perfectly, the first time. "Not his greatest work," he pronounced, "but nice enough, I suppose."

"Oh, you suppose!" I said coolly.

"Now perhaps you would be good enough to sing, Baroness," he said. "I want to hear how you sound."

"You—want to hear how I sound!" I exclaimed. "You are rather impudent, young man!"

He squinted at me through his thick glasses. "Why do you say that? I certainly can't play for you if I can't bear to listen to you." He thumbed through a pile of music and pulled out a killing aria by Mozart. "Try this."

I sang it through. He played beautifully, without even looking at the music. In fact, he had his eyes closed!

"Not bad," he said glumly. Not bad! "Your top is a little shrill." Shrill! "And you lost control on some of that coloratura stuff." Lost control!

"You didn't tell me that you were a vocal coach as well as a pianist," I said coldly.

"Didn't I? I coached Lind for her performances in Vienna in '46 and '47. She made a lot of progress."

"Did she!" My eyebrows couldn't go up any higher. "Well, what are you doing in New York, if I may ask? Waiting for the Taylor Agency to find you a job?"

"I am not with the Taylor Agency. I saw an article about you in the newspapers and decided that if you didn't want to make a complete fool of yourself you would hire me. I left Europe because I found conducting too taxing. I am not a strong man, but neither am I a rich one. I would say that we needed each other. When is your concert?"

"Five weeks," I said faintly. "In mid-September."

He shook his head. "You can't possibly be ready by then. And it will still be much too hot here. The really important people won't even be back from their summer homes yet. We'll re-schedule the concert for the first week in October. Now let's get down to work. I'll come here five days a week until two weeks before the concert, and then we'll reduce that to three. I don't want you to sound tired."

"Tired!" I sniffed. "I don't get tired!"

"No, but your voice does." He saw me pouring myself some champagne and he frowned. "And no more of that until after the performance. It places a strain on the larynx."

No more champagne! A strain on the larynx! He was impossible. What could I do? I hired him.

We fell into a routine. I slept until ten or eleven o'clock in the morning and then had a large lunch. David came at precisely one o'clock and we worked for two hours, exercising my voice and preparing songs. Then I received callers or shopped or explored the city. I hired a light curricle and a team of fine chestnut horses and drove myself all around town, alone. Crowds gathered to watch and shout and point and the newspapers had a wonderful time.

"Bavarian Baroness Bests Beston!" trumpeted one

headline about a week before the concert. Alfred Beston was a grandson of the American Revolution, a bored, wealthy bachelor who liked horses. He drove his own team around the city and one day we met and engaged in an impromptu race. I won and he invited me to dine with him.

"I cannot go out in the evening now until after my concert," I told him. "My pianist is a tyrant! But afterwards I shall be available for all sorts of jollity. Of course you will buy many tickets!"

He bought a block of tickets and promised his friends would show loud, enthusiatic support.

"Oh, I don't need a hired claque!" I laughed. "When they hear me sing they will willingly leap to their feet, shouting with joy!"

David Thatcher and I quarrelled every day. "Listen to me," I said firmly one afternoon, about a week before the concert at the Lyceum, "I want you to write accompaniments for two more Gypsy songs. I will do Liszt's, of course, but I want these for encores. I shall sing one slow—full of sadness and longing—and the other happy, celebrating the Gypsy way of life."

David regarded me solemnly over the tops of his spectacles. "I will not compose drivel for you," he announced. "I have prepared some very nice songs by Brahms for your encores—"

"Brahms! You have prepared!" I shouted, banging my fists on the top of the piano. "I am the singer, not you! This is my concert, mine! I prepare, I decide what to sing and then I tell you and you play for me! Give me the settings for these songs tomorrow or I will find someone else to play for me, do you understand?"

"Perfectly." He stood up and closed the lid over the piano keys.

"Where do you think you're going?" I demanded as he walked out of the room. "Have you forgotten that we have a concert in just one week?"

"I haven't forgotten anything," he said mildly. "But I will not betray my standards."

"Standards? What do you think this is—a command performance for royalty? These people are paying to see a show! They want to hear songs they can understand, not—Brahms!"

"You are wrong, Baroness," David Thatcher said coldly. "If you want to be part of a sideshow then I suggest that you get Mr. Barnum to promote you. He understands the deplorable tastes of the American public. If you want to cheapen yourself, if you want to cheapen your association with Franz Liszt and Signor Loccatelli and King Ludwig, then just continue in your present spectacular vein. But you will simply have to hire another pianist. In the long run, if you keep your performances tasteful and concentrate on the beauty and integrity of the music—"

"Tasteful is dull!" I cried. "Integrity is boring!"

"Please let me finish," David snapped. I subsided and pouted at him. "If you do justice to your music, you will attract more listeners and more followers than you will if you act the seven days' wonder in beaded gowns and feathered headdresses."

"Well!" I sat down heavily. He started to leave. "Come back here!" I shouted. "You are a good-hearted man, David Thatcher, even though I find you stubborn and stiff-necked. Do you think I don't love music as you do? It's in my blood, in my viens! I am Gypsy, and for a Gypsy all of life is a song! I tell you, I would sing every day for nothing—only it wouldn't earn me anything. I have to think of money as well as enjoyment. I sing because I like to sing, and why shouldn't I sing the songs that make me happy? It makes sense, no?"

"No. If you want to attract the right kind of people to your concerts—the rich and the well-born—you will have to set a very high standard for yourself. It takes a lot to impress these people. They won't be fooled by shining

337

dresses and Gypsy folk songs."

"Just one?" I said meekly. "The other I will do without piano, the way I would sing it in the Gypsy camp."

"No," he said adamantly.

"Please! It is really a very tasteful song, David. Liszt himself loved it. Please, let me sing it for you."

We compromised. David planned the program and I chose the encore pieces. He wrote settings for my two new Gypsy songs and I decided to include a couple of folk and popular songs in English, like "Barbara Allen" and "Home, Sweet Home." The audience would love it.

Our preparations went forward. I put advertisements in the newspapers: "Newly Arrived from the Continent! The Baroness of Ravensfeld will Appear for the First Time on these Shores! Direct from the Court of King Ludwig of Bavaria!"

The night of the concert arrived. The Lyceum Theater was jammed and crowds blocked the approaches and had to be dispersed by mounted policemen. New York had never seen anything like it. The day before the performance I rode a white stallion up and down Broadway, smiling and waving to everyone I saw, like a one-woman parade. It worked wonders. Every seat in the house was sold and the standing room was filled an hour before curtain.

My dark blue velvet gown was tasteful enough to win David Thatcher's approval, although he had some misgivings about my low decolletage.

"But I need room to breathe, David," I explained. I inhaled deeply, to demonstrate. My white breasts rose under his nose like twin balloons. His eyes widened behind their little panes. He blushed and fled the dressing room.

When I swept onstage, followed by my lanky young accompanist, the audience drew a collective breath and burst into spontaneous applause, on the strength of my looks alone! What a country! And they liked my singing, too. The next morning, even the harshest newspaper critics confessed that my voice had power and beauty, and that my performance was dazzling. Headlines hailed the arrival of a new star: "Baroness Brilliant in Two-Hour Concert. Lyceum Shakes with Applause. Poet Longfellow Lavish with Praise."

When David appeared at one o'clock that next day for our daily practice session, he found me propped up in bed with maps of the United States spread over my lap. I was sipping the first of my countless daily cups of tea.

"Hello, David!" I greeted him ecstatically. "Where shall we go next? Philadelphia? Boston? They say that it gets very cold north of here. Let's go south! And then west. And we'll perform in the north in the springtime!"

"You sang beautifully last night," David said. "Better than I've ever heard you."

"What did you expect? I don't waste my energy on rehearsing. Why should I sing to the walls? They don't pay. But you!" I jumped out of bed and threw my arms around his neck. He looked terrified. "You played so beautifully that I wanted to weep! I have never heard the 'Five Gypsy Songs' played better, not even by Liszt himself!"

"That's strange," David remarked, detaching my arms. "He wrote them."

"Pooh. Does that mean he knows how to interpret them? Look, I have something for you." I handed him a small box. Inside was a gold pocket watch set with diamonds. "Nice, isn't it? Very tasteful."

"It's beautiful," David agreed. "Thank you, Baroness."

"It's nothing," I said modestly. "We Gypsies are generous people. Look under that pillow. There's a little money there. Take a handful as a gift, please.''

''There are thousands of dollars here!'' David gasped.

''I do not trust banks,'' I told him. ''Anna, bring another cup! Our David wants some tea!'' Anna was three rooms away but I know she heard me without difficulty. ''Now to business, David. If you want to stay with me, well and good. I would like to have you. But if you are nervous about travelling and giving concerts in different cities, or if you think it will make you ill, then you should not come. I will understand. What do you say? We leave for Philadelphia in two days.''

''I—but this is rather sudden, Baroness,'' David said. For the first time I saw him flustered. ''I thought you'd be staying here. After all the attention Mr. Beston has paid—''

''He is too short and his breath is bad,'' I said, dismissing the erstwhile millionaire. ''Why don't you want to come? You have a girlfriend, perhaps? You can bring her along.''

''Certainly not!'' David was shocked.

''What's so bad about having a girlfriend?'' I wanted to know. ''You're not too young or too old. How old are you?''

''Twenty-nine.''

''Is that all? Sometimes I think you are eighty-nine. Philadelphia, I think. Then we'll go to Baltimore and Washington and there I will sing for the President! Is that a good idea?''

''Splendid,'' David mumbled in a dazed voice. ''You are an amazing woman, Baroness.''

''Not amazing. I'm Gypsy. I've been in this city too long and I want to travel. Why shouldn't I? I am young, I am free, and I want to have fun!''

Terrible snow and ice storms plagued the eastern coast of the United States during the winter of 1848-49, but they were nothing compared to the storm I caused. I travelled in a huge, custom-made coach, extra-large to accommodate my retinue, which included Anna and David and a mulatto cook named Dora and the driver and his brother, as well as a fat white puppy named Kalinka. My coach was drawn by six perfectly matched white horses, gifts from a disappointed lover, Alfred Beston. In addition to the passengers and drivers, my coach had to hold a half-ton of luggage. David suggested half in jest that I get myself a private railroad car, but unfortunately the country didn't have tracks that went everywhere I wanted to go.

I earned a lot of money from my concert appearances, and it disappeared almost as soon as I made it. Six horses and a dog and six people eat a lot, and I needed gowns and coats and shoes—all the paraphernalia that you must have if you're a Baroness and a public figure. I believe it's called "keeping up appearances." I admit that I didn't spend all the money; I gave away a good bit, too. I was a soft touch for anyone who had a sad story to tell. Half the time I sang for free, giving benefits for crippled children or palsied musicians or widows and orphans.

Naturally I did not receive anything for singing at the White House in January, 1849. I was supposed to be grateful for the honor of being invited at all. I wore green velvet that night, with long sleeves and a very modest neckline. Chunks of sparkling diamonds at my ears and throat made up for the plainness of the dress. President and Mrs. Polk seemed delighted with my short recital of songs by Beethoven, Schubert and Liszt, but everyone was most pleased with the songs I sang by Stephen Foster. I like to watch David Thatcher's face while he played those songs: he looked as if he had eaten bile soup.

A tall, handsome gentleman with a mane of white hair danced with me at the reception afterwards. He introduced himself as Garth McClelland, and I found out later that he was Vice-President.

"McClelland? Do you have a son named Steven? Tall and good-looking, like yourself?"

"I do have a son by that name," he admitted. His eyes were blue and merry, and his smile was devastating. "Have you met him?"

"Oh, yes! He rescued me after the revolution in Munich. He was as fierce as a lion. Very brave!" My partner looked incredulous. "You think I am fooling? I assure you, it really happened. He was a secret agent for King Ludwig."

"I don't disbelieve you, Baroness," Garth McClelland said, "but it hardly sounds like my son. He's a little dry and stuffy. A lawyer."

"Yes, I know. I'll tell you about it." And I did. "He didn't want to be a secret agent. He just did it as a favor for the King. But perhaps I shouldn't talk about it? Do you find it embarrassing, politically?"

"I find it delightful!" he said warmly. "I can't wait to tell my wife." Our dance ended. "Perhaps we shall meet again, Baroness," the Vice-President said gallantly. "You should go to New Orleans. That's a city that knows how to make a beautiful woman feel at home. And my son might even have returned from Europe by then. I know he'd love to see you again," he twinkled.

In late spring we arrived in Vicksburg, Mississippi. We found a hotel, and Anna and Dora set about making my rooms comfortable. Dora littered the bedroom floor with colorful pillows and hung yards of gaily printed fabric all around the bed. Anna filled the samovar with water, dropped red hot coals into the cylinder in the center to bring the water to a boil, and then she made strong tea to steep in a little pot that she put on top. They both unpacked my trunks—a three hour job. David found a fairly decent piano in the building and persuaded the management to move it into my sitting room. Kalinka ran in circles and barked and chewed the pillows.

"Gypsy caravan!" I sighed contentedly, falling onto the bed. "Home!"

My concert in Vicksburg was a great success, and I gave a benefit for The Blind Widows of Men Drowned at Sea. The newspaper praised my generosity and some women even asked me to sing in church on Sunday. I was becoming almost respectable!

After the benefit I threw myself down on my bed and moaned, "I am tired. I am irritable. I am sick of the sound of my own voice."

Anna moved silently around the room, arranging cushions, hanging up clothes.

"Do you know what I did this morning, Anna? I kicked Kalinka because he was underfoot and I scolded Dora because the coffee was cold and I shouted at David because he came to our practice session five minutes early! I am going mad. I need rest, quiet."

Anna gave me a sour look and rubbed the fourth finger of her left hand.

"A husband? I don't want a husband. Just one more person underfoot."

Anna shook her head and traced a large "S" in the air with her finger.

"Steven? Yes, he was nice, very nice. I think I miss him. His quiet voice, his sympathy. Those lovely strong arms. Ah." I rolled over and buried my face in the pillows. "I'm getting as mean as a spinster in my old age, Anna. But what do I do? Most of the men I see just don't interest me. I have slept with rogues and kings and I have a right to be choosy."

I sat up again and accepted a cup of tea. Anna locked her arms together and rocked them back and forth.

"Babies," I said.

She nodded and mimed an old woman with a bent back and palsied hand.

"I should have babies before I get too old! You think what I really want is a husband and a family!"

Anna waved her arms at the ceiling.

"And a home! You're saying that I want to be like every other woman with a husband and a home and lots of babies! Oh, Anna, sit with me." I put my arms around her. I can't help touching people I like. "Are you tired of all this travelling and all this fuss?" She nodded. "Are you scolding me because I'm trying to keep busy and I'm not thinking about what I really want out of life?" Anna nodded more vigorously. "But I'm having such a wonderful time!" Anna sat immobile. "They love to hear me sing, everywhere I go! And I love to sing for them, Anna. I do! They—they need me." No reaction. "Bah," I said impatiently, "sometimes when I talk to you, Anna, it's like talking to myself. Everybody always thinks they know what's best for me. David wants me to sing Brahms, Dora wants me to eat cornbread instead of blintzes, Kalinka wants me to walk with him all the time. Oh, God, I'm tired. Where are we supposed to go next? Natchez? We won't go," I decided suddenly. "We shall go straight to New Orleans instead! And I'll buy a house and sing in my own living room for the people I like and rest and grow fat—. And maybe I'll even find someone to marry down there, eh?"

Anna hugged me warmly. Then she sat up and frowned. "What is it? What's the matter?"

She rubbed her ring finger again and drew another "S" in the air.

"Steven?" I asked. She shook her head, bounced off the bed, and walked across the floor, limping and leaning on an invisible stick. Her imitation of him was so perfect it made me shiver. "Ṣeth? What about him? You think I can't marry anyone because I'm already married to Seth."

We sat quietly for a long time, remembering Vienna, remembering his betrayal. Then I lifted my head.

"But that was a long time ago, wasn't it? He might even be dead. I hope so! And if I married someone here, in America, he would never know. And my husband would never know about him. Isn't that so?"

Anna looked doubtful.

13

New Orleans Reverie

THE TEMPERATURE OUTDOORS was in the nineties. Indoors it was slightly cooler because of the tall live oak trees that shaded the house, but tempers in my music room on the second floor were still frayed and short.

David had arrived promptly on the dot of eleven for our daily session. We still worked every day even though I was not planning to perform soon. We had found that the intense heat in New Orleans in the summertime made work impossible after noon, and by the time the days cooled off, in the evening, I had other things to occupy my time.

But at eleven-fifteen on that particular day I still had not sung a note. Yet another Theatrical Consultant had come to pester me. This one, a Monsieur Legrange, said he would be satisfied with only a third of the profits after each concert, instead of the half I had come to expect.

"And how do you propose to earn your third?" I asked him.

"I would arrange everything for you, Baroness!" he said eagerly. "Hotels, food, rehearsal space, the finest pianos, the best theaters, advertising, interviews!"

Anna came in with another calling card on a silver salver. I put it aside without even reading it. Where did these people come from?

"After you sing in New Orleans," Legrange went on, "we'll travel up the river by steamboat, playing every little town—"

Anna pulled at my arm. I shook her off and said impatiently, "For Heaven's sake, Anna, can't it wait until later?" She shrugged and went out, casting me a smug look over her shoulder.

I turned to Legrange. At the piano, David Thatcher was scribbling notes on an opera score. I took a breath.

"What if I don't feel like playing in these little towns?" I asked Legrange. "Suppose you make me an engagement three months from now and in three months I do not feel like singing? I came here not to perform but to rest. If I had signed some stupid paper and agreed to do a concert here, I would not be resting. I would be working, working, working. Isn't that right, David? I work, work, work anyway because I love to sing, but nowadays I sing for myself and for my friends, not for strangers. Perhaps I shall never perform in public again. Who knows?"

"Oh, Baroness," moaned Legrange, "that would be a great tragedy!"

"Yes, you think so because you can see your third of the gross receipts flying out the window. If I do not work, you do not get your share, right? But for me there is nothing tragic about living in this beautiful city and meeting its people in my home and not having to look at them from the stage. I like this city. Suppose I decided I want to stay here for the next three months or the next three years? What would happen to my engagements then?" I demanded.

Legrange stuttered an incoherent reply. David plunked at the piano keys and hummed to himself.

"I will tell you, Monsieur Legrange, ever since I came to this country I have sung where I wanted to sing. I arrange these things myself, with David's help, and I do not get thirty-three and a third percent, Monsieur Legrange. I do not get fifty percent. I get the whole thing! Why should I pay you for doing things that I can so easily do for myself? Do you think I pay for space in the newspapers? Only for the smallest box to announce the date and time of performance, and the reporters take care of the rest. I pay nothing for that. Do you think I cultivate notoriety because I like to be stared at and pointed at and jeered at? Of course I don't mind because this notoriety attracts people to my concerts who would not otherwise come. Isn't that right, David?''

"Yes, Baroness." Plunk, plunk. Scribble.

"And once these people come they are treated to the most beautiful music man has composed and woman has sung. I am performing a great public service! I am bringing Art to people in this country who have never seen Art! And Beauty! These people go away from my concerts and they feel as though they have seen a fairy princess. A Baroness! A real, live Baroness has touched their lives! A beautiful woman who sings better than the nightingale!"

"That is true, Baroness, that is true!" Legrange quickly agreed.

"Besides," I said bluntly, "I cannot afford you. I do not have a third to spare. I am a poor woman, Monsieur, with many obligations. So many mouths to feed, a house to maintain, a staff—! There is nothing left! You have taken up enough of my time, sir. Good day to you."

He bowed and stumbled out of the room. I forgot all about the visitor who was waiting in the hall. I rubbed my temples.

"Ah, these people will drive me mad. Always someone who wants to take. Is there no one in this world who gives except me? My God, I have a headache already. What would you like to work on?"

"Beethoven." David rooted through a pile of music.

"Beethoven," I grunted, "in this heat! You really are crazy."

I went over to the piano and studied the music through a pair of pince-nez spectacles. David started to play the song, "Adelaide," which was one of my favorites. Music filled the room, the brightest and happiest place in the house. The curtains and upholstery were yellow chintz patterned with lots of birds and flowers. Pillows of many colors were scattered around the floor. Potted palms and ferns stood on pedestals in the corners. Cheerful pictures in gilt frames hung on the pale yellow walls. On a table in the center of the room stood a large brass samovar.

"Forgive me for interrupting," said a masculine voice from the doorway.

"Great Heaven, another pest!" I said, exasperated. I whirled, ready to give the intruder a piece of my mind.

And there stood Steven McClelland, looking cool and immaculate in a white linen suit. His face was deeply tanned, and his blue eyes looked like inviting pools. His hair was lighter than I remembered, sun-bleached.

With a glad cry I tossed my music and spectacles onto the clutter on top of the piano and went forward to greet him.

"Oh, my dear friend! What a wonderful surprise!"

We clasped hands warmly and stood silently for a whole minute, just grinning and admiring each other. I wore a pink dressing gown with thousands of ruffles at the neck, hem, sleeves—all over. Dora had told me that morning that I looked gorgeous, like a giant camellia.

"You are more beautiful than ever," he said in his straightforward way. "How do you do it? Work, work, work?"

I laughed and said, "So you were eavesdropping on my tirade to that man—what was his name, David?"

"Beethoven," growled my accompanist. I performed introductions, then David said, "I'm going down to get some coffee. Do you want some?"

"You drink too much coffee," I scolded him. "Have tea instead."

"I loathe tea." He shambled past the samovar. "I hope that thing blows up someday."

"He's really going to smoke one of his filthy cigarettes," I confided to Steven when David had gone. I took his arm and led him to a plush settee near the samovar.

"He says he didn't have any vices before he met me and now he has hundreds! He even drinks champagne! At least let me offer you some tea, Steven. I know it's dreadfully hot today, but I find it so refreshing." I poured two cups of tea from the small pot on top of the samovar, then diluted them a little with hot water from the spigot at the bottom of the urn. "Ah, it is so good to see you! And you are looking so well, too. Not a bit tired. But listen to me, talking too much!" It was true, I felt as nervous and fluttery as a debutante. I handed him his cup and settled back against the cushions. "How do you like my house? Isn't it grand? I do love it. I was so tired of travelling."

"You're quite famous, I hear," Steven smiled. "I'm very proud of you."

"You are wonderful," I said, pressing his hand. "I knew you would call on me when you came back. How are your children? And your parents? Did your father tell you I danced with him at the President's house? To think, he is Vice-President of the entire country! What an honor!"

"He's no longer Vice-President," Steven told me. "There's a new party in office now. Zachary Taylor is President instead of Polk."

I stared. "So quickly? A new president? Was there a revolution?"

He laughed. "No, there was an election."

"You will think me very stupid. The only things I read in the newspapers are the pieces about me. Ah, your father is so handsome. Like you!"

"He's looking forward to seeing you again," Steven told me. "I'd like everyone to meet you." He grinned suddenly.

"And I would adore to meet—but what are you laughing at?"

"I've found you out," he said. "I read in the newspapers this morning that you can't read a note of music and that you have to learn all your songs by ear. When I came in you were not only reading music, but reading it through spectacles. Dear, dear!"

I laughed merrily. "Yes, it's so silly. I can see a bee on a lamppost at a hundred yards, but those wretched little dots—! I will soon be as blind as David Thatcher. And I tell people that I can't read music because when they hear me sing they will marvel all the more at how wonderful I am. Isn't that wicked?"

"Terribly wicked." He gave me a searching gaze and then dropped his eyes.

"What is it, Steven? Something is bothering you. Please tell me."

"It's not important," he said softly. "I don't want to spoil your fun."

"No, Steven. I couldn't be happy knowing that you were unhappy. Tell me why. I'm so selfish, prattling on like an idiot when you were trying to tell me something."

He sighed deeply. "You've been here three months, since July. And you've received lots of visitors, crowds of admirers. It's been open house. You're so generous you can't turn anyone away without seeing him, like that idiot Legrange. You're very popular with the young bloods of the town, and with their elders, too. You give them music, some food and champagne, and you even have a little gambling, I've heard."

"You're disappointed with me because I've taken up gambling again," I said quickly. "Oh, Steven, I had to! I was spending so much and earning so little. I've even had to sell some of Ludwig's jewels. But it displeases you. I will stop, I promise."

"No, Rhawnie," Steven said reassuringly. "I'm not much of a gambler myself, but I can understand the attraction it holds for you and for other people. Just let me finish.

One of the young bloods who is so smitten with you is my younger brother, Sean."

"Your brother!" I exclaimed. "I didn't even know. There are so many faces, so many names. Sean, you say? He is like you, fair-haired?"

"He's dark, more like—but I'm not concerned about Sean. He's old enough to enjoy himself without hurting anyone. But the last few times he's been here, he's had a young girl with him."

"An undesirable match!"

"Not at all. Our sister, Gabrielle. And my mother feels—we all feel—that the drawing room of a worldly, sophisticated lady is not the most suitable place for an impressionable girl to meet people." He stopped, embarrassed.

"Of course it isn't," I said sympathetically. "I don't blame you for coming to me. I never dreamed—"

Steven said, "We think she's meeting someone here. Sean has helped her—he thought it was a lark—telling us he was taking her to this affair or that play, or to call on some friend or other. But all the time they've been coming here. It's not your fault, Rhawnie. He's a young fool and he won't do it again, or so he says. But we can't keep them prisoner—"

"Who is he?" I asked. "The man she's been seeing. Do you know."

"A Russian. A Prince Boris something—"

"Boris Leontovitch Azubin," I said. "I know him. He's no more a prince than I am a baroness. He's a gambler, and cruel. Oh, this is terrible. Dreadful! Oh, Steven, I am so sorry!" I jumped up and paced the floor. "It will be easy enough to put an end to their meeting here. If it is difficult for them to see each other, the infatuation may just end. We must try. I shall close my house to visitors—to all but the most special people. You must speak sternly to your little brother about his responsibilities to his sister. Azu-

bin, of all people! He is a rogue, that one. I have heard—''
''What?'' Steven urged me. ''What have you heard?''
I shrugged. ''Just a rumor. That he—killed a girl in Paris.'' I saw the stricken look on his face and I ran to him. ''Oh, Steven, it was just a story! A lie, I'm sure of it! Do not worry. Listen, I shall speak to Boris myself, and find out just what his intentions are. I know that kind—he will get bored soon and want to move on. Perhaps I could even buy him off—or seduce him myself!''

Steven laughed and the worry left his face. ''You're a terror, Baroness. I beg you, don't do anything drastic. I'm sure we're worrying about nothing.'' We rose together. ''I'll see you again?''

''You are welcome at any time,'' I said, feeling disappointed that he had to leave. ''And do not worry about Gabrielle. Everything will be fine, I promise.''

After he had gone I rang the bell for Anna. ''From now on I am not at home to anyone, do you understand, Anna? Only to Steven and members of his family. Tell everyone else that I am preparing to sing and that I need rest and privacy. But if Prince Azubin should call—I am home to him.''

I sighed and walked to the window. I had forgotten how really handsome Steven was. And so kind and gentle.

''I wonder,'' I murmured, ''if he would have come to see me if he hadn't had that trouble with his sister. I think not. That chateau was far away, and he was not himself. He was playing at being a secret agent, an adventurer. But here he is himself again, a respectable man with a family and a good name and duties and responsibilities. He won't want to associate with the Baroness of Ravensfeld now. Well, Anna,'' I said aloud, ''no more gambling. I'll have to work for my living again. Send David up and send for my dressmaker. I must have a new gown for the concert. Something really special.''

David shambled in five minutes later. ''You mean you really are going to sing today? I don't believe it. Your friend didn't stay long, did he?''

"I am going to do a concert here after all," I announced. "After Christmas, I think, when the social season begins. And I want the program to be brilliant, is that clear? These people are cultured, they appreciate fine music. They have had opera here for centuries! I want Beethoven, Mozart, Brahms! Only the best!"

"You mean you aren't going to thrill them with 'Home, Sweet Home?' " he asked sarcastically. "That's the best part."

"I will do Liszt's 'Five Gypsy Songs,' but no more. You don't have to mock my show of good taste!"

"I'm not mocking. I'm just astonished that I've taught you something after all this time." He sat down at the piano and rippled off some quick arpeggios.

Prince Boris Azubin called on me two days later. I received him in the drawing room downstairs and ordered tea. He was no longer young, about thirty-five, and his face reflected his dissipated life-style. His blond hair was thinning at the crown and at the temples. He had deep creases in his cheeks, like jowels. And his pale grey eyes were enmeshed in a fine red web, the result of hours of peering at playing cards through a fog of cigar smoke. Even though I did not feel attracted to him myself, I could see how a young girl like Gabrielle McClelland might find his bored, worldly air fascinating.

"You have gone into seclusion, I hear," Boris said. "A shame. Everyone will miss the brilliant evenings spent in your charming company."

"Ah, yes," I gave a martyred sigh. "I'm afraid I must deprive myself of these diversions for a few months."

"I am sure you won't deprive yourself unduly," he said dryly.

"I was surprised to find such a fine gentleman as yourself in a provincial city like this. Don't you find it dull?"

"I could never find any city dull where you are, Baroness," he said with glib gallantry. "You are the most charming woman I've met since I came to America. It didn't surprise me to learn that you were Russian."

"Half-Russian," I corrected him. "But enough to make me charming, eh? Well, now that I have closed my house to you immoral revelers, what will you do with yourself? Shall you move on, to a new city?"

Boris shrugged. His eyes were hooded, like a turtle's, and his lashes were as pale as his hair.

"I take my amusement where I can find it," Boris said wearily. "I confess I have found other attractions in this city besides yourself, Baroness."

"Have you? Tell me about her."

Azubin grinned. It gave his face a beaky look. "I didn't think you would be interested in my little conquests. But as a matter of fact, I have captured the heart of the only daughter of a very prominent citizen—a man who used to be Vice-President of the United States!"

"Really!" I tried to sound impressed. "How clever you are, Prince. But surely she is only a dull, provincial girl with little conversation and experience. I fear you will tire of her rather soon."

"I could never tire of her fortune," the Prince grinned wolfishly. "Her esteemed parent has vast wealth."

"Ah," said I, enlightened at last, "so you want to marry her! Admirable, Prince. I congratulate you."

"You know better than that. But surely a Vice-President would be willing to part with a little of his wealth, just to keep an unwelcome suitor from forcing his attentions on his daughter. Wouldn't you think?"

"I think you'll be lucky if her brothers don't kill you," I said.

"Fortunately duelling has been outlawed here," he said smugly. "You know her brothers, do you? And you were the lucky recipient of a visit from that prig, Steven. He is following in his father's footsteps. They say he could be the governor of the state in a few years."

"You say he was here? I do not recall. So many—I don't even know their names."

"Yes," said Boris, moving closer to me. "He called a couple of days ago, and after he left you issued your edict banning further hospitality under your roof. Quite a coincidence, that. I don't suppose he mentioned me?"

"Why should he?" I asked coldly.

Boris picked up my hand and lifted it to his lips. "I thought he might have confided his concern about his sister to you. Did he say how much they would give to buy me off?"

I snatched my hand away. "I don't know what you're talking about!" I snapped. "Listen to me, Prince, no true gentleman would pursue a girl, knowing that her family did not approve. Why don't you spare her this trouble? Leave New Orleans, please. Do it—for me?" I looked at him alluringly from under my lashes.

"For you, Baroness?" he leered at me. "You know I would do anything for you." He boldly put his hand down my bodice. I sat bolt upright but said nothing. "And what will you do for me in return?" he whispered thickly. "Will you give me—this?" He squeezed, hard.

I pushed him away and said angrily, "How dare you! Leave at once!" I was breathing hard. The man revolted me. I could not seduce this creature to save Gabrielle; I couldn't do it to save my own sister. "Get out. You sicken me!"

Boris Azubin stood up and stretched lazily. "I'm sorry we couldn't come to some sort of agreement, Baroness. There might have been circumstances under which I might have been persuaded to give up my lovely Gabrielle."

"How much do you want?" I asked through gritted teeth.

"Ten thousand dollars would do for a start," he said with a casual shrug. "Not too much to ask for the virginity of a beautiful girl."

"I won't have any money to spare until after my concert in December," I said truthfully. As it was I would have to

359

pawn or sell some jewels to get enough money to live on until then. "But you shall have the money then, I promise you. Just pledge to me that you will not try to see her again."

"What? Deny myself the pleasure of her company for over two months, on the strength of a promise from a woman like you? A Gypsy whore?"

I leaped to my feet and slapped his face. He lunged at me and put his hands around my throat. His thumbs dug into my larynx.

"I could fix you so you'd never sing again," he said angrily. "Not even a note. I could make you mute, like that servant-girl of yours." His eyes burned.

"Listen, Boris Leontovitch," I said in a gagging whisper, "I'll get the money sooner—in just a few days—ten thousand!" I would go to Steven, he would help me.

"I don't want your money, Baroness," he sneered, pushing me back so that I fell against the tea cart. China smashed, tea and cream spilled. "I'm having too much fun with little Gabrielle to give her up so soon. She is beautiful and headstrong and impetuous. What she has to give me is beyond price."

"Devil!" I croaked. I put my hand to my throat. My neck ached and I wondered if he had hurt my voice. "Get out of here before I murder you!"

He laughed lightly and made a mocking bow. When he was gone I sat down wearily and rubbed my throat. Boris was a devil, thoroughly corrupt, completely amoral. I had underestimated him. I had failed utterly and miserably. I was a fool. I hoped Gabrielle would act like a sensible girl and listen to her parents' counsel. I had done all I could.

I tried to sing, to test my voice.

"Come away, come away—." I sang softly at first, then more loudly. "Come away, Little Paprika, with me!"

I closed my eyes and sighed deeply. My voice was all right. The swine hadn't done any harm.

I was rather surprised to receive a note from Steven the

next day, inviting me to dine with him. I made David handle all my correspondence because I had great difficulty reading script in English. We met at Felix's, one of the city's finer restaurants. I felt constrained with him and a little nervous. I was sure that he really didn't want to have anything to do with me, that he just wanted to find out how I had fared with Boris.

We chatted about inconsequential things. I told him about my small victory over the managers of the French Opera House, who, "as a rule," didn't permit solo recitalists to appear on their stage but who made an exception because I was such a "well-considered *artiste*." I drank a lot of champagne but it had no effect on my spirits. I wanted to ask Steven if he ever thought about our nights together at the chateau, but I didn't dare. I didn't want to be rebuffed, and I didn't want him to know that I thought about them—with longing.

"You're rather subdued this evening, Rhawnie," Steven observed. "I hope you're not concerned about your reception here. Don't be. You'll conquer New Orleans as you've conquered the rest of the country."

So kind, so sweet. He always said the right thing.

"I talked to Boris Azubin the other day," I said, twisting my wine glass by the stem. The candlelight gleamed on my filigreed gold bracelets. I wore a high choker on my neck to hide the blue bruises Boris' fingers had left. "I'm afraid I made rather a mess of things, Steven," I confessed glumly. "He was—unreceptive."

"Did he hurt you?" Steven asked quickly, putting down his knife.

"Oh, no! He was just rude, that's all. But he refused to stop seeing Gabrielle. I might even have fired his determination. He will continue to behave badly now, just to spite me."

Unselfconsciously I put my hand to my throat. Steven saw the movement, and reaching around behind me he unfastened the choker, which fell into my salad dish. I tried to cover the vivid purple marks with my hand.

"An accident," I explained lamely. "David Thatcher and I were trying to discover the exact location of the upper register—"

"Swine," Steven said darkly. I knew who he meant. His lips tightened with anger and he threw down his napkin. The waiter cleared and brought dessert, but a pall had descended over us that not even trout *meunière* and *mousse au chocolat* could dispel.

"Was anything wrong with the meal, Monsieur McClelland?" the headwaiter asked anxiously as we stood up to leave.

Steven assured him graciously that everything had been perfect and that we would return when we could do justice to the cuisine. As we stood on the sidewalk outside the restaurant, waiting for Steven's carriage, Boris Azubin strolled by, swinging his cane and whistling cheerfully as though he didn't have a care in the world.

"Well, well," he said lightly, "the two conspirators, caught in the act. You really shouldn't associate with her, Monsieur McClelland. You'll damage your reput—"

Steven snatched the cane out of Boris' grasp and started to thrash him with it. The slender ebony stick snapped on the fourth or fifth blow, and then Steven used his fists. He was like a different man when he was enraged, and he was terrifying in his violence. Boris squealed like a pig and cowered like a dog.

"Stop him! Stop him before he kills me!"

I put my arms around Steven's shoulders and pulled him away. "Let him go," I implored. "You will only make trouble for yourself, Steven. Let him go!"

Steven allowed me to drag him away from the snivelling Boris. "If you ever touch this woman again I'll murder you," he said slowly. "And if I catch you near my sister—"

"You'll have me arrested?" Boris sneered. Now that the

danger was past he could afford to be flippant. "On what charge?"

"Don't worry about the charge," Steven said. "A man doesn't need an excuse to exterminate vermin."

A crowd had gathered. I heard scandalized whispers: "It's Steven McClelland! What happened? Who's that with him? Not that singer!"

Boris limped away through the crowd and Steven's carriage pulled up. We climbed inside and rode in silence back to my house on Esplanade Street, not far from the Mississippi. The carriage drew to a halt.

"I meant it," Steven said, breaking the silence. "I will kill him if he bothers either of you again."

I touched his hand. "He's not a complete fool, Steven," I said gently. "He's a coward. He'll go away, I'm sure of it. It's over now and your sister is safe. He's such a villian— she could never love him." I could see that the incident had disturbed and upset him. He was unaccustomed to violence. "Will you come in with me, for coffee?"

He shook his head. "Another time, Rhawnie. I still have work waiting for me at home." He walked me to my door and saw me safely inside. He seemed preoccupied and distant. We wished each other good-night and he turned to go. He looked back at me and said unexpectedly, "I'm glad you're here." And then he went away.

We saw each other a few times after that. We dined together and went to the theater. But he always made excuses when I invited him to come into the house, and the only kisses I got were sweet, sisterly pecks on the cheek. I was in agony. I wanted to throw myself at him, and kiss and caress him until he shouted for mercy, but I didn't. I was certain that he would be put off by a brazen show of lust. It was only logical: nice women don't behave like whores; nice men don't patronize whores. Steven McClelland was a nice man; if I behaved in too forward a fashion, he wouldn't want to see me anymore. I liked seeing him, if only to admire him and torment myself because I couldn't have him. Therefore: I had to behave—nicely.

One night as we were strolling arm in arm along the levee near my house, after a very satisfactory meal at Felix's, he said.

"I ran into your friend last night, on Royal Street. After midnight."

"Which friend? Boris?"

"No, your pianist. David Thatcher."

"Ah. I wonder what he was doing, prowling around after dark like a cat? I have often thought of following him when he left the house, just to see what he does in his spare time. He's very secretive." I shrugged. "Perhaps he takes a constitutional after dinner. He wasn't with a young lady, was he?"

"No, he was alone. "I'm—confused. I thought he lived—in your house?"

"David?" I laughed. "No, no. He says that the two or three hours we spend together each day are all his sanity can take. I asked him once, in jest, of course, how he kept himself from falling in love with me. He said that not only was he smarter than most men, he was more near-sighted. He's very insulting, but I keep him because he plays better than anyone, except Liszt. I tell him he plays better than Liszt, though, because men like flattery. And there isn't anything else about him that I can flatter believably—oh!"

He pulled me around and kissed me soundly.

"What was that for?" I asked weakly.

"For being yourself. And because I'm an ass and an idiot. I won't say any more."

Then he slipped my arm through his and we continued our walk, as if nothing had happened. My little imp of desire kept shouting at me to do something, but I couldn't. His closeness paralyzed me, and only after he had left me and I was preparing for bed did I kick myself and curse myself for not taking advantage of an opportunity when it presented itself.

"He was jealous!" I said amazed. "He was jealous—of David!" And I hugged myself and buried my face in my pillows.

I didn't hear from him for two weeks. Then in late October I received a charming note from his mother inviting me to spend a week at Highlands, their plantation upriver. She said that Steven and I would be coming up together.

We travelled on the steamboat *Eulalie*, which was about a hundred feet long, decorated with freshly-painted, elaborately carved woodwork, with promenade decks and lushly-appointed salons and staterooms. Anna and I agreed that travel on the river was much superior to ocean travel. The trip to Highlands took only a few hours, and as we rounded a bend in the Mississippi, Steven pointed out a red brick mansion perched on a knoll above the river.

"The only house like it in Lousiana. My great-grandfather was a stableboy who wanted to be an aristocrat. He grew up in England. This house is an exact copy of his master's house. It's very plain, don't you think? But rather beautiful. Simple, symmetrical and beautiful."

He rested his elbows on the railing and turned his head so that he could look under my broad-brimmed hat. I smiled down at him and the breeze on the river whipped my shirts and sent my ribbons streaming. The sun still felt warm, but not so warm as Steven's smile.

The steamboat anchored at a wharf at the bottom of the knoll and put out its gangplank. A crowd of black men shouted greetings to Steven, and they rolled enormous barrels up the ramp to the boat.

"Molasses," Steven explained. "We had a fine sugar cane crop this year. Some of those barrels will go as far as New York."

"And those are your slaves?" I asked. Two black men in livery smiled to us and carried our luggage up to the house. Steven and I followed at a slower pace, and Anna brought up the rear.

Steven said, "All our workers are free men. My mother refuses to have a slave on the place, and whenever she hears about a fugitive, or a slave who is mistreated by his owner, she shelters him and buys him and then gives him his freedom. They all adore her. We pay them a wage and provide living quarters. Most of them grow their own food in small plots near their houses. Those little cottages over there." He pointed. "My Uncle Phillippe lives near here—he's the one who owned the chateau at Lesconflair, remember? His plantation is La Rêve. We passed it just before we docked. Philippe is married to Colette who is the sister of mother's first husband. It's rather complicated. I'll let Mother unravel the family history for you."

The grounds were well-shaded and beautifully landscaped. A small white gazebo stood at the highest point overlooking the river. As we sauntered up to the house we heard a shout and Sean McClelland raced towards us from one of the outbuildings. He was about nineteen, thin and dark but with flashing blue eyes, like Steven's. I remembered him from my soirees. When he greeted me his expression became calf-like and he blushed a little.

"Monsieur Sean," I said sweetly, "it is such a joy to see you again! Will you take my arm? I am feeling rather fatigued." He looked as if he would die of pleasure. My eyes caught Steven's and he winked at me.

A butler opened the door for us and when we stepped into the cool interior of the house Sean bellowed, "They're here, Mother!" He gave me an apologetic look and said, "Excuse me, Baroness. I'll go and get her. We expected you on the afternoon boat, Steve. You might have told us. The Guv'nor's not even here now. He went down to La Rêve a couple of hours ago."

Steven laughed and said to me, "Would you like to see your room or shall we have some refreshment first?" I opted for tea. Sean darted away, shouting, and George, the butler, said he would show Anna where she and I would be sleeping.

Steven led me into a drawing room. The ceilings were high, the walls a creamy white, and the furnishings were old but elegant, and highly polished.

Gabrielle came in while Steven and I were admiring the view. She threw a stranglehold around her oldest brother's neck and hugged him tightly. When she saw me she dropped a curtsy and made a short formal speech of welcome.

I took her hand and kissed her on the cheek. "It is wonderful to see you again, Gabrielle. I am so glad that I will be able to know you better. What a pretty dress! I wish I could wear yellow, but on me it looks vile. You are fortunate to have such vivid coloring."

She looked pleased. She was small and dark, with curling black hair and large brown eyes, which looked suspiciously as if they had been weeping. I didn't doubt it. She was sixteen and at sixteen *gorgio* girls cry a lot.

We heard a musical laugh and a small woman came briskly into the room. "Every day Gaby says, 'Mother, why isn't my hair yellow and straight like Steve's?' I hope you can talk some sense into her. How do you do, Baroness? I am Elise McClelland."

She embraced me warmly and then stood back and said, "You're right children, she is beautiful! You know, my dear, ordinarily I detest tall women. My husband's first wife was tall and blond."

Gabrielle groaned, "Oh, Mother!"

"I know, isn't it awful to be so prejudiced?" said her mother cheerfully.

I said, "I have always felt sorry for short women, until now. I envy you your beautiful family, Madame."

She laughed merrily and led me to a sofa. She was energetic and humorous, and she still looked very young. There were only a few grey strands in her dark hair, and fewer lines in her face. She must have looked a lot like Gabrielle does now, I thought, when she was young. She could have been one of her own children, so easy and relaxed was her manner with them.

George served tea. As she poured, Elise said eagerly, "I must know the truth, did you really ride a white charger bareback down Broadway in New York?"

"Not at all, Madame," I replied. "The horse had a saddle."

We all laughed. Sean entered. He had put on a coat and he had tried to plaster down his dark curls with water. As his hair dried the locks sprang up, willful and unruly, and he kept trying to crush them down with the palm of his hand. Finally Garth McClelland returned from his ride. He had with him a little girl of eight or nine, who launched herself into Steven's arms with a happy cry.

"This is Marie," he told me. "The boys are in school in Massachusetts, but they'll be home for Christmas. This is the Baroness Rhawnie, dearest."

"How do you do, Baroness?" Marie said politely, dropping a curtsy. I did the same, and we shook hands. "Welcome to Highlands!"

Garth McClelland came forward. "I reiterate, Baroness. Welcome to Highlands!"

"It is good to see you again. Your son tells me you have lost your job. I'm so sorry."

Everyone laughed and Elise McClelland said. "I'm not a bit sorry. I have him all to myself now." She put her arms around her husband's waist and hugged him and kissed the top of her head.

"I haven't told you," Garth said, "I've decided to run for President."

"I won't hear of it!" Elise cried. "Not that you'd stand a chance of being elected. You're a threat and a troublemaker to the people down here."

"You're the threat and the troublemaker," her husband corrected her. "I'm just guilty by association."

They obviously adored each other. Elise never left his side, but fussed over him and kissed him frequently. I saw Gabrielle squirm and turn scarlet at her parents' open display of affection, but none of the rest of us minded. Steven gave me a look that made me feel warm, too. We could be like that, I thought wistfully. And then I buried the wish deep inside me. It could never happen.

Sean asked his father if he could live in town. "Things are pretty dull around here this time of year, Guv'nor."

"You should be preparing yourself to go back to school," Garth said. "You're going to the University of Virginia after Christmas, remember?"

"They'll only send me home again," Sean said airily. "Old Palmer at Harvard says I'm a hardened case."

"Make an effort to reform," Steven advised his brother. "Perhaps you can impress the Baroness by being a steady, serious college man."

Sean looked at me and blushed slightly. "You wouldn't care about that, would you, Baroness?"

I said, "To the contrary, Monsieur Sean, I am most impressed by learning because I have so little myself."

"Not so!" protested Steven. "You speak four languages fluently, plus Romany; you know more about music and art than any woman I've met, and you can quote the classics. I'd say that Sean had a lot of catching up to do."

"And you can play faro like the devil," Sean said reverently. Clearly that was the accomplishment that he valued most. "I wish college could teach me that."

"No more town for you until we move back at Christmas," Garth told Sean. "You can't possibly get into trouble in the canebrake and the swamps."

Sean cast a furtive look at Gabrielle and said, "That wasn't my fault."

The girl's cheeks flamed. She stood up stiffly and said in a voice that threatened tears, "Please excuse me. I promised Aunt Colette that I'd finish that embroidery—" She pressed her knuckles to her mouth and ran out of the room.

"Oh, Sean," said Elise reproachfully. She turned to me. "I'm sorry, my dear. I thought that with three boys I had suffered all that a mother could suffer when it came to raising children. And then I had a daughter."

"Three?" I murmured, surprised.

But before she could explain Sean said, "I don't know why everybody treats me like a cad; it was all Gaby's idea from the beginning!"

"That's enough, Sean," said his father wearily. "Where is that devil now, I wonder?"

I said, "I heard yesterday that he had left the city on a steamboat. After Steven beat him—" David had told me. He was a mine of information sometimes.

They hadn't heard about that. A servant came in and took Marie away to clean her up after her ride with her grandfather, and then Steven explained what happened.

"Damn, Steve!" said Sean admiringly. "I wish I'd done it!"

"Watch your language, Sean," said Elise mechanically. "Well, it's over. Don't tell her, anyone. She'll just have to get over him in time. But if he should come back—" She paused and sighed, "She's so stubborn!"

Garth McClelland chuckled fondly. "Like her mother."

"I feel dreadful about the whole business," I said unhappily.

"But it's not your fault, Rhawnie!" Elise assured me. She pressed my hand fondly. "If she hadn't met him at your house she would have found some other place to meet him—at the opera or at the house of a friend. You mustn't blame yourself."

"She looks so thin," Steven said worriedly. "She's breaking her heart over him!"

"I know," his mother said. "I've tried to speak to her about him. But you know how it is with mother and daughter. She's convinced that I'm cold and heartless and that I don't have any understanding and sympathy." She turned to me. "Gabrielle is fond of you, Rhawnie. She adores you and wants to be like you. Do you think—"

"You want me to talk to her?" I said. "I will try,

370

Madame. I have known other men like Boris. They're not worth the pain— Yes, I will try.''

"Thank you," she said. "I don't blame my entire family for falling in love with you. Even my husband! You should have seen the letter he wrote after you sang in Washington!"

"At least I wasn't evasive, like Steve," Garth replied. "Because I had nothing to hide."

We all looked at Steven, who grew red. Then Sean started to laugh, and we all joined in. The mood in the drawing room grew light and happy again.

I found an opportunity to be alone with Gabrielle the very next day. I found her sitting at the piano in the drawing room. She rested her cheek on her left hand while with her hand she picked out the melody of a very sad love song. I put my hand on her shoulder and said softly,

"You are sad about your Boris, aren't you?"

She stopped playing and put her hands in her lap. "What do you mean? I wasn't thinking about him at all."

"He went away very suddenly, didn't he? And you have heard nothing from him."

She jumped up. "I know he would have written or called here, if he could. It's not like him to behave like this! I think something must have happened to him." Then she straightened her back and tossed her black curls. "But why should I care? I'm not in love with him. I know what you're thinking! And—and you will excuse me for saying this, Baroness, but I really don't see that it's any of your affair."

"It is my affair because I can see your pain, and I feel deeply for you," I said gently. I took her hand and led her to a sofa. "Oh, Gabrielle, I know Boris. You mustn't make yourself unhappy over him—"

"Everyone is against me!" she cried, pulling her hand away and twisting around to confront me. Her cheeks burned. "Everyone! Mother and Father, and Steven—and you! Only Sean has shown the slightest feeling and understanding for me!"

"That is because your brother is a fool," I said crisply. "He thought it was a lark, but he doesn't think so now. We love you, Gabrielle, and we know—"

"You don't know Boris! No one knows as I do. I love him, Rhawnie! Oh, why do I feel this way," she said despairingly. "Why does it have to hurt so much?"

She covered her face with her hands. I waited until she was calmer."

"Listen to me," I said intently. "I must speak, even though you will be angry with me and probably hate me for it. I have seen a lot of the world. I have known a lot of men. I know people. From my very earliest childhood I have made it my business to observe them and study them and know all about them. And I know Boris. No, we have not been lovers," I said quickly when I saw the fear and suspicion in her face, "never that. But when I was very young, when I was your age, I gave my heart to a man who was like him in every way. Do you know what happens when you do that, when you give your heart to a man who has no heart? He destroys you. He has never known love and he sneers at it and says it doesn't exist. I was warned about him, by someone who knew men. And in my heart I knew what he was. But I didn't listen.

"Boris is a gambler, as my man was. Boris has slept with hundreds of women in his life, as my man did. You don't believe me? You are shocked? I am sorry to shock you, my dear girl, but facts are facts. How can a man love one woman, who has known so many? What can one woman's love and sacrifice mean to him? Nothing. Nothing!" She started to rise and I pulled her back. "Oh, Gabrielle, I want to be your friend! I know what you are thinking and feeling. You burn for him, and you tell yourself that if he ever comes back to you, you will follow him anywhere. You tell yourself you don't care about the cost in terms of pain or shame. Won't you let me tell you the cost? He won't marry you. And if he does, he won't stay with you. I know! He will take away your youth and your beauty. He'll revel in them, and he'll leave you. Did you know that this wonderful Boris of yours tried to make love to me?''

She went white, then red. ''I don't believe you,'' she said in a low voice. She stood up and stared down at me coldly. ''You're lying. Everything you've said to me has been a lie. Mother put you up to this! And Steve! I suppose you thought that you could worm your way into the family if you did this little favor for them. I know what you're up to, Baroness. You have your cap set for Steve, only he's too blind and stupid to see it. He doesn't know what kind of woman you are. He doesn't know how you lie—''

''What do you know about anything, you silly child?'' I was on my feet, too, and I was angry. ''You're a child, a baby. What your brother does is his affair, not yours. He's a good man, the best. I haven't lied to him about myself and I'm not lying to you now. Why should I? I have nothing to gain by turning you against me. Yes, your mother asked me to speak to you. But if she hadn't I would have spoken anyway, if only to spare you some of the pain and torment I have known. Think about what I have said, Gabrielle. Boris doesn't love you, he told me so.''

''No, no, no!'' She covered her ears and closed her eyes. ''I won't listen to any more lies from you! I won't! He loves me, he loves me!''

She ran clumsily out of the room. I could hear her pounding up the stairs. I knew she would cry and cry until she was weak. And I knew she would never believe a word I had said. I doubted that I would, either, in her place. Love is stubborn, and single-minded. I sighed. I had failed with Gabrielle and I had failed with Boris. My luck was not running very well.

On the day before we planned to return to the city, Steven invited me to go boating with him on the river. The cook packed a picnic for us and we set out. Steven rowed towards an island in the middle of the river and I sat in the bow like a blond Cleopatra, dragging my hand in the water.

"It's a wonderful, beautiful day," I breathed.

Our little boat bumped up against the shore of the island. Steven jumped out to secure it and then he helped me onto dry land.

We found a grassy spot shaded by a tall live oak. Steven spread out a blanket and I bent over the hamper.

"Shall we have a look inside? Your mother told me there was something very special for us. Ah, champagne! And a cord! Wait, there's a little note attached. I will try to read it: 'Tie one end of rope to bottle; fasten other end to tree,' " I read with laughable slowness. " 'Im—immerse bottle in water for one hour.' " I laughed and carried out the instructions. Steven stretched out on the blanket, his hands locked behind his head. He watched me. "Now," I said when my task was finished, "what are we supposed to do while the champagne is chilling?"

"Come and sit with me." He rolled on his side and patted the blanket. I obeyed him. He leaned on his elbow and looked up at me. After a moment he reached up and removed my hat and tossed it aside. "That's better. It hid your face in shadow."

I felt the color rise to my cheeks. "Isn't this silly?" I said. "I have stood up in front of thousands of people and sung for them and never felt a qualm. But when you look at me like that, it terrifies me."

"Why?" he asked gently.

"I don't know," I whispered.

He took my hand and planted a soft kiss on the palm. The cuff of my sleeve slid up, exposing my scar, and I tried to jerk my hand back. But he held it tight and kissed the scar, too.

"I've been composing a speech for days," he said without looking at me. "Especially for this occasion. And I can't remember a word of it. So I'll have to improvise."

My heart stopped. I held my breath. He looked into my eyes and said, "I love you, Rhawnie. I want to marry you."

Tears came to my eyes. When I found my voice I said brokenly, "No, Steven. No. It's impossible! I'm married already, you know that."

"It is possible," he said evenly. "You'll get a divorce." He sat up and spoke confidently. He was back on solid ground now, in the realm of Law rather than Love, and he didn't have to grope for words. "It won't be difficult. I have friends abroad, lawyers, in England and in France. We can get to work on it—"

"But I don't even know where he is," I said weakly, "or if he's alive or dead!" My hands were trembling, like my voice, and I kneaded my skirts. "I feel—so strange. Oh, Steven, hold me!"

I put my arms around his waist and rested my head on his shoulder. He held me tight and I could feel his breath on my hair.

"It's not right, Steven," I said, "you know what I am. You are ambitious. You could go far. But not if you're married to a woman like me. And if I were divorced—! People in this country have very strong feelings about that."

"If we can't find this man we can work on an annulment. That would negate the marriage completely. It would be as though it never existed. Even a French court wouldn't hesitate to dissolve a marriage like yours. You were young, he was a notorious rogue, he deserted you and your infant. It can be done, Rhawnie. Honestly. Just leave it to me. Do you think I care what people think, what they say? I know what kind of woman you are, and I love you. Not in spite of these things, but because of them. Because they're part of you. Scandal is nothing; scandal is—air. Stories, gossip, rumor. It's cruel and it hurts, but it can be weathered. If you don't believe me, ask Mother. Scandal might have slowed Father's career a little, but it didn't stop him. And it won't stop me."

I shook my head, dazed. "You are a tiger, Steven! You are irresistible!"

He laughed and kissed me lightly. "I'm glad to hear it. I

have an idea about what we can do while we're waiting for the champagne to cool. I'm sure it's just what my mother had in mind.''

''Your mother is a most remarkable lady,'' I said.

He laughed. ''She's a pirate!''

I blinked at him. ''What did you say? A pirate? You're joking—''

''No, I'm not,'' he said laughing. ''The scourge of the Gulf, before the War of 1812. She sailed with Jean Lafitte. You see what I mean about scandal.''

''Before she married your father. That's remarkable,'' I said lamely.

I should have pursued the matter right them. I should have said, ''You have another brother named Seth.'' But I didn't. I told myself that it was a coincidence, nothing more. I didn't want to know anything beyond what I knew already: that Steven loved me and wanted to marry me. He was a good man. It seemed at that moment that all I had ever wanted in my life was marriage to a Good Man. And now it was happening. And I didn't want anything to spoil my chance. I pushed my worries away, Gypsy fashion, and gave myself up to the enjoyment of the moment.

We fell back on the blanket, laughing together, caressing each other.

''This is the only time of year when outdoor trysting is possible,'' Steven informed me. ''Too late for bugs and too early for winter.''

''You are very devious and clever,'' I said. ''You brought me out here deliberately to seduce me!''

''No, the seduction was to take place only if you consented to be my wife. Do you consent? If you refuse I'll pack you back into the boat and take you home.''

''No more kissing?'' I sighed wistfully.

''None.''

''I'm not very honorable,'' I said. ''I take bribes. Yes, I will marry you.''

"Then you shall have your reward."

"A while later I said," I have bewitched you. You never would have asked for marriage if I hadn't wanted you to. You are in my power."

"Absolutely, irrevocably, and forever," Steven agreed. He pulled me down on top of him. A curtain of golden hair blocked out sunlight. "Perhaps you're right," he said. "You have bewitched me. Steady, reliable, serious-minded Steven McClelland has fallen in love with a Gypsy singer!"

We toasted each other with champagne. "I thought you were embarrassed about what happened in France," I told him. "I thought you didn't want to remember—I've been very foolish, too. But you never referred to that time until today! How polite he is, I said to myself. I was very irritated with you. Will you come and visit me when we get back to the city? Will you spend whole nights in my bed and slip away before dawn so that we can keep our love a secret? Will you stop being so good and be a little wicked?"

"I'm leaving for Washington the day after tomorrow," he said regretfully.

"Lawyers!" I made a face. "Bah! When are you coming back?"

"For Christmas, of course. What do you think? Shall we tell them now?"

I shook my head. "No, Steven. Let's wait. Until Christmas."

"Until Christmas."

14

The Prodigal Returns

ON CHRISTMAS EVE, 1849, the McClelland family assembled in their big house on St. Charles Avenue. Steven and I told them that we wanted to marry. We had no intention of making a public announcement because we couldn't marry soon anyway, but we wanted them to know, and to share our happiness.

Garth and Elise seemed genuinely delighted. Sean pretended to nurse a broken heart. Gabrielle gave me a wan smile and a cool sisterly kiss. She still hadn't forgiven me, but she seemed a little friendlier and happier than when I had seen her in October. Her mother and I agreed that she was finally learning to forget Boris. We were as blind as Gabrielle was clever.

Steven had returned from Washington only two days earlier, looking tired and travel-weary. But he had his sons with him, John and Philippe. Both boys resembled him, with their fair hair and blue eyes, but John, the older, was serious and reserved, and Philippe had devils dancing in his eyes. Steven and I had only the briefest time together, but we promised ourselves that after my concert, which was scheduled for December 31, we would go away together, to the country perhaps. I had been very lonely while he was away, and I threw myself into my work so that I wouldn't miss him too much. Steven confessed to me that he had done the same.

Elise McClelland despised the custom of leaving the men to their port and cigars after a meal, and after dinner that night we all went into the drawing room together. A butler passed the port, and Steven and his father smoked happily in the company of their ladies.

"You have such a wonderful family," I said to Elise McClelland.

"We're your family now, my dear," she said happily, squeezing my hand. "I'm so delighted for Steven. He really needs to marry again."

"What about the children?" I asked. "Do you think they will mind—having a stepmother?"

"Oh, no! Marie loves you already, and the boys were very impressed with your coach and six. Those magnificent horses! They were so young when Julie died. They hardly remember her."

"She was a good mother to them, wasn't she?"

"A wonderful girl. Steven has told you about her?"

"Oh, yes. They were happy together. I hope I can make him as happy. He is so good, so kind."

"Do I hear my praises being sung?" Steven leaned over the back of the couch where his mother and I were sitting, and kissed my cheek.

"None of that," said Garth McClelland sternly. "You have to wait until you're married."

"Why should they?" Elise demanded. "We didn't!"

Everyone laughed except Gabrielle, who blushed and wailed, "Oh, Mother!"

"I say, Guv'nor," said Sean, "I think it's a mean thing to send a fellow away just when things are getting lively in town. What ever happens in Charlottesville, Virginia?"

"Boys become men," his father scowled. "At least I hope that's what will happen to you."

"Please try and persuade David to come to our ball tomorrow night," Elise said to me. "Did you know that his father is the governor of Massachusetts? Garth knows him very well. He even studied law for a while—David, that is—but gave it up for music. He's so bohemian!"

"My goodness, Madame," I said astonished, "you have found out more about David Thatcher in one night than I did in nearly two years!" I had dragged David to a dinner party at the house the night before, and Elise had taken him in hand.

Elise slid closer to me and said under her breath, "And I think Gabrielle likes him a little. He certainly seemed taken with her!"

"You're really incorrigible, Mother," said Steven. "Stop matchmaking."

"Why should I? I brought you two together, didn't I?"

"If you mean your transparent little trick with the champagne—"

"I mean that when you got back to New Orleans and heard that Rhawnie was living here, you were reluctant to see her. Weren't you? And so I asked you to go and talk to her about the Gabrielle-Boris thing, and you went, and here you are!" She beamed triumphantly.

"Is this true, Steven?" I twisted around and smiled up at him. "Were you afraid to come and see me?"

He grinned and said, "You were certainly eager to get away from me in France, remember? All that stuff about trying your wings. Well, what about your wings now? I'm about to clip them, and you don't seem to mind."

"No, I don't mind. I'm glad." He put his hands on my shoulders and I pressed one to my cheek.

It was such a happy evening. I really was part of a family again. I was loved. I was wanted. Nothing could go wrong, I was sure of it.

After we had our coffee, Elise persuaded Gabrielle to play the piano while we all sang Christmas songs. Steven had a really fine baritone. We sounded so good together that the rest of the company applauded our rendition of "En Flambeau, Jeannette, Isabelle," one of Elise McClelland's favorite French carols. After the singing Steven and I moved away from the rest of the group. I stood with him in front of the fireplace, my back to the room. We laced our fingers together.

"Everyone was so pleased about us. Are you happy, Rhawnie?" he asked tenderly.

Outside a horse clattered up to the house. Sean wondered who it could be, on Christmas Eve. I think he must have looked out the window, because he shouted something incoherent and ran out of the room.

"I am so happy I could cry," I told Steven truthfully. "To have a family again! It's a wonderful thing, all this love."

"You haven't bought him a new horse, have you?" Elise asked Garth.

"Certainly not. It's the last thing he needs. Have you?"

"You'll never believe it!" Sean shouted from the doorway. "Look! Just look who's here!"

Steven sucked in his breath and grabbed my hands tightly. His face turned pinched and hard. I heard an uneven step and the tap of a cane on the floor. I stopped breathing. I did not have to look around. I knew who had come.

"Seth!" Gabrielle shrieked. "Oh, Seth!"

I was grateful for the commotion produced by his arrival. Everyone crowded around him, laughing and talking and crying. Except Steven, who steadfastly maintained his position beside me. He put his arm around my shoulders as if to protect me. He knows, I thought. He knows, but how?

Then Seth looked up and saw us. His eyes met mine for a moment and I felt my anchor in reality sliding away. I was engulfed by a flood of memories. Memories that swirled around my mind and soul like a poisonous gas, smothering me, sweeping me away from the warm drawing room in New Orleans into another time, another world, where Seth and I had been locked together in a prison of passion.

Once again I felt stripped and naked under those eyes. I was sure that he could read my deepest thoughts and most secret dreams. A chorus of "No's!" thundered inside my head. I should have known that he would sense my new happiness, and that wherever he was in the world, he would come to find me and take it away from me. I wanted to shout at him, to shout out my anger and loathing.

But I didn't shout. I smiled serenely and said, "Will you introduce me to your visitor, Steven?"

I saw Seth's eyebrows lift, ever so slightly. He was thinner and harder looking, clean shaven, without even the mustache he had sported in Europe. There was more grey in his hair. His eyes—his eyes were just like Steven's. And the line of their jaws was identical. Even their noses were similar. Steven had seemed familiar to me. Of course I felt that I had known him for a long time. I had known his opposite number. For they were like opposite sides of the same coin: one fair, the other dark; one kind, the other cruel. Light and shadow. Good—and evil.

His eyes flickered over me appraisingly. He smiled and approached us.

"Welcome home, Seth," Steven said. I was surprised to hear in his voice an echo of my own feelings towards the arrogant, black-hearted devil who stood in front of us. "Rhawnie, this is my younger brother, Seth. Seth this is my fiancée, Rhawnie, Baroness of Ravensfeld."

I extended my hand. "How do you do, Monsieur?" What would he do? What would he say? He would unmask me, I was sure of it. He was a spoiler.

"This is a pleasure and an honor, Baroness," he replied. He lifted my fingers to his lips and his kiss was too long, too lingering. I snatched my hand away as soon as I felt his hold ease. "Well, your fiancée, I congratulate you both. When is the happy day? I'd like to come to the wedding."

He wasn't going to expose me. Not yet. That gave me a little time, a little breathing space.

"We haven't set a date yet," Steven said. "And we haven't made a public announcement. But I thought you should know."

"I appreciate that," Seth said with a little mocking nod. The air between them was electric with feelings that I couldn't understand. I was suddenly aware that while this encounter had been taking place everyone else in the room had fallen silent, watching us—and waiting. But for what?

Then Elise began to laugh and the tension in the room dissolved. She berated her son in good motherly fashion for not writing and remarked on how thin and tired he looked. Garth asked where he had been keeping himself.

"Various places," Seth replied. "I've been gold-mining in California and fomenting revolution in Nicaragua and Cuba lately."

"With old Lopez's boys!" Sean shouted. "You see, Guv'nor, I told you I should have gone with those filibusters! I would have met Seth!"

Steven told me later that the filibusters were adventure-seeking no-accounts who gathered at the Maspero Slave Exchange in New Orleans to plot against the government, to trade tales, to collect money for causes like the liberation of Nicaragua and the annexation of Cuba.

Garth McClelland snorted. "Revolutionaries in short pants."

"Tell me about California, Seth," said Sean eagerly. "Is it true what they say, that the gold's just lying on top of the ground, waiting to be picked up? Oh, I say, Guv'nor, let me take just one more year off from school! I'll make us all rich!"

Seth grinned at his little brother. "You'd have to dig the gold out of the ground first, Sean. Then you'd have to keep yourself from being killed to hang on to it—and your claim. You'd probably come down with scurvy or malaria or dysentery, too."

"It sounds just horrid," Elise declared. "Gold indeed! Just another excuse for men to leave their homes and families to go off gambling and whoring—"

"Mother!" Gabrielle said.

I didn't join the laughter. Garth hugged his wife, who came no higher than his shoulder, and said, "Sounds like just the thing for a man newly retired from politics. I'll hop the next boat—"

The conversation swirled around me. I felt sick. The heat in the room seemed overpowering. Steven and I sat apart from the rest, listening silently to the stories of Seth's adventures. I wondered later how I managed to keep from leaping out of my seat and running from the room. Every so often Seth would shoot a look in our direction. I tried to meet his gaze squarely, without blinking, just to show him that I wasn't afraid. I sensed that Steven, too, was tense and on guard.

Sean was enthralled by his older brother's exploits. He hung on Seth's every word, asked a hundred and one questions, and groaned loudly when his father reminded him that would be time enough for adventure when he had finished his education.

"But why, Guv'nor?" Sean demanded. "Look at Seth. He qualified as a doctor and he's not using his education at all. If you ask me, he paid off those coves at the Sorbonne and in Heidelberg to say he'd done his work and he spent his time having fun."

"Oh, we can't be sure of that, Sean," Steven spoke for the first time. "Maybe Seth's been nursing the miners in California and helping the afflicted in Cuba. Good Dr. Seth."

Seth gave his brother a lopsided grin. "That's right, Steve. I'm one of the world's great humanitarians."

My head was spinning. Seth, a doctor? I would never

have believed it, never. Well, why not He had saved me when I cut my wrists and he had delivered my baby, hadn't he? But I thought doctors were supposed to have more reverence for life, and more compassion. He was such a fraud. If only they knew, these people. They had missed him. They all adored him—except Steven. If only I could tell them the truth.

Gabrielle sat very close to Seth, who petted and teased her and told her how pretty she had become.

"I suppose you have a pack of admirers, Gaby?" I could see that he was fond of her. I had never known him to behave so tenderly towards anyone.

"She could have," Sean put in, laughing, "but she's pining away from love for some Russian cove named Boris. Steve thrashed him and he left town pretty quick."

Gabrielle jumped up, her fists clenched. "Steve!" She looked over at Steven. "You—didn't! How could you! How could you do such a thing? Why didn't you tell me? Oh, I hate you. I hate you!"

Elise put her arms around her daughter and cooed, "There, darling, it's all right. Steven only acted in your best interests. You know how we felt about Prince Azubin. He should have called at the house. His behavior was insulting, to all of us."

Gabrielle pushed her mother away. "You don't understand, any of you! I can't bear it, living with you all!"

Steven stood up and looked at his pocket watch. "It's twenty past eleven. I don't suppose you still want to go to midnight mass, Gaby?"

"Yes," she cried. "I do want to go! Please, Steve?"

"Then you have just enough time to run upstairs and wash your face. Anybody else want to come? Seth?"

Seth declined. Sean decided he would stay home, too, but his mother told him to go.

"To keep Gabrielle company. She's feeling particularly left out tonight, because of Rhawnie and Steven." She turned to Seth. "We're so excited, Seth! I'm glad you are home, so glad. Everything will be fine now, won't it? And you'll get to know Rhawnie and to love her as we do. I'm so happy, darling. This is the most wonderful Christmas present of all!"

He hugged his mother and looked over her head to me. I couldn't read anything in his eyes. He was too good a gambler to give himself away. But I wanted to die on the spot. No good could come of the situation. Someone would be hurt—Steven or his mother or me. It was an intolerable mess.

If I were really brave, I said to myself, I'd speak. Now. But a Gypsy's first impulse is to run from trouble. So I kept silent and bid them good-night, Seth and Elise and Garth, and allowed myself to be marshalled into the carriage with Gabrielle and Sean and Steven. When we had gone half a mile I turned to Steven and told him that I had a headache. He directed the coachman to go to the house on Esplanade Street first.

"I'll come in with you," he said. He asked Gabrielle and Sean to stop for him on the way home from mass. They drove off. I thought that Gabrielle's spirits had recovered rather quickly. She even gave me a little hug before I left the carriage.

Anna opened the door. She was beaming, happy about our engagement, but when she saw our faces she became anxious. I kissed her and asked her to bring some brandy up to the music room and to prepare the samovar. Then Steven and I went upstairs.

I had decided that I had to tell him. I couldn't live, knowing that Seth could expose me at any time. I had to be free of them. I wasn't sure if Steven would still want to marry me after he knew the truth, but I would leave that to him. I had to tell him.

Steven paced the floor. I kneaded my hands. We hardly looked at each other and we didn't speak until after Anna had brought the brandy and started the tea brewing. Then Steven poured himself a large measure of brandy and downed it in one swallow. He followed that with another. This was a bad sign: Steven was not a heavy drinker.

"You didn't tell me about this brother," I said. My voice sounded shaky and out of control. But he didn't seem to notice. "I find it strange that no one in your family ever mentioned him before."

"Not so strange." Steven sipped his second brandy. "The prominent families in New Orleans don't talk about their black sheep. They grieve for their strays, sigh for them, pray for them. But they can't brag about them and so they don't talk about them at all. It's very painful for Mother. We went through a bad time with Seth. She cried a little whenever his name was mentioned. So we just got out of the habit of talking about him, even of thinking about him. It wasn't hard. He wasn't there. We never knew where he was, if he was alive or dead. Like a tom cat that keeps straying farther and farther from home until one day—you never see him again. That's Seth. Never writes. Never sends word. Nothing. But every seven years or so, like the plague, he turns up to cause trouble, to awaken old memories and to reopen old wounds."

"You sound so bitter, Steven," I said wonderingly. "I don't understand. It isn't like you. The minute he came into the room tonight, something happened to you."

Steven put his arms around me. "I love you so," he murmured. "It spoiled your evening, too, didn't it? You feel everything so deeply. Poor darling, your heart is racing."

"I suppose I was rather surprised to see him," I said with greater truth than he knew. Steven, there is something I must tell you," I began.

But he wasn't paying any attention. "Did you see the way he looked at you?" he said angrily. "Arrogant bastard. I wanted to punch his face in." He broke away from me and looked down at his clenched fists. "Look at me," he said disgustedly. "That's what seeing him does to me. Good old steady, reliable Steve McClelland turns into a snarling dog when his own brother comes into the room. Kill the fatted calf, bring out your best wines. Greet the prodigal with open arms! It's laughable, isn't it? And sickening."

He was really distraught. I fussed over him and made him sit on the plush settee near the samovar. I put another glass of brandy into his hand and said, "Why, Steven? Tell me about it, please. What has he done that is so terrible? What is so awful, so dreadful that you can't forgive after many years? Whatever is past is past. It is a weak and foolish thing to carry resentment from year to year. Leave it. Forget it."

He groped for my hand. I sat close to him. "I know I'm a damned fool. Blast him! Why did he have to come back now?"

Silently, secretly, I echoed his sentiments.

He said, "Seth is three years younger than I am. We've always been in competition, as far back as I can remember. He always instigated it, though. He was always daring me, challenging me. He had to prove that he was as good as I was at everything, even though most of the time we were growing up he was a couple of inches shorter and a few pounds lighter. He had to run faster, play harder, take greater chances. We were devils, both of us. I don't know how Mother put up with us."

I smiled thinly. "That's what mothers are for, dearest."

"You saw how he limped?" Steven asked. I nodded. "It was my fault. He'll have that limp until the day he dies. And I did it to him.

"We were still very young," Steven said. "It was the summer before I went off to Harvard. I was sixteen, Seth was thirteen. We were riding together at Highlands and he challenged me to race. We headed for a fence first and both cleared it all right. Then he spotted a tall hedge. It must have been at least seven feet high. He dared me to take it, and then he whipped up his horse and raced towards it. I shouted at him not to be a damned idiot. He didn't listen. It had been raining. The ground was soft and my horse slipped a little and I fell behind. But I was determined not to let him show me up—he being only a kid and me a big college man—or almost. I saw him clear the hedge. But then I heard his horse scream. I knew he'd gone down. I was only a few yards away. I should have pulled my horse up short, even if it meant falling myself. But I didn't do it. I was damned if I was going to let him think that I was afraid of that hedge.''

He was very tense as he spoke, so taut that he was trembling slightly. I put a reassuring hand on his arm. He felt as hard as steel.

"I shouted for him to clear out, that I was coming over, too," he said in a low voice. "My horse cleared the hedge without any difficulty. And we came down right on top of Seth."

I gasped and my hands flew to my mouth.

"Her hooves cut into his left leg," Steven went on grimly. "We all went down in a heap then. He'd struck his head and he hadn't heard my warning. It was a mess. Mud and blood everywhere. Seth was white as a sheet. His leg was bleeding badly. I strapped my belt around his thigh and somehow I got him up on my horse and back to the house. His horse had broken two legs. We had to send a man back, to destroy it. Seth was unconscious by the time I got him home. I rode for the doctor. I was sure that he would die. I felt sick and scared.''

"It wasn't your fault. You didn't know—"

"I shouldn't have tried the jump," he insisted. "Later, after they patched him up, they asked us how it happened. Seth told them it was his doing. He said his horse had slipped her stride as they got up to the hedge, that he'd gone over her head and she'd come down on top of him. I was there while he was telling them. He looked very cool, very sure of himself. I didn't know why he wanted to lie about it, but it made me look less of a fool and so I let his story stand. Until I saw that he'd done it to put me in his power. It's hard to explain. He wanted something, a secret, something he could use, something to hold over me. He needed to make himself feel equal to me, or even superior. I know it sounds incredible, that a thirteen-year-old boy—"

"No, I can believe it of him," I said wearily.

"Well, as soon as I caught on to his game I told the truth and took my well-deserved lumps. I felt a little better, and at least I'd thwarted his devious little plan, whatever it was. It's not a good idea to let someone like Seth know your secrets, Rhawnie."

"I know that, Steven. Steven," I shifted around in my seat, "I want to tell you—"

"But every time I saw him walk, saw him limp, it hurt. He never said anything, never blamed me. But we both knew that I'd maimed him, marked him for life. It was a long time ago," Steven laughed softly and bitterly. "Nearly twenty years. After the accident he tried even harder to excel, to make up for his bad leg. He never let it interfere with anything he wanted to do. He learned to fence, to dance, to raise hell. And he was still competing. I went in for law. The Church didn't appeal to him—God knows!—and so he went in for medicine. He was a lot like Sean in those days; got himself thrown out of the best schools in the country. So Father packed him off to Europe, to Paris and Heidelberg. He surprised us. Came home from Heidelberg with a good degree and that duelling scar on his cheek. He was twenty years old. A qualified doctor. He could have had anything. The world was open to him."

I was almost afraid to ask what happened next. I thought I knew. "A woman?" I said softly.

"Julie."

"Your wife!" My eyes widened.

"She wasn't my wife then. She was Aunt Colette and

Uncle Philippe's daughter, our first cousin. We'd always liked her, of course. But I never noticed that Seth was any fonder of her than I was. But when he came back from Germany he proposed to her. She was only fifteen. Still a child. Mother and Aunt Colette advised them to wait a year or two, with good reason. At twenty Seth was already a man of the world. We'd both had our share of women, but he was insatiable. He seemed to want to make a career of whoring. He got a reputation among the bloods of New Orleans as the one to watch and emulate. He'd picked up some fancy tricks with the blade in Heidelberg—when he should have been studying, I'm sure—and he could beat any fencing master in the city, and New Orleans had the best. I think Julie was a little frightened of him, the way he swaggered and carried on like a true cove, as Sean would say. She accepted our mothers' advice and told him that she wasn't ready to marry yet. He took that as an affirmative answer. But he shouldered his disappointment and marched off to war with Mexico.

"He impressed Sam Houston and was lucky enough not to be at the Alamo when the slaughter came, and he came home a year and a half later, covered with glory. I'm sure he hadn't done a lick of doctoring out there. He found killing more to his tastes. And when he got back, he found that Julie and I were engaged. We didn't do it to spite him—we didn't give him much thought. After all, she didn't say that she would marry him, only that she wasn't sure and wanted to wait. Maybe we felt that his proposal was one of the crazy impetuous things he did on the spur of the moment. It's just that—while he was away—we discovered that we loved each other."

Steven was silent for a few minutes, remembering. He didn't seem to be aware of me at all.

"No one dreamed that Seth really cared about Julie. But he did care, more than we knew. He was beside himself. I'd never seen him so angry. And he was furious with me.

Accused me of playing up to his girl while he was off fighting for Old Glory. Young fool. I wasn't impressed by his heroics and I told him so. I can understand his feelings. He'd been competing with me all his life, and while he was off in Texas blowing holes in Mexicans and carving them up with his sword, I was safe at home, making love to the only girl in the world that he really wanted. And so he did what any disappointed lover would do under the circumstances. He kidnapped her.''

"You're joking!" I gasped.

"No, I'm not. He rode down to La Rêve and carried her off in the dead of night. I thought that it was his intention to dishonor her, to force her to marry him. I still think so. But Julie said no. She always maintained that he was just disturbed about the whole business and that he wanted time to talk to her in private, an opportuniy to renew his proposal and to convince her that she should marry him, not me.''

"I think you are right," I said. "He has no honor. Your wife must have been very good, very trusting.''

"She was an angel," Steven said. He rested his elbows on his knees and clasped his hands together. "But whatever his intentions were, he failed. Julie's maid discovered her absence almost immediately and alerted the household, and Uncle Philippe rode up to Highlands to tell us. Father and I went after them and brought them back. Julie was still wearing her nightdress. He'd thrown a cloak around her to keep out the damp. She was crying. I remember that. Not sobbing loudly, but her face was wet. I didn't touch him then, in front of her. I didn't say a word. But when we got home I did what any outraged bridegroom would do under the circumstances. I called him out.''

"You challenged him!"

Steven nodded grimly. "We didn't tell our parents, of course. Kept it a dark secret. It was the classic confrontation. We met under the Duelling Oaks outside New Orleans one misty morning. Two brothers thirsting for each other's blood, each convinced that the other was a swine who deserved to die. I swore that I was going to kill him. I wanted to hack him to pieces and throw him to the alligators. Loving brothers, weren't we? You remember when I horsewhipped the Prince in front of Felix's that night? I felt the same way about Seth, that he was a cad who didn't deserve to breathe the same air as the rest of us. Men like Azubin—and Seth—bring out the worst in me. That duel with Seth showed me a side of myself that I hadn't known existed. I was full to the brim with anger, and a hatred that went deeper than just that kidnapping nonsense.

"And he wanted my blood, too. He really thought that if he killed me he could have Julie again after the fuss died down. He couldn't get it through his head that she didn't love him. Poor child. She was distraught about it. But she never said a bad word about him. She was always ready to understand and to forgive. She always had an excuse for the way he behaved."

"What happened?" I asked excitedly. "Did you fight?"

"Oh, yes, we fought. He chose broadswords. He fancied himself the best swordsman in the country, remember, and I let him think so. But I'd always loved fencing. And when Father and I were in Washington together—I spent some time as his aide soon after college—we met regularly, just for fun. Mother was down here at the time, and Father said he had to do something to keep his mind off other women. Father could wipe the floor with any of those Royal Street monkeys in their fancy academies. He was the best I'd ever seen. But I worked hard and I got to the point where I could beat him sometimes.

"Well, Seth and I squared off and took stances. He was grinning all over his face. I could tell he thought this was going to be an easy fight. But I didn't want to toy with him. I lit into him with everything I had, and the grin left his face pretty quickly. He was fighting for his life, and he knew it. Neither of us gave an inch. He cut me pretty badly under the ribs. But when he was pulling back I lashed out and chopped at his bad leg. It caught him off balance and he went down. I stuck the tip of my sword into his throat. He dared me to kill him. But I couldn't. I thought of Julie and Mother—it would have broken their hearts. He sneered at me and called me a coward, but so help me God, I heard these words ringing in my ears: 'And Cain slew his brother Abel.' And I thought, 'What the hell am I doing. And I threw down my sword. Just then Father rode up. I've never seen him so angry. He shouted at me, called me every name he could think of, and I swear if Seth hadn't been hurt he would have pounded his face in. Seth left the city soon afterwards. We didn't see him again for seven years, until just after Julie died."

"Oh, Steven." I put my arms around him. "If things had happened differently, if he had had the chance to kill you, he would have done it."

"I don't know," he said. "I've often wondered about it. But it was a bad business, all the way around. I couldn't even take pleasure in knowing that I'd fought fair: I'd struck him in his weakest spot, taken unfair advantage. It caused a terrific scandal. Everyone was hurt by it: Julie, Aunt Colette and Uncle Philippe, Mother, Father. Especially Mother. It broke her heart, the fact that her two oldest sons hated each other and that one of them had been driven from his house."

"You blame yourself still," I said sadly, "for no reason. Oh, Steven, he has a demon inside him. A hundred demons! They have always been there."

"That's what Julie said. That he was driven and desperate. But driven by what, I'd like to know? Not ambition. He gave up medicine, called it a fool's game. And desperate? Why, because he wasn't born first? I don't know how he lives. I don't want to know. As far as I'm concerned he can roast in his private Hell, the one he's made for himself. Along with his fellow gamblers and his women.''

I froze. His voice was thick with loathing. He hated his brother and everything associated with him. I had an impulse to shout, "I know him! I know how he lives! I was one of his women! I was his wife!''

But I said nothing. If I told Steven the truth I would lose him, I was sure of it. He would lose me. He would lose and Seth would win. I couldn't do it. It was up to Seth now, whether he would spare me more agony and keep silent, or whether he would tell his brother that the woman he wanted to marry was his wife. And then—I hated to think about what would happen then. We were in his power, both of us, Steven and myself! Oh, God, I thought despairingly, will I never be free of him?

Impulsively I threw my arms around Steven's neck and hugged him tightly. "I want to be a good wife to you, Steven!" I whispered. "I don't want to hurt you!''

"You could never hurt me, darling," he said. He pulled back and looked at me fondly. "I'm so glad, Rhawnie. So very glad I found you.''

We heard sounds of a carriage below. "They're here. Mass must be over," I said.

"I want to stay with you," he said. "Please, Rhawnie.''

"No, no, Steven, not tonight! We don't want—scandal. Later, after my concert, we'll go away. Far away!" I hugged him again. "Go now," I said softly. "It's very late. I love you.''

"I love you.''

As soon as he had gone I rang for Anna. I paced the floor. I stood in front of the piano and banged at the keys. I twisted my hands and clutched my hair like an old-fashioned tragedienne.

Anna came in, her eyes full of questions.

I said in a dead voice, "He is here, Anna." She knew at once who I meant. She ran to me and put her arms around me. "I must think!" I said frantically. "I cannot marry Steven now. Seth is his brother, Anna! Yes, his brother! Oh, dear Heaven, what can I do? I can't tell him. I tried, but I couldn't. They hate each other! It would kill Steven to know the truth. He knows all there is to know, oh, yes, but so long as this 'husband' of mine was a faceless stranger, it was somehow all right. But this devil is his own brother! I am at my wits' end. It is hopeless, impossible! I—I'll leave here at once!"

I started to pace again.

"Pack my things, Anna! We'll leave at once, go far away! I'll get out of their lives and never see either of them again. Well, what are you waiting for?" Anna stood motionless. "Do as I say!"

She shook her head and pointed to her throat.

"I know I have to sing," I said impatiently. "I haven't forgotten everything. But this is more important! And how could I sing, knowing that he was there, listening, listening and laughing at me!"

Now Anna looked impatient and wagged her head.

"Yes, he would too laugh!" I averred. "He has nothing but scorn for me and the things I can do. He is a monster! Of course I must leave. It's the only solution. Do you want me to stay and be humiliated?"

A shrug.

"Ha. No matter what I do, I am lost. Oh, if only I could persuade him to keep silent!"

Anna grinned unexpectedly and mimed slicing her own throat.

"This is no time for jokes!" I shouted. I threw up my hands. "Do you think I haven't wanted to kill him, a hundred, a thousand times? Oh, if only he would die. Devil! Bastard! I just don't understand how he could be born to a woman like Elise McClelland. He is a changeling!

That's it! He's not her son at all, but some evil thing the Gypsies put in the cradle when they stole the real Seth. Oh, will you listen to me? I am so crazy that I'm starting to believe the lies they tell about my own people! Mad. I am going mad. Oh, what am I going to do?''

Quickly, Anna signalled to me that I must stay, that Seth was sure to come and that I must convince him to leave me in peace.

"Yes, Anna, you're right," I said. "He will come to sneer and to gloat. Oh, if only I had a weapon. Something — like a secret. Something I could use against him!"

Anna grabbed my arm and shook me. She made motions that I couldn't understand, and looked pained and frustrated when she saw my incomprehension.

"What, Anna? Seth—and Steven—their Mother? I don't understand. We will talk later, Anna. Be calm. I will be calm." I stood stock still in the middle of the room. "You see? Calm. I will make myself ready. I will talk to him calmly and rationally. I will not shout or scream. I will try to—persuade him."

Anna helped me out of my gown and corsets. I put on a green silk nightgown and on top of that a Chinese-style dressing gown with flowers and dragons woven into the fabric. Then I sat at the dressing table in my bedroom, which adjoined the music room, and Anna brushed my hair a thousand strokes.

"Why did I marry him, Anna?" I wondered. "I must have been out of my mind. Perhaps it's illegal to marry while you're insane? What do you think, Anna? Do you think we're really married? Steven would know, but I can't ask him. Bah, I know why I did it! Because he willed it! I was his puppet and I danced when he pulled the strings! But no longer, Anna." I turned around on the low bench and gripped the small woman's wrists. "No more," I said huskily. "He is not my master now. I am free of him.

My hatred has freed me. Once I loved him, but now I hate him, I hate him for what he did to me in Vienna. And my hatred will make me strong! I will defy him, Anna, and I will win. This time I will win!''

Anna stopped her brushing and braided my hair loosely. I wore it braided to bed so that it wouldn't tangle too much while I slept. She was just finishing when we heard a tapping on the path in front of the house. Step, step, tap. We both froze. Anna clutched my arm.

"Don't be frightened, Anna," I said. "I'm not afraid. Go downstairs and let him in. Bring him up. I should have known that he would come tonight. He couldn't wait. But he can't hurt me now, Anna. I really believe that. Ah, look at these braids! I look too young, too vulnerable. Like a little girl. I'll pin them up myself. Listen, there's the knocker! Bring him, Anna." I wound my braids around my head and jabbed at them with pins.

Anna left the room and went downstairs to admit our visitor. I went back to the music room and poured myself a glass of tea. I laced it with brandy and drank it down. I would not fail.

He followed Anna into the room. The three of us stood there for a moment. No one moved or spoke.

"It's all right, Anna," I said. "Leave us."

Filled with misgivings, yet reluctant to disobey, Anna backed out of the room and closed the double doors.

Seth leaned on his cane and looked around. A small fire in the grate, just enough to take the dampness out of the air, cast a warm light on the gold fabrics and furnishings in the room. On top of the enormous grand piano in the corner a candelabrum hung with glittering prisms held eight burning candles, and another stood on the table that also held the samovar and the brandy. It was a beautiful comfortable room, made for pleasure. I wondered if he approved.

He was wearing evening dress—black cutaway coat,

white shirt, white stock, black cloak. He looked as he always did when he was on his way to gamble and to wench in style. It may have been nearly two in the morning on Christmas Day, but in certain parts of New Orleans the fun was just beginning. He tossed his cape over a chair and laid his stick on the round table, next to the samovar. He looked around again, seeing everything saying nothing. Then his eyes rested on me.

I watched him suspiciously. I had my arguments ready, but I wanted to wait for him to make the first move.

He did. He came over to me and touched my cheek lightly with the back of his hand. His eyes gleamed wickedly.

I jerked my head up. My nostrils flared. "Stop that!" I pushed his hand away. He moved closer. I stood my ground, refusing to back down and show him that I was afraid of him. He put his hand on the back of my neck and tried to kiss me. I twisted my face away. "No!"

He held my head and pressed his lips down on mine. I went stiff as a board. Tides of hatred and fury rose in me. His arms closed around me. He slid his lips slowly along the line of my jawbone to my ear, then down my neck to my throat. A shock of pleasure as strong as an earthquake and as debilitating as a bolt of lightning struck me. I tried to collect my wits, to push him away, but he pressed closer, kissing and licking my throat lightly. My hands fluttered ineffectually in front of my bosom, like frail, helpless butterflies beating themselves to death against glass.

He opened the sash of my robe and slid his hand under my nightgown. He cradled my breast in his palm and manipulated the nipple expertly with his thumb. He kept his other arm securely around my waist, but he needn't have. My legs were so weak and rubbery that I couldn't have run if I wanted to. I felt myself sinking and swirling. I reached up and touched his cheek. Flashes of heat danced down my spine, pierced my flesh.

I gulped air and cried, "No!"

I wouldn't let him do it. I broke away from him and ran into my bedroom. I slammed the door and fumbled with the key. The damned thing had never been used since I'd been in the house and it jammed in the lock. I cursed. I heard him coming and I fell back just as he swept the door open.

"Stay away from me, damn you!" I cast about desperately for some kind of weapon. I wished I had an axe: I would split his grinning head in two, right down to his belly. He moved forward, unsmiling now, slowly and relentlessly, like a snake intent on capturing its meal.

"I won't let you—" I gasped.

He grabbed my wrist and hauled me into his arms. Jerking my head back, he pillaged my mouth with his tongue, hurting me, pressing in on me until I was dizzy and breathless. I kept shaking my head, trying to clear away the thick mist that enveloped my brain. I was like a drunk trying to view the world soberly. He fondled my face, his hands swirled around my breasts. They felt cool and dry. I was hot, burning, sweating.

I sagged limply against him, sighing, and he slipped off my robe and gown and carried me to bed. I moaned softly and covered my face with my arms, giving myself up to his caresses. He covered my long body with a hundred kisses, like shooting sparks. They burned my throat and my breasts, my abdomen and thighs, and finally the soft feathery region between my legs. I was helpless. How could I fight him when he attacked me this way, knowingly and lovingly? My buttocks filled his strong hands and he buried his face in my softness, fondling the tiny fleshy mound there with his lips, darting his tongue in and out. Again and again his touches sent jolts of yearning through my body, into my fingertips, into my toes. I sobbed and clutched at his thick hair with my hands, trying at the same time to deter and to encourage him.

He moved away from me and undressed in the dim light shed by the lamps in front of the dressing table mirror. I couldn't look at him, naked. I closed my eyes. I felt him ease himself down beside me.

"Look at me," he said.

I opened my eyes. His face hovered over mine, dreamlike. I knew it so well, every crease, every pore, every shadow. Sorrow and anger were forgotten, shed as easily as the flimsy garments that lay in a pile on the floor near the bed. I gave myself up to the ancient passion that had lived in my body since I had known him. I opened my arms and my soul to him. His shaft felt as hard and as slick as steel. We crashed together and I returned his kisses with a greed that matched his own. I let my long fingers skim over his body, remembering. I knew every contour, every scar, every depression and hair, every sinew and bone. He drove himself into me, taking me swiftly and hungrily, as though he wanted to capture some essential magic of my womanhood before it slipped away, before it eluded him.

Each fierce thrust sent hot arrows fleeting through my heart to my brain. I felt myself sliding backwards, plummeting headlong into a molten sea, without air, shivering, shrieking, shaking. With a roar he released his fire and at the same instant the soft petals of an elusive dark flower captured him and held him fast.

It had never happened that way with us before. A shattering, draining moment when we merged in sweetness and were really one. I wanted to lie forever welded to him in an infinite embrace. I wanted the world to end, there and then, so that we could die together before we began to act and speak again. Before we could spoil the magic.

Seth quivered. We were both wet from exertion and the room was chilly, but neither of us wanted to make a move to pull up the coverlets. Slowly, the world righted itself. I lay absolutely still, listening to the music of his breathing and the soft drumming of his heart. I could hear the rustle of leaves against the window pane and the small noises of the house settling itself into sleep and darkness. I drew my arm up and turned my face away from him, into the curve of my elbow. A tear slid down my cheek into the satin pillow under my head.

His hand came up to the side of my face and found the tear. He said my name, so softly that I thought I dreamed it.

After a while he groaned and rolled over on his back. He hitched up one leg and spread his arms out. I moved out of the way and sat on the edge of the bed. I noticed a new scar on his upraised thigh, and another round one, a bullet hole, on his upper arm. Signs of battles fought. His little victories in his war against life. A few demons exorcised through the ritual of danger and death, but hundreds remaining. He moved and tossed. I grimaced. He even sleeps aggressively, I thought.

I started to get up. His eyes flew open and his hand whipped out to close around my wrist. "Where do you think you're going?"

"The next room. I don't want to sleep with you."

"Stay here." He pulled me down next to him and flung his arm over me.

"I don't want to." I twisted around. I felt stiff and dead inside. The magic was gone.

"Wife's place is with her husband," he said drowsily. "Be a good girl and close your eyes."

"I am not your wife!" I said, throwing off his arm and sitting up again. "What a farce. You weren't even using your legal name. It can't possibly be legal!"

"Why not?" he grunted. "If you can go around calling yourself the Baroness von Ravens-toenail, I can certainly call myself Garrett. I can call myself Seth Garibaldi, if I like. Who's to stop me?" He folded his arms behind his head and grinned at me. "I knew I must have had a reason for marrying you. I've given it a great deal of thought—as much thought as I give anything. Insurance. You are—my wife. My property. Mine. And you'll stay mine, my dear. I won't give you up."

"You—won't give me up!" I laughed bitterly and gave him an incredulous look. "Where have you been for the past four years? What do you call what you did in Vienna? You deserted me and my baby. You left us, with hardly enough money to live on." My voice shook and I shrugged to get it under control. "Don't you remember? Give me up, indeed! You gave your son up very easily. Do you know what happened to him? He died. Three weeks after he was born, in a hotel room that was small and cramped and cold. I wrapped the body myself and walked behind it to the grave." I jumped off the bed and pulled on my wrapper. "Don't you dare try and assert your mastery over me. I won't stand for it, do you hear? You think a few words spoken in front of a man neither of us had ever seen before means that we are married? Marriage means love and caring and responsibility. And you aren't capable of any of that. Steven is. You may be able to stop me from marrying him, but if you think that I would ever, ever live with you again and endure your cynicism and your callowness and your infidelity—well, I won't! You remember these?" I bent over the bed and shook my upturned wrists under his nose. "The child who did that to herself because she couldn't think of any other way of escaping you no longer exists. But I tell you, Seth Garrett McClelland whatever-your-name-is, she is just as determined not to let you control her. Now why don't you get out of my house before I get really angry!"

He nodded approvingly. "Wonderful speech, Rhawnie. I congratulate you—your English has really improved."

"You—bah!" I glared at him.

He laughed lightly. "And now you've gotten yourself engaged to Steve. I could hardly believe my eyes. I walk into the house after six, seven years, and there you are,

406

stuck like a leech to my brother, looking like the cat that stole the cream. What a joke! What a damned, funny joke!''

"Don't make yourself sick laughing too hard," I said through gritted teeth. I tightened my sash with an angry jerk and walked into the music room. I poured some tea into a glass, added some hot water from the samovar, and popped a sugar cube into my mouth. Blast him. God damn and blast him!

He strolled out of the bedroom. He was wearing his ruffled shirt and trousers. His feet were bare. "May I?" He helped himself to brandy.

"I hope you choke." I sucked my tea loudly.

He grinned. "More likely your faithful little Anna has slipped poison into the decanter." He lifted the snifter to his nose. "Excellent! I'm happy to see you've retained some of the things I taught you. Some of the important things." He put his hand on my rump.

I moved away from him and plopped myself down on the settee. I slurped my tea. He sat next to me.

"Your performance tonight was really remarkable," he said. "Can Steve be such a failure as a lover? I wouldn't be surprised. All those years of fidelity. Really takes the edge off. But maybe he's been neglecting you. He's a fool. I'll have to tell him about you and your needs."

"Why do you talk this way?" I asked. "Why, why do you want to hurt me? Haven't you done enough? Why can't you be kind to me?"

He set down his glass and looked at me. "Because I'm not Steve," he said in a harder voice. We didn't speak for a while but watched the fire die. He cocked his head and looked around. "My brother is a generous man. I congratulate you. You've done well for yourself."

"And I have done it for myself," I said. "Your brother has given me nothing. Haven't you heard, I'm a concert singer now. I'll be singing at the French Opera House next

Saturday. Please don't feel as though you have to come."

"Wouldn't miss it for anything," he said. "Tell me how you got your hooks into Steve? Mother had some fantastic story about his rescuing you from some German baron."

"You might have asked how your brother got his hooks into me," I said. "I didn't propose to him. It was a complete surprise to me. But it's what I want, Seth. And you want to spoil it."

"Want to—!" He laughed. "My dear, we are married, like it or not! It's not what I want or don't want. It's a fact."

"Give me a divorce, Seth. Please! I'm sure it can be done without Steven's finding out who you are. I'll hire a lawyer in England—far away from here. I'll find some excuse to go abroad!"

Seth shook his head. "He'd find out. Lawyers are very clubbish. He'd poke around and learn the truth. Why don't you tell him I'm dead? Your husband, I mean. He'd believe that."

"And then you'd appear on our seventh wedding anniversary with a startling revelation," I said bitterly. "I know you. No, what I need is some insurance, as you call it. I want you to help me, Seth. I want you to promise me that you won't spoil this, that you won't tell them. Give me your word."

"What an outrageous suggestion!" Seth looked shocked. He's really enjoying this, the bastard, I thought. "You want me to suppress the truth about us so that you can marry my brother! There is such a thing as bigamy, my darling. It means—"

"I know what it means. And I don't consider myself married to you. What's a *gorgio* wedding anyway? What's the harm in it? We were married only a few months before you left me, and I haven't seen you in four years! Please, Seth. I'll make him happy, I swear it!"

"I don't doubt it," he said quietly.

"I want to be married to him," I said quickly. "He's

good and kind and—respectable. Please, don't laugh at me, Seth. All I've ever wanted in my life was a husband and a family. Babies, three or six or a dozen. And a good man to take care of us all. It's not such a big thing. Millions of women have just that—a family. I'd give anything for a chance like this. I could be a great singer. You don't believe me, but it's true. The best people in Europe have said so. But I wouldn't want to sing for money if I could sing for my own babies at home. This concert business is a game I play. I would throw it all away for Steven. Please, Seth, I have never asked you for anything. I never made demands of you, never whined for carriages and dresses and baubles the way some women do. All I ever wanted from you was my freedom. And that's all I want now. Don't tell them. Please. Do this for me. You owe me this! Do it and I will thank you all my life."

He reached over and brushed a strand of hair from my face. "You haven't said that you love him."

"I do love him!" I said passionately. "He is good and kind and—"

"Yes, yes," he waved his hand impatiently. "I know all that. Steve the paragon. Steve the model husband and father. Steve the upright example to us all." He made a sour face. "Good old Steve. But tell me, Rhawnie, what do I get out of all of this? Will I be entitled to special attentions when I come to town?" He sat closer and put his arm around my shoulders. He fondled my breast through the silk of my robe. "What fun that will be. A family picnic at Highlands. Daddy Steve and Grandpa Garth take the tots for a swim, and Mother Rhawnie and Uncle Seth sneak off into the shrubbery."

"Please stop that!" I twisted away. "You're treating it like a joke and it's not a joke! I am serious about this!" I whirled back again and grabbed the ruffled front of his shirt with both hands. "Listen to me, Seth. I won't be blackmailed by you for the rest of my life. You will either do this for me or you won't. But you must decide now. One thing more: if you tell them about us, I will tell them about you. About how you live and the way you used me and deserted me. It wasn't a very honorable thing to do, was it, Seth? Think of how disappointed your parents would be—and Sean! He worships you. But even he, in his youth and callowness, would think less of you for doing that. And Gabrielle. You love her, don't you? And she loves you. But if she knew what you were, what you are, what would she think?"

I knew I was grasping at straws but I had to try anything. I pressed on.

"I'll tell her how you killed Martin de Vernay, and how you used my talent for faro to cheat people all over Europe. I know you so well, after all. Why shouldn't I use what I know? And if it wouldn't hurt you—it would hurt them. And I wouldn't care! By that time I'd have nothing to lose anyway. I'd have lost Steven and my new life. Think about it, Seth. Tell Steven. He won't have me, but you won't have me, either."

"You're being ridiculous," he said curtly. "To think that you had any kind of power over me—"

"I have seen you with your family." Yes, family! That's what Anna had been trying to tell me: I could get at him through his family. "I used to think that you didn't care about anything in the world. But you care about them, don't you? You changed your name so you wouldn't embarrass them. You came home on Christmas Eve to be with them. I think you even care about Steven. If you really wanted to hurt him you would have stayed after the duel. I think I do have a weapon I can use against you, Seth. If you destroy my dreams," I took a breath, "I will hurt you, through them. I swear it. I swear it on the body of my dead baby."

I must have looked like a madwoman. My braids had fallen down and become unravelled and my hair swirled around my face like a golden cloud, now concealing, now revealing. And my eyes were wild and bright with anger. And he must have believed my threat, for he said.

"You damned crazy Gypsy lunatic. I'd kill you before I let you—"

"Then kill me now," I said passionately. "I'm not afraid of your threats. I fear nothing!" I held up my wrists. "And I certainly don't fear Death!"

I watched a variety of emotions play over his usually impassive face: anger, frustration, and finally, after a struggle, calm.

"I don't strike bargains with madwomen," he said. "The whole thing is ridiculous. You and Steve! Ha! That's a match for you! By God, I ought to let him have you! What a fine joke! I suppose he told you about Julie?" I drew back a little. "Of course he did. Dear Julie. So saintly, so good. She married Steve because that's what her parents wanted for her. I wasn't good enough, but he was. But before she was his, she was mine. Do you understand?"

My mouth felt dry. "You—ruined her."

"That's what the pious blockheads around here would call it. Ruin," he sneered. "But I didn't have to force her. She wanted me. She was very willing. We had quite a nice little time in a deserted cottage. If it hadn't been for that delay Father and Steven never would have caught up with us. Little Mademoiselle Julie was no saint, I can tell you."

I closed my eyes and put my hands to my cheeks. I could picture the scene—I had played it myself. Julie, young and sweet and innocent—even more innocent than I had been. And he took her away from the protection of her home and worked his vile magic on her, his sweet, vile magic. She couldn't resist him. No woman could, even a woman who had fallen victim to his will a thousand and one times, as I had. He took her, knowing she would never tell, knowing that she would marry Steven and live in the shadow of a lie for the rest of her life. Poor child. Poor woman.

"Steven should have killed you when he had the chance," I said bitterly. "You think you've beaten him, don't you? Beaten him at whatever crazy game you've been playing since you were children. He has loved two women in his life—which is two more than you've loved—and you have spoiled them both for him. He doesn't know anything about it, and so you laugh at him and call him dull and make fun of his kindness, because you have your dirty little secrets and you can use them any time you want to destroy him. It's the same thing you did when you were thirteen and you lied about the accident that made you lame. Secrets. Dirty secrets that make people afraid. I'll tell Steven myself. And then you can deal with his anger. I hope this time he doesn't let you go."

"I'm not afraid of him," Seth growled.

"You should be afraid. I've seen him when he's angry. He would surely kill you." I stood up and sighed deeply, and said in a lighter tone. "But perhaps you will kill him. And it will break your mother's heart all over again. And Gabrielle, who was too young to know what was going on when it happened the first time—her heart will be broken, too. And your whole family will be in disgrace. But Fate has done this to us, hasn't it? Fate has sent me here to destroy you all!" I threw back my head and laughed. "You're right, Seth, it is a joke! Jove has married the beautiful Venus to the ugly Vulcan, who is a brute and a beast. But she loves the fair Apollo. And so there is war in the heavens!"

Laughing and crying, I sank down onto a cushion at his feet. He gripped my shoulders and shook me, hard. "Stop that," he said sharply.

I looked up at him beseechingly. My cheeks were wet with tears. "Don't tell them," I begged him. "Please, Seth. You can make up for all the sorrow you've caused. Promise me, promise me—"

"You're hysterical—"

"Please, Seth," I whispered. I put my hands on his

chest and leaned forward. I touched his cheek with parted lips. "Please?" I kissed him lightly in a half-dozen places and felt him shiver. "You have no choice—and neither do I," I murmured. "You will do this for me—I know you will. You will let me be happy, Seth." I rested my hand on the bulge under his trousers. He was huge—and ready. "Promise me—promise—"

I let my dressing gown fall open and I took his hands and placed them on my breasts.

"I won't—," he started to speak. I covered his mouth with a soft kiss.

"You will," I said knowingly. "Say yes, Seth. Just—yes. That's all. One word. Yes. Yes."

His heart was racing and he was breathing heavily. I let my robe slide off my arms and gently I pulled him down, down on top of me. He buried his face in my hair.

"Yes, say yes," I coaxed him. "Promise me, Seth." I moved under him, slowly, like an ocean wave on a calm day. "Promise—yes—"

"Damn you—"

"Yes, Seth—oh, Seth—ready—now—yes—"

He drove into me—mercilessly—I was his hated enemy.

15

"No," Garth put his hand on the boy's arm. "I might be wrong about this. It's possible that they've gone in another direction, or they might even be in town yet. I'll need you here, David. Keep asking around the Quarter, you might hear something important. If you do—if they're not on the *Valerie Jane*—send a wire to Seth in St. Louis and he'll come back. Don't worry, lad. She'll be all right. Seth, I'll send word to the house for George to pack a valise for you and send it down to the dock. You go see what kind of deal you can strike with Seward."

Then the three of them left the room, with nary a backward glance at me.

"So foolish, so young," I sighed. "Why, why wouldn't she listen to me, Anna? No good will come of this, no good at all. I'm afraid for her, Anna."

I thought of how desperate and sad I had been when Seth had left me, and how I might have died of sorrow if it hadn't been for Anna. Somehow, having another woman there, to talk to and commiserate with, had helped me.

I said, "Anna, I am going with Seth! On that boat, the *Delta Belle!* Pack a large valise for me. Some medicines and tea, some brandy and vodka and a little food. One dress will do, something sturdy and plain. Underthings and a warm cloak—but I'll wear that. And rip the last of my jewels out of that petticoat! I may need them."

Then I sat down at my desk in the music room to dash off a note to Steven. It was the hardest thing I had ever done in my life—not because I didn't know what to say, but because I had never written a letter in my life, and it had been a long time since my lessons with King Ludwig.

"Deer Stefan," I wrote, spelling the words the way they sounded to my ear. My pen made a fat blob on the page. I tore it up, cursing, and started again. "I now yu vill unterstend." The pen nib broke, I was pressing so hard. I didn't know what to do next. David did all my writing for me, and God knows where he was at that moment. Clearly I was not meant to write to Steven. He would have to hear the details of our departure from someone else, and I hoped he would understand. And perhaps when I returned I would have the courage to tell him the truth.

The dock in front of the *Delta Belle* swarmed with activity. A crew of black men was unloading every piece of freight and every article of furniture that would add to the weight of the boat. A man on the bridge kept shouting at them to hurry. I decided he must be the captain, Farley Seward. I caught a glimpse of Seth pacing the deck behind him. Of course he was burning to be under way.

"Rhawnie." I felt a hand on my arm and looked around. It was Garth McClelland. "What are you doing here?"

"I must go with him," I said. "She'll need a woman when we find them. I want to help. Please, don't try to stop me."

"I won't. Are you really doing this for Gaby? Or for yourself." His blue eyes were kind, like Steven's, and very shrewd.

I felt myself blushing. "I don't know what you mean."

"I think you do."

"Things are very confused for me right now," I said in a rush. "I don't know who I am or what I want. I need to get away—can you understand? Everything is happening too fast. I love him—I don't want to hurt anyone. I must tell you—oh, Monsieur!—I cannot marry Steven even though I love him because I married Seth a long time ago." I hung my head. "You think I'm terrible, don't you? I had to tell someone. I don't know what to do."

His arms closed around me and he said, "You're on the horns of a dilemma, aren't you? And you're afraid to tell Steve."

"I can't," I said into the front of his coat. "I tried and tried, but I can't!" I looked up hopefully. "Maybe—you! You will tell him!"

He shook his leonine head. "It has to come from you

and Seth.'' The *Delta Belle's* whistle sounded. Garth gave me an encouraging smile and said, "You'd better get on board. They're about ready to cast off. Don't worry. Messes have a way of straightening themselves out. Good luck, Rhawnie. To both of you.''

I gave him a quick hug and a kiss and wiped my eyes. Then I instructed one of the workers to take my valise on board and I ran up the gangplank just as the deckhands were getting ready to pull it in. A burly sailor barred my way.

"No passengers today, Ma'am," he said. "We're runnin' a race and—"

"I know what you're doing," I said crisply. "And I'm going with you. It's all right. If anyone asks you—I'm Seth McClelland's wife."

16

The Chase

THE GREAT PADDLE wheel churned the river to froth and the *Delta Belle* moved swiftly upstream, past Baton Rouge, past Natchez and Vicksburg and Greenville and Memphis. Past the point where the two great rivers, the Mississippi and the Ohio, came together in a torrent of swirling, muddy water at Cairo, Illinois, and where the river was so broad that if you stood on one bank you couldn't see the other side. Or so they told me.

Huge twin funnels belched double columns of thick black smoke. The captain of the *Delta Belle* shouted down to the firemen to pile on more wood. The river was swollen with rain and melting snow, and the current was swift. We had to fight for every mile. Fortunately the rains had deepened the main channel and we stood little chance of running aground. The pilot kept checking our depth, and his cry rose over the din of the boiler and the banging of pistons: "Four fathoms five! Five fathoms! Four fathoms ten!" Chunks of floating debris struck the hull and some became caught in the paddles of the wheel and were crushed into powder. Thanks to the pilot's keen eye and the captain's knowledge of the patterns of the river's flow, we were able to avoid more dangerous obstructions.

It was noon on the seventh day out of New Orleans. We were about fifty miles downstream of St. Louis. Any minute we expected to see the smoke of the *Valerie Jane*, and our chase would end. Captain Seward and Seth had estimated that it would take that long to catch up with her, for although the *Valerie Jane* had a week's head start, we were travelling at twice her speed and not making stops to pick up passengers and freight. After the supply of logs the men had loaded in New Orleans ran out, we stopped only to pick up more fuel.

Seth and I stood in the pilothouse with Farley Seward. We all strained our eyes, hoping to catch sight of our quarry. Seth looked drained and exhausted, his eyes bleary and sunken. He had hardly slept or touched food since we had been on the river. A cigar hung limply from his lips; he had chewed on it until it was a pulpy rag. I saw him pressing his body forward, as though he could make the *Delta Belle* go even faster. In just a short time he would have his sister back, and Boris Azubin would be lying dead at his feet. Neither of us doubted that for a minute.

Seth had been furious with me for coming aboard. He ordered me ashore and when I refused to obey, he threatened to toss me overboard into the Mississippi. I gave him my reasons for wanting to come, stressing my own experience with Boris' cruelty and particularly Gabrielle's need for a woman companion on the way home. I even suggested that we might be able to salvage her reputation by inventing some lie to explain her absence from New Orleans—but only if she returned in my company. I would be her chaperone.

"Of course your own reputation is beyond saving," he snorted. "Steve isn't going to like this—his bride running off with the wicked black sheep of the family."

I pushed down my anger. "He will understand. His mind isn't corrupt, like yours."

"That's true. He doesn't have my vast experience with Gypsies."

He hardly looked at me when we were together. His resentment and dislike of me showed plainly in the expression on his face and in the set of his body. He had been hostile towards me since the concert, and now in spite of my repeated denials he still believed that I was responsible for what had befallen his sister.

I told myself I didn't care. Even though the nature of our quest was urgent and desperate, I was delighted to be travelling again. As the distance between me and New Orleans widened, I felt my burden of confusion and doubt begin to lighten. The future would resolve itself, I thought. If I am destined to marry Steven, I will marry him. But now I felt free again. Freedom. Freedom. I could feel the rhythm of the word in the pounding of the engine and the roar of the furnace and the slap of the paddles against the surface of the water.

"More wood!" Seth had offered to pay Seward a thousand dollars for this run, with a thousand dollar bonus if we caught up with the *Valerie Jane* before she reached St. Louis. One of the firemen warned the Captain that the boiler would explode if he pushed it too hard. "Explode!" Seward cried. "My boiler can't explode! She was cast in Hell, boy! She can't never explode!"

"We got to stop for more wood, Cap'n!" a hand called out.

"We ain't stoppin' 'til we git to St. Louis!" Seward shouted back. "Or 'til we catch the *Valerie Jane!* Tear up the floorboards! Rip off all these fancy trimmin's!" He was referring to the lacy wooden gingerbread that adorned the roofs and the uprights and the railings, every visible surface of the boat.

We all caught the excitement. Seth joined the dozen crewmen who had been permitted to stay on the boat in tearing up the woodwork and flooring for fuel. I offered to help but he told me curtly to stay out of their way, With a shrug, I retreated to a quiet corner and sat there until my wooden bench was ripped out from under me.

"I see her! I kin see her smoke!"

We dashed up to the pilothouse. The Captain peered through a long telescope while Seth and I squinted at the tiny speck that wavered on the distant horizon. Then the *Valerie Jane* disappeared around a bend in the river.

"That's her, all right," Captain Seward said with jubilant satisfaction. I could see his fingers twitching in his pockets and I knew he was counting his chickens. "Pour it on, boys! Give her everything she's got! I want to catch that tub now, not in St. Louie! More fire! More steam!"

The pistons pounded, the stench of smoke and sweat filled the air. Black deck hands, their muscular backs gleaming with perspiration, wielded their crowbars with a vengeance, redoubling their efforts as the Captain promised them a share of the money.

Seth had stripped to the waist. He was drenched with sweat. His curly hair was straight, like Steven's, and plastered to his forehead. He worked like a madman, wrenching up boards, tearing off woodwork, carrying armloads down to the furnace. Every so often he would come up to the pilothouse and watch the river in front of us. The plumes of smoke from the *Valerie Jane* were growing larger as we grew nearer. We would catch her.

I put my hand on Seth's arm. "Won't you rest?" I asked him.

"Get out of my way," he growled, pushing past me. Down he went to the furance again, grim Vulcan to his forge.

Then it happened. Without any warning. I heard horrid screams from below as the boiler sprang a leak and sprayed two deck hands with scalding steam. There was a deep rumble, then a deafening explosion and a sickening splintering sound. The pilothouse tipped crazily and Seward and I skittered across the slanting floor. Flames sprang up in front of us, behind us, all around.

I ran towards the little door and plunged through a

curtain of flames. Immediately I smelled singed wool and hair. I hurled myself over the side of the steamboat, and as the cool waters of the Mississippi closed over my head I heard still another explosion. The echoes seemed to follow me down, down to the bottom of the world.

When I bobbed to the surface my ears were ringing. The *Delta Belle* was in flames. She burned quickly, and soon she was a cockeyed blazing skeleton listing into the voracious maw of the river. Over the crackle and hiss of the fire I could hear shouts, and my nostrils were filled with the reek of charred wood and flesh.

Treading water, I looked desperately around for Seth and called his name hoarsely. I searched for him, moving through the thick smoke that hung over the water, pushing past flaming chunks of floating debris. With each passing minute my conviction that he was dead grew stronger. I could see no survivors.

Then his head surfaced not ten feet away from me. His mouth was open and he gulped air and water. He sank again. I swam to the spot and dove, trying to see him through the stirred-up silt and mud. I found him at last by groping rather than seeing. He felt limp and heavy in my arms as I pulled him up with me and our heads broke water.

The shore seemed miles away. I was weak and tired, and my burden felt almost unbearably heavy. But somehow I managed to drag him along towards the distant fringe of trees. My arm was tight across his chest, and I tried to detect the flutter of his heartbeat, but I couldn't.

I dragged him up on the bank. The ground was muddy and slimy, but the earth had never felt so good under my feet. I flopped him over on his stomach and twisted his face sideways to the air, then I threw myself on top of him and started to pump the water out of his lungs, the way I had seen Lyubov do to a Gypsy child who had fallen into a pond. We all had to learn to swim after that. The child

445

lived, and I was determined that Seth Garrett McClelland would live, too.

"Come on, damn you!" I grunted. "Breathe! Live!"

Water spurted out of his mouth as I worked, but I could detect no signs of life, no weak currents of air around his nose and mouth.

And then he gagged. And choked and coughed. And gasped. He was breathing. My face was wet, with tears or river water or sweat I don't know. But I was filled with an almost holy joy. He was alive, and I had saved him.

I continued to pump until he could breathe by himself, and when he began to stir I lifted him in my arms a bit so that when he vomited he would not choke. He did vomit, half the river, and when he was exhausted and empty I rolled him over and cradled him against my breasts. He opened his eyes and blinked to focus them.

"Gypsy," he said weakly. "You're—a mess."

I laughed down at him. Of course I was a mess. Hair streaming and mud-caked, face streaked with smoke and tears and filth, stinking of vomit and river sludge. I grinned and said, "You should see yourself, *gorgio*. But we're alive, eh? It feels good!"

He closed his eyes again and moaned. I looked him over. There was a bloody cut on his head—a falling spar had probably knocked him unconscious—and his maimed left leg was red and blistered. He was burned, and badly. His hands, too, were raw and burned and he was beginning to shiver. He was alive and I had rescued him from drowning, but I might lose him yet.

I dragged him off the mud, onto a higher grassy bank near some pine saplings. There wasn't a house, a wharf, or a sign of civilization to be seen. I took off my own sodden cloak and wrapped him in it. Then I went back to the river to search for more survivors. We had gone down in the middle of the river, and I hoped some others might have made it to the opposite bank.

A brown lump bobbed in the water about twenty feet from shore. I peered at it. My valise! With a joyous shout I plunged into the water after it. I got it back to land and opened it. Yes, yes, dry clothes and a blanket and medicines and liquor! I rushed it back to Seth and covered him with the blanket and a shawl, and then I looked more closely at his wounds.

The head wound was more of a bump than a cut, and beyond cleaning it and putting a cool rag on it to keep the swelling down, there was little I could do. I turned my attention to his burns. I knew that burns were the most dangerous of all wounds, for the tender raw skin underneath is very susceptible to disease and infection. I built a fire, using the matches I found in the valise, and piled it high with driftwood and dried grass and whatever I could find until it blazed like the hulk of the *Delta Belle* herself. It warmed us both and in the fading light of day gave off enough glow to see by. Seth's wounds couldn't wait until morning.

I cleaned the burns as best I could with water and vodka and covered them with some special Gypsy ointment and clean strips torn from a chemise. I was thankful he was unconscious, for even so the sting of the alcohol on his open sores made him cry out. When that was done I piled more fuel on the fire, wondering fleetingly about how flames could be the tools of destruction and devastation one moment and a saving source of warmth and comfort the next. Then I lay down beside him and held him in my arms. We both slept soundly until morning.

I found another body on the shore the next morning—Captain Seward. I stripped him and buried him, then washed his clothes and dried them in the sun. At least Seth would have something to wear. They were about the same size. I foraged for food. Aside from many charred chunks of debris, the riverbank yielded only a half a bottle of bourbon, a square of tattered canvas awning, and a few bits of rope. I salvaged them all.

My patient was feverish and delirious. I bathed his whole body with cool water and hoped that he would be strong enough to fight off the sickness. I doubted it, because of the way he had been driving himself the past week. No food, no sleep, no resistance, I thought mournfully. I was hungry myself, but I didn't want to leave him for very long. So I told my rumbling innards to be quiet and patient. I had a few jars of cavier in my valise, but caviar did not strike me as particularly appropriate.

I changed the dressings on his burns frequently, watching them closely for signs of infection. By noon I had to use the canvas to shade him from the sun, which if not intense was still warm enough to make him uncomfortable in his feverish state. And I waited, telling myself that it was no good to hope for this or that or to have regrets about one thing or another. I would simply have to do my best with each hour that passed.

I gave no thought to loving him, and I even told myself that I would do as much for any human being or any animal. But of course that wasn't true. While he was ill I felt that part of me was ailing, too. When he stirred or moaned or cried out, I felt searing pains in my leg and hands and body. He was part of me as I was part of him. That's just the way it was with us.

A savior appeared in the afternoon in the person of a farmer who was on his way to St. Louis to buy grain. I heard the rattle of his wagon and raced towards the sound. I found myself on a road—a dirt track, really—and I'm sure I scared the wits out of the poor man when I materialized in front of his mule. I waved my arms like a demon-woman and shouted for him to stop. He followed me back to my small campsite and agreed that we should take Seth back to his farm at once. It was a three-hour ride and we could make it before dark.

I sat in the back of the wagon, holding Seth in my arms,

trying to absorb the jarring bumps and jerks as we lurched along the rutted roadbed. I crooned and whispered to him, much as I croon to horses, and it seemed to soothe him.

The farmer's name was Kurt Geller. He was silent, spare, and mournful. But he was kindly and generous, as was his wife. They took us in, praising God on our behalfs that we had been spared in the catastrophe. They were German immigrants and they were delighted that I could speak their language.

When they asked if this man was any relation to me, I told them the truth, that he was my husband. And they kindly let Seth and me have their own small bedroom during the period of his convalescence.

Herr Geller rode thirty miles for the doctor that same night, and thirty miles back again. There wasn't much the doctor could do that I hadn't already done. He left some more ointment for the burns, and told us that Seth would probably live if he could survive the next few days.

They were anxious ones for me. Frau Geller relieved my vigil from time to time so that I could get some sleep, but most of the time I tended him myself, washing and soothing and watching over him. Then the fever broke and we knew he would be all right. I cried a little, because I was so relieved.

His first words to me were, "What are you doing here? Why didn't you go after them?"

I sighed. What can you do with a man like that? Naturally he was eager to resume the chase, and he fretted because he was too sick and weak to travel, because he couldn't bend his fingers, because his leg throbbed, because he couldn't sleep with me in the same bed.

"Why in hell did you tell them we were married?" he growled one night.

"Because it was the truth," I said. "You know these God-fearing Christians, if they thought we weren't married they wouldn't let me touch you." I undressed, slipped

449

a warm nightgown over my head, and crawled into bed beside him. "Don't worry," I said archly when I saw him stiffen, "I won't rape you. But I'm not about to sleep on the floor, either."

"Damned bitch," he muttered darkly. "This is all your fault."

"My fault!" I bounced angrily. He sucked in his breath. I knew I had bothered his wounds but I didn't care. If it hadn't been for me he wouldn't be alive and capable of experiencing pain. "I should have left you in that river," I seethed. "Should have worried about saving myself and not given you a thought. That's what you would have done if you'd been in my place, isn't it? I should have left you for the fishes! What an ungrateful fiend you are. I bring you to life with my two hands, after you have no life. I nurse you and feed you and clean up after you as if you were a giant baby! Bah! I hope your leg rots and your hands fall off. I don't ask for thanks, do I? I don't even ask for kindness. But to blame me—! It is unfair and unjust. But what could I expect from you. I can't stand being close to you." I hopped out of bed and dragged a blanket with me. "I wouldn't sleep with you if you were the King of England!"

I rolled myself up in the blanket and lay down on the floor. I heard him cough, then sigh, then snore. And I was almost certain that I detected a grim chuckle in there somewhere.

He grew stronger day by day and he chafed at our delay. Finally he persuaded Herr Geller to take us to St. Louis. I kissed Frau Geller's weathered cheek and pressed one of Ludwig's baubles into her hand. Even if she didn't need to sell it, she would have something bright and shining to look at on her dreary farmstead.

Every bump and jerk on the road pained Seth, I could tell. But this time I made no effort to soothe or to cushion him from the punishment. I sat on the opposite side of the wagon bed from him, arms folded across my chest, glaring at him. My valise stood between us like a low wall. The pain of being jounced around like a pea in a bucket turned his skin white, and beads of sweat broke out all over his face. I steadfastly ignored his discomfort until he fainted, then remorse flooded over me and I sprang to his side like a mother rushing to her wounded child. His leg had knocked against the crudely-hewn upright at the side of the wagon, and his bandages were blood-stained. I shouted to Herr Geller to stop and we discussed the problem. There was a tiny settlement upriver about ten miles. We decided to stop for the night there, and to try and finish the journey to St. Louis the following day.

St. Louis was crude and raw and bustling, not sophisticated and well-established and beautiful like New Orleans. But it had an excitement and energy all its own. I checked us into the Grand Palace Hotel, which was neither grand nor palatial, and after I had bathed and changed I went off to see if I could learn anything about Boris and Gabrielle. Everywhere I went the talk seemed to be of California and the gold strikes. The streets were clogged with men from all over the east—Boston and New York and Philadelphia—who were eager to exchange their broadcloth suits for the rough clothes of a miner. I didn't have to see California to know what they would find: blistered hands and dysentery and back-breaking work that was harder than any they had ever known. I was willing to wager that there wouldn't be many Gypsies in the gold fields. Gypsies and hard work are like oil and water, as they say. But I decided that there could well be Gypsies on the fringes of the work areas. They would be telling fortunes, trading horses, even stealing a little.

Late that afternoon I returned to the hotel. My arms were filled with packages. I found Seth limping around our room, holding on to pieces of furniture for support.

"What are you doing! Do you want to tear that wound open again!" I cried. "What a big idiot you are. You'd think a doctor would know better, but not you. Sit down at once." He started to give me an argument but I wouldn't let him. I pushed him into a chair and slid a low stool under his bad leg.

"Where have you been?" he growled. He looked terrible: gaunt and pale and unshaven. His blue eyes were sunk deep into his skull, and the scars on his face were vivid and evil-looking. "You couldn't wait to get away from me, could you? Shopping," he sneered, eyeing my purchases. "Women!"

"I only permitted myself to shop after I had finished my detective work," I informed him. "Most of these things are for you anyway. Look!" I tore open the packages and displayed shirts, a fine pair of riding breeches, warm underwear, and a beaver hat with a low crown and a broad brim. Then I unwrapped my prize: a carved oak walking stick, not fancy but serviceable, sturdy and straight, with a lion's head carved at the top. "Isn't it wonderful? This nice man was walking down the street, swinging it, not even using it properly, and I bought it from him! He asked me to have dinner with him, but I refused. Don't look so cross. I haven't been out seducing every man in St. Louis."

"You might get me a drink," he said.

"Yes, I might. Or I might not." He was so rude, so surly. I bustled around the little room, putting things away, finding the cigars I had bought him, wiping a glass with the hem of my skirt. I poured him a large bourbon and then a smaller one for myself, lit a cigar and shoved it into his mouth, then sat on the floor at his feet and told him what I had learned.

"You'll never guess what I saw when I went down to the docks," I began. "The *Valerie Jane*!"

His eyes widened and he leaned forward quickly.

"What do you mean? Where? How long—"

"Don't get so excited, Seth. Let me tell the story in my own way. Well, I couldn't believe my eyes. Two weeks and she's still here! She had boiler trouble. I went on board and talked to her captain. He got out his passenger list, Boris and Gabrielle weren't on it. So I described them to him and he thought and thought and finally he said, yes, there was a couple named Anderson who had come up from New Orleans. The man gambled a lot and the girl spent most of her time in their stateroom. It's them, Seth, I'm sure of it! Of course he didn't know where they'd gone after they docked here, and so I asked some more of the people on the boat if they knew anything. One of the waiters said yes, he was sure he had heard Mr. Anderson asking someone if there was anyplace in St. Louis where he could win back the money he lost on the *Valerie Jane*. Finally I found that person and he told me that he had recommended the Washington Hotel. There *is* a gambling room there. Very fast play, just Boris' style. Are you comfortable? Warm enough? Let me get you a pillow."

I jumped up but he grabbed my hand. "Finish your story. What else?"

"Well." I settled back down and took a sip of my drink. The bourbon was foul, but the best I could find in a city overrun with thirsty men. "I hurried over to the Washington. And the Andersons had been there! But they stayed only three days. Boris won a lot of money at the faro tables, though. And Mr. Belcher—that's the manager—remembers that he asked where he could make arrangements to go to Independence."

"Independence!" Seth sat up straight and winced a little. "Why in hell does he want to go to Independence!"

"For the gold," I explained. "I heard all about it today. They are calling Independence the Gateway to Gold. Men are gathering there from all over the country and forming trains of wagons to go west to California. Boris and Gabrielle left over a week ago, so they're probably there by now. It's three hundred miles. A long way. But a steam packet is leaving tomorrow. And if it doesn't blow up we can be there in just a few days."

"You got us on it!" He grabbed my shoulder. His fingers dug into my flesh.

"Certainly." I firmly pushed his hand away, being careful not to hurt him though. I was still angry with him for his behavior towards me, and after all I'd done for him! "It wasn't easy," I went on. "Every man in St. Louis wanted to be on that boat. But I found a man who had reserved a cabin for himself and his friend, and I played a little faro with him and won the tickets."

Seth sat back in his chair with a sigh. A frown distorted his already battered countenance. His eyes looked too bright and I knew that he was feverish again. I gave him another generous shot of bourbon: if he got a little drunk he would sleep soundly.

I stood up and shook out my skirts. "Well, I have done the best I could. I didn't expect you to fall on my neck with kisses, but you might at least tell me that you're satisfied with what I've done. If we're lucky they'll still be in Independence. I'm sure they're heading for California. Boris is just the kind of greedy pig who would like to take gold away from the miners at the faro table without even digging for it himself. And from what I hear, Independence is a madhouse. Men are waiting for weeks with their horses and wagons, just for a chance to take the ferry across the river into Kansas! These 'Andersons' will have great difficulty in finding horses and supplies. I'm sure we'll find them there."

"I'll go after them myself," he said. "You're going back to New Orleans on the first boat."

I looked at him. It would have been a good moment for a glorious prima donna rage, but he was a sick man, after all.

So I squelched my anger and said calmly, "I know you are eager to get rid of me, and believe me, I would like nothing better than to get away from you and back to my house and the ma—the people I love." I thought of Steven and suffered a fleeting pang of guilt, but I ignored it. "But I came here not to be with you but to help Gabrielle. Remember that. I will not go back until I have her with me, is that clear?"

"This is no place for a woman," he began with as much aggression as he could muster.

"Faugh! Your sister is a woman, isn't she? Or if she wasn't a woman before she left New Orleans she is now," I said bluntly. His eyes flashed dangerously but he held his tongue. "And I need not remind you that you are still in no condition to travel, and that if I hadn't come along you'd be lying in the silt at the bottom of the river, along with the rest of the crew from that accursed boat. So far I have been a greater help than hindrance to you, haven't I? I won't hold you back, don't worry. The way you are now, you're the one who will slow us down. I'm very strong. I know what it is to sleep under the stars on frozen ground. And I can ride better than any *gorgio* man. As your President Jackson said of Chief Justice John Marshall: he has made his law, now let him enforce it. I can see that you think you have made your law. But I defy you to enforce it!"

I swirled away from him. You see what you can learn when you fraternize with lawyers? We both knew that he would take me. He was still as weak as an infant and he needed me to look after him.

Was ever a journey so plagued with misfortune as that chase of ours? Our steam packet ran aground on a sand bar about halfway to Independence and we sat there for two days, stranded, waiting for the current to wash away the obstruction. I left Seth sleeping in our cabin and passed the time in the main saloon with the men, gambling—and winning. I really liked faro, and my old gift didn't fail me. At first my presence created rather a stir among the men, who were accustomed to ladies sequestering themselves in thier own saloons on treacherous journeys like this. But I did not lack partners for play, and once again I noticed that men who most resented losing to other men didn't seem to mind so much when I relieved them of their gold.

We passed a whole night and day on that sand bar. Then as day melted into night again, there came sounds of disturbance from the lower deck. I heard a deckhand cry, "Bandits! River pirates!"

While the others in the saloon smoked their cigars and drank their whiskey and wondered idly about what was happening, I snatched up my loot and dashed back to our cabin.

I burst into the cabin and roused Seth. "Wake up! We're being attacked!"

Sick as he was, his instincts didn't fail him. He leaped out of the small bunk and snatched up the revolver that was never far from his hand now. He made sure it was loaded and he cocked it. I tossed our things into our valise. I could hear shouts, gunshots, a woman's screams. Then the acrid odor of smoke seeped into the cabin.

"They're firing the boat," Seth said, voicing my own grisly thoughts. I helped him into his coat and threw on my own cloak. Then I picked up the valise and Seth grabbed his cane, and we slipped out into the narrow corridor. Above us we could hear sounds of battle. The bandits must have been numerous and bold, to attack a boatful of men, most of whom were armed.

A bearded ruffian appeared in front of us. He shouted at us to stay where we were. Seth raised his pistol and shot him dead.

We clambered over the body and moved up a short flight of steps to the lowest deck. A battle was raging in the gambling saloon on the second deck—the pirates knew where most of the ready money could be found—and the pilothouse was in flames.

Seth handed me his cane and slipped over the side of the boat into the water.

"It's not deep," he whispered. "I can stand."

I handed down our valise—ours because it contained everything we had—and then I picked up Seth's cane and slung my leg over the rail. Meaty hands grabbed me from behind.

"Where do you think you're going, little lady?" a whiskey voice wheezed.

"To the devil, like you!" I cried. I gripped that cane tightly and swung it at his head. It struck his skull with a satisfying crack and he fell away from me, moaning and clutching at his hair. I tossed the stick to Seth and followed with great speed. The water really was only waist deep, until we left the sand bar, then we had to swim for it. We let the current carry us downstream. We pulled ourselves ashore about half a mile below the blazing packet. In the glare of the fire I could see men leaping over the side of the boat. They were black specks silhouetted against the flames, hopping around like fleas in a frying pan.

Seth and I were both soaked and shivering. It was January, and cold enough that we could see our breaths in clouds, even in the moonlight. Fortunately everything in that trusty valise was dry. We changed our clothes and I wrapped Seth in a blanket. My own cloak was sodden.

"What smart people we are," I said cheerfully. "To get away before things on that boat got too hot."

"Damn," my companion said. "My cigars are wet. Where's the brandy?"

We both drank greedily, passing the bottle back and forth. Then we found a sheltered spot under some pine trees and settled down for sleep. I snuggled close to Seth and he didn't object. He needed me for my warmth, if for nothing else.

In the morning we set out on foot to search for a settlement or a farm where we could purchase a horse or two. The best we could do was a mule. One enormous jackass who was as stupid and thick-headed a beast as I have ever come across. Not even Gypsy magic could make that one go faster. We did only ten or fifteen miles that day—snail's pace. Seth was tired and irritated by our lack of speed. He was impatient to get to Independence before Boris and Gabrielle left for the west. His hands were too tender to hold the reins and so he rode behind me with his arms around my waist. We tried to tie the valise to the side of the animal with a girth of rope, but the thing kept slipping down and getting tangled in its legs. That trip was a farce. Finally I walked in front, leading the mule with one hand while I carried the valise with the other. And Seth rode and dozed, like a pampered potentate.

That night I was so tired that I fell asleep without even thinking about food. I suppose Seth made do with whiskey and cigars.

In the morning I was ravenous. While Seth was sleeping I scouted around our campsite and came upon a farmstead not too far away. The morning breeze brought the pleasant squawking of hens to my ears. It was time to put my childhood training, long unused but not forgotten, into play. I stole through the pine trees and the winter-browned underbrush towards the henhouse. I squatted behind a smokehouse and made little "chick-chick" noises to attract the hens' attention. One dim-witted bird actually thought that I had something special for her, and she was right. She moved toward me, making little clicking noises and singing to herself the way a contented chicken will. When she was three feet away I lunged at her with my arms outstretched and I felt the reassuring softness of feathers in my hands. Victory! With a quick, practiced twist of my wrist I put an end to her young life.

Then I heard a frantic barking and an angry shout. There

was an explosion and a piece of the smokehouse splintered over my head. I tucked my chicken under my arm and ran back to the camp as fast as I could go.

Seth was awake. "Where have you been?" he demanded. "I'm ready to go."

"So am I," I gasped. "There's an angry farmer with a gun after me!"

We roused our mule and cleared out fast, somehow managing to hang on to both the valise and the dead chicken until we were at least five miles away from that irate farmer.

We stopped to catch our breaths. I helped Seth dismount. I felt that he was trembling, but when I looked anxiously into his face I saw that he was laughing. He laughed until tears streamed down his cheeks. He clutched at his sides in the time-honored fashion and fell to the ground, roaring and shouting until he was limp. I stood over him and when he was more quiet I demanded furiously to know what was the matter with him. Had he gone mad? Had his illness turned his brain?

"The—the chicken!" he managed to gasp. "Never—never will I forget—! You, running out of the woods—with that chicken!" He collapsed into inconherence again.

I wanted to be angry with him for laughing at me, but as I stood there watching him, I felt my lips twitch and my cheeks swell, and in short order I was laughing, too. We decided to roast the bird at once, on the spot, just to dispose of the evidence.

Later that day we hailed a flatboat and offered them fifty dollars to take us to Independence. Even poling along at five miles an hour was better than trying to cope with that mule of ours. It went against every ounce of my Gypsy blood to leave that beast tethered to a tree near the river. But Seth insisted.

"Somebody will find him and take care of him," he said.

"I know," I said glumly, "but I could have traded him

459

for a third-rate horse!''

The situation in Independence was everything we had been led to expect, and worse. The muddy streets were jammed with hopeful prospectors, willing to sell their souls for a shovel or a spade, or even a coil of rope. There were no rooms to be had. No hotel rooms, boarding house rooms, rooms in private houses, not even floor space in barrooms. Men drank, gambled, patronized the few whores that were available, fought and tried to go west. That wasn't easy. The town was like a funnel. Hoards of men poured into it, bumping and jostling each other and clogging the narrow opening to the west, which was the ferry to Kansas City.

Seth told the proprietress of a boarding house that we were on our honeymoon; that lie plus a hundred-dollar tip got the present tenant evicted and us installed in a room. We plotted our strategy: I would ask about Boris and Gabrielle, the 'Andersons,' in the various rooming houses and hotels, and Seth would haunt the saloons and tent games. We would meet in the evening to exchange information.

We discovered that the Andersons really had come to Independence. They had stayed at the Clark Hotel near the river, a truly ramshackle establishment. Boris' luck at cards must have been very bad. But they had given up their tenancy after only a few days because of a quarrel with the landlady. I wasn't surprised at that; I had her pegged as a thief from the moment I laid eyes on her. From there they seemed to have moved to a tent near the north edge of town. Boris must have restrained his impulse to gamble. Seth couldn't find any signs that he had wagered so much as a dollar on a horse race or taken part in any games, be they poker, nickel-toss, or faro.

A week passed and we did not find them. Worse, we had no place else to look. We had turned Independence upside down, quizzed every would-be miner, every card sharp and faro dealer, every hotel worker and tart. Where had they gone?

Then finally we heard that a wagon train had left Independence two weeks earlier, only a week after Boris and Gabrielle had arrived in town. One of the two men who owned one of the wagons was killed in a fight, and his partner had lost heart and sold his wagon and team and all his equipment. The purchaser had been a thin man with blond hair. He had a wife, who was small and dark. Boris and Gabrielle.

Trying to find decent horses in Independence was harder than finding an honest woman in a whorehouse, Seth said. Just to hire two horses for a few hours so that we could go out of town to look over some Indian ponies we had heard about cost us seventy-five dollars, and even then I had to leave my valise behind as a gesture of good faith. The horses we saw were Indian only by their association with their swarthy, black-haired captors, who had snatched them off the plains only a few weeks before. I had never seen such wild beasts. They seemed maddened by their captivity and they raged at their confinement in pens. I sympathized. Other buyers came to look and went away within minutes, shaking their heads.

"Those devil's 'll kill you, son,'" one man told Seth. "You can't git nearer 'n twenty feet to 'em! They're plum crazy!"

"He's right," Seth said bleakly. "I could try to break them, but with the shape I'm in it could take weeks. Damn. We need at least three of them. I'd only need one if you weren't along—"

"No," I said automatically. My eyes were shining and I warmed to the challenge. "I will have them ready, the three best, in three days. I can do it: three horses, three days!"

"Ready for what?" he wondered. "The buzzards?"

"Ready to ride, of course," I said patiently as if I were talking to a child. "Let's see." I looked them over. "I'll take that little mare right over there, the roan. I shall call her Fire, to commemorate our trip on the *Delta Belle*. See how she shines in the sun? And you, dear husband, should have that black stallion, the biggest one. He will be Blaze."

"You can call them what you like. But it doesn't mean you'll be able to ride them." He turned and limped away from the paddock.

"You have no faith in me!" I called after him reproachfully. I asked one of the impassive Indians for a length of rope. I sat on the top rail of the fence and made a coil. Then I began to sing a soft, come-hither tune. I kept my eyes on the black stallion and I beckoned to him. He caught my look and stood stock still, watching me warily. I dropped down into the arena inside the fence and approached him slowly, very slowly, speaking to him all the while in Romany, the language of the Gypsies and the one human tongue that horses everywhere understand. I clucked and sang and I swung a loop of rope slowly and regularly, mesmerizing him.

"Rhawnie, come back here!" Seth shouted. I heard a gabble of masculine voices. A Mexican said, "Loca." Seth ordered me again to come back. I didn't answer them. To bark back a reply would have broken my spell over the horse. So I ignored them. What did the *gorgio* know about horses? About anything?

"Blaze, Blaze, brave horse," I sang in Romany. "I am your friend. Come, Blaze. Come."

He quivered and pawed the dusty ground. When I was ten feet away from him I held out my hands to show him that they were part of my body. If I brought them out of nowhere to touch him, he would be frightened. The loop of rope swung rhythmically and I never stopped my talking. His eyes were wide and wary, but he wasn't frightened.

At five feet I lifted the rope as high as his head but kept moving it. In my left hand I held a lump of sugar, purloined from the breakfast table that morning for just such a purpose. He sniffed it, licked it, and I slid the rope over his head and tightened it ever so slightly.

He started and pranced away, and I let him go until the rope was played out. I kept speaking to him in reassuring tones: Dear Blaze, good horse, good friend. I am Rhawnie, Queen of the Gypsies. I am your friend. I led him around me in an ever-tightening circle. The distance between us narrowed until my shoulder touched his withers.

I boosted myself up on his back and straddled him. He was so surprised that he stood frozen for half a minute, trying to decide what to do next. Should he rear? Should he pitch me off? But I was his friend. It was very confusing for him. I laughed at him fondly and called him pet names, then I kicked his sides and made up his mind for him. I told him that what he really wanted to do was run. That sounded like a good idea to Blaze. After dancing and bouncing a little, he reared up and kicked his feet in the air. I clung fast to his mane and the rope around his neck. When he came down he bolted straight at the fence where all the men had gathered to watch.

"Up, up," I urged him. I hoped he wasn't silly enough to think he could run right through that fence. But I should have trusted Blaze. He put on a burst of speed, tucked his legs up and cleared that fence with a foot to spare. I laughed aloud and when we were at the zenith of our leap I looked down. The men had scattered, shouting. Blaze and I hovered in the air for the merest fraction of a second, and I saw their amazed faces looking up at me. Seth's was among them. I was flying, really flying at last. My old dream had come true.

We raced across the barren fields outside the paddock. Free together. I let Blaze run until he slowed of his own will. That meant he was tiring. Then I kicked him and made him gallop faster, faster. I suppose he thought that if he ran fast enough he could run right out from under me. But finally all his pent-up energy was spent, as was his anger and frustration. I turned him and we cantered sedately back to the others.

After that it was easy. I showed him a saddle and we walked around and around it until he knew it as a harmless dead thing. He didn't resist when I put it on his back. He didn't like the bridle, but I could understand that. I would have hated it, too. By sunset he was mine, my friend and my servant. He trusted me and he knew I would not betray him.

I made sure that he was well-fed, then it was time to go back to town. I felt exhilarated by the workout and delighted with my success. You would have thought that Seth would have been excited, too. But he just looked sour and said,

"Don't you think one of us should guard him tonight? Someone will try to steal him."

"A thief wouldn't have a very easy time," I said wearily, swinging myself into the saddle of my rented horse. "He doesn't trust anybody but me. He'll kill anyone who comes near him."

"Like a well-trained guard dog," Seth remarked.

"Yes. Before we leave you'll have to show them that you are a friend, too. Bring some sugar for them tomorrow and I'll show you how."

We rode back to Independence in silence. When we got back to our tiny room Seth stretched out on the little bed. He acted like he had had a very wearing day. I stripped to the waist and splashed some cold water from the pitcher into our washbowl. I was too exhausted to care about covering myself up in front of him. If he wanted to be as silent as a chair, then I would treat him like one.

"Why do you hate it when I show you that I can do things?" I asked him. I looked up and our eyes met in the cracked glass that hung over the washstand. I scrubbed my face and neck. "It's true, isn't it?" I went on. His expression didn't change. "In the old days I was your slave, your puppet. You allowed me to play cards and make love, but that's all you wanted me to do. You didn't want me to know anything that you didn't teach me, like how to read and write." I bent over the basin and sloshed water on my face. "It made you angry when I tried to be independent. I think it's interesting that you wouldn't have anything to do with me after I got pregnant. And then, when you saw me with that baby in my arms, you hated me because I had another human being to love and I didn't need you anymore. And so you ran away, to punish me. To show me how much I needed you."

His face was pale and grim, but still he did not speak. I should have stopped right there, but I felt annoyed because he hadn't given me a single word of praise, or even thanks, for finding a solution to our need for horses. I think, too, that I wanted to see how far I could push him.

"It nearly killed you when you saw me in New Orleans, didn't it?" I said, shaking the water off my hands and reaching for a towel. "Not so much because I'd managed to get myself engaged to your brother, but because I had survived Vienna. And not only had I survived, but I had become a great lady without your help." He gave a snort at that. I rubbed my face and chest with the towel and turned around to look at him. I held the towel over my breasts and leaned back against the washstand. "I was a great lady and a great artist. My success as a singer rankled, didn't it? You couldn't even sit through my concert. Your dirty little Gypsy had blossomed into a beautiful butterfly. She didn't need you. She didn't need anyone. You hated me for not failing, didn't you?"

"That's enough, Rhawnie," he said softly. There was a dangerous light in his eyes but I ignored it.

"And now we come to this business with the horses. Why are you angry with me? Are you humiliated because I showed the world that I knew more about horses than you did? It's no disgrace. I know more about them than most people. But you don't want me to have any skills that you didn't teach me. Playing cards. Making love. That's all I'm good for in your mind. You haven't changed. You still want life on your own terms, everything in your own time, your own way. I pity you. You're not like Steven; you haven't—"

He sprang off the bed and lunged at me. I stumbled against the washstand. The pitcher and bowl slid off and smashed on the floor. He put his hands on my throat and pressed so tightly that I couldn't catch my breath. I shouldn't have pushed him, I thought with regret. Now he is going to kill me and everything I've done will have been for nothing. My eyes bulged at him. His face, so full of anger and loathing grew clouded and indistinct, then it disappeared altogether. The pressure on my throat eased and I slumped to the floor.

The next thing I knew, I was on my back and he was on top of me. He shoved my thighs apart and drove his great angry bludgeon deep up inside of me. He pounded at me furiously, as if by hurting me like that he could drive away the things I had said to him and chase them into oblivion like so many evil vapors. In two minutes he was finished. He was panting and sweating. His breath on my face felt like a searing wind that dries the land and kills everything that grows. I pressed my forearm over my eyes so that I couldn't look at him. Finally he withdrew and stood up.

"You've got me where you want me," I said thickly. "Why don't you throw in a kick or two for good measure, just so I'll know you're a real man."

"Damn you," he whispered. He limped towards the door and went out.

I opened my eyes and sat up. I ached in every part of my body. First a wild stallion, and now this. And I didn't know but that Seth was stronger and wilder than that horse.

He didn't come back that night. The next morning I took my things and went out to the paddock. I would sleep on the ground and eat hay rather than stay with Seth.

The other two horses presented no real problems. Fire was a fine mare, strong and spirited, and the third horse I chose, whom I called Venus, was a fairly passive little mare who would be a good pack and relief horse. Two mares and a stallion is a safer combination than two stallions and a mare. I knew that from experience.

Seth turned up on the morning of the fourth day, when he knew my work with the horses would be finished. He brought supplies and gear for a long trip over prairies and mountains. He informed me that we would be leaving at once. I had made no preparations for myself. I wanted to buy a few things like shirts, trousers, a broad-brimmed hat and a warm coat, if I could find one. I told him coolly that I wouldn't be ready to leave for another day.

"That's too bad," he said. "I can't wait that long." He picked up a saddle and moved towards Blaze.

"You can use the time while I'm away to show the horses that you are a friend," I advised him.

He gave an unbelieving sniff and proceeded to saddle Blaze for the trip. The big horse took it well enough until Seth lifted himself into the saddle, then he reared and bucked as though a demon possessed him. Seth flew through the air and landed hard at my feet in the dust. I had no wish to laugh at his stubbornness.

"You'd save yourself a lot of broken bones if you do as I say," I remarked. "You'll just have to break him all over again, and believe me, he's even more stubborn than you are." I caught Blaze and spoke soothingly to him, then led him over to where Seth was standing and brushing himself off. "This man is a friend, Blaze," I said in Romany. "He is a monster and a beast sometimes, but then so are you, eh? I have seen him with horses and know he understands them and loves them. He will be a good friend to you."

You might laugh and say that Blaze didn't understand any of this, but horses are no fools. He snorted and blew out his breath noisily.

"Well," I turned to Seth, "did you bring him anything? A treat?"

"No." He looked bruised and sullen. He had taken a hard toss.

"Give him this then." I dug in the pockets of my skirt for some sugar. "Talk to him for an hour or so, walk with him, and give it another try. If he trusts you he will let you ride. Then do the same with the other two. It won't be so hard because they are not so smart as this one. I'll be back before you're ready to go at sunrise."

"I gave up our room," he said. "You won't have any-place to sleep."

"I can take care of myself." I walked away without looking at him again.

I spent the night on the prairie, not five hundred feet away from where he lay sleeping. But he didn't know that. When I appeared at dawn he said nothing. He probably thought I had bedded half the men in Independence and even taken money for it. What did I care? I hadn't come all that way just to prove to him that I loved him. I had come for Gabrielle's sake. Well, hadn't I?

We rode out and forded the Missouri River just as the sun was beginning to spread its orange glow across the horizon. I rode Fire, he was mounted on Blaze. He didn't speak to me, I didn't speak to him. It promised to be a thrilling journey. Before we had gone five miles I decided that I would turn back: I couldn't endure his moods another minute.

But that was just what he wanted, to be rid of me. I couldn't give him the satisfaction. And so I kept my mouth closed and my eyes glued to the trail in front of us.

17

We Cross the Great Plains

WE CROSSED THE immense prairie in early March, in torrential rains. Deafening thunder crashed around us. Lightning shimmered and flashed, and at night it illuminated the whole bleak landscape so that we could see for miles, as if in daylight. Nothing disturbed the horses, though, not storms or mud or fierce winds. They were tough and strong, and we nearly always tired before they did.

Seth pushed us relentlessly. We had learned that the wagon train we were following was under the leadership of a man named Murray, who had taken half a dozen parties across the plains to California. The route Murray always took was the northermost one, along the Platte River to Fort Laramie and through the Rocky Mountains at South Pass. Seth seemed to know just where these places were. The wagon train had a little less than a month's head start or about one hundred and fifty miles. Assuming they could do twenty miles a day, which Seth doubted. Seth and I, travelling lightly with only a single packhorse and no cumbersome wagon, could easily manage thirty-five or more miles a day without overtaxing the horses.

His sullen silence soon gave way to the most unbearably autocratic behavior. From the outset I took care of the horses at the end of the day, because I much preferred their company to his. I fed and watered and groomed them at night, and I spoke to each one in turn and praised it for a good day's work.

The rains had driven most of the small game under cover, and for the first week Seth and I lived on dried meat and the supplies we had brought from Independence.

One night, after a particularly wearing day on the trail, I finished with the horses and then joined Seth at the campfire.

"What's for supper tonight?" I asked jokingly. "Squab under glass?"

He was smoking, lying on his back. "Whatever you decided to fix," he said lazily.

"Me!" I straightened up fast. "I've just spent the past hour with the horses! Why don't you shoot something? It could have been cooking all this time."

"You take the rifle and see what you can find," he suggested.

"I will not! I hate guns! You know I hate them. I've never fired a gun in my life!" Indeed, the only weapon I carried was a fine new Bowie knife which I stuck down in the top of my boot, just like a real Indian fighter. "Well, let's not argue about this now. I'm famished. I'll get out the last of the dried meat and cheese. Where's the food sack?"

"I'm lying on it," he said. And so he was, using it for a pillow.

"Please get up," I said, standing over him.

"I don't feel like getting up. Help me with my boots, will you, Rhawnie? My leg's very stiff tonight."

He actually raised his left leg a foot off the ground, as if he expected me to comply. I slapped at his boot angrily and said, "I won't help you with anything! At least not until you come to your senses and stop acting like a silly child. For Heaven's sake get up and let me have something to eat."

"This is my food," he said. "I very thoughtfully provided for my own needs on this trip, and I expected you to do the same. You had your shopping spree in Independence. It isn't my fault you didn't have the foresight to stock—"

I pulled my foot back and aimed a hard kick at his side. There was nothing wrong with his reflexes. He grabbed my ankle and lifted at the same time as he stood up. My other foot slipped out from under me and I went down, hard.

"Now don't be childish, Rhawnie," he said in a bored voice.

"Me! Childish!" I yelled. I pulled myself together and faced him squarely, half in a crouch like a fighter. "I suppose this is your way of taking revenge on me for the things I said to you back in our room in Independence." I balled my hands into fists and shook them in his face. "What a goddamned bastard you are! I would never, never in my life believe that you and Steven were born of the same mother—"

"Let's leave Steve out of this dispute," he said coldly.

"No! It's my dispute and I'll drag in anyone and anything that I please. You think you can intimidate me and terrorize me and starve me and make me your slave again, but it won't work! It won't work!"

"You should have stayed behind," he said. "It's not too late for you to turn back. I'll even take you back myself, as far as Kansas City. To protect you from harm," he added smugly.

"Oh? And who will protect me from you, answer me that?" I demanded furiously. "What's the matter with you? Are you afraid that I'll think less of you if I see you cooking and washing your own shirts, or if you behave towards me like a human being instead of a—a gorilla?

475

Listen, you couldn't possibly sink lower in my estimation. I know everything about you that there is to know—"

"Do you?"

"Yes, everything that I need to know to know that you're a blackhearted, evil scoundrel! You think you can break me, Seth Garrett—McClelland!—but you can't. You tried before, over and over, and you failed. No man can bend me to his will! I'll keep up with any pace you set. I'll let you browbeat me. What do I care for your food? I'll catch my own supper, damn you, and I hope—I hope you choke on your rotten dried meat!"

When I stopped ranting, I realized that I had been shouting at the top of my lungs and that I was even hopping up and down in my rage. Seth regarded me with silent interest, as if I were a curiosity at a sideshow, then he said, "Very impressive, Rhawnie. By all means, keep your voice in shape by shouting at me. There's nothing more stimulating to the appetite than witnessing a nice prima donna rage, is there?"

I slapped at his face and he ducked, laughing. I stalked away to tell the horses my troubles, but they had eaten their fill and were dozing and they really weren't interested. I threw myself down on the ground about fifty feet from the campfire and I fumed. I could hear him rustling around in the sack for his dinner, and my stomach growled. Of course I had provided myself with some food staples. But that wasn't the issue. His selfishness, his refusal to share, his attempt to dominate me—"Rhawnie, take off my boots!"—that was the issue! Bah!

As I sat there, absolutely motionless but raging inside, a large fat rabbit hopped into view. He came closer, so unsuspecting, and he stopped only three feet away from me. Surprised, he blinked at me. Also surprised, I blinked at him. Then I made a fast dive, and I caught him. Poor little creature. How was he to know that he had crossed the path of that most deadly of all hunters, a hungry Gypsy?

I wrung his neck—a quick, merciful death—and I sat for a long moment savoring my good fortune. Then I pulled out my new knife and slit his belly, wishing it were Seth's belly. I gutted and skinned him, throwing the pelt and the entrails to the coyotes and the vultures but reserving the heart and the liver for myself. Then I carried my prize, fully dressed, back to the fire.

Seth looked up, surprised. Of course he was surprised. There had been no shot, nothing. I gave him a quick, sneering glance, then I unpacked my cooking pot. I disjointed the rabbit, added an onion from my provision bag, a little salt, some wild garlic, and a bottle of Bordeaux that I had brought in St. Louis and somehow managed to keep Seth from drinking. Soon a fragrant *lapin au vin* was simmering over our stinking little fire of buffalo chips. The rabbit wouldn't be ready for an hour, maybe two, but I could wait. I would be glad to wait and to savor that delicious aroma. I stole a look at Seth, who was still trying to chew his tough beef jerky while he pretended that it was the finest sirloin. Yes, I could wait. The longer the better.

He didn't relent. The next day he roused me before dawn and ordered me to pack up and get ready to move out. We rode without stopping for close to fifteen hours. After I had eaten a little cold rabbit and had some wine, I wrapped myself in my cloak and blanket and went to sleep. The next morning the routine was the same. I really believe that he had decided to test my mettle by choosing the hardest trails over the roughest terrain. But I had bragged to him that I could take any punishment, endure any torture, and I would not back down.

Two more days passed like that, grueling, exhausting days. Then we caught up with a wagon train. My excitement mounted. Perhaps this was the end of our quest. We approached them. We hadn't gotten very close when a rifle report sounded. Two dark figures appeared from behind a wagon and we pulled up our horses.

"Sorry, men," one of them called. At that distance he could be excused for thinking me a man; after all, I was dressed like one, in high boots, cord breeches, a shapeless cloak and a floppy felt hat. "We can't let you come any closer."

"What's the matter?" Seth shouted. "Sickness?"

"Cholera. It's spreading through the wagons like wildfire."

I felt a sinking sensation in my middle. Oh, Gabrielle! I looked over at Seth. He also looked worried.

"Is this the Murray train?" he asked. "We're looking for a couple named Anderson."

"No one here by that name," one of the men answered. Seth described the fugitives, thinking that perhaps they had changed names again. But the answer was still the same. We breathed a sigh of relief.

"One of you isn't a doctor, by any chance?"

Beside me, I could feel Seth stiffen slightly.

"We could sure use a doctor here. We've lost fifteen people already half of 'em women and children."

A light wind blew up, carrying the echoes of suffering from the bunched wagons. I heard moans and shrieks, the sounds of people in mortal pain. Our horses shifted nervously.

"Well?" I said to Seth. "Here's your chance to do something for someone other than yourself."

"Don't be a little fool," he snapped. "Sorry!" he shouted back. "Good luck!" He raised his rifle in a farewell salute and wheeled Blaze around.

"But you can't leave them to die!" I cried. The screams of the dying tore at my heart. There were children in there. I urged Fire forwards and we trotted towards the wagons. I heard Seth's angry shouts but I ignored them.

I was only a dozen yards from the outermost wagon when he came abreast of me and caught Fire's reins.

"You can't go in there," he said angrily. "You couldn't help and you'd probably catch it yourself. Do you know anything about cholera? It can kill a strong man in two days. It's fatal half the time. And without medicine there's no hope. You'd go in to nurse and stay to die."

"Is that why you don't want to help? Because you're afraid?"

He shook his head impatiently. "Without medicine there's nothing I could do for them that they can't do just as well themselves. Believe me, Rhawnie, I only—"

"I don't believe you. I don't believe anything you say!"

I tried to pull the reins out of his hands. He held them fast. I began to fight him, to claw at his face and to beat at him with my fists. He pulled me off Fire's back and we rolled on the ground. I screamed incoherently and cursed him in half a dozen languages.

"Coward! Beast! Selfish greedy animal!"

He held my wrists firmly and tried to talk calmly to me, to quiet me, but I wouldn't listen to him. Finally his fist shot out and caught me under the chin. My head snapped back and the world went black.

He must have slung me over Fire's back, for when I awoke I was lying on the prairie grass with the warm sun on my face and my stomach muscles ached like fury. I sat up and rubbed my swollen jaw. There wasn't a wagon to be seen. Seth was near, at Blaze's head. He stroked the horse's nose and watched me.

"You didn't have to do that," I said groggily.

"I had to do something to get you away from there and to quiet you down," he said without any hint of apology in his voice. "You wouldn't listen to reason."

"No," I said bitterly, "I wouldn't. And besides, it gave

479

you a good opportunity to hit me. Seth McClelland, a great big fighting man, takes out his anger on weak, defenseless women!"

He grinned suddenly and said, "Well, you're certainly a woman. But as for being weak or defenseless—"

"Shut up," I growled, getting up and staggering over to Fire. "I'm in no mood to quarrel with you."

"I never would have guessed," he replied.

We pushed on, not stopping until well after sunset. The next morning we awoke to steady rainfall. I was limp and tired from a bad case of diarrhea, and I didn't even try to keep up with Seth, I had to dismount frequently.

At one point, Seth came back to harangue me for slowing us down.

"What do you know about anything?" I snarled. "You're not a woman!"

"You're not pregnant, are you?" he asked.

"No, thank God. Go ahead. I'll catch up." I waved him away.

The rain penetrated my cloak and soaked me to the skin. I felt cold and miserable. The horses dragged their feet on the soft turf. Thunder rumbled over our heads and once lightning struck so close to me that I could smell the scorch of the earth. I wished we could stop, but I didn't want to ask. We plodded on. The terrain grew a little harder and rockier. We had reached the Platte River, three hundred and sixteen miles from Independence. Compared to the Mississippi the Platte wasn't a river at all, but a swamp, a mile wide and unfordable because of quicksand.

But what did I care about quicksand? I felt awful, so weak and drained from my diarrhea that I could hardly sit up in the saddle. When next I dismounted it was to vomit. I straightened up and leaned heavily against Fire's flank.

Seth rode up. "More nature calls?" he asked sarcastically. "Listen, Rhawnie, if you can't keep up—"

I could barely hear him over the pelting noise of the rain and the roar of thunder, but I said as loudly as I could, "I'll die in the saddle before—"

A bad cramp in my middle made me double up. I fell on my knees and vomited again. No food, only milky-colored water that the rain washed away at once.

Strong hands under my arms lifted me easily to my feet. A voice like the Day of Wrath boomed in my ear: "Have you had diarrhea? Well, have you?"

Sick as I was, I blushed and said with all the dignity that I could muster, "What kind of question is that? It's none of your damned business."

"It damned well is my business!" he shouted. I swear, his voice was louder than the loudest thunder. "Yes or no? Come on, answer me!"

"Yes." I squirmed. Sure, the man had delivered my baby, but that didn't give him any right to—

"When did it start?"

"Last night. I didn't sleep at all."

"Jesus. Why didn't you tell me?"

Foolish question. Before I could reply the most excruciating pain seized my left leg while another grabbed my middle. I fell on my knees in the mud, and I bit my lower lip hard to keep from crying out. I vomited again and again.

I was dimly aware of Seth moving around, putting up our small canvas tent, building a small fire. I had to give him credit there. I have seen many a Gypsy trying to start a fire in the pouring rain, and Seth did it in an impressively short time. Of course he was so efficient that he probably carried a few dried buffalo chips inside his coat for just that purpose. He knew how to pitch a tent, too, on the highest point of the plateau, so that we wouldn't catch any run-off from other slopes.

Within half an hour he had me tucked up inside that tent.

481

It was four feet high at the center, tall enough for a man to kneel up fairly straight.

He started to strip off all my clothes, everything, even my flimsy chemise and lacy pantaloons.

"What are you doing?" I asked. My voice sounded odd to my ears, husky and harsh and not a bit musical. And my mouth felt as dry as old bones.

"It will be easier to keep you clean if you soil yourself," he said with ruthless matter-of-factness. I cringed. Where I came from men didn't discuss a woman's bodily functions like that. At least not in front of the woman. "Also you'll be sweating profusely and everything you have on will be wet—and cold."

"Soil myself?" I muttered. "That's a laugh. After last night there is nothing left. Only water. I am very thirsty. It must have been the *lapin*. Take my advice, Seth, don't waste even cheap Bordeaux on these prairie rabbits. They're as tough as old boots."

"It wasn't the rabbit," he said, wrapping me in a blanket. "You have cholera."

"Oh." I thought about this and then I had a bad seizure, followed by vomiting. Seth held me under the shoulders and braced my forehead, and he wiped my mouth when I was finished. He helped me to lie back. "Am I going to die?"

"Maybe. Maybe not. I told you, there's a fifty percent mortality rate."

Another cramp struck my abdomen. I screwed up my face and turned away from him so that he couldn't see how I was suffering.

"Leave—me," I grasped. I felt ashamed that anyone would see me like that, sick and weak and vulnerable and distorted by pain.

"Why don't you scream?" he suggested. "You might feel better."

"Me—Gypsy—scream?" Sweat poured off me. I waited for the seizure to pass. "No, *gorgio*. I cannot!"

He tried to take my hand but I wouldn't let him. More cramps in my legs drove everything else from my mind. I was being crushed in a vice of pain. I felt hot, burning up, and so thirsty that I wanted to rip away the tent that sheltered us and drink the rain.

"Water," I begged. "Please, Seth, water. So—thirsty." I vomited again.

Seth helped me rise a little and to drink from a tin cup. He let me have only the smallest sip. I wanted more but he refused.

"You'd only vomit it again," he said reasonably.

"So—cruel!" I gasped. "You are—oh!" More cramps, more vomiting.

"Listen, Rhawnie, do you have any drugs in that bag of yours? Any opium or laudanum? Something to arrest the—"

"What would I—be carrying stuff—like that for?" I moaned. "I am not sick. There is—Gypsy ointment."

"No good. There's got to be something," I heard him mutter. "We've got to stop the vomiting."

He moved around the cramped tent. It took all my strength not to cry out. I didn't want to show weakness or cowardice. After a while he raised me up slightly and made me swallow some powder. That was followed by a small sip of water. The taste of the stuff was unbelievably foul.

"What—was that?"

"I saw some hemp plants growing along the river," he said, wiping my mouth and swabbing the rivulets of perspiration away from my face and out of my eyes. "The Indians use it as a sedative as well as a stimulant. And there were a couple of camphor balls in the bottom of your valise. Taken together, I hope they'll have a mild, narcotic effect that should help arrest the vomiting. Try and keep it down as long as possible. Ah!" I vomited. "Come on, try again."

I ate some more of his concoction and choked on it. He gave me a sip of water to wash it down.

"You sound—like a medical textbook," I said.

"And where would you have seen a medical textbook, Gypsy?" he asked soothingly and mechanically as he wiped the sweat away. I decided that one of the aspects of his medical training had been, "Humoring the Patient." I wondered why some of that hadn't stayed with him and carried over into his private life.

"Couldn't read—it anyway," I rasped. My voice sounded ugly, so hoarse and scratchy. "Thirsty. Water, please."

"Don't talk so much," he advised gently. "No, you can't have more than a sip."

"More," I begged, "please, Seth."

"No," he said crisply. "It's not good for you. I know it's hard, but too much water will only irritate—oh, never mind. Just believe me when I tell you that I can't let you have more water because it's not in the prescribed treatment. Now take some more powder."

"Doctors are fools," I said. You hate me—because of Steven. Don't you? Listen, Seth." I grabbed feverishly at his shirtfront and looked up at him beseechingly. "I may be—dying. I will not lie to you. What—would be the point? I had lovers—after you left me. Not many. Before I met—Steven. But he—he was never my—lover. I swear this, Seth. May the hands of my dead—reach up and take me to Hell—if I do not speak the truth. Your brother—too much of a gentleman. He didn't believe—in it, before marriage." I released him and fell back. My mouth was so dry I could barely whisper. "Do you—do you believe me? I want you to understand—to make things better between you—before I die. Do you—believe?"

He gave a weary sigh and said, "Yes, Rhawnie. I believe you."

"I wouldn't lie," I insisted. "Only a fool—would tell lies—on her deathbed."

So why was I lying like a Gypsy, with my death only a few short hours away? I'm not sure. I really did want to make things better between them if I died. And if I lived, Seth wouldn't resent me so much. He wouldn't have to torment himself with thoughts of me in bed with his brother.

I had more severe pain and more vomiting. Seth forced me to take more medicine and then just a bit of water. I was drenched with sweat, and when I looked down at my hands and arms I saw that they were blue and shrivelled, like a washerwoman's. And my thirst, my thirst was so great that I would have given my soul for water. I had visions of myself floating in a vast freshwater lake. I opened my mouth and let the blue waters of the lake flow into my body, down my throat and into my stomach and out into my dried up tissues, which absorbed the water like a balloon fills with air, and grew plump and firm again. I was drinking, drinking, as much as I could hold.

Every time I vomited, Seth made me take more foul medicine, then a taste of water to wash it down. But after my stomach warmed the liquid I was sick again. The miserable business went on and on.

"When—will it end?" I asked him.

His arms felt so strong and steady under my shrinking frame. His face was kind, full of care and concern. It was so beautiful to me, with its straggling mustache and bristling beard—he didn't like to shave on the trail—and its silly bumps and scars. I wanted to cry.

"It will be over when the vomiting stops," he said. "Then you'll be able to rest quietly."

"Or when—I die." He didn't say anything to that. I

knew there was a very real chance that I wouldn't live to see another morning. "I'm not afraid—to die," I told him honestly. "I haven't been afraid of Death—since London. Remember? You saved me then, too. Remember, Seth?"

"I remember."

"I was—very young, then. Eager to prove—how brave I was. It was—foolish. Life is too precious—to throw away. But I do not fear Death. He is an—old friend now. You know him—"

"We've met," he said. I was sick again. He held my head and then wiped my face and mouth. "Many times, in fact. But I've always beaten him up to now. And so will you."

"Perhaps, but if not—will you forgive me? I cannot die—without your forgiveness. Please, Seth. Please." I reached for his hand. He held mine tightly.

"I forgive you," he said softly, "for all the wrong you have done in your life. And I ask you to forgive me." He paused, and I remembered all the things I held against him: different cities, different sins. Paris. London. Vienna. "Do you forgive me, Rhawnie?"

I closed my eyes. Could I really forgive all that? I had to, if I wanted my death to be peaceful and happy. "Yes," I whispered. "I do forgive." His hand moved on mine, caressing, reassuring. "One thing more. One more—truth," I said. "I love you. Always. And forever. You are—part of me. And I—love."

My heart swelled and tears mingled with the sweat on my cheeks. I hoped he wouldn't see my crying. I felt something warm and dry brush my forehead. A kiss.

The spasms of pain and vomiting continued throughout the night. Then I entered a new phase of the disease. I had great difficulty breathing and I felt cold, very cold, particularly in my hands and feet. Seth told me later that the dehydration caused by the sickness causes the blood to thicken, and that impairs circulation. But I didn't know any of that then. I knew only that I was sicker than I had ever been in my life, and I felt so wretched that I would have welcomed Death as a release from the discomfort and pain.

The rain stopped. Seth moved me outdoors, into the sunshine. He built a bigger fire and he chaffed my limbs to encourage movement of blood. He forced me to drink, even though I was barely conscious and I choked and gagged on the water. And when night came again he lay beside me to give me his warmth. That was only fair; I had done the same for him.

Another dawn broke. I awoke to find myself nestled in the curve of his arm. He was sleeping soundly. I didn't want to wake him. But after a while I felt him stir and I said, "May I have some water, Seth? I'm terribly thirsty."

He cradled me in the crook of his right arm and held the cup for me to drink. This time he let me have as much water as I wanted, as much as I could hold.

I looked down at myself. I was utterly emaciated. Skin and bones! I looked like a pale, plucked chicken and I must have weighed only ninety pounds.

"Is it over?" I asked him.

"It's over," he said. His voice held a note of triumph, as if he alone was responsible for my recovery. And he probably was. He had a right to be proud of himself. "You're alive, Gypsy. To torment me and irritate me and dazzle me with your beauty and your stupid lies." He grinned at me. "You're going to have to drink a lot to make up for what you lost. I'd like to get some salt into you—"

"Caviar," I suggested weakly. "In the bottom of my valise. I have two jars left."

"You would!" he laughed.

My recovery was remarkably speedy. Two days later I felt as though I had never been sick. I was still weak, and I suspected that my endurance on the trail wouldn't be what it was, but I felt like myself again. I was alive!

"Camphor, Canabis, and caviar," Seth said with a shrug. "Never fails."

"But you," I asked worriedly. "Will you get it, too?"

"I don't know. Maybe not. Cholera is strange that way. Very often the ones that are closest to the victims are spared, never get it at all, while it strikes a group of people miles away who have had no contact with a human carrier. It seems to travel on the wind."

"Like scandal," I sighed. "Well, I hope you don't get it."

"Why, don't you want to nurse me again?" he asked, giving me a devilish grin that made my heart bump. "We've each had a turn now; I think we should call it quits with medicine. No more accidents, no more illness. Fair?"

"Fair." I looked at him, standing hatless under the sun, his shirt open to the waist and his sleeves rolled up over his brawny forearms. The sun brought out warm red lights in his hair. Funny, I had always thought that his hair was black as pitch.

I wanted to ask him why he had abandoned medicine, if it was because of Julie. But according to Steven he gave it up before that debacle, before he went to fight the Mexicans in Texas. He would have been a fine doctor. But I knew if I said anything I'd only get a flippant, evasive reply, so why bother? I contented myself with musing on the question in my spare time—when I wasn't preoccupied with disliking him for one reason or another.

"I've loaded the horses and we're ready to ride," he announced one morning four days after my illness had abated. "We'll go as far as we can until we get tired. No false bravery. If you feel like you want to rest, tell me. I won't hold it against you. We don't have much farther to go anyway. We're sure to catch up with that wagon train at Fort Laramie."

Neither of us mentioned that touching scene at my death bed. After all, I hadn't died, and I decided that all those forgivenesses didn't count. But I looked into my heart as we rode along—with Seth's protracted silences and the monotonous scenery along the Platte there wasn't much else to do—and I discovered that I really had forgiven him for most things; for everything, in fact, except his desertion of me and our baby in Vienna. I didn't care what demons drove him, what ghosts haunted him: that had been a wretched and heartless thing to do. Well, I sighed inwardly, maybe by the next time I'm dying I'll be able to forgive Vienna, too. If he hasn't added a batch of new sins to his roster by that time.

The trail rose steadily. We left the Great Plains. The long waving grasses of the prairie became short, tough shoots that could survive the blistering heat of the summer and the parching dryness. We crossed the South Platte River and passed Court House Rock, aptly named and looking like it could easily accommodate a thousand dusty bureaucrats. We saw Chimney Rock, which rose out of the flat, dry plain and shot up forty feet in the air. And we rode under the wind-eroded faces of the rocks known as Scott's Bluffs.

As Seth predicted, we caught up with the Murray train at Fort Laramie. As I saw the band of wagons clustered around the thick adobe walls of the fort, I panicked a little. I felt frightened and nervous. This was the end of our quest, the end of my time with Seth. It was over. I would have to go back to New Orleans now, and face Steven with the truth about us. The prospect unsettled me. I felt that I wasn't ready. I was a coward.

Seth and I found Murray, who was sitting in the shadow of the fort's walls with his guide, a hirsute mountain man named Blythe. It was noon, and even in March the sun on those plains was hot and devitalizing.

We exchanged greetings. The men never took their eyes from me.

"I'm looking for a couple named Anderson," Seth told them. "They might be using a different name, but I'm sure they're with you." He started to describe them but Murray stopped him.

"They was here, but they ain't here no more," the man said, spitting a wad of tobacco juice out of the corner of his mouth without even turning his head. His bright eyes never left my face. "Left the train nigh on two weeks ago, warn't it, Blythe?"

Blythe, too smitten to speak, drooled assent.

"What do you mean, they left you?" Seth said. "Who did they leave with? Another train? Why? Which way were they headed?"

"One question at a time, young fellow," Murray said slowly. "Young varmint never could see eye to eye with any of us. Most argumentative, stubborn fellow I ever met up with. Ain't never seen the other side of the Mississippi and he kept tryin' to tell me I was takin' the wrong trails. He had this book with him, you know. By that fellow Hanson. *Hanson's Guide,* warn't it, Blythe? Told all about easier passes through the Rockies, how you kin git to California in two weeks less time. Now, boy, you and I both know that book is a load of—you'll pardon me, Ma'am—buffalo pies. That varmint Hanson ain't never even seen the Rockies! But I couldn't talk sense into him, and neither could Blythe here, who knows these mountains like the backs of his very own hands."

Blythe acknowledged the compliment with a grunt.

"So this Anderson took his wagon and lit off by himself. Said that if any of us tried to follow him he'd blow a hole through 'em. I say if a man's that eager to play the fool, it ain't my business to stop him."

"What about his wife?" I said eagerly. "Is she—was she all right?"

Murray shrugged. "I guess so, Ma'am. We didn't see

too much of her. Stayed in the wagon most of the time, sick-like.''

''Sick?'' Seth said quickly.

''Mornin' sick. Green sick.'' I thought I detected a faint blush under Murray's abundant facial hair. ''She was real poorly for a while, I heard. Too bad. Purty little thing, Miz Anderson. Real purty.''

Blythe grunted enthusiastically. Seth turned on his heel and stalked away.

''It's all right,'' I assured him. ''Don't worry. Women have babies every day. She can't be very far along, only a few months. We could even get her home before the baby is born, don't you think?''

''Be quiet,'' he said. ''I have to think. They won't make any time in the mountains, not with the wagon they're hauling. We shouldn't have any trouble finding them. We'll stay here a couple of days, to rest the horses and pick up some supplies.''

It felt good to wear a dress again. The soldiers at the fort made much of me, and I had a good time visiting with the other travellers and gold seekers and pioneers who were staying there. I caught up on my laundry, replenished my supply of brandy, and even won a few dollars at cards. The captain of the fort invited Seth and me to use his room and his bed. Seth declined and told me to go ahead. Our relationship probably baffled that poor captain, but I didn't feel that I wanted to explain. On our last night at Fort Laramie the members of the Murray train gave a square dance and invited Seth and me.

I had a wonderful time. I learned new dances and new songs and I even got a little drunk on some powerful applejack. Seth didn't dance, but he watched me closely from the sidelines.

After a particularly exhausting reel, I joined him. He was sitting on top of a large trunk and when I came over he shifted to make room for me.

"You picked that dance up quickly," he said.

"It's not hard," I said breathlessly, fanning myself with my hand. "Not so different from Gypsy dances."

"Only the men and women dance together," he said mischievously. Then, "Tell me how you met Steve."

"You mean your brother?" I said stupidly.

"The same."

"Why, in Munich. Your mother told you. Steven helped me to escape when the revolution broke out."

"The revolution that you caused," he said playfully.

I tossed my head. "Some would say that. But it's not true. While I was in Bavaria I made some very powerful enemies. One Baron in particular. He used me to start that revolution himself, just so he could throw my dear Ludwig out and put his own man in. The whole affair was a disgrace. Von Zander was a greedy, opportunistic fiend. Utterly ruthless!"

"Sounds like a man after my own heart," Seth grinned. "And Steve got you out in the nick of time, eh? How? I want to know the gory details."

I gave him a fairly accurate account of our escape and our journey to Le Havre, expurgating, of course, the story of our night of love at the Chateau Lesconflair. That tale, I was sure, would never leak out. Steven was far too polite and discreet.

"So you see," I concluded, "your brother is not the dry stick you think him. He is brave and resourceful. A man of action!"

"That's not the kind of action that interests me right now," he said. "Do you mean to tell me that you spent over a week in each other's company and you didn't seduce him?"

"Is that so strange?" I said stiffly. "You and I have been together for two months—longer!—and I haven't tried to seduce you."

"Why not?" he wanted to know.

I flushed. "I really don't want to discuss it. I—I'm engaged to Steven, remember?"

"I remember. But you love me. Always—and forever." His voice was caressing, soft. He took my hand. I pulled away quickly, as if he had burned me. "Don't you remember saying that?"

"Oh—I—I was sick and delirious!" I answered quickly. "I was delirious! I lied!"

"You weren't delirious. You thought you were dying. You were telling only truths that night."

"I think it is very mean of you to hold that against me!" I said tartly. I hopped off the trunk and rejoined the dancers. I felt angry with him, but even angrier with myself. The minute he had started talking about love and seduction the little imps inside me started racing around, making trouble.

We left the fort early the next morning. I thought Seth looked particularly handsome as he rode along. He sat his horse so well, so easily. The muscles of his broad back and shoulders swelled under his coat, his thighs bulged inside his breeches, and they looked firm and hard on the saddle. His beard was neatly trimmed, and he narrowed his blue eyes slightly against the glare of the sun.

A vast herd of buffalo crossed the prairie in front of us, and we had to wait for them to pass. They moved in thick clouds of dust, and even from miles away we could hear the low thunder of their hooves on the hard ground. The rains had stopped long ago, and the grass under our horses' feet was dry and crunchy.

"Do you want buffalo steak for dinner?" Seth asked.

"They are so big," I said. "So much waste!"

"We could take a couple of days out to dry some meat. There aren't any more herds west of the Rockies. Food may be scarce. I hope we don't have to go that far." He gave an amused grunt. "I haven't killed a buffalo in years."

"Leave them," I said. "It would be dangerous to get too close."

"Easy enough to drop a straggler with a rifle. Last time all I had was a bow and arrow."

"How brave you were!" I marvelled.

"Foolhardy," he grinned. "Nearly got myself killed."

That night when I was talking to Fire he sneaked up behind me. I was finished with the horses for the night but I didn't feel like joining him at the campfire yet. And I liked telling the horses my problems, in Romany, of course. They always listened politely and never talked back.

I didn't even hear him approach. He could be as quiet as an Indian when he wanted to be. The bastard. He slid his arm around my waist and cradled my breast in his hand. He kissed the nape of my neck and sweet pain consumed me, flowing from the top of my head to the soles of my feet. After a minute of that, he turned me around and held me close, then he kissed me slowly and deeply. Shocks of pleasure shook me to my core. Only by the greatest act of will did I stop myself from giving in to him then and there. Instead I kept my head and remained unresponsive and stiff.

He released me and stepped back slightly, still holding my arms. I wiped my lips with my fingertips and said, "If that's an invitation to something better, I will have to refuse."

"Why?" he asked softly. "Do you have somebody better waiting in the wings tonight? You're just trying to stay faithful to your betrothed, is that it? Admirable, darling. I take note, and I'm duly impressed. But Steve is a couple of thousand miles away. And we're here. Now. And I want you."

"I don't trust you," I said with perfect truth. "And I don't trust myself. We were finished with each other a long time ago. It's better if we stay finished. I do have some pride, you know. A Gypsy's pride doesn't mean much to

494

you. But it's important to me, Seth. It's not easy for me to keep my self-respect when you start manipulating me like this. It's not fair. You tried to subjugate me by harsh treatment and harsh words, and you failed. And so now you'll change your strategy. You'll dominate me by desire, because you know that way you're assured of success. I don't want to be hurt by you anymore. Please, Seth, just leave me alone."

He stepped away and lit a cigar. "Well, if that's the way you want it. What a waste. What possible harm could there be in having a little diversion on the trail? After we catch up to Gaby it won't be so easy."

"There's no harm in it for you," I said, "because you don't care about me. Oh, I think you have some feeling for me, because we've known each other for a long time and we've been through a lot together. But you don't love me, not the way I love you. I don't know why I love you. I just can't help myself. And every time you touch me, it's like you were reopening old wounds and pouring vinegar into them."

"So that's why you came along on this little adventure," he said. "To torture yourself?"

"I came to help Gabrielle," I said stubbornly. "Or that's what I told myself at the time. Oh, hell. I don't know why I came! I wish I knew what makes me do the things I do! I don't think about my reasons. I just act! I live! What do you want from me? I'm a Gypsy!"

"I think you're using Gaby as an excuse to get away from Steve," he said shrewdly. "It's an easy way out of your situation. You don't want to hurt him by breaking it off yourself, and so you run off with me, giving him a fine excuse for breaking with you. No man likes to be made to look a fool. No one would believe that you and I spent months in each other's company without succumbing to the inevitable."

"You're wrong!" I cried. "You know perfectly well that

495

we didn't expect to be gone more than a couple of weeks. As it is now—except for that incident in Independence—we can truthfully say that nothing happened between us. Nothing! That we were like—brother and sister. I intend to tell Steven the truth about us when we go back. And then I'll let him decide if he still wants to marry me. I still want to marry him. And you still want to spoil it!''

He sighed and shook his head. ''You're hopelessly confused, Rhawnie. You've been a liar for so long that you wouldn't know the truth if it reared up and kissed you on the mouth. You say you love me. You come two thousand miles with me even though you could have turned back at any time, as long ago as St. Louis. You admit that you want me as much as I want you. But you tell me that I'm not supposed to touch you because you have some crazy idea about saving yourself for Steven. Why? You just finished telling me that when you told him about us your engagement to him would be in trouble. You really think that he'll be willing to marry you when he knows? Then why didn't you tell him long ago? Because you know that he's going to be appalled and sickened when he learns that the woman he loves belonged—no, *belongs*—to the man he considers the world's biggest moral cretin. You—''

''No! No!'' I covered my ears with my hands. ''I can't listen to any more! You're just trying to get me mixed up!''

He threw up his hands. He tossed the stump of his cigar down and ground it out with his heel. I ran back to the campfire and crouched with my palms extended, warming them. The sky was a vast gleaming canopy of stars. A chill wind blew down from the north. A coyote howled in the distance, but inside the circle of fire I felt safe, secure.

I sat with my arms wrapped around my knees. I heard Seth come up behind me. He sat on the ground beside me and lightly touched the fine hairs at the nape of my neck.

"Take your hair down," he whispered.

I lowered my face onto my arms and shivered. I tried to summon my strength but it had deserted me. He sensed that I had been teetering on the edge of a precipice, and that at the slightest pressure from him—over I'd go. He knew the wanton in me; he had created her. He knew that when he touched me, the wanton would yearn for more than a kiss. And he knew that when he murmured sweet words and accompanied them by a deft caress, the little imps of desire that lived in me would clamor for more. He didn't want rape. He wanted surrender.

I sighed deeply and tumbled over the precipice.

He took the pins out of my hair and unlaced my braids His mouth did terrifying things to my neck and throat and lips. With a groan I lay back in his arms and pulled him close to me.

He spread out a blanket near the fire and we undressed each other. I shivered a little. But his hands and mouth and fine strong body worked their magic and I soon forgot the cold. The wanton took possession of me. I stroked his velvety smooth manhood, source of so much delight, so much distress. I lifted my body to receive him. He gasped with pleasure and he descended into sweet darkness. He moved slowly and knowingly. I writhed ecstatically, rejoicing in the disarming sensations that washed over me. He drove deeper, harder, straining to possess me. He took my buttocks in his great hands and palpated my flesh, and he lowered his dark head over my breasts, kissing and exciting them. I nearly went mad. I was his slave, his—

Something happened. I began to scratch and beat at him, to dig my nails into his flesh and to bite the shoulder nearest my mouth.

"Stop it!" I cried, wriggling out from under him. "Let me go! I don't want you!"

He swore at me and told me to calm down. I couldn't. I

tore at him, hating him, hating myself for falling so easily into his snare. All the tenderness between us vanished and the wind felt cold again. I struggled desperately to get away from him. He pinned my hands above my head and tried to kiss me. I tossed and rolled my head.

Tears flooded my cheeks. I craned my neck forward so that I could savage his flesh with my teeth. He pulled back, out of reach. I wept with anger and frustration and fear. I didn't want to lose my heart to him again, and have him return it to me looking like it had been battered in the paddles of a steamboat wheel.

"I don't want you!" I sobbed. "I hate you! Get away from me!"

"You crazy bitch," he growled. "What's the matter with you?"

I raved on and on, and fought and twisted and kicked. Then he slapped my cheek, rather lightly. The blow stung me and shocked me and stopped my ranting in mid-curse. I gazed at him for a long moment, my eyes full of surprise and hurt wonder. Then I started to cry, awful wrenching sobs that tore me apart. Never in my life had I cried like that, and certainly not in front of him.

He lifted himself off me. I rolled onto my side and drew my knees up and cried and cried like an hysterical child. I would have expected him to slink away, feeling angry and thwarted, to drink whiskey and smoke sullenly. But after a minute or two he knelt beside me and gathered me into his arms. I clung to him. He smoothed my hair and whispered softly and soothingly to me. He said my name over and over again, and he told me to be quiet and he said that everything would be all right.

I tightened my arms around him and drew on his great strength. Finally the tears stopped flowing. Sobs like shudders wracked my body for a long time afterwards. I wouldn't let him go. As long as I could cling to him like that

I could pretend to myself that he loved me. And that night I needed the pretense. It made me feel a little better about betraying Steven's trust, about the mess I'd gotten myself into. I did love Seth. Just as I told him, always and forever. And only a simpleton would believe that I had come all this way with him just to help him search for his sister. No, I had wanted to be alone with him, to make him love me, to win him forever. Only it hadn't worked that way, and it wouldn't. I had just presented him with one more blazing opportunity to make a fool of me.

He said, "I'll leave you. Try and get some sleep."

But I pleaded with him to stay with me. So he drew another blanket and my wool cloak over us and lay down beside me. I rested my head on his shoulder and put one hand on his chest. Time passed and the stars wheeled in their orbits. I grew quiet and warm. I moved my hand lower, to his stomach. Nice. And to his abdomen. As tight as a drum head, even when he was relaxed. Still lower— he caught my wrist.

"No," he said sternly. "After that disgusting exhibition I just witnessed?"

"I don't know what came over me," I said humbly. "I can never again boast to you about how brave I am, about how I never cry. You—you won't tell?"

"I'll tell everyone I know," he assured me. "And when we get back to civilization, I'll publish the truth about you."

"I'm ashamed of myself."

"You should be. Go back to sleep."

"You think I'm bad."

"I think you're the world's second biggest moral cretin. Now shut up and go to sleep."

My hand began to stray again. This time he didn't try to stop it. I found his sleeping member, no bigger than a new kitten. I stroked it lightly until it swelled and throbbed under my hand. I covered him with my body and kissed his eyes and his ears and his mouth and his throat. I licked his small flat nipples until they were hard, and then I buried my face in the soft fur of his belly while I kneaded his thighs and buttocks with long, strong fingers. He twitched and moaned. From the tightness in his body I could tell that he was trying not to abandon himself to pleasure.

I slid down and barricaded myself behind the low wall of his open legs. His breathing became deep and rapid. I worshipped his swollen idol with my fingers and my lips, loving it, tasting it, taking it into my mouth, into my soul. Taking it all. He clutched at my hair and strained against me. I sank my fingernails into his hard buttocks and heard him suck in his breath. He couldn't hold back any more. He gave a great moan and a convulsive heave, and he was mine.

I lay quietly between his legs, my head pillowed on his belly, my hand covering his shrinking trophy. I felt victorious. Over him, and over myself. I had taken him. He had not taken me. I had rendered him helpless. And I had subjugated him not by force but by desire. He was in my power, and I had done it in my own time, in my own way.

The object under my hand awoke again and stirred and stretched, growing strong and straight. Seth lifted me up so that our eyes were even once more. He touched my face lightly.

"You're beautiful," he murmured softly. "Completely crazy. But completely beautiful."

He turned me on my back and lowered himself onto me. I welcomed him, and I let him know it, but not with words. Our bodies moved together, softly as a sigh. And the stars looked down. . . .

In the morning, even before the sun came up, he prodded me with his boot.

"Time to get up. We can make it to North Platte crossing

by nightfall if we ride hard today and don't waste time."

"North Platte Crossing?" I grumbled. "Why on earth would anyone want to go to North Platte Crossing?" I pulled the blanket tighter around my shoulders. Mercilessly, he stooped down and ripped it off me. I shivered in the cold pre-dawn air. "All right, all right," I said irritably. "I'm coming."

I dressed quickly and brushed and braided my hair. I groped in the darkness for my pins, on the ground where I thought Seth had left them, but I could find only two. I had to let my braids flop. The day didn't get any better. The girth on Fire's saddle snapped when I was tightening it, and rather than take time out to fix it, I decided that I would ride bareback that day.

We rode out. Seth was wrapped in silence. It wasn't morning too-early-to-talk silence, but the kind he used for a retreat when I had annoyed him in some way or when he wanted to think.

I didn't care about his mood. I grinned and sang a little Gypsy song to Fire, who liked music. I felt free again. I wasn't afraid of Seth anymore. The business with Steven would straighten itself out. What was I worried about?"

I kept my distance from Seth, sometimes letting him get a quarter of a mile ahead before I put on a burst of speed and caught up with him again.

Seth rode Blaze and led the packhorse, Venus. The Rocky Mountains lay in front of us, distorting the evenness of the horizon. The sky was brilliant, dazzling. A lark sang. A grouse chipped. Rabbits and deer scurried along.

We reached the mountains and searched there for a week, to no avail. Then in some obscure pass near the Sweetwater River, we found a dead horse blocking the trail. We examined it.

"He's wearing shoes. Not a wild pony," I said. "I think he died of exhaustion."

"Well, they can't get far with one less horse. He hasn't been dead too long. A couple of days. Rigor passed off long ago."

I saw their wagon first, at the bottom of a precipice. Vultures circled lazily overhead. I shuddered and closed my eyes.

Seth and I went down on foot to look. A horse with two broken legs gasped raggedly under the rubble. Two other horses lay close by, already dead. Seth shot the horse who was still alive, to end its misery. I cursed Boris. Any fool could see that the trail around the cliff was too narrow for a wagon.

Then I saw a foot jutting out from under the wreck. A man's boot. I touched it. He was dead.

Seth and I lifted the crumpled wagon off him and dragged him out. There was no sign of Gabrielle. The corpse's blond head was matted with blood.

"She's got to be around here someplace. She's not in the wagon." Seth looked around anxiously.

"Perhaps she was following on foot," I suggested hopefully. "She might not have gone over at all."

We shouted for her. Our words came back to us.

"We'll search," Seth said. "She might have been hurt and crawled away to a sheltered place. Take the south side and I'll—don't bother with him. Let the vultures have him."

I was trying to turn the body over so that I could see his face. I had a peculiar feeling. Something was wrong. The body was too big, too clumsy-looking. Boris would never have worn such ugly boots.

"Seth!" I called. "Come here, quickly!" He joined me and I looked up at him. "It's not Boris," I said.

He turned pale under his tan. "You're lying," he said quietly. "You're lying! It's got to be!"

502

"It's not," I said gently. "I knew Boris, remember? This man isn't Boris Azubin. He's too big, too heavy. He's—he's not Boris!"

Seth's fingers dug into my shoulder. I winced. "If this is some kind of joke," he said dangerously, "I'll—"

"No, no!" I cried, "I swear I'm telling the truth! We'll—we'll search the wagon. Maybe we'll find something!"

There were a few personal objects buried under the welter of canvas and wood that had been the Andersons' wagon. A Bible, with a flyleaf that bore the names of a dozen Andersons and their brides and their children. A new-looking photograph of the dead man and a pretty dark-haired girl with wide eyes. A letter to Mary, signed "Bo." A locket, with his face on one side and a pale lock of hair on the other.

We had been chasing a dream. I had an impulse to laugh—I know it was just nerves—and I stifled it swiftly. But the situation really was ludicrous. We had come well over a thousand miles, chasing people we didn't even know. All of that suffering, all those days and nights on the trail, the rain and the cold and the sickness—it had all been for nothing.

I looked at Seth. His face was suffused with anger. His body was taut and tense, ready to snap. He seized my arm and twisted it behind my back. The pain was agonizing.

"This is your doing, I know it is!" he said through his teeth. "A wild goose chase! Almost two thousand miles! Where is she? What have you done with her?"

"I haven't done anything!" I gasped. "Let me go, Seth. For the love of God, stop and think a moment! It wasn't my idea to go chasing after the *Valerie Jane*. It was your father's suggestion, remember? You can't blame me for this mess! Blame your father!"

Why not? He wasn't there to bear the brunt of Seth's wrath, and I was.

"He was going to send a wire to St. Louis," Seth said. "Did you check? Did you remember to go to the telegraph office and ask for a message? No, of course not." He shook me. My shoulder strained in its socket. He let me go and gave me a little push. I fell on my knees and rubbed my aching arm. "You didn't want to know the truth. It didn't matter to you who we were chasing. You just wanted to get me out here so you could seduce me at your leisure! The biggest damned whore—"

"Me! Seduce you!" I shouted. "Why don't you just slow down a little? You can't blame me if I didn't ask for a message in St. Louis. I did the best I could and I didn't get any help from you, remember? And I talked to the captain of the *Valerie Jane* as he told me that Boris and Gabrielle were on the boat from New Orleans. The description fit these Andersons perfectly! It's just a horrible coincidence that they happened to be on that boat, that's all. This man even gambled, just like Boris! You can't blame me!"

"This Boris of yours was Russian, wasn't he? Did it occur to you to ask anybody if Anderson spoke with a foreign accent like yours?"

"Accent!" I shouted. "What do you mean, accent?" It came out sounding like, "Vat do you mean, agzent!" I took a breath. "My English is as good as yours!"

He spun around and slammed his fist into a tree. I might have felt sorry for him if I didn't hate him so much then. He really was the most pig-headed monkey I had ever known. It wasn't my fault the *Delta Belle* blew up and wounded him so that he couldn't ask his own damned questions. I hoped he smashed his hand to pieces.

"We'd better look for the girl," I said after a few minutes of silence. "She might still be alive."

He didn't move. I searched through the trees at the base

of the cliff. I found her huddled under a large overhanging rock. She was barely breathing.

"Mrs. Anderson," I said softly. "Mrs. Anderson, can you hear me?"

I shouted for Seth. No answer. I shouted again. One of the woman's legs jutted out at an awkward angle. I felt her bones gingerly and decided that not only was her leg smashed but her pelvis as well. If she was carrying a baby it was probably dead.

"Bo," she moaned. "Bo."

Seth came up. "She is very badly hurt," I said softly without looking at him. "The best we can do is make her comfortable."

She opened her eyes and stared into my face. I held her shoulders and clasped her hand reassuringly. "Where is Bo?" she asked weakly but lucidly. "Is Bo all right?"

I looked at Seth, who signalled that I was to tell her yes. She wouldn't live long enough to find out the truth.

"He's all right," I said. "Just a little banged up from the fall over the cliff. He's awake and he's asking for you."

She closed her eyes. "I'm so glad. He wanted to see— California. It doesn't matter—about me. But he—"

She died in my arms. Seth and I buried them both, marked the graves with rocks, and left the spot forever.

Seth wore his anger like a shield and his silence like a cloak. I knew I couldn't penetrate the barrier of resentment and fury that he had thrown up between us. I didn't even try to talk to him. I wondered where Boris and Gaby had gone, what had happened to them if they hadn't come upriver? And what about us? Where would we go now, what would we do? How could we continue to search, knowing that they might well have been found, closer to New Orleans?

That afternoon we met a wagon train in the mountains, just below the pass where we had found the dead horse. A group of men and women hurried forward to meet us.

"Can you help us, friend?" their leader asked. He was a tall man, fully bearded and soft-spoken, with grey tufts of hair in his ears and nose. "We are lost. We have been looking for a passage through the mountains—"

"Why didn't you take the South Pass?" Seth asked curtly. "It's clearly marked on all the maps and it's the easiest and fastest way through."

The man searched through his pockets and brought out a well-worn book. "We have this guide," he said. "By a Mr. Hanson. He says—"

Seth snorted. "That man never came within five hundred miles of the Rockies. He never got out of New York City. All his information is third hand. Or worse."

The bunch looked crestfallen. "We've been wandering up here for days," said one woman. "We hoped that God would show us the way."

"God didn't help the couple we found a few miles back," Seth said. "We just buried them."

"Sir," said the first man deferentially, "you seem to know these parts very well. Perhaps you could show us the way? Be our guide, at least until we get out of these mountains. We are going to Deseret, to Zion. We will pay you. We have some money—"

"I don't want your money," Seth told them. "Why in hell do you want to settle out there? It's a desert, a hell hole. A blast furnace in summer, dry as bone dust."

The ladies flinched at his rude speech, and one of them said nobly, "We are Mormons, sir. Members of the Church of Latter Day Saints. We have come over a thousand miles, all the way from Missouri, to escape persecution and to find rest and peace in a land that no one else in the world would want. Our noble leader, Brigham Young, has—"

"I know all about Brigham Young," Seth said. "Go

back to your wagons. You're going to have to back your horses up until we get to a place that's wide enough to turn around in. But your troubles won't be over when we get clear of these mountains. The real fun starts on the other side, in the desert.''

''We are used to hardship,'' said a lady piously.

''That's what you think.''

Those Mormons were a tough and holy group. They didn't spare themselves. A bugle sounded at five in the morning. While their animals grazed they prayed and ate a hearty breakfast. They invited Seth and me to join them, but we never did. When Seth told me that these people were God-inspired and fanatically religious, I decided to avoid them. Devout believers in anything but selfish opportunism made me nervous. At six-thirty the bugle sounded again, and we would start our trek of the day. Seth rode at the front, sometimes ranging so far ahead of us that I lost sight of him.

The Mormons had nothing against music and they sang as they plodded along. They were rarely silent, and I found their company pleasant after a while. The leader's wife, Lucy Ashbaugh, invited me to ride in their wagon to rest Fire. After a couple of refusals, I accepted. Seth wasn't interested in me, even though we slept near the same campfire outside the circle of wagons. He hadn't touched me in days, not since we found and buried the Andersons. I didn't know why he had consented to lead these people to Uta or Deseret, as they called it. It didn't matter. Nothing mattered now. And obviously neither of us had anything better to do.

There were two younger women in the Ashbaugh group besides Lucy, and several small children. I asked Lucy if they were all her children.

She laughed. ''Oh, no, these are Orson's wives, too. And the boys and girls are his children by them.''

I was speechless for a moment. "But you are his wife!"

"We are all his wives," she said gently. "And he is our husband."

"Our" husband! "Don't you—don't you quarrel?" I wondered.

"Why should we quarrel? We accept the will of God and rejoice in it!" She gave me a sweet, forebearing smile. That's right, I thought irritably, when life deals you a bad hand, blame it on the will of God.

"These men have many wives!" I told Seth that night. "I could not believe it when Mrs. Ashbaugh told me. That old man has three women! What do you think of that? Three wives!"

"I told you they were fanatics," he said with a shrug. "I feel sorry for the man who's saddled with one."

I felt stung and sad. Why did he have to say things like that? Two days later we reached the Little Sandy River and began our descent out of the mountains to Fort Bridger, which had been built by a Mountain Man named Jim Bridger. He welcomed Seth like a long-lost son.

"Seth boy!" Jim Bridger cried, pounding Seth on the back. "Seth boy! It's good to see you! I thought a wolf or a woman had got you, I hadn't seen you in so long." I came forward and he grinned. "And who's this lovely lady? How do, Ma'am! This is a great day for Fort Bridger!"

I started to say, "I'm Seth's wife," but Seth said quickly, "This is the Baroness of Ravensfeld. She is travelling with us."

A few of the Morman women trilled excitedly in the background. It was the first they had heard of my titled status, and they were impressed. They wouldn't have been so impressed if they knew how I had come by that title, I thought dryly.

We spent only one night at Fort Bridger before moving on, into the Wasatch Mountains. Once we had crossed those arid humps we would be in Salt Lake City. From what I had heard, it didn't sound like my kind of city. I knew that Seth and I wouldn't stay long. I was getting anxious to be shed of the Mormons anyway. Their goodness and piety made me uncomfortable, and when I was around them I had an inexplicable impulse to be wicked.

The Mormons in Salt Lake City made us welcome. Seth and I, as man and wife, were given a room in the home of one of the more important elders, a merchant named Zebulon Pratt. I was delighted. At last we could be alone together, without the distractions of the trail. I felt we needed to talk, to straighten out our differences, to plan our next move.

On our first evening in the town we were invited to dine with Brigham Young at his home. Elder Pratt, Elder Ashbaugh, and a handful of their wives would be there also. Neither Seth nor I enjoyed that meal very much, even though the food was excellent and the conversation interesting. Seth looked annoyed because there was no wine, and I was so eager to be alone with him that I couldn't absorb more than half of what was said.

Brigham Young might have been a fanatic, according to some, but he was also an intelligent, efficient planner and a charismatic leader. He had actually persuaded these people to give up individual ownership of land for the good of the community. Each family was given only as much land as it could efficiently farm. The Saints had devised an irrigation system, the first of its kind in the world, that had brought water to their crops and turned the arid desert into a blooming, green valley.

Brigham Young was also a courtly, courteous gentleman who had an eye for feminine pulchritude. He beamed at me approvingly. I wore my only dress that night, a rose silk gown with a less than modest decolletage.

"I've heard of you, Baroness," said the great Mormon

509

leader. "One of my wives heard you sing in Germany, a long time ago."

"Surely not that long ago," I smiled brightly. "But how did she come to do that?"

"Her parents immigrated to this country soon afterwards, and became converted to the Saints' religion," he explained. "Perhaps you would honor us by singing for us this evening?"

I started to decline graciously but the rest of the party—except for Seth, who looked as though he couldn't be less interested—set up such a clamor that at last I had to consent. I just hoped they wouldn't make me sing any of their tedious hymns. But one of the wives came up with a book of songs by Franz Schubert. King Ludwig had loved Schubert so. After dinner everyone adjourned to the living room. I stood next to the upright piano while one of the wives—the younger one who had seen me in Munich—pounded vigorously at the keys. I chose songs that weren't too difficult for her: "What is Sylvia?" "The Nightingale." And the last song I sang was "Guten Nacht," or "Good-night." I sang all the songs in German. I knew Seth could understand the lyrics:

> Love likes to travel
> From one to the other,
> God has made it so;
> My fine lady-love, good-night!
>
> I will not disturb you in your dreams;
> 'Twere pity to spoil your rest.
> You shall not hear my footsteps . . .
> Softly, softly I closed the door.
> As I go out I will write
> "Good-night" to you on the gate,
> So that you may see
> My thoughts were of you.

I don't know why I chose that song. Perhaps I had a premonition, or foreboding. I watched Seth as I sang. His eyes were cast down and he looked very thoughtful and brooding. I told myself not to imagine things. He was probably just wishing he could smoke in Brigham Young's parlor.

We walked back together to Elder Pratt's house, which was at the north edge of town. As usual, Seth was silent. We undressed without speaking. I had exhausted my fund of amusing small talk at dinner, and he didn't want to hear it anyway. As I lay beside him in the darkness, my heart grew full of sorrow and an ancient fear possessed me. I was soothed and relieved when he turned over and took me in his arms. But there was no real love in his touch that night, no enthusiasm. He was quick and heedless of my pleasure. We might have been a long-married couple seizing our opportunity while the children slept next door, trying not to awaken them by making the bedsprings squeak too loudly. He finished in five minutes and then he rolled over on his side and snored loudly. I started at the pale shadows on the ceiling. I felt cheated and resentful and more fearful than ever.

When I finally got to sleep, I slept deeply. And when I awoke I saw that my fears had come true: Seth was gone. His things were gone. I dressed quickly and went out to the stables in the back. Of the three horses that belonged to us, only Fire was left. Gone. Seth was gone. Without so much as a "good-night" scrawled on the gate.

I ran into the house and back up to our room, which was at the rear on the second floor. I tossed my things into my valise, and I noticed that the wadded chemise that had held the last of Ludwig's jewels was gone. I searched everywhere. The *gorgio* bastard had absconded with them, too! I sat back on my heels, stunned and sick. He had done it again. Deserted me. Abandoned me. Left me with nothing. Well, he wouldn't get away with it.

I dressed in my trail clothes and finished packing. I picked up my valise and opened the door. Elder Zebulon Pratt stood there, his gross body filling the doorframe.

"Good morning, Mistress McClelland," he said sweetly, emulating his leader in courtliness, even at seven o'clock in the morning.

"Please excuse me," I said brusquely. "I must leave at once. Thank you for your hospitality—and for caring for my horses—".

I tried to push past him but he wouldn't move. He was a burly, overweight man, more fat than muscle. He had grown fat on the troubles of the gold diggers and maybe he had stolen from his fellow Saints to boot. He had the look of a cheat about him: small eyes, ready smile, soft hands.

"Now, now, don't be in such a rush, Baroness," he said in a voice like strained honey. "As for carin' for your horse, it was a real pleasure. She's a right fine little filly. Like yourself. She'll make a nice addition to my stables."

"What do you mean, to your stables?" I said impatiently. "She's mine."

"No, Ma'am, she's mine," he corrected me apologetically. "Your husband sold her to me. Along with your saddle and bridle. And a pocketful of some bright and shiny stones."

"Stones! Jewels!" I cried. "Those things are mine! That horse is mine! That saddle is mine! How dare he! How dare you! Let me pass at once or I'll scream the house down, I swear it. You have no right to keep those things. I order you to return them to me at once. Thief! Scoundrel!"

I got myself very worked up. It didn't occur to me then that this fat, greasy merchant was lying, that Seth hadn't sold him the things at all. In my mind they were equally despicable. But Seth was gone, and I had to take out my anger on the grinning Elder. I was a head taller than he but he outweighed me considerably. When I became too boisterous he simply put a meaty hand on my shoulder and pushed. I reeled backwards and fell hard against a dresser, bumping my head. While I sat on the floor, trying to collect myself, he came into the room and stripped the sheets and blankets off the bed. Then he walked out and shut the door. I heard a key grind in the lock. I was his prisoner.

I hammered at that door until my fists were black and blue, and I kicked it until the house shook. No one came to let me out. Not a wife, not a child. I know they heard me—Seth McClelland himself probably heard me, wherever he was—but so cowed were the women by their husband, so much under the spell of obedience to their master, that not one even bothered to come up and ask if I wanted a glass of water.

There was no way out of that wretched room. It was a sturdily-built adobe house. My room had only one window. I looked out and saw to my dismay that although I was only on the second floor, the house had been built on a rocky plateau, and from the window to the ground was a sheer drop of twenty-five or thirty feet, without so much as a shrub or a rosebush below to break my fall.

I indulged in a screaming fit. I shouted and pounded and tore at the bed and pillows until the air was filled with feathers. I smashed the mirror. I smashed the washbowl and pitcher. I wrecked a spindly-legged chair, and I used the legs to club at the washstand until it fell apart. And when I was exhausted I threw myself down on what was left of the mattress and cried my eyes out.

The day wore on slowly after that. I was sorry to see that my tantrum had taken up only a few minutes. Even so, it had made me feel better. I had no food that day. No water to drink. Fortunately in my rage I had forgotten to look under the bed, and so at least I still had a chamber pot. With my energy spent, I could only rage inwardly now at Seth and his treachery. Why, why couldn't I learn that to throw your heart to a man like that is to throw it into a pool of quicksand? He would take and take and never give anything back. Oh, he could give his precious body and the skills he had learned from a thousand and one women, but nothing, nothing of himself.

The night passed. I was wakeful, desperate. They would leave me here to starve, the swine. In the morning Zebulon Pratt appeared again. I heard the key turn in the lock, but I was too limp and listless to get off my mattress. I folded my arms across my chest and glared at him.

He clucked his tongue at the mess and said, "You must learn to control your temper if you are going to be good Saint, Ma'am. Learn to accept what God gives you: don't resist His power. In His divine wisdom—"

"Go to hell," I growled. "I'm hungry and thirsty. Bring me food and water."

"In time, in time," he said smoothly. "First let me make my offer. If you marry me you—"

"Marry you!" I laughed derisively. "You ass! Get out of my room and leave me alone!"

He gave a little chuckle. I wanted to smash his face. "I hope you'll come to see reason, Ma'am. I'll talk to you later, when you're feeling—hungrier."

I snatched up a chair leg and threw myself at him, but he ducked out the door and slammed it in my face. The key turned. I wrestled with the knob until it came off in my hands.

My innards growled, demanding sustenance. I had to think. At this rate, depriving me of food and water, he could break me down in no time. I wasn't a complete fool—only where Seth was concerned—and I knew how desperate a man can become after only a few hours without water. Out here, where the air was hot and dry, I couldn't last too much longer.

The second day of my captivity wore on. I grew weaker

and weaker. In the afternoon I even heard a whistling in my ears. I bobbed my head a little to see if I could make it go away, but it wouldn't stop. I looked around. The sound was coming from outside. I leaned out the smashed window. A lean, white-haired man was raking the area behind the house. He wasn't working very hard, just dabbing at the ground with his tool, and whistling.

"Psst, you, man!" I hissed. He looked up. I said formally, "If you have any Christian love in your heart at all, brother, I beg you to throw me a rope and help me get out of here. I think brother Pratt has been out in the sun too long. He is holding me prisoner—"

He looked around furtively and said in a harsh whisper, "You don't have to talk like that with me. I'm kind of a prisoner here myself." His face was doggy-looking, pulled down at the corners of his wide mouth into sagging jowls. His eyes were big and brown and childlike. He had a rather pathetic and hapless air about him. He looked around again and feigned work. He said as he pretended to rake, "If I help you get out, what will you do then?"

"What do you think?" I snorted. "I'll steal back my horse and get out of this town."

He looked up. A shrewd light burned in his eyes. "Will you take me with you? Please? I—I won't help you if you don't!"

I frowned down at him. What kind of man was this? Why didn't he run away if he was a prisoner here? He was still free to walk around, wasn't he? Why did he have to wait for a woman, especially one who was a prisoner, to help him? But I said nothing. I didn't want to antagonize him now. Later, maybe, but not before he helped me.

"What's your name?" I asked him. "How do you come to be here?"

More furtive looking around and desultory raking. "They call me the Professor," he said guardedly. "At one time I was very prominent in my field.'' I nodded, impressed. I guessed he told people that to help save his sagging pride. "But the lure of the gold fields was too strong for me," he sighed. "I gave up everything to come out here. But when I got to Salt Lake City I needed a new horse, some food, some equipment. It took all the money I had just to buy supplies, and then I couldn't afford a horse. Elder Pratt said that if I worked for him awhile he would let me have one. But he's only paying me a dollar a day and he's charging over two hundred for the horses.''

What a fool, I thought.

"Professor!" came a screeching voice from inside the house. "Ain't you finished out there yet? I want you to haul some water fer me!"

"Almost finished, Miz Pratt!" he called, and he raked furiously. After a minute he looked up and said, "I have to go now. I'll talk to you later."

"Wait!" I leaned out the window. "He hasn't even given me a drop of water. Look, I'll lower a string. If you could tie on a jug—''.

He hesitated but finally he consented because he needed me as much as I need him, to escape. I hurriedly made a slim rope of strips torn from a chemise. In fifteen minutes I was hauling up a sweating stone jug. I hoped that I could keep from knocking it against the side of the house and I prayed that my rope would hold. I drank thirstily and blessed the Professor. I could see that he was a kindly if spineless man. That was all right. That kind of man was easy to manipulate.

We formulated our plans. Or I did, after quizzing him on the lay of the land. After dark he tied the end of a sturdy rope to my string and I pulled it up and brought it inside, saving it for later. I had just finished stowing it under the remains of my mattress when I heard the clink of Elder Pratt's key. I looked around. The jug! I tossed it into my valise and covered it with a petticoat.

"Well, I see you're still on your feet," Elder Pratt said cheerfully.

"God is giving me strength to endure this torture," I said coldly. "I can hold out as long as you can."

He chuckled. "We'll see about that!" And he left me. It never occurred to him that I would get a confederate on the outside. He probably never even gave the Professor a thought, except to rub his fat hands together and laugh at the way he was rooking him. Pratt would certainly never credit him with having the guts to escape. All to the good, I thought.

The Saints retired very early so they could rise early and work that much longer. At midnight I heard the Professor's signal:

"Pssst!"

I darted to the window and motioned for him to be absolutely silent. First I lowered my valise on the rope, which I tied to the leg of the bed. Then I lowered myself. I climbed down the wall of that house as quietly as a fly on a wall. My feet were bare: I wouldn't put on my boots until we were well away from the house.

"Where are your supplies?" I asked the Professor when we were well away from the house. "You have water containers, blankets, food?"

He nodded. "But they're all locked up in Elder Pratt's storeroom, right off the kitchen. Do you think—do you think we'll have to start out—with nothing?"

"Don't worry," I patted his hand, "I'll get what we need. Listen, where does he keep his money? Does he have a safe or anything like that? He has some jewels that belong to me."

The Professor frowned. He wasn't used to thinking about such mundane considerations as survival. I waited impatiently. Finally he said slowly, "There's a box in the storeroom. I don't know what's inside. Elder Pratt doesn't even know I know about it. He hides it under a floorboard and I saw him through a crack in the wall one day as he was putting it away.''

"Wonderful!" I congratulated him. "First I will tend to the horses.''

Fire was stabled with a dozen other horses. I had no doubt that when he discovered our flight Elder Pratt would give chase. And with a liability like the Professor along I would need every advantage to escape him. I had asked the Professor to get me some salt, and I mixed up a special batch of oats for the unsuspecting horses and salted it heavily. In the morning they would be so waterlogged from drinking to quench their thirst that they wouldn't be able to go five miles without becoming cramped and exhausted. I hated to do it, and I apologized to them, but I had no choice. Only Fire and a couple of other sturdy specimen were spared the treatment. I blindfolded the three horses and muffled their hooves with rags. I told the Professor to lead them away from the Elder's property and leave them there. Blinded they wouldn't stray or spook at anything. Then he was to come back for the saddles and saddle blankets. By that time I expected to be finished in the storeroom.

A hair pin made short work of the padlock on the storeroom door. Inside, I lit a candle and scrounged around for everything I thought we would need: dried meat, some hunting knives, a rifle, rope, blankets, matches. Even a couple of bottles of whiskey, one of which was half empty. The good Elder Zebulon was no model Morman.

Then I probed around on my hands and knees for the loose floorboard. It wasn't hard to find. The Professor's box was there, all right. It was as big as a baby's coffin. The lock was more difficult than the one on the door but hatred and excitement lent sharpness to my skills and soon I had it open. My little wad of baubles was nestled right on top of two of the fattest sacks of gold I had ever seen.

I didn't hesitate a second. I calculated at least one gold piece for every minute of suffering I had endured in that arid, airless room. I dropped both sacks into the blanket I was using to collect my booty, restored the box to its resting place and replaced the board. I hoisted my burden on my shoulders, and left. Towards California. And revenge.

18

The Golden Gypsy

I .CAME DOWN the narrow, red-carpeted stairs. Two Chairmen, who were washing the prisms of the big chandelier in the entrance, bobbed their heads and wished me good morning. I wished them the same. Two more were sweeping out the big gaming room to the left. On the other side of the entrance hallway was the smaller gaming room, for faro and poker. Both rooms had long bars. Behind the Little Salon was the Member's Lounge, carpeted in red and richly furnished with dark tables and soft chairs that were conducive to long hours of sitting and talking and spending money on my overpriced drinks, twice the price of those served at the two bars. Anyone could be a member, provided he paid a thousand-dollar membership fee. Membership that November was twenty, and I had a waiting list of fifteen more. The Golden Gypsy had no restaurant—that would come later, I promised myself—but I did have a cook. The Members were entitled to order snacks with their drinks, goodies like caviar, shellfish, broiled oysters, Russian piroshki, and small smoked sausages that were sent up every week from a German farmer who lived down the coast.

The Professor and I had living quarters on the second floor. Customers were not permitted above the first floor unless invited by the management. I seldom invited anyone. I had a nicely furnished sitting room that doubled as my office, and my bedroom was large and comfortable. The Chinese cook who prepared hors d' oeuvres for the Lounge also cooked for the household.

"Have my horse saddled, will you, Wang?" I told one of the Chinamen. "I'll be going out for breakfast."

I strolled into the Lounge. The Professor was already up. A closer look told me that he hadn't been to bed at all.

I joined him and called for coffee and black bread. "You're looking a little washed out this morning, Professor," I observed cheerfully. "I've warned you about vodka. It's dangerous stuff." All the other casino owners were furious at me for buying up the entire stock from a Russian trading vessel. Why not? I got there first. I rowed out to the ship and greeted the captain and crew in Russian. I had money with me and I closed the deal in less than half an hour. I invited the captain and his men to visit the Golden Gypsy, and we parted, friends for life. That vodka was wicked and potent. Even watered down it was stronger than anything else they were serving along Washington Street that fall.

The Professor groaned and massaged his temples. "Head aches," he moaned.

"Have some coffee," I suggested. Kim, the cook, brought in a tray and set it down in front of me. I tipped the pot and passed the Professor a steaming cup. "You will be pleased to know that we're doing even better this month than we did last month, and I expect December to be even better. When the weather in those hills gets too damp and cold, those miners will want a warm place with lots of whiskey and lots of action. You see? All your misgivings about the business were for nothing.''

"I'll never get to dig any gold for myself," he said sullenly.

"What are you talking about?" I said impatiently. "What do you call this, if not digging gold? You have more money now than you ever dreamed of! And the future—!'' I opened my arms wide to indicate the enormous potential of the future. "When we get the restaurant going, and enlarge the Big Salon—ah, it will be wonderful! And you still want to go off and grub in the dirt with your hands, and break your back and get hit over the head and robbed. Bah! You are a child. You have a one-track mind."

"We'll, at least that's honest work," he said into his cup.

"Oh? And you are implying that what we are doing is dishonest, I suppose. Where do you think those men would go if they didn't come here? Answer me that? To the other gambling hells in this town, that's where. I run the only straight, honest, clean games in town. Every dealer is honest, every game, every card. I even have you at the big faro table, don't I? And you're the most pathetically honest creature I have ever met in my life. I would have thought that after five whole months in my company a little of my larceny would have rubbed off on you. But no. You still feel guilty about the gold we stole from that pig, Pratt!"

"I didn't steal it, you did! It wasn't ours to take!"

"You are the biggest idiot I have ever met." I bit off a hunk of black bread and chewed furiously. The Professor was shy of girls, scared of gambling for high stakes, afraid of fast horses, terrified of getting sick. But he liked his drink. "Anyway, you're not the thief, I am. Sit back, enjoy yourself. Isn't this better than teaching a lot of silly boys a language that no one speaks?'' The Professor had confided to me that he had been a teacher of Latin at ''one of the better Eastern colleges.'' Some nights it was Harvard, others Princeton. I doubted that it was either.

That poor man. What I must have put him through! I bullied him across the deserts of Utah and Nevada. I forced him to go on even when he cried and complained and swore he couldn't go another mile. I cajoled and tormented and shouted at him. I dragged him away from the little mining camps in the mountains east of San Francisco and told him he'd be a fool to break his back for a few dollars when we had ten thousand in our saddlebags.

I was so angry with Seth and Elder Pratt that I probably could have crossed those deserts on foot, in the full heat of the broiling sun if I had to. But the poor Professor. It was just his bad luck to have fallen in with me when I was at my worst, possessed by such passionate fury that I was irrational, obsessed by the idea of revenge. After a month of travelling over the most hideous and desolate terrain we finally reached San Francisco, I persuaded him to be my partner in a gambling venture. He couldn't refuse. He didn't dare.

My plans after I reached the town were not to stay, but to leave at once for New Orleans by ship. This was the height of gold fever in California, and the town was full of prospectors, merchants, gamblers, men who had come to mine the mines and the miners. Boats anchored in the bay and whole crews deserted for the gold fields, leaving cargos unloaded and whole ships rotting. A lot of the early buildings in San Francisco were built of ship timbers. I saw immediately that it wasn't going to be easy to get back. I heard horror stories about voyages around the Horn that had ended in disaster, and I wasn't a good sailor to begin with. I certainly didn't want to travel over land again. I kept deferring my return, putting it off and putting it off—

Then a chance came up to buy into a little gambling den

down on Kearney Street, just north of Washington. The Professor and I bought out the owners and we prospered. I am not being immodest when I say that the success of the Golden Gypsy as we named our casino, was due largely to my own dazzling presence. In 1851 women were still enough of a rarity so that just the appearance of one on a crowded street was enough to cause a commotion. Of course every boat from Europe and South America and Australia brought a few more harlots, come to make their fortunes, just as every boat from China brought scores of young girls and women to be sold into prostitution.

But in the early summer of 1851 I was a novelty, and men flocked to the Golden Gypsy to see me. And the novelty didn't wear off. I became an institution, a tourist attraction. I called myself the Baroness, of course, and I reigned as Queen of the Casinos. When I presided over the faro table at the Golden Gypsy, men were so eager to lose their money to me that sometimes fights broke out when a seat fell vacant and a dozen men tried to fill it at the same time.

"Horsey ready, Missy," Wang said, bowing. I stood up and patted the Professor on the shoulder.

"Take heart," I said cheerfully. "Your headache will be gone by evening and you can start all over again. Something to look forward to."

I picked up my gloves and my riding crop, and walked out into the misty San Francisco morning.

"Mornin', Baroness."

I looked around and saw Black Jack MacDaniel, owner of the Golden Eagle next door. I greeted him and watched, amused, as he appraised my outfit: a tailored riding costume, dark grey wool trimmed with red, with a short split skirt, tightly-fitted jacket that flared over the hips, and flat-topped hat with a very wide brim. My boots were red leather, like those the Grandfather had given his little Gypsy so long ago. There were only two dressmakers in

527

San Francisco, and one of them worked almost exclusively for me. She charged the earth, of course, but what did I care? I had plenty of money.

"Well, Mr. MacDaniel, do you like what you see?" I asked archly.

"You know I do," he grinned broadly. "I'm really angry with you, Baroness." He had a slow drawl that I liked.

"Oh. Why?"

"Because I'm losin' business on account of you. The Golden Eagle was the finest casino in San Francisco 'til you come to town. Now it's only the second finest. Do you want to sell?"

I laughed and mounted Fire who was waiting patiently for her daily outing. "Thank you for the compliment, but no thank you to the offer."

"Then how about we play a little poker for her?" he suggested. "You're a gambler at heart."

"A gambler but not a fool," I reminded him. "Besides, poker is a little slow for me. I prefer faro. Quick and dangerous. Do you want to play faro for the Golden Gypsy?"

"No, thank you," he said, shaking his well-pomaded head. "I know you never lose. I tell you, Baroness, I've been around this town a long time, since before Sutter struck gold. I've seen fires and hoodlums and gold nuggets as big as your fist, but I've never seen anybody like you. As they say back home, you sure do beat all."

"You've been here that long? Did you ever meet a man named Seth McClelland? Or Seth Garrett? He's a gambler, too."

MacDaniel laughed. "Sure I know him. Seth Garrett. He passed through here a couple of years ago, I guess it was. Took me for everything I had. Why?"

"I have an old score to settle with him," I said. "I would consider it a great favor if you would inform me, if you should see him."

"A pleasure, Ma'am. I mean, Baroness." He bowed and grinned again. Like a lot of the professional gamblers I had met he was dressed in sombre black from head to toe, with only a frilly white shirt front to keep him from looking macabre. I kicked Fire lightly and trotted off.

San Francisco was little more than a shanty town in those days, with a few adobe buildings here and there to remind the visitor that it had once been Mexican territory. The streets were deeply rutted tracks, virtually impassable for vehicles in most weathers. There was hardly any law except what the citizens themselves made and enforced. Lately a group of vigilantes had been formed to combat the Sydney Ducks, convicts and cutthroats from Australia who had entered the country illegally. They were now terrorizing the city. Their moves were becoming bolder: they would rob a building, a bank, or a warehouse, then set fire to it to destroy the evidence. I avoided Sydney Town in the afternoons and evenings, but in the early morning, before noon at least, most of the brutes were still sleeping, resting from their troublemaking.

A few children raced after me, waving and shouting. I hailed them and pulled Fire to a halt. They were mostly the unwanted offspring of the harlots, or children of white soldiers and Indian or Mexican girls, children of two worlds who belonged to neither. I talked to them for a few minutes, then gave them a few coins and told them to run back to the Golden Gypsy and ask Kim for something special to eat.

They scampered away and I rode northwards, not paying very close attention to where I was going. I saw that I had turned down Broadway and was wandering towards the Bay. Conditions in that part of the city were unspeakably squalid. I passed a line of cribs, which were really just mean sheds where the lowest grade of prostitute worked for virtually nothing, enslaved by a master who took everything she earned. Those women were poor, miserable creatures who rarely lived to be more than twenty years old.

A few of them were already awake and waiting for customers. They stared listlessly at me as I rode past, and I tried not to stare back. I left the area quickly, and I felt sick and sad. A city being born, a city without laws, without leadership, shows man at his best and at his worst. I compared the opulence of the Golden Gypsy with what I had just seen. It hardly seemed fair. But on the other hand, I had been trained from birth to use my wits, to survive. And these poor girls—

I was shaken from my dismal reverie by angry shouts and shrill screams. I twisted around in the saddle. The sounds seemed to be coming from a ramshackle building on Sansome Street, very near the docks. I dismounted, gave Fire's reins to a child and told him he could earn a dollar by looking after her. I went inside, riding crop in hand, and my Bowie knife stuck in the top of my boot.

I followed the screams to a room on the second floor. I pushed the door open. A burly Sydney Duck, a man who reeked of whiskey and filth, was savagely beating a young girl. She was sitting on a low bed and cowering, trying without much success to protect herself with her thin arms.

I threw myself at the man and dragged him away from her. "How dare you!" I cried. "Leave her alone! She's just a child."

He turned on me, arm raised to strike. I held my knife under his chin.

"Get back!" I snapped. He obeyed. "And get out of here! If you come near her again I'll have you shot, do you understand?"

"Ya got no right—"

"I have every right! It's you who have forfeited your rights because you can't act like a civilized human being!"

Imagine me, the dirty little Gypsy child who had so strongly resisted her uncle's attempts to civilize her, preaching to some thick bastard about social responsibility. "Now get out!"

"She's me wife," he said. He reeled slightly. He was very drunk, and I knew it wouldn't take much to get rid of him. "Ya got no right—"

I sprang at him, knife extended, hoping to frighten him away. But in stepping back he stumbled and fell, knocking his head against the doorframe. I bent over him. He was alive, but he would sleep for a while. I turned my attention to the girl.

She lay back on the filthy bed. As I crouched down next to her she turned her head into her pillow and coughed. She was breathing hard. I touched her arm. She was hot, feverish, and very, very sick.

I leaned out the window. A man was leading an empty cart down towards the docks. "You!" I shouted. "The man with the cart!" He looked up. "Yes, you. I want to hire your cart. Right now. Bring it over here."

"What for?" he asked suspiciously.

"What do you mean, what for? Because I say so. I'll pay you fifty dollars. Come on, hurry up. And then come up to the second floor. I need some help."

I crouched on the floor next to the girl. She opened her eyes and stared at me. Her face was pinched and white. Her lips were swollen and both eyes were ringed with bruises. Her black hair was matted and dirty. She stretched out her hand to me and then dropped it again. She had no strength.

"Rhawnie," she said weakly. "Rhawnie."

My hair stood on end. My mouth opened but no sound came out.

"You—don't know me." Tears welled up in her blackened eyes.

531

"Oh, yes, darling," I said, trying to hold back my own tears. "I know you. Oh, Gabrielle. Poor Gabrielle."

I held her in my arms and we cried together. She had no flesh left, no meat. And she was burning with fever.

"I'm so sick, so tired. Oh, Rhawnie."

"It's all right now, Gabrielle. It's over, all over. I'm taking you away from here, to a fine, bright place. My casino, the Golden Gypsy. And we'll make you well and strong and beautiful again. Oh, my poor darling, my poor sweet Gaby. Don't cry anymore. Don't cry. I won't leave you."

Then I heard a feeble mewing sound. A rat? "My baby," Gabrielle sighed. "My baby. My Adam."

The infant Adam was lying in a wooden crate in the corner, on a pile of rags. He was naked and cold and as thin as a starved kitten. He wasn't very old. Two weeks? Two months? It was impossible to tell. I picked him up and brought him over to her. She held him to her breast to suckle him but she had nothing to give. Poor little mite. Poor Gaby.

The clumping of boots on the stairs drew me to the doorway. The carter was there, with two of his friends.

I said, "There's a sick woman in here. I'm taking her to the Golden Gypsy on Washington Street, but I need a few more minutes to get her ready."

I searched the room for clothes but found none. I wrapped her in the dirty blanket that was on the bed and called to the men. One of them lifted her and carried her down the stairs. I followed with the baby. We all had to step over the unconscious man who lay snoring on the floor.

I rode in the cart with Gabrielle while one of the men walked behind, leading Fire. The baby squalled weakly and subsided quickly. He didn't even have the energy to cry when he was hungry. Gabrielle clung tightly to my hand the whole way.

When we got to the Golden Gypsy I paid the men and alerted the staff. I sent Wang for a doctor at once. We got her upstairs to my room and I called for hot water and soap and scissors.

"And someone find a wet nurse!"

I had finished bathing her and was trimming the knots out of her hair when Doctor Clement arrived. I sighed with relief when I saw that he was sober. Then Wang appeared with a short, rotund Mexican-Indian woman in tow. She took one look at Adam and opened her blouse. The little fellow ate until he looked like a stuffed hen.

"What's your name?" I asked her.

"Maria," she shrugged.

"Are you a whore?" I had to know. Whores get diseased and I didn't want Adam to catch anything he didn't already have.

She gave me an incredulous look, then looked down at her bulky figure, then looked me in the eye again. "Nobody pay for thees," she said, shaking her head. "I wash the clothes."

We talked and came to a quick understanding. Maria would work for me as wet nurse and laundress. She and her own two children would live in the empty room down the hall, near the Professor's rooms. And she would help in nursing Gabrielle.

The Doctor Clement came out of the bedroom. "Advanced consumption with some bronchitis. Easy diagnosis. Good care. Constant nursing. She'll probably die anyway."

I already knew that in my heart, but to hear your fears voiced is hard to take.

The doctor instructed me in the care of the consumptive: good food, pure air, lots of rest, freedom from worry.

"You know her?" he asked before he left.

"Yes, I know her. And her family. Goodbye, Doctor."

Kim had prepared the samovar. I poured myself a cup of

533

tea and sat at my desk. Gabrielle was dying. I had found her, but not soon enough. For a moment I almost wished that I hadn't wandered into Sydney Town. Wouldn't it be better not to know? It hurt so to see her like that, weak and sick and beaten-looking. Then I pulled myself together and vowed to do everything I could to make her well. Something, some force had led me to her, and I was glad. Glad that she wouldn't have to die alone and in squalor.

Gabrielle was pathetically grateful for everything we did for her. She apologized over and over again for being troublesome.

"What rubbish you talk," I said gruffly as I straightened her sheets. It was two days after she came to the Golden Gypsy. "As if you could ever be a trouble! Oh, you've hardly touched your egg nog. How can you get strong if you don't eat?"

"I'm not hungry," she said meekly. Sometimes I could hardly believe that this was the girl who had defied everyone, society and her family, to run off with a Russian adventurer. She had no fight left, no spirit. A man had done this to her, a man like Seth. I hated him. I hated all of them.

I never mentioned Boris. I knew it would be painful for her to talk about it, and that she would have to tell me in her own time.

"How—why are you here, Rhawnie?" she asked me.

"I came west with your brother to look for you. No, not Steven. Seth."

She looked surprised. "But how did you know we were coming—?"

"We didn't, I said ruefully. "We were chasing another couple that we thought was you." I told her about the Andersons, everything except their unhappy end. Soon after we got to Salt Lake City, Seth and I, ah, parted

534

company, as they say here. I think he must have gone south to look for you, or perhaps he returned to New Orleans. I don't know."

"He's wonderful, isn't he?" Gabrielle sighed. "I suppose I don't really know him very well. I was very small when he left New Orleans for the first time. But there's always been something special between us. He used to send me things from far away. He's so kind."

I ducked my head and pretended to adjust her blankets so that she wouldn't see my face. "Yes, darling," I said briskly, "he is a veritable prince. Very nice, very kind. Now try to sleep, and I'll bring Adam in a little later for a visit."

She looked forward to Adam's visits eagerly. He was growing fat in Maria's care, and he seemed healthy enough for all he'd been through. He certainly shrieked like a steamboat whistle when he was hungry. But Gabrielle wasn't getting any better, in spite of the care we lavished on her. Kim made tempting dishes, custards and soups and light stews, but she hardly ate anything at all. I suspected that she didn't want to prolong her life.

Soon after I found her I heard about a man who was planning to travel east, to St. Louis. I decided to give him a letter for Steven. I didn't know how long it would take for the letter to reach New Orleans, months perhaps, but I felt I had to tell someone in the family about Gabrielle. I knew better than to attempt to write it myself. I sought out the Professor.

"I want you to write a letter for me," I told him. "You know how to read and write, don't you? It's for Mr. Steven McClelland in New Orleans. And I don't want you to breathe a word of this to anyone, is that clear?"

I dictated and he scribbled:

"Dear Steven, I am sorry that I could not write before I went away. I tried but it was no good. Your brother and I

535

followed Gabrielle and Boris to St. Louis, and all the way to the Rocky Mountains before we discovered we were chasing the wrong people. From Salt Lake City, we went our separate ways, and I came to San Fransico. I have found Gabrielle. She is safe now but she is very ill. She has consumption. I am taking very good care of her, but the doctor thinks and I agree with him that she will proabably not live through the winter.

"Please forgive me for going away so suddenly. I still think of you fondly, but marriage between us is no longer possible. Someday perhaps I can explain things in person. I wish you the very best and I will always remain your dearest and most loving friend, Rhawnie. P.S. Your sister has a fine son, very strong and healthy. His name is Adam McClelland."

When I finally got the thing sealed up and saw my carrier on his way, I felt as though a load of logs had rolled off my shoulders. I had done my duty as a friend of the family, and at the same time I had ended my engagement to Steven. It wouldn't have worked. I had just been fooling myself.

I gave no more thought to Steven or the McClelland family until two days later. Right before I went downstairs to the gaming rooms that night, Gabrielle called to me. She held my hand tightly.

"Rhawnie," she said weakly. Her eyes were large and dark, full of pain and sorrow. "Rhawnie, I don't want them to know about me. I would rather they never knew—what happened to me. I'm so ashamed, Rhawnie!" Tears rolled out of her eyes and spotted under her head. "Please, please don't tell them."

"Of course I won't tell them, darling," I said reassuringly. I knew whom she meant by "them": her family. "This is our secret, eh? Just us. I have made everyone here swear not to tell about you, so that that bully won't

536

find you. They won't tell, I'm sure of it. No one will ever know, ever."

I didn't tell her about my letter. The doctor had warned against needless worry.

"Seth," she said, tightening her grip on my hand. "Especially Seth! Swear to me, Rhawnie. If he comes—you won't tell him! I don't want him to know what happened to—his little Gaby. He would be so disappointed and he would hate me—!"

"But he is your brother, darling," I said reasonably. "He could never hate you. He loves you and he would understand that it wasn't your fault. A brother will always love, always. And he will forgive."

"No, no!" She struggled to sit up. "You mustn't tell him! Promise me, Rhawnie, please! I would die if I thought he knew—! Please, please!"

She became more and more worked up. I tried to calm her, and in the end I had to promise that if Seth appeared in San Francisco looking for her I wouldn't tell him a thing. And as if that weren't enough, she made me swear it again on the small Bible she kept by her side. Only then did she relax and grow calm.

"I'm so ashamed," she sighed. "It was awful. He—he wasn't the man I thought. You remember—you remember what you told me, that time at Highlands? You said he would use me and break my heart. I should have listened to you. Oh, why, why didn't I listen?"

"Love has no ears," I said sadly. "No one will blame you, Gabrielle. Boris was quite a charming man when he wanted to be. And you had no experience with men like that. I didn't know, when I was your age. I believed in love then, as you did."

"He's dead," she said dully. "I saw him die. And I was glad."

Customers began to straggle in downstairs. Unlike most

of the other casinos the Gypsy didn't stay open twenty-four hours a day. I opened at six and closed when they got tired and went away, but I had to close for a few hours, just to have some peace and quiet. I heard shouts of raucous laughter. Ordinarily I was downstairs by that time, watching over things, greeting the patrons as they arrived eager to be fleeced. But the Professor would have to cope alone tonight. Gabrielle was ready to talk, and she needed me.

She and Boris had set out for California, all right. But they hadn't taken the route that Seth and I followed. Instead they boarded a ship bound for Panama. Boris had heard that the quickest way to the gold was to dock at Colón, to cross the Isthmus to Panama City, then to take another ship to San Francisco. From Panama City it was a sail of only a month or more. So the pair hired a guide and crossed the Isthmus on foot, hacking their way through jungles and wading through swamps.

"Boris was very sweet to me for the first few days," Gabrielle said. "I thought I was in love with him, and I wasn't a bit sorry I ran away. But as soon as our ship reached the Gulf of Mexico he changed. As if when I was out of the reach of my family, he didn't have to be nice to me anymore. He shouted at me, and he hit me. I'd never—I'd never been hit before, never in my life.

"It only got worse after we docked in Colón. He treated me like a low creature. He used me, and he got drunk and beat me." She coughed into a handkerchief and struggled to get her breath.

"You don't have to tell me everything now," I said, smoothing her short hair away from her face.

"Yes, I want to," she cried. "I must tell someone! Please, let me finish."

They had to wait for over a month in Panama City for a ship to take them to San Francisco. Boris gambled and lost. They quarrelled. He drank.

"Then finally a ship came. We had terrible storms all along the Mexican coast. I was so sick, even though I'd been a good sailor before then. I was pregnant with Adam and I didn't even know it. Then we were shipwrecked. The ship hit the rocks and broke up in a matter of minutes. I climbed up on a piece of board, a door I think it was, and then I saw Boris. He was shouting to me that he couldn't swim. I lay face down on the door and I looked at him. He was so close—that if I stretched out my hand—but I didn't. I didn't want to save him. I said, ''I hope you drown.' And he did. He slipped under the waves and I never saw him again. I killed him, Rhawnie."

"What nonsense," I said briskly. "If you had tried to save him, you might have drowned yourself. Besides, if ever a man deserved to die, he did. Stop torturing yourself about it. You did the right thing."

"I wish I could believe that," she sighed. "I'd never seen a man die before. There was a lot I hadn't seen. I was so simple, so ignorant. I just didn't know—that life could be this way. I wish I had drowned. I would have been spared so much—the worst things that could happen to a woman have happened to me, Rhawnie.

"There was another ship in the area that saw our distress flags. They made a great fuss over me. I told the captain that I had no money to pay my fare, and he said I shouldn't worry about it, that we could work something out. Well, when we got to San Francisco he sold me at auction to get the money I owed him.''

A drunken miner paid the captain one thousand three hundred dollars for Gabrielle. He took her to his claim near Mariposa, and he worked her and used her until she dropped. He was killed in a brawl one night, and she ran away. She made her way back to San Francisco, hoping to find someone there who would take her in and care for her until she got word to her family.

A Sydney Duck named Ratbane, a convicted murderer from Leeds, England, who had come to San Francisco by way of Australia, found her wandering the streets of the city, and he took possession of her. The baby Adam was born in October in the filthy room in which I found her. A Mexican whore helped her deliver him. Ratbane beat her and insisted that she make his friends feel "welcome." Her refusal didn't daunt him. She had no choice. Ratbane's friends made themselves at home and he turned a profit. And then I appeared, her deliverer.

"I couldn't deceive you any longer," she said, turning her face away from me. "You won't be so nice to me now that you know— I'm the worst woman in the world, the lowest thing that lives."

"You'd better not say that too loudly," I told her. "You have a lot of competition in this town and they'd give you an argument."

"How can you laugh at me," she said in a hurt voice. "How can you—!"

"Because it's stupid of you to carry on like you're the only girl in the world who let a man take advantage of her and then had to pay the price," I said sharply. "There are a hundred more like you out there in the streets, girls from nice families, rebels like you, girls who were too pigheaded to listen when anyone warned them. What good does it do to punish yourself? You have suffered enough. Why add to it? You cannot change what happened. And whatever happened, you're still the same Gabrielle you always were. I suppose you feel guilty because you liked it when Boris made love to you, even after he treated you badly?"

Her deep blush told me I was right.

"Silly girl. You felt like a whore and a wanton, didn't you? And you told yourself you would never give in again, and then the next time he put his hands on you and you felt yourself melting inside like a piece of ice in a frying pan, you told yourself that you must be wicked and evil. Oh, I know. I've been through all of that, and I know that where a certain man is concerned, I'll always be a wanton. I can't help myself. But I'm not wicked because I'm that way. Foolish, maybe. And silly, like you. But not wicked.''

"Oh, Rhawnie!" She started to weep softly.

"I've upset you," I said, "but I'm not sorry. It's time somebody talked some sense into you. You didn't have any brains when you ran away with that devil, but that doesn't mean you can't have some now. You lie here day after day and wish for death, don't you? You think I don't know what's in your mind? But death doesn't solve anything. It's only a shortcut, a coward's choice. I found that out long ago. I didn't think you were a coward, Gabrielle. But now I'm not so sure. Life is so precious, so easy to lose. Live, live, if only for Adam's sake!"

"But I'm dying!" she sobbed. "I know I'm dying! I'm not a complete fool. I know I'm sick and that you only tell me I'm getting better because you're trying to cheer me up. There's nothing anyone can do!"

"Then be brave and accept your fate. Die a good death instead of a bad one. You can have peace instead of anguish, but you have to do it for yourself. Conquer fear. Gain wisdom. Help the rest of us to become wiser and better because we knew you. What do you think will happen when your parents hear about it? And they will. I will tell them myself because it would be cruel to let them go on thinking that someday you will come back to them. How do you think they will feel if they hear that you were desperate and alone and unhappy when you died? But if they knew that you were at peace with the world and at peace with yourself—can't you see how much better it will be for them? And for your son? Babies know more than we think, they feel everything. He senses your despair. Well,

541

I've scolded you enough. I must get down there before those apes tear the place apart. They don't know how to respect a woman's home. We will talk later.''

"Rhawnie, help me, help me to be brave, like you."

"I don't have to help you," I said. "You are brave, or you never would have survived this long. Well, good-night, darling. Try and sleep. I'll come up a little later, to look in on you."

She smiled weakly and closed her eyes. Her skin was blue and transparent, her breathing labored. The air felt damp and chilly. As winter closed in, thick fogs rolled into the Bay area from the sea. She would never get better if she stayed here, I knew that.

I started down the stairs to the music and the drinking and the laughter. This is no place for her, I thought. So noisy, so rough. And Adam. A child shouldn't grow up in a place like this. But where can I take them? I sighed and pasted a professional-looking smile onto my lips, then I sallied into the Big Salon. These things would have to take care of themselves for the moment. I had to go to work.

Some providential spirit was watching over us that night. I played faro with a miner who wasn't happy until I had won all his gold, and even then he didn't want to stop. He pulled out a piece of paper from his pocket and threw it on the table.

"It's for a farm," he said. "I was gonna bring the wife out, and the kids. I bought it from a greaser—a Mex—fair and square. Will you take it as a wager?"

My desk was stuffed with deeds for claims in the mountains, corner lots in San Francisco, acres of land in the desert. Of course I took his wager. After I had won and he had gone away feeling cleansed and relieved and ready to start over, I took the deed over to the Professor and made him read it to me. I had a feeling about that farm—he told me I had won a house and fifty acres of land near San Mateo, south of San Francisco. But that's all he could tell from the deed. I decided to see for myself.

I rode down the peninsula very early the next morning to inspect my property. I didn't tell Gabrielle about the farm because I didn't want to raise false hopes. I found a man in the village who knew the property well; he had worked for the former owners, the Mendozas. Juan was garrulous and happy, and eager to show me around my farm.

I was delighted with it. In addition to the house, which was perfect, I had won about two hundred olive trees, a hundred lemon trees, and a little stretch of vineyard. The house was only one story high, but it was built around an open courtyard that had a pool and a fountain in the center. Its red tiled roof flamed in the afternoon sun. The adobe walls would provide splendid insulation in winter and summer, and there were fireplaces in most of the rooms, something that the hastily-built structures in San Francisco lacked.

"Why did the Mendozas sell out?" I asked Juan.

He shrugged. "They did not like the Americanos. They did not want to live in America. So they go back to Mexico. Me, I like it here. I stay. The Americans are not too bad. You like this place? You will live here, Señora?"

"Yes, I like it very much." There was no furniture in the house, and squatters had left the house in rather a mess, but there wasn't anything wrong that couldn't be remedied quickly and easily.

Juan showed me around the buildings and stables. There was a smokehouse, a barn, some little houses for workers, all empty and deserted.

"Listen, Juan," I said, "I need some people to stay here, to live here and make it a good farm again. Do you know anyone who would like to work for me?"

"Yes, Señora!" he said happily. "I would! And my wife and my fifteen children and also my brother and his family.

543

It will be a pleasure Señora!''

I gave him some money to hire men and to start repairs on the house. I planned to bring Gabrielle down within the week, along with Maria and her two children and of course, baby Adam. Gabrielle would like it here. And perhaps she would even get stronger and better. I didn't want to give up hope for her completely.

The move wasn't too difficult. I hired three wagons and filled two of them with furniture and bedding and foodstuffs. Gabrielle was truly delighted with her new home.

"I will try to get well," she promised me. "I really will. I want to live, to see Adam grow up."

I spent a week on the farm, getting things organized and making sure that my charges were settling in all right. Maria showed an unexpected flair for cooking. Kim had taught her to make some Chinese dishes, and once I broke her of the habit of putting hot peppers into everything, her cuisine was quite acceptable.

"Why do you have to go back?" Gabrielle asked. It was the day I planned to return to San Francisco.

I laughed. "Because the Professor simply cannot cope without me. He hates running the business alone. He's terrified of being cheated by the customers. And of course the staff takes advantage of him when I'm not there. That's all right—they take advantage of me, too. But asking Professor to look after things for more than a week is like telling a child to sail a ship. He's petrified."

I stooped over and threw another piece of wood on the fire in her room. There were no curtains on the windows, only shutters; no rugs on the floor, no furniture other than a table near the bed and a couple of hard chairs. Nothing soft that could incubate more disease. But Juan had brought her a cactus in a pot, and it stood like a spikey sentinel near the door. A few pictures on the walls and a

544

few other plants made the bare room seem more cheerful. It was December now, and the air was damp and cold at night. We kept a low fire burning at all times, to keep Gabrielle warm and dry.

"Rhawnie?" Her voice sounded small and thin, like a little girl's.

"Yes, dearest?"

"Rhawnie, do you ever think about that man, the one you told me about? The one you met when you were young like me?"

"Oh, yes," I answered with perfect truth. "I think about him all the time." I thought about him and wished him in Hell, but I didn't tell her that.

"Do you ever want to stop thinking about him?"

I shrugged. "I suppose so. But his memory is a warning to me never to be foolish about love again. I know I'm a Gypsy and that Gypsies aren't suppose to dwell on the past—what's done is done. Except my business with him isn't finished. And he has had too great an influence on my life for me to be able to forget him easily."

"I think about Boris," she admitted. "It's very hard not to sometimes. Compared to some of the others, like Ratbone, he was an angel."

"No, he was just a smaller devil. But a devil nonetheless. But you have too much time to think. Hurry up and get strong so that I can put you to work in my vineyards. There's plenty to be done! Well, I will say goodbye to you now. I need to start back at once if I'm to make it before dark. You know what that city's like. But I will visit soon, I promise. And I'll bring baskets of good things to eat and drink, and some newspapers and books, if I can find them. They will make the time pass more quickly for you."

I rode back to San Francisco. The trip took about three hours. I arrived early in the evening, but the Golden Gypsy and the other casinos were already in full swing. I dis-

545

mounted and handed the reins to my doorman, then I went inside. A few of the miners cheered my return and I greeted them gaily. I didn't stop to change my clothes. I went into the Little Salon to the left of the doors and said,

"Hello, everybody, I'm back!"

The bartender shouted a greeting, as did the croupiers, and a dozen men actually cheered. I went to the big faro table to say hello to the Professor. And there, in the dealer's chair, sat Seth McClelland.

I didn't even pause for breath. I whipped my knife out of my boot top and hurled myself at his back.

Something warned him of the danger. He leaped up, sending his chair flying across the room, and he caught my wrist and twisted. I dropped the knife.

"Let me go, you filth!" I gasped. "I'm going to kill you, right here!"

Drunken miners crowded around us, cheering. Fools. They liked anything exciting.

"Now, Rhawnie," Seth said with a slightly wounded tone in his voice that suggested that I should have been happier to see him. "This is no way to greet an old friend."

"It's the only way I know to greet a liar and a traitor! Filth! Deserter! You left me—with those monsters out there! You stole my horses and my jewels and—"

"Calm down," he said. "I didn't steal anything. You're imagining—"

"I'm not imagining anything! Oh, let me go! Let me go and I'll tear your heart right out of your body with my teeth!"

He scooped me up and slung me over his shoulder. The miners cheered and parted to let us pass. He hardly seemed to notice as he carried me up the stairs that I was flailing and kicking and shouting like a wounded banshee. He kicked open the door to my sitting room and carried me inside, then set me down. I threw myself at him again, but he caught me in a tight embrace and kissed me. When he finally released me I was breathless and panting and still furious.

"You get out of here," I said, wiping my mouth with my hand. "This is my place. Mine! I'm going to have you thrown out of here so fast—"

I went to the door but he neatly blocked my way. "It won't do any good to call for help," he said reasonably. "Your staff wouldn't be very likely to throw out their new employer."

"What are you taking about?" I demanded. "This place belongs to me. And the Professor. We're partners."

"You were partners," he corrected me. "The Professor sold his interest to me. He had a real yen to see the gold fields. You were away and he grabbed the opportunity to get out. I'm afraid you had the poor fellow rather intimidated, my dear. He admitted that you were a hell of a woman, too much woman for him."

Then he sat down in the chair in front of my desk, put his feet up on its cluttered surface, and lit a cigar.

"Welcome to the Golden Gypsy, San Francisco's finest!" he said, exhaling a plume of smoke. "Mister and Mrs. Seth McClelland, proprietors."

19

The Golden West

I STARED AT him, completely dumbfounded. I sank down
on a chair at the other side of the room from him.

"You're a rotten liar," I said. "You've killed him,
haven't you?"

"Rhawnie," he gave me a reproachful smile," I
wouldn't do a thing like that. I paid the Professor ten
thousand dollars for this place. A lot more than you paid
for it, I understand."

"It's worth five times that much," I sniffed. "How did
you get the money?"

"Won it at poker. From Black Jack MacDaniel, next
door. A friend of yours, I understand. He speaks very
highly of you, Baroness."

"You are the lowest, most arrogant creature," I said
through my teeth. "Well, I can't tolerate this. I won't! I'll
buy it back from you, right now. Ten thousand dollars, just
what you paid."

He grinned and studied the glowing tip of his cigar. "No," he said. I started to rise out of my chair but he put out a hand as if to say, hold on a second and let me finish. "It's not that I don't want to deal with you, Baroness. But I have examined your so-called records."

He waved his hand over the welter of papers on my desk. Since Gabrielle had been with me I hadn't had a minute to spare to attend to the details of the business. Not that I would have attended to them anyway; paperwork wasn't my strongest suit.

Seth went on. "Such wanton extravagance! Such wild spending! I've seen enough to know that even though this place is turning a fine profit, you owe everybody in the city and you continue to spend the money as quickly as it comes in. My dear, you don't have a loose dollar to your name. Ten thousand dollars? You'd have trouble raising half that amount. But all that will change. I'll take over the bookkeeping. I'm sure you won't have any objections. Amazing." He shook his head unbelievingly. "All that money. Where has it gone?"

"Things are ridiculously expensive here," I said defensively. "Oh, what's the matter with me?" I jumped up and waved my arms. "Get out of my room and don't you ever come in here again! I don't care if you do own half this place now, you have your own rooms, right next door. This is my sitting room and you are not welcome! Out!" I threw open the door. Then I started to gather up armfuls of papers and I threw them out into the hall. "And take this stuff with you! I don't want any part of it—or of you!" I faced him angrily. "I intend to have as little to do with you as possible, is that clear? I will continue to gamble with whomever I wish and I will attract crowds—and don't fool yourself into thinking that anything else attracts these men to this place—and I will continue to spend my share of the profits as I see fit. What you do with yours is your own business. Now leave me alone, Seth McClelland. Just leave me alone!''

I ran to my bedroom and slammed the door. I was shaking from head to toe. He was such a bastard. Every time my life seemed to have straightened itself out a little, he turned up and bent it into a pretzel. But I was determined not to let him best me this time. I was finished with Seth.

And what about Gabrielle? He hadn't asked me about her. He had probably searched everywhere and given up hope of finding her. Clearly no one had told him about the sick woman I had been nursing in my rooms for the past four weeks. I should tell him, I thought. But I knew I wouldn't. Not only because of my promise to her, but because he had earned no favors from me.

The next morning I found him in the Lounge. He was having his breakfast, reading the *Alta California*, San Francisco's first newspaper. He looked tanned and fit and utterly in command.

He handed me a ten-dollar gold piece.

''What's this?'' I asked him. ''A tip for the laundress?''

''Your share from last night's take,'' he told me. ''Don't spend it foolishly.''

''What do you mean, my share?'' I flared. ''I saw how busy those tables were last night. I'm not that much of an idiot. We must have taken in three thousand dollars or more!''

''Ah, but I have deducted your share of the operating expenses and the outstanding debts,'' he said. ''Both of which were considerable. You don't want to lose your credit, do you?''

''Credit!'' I shouted. ''What do I care for credit! These fools can wait for their money. But I can't wait! I need some new dresses and—''

''Your finery will have to wait,'' he shrugged. ''You'll be

happy to know that my share was the same. Do you know that your staff hasn't been paid for over a month? They didn't walk out on you because they trust you, but that's no way to run a business. And this hors d'oeuvres nonsense is out, too. No more food. In fact, I'm turning this lounge into another gaming room. That's where the real money is."

"No! I forbid it. What do you mean, no more food? It's a very important part of the Golden Gypsy. What about the members? The most important men in the city meet here and drink and talk and eat my food!"

"No," he corrected me, "the most important men are the ones who come here to gamble. Keep Kim—he's a fine cook—but no more food for public consumption. It's much too costly."

"But we were going to add a restaurant!" I cried. "This was a way of building up interest—"

"No. Restaurants are notorious money-losers. Great potential for waste. We're here to gamble, Rhawnie. And to sell liquor. No food. At a hundred and fifty dollars for a barrel of flour and ten dollars for an egg, it's a wonder that anyone can afford to eat these days."

I couldn't listen to any more of his fatuous explanations. They turned my stomach. I stormed out into the hall, shouting for my horse. Outside the Golden Gypsy I ran into Black Jack MacDaniel.

"Mornin', Baroness," he said politely. "You asked me to tell you if a certain party appeared in town—"

"I know very well who has come and what he's doing," I fumed. "And I won't let him get away with it!"

But what could I do? From that day on the Golden Gypsy didn't belong to me. He took over. It wasn't fun for me any longer. All I had to do was appear at the tables in the evenings and look beautiful. He took care of the rest: hiring and firing staff, paying bills, remodeling the lounge, ordering supplies, dividing the evening's take. I was so angry with him, so upset at the shape things were taking, that I could hardly bring myself to speak to him except when I couldn't avoid it. Then he talked and I listened in silence. I didn't even quarrel with most of his decisions because he was right: the bookkeeping was a mess and it really wasn't fair to the staff to forget to pay them, and I knew that I couldn't depend on my whiskey suppliers to deliver if they weren't paid.

One day he said, "We're hiring more girls."

I jerked my head up. We were getting ready to open and I was pulling on a pair of long white gloves. My costumes changed with my moods: some nights I wore lavish finery, beautiful gowns, lots of jewels. Other times I appeared in dazzling Gypsy garb; colorful skirts, boots, a low-cut blouse, lots of noisy gewgaws.

"What do you mean, more girls? There aren't any to hire."

"A ship arrived today from France. I hired three. They'll be here in a few minutes."

"You—hired—French—whores!" I rasped in a strangled voice. "To work here, in my place?" My voice grew stronger. "To live under my roof?" I shouted.

"No," he said calmly, "they're living at the Palmer House for the time being. There's no room for them here. And whatever kind of business they engage in after hours is their affair, not yours, not mine."

I tore off my gloves. "Well, that's that. If you have them you won't need me." I threw the gloves at his feet and unpinned the swaying plume from my hair. "I'll be leaving tonight. You can run this place into Hell, for all I care. Just be sure and set aside half of everything for me."

"As you please," he shrugged. "But you won't get a nickel that you don't earn.

"Earn?" I squawked. "What do you mean, earn? I

don't have to earn. I'm a partner here, remember? Not a worker. I get half—''

"It doesn't work that way," he informed me. "You're the main attraction, Rhawnie. The Golden Gypsy in person. If you don't show up, we lose customers. If you share the profits, it's only fair that you share the losses as well. And I'll deduct that percentage of loss from—'' He saw that he wasn't getting anywhere and he stopped and said in a different, placating tone, "I had to hire them, Rhawnie. If I didn't, MacDaniel would have. Now I want you to train them—''

"*You* train them to do your devil's work," I spat. "After all, you taught me! So you train your whores to cheat and steal. Oh, I will not endure this. I will not!"

But I had to endure it. The three French girls brought in even more business, and I found that Seth was true to his threat: when I stayed in my rooms and sulked and didn't show up at the tables, my share of the take shrank drastically. Suddenly, I had no money to spend. And I needed that money, for the farm. For Gabrielle and Adam. For Juan and his wife and his brother and their squad of children. I had dependents now. Lots of them.

I had no choice. I steeled myself and presided over faro while the girls ran roulette and blackjack and Seth played poker. The money poured in. Seth took money out of our profits and bought the lot in back of the casino, and he began to work on a design for expansion.

I began to use the farm as my escape, my haven. I didn't care if I lost money because of my visits there; I couldn't bear life at the Golden Gypsy any longer. The sight of those French doxies made me white with anger. I never spoke to them, never even acknowledged them. I thought, just let one of those jades try anything other than gambling on my time and I'll break her hands. And I couldn't stand the smug look on Seth's face. I needed to get away, and my visits grew longer and more frequent.

Gabrielle sensed that I was disturbed about something and asked me about it. I lied and told her that the Sydney Ducks were making life in San Francisco rather difficult and that I was a little worried about the danger to the city.

"Why don't you leave?" she said. "Come and live here with us, forever. I know you can find a buyer for the Golden Gypsy. Mr. MacDaniel—"

"It's not so easy as that," I said smiling. "But don't you worry. Things will work out. They always do. I got us this place, didn't I? It's so quiet here, so calm. And how big our Adam is getting! He will be tall, eh? You see, if I measure him against my forearm, as Lyubov measured me—."

We laughed and I hugged the baby, who squirmed and giggled.

"You love him, don't you?" Gabrielle smiled.

"Of course I love him! As if he were my own son. And I love you, too." I kissed her pale cheek. "You are my dear sister."

They were wonderful days. I loved the baby and passed the time of day with Gabrielle, and I planted roses and watched the women at their work and made trouble in the kitchen. Juan taught me about wine culture and olive culture. Our grapes never did well, Juan told me. But Mr. Mendoza never gave up trying to produce a good wine like Spanish sherry, and neither would I. I was happy at my little hacienda. I dreaded going back to the Golden Gypsy, and to Seth.

One night I heard feminine laughter coming from his room. In the morning I confronted him.

"You had one of those women in your room last night," I said evenly, trying not to fly off the handle. "I cannot allow that. You can bed your whores someplace else, but not here, not under my roof."

"It's my roof, too, remember?" he said. "And I'll bed

whomever I please, wherever I please. On the faro table, under the bar—''

"You are disgusting," I said in a low voice. "'No better than an animal.''

He stroked my arm. I jumped a foot and glared at him. He laughed. "You're a bundle of nerves, Rhawnie. Your little trips out of town don't seem to be doing you much good. You might as well stay here and earn some money instead of running off. Where do you go? To ply your trade in the gold fields?''

"That's my business. And as for plying trade, those girls are out, as of now! You said you wouldn't let them carry on their profession here!''

"There's no commerce going on," he said innocently. "I've never paid for it in my life, dear heart, and I certainly don't have to start now. My free time is my own, and so is Yvette's.''

"You and Yvette can go to the devil!" I snapped.

"If you really don't want her around," he suggested, "I know what you can do. Take her place in my bed.''

I flushed, and I was annoyed at the sharp stab I felt under my ribs. "You'd like that, wouldn't you?" I sneered. "You'd like to start that all over again, making me your mistress and your slave. But I tell you, Seth, the very sight of you makes me ill. If you try to lay a hand on me, just once, I'll cut your throat. I swear it!''

He tried his tricks—light kisses, tender caresses, whispered endearments—but for once I felt immune to his approaches. Was it possible that I was really cured of him? Free of him at last?

I was under a terrible strain. Life at the Golden Gypsy was bad enough, but the burden of my knowledge of Gabrielle weighed on me like a stone. I couldn't tell him about her, and I couldn't tell her about him, because I knew it would upset her. Yet as her brother, he had a right to know. Whatever he was, whatever he had done to me, he loved her. I had seen that. And yet I kept silent, because of my promise to her, and because of my anger towards him.

Whenever I rode down to San Mateo, I left the casino very early, just after dawn. I generally slept very late, until eleven o'clock most mornings because we stayed open until three in the morning or even later. But I liked to get an early start so I could have a long day to spend with Gabrielle and Adam, to walk in the hills and forget about my problems.

The morning after our argument. I left the Golden Gypsy at about seven o'clock, just as the sun was coming up over the sleeping city. I wasn't aware of it, but I was followed.

I was sitting with Gabrielle in her room when we heard sounds of arguing in another part of the house. I went out to investigate, and I saw Maria, all four feet ten inches of her, trying to keep Seth from coming in the front door. She was doing a pretty fair job of it, too.

"It's all right, Maria," I said. "I'll handle this."

"He break in! I cannot stop him!" she cried.

"I don't blame you, Maria. He's very hard to resist sometimes, and he has no manners." She went back to her kitchen, casting black looks over her shoulder. "Well, what do you want?" I asked him when we were alone. "Is there trouble at the Golden Gypsy?"

"No trouble except what you stir up," he grinned. He leaned on his cane and looked around at the cool interior with its arched doorways, woven rugs, sturdy furnishings. "Nice," he said. "Very nice, indeed. I wondered what was the big attraction that kept pulling you away from San Francisco."

"So you've discovered my little home away from home," I shrugged. "My dreadful, guilty secret. Can you blame me for wanting to get away from you and your whores? Well, now that you've seen where I go, you can just turn right around and leave. It's a long ride back to the city. I don't want to detain you.''

He tossed his hat onto a chair. ''I wouldn't want to leave before I see the rest of our house. Why don't you give me a tour?''

''What do you mean, our house? This house is mine!''

''You won it at the Golden Gypsy, playing faro. That's right, isn't it? I found the deed, among others, in that pile of rubbish you call a filing system. And, if you recall, part of your original agreement with the Professor was that you share equally in all profits and losses. Just as we do now. So, my darling, this beautiful place is half mine.''

''Are you so selfish, so grasping that you won't let me have my island of peace?'' I cried.

''It takes two to make a desert island a really attractive place,'' he remarked. ''Where is he?''

''Where is who?''

''Your lover, of course. The real attraction. You can't blame me for being curious. I'm not a fool, Rhawnie. There's something else. There's got to be—you're not interested in me anymore. I wonder where he's hiding.''

He walked through the living room and dining room, through the kitchens, into the central courtyard. I skipped around in front of him and said breathlessly, ''Listen, Seth, I'll go back to the city with you if that's what you want. I'll limit my stays here to three days, no more. You're angry because I've been neglecting the business, aren't you?''

''No,'' he said, easing himself down on the low wall around the fountain and resting his hands on the knob of his cane. ''Business is better than ever. Profits are so good that you might even have a little money waiting for you when you get back. Why are you trying to rush me out of here, Rhawnie? Just tell me who he is. You're not ashamed of him, are you?''

Just then in another part of the house little Adam started to cry. Seth watched my face carefully.

"Ah, a baby, eh? Is he ours? Come on, out with it. I won't hold it against you."

I couldn't speak. I couldn't even move. He got up and started toward the doors on the courtyard, the bedroom doors. I ran to stop him.

"He's not my baby," I said hastily. "He's—Maria's! You met Maria, at the door, remember? Little and fat? Oh, why don't you go, Seth? A baby is a baby. They all look the same. Please, just go away and leave me in peace!"

He opened the door to my bedroom. He knew it was mine because of the riding habit thrown on the bed. He backed out of the room—without checking for a stray lover under the bed—and went on to the next door. Another empty bedroom. The next would be Gabrielle's room. I had to stop him.

I put my arms around him. "Please, Seth," I begged, "don't look anymore. There is nothing for you to see here, I swear it. Just go, now. If you ever had any feeling for me at all, you will do as I ask. Don't—"

He picked me up as if I were a piece of lint and set me aside. He opened the door to Gabrielle's sickroom.

"Who is that?" I heard her ask. He walked to the bed.

I watched from the doorway. "I'm sorry, darling," I said dully. "I didn't tell him, honestly. He followed me. I couldn't keep him out."

"Gaby," he said. Her name caught in his throat. He sank down on the edge of her bed and took her hand. "Oh, Gaby. Oh, my God." He dropped his head and she whispered his name and stroked his hair, her white hand looking like a white bird against the background of his darkness. After a moment Seth lifted his head and turned blazing eyes on me. "You knew," he said accusingly. "You knew all the time, and you didn't tell me."

"Oh, no, Seth," said Gabrielle. "No, it wasn't Rhawnie's fault! I made her promise never to tell any of you. I made her swear it on the Bible. I made her. Don't be angry with her. She's been so good to me, so good. I love her so much, like a sister. Please, don't be angry with her," she pleaded again.

I couldn't listen to any more. I backed out of the room and closed the door. I sat on the edge of the fountain. After a minute I called to Maria and told her to take Adam in to his mother.

"That man is gone?" she asked.

"No, the man is still here. He is the baby's uncle. And he might as well know the worst, all at once."

Maria carried Adam, still squalling, into Gabrielle's room and closed the door behind her. I stared at the three fat goldfish in the pool under the fountain. Lucky creatures who didn't have a care in the world. Then I heard Seth limping towards me. I didn't look up.

"You had no right to keep it from me," he said.

"I wanted to tell you," I said. "But I gave her my word."

"I'm her brother," he said. "No matter what you think of me, you should have told me. For Gaby's sake."

"She's not supposed to have any excitement," I said lamely. Finally I met his eyes, as cold as flint. I wanted to tell you, I really did. But I haven't had a very easy time communicating with you lately."

"She's very sick," he said.

"She's consumptive. She probably won't live through the winter," I said brutally.

He raked his fingers through his thick hair. "She needs care, the best of care!" he muttered frantically. "We've got to call in a specialist—"

I looked at him pityingly. "This isn't London or New York," I said. "There are no specialists around here. I was lucky to find the doctor when he was sober. And as for care," I stood up and faced him squarely, "she and Adam have everything they need. I've seen to that. She had the best care, right here. Don't think I'm doing it for you. I'm doing it for them. I love them, both of them, as if they were my own flesh."

"This is your idea of revenge, isn't it?" he rasped. "You wouldn't even have told me if she had died. You wanted to keep me wondering—"

Just then Maria came out of Gabrielle's room. She was carrying Adam, whose cries had stopped.

"If your way of wondering was to buy out the Professor and install yourself in my casino, then you weren't wondering about her very hard. I *would* have told you when she died, because then my word to her wouldn't have mattered. And don't try and make me feel guilty for any of this. You can't. I have done what I could for her, but I'm not the one who seduced her and stole her away from her family. I'm not the one who raped her and beat her and turned her into the pathetic creature she is now. Men did that to her. Men like you, Seth, without hearts and souls, who think they can use a girl and leave her and break her heart because she's just a woman. You'd like to kill them, wouldn't you? The men who did this to her? Because she's your sister, your precious Gabrielle. But what about the women *you've* used, Seth? What about me? I was sixteen once, as fresh and as green as Gabrielle, remember? Did you have any more compassion for me than they had for her?"

Maria came through the courtyard again. She was carrying a basin this time. I heard the door slam as she went into the sickroom.

"What's the use of talking to you?" I sighed wearily. "The only person who's important now is Gabrielle, and we must use the time she has left to make her happy. You may stay, now that you are here. She needs to have her family close to her. It isn't going to be easy for her. She's afraid to die. But you can give her courage. You can help her. She thinks you're wonderful; she thinks you can do no wrong. She didn't want me to tell anyone about her, but especially not you. She felt you would be ashamed about her. She can take her illusions about you to the grave. I don't care.

"But I tell you this: if you upset or distress her in any way, I'll drive you away from here and I won't let you come back. I won't let you undo any of the good I've done for her."

He didn't say a word, just scowled at me under his black brows. He was so shaken by his discovery and by what he considered my treachery that he couldn't even speak.

"Well, I've said enough, I guess." I stood up. "Except that there are some rules I expect you to observe while you're here. You are not to touch the baby or anything else after you have touched her unless you have washed your hands thoroughly. There is a basin in that room for that purpose. You may not smoke in her room, and I cannot allow you to take your meals with her. Also—"

"I know all that," he growled.

I left him alone at the fountain and went in to see if Gaby needed anything. Maria left the room when I entered. I didn't say anything right off. She didn't speak while I stoked the fire, plumped her pillows, and opened the shutters to admit the warm afternoon sun. She just lay there, watching me through her big dark eyes.

"Seth is the one you were in love with long ago, isn't he?" she asked.

Prickles of fear ran down my spine. "Why do you say that?" I said.

"Maria left the door open when she took Adam out."

I sat down on a hard chair and buried my face in my hands, the tears flowing. I was so tired, so very tired.

"Rhawnie, come here," she said. I dried my eyes and obeyed. I sat next to her and she held my hand. "I'm sorry. He's angry at you because of me. I shouldn't have made you promise. I didn't know how hard it would be. But what about Steven? I thought you loved Steven?"

"I did," I sniffed. "I do. But you know how it is, with a man like Seth. You know better than anyone. It's as if he put a brand on my heart."

"Poor Rhawnie," she said. "Did he treat you badly, as badly as Boris treated me?"

"Oh, no, darling!" I said quickly. "Nothing like that. He—we—well, you know how foolish young girls are about love. I loved him more than he loved me, that's all. And I couldn't understand it when he left me. I still can't understand it. I know him better now, though, and I know he's not really the evil ogre I thought he was. He's been hurt, too, and he's just being—overly cautious. The hurt was my fault, not his. He was very kind to me," I paused to wipe my streaming eyes. I couldn't seem to stop crying. "But you know how men are. He—he taught me a great many useful things!"

Gabrielle said, "Oh, Rhawnie," in a voice that told me she didn't believe a word of it. "And you still want to marry Steve?"

"No!" I said. "Yes, I do. But I can't! No, I don't want to marry him. It wouldn't be right, you can see that. I love Seth, even though I hate him, and that wouldn't be fair to Steven, not after—Seth was first, you see, and—oh, it would be hard, and bad, very bad for all of us. I should just look the truth in the face and accept it. I can't have either of them. But what does that matter?" I said with a feeble show of bravery. "I still have you, and our big boy, Adam."

"Oh, Rhawnie," she sighed. She looked thoughtful.

Seth stayed for three days. He was very sweet to

Gabrielle—I even heard her laugh once or twice, something I hadn't heard since I'd found her. He talked to her, read to her, played with little Adam and praised him like a proud uncle. On the second day of his visit Gabrielle asked me to send for the priest from San Mateo.

"It's not for me," she said, reassuring me. "It's for Adam. I want him to be baptized. You and Seth are to be his godparents. If anything should happen to me, you will both take care of him."

"Oh, darling, nothing will happen," I said. "You're getting stronger every day, you know that. Even Seth has noticed an improvement."

She smiled. "No, it's all right, Rhawnie. Don't lie to me anymore. I know it's coming, and I'm trying hard not to be afraid."

"You are very silly," I said gruffly, gulping back tears. "And as brave as a Gypsy."

"Do you think so? I know that it will be easier for everyone if I'm brave, and I really am trying. Sometimes, late at night, when I can't sleep because of my cough, I lie here and wonder what it will be like. And I'm frightened, a little. But you know, lately I've been feeling more tired, tired of being sick. And I feel—eager. It's hard to explain." She turned her head and looked out the window. "I want to see the spring, Rhawnie. I want to see the olive trees in blossom, and the lemon trees. And the roses you planted. And wildflowers. And the new lambs. I want to see the spring, just once more." She turned back to me. "About the priest, Rhawnie? Please?"

I nodded. The priest came that very afternoon and he baptized Adam in Gabrielle's room. The household gathered to watch. We made it a festive occasion and Maria produced a very creditable feast on short notice.

I held the baby while Seth stood close at hand. The priest poured water on Adam's head and muttered prayers in Latin. Adam cried lustily, and everyone laughed and said that he had fine lungs. While I was holding him and patting him on the back I met Seth's eyes. I had to look away. It was very painful for me. Our own baby had had such a short life.

Later I said to Gabrielle, "I know what you're trying to do, and I don't like it. And neither does your brother."

"What?" Her eyes widened innocently. "What am I trying to do?"

"You're as cunning as a Gypsy," I told her. "You're trying to matchmake from your deathbed!" She giggled. "Well, it won't work. He doesn't love me. He never loved me."

"Yes, he does," she said. "I know. I've seen him looking at you. And besides, I asked him."

"You did what?" I felt myself growing warm. "Well, come on, what did he say? He said no, didn't he? And you interpreted that to mean yes. You're still a silly little schoolgirl, Gabrielle McClelland."

"He said yes, Rhawnie. He said he loved you very much, but that the two of you couldn't seem to work things out. He was very honest. He even told me you were married. And that you had a baby but it died. And that you held it against him."

I felt hot, then cold, and I blushed all over. "He would lie to you, just to make you happy," I mumbled.

She smiled and held my hand. "Not everyone is a Gypsy, Rhawnie. Not everyone lies all the time, like you. Seth's not a liar, I know that. And he respects and loves me too much to lie to me, now. Talk to him, Rhawnie. Please, for me?"

I shook my head. "I can't. Not now. I never could. I always seem to end up shouting at him or making love to him. It's hopeless."

Seth announced the next morning that he was going back to town.

"I'll come with you," I said.

"That won't be necessary," he said quickly. "I won't dock your share of the profits anymore."

"That's very generous of you," I told him, "but I need to order some things for the farm. And besides, Gabrielle rests better when there's no one here but Adam and Maria. But if you'd like to stay a little longer, I can look after things at the Golden Gypsy for awhile—"

"No, I want to go back," he said in a bored drawl. "Life in the country has never agreed with me."

His coolness didn't fool me. It was the sight of his dying sister, and his own helplessness that didn't agree with him.

No one looking at Seth McClelland in the next few days would have guessed that he carried a private sorrow. He drank too much and laughed too loudly and took the most extraordinary chances at the tables. I knew the signs, but everyone else thought he was just a gay fellow. And while he didn't bring Yvette or anyone else to his room again, I was sure that he was bedding every whore in San Fracisco. There were nights when he went out after the place closed and didn't come back until mid-morning.

I hated him, I love him, I pitied him. But I couldn't do as Gabrielle asked, I couldn't talk to him. I didn't trust him.

After that time we never went to the hacienda together. I told him when I was going and when I would be returning, and I left it to him to plan his own visits. The winter months slipped away. Gabrielle grew stronger and even gained a few pounds. Her cough eased, and I hoped anew.

In late March the winter rains stopped periodically. On the slopes near the house I could see tiny wildflowers blooming, and I ran out to gather fistfuls to bring to Gabrielle. She could sit up now, and she spent a few hours a day in the courtyard, watching Adam crawling around near the fountain.

"You will get well," I told her. "I'm sure of it."

"If God wills it, I will," she said with a serene smile. "Thank you, Rhawnie."

her eyes. Seth continued to hold her and to stroke her cheek. His face was wet, too. I left him and went out to the courtyard. Maria came up and we held each other and cried.

An hour later I went back. Seth was still holding her.

I put my arm around him and said gently, "You must let her go now, Seth. We must get her ready. Come with me. I'll take you to the kitchen and we'll have some of Maria's dreadful coffee. Come."

He permitted himself to be led. He was like a man in a trance, like a stunned child. I pressed a cup of coffee into his hands and sat him down at the table. Maria and Juan's wife prepared Gabrielle's body for burial. They dressed her in a pretty blue gown that I had had my dressmaker sew for the day when she got better. She had liked it. Seth and I went in to look at her. She looked peaceful and almost pretty again.

Then Juan brought in the coffin and we had our funeral. Juan and his brother and his sons carried her to a spot on the hill. She had chosen the place one day when we were sitting together. She had pointed out a bird sitting on a rock near the olive trees, and she told me that was where she would like to be buried. She tried so hard to be brave. Seth and I followed the coffin. I carried Adam, who was sleeping.

They lowered the box into the ground. I turned to Seth. "Say something."

He shook his head. "I can't. There is nothing to say."

"Yes, there is," I said. I looked at the flower-strewn coffin. "You have started on your journey, sister. Your pain and suffering are over, and we are glad. We will always remember you fondly, and with laughter, as you would wish to be remembered. And when your son grows to be a man, we will tell him about your courage. You showed us how to live, graciously and lovingly, with no malice in your heart and no hatred. And you showed us how to die. We are very proud of you, Gabrielle.''

I made Seth hold the baby. Then I took off my bracelets and my earrings and threw them into the grave. I tossed some coins after them. Then we all went back to the house in silent procession, except for Juan and his brother. Adam woke up and started to scream. I took him from Seth and held him close. He knew, that little one. He knew his mother had gone.

We made a pile and burned her things, everything she had owned since coming to live at the hacienda. Her books, her bed and bedding, her pictures, her clothes. We did this not only for reasons of health and sanitation, but because Gypsies believe that when a man dies everything that he has owned should be destroyed, even his caravan. This spares the living being reminded of their loss. We then stripped her room and scrubbed it thoroughly. I was grateful for these tasks. Even a Gypsy will agree that there are times when work is a blessing.

In the early evening I looked up from my work and saw Seth riding away from the farm. I saw him rein in his horse near the grave for a moment, then take off over the hill, towards San Francisco. I stayed on for a few more days, then I, too went back to town.

Seth drank heavily and stopped paying such close attention to the business after that. His heart wasn't in it. His behavior towards me didn't alter drastically; he still didn't speak to me unnecessarily, and he looked through me most of the time, as though I wasn't there. It was as if there was a glass wall between us a foot thick. I could see him, but I couldn't touch him or reach him or talk to him. We were farther apart than ever. Yvette didn't come back, even to work the tables, and Seth didn't bother to replace her.

A month passed. My sorrow over Gabrielle's death eased and I felt that I could enjoy life again. A lot of burdens had been lifted from my heart, among them the burden of my love for Seth. Not that I stopped loving him. I had never loved him more, and his unhappiness and inability to express his grief made me feel wretched. But I knew that a lot of things were happening inside him, where I couldn't see them, and I wouldn't have been a bit surprised to wake up one morning and find that he had left me again. That was the pattern of his life so far, and I expected him to follow it.

Then one night, as I lay awake wishing that I could go to him or that he would come to me, I discovered a great truth. To love someone is to want what is best for them. I had no right to expect him to stay with me if he didn't want to stay. He was free, as I was. And to keep him, to bind him to me with the snares that women use, would be like hobbling a wild horse. Seth had to come to know me and trust me in his own time, and if he never learned, if I never tamed him, then I would have to live with it. And having come to this simple realization, I was able to sleep and to awake in the morning and all the mornings after that without fear.

One night my Russian sailors appeared, the ones who sold me all that wonderful vodka. I greeted them joyously, and after the captain and I had made a good deal on another shipment, I announced that drinks were on the house. One of the sailors produced a guitar, and another a concertina, and a third pushed my piano away from his tinny upright. I was wearing Gypsy garb that night: lots of skirts and a peasant blouse and hundreds of beads and bangles and ribbons. The Golden Gypsy was joyous that night with song and laughter. The sailors danced athletically, impressing the Americans with their strength and grace and stamina. I sang for them, songs I hadn't sung for years, since I left Russia. I sang about love and loss, sadness and joy. And I drank a lot of vodka and didn't feel a thing.

Seth sat at a table with a bottle of vodka in front of him and a glass. He didn't seem to hear the music or to see the dancers. He was immersed in his own silent depths.

I put my arms around his neck and kissed him. "What is the matter, Partner?" I asked him. "Are you angry with me for spending so much money? Money is for fun. But maybe you don't like our music? Is it too soft? Brothers!" I shouted to the Russians. "My friend says he can't hear the music! We must sing louder!"

The walls shook. I decided that I would dance. I ripped off my boots and took the pins out of my hair, tossing them to the miners who fought over them as if they were made of gold. Then I shook out my braids and shouted to my musicians to play a Gypsy song that every Russian knew: "Two Brothers."

The two brothers in the song love the same girl and she cannot make up her mind between them and so she marries another man, a different one entirely. It is a fine song with lots of verses, lots of clapping and laughter. I threw back my head and lifted my arms to the ceiling. I started to sway and whirl. The music grew louder and the men all clapped in time. I laughed out loud, because I loved song and dance and life and I didn't care anymore what was preying on Seth's mind because I loved him and I wanted him to be free, as free as a Gypsy.

I danced up to Seth. He didn't lift his head.

"Come, come, Monsieur Seth," I said in a barbarous combination of Russian and French. "I want to dance for you and you're not even watching. I want to dance for you alone! Stand up, I say! Stand and watch me dance!" I pulled at his hands until he stood in front of the table. "Now, watch me carefully," I ordered him. "You, men, make sure he watches me!"

Two obliging Russians stood on either side of him and held his arms so that he had to look at me. I danced then. I was sixteen again, dancing for him on the veranda of the Delacroix mansion in Paris, with music and laughter ringing in the background. I swayed from side to side, moving my arms and upper body in a different direction from my hips. My blouse slipped down over my shoulder and I made no attempt to pull it up.

I whirled faster and faster, coming ever closer to Seth so that my flying hair swept across his face. I laughed at his impassivity, his expressionless immobility. I wanted to create a maelstrom of movement and joy that would suck him in.

I danced until the din of the miners' approving shouts was deafening, and finally I could dance no more. I stopped abruptly, in front of Seth. I felt dizzy. The room tilted sharply. I felt myself falling. And then I was floating. Seth lifted me up and carried me out of that noisy, smoke-filled room and up the stairs to bed while the miners cheered and the Russians toasted us and shouted encouragement. I was as limp as a doll in his arms. I laughed and sang a little tune while I floated up, up to the sky.

He took me not to my room but to his. I wanted him so badly that I could feel the imps of desire dancing wildly in every part of my body, even in my fingertips. I longed for his lips and his arms and his thighs and his mastery.

He set me down very gently on top of the coverlet, then he sat next to me and pushed the hair out of my face with both hands. His touch was soft and tender. I reached up and cupped his face in my hands, and I looked into his eyes. They were bright now, and sure. Full of life. He lowered his head and kissed me. I pressed close to him, losing myself in his arms. I wanted to let him know that I wanted him, that I loved him. He pulled back a little and looked intently into my face. He seemed to be searching, wondering, remembering.

Then he stood up abruptly and walked out of the room, closing the door firmly behind him. My arms still jutted up in the air, as if I had been embracing a wraith.

I was so shocked that I lay there for minutes, staring up at the ceiling like an idiot, wondering what I had done wrong? Then I sat up and tossed my legs over to the floor. But when I tried to stand, the room tilted like the deck of a ship in a storm and I sat down fast. I fell back and rolled over on my side. The room settled down again.

I felt some confusion the next morning when I awoke to find myself in a strange room. Then I remembered what had happened and that confusion gave way to embarrassment and shame. I had gotten drunk and made a perfect fool of myself. Again. Well, I thought, if he's still here this morning, I'll go myself. I can't take much more.

Seth wasn't in my room when I went in to wash my face and hands and change my clothes. I went downstairs. The Chinamen were sweeping up. The floors were littered with bits of broken glass.

I found Seth sitting in the small private dining room off the kitchen, the only part of the lounge that remained after the remodeling. He was eating heartily and reading the *Alta California*.

"Good morning," he said. I frowned at the unexpected greeting. He had spoken. Voluntarily. Even cheerfully. "Did you sleep well?"

"No," I grumbled, "the room kept pitching. It kept me awake all night. Must have been earthquakes." I shouted for coffee. My voice sounded hoarse and faraway. Seth smothered a grin. "Take my advice," I said, "never drink with Russians. They're maniacs, all of them."

"I'll try to remember that." He was silent for a moment, then he said, "I don't suppose this is a very good time, and I should have done it sooner, but thank you, for helping Gabrielle."

"You don't have to do that," I said. "I told you, I did it for her and the baby. Not for you."

"Yes, I know that." He pushed his plate away and tossed down his newspaper. "And I'm sorry about it."

Something in his voice made my heart fly around under my ribs like a panicked bird in a cage. I sat up straight and said, "How would you like to play a little faro with me?"

"For what stakes?"

"The Golden Gypsy. Or what's left of her after last night. We'll play right now, one card. Will you?"

He frowned at me. I forced myself to meet his gaze. I had made my decision and I would stick to it. I didn't want to set myself up, only to be knocked down again. It had happened too many times. I needed to be rid of him if I wanted to be free.

"And if you win?" he said.

"If I win—I'll stay, I guess. Or I'll sell my share to MacDaniel. Unless—you want to put up your half—"

"No." He reached into a side pocket and brought out a fresh deck of cards. That was a gambler for you. Ready for anything. "What card?" he asked.

I closed my eyes. I hoped my Gypsy magic wouldn't fail me now. I saw Gabrielle's face. "The queen of hearts," I said. "And don't try to cheat me. I know every trick there is. You taught me, remember?"

"I remember," he said, breaking the seal. Wang came in and cleared away the breakfast things. Seth shuffled the deck, offered it to me to cut, and turned up the first card. The next card was my win, a nine of diamonds. He turned over a jack of spades on his own pile. He delt swiftly and honestly, no tricks. "My win," was a three of clubs. "Your win," a four of spades. "My win." I caught my breath. The queen of—diamonds. "Your win." A black seven. "My win" was an ace of spades. And finally there she was, on my stack, the queen of hearts. I had successfully lost the Golden Gypsy to Seth.

I breathed a deep sigh of relief and pushed back my chair. "Congratulations, Seth. She's yours now."

He shuffled the deck absently. "What are your plans?"

"Oh, I don't know." I stood and stretched. "Maybe Europe again. Maybe I will go back and take up my singing again. But I'm a free agent. I don't have to plan. I'll just travel first."

"And what about Adam?" he said without looking up.

I felt deflated. Adam. I had given no thought to Adam. I couldn't give him up! He was like my own son.

I sat down again. "I don't know," I said. "I'll take him with me."

"No," Seth shook his head slowly. "He's my responsibility, too, remember? My nephew. Which gives me a legal claim over him. And I did promise Gaby."

"But you don't care for him!" I cried. "Oh, it's just like you to use a baby you don't love as a—a weapon to work me around, to bend me to your will. You think I can't see what you're doing? You know damned well you don't want to be bothered with a child. A child needs a woman, Seth. A mother. I am his mother now! He doesn't mean anything to you!"

"Now there's where you're wrong," he said softly. "He means a lot to me."

I slammed my fists down on the table. "Why, why did she do this? Why did you have to come back? He could have been mine, and now you're going to exercise your 'legal rights' and take him away from me, just to spite me!"

"We could take care of him together," Seth suggested. "That was what Gaby wanted. It's the rather obvious solution, don't you agree?"

He looked at me squarely. I felt myself blushing softly. There was something in his eyes—

I shook my head vigorously. "No. Not that. I don't trust you. I can't! You don't want to be tied to a wife and family. You didn't before, why should you now?"

"Because things are different now," he said gently.

"Everything is the same!" I insisted. "You haven't changed. But maybe I have. Maybe I'm tired of wanting you and getting nowhere. Why can't you just let me get out of your life and put you out of mine? Why?"

"I will not give you a divorce to marry Steven," he said evenly. "Or to marry anyone. I'll stop you. And you'll never have the boy."

I stood up and said coldly, "You've beaten me, then. I'll pack my things. You'll want the room for—Yvette!"

"Rhawnie." He stood in front of me and put his hands on my shoulders. "Rhawnie," he said again, very softly. I turned my head away from him. I couldn't trust myself to meet his eyes. "This isn't like you, worrying about the future, running away from me. You're not a coward."

"No," I said bitterly, "and I used to tell myself that I wasn't a fool, either. But every time I'm with you I do foolish things and I break my heart over and over again. Why shouldn't I run away this time, instead of you? I love you and I want you to be happy. And obviously you're not happy being around me too long. By getting out of here now I'm saving you the trouble. You ought to thank me."

"Crazy as ever," he said in a slightly exasperated tone. "Rhawnie." His voice could have melted rocks. "I love you. I want you to live with me, as my wife."

I moistened my lips and looked squarely into his face and said, "And that's why you left me last night? Because you love me?"

"Yes," he said. "And because I was remembering a slim girl with long legs and incredibly long hair whose eyes were full of trust and love. I didn't want to betray her again. I love her too much."

"Stop it!" I said sharply. "I'm not that girl now. I knew what I was doing!"

"But I didn't," he said. "I needed a chance to think. I didn't sleep last night. I took a long, hard look at things—at myself, at you, at us. I'm not going to leave you, Rhawnie. If I were, I'd be gone by now. I'm staying with you, because I want to be with you. I love you, Rhawnie."

I broke away from him and faced him angrily. My eyes were full of tears and my voice shook.

"I don't play with fire anymore, *gorgio*," I said. "Not two minutes ago you were threatening me, remember? You were using that little boy as a club! Remember, Seth? Oh, I know you so well. Rule number one in your book is: if all else fails, make love to her and she'll come around. You have to have your own way. Always life on your own terms and not anybody else's, right? Well, Seth, I may regret the first day I set eyes on you, but I don't have to go on regretting it for the rest of my life! You have hurt me over and over again—and I'm afraid! I'm afraid of you!''

I started to walk away but he pulled me back. "Listen to me, Gypsy,'' he growled.

"Let me go!'' I said sharply. "I'm through listening to you. You have what you want, the Golden Gypsy and Adam. Let me go!''

"You're the damndest most stubborn little bitch—''

"Me, stubborn? I've been more than generous, Seth. I've given you chance after chance. I won't give anymore!''

"You're not leaving here!'' he said loudly. "And if you do—''

"Take your hands off me!'' I started to wrestle with him.

"Stop that and listen to me!'' Seth shouted in a voice like thunder.

And then we heard a cool voice, like spring rain.

"I hope I'm not interrupting.''

Steven McClelland stood in the doorway.

20

Two Brothers

SETH AND I stood frozen in our combative posture: Seth gripping my wrists tightly while my right knee was hitched up to kick him in the groin. We came to our senses at about the same time and pulled away from each other. The three of us were silent for a long moment. I gaped at Steven while Seth shot me hostile glances.

Steven looked lean as ever, tanned and bearded. My heart gave a queer twist; I had forgotten how handsome he was. He was dressed for the trail in heavy boots, cord trousers and sheepskin jacket. His clothes were covered with dust.

I spoke first. "Ah, Steven, what a surprise. We—didn't expect you."

He smiled. "I can see that." He glanced at Seth and gave him a cool nod. "I'll leave and come back a little later, if you like."

I sprang forward and said, "Oh, no, you mustn't do that! No, no, come in and have some coffee, something to eat. We were just having a little discussinon about the business, that's all. We—Seth owns this place. I used to, but I don't anymore." I called out to Kim to bring coffee for one. "You look so tired, Steven! Please, sit down, sit." I pushed him into a chair. I kept bubbling like a fool; I couldn't help myself. "We are such poor hosts, Seth and I. What a welcome for you!"

"Tell me about Gabrielle," he said. "Is she—?"

I sat next to him and took his hands in mine. Seth leaned against the doorframe with his arms crossed over his chest.

"Oh, Steven, she lived to see the spring," I said gently. "But she couldn't hold out any longer. It was a good death, very peaceful. She had the priest before she died, and Seth and I were both there at the end. There was no pain. She was very brave, braver than any of us. I'll take you to see her grave tomorrow. It's a little farm south of here. She was happy there."

"And the boy? Adam?" Steven asked.

"Oh, Adam is fine, just fine!" I said happily. "So big for his age, and smart! He looks like his mother. *Yes*, He's just fine. We even had a baptism for him, on the farm. Seth and I are—godparents." I swallowed.

"I see," said Steven softly.

I told him a little about what had happened to Gabrielle, and how I had found her. Kim brought coffee and brandy and I helped myself to a big dose of the latter. I needed it. I was still feeling seedy from my exertions of the previous night, and all this excitement and tension weren't doing me any good. Steven sipped his coffee and told us that he'd been on the trail for two months, since the end of January.

Then Seth spoke for the first time since Steven came in.

"How did you know about Gaby? And the baby?"

I said quickly, "How do you think he knew? I wrote to him as soon as I found her."

"And you still didn't tell me." He looked grim.

"No, I didn't. Do we have to go all over this again? I didn't tell you because she specifically asked me not to, and because you were being so horrid that I—"

"Please, Rhawnie," Steven said softly. "It's over now. No need to fight about it. Mother and Father are coming, too, by the way. They're taking a ship around the Horn. It's impossible to tell when they'll arrive."

"Oh, Steven, how sad for them," I said. "It will be lovely to see them again, but under such circumstances—"

"They'll be all right," Steven said, pressing my hands. "They will understand that you did everything you could, and they'll be grateful to you, as I am."

From the doorway Seth continued to glower at us.

Then Steven said, "Rhawnie, in your letter you said that marriage between us was no longer possible. What did you mean?"

I stiffened. "We don't have to discuss that now, Steven, so soon after— we will talk about it later."

"I'd like to talk about it now," he pressed me. "Why won't you marry me?"

I looked up at Seth, whose face was impassive.

"Well," I said coolly, "do you want to tell him? Go on, here's your chance to make good your threats. Tell him!"

Seth scowled and kept silent.

"What's the matter?" I asked him. "Suddenly it isn't so important to you to hurt me? Very well, I'll just have to tell him myself." I turned to Steven and said, "I cannot marry you because I am already married. To your brother."

Steven did not react with surprise, hurt—anything but utter self-control. "When?" he asked. "Recently?"

"We were married in Scotland, many years ago." I said

quietly." Your brother—is the one I told you about." I hitched my chair close to his and said anxiously, "Oh, Steven, I didn't want to hurt you, I never intended to hurt you! And I wanted to tell you, but I couldn't, can you understand that? I swear I never dreamed that Seth was your brother and then he came and I could see my dream of happiness with you just—evaporating! You mustn't blame him—I made him swear not to tell you. I know it was a foolish idea, and I realized that it would be very wrong to deceive you, but then it just got worse and worse and harder and harder to tell the truth and I needed to get away for a while and so I followed Gabrielle with Seth and—"

Eventually I ran out of steam. Steven wasn't listening anyway. He was watching Seth intently, and there was a glint in his eye that spelled trouble. Seth glowered back at him. He never moved from his place at the door but I saw him tense up a little.

Steven stood up slowly and went over to his brother.

"You goddamned bastard," he said in a low voice. Then he let one of his fists fly.

Seth reeled back and struck the wall. He shook his head to clear it and put his hand to his chin. Blood trickled down from a cut on his lip.

"Feel better, Steve?" he asked thickly. "You've been wanting to do that for a long time."

Steven said, "That's right, brother." He stripped off his coat and rolled up his shirtsleeves. "That and more. I never should have let you go after what you did to Julie. You thought I didn't know? Damn you. I'm not a complete fool, Seth. She lied for you until the day she died, but I knew the truth."

He knew? I thought. He knew what they had done, and he had married her anyway. Because he loved her, and because he didn't want to shame her. And he had gone on loving her, in spite of everything.

"I'm going to kill you, Seth. I'm going to tear you apart. I should have guessed when Rhawnie told me about this husband of hers. I should have known that there was only one man on this earth cold-blooded and egotistical enough to treat women the way you treated Julie and Rhawnie. Come on, Seth. I want to finish you, once and for all."

Seth straightened up and said, "Look, Steve, I don't want to hurt you. But don't push me—"

"I'm pushing you," said Steven grimly. "And don't worry, I'm not going to get hurt. You are."

I threw myself at Steven and wrapped my arms around him. "No, Steven, no! You mustn't! You can't undo the harm he's done, so what's the point in fighting him? The past is done—"

"Don't interfere, Rhawnie," he said. "This is between Seth and me."

"No, no, we're all involved—you and Seth and Julie and me! Forgive, Steve, please. Julie forgave, and you forgave her because you loved her! Don't—"

"And what about you, Rhawnie? Can you forgive him? Everything?"

I was speechless for a moment, and Seth said, "Leave her out of this. I don't have to hide behind a woman, Steve. Come on, I'm ready for you."

Steven pushed me aside, not very gently. He swung first. Seth ducked the blow and brought up his right fist under Steven's jaw. The force of that punch might have cracked Steven's head if it connected, but it didn't. Steven dodged to the left and countered with a hard punch to Seth's middle. Seth grunted and sprawled backwards, into the table. The table tipped noisily, and coffee cups and brandy glasses shattered.

Seth bounced up, undaunted, and threw himself at Steven. He got in close and pummeled Steven's body. Steven wrestled him to the floor and smashed his fist into Seth's face. Seth's eye swelled shut immediately. His lip was bleeding profusely. They rolled around on the floor, knocking into chairs, kicking at the walls and door.

I pressed myself into a corner, out of harm's way. I didn't want to watch the carnage, but I couldn't tear myself away.

They got to their feet and grappled with each other. Occasionally one of them would break away long enough to throw a powerful punch. They fell through the doorway into the gambling room, the Little Salon. Now they had more space, a bigger battlefield, and they widened the scope of their battle. Seth picked up a chair and swung it at Steven's head. Steven ducked quickly and the chair smashed into a table and shattered into toothpicks. Steven snatched up a chair of his own and hurled it at Seth's head. Seth stepped aside and the chair flew into the big mirror over the bar. Glasses and bottles came tumbling down with a deafening crash.

My workers crowded into the doorways to watch. The Chinese chattered excitedly and started to place bets. I wouldn't have known which way to bet. It seemed to me that Seth had the advantage in weight and strength. But Steven was driven by an obsessive madness, a thirst to punish and destroy the man who had hurt the two women he had loved in his life. Seth's fighting edge was dulled by his soft life at the Golden Gypsy. While Steven was fresh from the taxing rigors of the trail. He was taut and alert. All in all, I decided that Steven's fury would probably win the fight for him.

Seth got into a boxer's stance and taunted his brother to fight fair. Steven squared off, fists raised, and the two of them battled conventionally for a while, feinting and jabbing and dodging. Both of Seth's eyes were almost closed now, and his face was streaming with blood and sweat.

The two of them were staggering wearily by now, but

they wouldn't give up. A terrific punch in Steven's stomach made him double up, and Seth pressed the advantage and started to rain blows on his brother's head and face. But Steven recovered quickly. He straightened up, uncoiling like a tightly wound spring, and drove his fist into Seth's jaw. Seth swayed and went down, then Steven threw himself on top of Seth and put his hands around his throat. He squeezed as he pounded Seth's head against the floor.

I screamed and tried to pull him off. "Stop it, Steven! Stop! You're killing him! Please, Steven, stop!"

Steven paused in his deadly work. Then he tightened his grip on Seth's throat and said, "Tell her you're sorry. Come on, tell her! Talk, damn you, or I'll strangle you!"

Seth gagged and said tightly, "I'm sorry, Rhawnie."

"Tell her you'll never hurt her again!"

"—never hurt you—again."

"And you're sorry for what you did to Julie. Tell me you're sorry for that!"

"Sorry," Seth choked out the words painfully. "Loved her—didn't mean—"

"Say, 'I'm sorry, Steve!' "

"I'm sorry—Steve."

Steven sighed heavily and released him. The Chinamen grinned and nodded at each other. It had been a good fight, and a close one. Money quickly changed hands.

I was crying and didn't know it. My body was shaking like a leaf.

Steven tried to stand, teetered, and then dropped like a felled oak. I asked the men to take the two of them upstairs and make them comfortable, and I sent Wang for Dr. Clement. Then I sat down at one of the faro tables, lowered my head onto my arms, and sobbed.

After about half an hour I pulled myself together and I went to see what I could do for them. Steven was lying on my bed. He was conscious and he gave me the weakest of smiles.

"He has a punch like a load of dynamite," he whispered. "Didn't think I could hold out much longer. Good thing he forgot to keep his left up. Never could remember."

I looked at the cuts on his face. They weren't too bad. "Where does it hurt?" I asked him.

"All over," he moaned. He moved on the bed and clutched his middle. He started to wretch and I held a basin under his head.

"Stupid fools," I muttered. "Like a couple of children."

"Don't be angry," he said, lying back and closing his eyes. "Did it—for you."

"You did it for yourself. Well, I hope you feel better. You've been carrying that hate around inside you for a long time."

"You said—you loved me," he whispered. "Was that a lie?"

"A lie! Oh, no, Steven!" I put a damp cloth on his forehead and let my hand linger there. "I lie about everything else, but never about that. Oh, no. I did love you. I do love you. Of all the men I have known in my life, you are the most deserving of love. I'm only sorry because I know this has hurt you, and that's the last thing in the world I wanted to do. Sleep now, Steven. We will talk later."

I started to walk away but he caught my hand. "Still want you," he said. "This doesn't change anything. Love you, Rhawnie."

I sighed and said, "Later, Steven. We'll talk later."

Wang appeared and told me that Dr. Clement was too drunk to come. I wasn't surprised. The way the day had gone so far, any kind of good news would be too much to expect. I went into Seth's room. He was still unconscious and snoring heavily. His face was a mess. He looked like he had been run over by a herd of buffalo. I washed away some of the blood and piled cold compresses around his eyes. That was all I could do for the moment. I started to tiptoe out the door.

"Rhawnie," Seth groaned. I looked around. He was tearing at the compresses and trying to sit up. "Rhawnie."

"Yes, I'm here." I went over to him and pushed him down. "Don't get so excited. And leave these alone." I replaced the cool cloths.

"I meant—what I said." His voice was muffled. His lips were so swollen he could hardly move them. It must have been very painful for him to speak at all, and I tried to stop him, but he was insistent. "I am sorry. Never should have treated you that way."

"It doesn't matter now, Seth," I said. "It's over and—"

"No. Can't let you go now. Love you too much. Can't stand to lose the thing I love—like Julie. Too damned stubborn, possessive. Married you so you wouldn't get away. You can't leave—won't divorce you."

"Oh, Seth," I said wearily, "I don't want to start this all over again. We'll talk about it later, all right?"

"No," he said stubbornly. "Now! Want to talk—about Vienna. I loved you then, I swear it. But I had to leave, for a little while. Think. Clear my head. Understand?"

"No," I said.

"I went back. You were gone. Hotel didn't know where."

I stared at his battered face. "What do you mean, you went back?" I said slowly. "I don't believe you—"

"True," he said. "Knew I was a damned coward. Couldn't live with myself. Drank like a damned fish but couldn't forget. Went back. Found out you'd gone to a boarding house. Lilienstrasse. Near the opera house. Damned ugly hole. I was—sorry."

His lips were dry. I gave him some water and helped him to drink. He gripped my wrist and told me to sit down, next to him. I obeyed.

"Landlady told me about the baby. Nicholas. Even found the doctor you'd called in. Dr.—Schumenheink?"

I caught my breath. Yes, that was his name. I'd forgotten it myself.

"Saw the grave. Sorry, Rhawnie. I thought if I'd stayed—you blame me. No more—than I blame myself."

"Oh, Seth," I said sadly, "don't talk about it anymore. Don't upset yourself, please."

He didn't listen. He had to talk, and I had to let him.

"No one knew—where you and Anna went afterwards. Looked everywhere. Checked trains. Nothing."

Of course he had found nothing. I hadn't bought tickets to Munich; King Ludwig had given them to me.

"Didn't know what to do next. You had—disappeared. Cursed myself. Thought I'd lost you for good. Couldn't believe my eyes when I saw you in New Orleans. And you told me you wanted Steve. Second woman I'd lost to him—wanted to kill both of you."

I smoothed the tumbled hair away from his bruised face. "I know," I murmured. "I know."

"Concert was agony. You looked so damned beautiful. And you belonged to him. Couldn't listen long. Too damned jealous. Always jealous of you, from the beginning. Remember? Wouldn't let you out of my sight. Didn't want any other man to have you, ever. Not de Vernay. Not anyone. You were my Gypsy. Mine."

He breathed deeply and fell silent. I knew he was asleep and I left him. I stood in the hallway and pressed my forehead against the cool wall. He loved me. He really did love me. Yes, he had abandoned the baby and me in Vienna. But he had come back. And I never knew.

I needed some air. I slipped into my room—Steven was

sleeping soundly—and I put on my riding clothes and went out. Fire and I left the city and rode down the peninsula, to the farm. I didn't intend to stay long. I just had to get away.

Maria and the baby were fine. Juan and his brood greeted me joyously. Maria scolded and told me I was too thin.

"That man," she said, looking at me shrewdly. "You marry him?"

I shrugged. "I don't know, Maria. I don't know anything anymore. I love him. I love his brother. Things are as confused as ever."

"You marry him," she decided. "He not too bad."

I rode back to town, arriving at the Golden Gypsy well after opening. The action was in full swing, even in the Little Salon. I went upstairs to wash and change. Steven was gone. I looked through my things and chose a gown of sky-blue satin. When I had finished dressing I tapped on Seth's door. No answer.

I found them both in the little dining room in back of the Little Salon. They had their heads together and when I came in they looked up. Seth's face was unreadable behind his cuts and bruises, but Steven looked guilty.

"Hello," I said with tempered cheerfulness. "What are you doing, deciding on the terms of your next fight?"

Steven said, "We both want you, Rhawnie. I meant it when I said this hadn't changed things. I love you and I want to marry you."

"Talk to Seth," I said. "He has first claim on me, legally."

Steven shook his head. "There wouldn't be any problem if you decided to divorce him. You have ample grounds. It's up to you. Will you?"

"No," Seth growled. "Don't listen to him."

"You're going to have to choose, Rhawnie," Steven said. "Make up your mind, one way or the other. If you decide to stay with him, I'll understand. I won't try to argue with you. You know best what he's like and you know what he's done.''

"Shut up, Steve," Seth rasped. "Said you weren't going to influence her."

"Well! So while I've been gone, the two of you have been sitting here, cooking up a solution to our problems, eh?" I crossed my arms. "You're ridiculous, both of you. You want me to choose? Very well, I choose—"

They leaned forward expectantly.

"—not to marry either of you. That's the only real solution. Remember the two brothers in the Gypsy song last night, Seth? You can tell Steven all about it while I go to work. I strongly recommend that you both stay back here, out of sight. You might scare off business."

I turned around and walked away from them. I could feel Steven's eyes boring into my back; Seth's were too swollen to do more than squint malevolently. I didn't know what to do and I was too tired of both of them to want to worry about the problems for very long. An answer would present itself if I stalled them long enough. I greeted the customers, took my place at the faro table, and started to play.

It was business as usual at the Golden Gypsy that night. The two remaining French tarts laughed and joked with the customers and fleeced them expertly. As the men drank more they grew noisier and the din was deafening. I even forgot that the Golden Gypsy didn't belong to me anymore.

Then two masked men with torches came into the salon and leaped up on the bar.

"Clear out, everybody!" they shouted. "We're gonna burn out this hell-hole of vice and sin!"

The girls screamed and broke for the doors. No fools they. All at once the place was in confusion, uproar. More masked men came in and started to attack the bar with axes. One of them set fire to the red velvet curtains at the windows. The occupants of the room started to surge towards the door.

I heard Steven shouting out my name, but we were separated by a crowd.

"Steven!" I shouted. "Seth!"

A thick pall of smoke descended over the room. I could hear the crackle of flames. The Golden Gypsy was only a frame structure; it would burn in no time.

"Wipe out the sources of evil!" a masked man shouted. "An end to the evil and the devil's own corruption!"

And another took up the cry: "Scatter the seeds of evil and they will grow no more! Burn the house of the harlot, the Jezebel, the witch!"

A faint prickle of recognition stirred in my brain. I knew that voice, I was sure of it.

Finally I managed to push my way through to the street. The mob in front of the building was so thick that I could hardly move. I made my way to the edge of the crowd, searching and looking for Steven and Seth. I didn't see either of them, and I prayed they had gotten out safely.

I could hear the roar and crackle of flames. I looked around. The dried timbers were burning quickly. In only a few minutes the Golden Gypsy was nothing but a black skeleton enshrouded in a veil of flames.

The fire was spreading to the Golden Eagle next door. Masked men rode in packs up and down Washington Street. All held torches and shouted about death and sin and retribution.

Strong arms pulled me even farther away from the conflagration. I looked around. It was Seth.

"You must have done somebody a bad turn," he muttered thickly. "Who are they?"

"I wish I knew," I said.

"Find the harlot, the Jezebel!" came a shout. I withdrew into the shadows and pulled Seth with me.

"I know who that one is!" I hissed. "That's Zebulon Pratt! The Mormon elder!"

"What? What's he doing here?"

I groaned and pressed closer to him. "I stole some money from him before I left Salt Lake City," I confessed. I spoke right into Seth's ear. "That's how I got the money to start this place. Ten thousand dollars."

"Righteous retribution," he grunted.

"Sons of Dan!" the masked men bawled. "Pay heed to the Avenger! Make way for the Sons of Dan!"

"Steven?" I asked Seth. "Is he all right?"

Seth nodded. "Saw him a few minutes ago. Ten thousand. Jesus. I'd be tempted to burn you out myself. Some people never learn."

"No, *gorgio*," some people never do." I felt my face broaden into a grin.

Two men came up behind us. They were unmasked, and at first I thought they were just watchers, like us. Then one of them raised a pistol, holding it by the barrel, and cracked the butt end down on Seth's skull. Seth dropped like a stone. I shrieked. Then something crashed into the back of my own head. The flames died into darkness.

The air smelled sweet. Sickeningly sweet. I moaned and opened my eyes. I found that I could not sit up because I was in a narrow space with only about three feet of headroom. But I could turn on my elbow and look out.

I was in a room, dimly lit by a couple of oil lamps suspended from the low ceiling. A haze of grayish mist hung in the air. The walls were lined with man-sized shelves. Most of them were filled with bodies. A few people were moving around. I could tell from their loose black pants and swinging queues that they were Chinese. They were carrying little devices with hoses on them to the bodies on the shelves. Around me I heard sucking noises, and some coughing and sighing, but no talk.

I felt dizzy and nauseous, but suprisingly I felt no pain in my head. Indeed, I didn't feel much of anything. My hands and feet were a little numb, and my whole body felt light and relaxed. Even my brain, which was barely awake.

Where was I? How did I get there? Then I remembered the fire. And Seth. Where was Seth?

I must have cried out, for a diminutive Chinese woman came over to me and spoke soothingly in her own language. She saw my agitation growing, and she called to a man. He came towards me, queue swinging behind him. He wore cotton pajamas and a little beanie of the same fabric. He spoke to the woman rapidly. She went away and came back carrying a glassful of liquid.

She held the glass for me to drink. I was very thirsty. The water tasted odd, flowery. I knew the smell. Of course, I had used the stuff on horses. It was laudanum.

I tried to tell them that I didn't want to drink anymore, but when I pushed the glass away, the man opened my mouth and the woman poured the remainder down my throat. It must have been a pretty strong dose, for I fell asleep almost at once.

When I awoke again I was still on my shelf in that room. Two men stood in front of me. The strangers who had attacked Seth and me.

One of them said in German, "It is time, Franz. The boat will be weighing anchor soon. It's almost daylight. They might be looking for her."

"That's your fault," the other one said. "I told you we had to get her away without being seen. I hope you had the sense to kill that fellow, Fritz."

"Of course I did," said the first man quickly. Kill? I thought hazily. Who? Not Seth! "I shot him in the head, Franz. Didn't you see me?"

"No, no!" I said weakly. I tried to sit up. The second man, who was tall and lean, pulled me out of the bunk and I landed on my face on the floor. I lay there, unable to move so much as an eyelash. My body felt dead, leaden. All I knew at that moment was that Seth was dead. And I loved Seth. These men had killed the man I loved.

They hauled me to my feet and wrapped me in a cloak. I couldn't walk unsupported, and they half-carried, half-dragged me out of the room.

We passed through a maze of dark corridors. Our only light was the lantern one of the men carried. When we emerged in a back alley, the sudden shock of breathing pure air after inhaling the fumes of the opium smokers nearly made me pass out. I knew I ought to try and get away, but I could no more have put my desires into action at that moment than I could have sprouted wings on my heels. A thick fog had settled over the city. Out in the bay I heard the muffled mooing of horns.

We passed down shadowy alleys and darkened streets. I looked over my shoulder once and saw that the sky over the Golden Gypsy was bright.

"Fire," I sighed. "Big fire."

"That's right, Baroness," the man on my right said. It was Franz. "Most of San Francisco has burned to the ground tonight. Come on, lift your feet."

They hustled me up the gangplank of a waiting ship. Another man took the lantern and led us to a cabin below decks. Fritz and Franz tossed me onto a bunk. One of them felt around under my gown to make sure that I had nothing concealed. Then they left me. A bar slid across the outside of the door. The ship creaked and swayed at anchor.

Vague phantasmagoric images floated around in the darkness in front of my eyes. I saw Seth, lying on the muddy street in front of the Golden Gypsy with a charred hole in his head. I closed my eyes tightly but that vision wouldn't go away. Finally I either fainted or slept, for when I woke again we were on the high seas, bound for God knows where.

The journey could have been worse. They kept me drugged so I wasn't as seasick as I would have been otherwise. The most incredible dreams and the most terrifying nightmares kept me company as I lay moaning in that wretched cabin for long days and endless nights. I seemed to have no will, no desire for anything after a while except that glass of laudanum they brought me every morning. I waited for it impatiently and swallowed it eagerly, greedily. I didn't know who my captors were or where they were taking me or at whose command. And worse, I didn't care. I wanted my drug. And if I didn't get it on time I became a crying, desperate maniac.

The ship docked, I don't know where. I was shunted into carriages and trains and wagons. Finally the last carriage took me through dark forests and across bridges that spanned treacherously deep ravines. Finally we arrived at a grey stone building that was grim and forbidding. Journey's end.

Fritz and Franz led me docilely up winding stairs, through damp, moldy passages, and into a enormous drafty room. The walls were hung with small tapestries and the heads of dead animals. Six-foot logs burned in a mammoth fireplace. They pushed me into a wing chair near the fire and left me. I dozed off immediately.

Cold hands slapped my cheeks. I opened my eyes and tried to focus them. I saw shiny black boots, white breeches on long legs, a scarlet coat belted with black with a revolver attached to the belt over the right hip, a chest hung with medals and ribbons. And then I saw the face. Vaguely familiar. Black handlebar mustache. Small

599

cruel eyes under menacing brows. A thin, prominent nose.

"Welcome back to Bavaria, Baroness," he said.

"Baron von Zander," I whispered.

"Yes. I trust you had a pleasant enough journey. I ordered my men to make you as comfortable as possible, within reason. Were you—comfortable, Baroness?"

Every time he said "Baroness" he placed an unpleasant stress on the word.

"Answer me!" he bellowed. He slapped my face again. My head snapped back. Strangely the slap hardly hurt. "Did you have a comfortable journey?"

I nodded a little. "Yes, quite—" My thoughts drifted away, into a vision of Gypsy camps and horses and flower-strewn fields.

"Good," he said, satisfied that I had answered his question at last. "You will be my guest for a while, Baroness. Would you like to know where you are? You are in Hohenschwangau Castle, in the Alps far south of Munich, very near the Austrian border. I use the place from time to time as a hunting lodge. No one ever comes here these days. Just me. And—my guests. I hope you will find the air invigorating.

"Why?" I sighed. I had some dim idea that I ought to be concerned about his reasons for bringing me to the castle, but as soon as that "Why?" was out of my mouth, I ceased to care. My thoughts drifted elsewhere.

But the Baron laughed. You want to know why I've had you brought here, eh? Well, I'll let you tell me, Baroness." Again that mocking stress on the title.

"I'm thirsty," I said. "May I go to bed now?"

He leaned over my chair and stuck his face right up close to mine. "You will listen to me!" he shouted. "And you will answer my question! Where are the pictures?"

I closed my eyes. I wanted to sleep.

He shook me. My head bobbed loosely on my neck.

"Where are the pictures! The ones you stole from my rooms at the Residence! The ones you are using to discredit me! You remember them. The photographs!"

I had a spark of recollection. "Naked man in women's clothes," I said slowly. "Hats. And masks. And—a dog."

"Yes, yes," he said eagerly. "Those are the ones. Come on, tell me. What have you done with them? Who did you give them to? Who is working with you to destroy me? Tell me! Tell me or I'll break your head right off your neck! Tell me!"

He started to slap me and beat me around the head. I squealed like a little piglet and covered my head with my arms.

"I didn't take them!" I shouted. "I swear, it! I didn't take anything! Stop! Stop! Let me go!"

"You must have taken them," he roared. "You were the only person who could have taken them. I saw you in that room myself! What did you do with them?"

"I can't remember," I mumbled. I dropped my head and slumped down in my chair. I felt so tired. I wanted my laudanum, my poison. I said so.

"No," he said. "No more laudanum until you remember what you have done with the pictures. You'll pay for this, Baroness. You have cost me dearly. Someone is working with you—someone is sending those pictures to Maximillian! And I know who is responsible! You, Baroness! You and your confederate. Is it Ludwig? Did you give them to Ludwig?"

"No, no one!" I said groggily. "Nobody. Didn't take any pictures. Never stole anything in my life."

"You are the root of everything evil in this country," he said harshly. "You are filth, vermin! Gypsy scum! You shall be rooted out and destroyed, all of you! Liars and beggars and cheats, all of you!" He hit me a few more times to emphasize his words. One of his blows knocked me out of my chair. My head hit one of the gigantic andirons in the fireplace and I knew no more.

They didn't bring me my laudanum that night. By the next morning I was screaming, hurling myself at the barred door of my room, tearing my bedding to bits.

The Baron came to the little window in the door and watched me. He must have decided that this kind of torture wasn't going to get him the answers he wanted, and so he ordered his men to bring me my dose of liquid opium. I drank it down and waited for the easiness to steal over my limbs and settle over my brain. Rest and peace. Rest and peace. That was what I craved. Sweet, sweet peace.

He stood over me. "Where are they? Answer me!"

"I don't know. Leave me alone. Go away."

"What did you do with them? Who did you give them to?"

"No one. I can't remember. Go away."

"You're sending them to the King yourself, aren't you? You're working alone! Aren't you?"

"I don't remember, I tell you. Stop pestering me. Go away."

"I'm not going anywhere until you tell me, Baroness. Think hard. I'll take away your opium again. You wouldn't like that, would you?"

"No, no!" I gasped. "Don't, please don't do that! I'm trying to remember, but I can't! I—I took them out of the drawer, I remember that much. And then—I heard you coming—and I hid under the desk."

"Ah, now we're getting somewhere." He smiled evilly. "You hid, then you heard me and Klaus. What did you do then? You came out from under the desk—you had the pouch with the pictures in it—what did you do with it?"

"I—I went to the window," I said slowly. "I looked out. Far down. Can't get out that way. I lean out—and I drop them. Rosebushes under the window. I drop them—into the rosebushes.''

"Well, what then?" he asked, grabbing my shoulders and shaking me. "What did you do after you left my rooms? Come on, think? Did you go down and get them?"

I frowned. "It was late. I was tired after—a concert. I sang. I was tired. And I went to bed."

He didn't get any more information out of me that day. After awhile I couldn't even remember my own name. He went away the next day, back to Munich. The guards at the castle relaxed a little. Franz and Fritz took turns watching over me.

I had no appetite for food. Only for opium. I lost weight quickly and I had no interest in my appearance at all. I hardly ever combed my hair. I wore loose-fitting night-gowns most of the time and slippers that were too large. I hardly spoke to a soul. I didn't care about anything. Only laudanum and the dreams it brought. One day I caught a glimpse of myself in a mirror. Cheekbones jutting out, eyes like charred, dead fire pits, with all the light gone out. Hair a tangled mass of straw.

The Baron returned. He badgered me with questions about the pictures. Apparently the situation in Munich was worsening. Everyone had seen at least one of those disgusting pictures, and von Zander's influence over Maximillian had dwindled drastically. He took away my opium for three days, and I went berserk. If I couldn't have opium, I wanted death.

He gave me my laudanum again and went away without learning anything new. Perhaps I knew, even in my deranged state, that to tell him the whole truth would be to condemn myself to death.

I tried to count the guards around the castle once. I got to thirty and gave up. They came and went, marching in little squads in the morning and again in the evening. For all I knew there might have been only ten soldiers who liked to march a lot. But I doubted it. I could see them from the small barred window of my room, high up in the castle. They looked like little rats scurrying around the courtyard below.

One day I saw a strange and unusual sight. A brightly-painted wagon came through the open gates and into the courtyard. A tall, white-haired man jumped down from the driver's seat and shouted out something. He wore baggy blue trousers and a red shirt and a blue scarf around the neck. A woman came out from behind the wagon. She was smaller and dark-haired, and she wore a red scarf on her head and a wonderful green skirt and yellow blouse. There was something very familiar about their appearance.

One of my keepers, the short one, Fritz, unbarred my door and came into my cell. "Come on, time for your walk," he growled. "Don't know why I bother with you."

"No, I want to stay and look," I said, holding onto the bars at the window. "Look at the funny people down there. Who are they?"

Fritz joined me at the window and grunted, "Oh, Gypsies. They come around from time to time, to peddle their junk and to take our old horses off our hands. Come to think of it, my horse could use a couple of new shoes. I wonder if they brought a forge? Some do, you know. Good thing the Baron's not here. He hates them like poison."

He dragged me away from the window and threw a shawl around my shoulders. The leaves were beginning to turn and the nights were very cold: even the days were chilly. The months were slipping away. I was hardly aware of their passing. Winter would soon be upon us. Then spring. Would I live to see the spring? I didn't care. It didn't matter to me one way or the other.

We went down long flights of stone steps and passed through the great hall and out into the pale sunshine in the courtyard. Fritz pushed me down on a low stone wall and told me to stay put, then he went to talk to the Gypsies.

I watched them listlessly, my interest in them gone. There were four men and one woman, all colorfully dressed. One or the other of them always seemed to be looking at me. One of the men, the darkest and swarthiest of the bunch, took a few steps towards me. The others restrained him. I noticed that he had a purple scar on his left cheek.

Then the Gypsy men unloaded an anvil and carted it over to a place near the stables. They built a roaring fire, a nice bright fire, and soon the clang of iron hitting iron rang through the courtyard. And they all shouted and laughed and talked at once, joshing the guards and Fritz, talking loudly about the merits of this horse or the other.

While they were busy at the forge the woman came over to me. One of the guards tried to stop her.

She laughingly pushed him out of the way. "I mean her no harm. I just want to tell her fortune, that's all. And I'll tell yours, too, if you're a good boy. I know you have lots of girlfriends, eh? You are a real devil with the girls!" She jabbed him in the ribs with her elbow and he shifted his feet and laughed shamefacedly. She kept up a steady stream of talk as she sidled over to me. After a while he let her pass without an argument.

She put her fingers under my chin and said loudly, "What a pretty girl! Ah, I have seldom seen a prettier!" She shouted over her shoulder to the guard, "What's the matter with her? Is she stupid or sick? What?"

He shrugged. "I don't know. I think she's mad."

"Ah, mad creatures are blessed," the Gypsy woman cried. "She is very close to God, this one. Come, child, don't be frightened of old mother Elise. She won't hurt you. Gypsies are good to poor creatures like you. Don't be afraid."

I stared at her. She wasn't young anymore but she had a pert, lively face and the brightest brown eyes I had ever seen. She sat on the wall next to me and took my hand.

"How warm it is here," she said gaily. "You are very smart to sit here. Now, let me see your hand. Maybe you, too, have a boyfriend in your future. Who knows?"

She cast a knowing look at the guard and cackled. He grinned and walked away. She tightened her grip on my hand and said in a low whisper, "Rhawine, listen to me. Rhawnie, do you know me? It's me, Elise, Elise McClelland, darling. Don't be frightened. Oh, Rhawnie, what have they done to you?"

The guard strolled back over again. The Gypsy cackled and said silly things about my husband and all the children I was going to have, and about how I had travelled far over big oceans, all the way from a big country named America. On and on she went, keeping an eye on the guard the whole time. I felt myself growing restless.

"I want to go back now," I said. "I want Fritz."

"Oh, Rhawnie, please try and listen to me," she hissed when the guard's back was turned. "Please, try. We want to get you out, but it won't be easy. How many guards are there here? How many? Think, Rhawnie. The men in the blue uniforms. How many are there?"

"Ten," I said slowly. "Ten. And they march all day and all night, around and around."

She gave an exasperated sigh and said loudly, "Ah, I see you have other talents, too! You are a fine singer! You sing beautifully, to shame the nightingale!"

I frowned. Singer? Nightingale? What was this crazy woman babbling about? The guard drifted away again.

She gripped both my hands in hers and said in a low intense voice, "Rhawnie, I beg you, pay attention to me! Listen! It's Elise, Seth and Steven's mother! Remember Seth? Remember, Rhawnie?"

"Seth is dead," I said dully, echoing some old distant memory.

"No, no, he's not! He's right over there, looking at you now. See him, Rhawnie? What have they done? They've given you something? A drug? What is it they give you?"

I sighed and wished she would go away and stop bothering me. But she had such a sweet face. And now she was irritated with me, like the Baron.

"Laudanum is nice, very nice," I said. "I have the most wonderful dreams."

She made a little moaning sound and closed her eyes briefly. Then she took the red scarf from her head and gave it to me. "Rhawnie, we've got to get you away from here. Can you understand what I'm saying? Where do you sleep? Where's your room?"

I shrugged. "Up there."

"Where? Which window? Point it out to me?"

I looked up. The glint of sunlight on glass hurt my eyes. "I don't know. All the same. Can I go in now?"

She pressed the scarf into my hands. "Take this scarf back to your room, Rhawnie. Tie it to your window, so that we can see where you are. Will you do that for me, Rhawnie? Please? Do it for Steven and for Seth. Tie the scarf to the window as soon as you go back."

The guard came back. The Gypsy laughed and stood up. "The poor thing took my scarf. I let her keep it. Such a pretty color, eh?"

"I'll get it back for you," the man said, taking a step towards me.

"No, no!" the woman said, holding onto his arm. "I want her to have it please. It will bring her good luck." She winked at me and nodded up at the windows. "And now you, my friend. Let me have a look at your hand. Ah, what a fine, strong hand this is! The best I have seen in a long time! Come over here, where the light is better.''

I stood up and walked slowly towards the forge. I wanted to get closer to the warmth and brightness of the fire. The swarthy Gypsy man with the scar ran up to me and said loudly, ''No, no, don't get too close to the fire, lady.'' Then he lowered his voice and hissed, ''Rhawnie, don't you know me? What have they done? What's the matter with you? It's me, Seth!''

I shook my head. ''Dead. Seth is dead.''

He started to say something else but Fritz came up and took me back to the castle and up to my room. I felt very tired and I lay down on my bed. As I opened my hand to ease myself down the red scarf fell to the floor. Yes, it was pretty, as the lady had said. I picked it up and held it to my cheek. It smelled like wildflowers and grass. Soft. Pretty.

There was something I was supposed to do. Something about the scarf. And the window. I remembered. I was supposed to tie the scarf to the window. And in order to do that I would have to get up and cross the floor and stretch up—no, I felt much too tired. I slept.

That evening when I awoke from my nap I went to the window. The Gypsies were gone. I stood at the window for a long time, watching the red sun setting over the mountains. I still had the red scarf in my hand. I held it outside the window. The wind caught it and fluttered it like a flag. And then I let it go and the wind carried it away.

Night came, folding its black wings around me. Fritz appeared with my medicine and he lit my lamp. I was grateful for the light. I saw horrible things in the darkness and I needed light to banish them. Fritz, who had a little compassion for me—usually brought a light for me. Sometimes he forgot, and those nights were hellish.

I dreamed of horses. Hooves clattered on cobblestones. The bar slid down away from my door and heavy boots thundered on the stone floor of my cell. I covered my ears and rolled onto my side. Noisy dreams, noisy enough to wake the dead.

"But why come now, so late at night?" Fritz whined. "Why couldn't you at least wait until morning?"

"Because the Baron is bringing a very important visitor down here tomorrow and he wants her gone," a man told him. The voice was strange and yet familiar. "Come on, hurry up, get her ready. We can't wait all night."

"She's ready now," Fritz told him. "You're welcome to her. You won't get any cooperation from her, though. She won't walk for you."

"Come on, woman, get up, get up," the voice said briskly. "We have a long way to go tonight, don't we, Colonel?"

"That's right, Lieutenant, hurry her along."

"Damn you!" an impatient voice hissed in my ear, "sit up! Come on, Rhawnie, we're trying to get you out of here! Try to stand. Come on!"

I flopped and fell like a stuffed doll. They pulled me to my feet and I slipped out of their hands. All I wanted was my bed, my dreams, my medicine.

"Don't want to go," I muttered. "Stop."

One of the two newcomers laughed heartily. "She's in a fog, all right. But a little ride in the night air will soon put that right."

"That's what you think," Fritz muttered, "Nothing will put her mind right again. Lift your feet, woman! Do as the soldiers tell you! Hurry up!"

Finally one of the soldiers, the tall one with fair hair, scooped me up in his arms and carried me down to a waiting carriage. Two more soldiers were waiting near the carriage. They threw open the doors. The man who carried me deposited me on the seat and slammed the doors behind me. Almost at once the carriage lurched forward.

The Gypsy woman sat beside me. Only she didn't look

like she did in the afternoon. She was wearing dark wool and furs. She wrapped a warm fur robe around me and wiped my face with a scented cloth.

"Oh, Rhawnie, you poor, poor thing," she cooed, "just look what they've done to you! Poor darling. But you're safe now. They won't hurt you ever again, I promise."

We rode for a short time and I dozed a little. All of a sudden the carriage came to an abrupt halt. I was awakened by shouts and the thunder of gunshots.

"Oh, God," said the woman beside me. She poked her head outside the window. "It seems to be a group of soldiers with the Baron in the lead." She opened her reticule and pulled out a revolver. "Thank Heaven for a full moon," she said. She pushed me down on the floor, crouched down under the window, and fired.

The fight and the noise raged around us. Soon the carriage jerked forward and we started to move. We careened through the night, leaving the sounds of the fight far behind. Then we halted again and one of the doors flew open.

"Out. Both of you!"

"Ah, you must be Baron von Zander," said my companion. "Please don't be impolite. This gun is pointed at your breast."

"Your gun is empty, good lady," the Baron retorted, "or you would have used it. Please do as I say. Get out."

She helped me out of the coach. I shivered. We were in a wooded glade. The moon was indeed bright and full, but occasional wisps of clouds crossed its face, giving it a surly and treacherous look.

"And now, Baroness," sneered the Baron, "and Madame, whoever you may be, it's time to put an end to your schemes, once and for all." I heard a click and looked at his hand. He was holding an enormous gun, and the dark eye of its barrel was pointed straight at me.

There was an explosion and the gun vanished quickly. The Baron looked surprised, and his hand went to the sword at his side.

One of the soldiers who had taken me away from the

castle stepped out from the shadows behind the coach. I recognized him, too, as the Gypsy with the scar on his cheek. But now he was in uniform.

"Good evening, Baron," he said. "I stowed away on the back of the coach. I hope you don't mind. Not the most comfortable way to enjoy the Alpine countryside, I confess."

"If you're going to shoot me," the Baron said, "then go ahead and do it. I don't like to waste small talk with interfering scoundrels."

"Unfortunately I have no more bullets," the soldier told him.

"Too bad," grinned the Baron. "Now I can dispatch you like a gentleman." He whipped out his sword and the other man did the same. "*En garde*, you devil. This will be the last time you upset anybody's plans."

"By the way," said the swarthy Gypsy-soldier, "I just want you to know that woman you have treated so badly is my wife. And you're going to die for it."

Wife? But I didn't even know this man.

Their blades clashed in the moonlight. The lady pulled me aside, well out of the way. The Baron moved as quickly as a cat, but the soldier was alert and ready for him. He parried every slash, blocked every thrust. Their blades moved so swiftly that they seemed to blur into one shining curved blade. The little woman at my side gripped my arm and sucked in her breath at every close touch.

"Oh, Seth," she murmured. "Be careful, son."

The duellists moved swiftly around the clearing, back towards the trees. The clang of their blades echoed off the rocks around us.

Then a dark cloud obscured the moon for half a minute, throwing the clearing into darkness. The din of clashing swords did not diminish. Just as the cloud passed there was a blood-curdling mortal scream.

The lady ran forward. "Seth!"

The moon grew bright. The Baron lay on his side on the ground, nailed to the earth by the sword that had pierced his vitals. He twitched and groaned. Blood trickled out of his mouth, and with a final gurgling gasp, he lay still.

Three men rode into the clearing. The pair went to meet them.

"Oh, Seth!" The little woman embraced the soldier. "Oh, thank God!"

I felt sick and weak and so very tired. With a deep sigh I sank to my knees. One of the men rushed over and lifted me in his arms.

"Rhawnie! Rhawnie, it's me, Steven. Do you know me? Are you all right, Rhawnie?"

I did know him. He was Steven McClelland, and I loved him. I had loved another once, but he was dead.

"Steven," I said weakly. "You have come for me. Hold me, Steven. Hold me."

He hugged me to him and buried his face in my hair. And at the edge of the clearing the man with the scar on his cheek watched stoically.

21

Two Gypsies

THE MCCLELLAND FAMILY took me to France, to the Chateau Lesconflair. Seth supervised my treatment. He decided that sudden withdrawal would be too cruel, and he decreased my daily intake of laudanum until I was taking only the smallest dose, and finally I didn't even need that.

I remember the day when the mists cleared away from my brain and I saw him standing at the window of my room.

"Who is that?" I asked. "Who are you?"

He came over to the bed. "Hello, Gypsy," he said with a little smile.

"It is you," I whispered. "I thought—they told me they had killed you. Back in San Francisco. I thought you were dead. Oh, Seth." I started to cry.

"Now, Gypsy," he said consolingly, "you know I'm

tough to kill. Like you. He put you through hell, didn't he?"

I tried to shrug. I still felt very weak. "Not too bad. Only when he took the laudanum away. Then it was terrible. I shall never forget the dreams, dreams of fire and death. Is he dead?"

"You don't remember?" he asked. I shook my head. I had only the dimmest recollections of that night. "Yes, he's dead. He won't trouble us anymore. How are you feeling? There are three men out there who are eager to see you."

"Steven?" I said. "Steven is here?"

His smile dimmed a little and he said, "Yes, Steve. And Sean and Father. Are you up to it?"

"Yes, I would like to see them. And your mother?"

"She's here, too. She's been helping with the nursing, remember?"

"I'm sorry," I said apologetically, "but I'm afraid I haven't been paying very close attention to what's been happening to me."

He patted my hand professionally, and felt my pulse. "You're forgiven," he said. "We're all prepared to be especially tolerant of you for a few days."

They crowded around the bed. Steven gave me a little kiss and held my hand while we talked. Sean tried very hard to restrain his natural high spirits. It was rather funny to see him trying to behave like he was in church. Elise sat on my other side and Garth, our patriarch, stood at the foot of the bed. Seth stood by the window.

"Before we go any further," Steven said, "I have to know: what was he after?"

"I stole something from him before I left Munich," I said. At the window Seth gave an amused snort. "Not money this time, but pictures. Photographs of the Baron himself in—doing rather unusual things." I looked up at Steven. "Wearing women's clothes," I whispered.

The men all laughed a little. "Anyway, he was angry about that and that's why he chased us after we left Munich, remember, Steven? But he didn't forget. He wanted them back. And he was angry because I wouldn't tell him what I had done with them. King Maximillian, Ludwig's son, had seen them, I think."

"We did some checking around Munich," Garth said. "The Baron had fallen from favor. He was barely hanging on. His reputation was in shreds and any influence he might have enjoyed once was gone. Apparently Maximillian is a bit of a prude."

"Yes, I know," I said.

"Well, what did you do with the pictures, darling?" Elise wanted to know. "Did you give them to Maximillian?"

"No, to his mother. I decided that she would know best. She was stronger than either her husband or her son. But why did she wait so long to use them?"

"The Baron was a fine organizer, whatever his faults," Garth said. "I suspect she bided her time until she felt he had exhausted his usefulness to her son and was becoming too ambitious for himself. That's when the pictures started to circulate. Damned clever woman."

"A good mother," Elise said. "You're a smart girl, Rhawnie."

I said, "I wanted to repay Ludwig for what he had done for me. He said that Maximillian could be a good king if he was out from under the Baron's thumb. But you? You came so far to find me? How did you do it?"

Seth said, "Wang—one of your men, remember?—had a brother who worked at the opium den where they took you on the night of the fire. That proved that the Sons of Dan had nothing to do with your disappearance. We traced you to the ship, and the rest wasn't too hard. The hard part was keeping Sean out of this. As you can see, we failed."

"I stowed away!" Sean said eagerly. "Just like them to keep a fellow from having a lark!"

"Then you went to California with your parents?" I asked him.

"Ha," grunted his father. "He came west on his own, with a pack of gold diggers. He's hopeless."

"I only wanted to see Gaby," Sean protested. "It's not fair to leave a fellow behind."

We were silent for a few minutes, thinking about the daughter they had lost. Elise took my hand and said, "Seth told us everything. We're so glad you were there to help her."

"I loved her," I said. "She was a sister to me."

"And now you are our daughter." She leaned forward and kissed me.

"You didn't make it very easy for us to save you, Rhawnie," Sean said. "We were all set to take you out of there in the Gypsy wagon and—"

"Fortunately we had an alternate plan," Garth grinned.

"You should have heard Seth when he found out you didn't even know him!" Sean exclaimed. "He wanted to tear the Baron apart with his bare hands!"

"Sean," Elise said warningly. "We'd better go. We'll talk more later, Rhawnie, but we don't want to tire you. We'll leave you in Seth's capable hands."

I gave her a grateful smile. And they went away. Two days later I heard hooves on the cobblestones outside my window and I went to look. Seth was riding away, around the fountains, down the drive, through the park. Elise came in.

"I thought you'd like a cup of tea," she said. Then she saw me at the window. "Oh, you're up!"

"Where is Seth going?" I asked her. "Is he going to get more medicine?"

"No, dear," she said coming over to me. "He's going away, back to Paris."

"But I don't understand!" I said. "He was here this morning—he didn't say anything! Why—why is he going?"

"Because you don't need him anymore. You're free of your addiction, and you're getting stronger every day. I'm sure he wanted to speak, but he couldn't. It's not easy for him, you know that."

"But I do need him!" I cried. "I need him so much—! He's done it again, left me without a word! Oh, I hate him, I hate him—!" I sat down and buried my face in my hands. "It's not fair," I sobbed. "He had no reason to treat me this way! Why must he behave like such an animal to me? Doesn't he know that I love him?"

"He thinks you love Steven," she said gently. "Because you remembered him and you didn't remember Seth. In the glade, after Seth killed the Baron? Steven held you and—?"

"But I thought Seth was dead!" I said despairingly. "I didn't know anything then! They told me Seth was dead and I believed them!"

"But before those men kidnapped you, Steven and Seth wanted you to choose between them, isn't that right? I suppose Seth thought you made you choice that night. He stayed here long enough to make you well, and now he's left you—to Steven."

My temper flared. "He is the stupidest, most stubbornly single-minded man I have ever met in my life. What does he know about what goes on in a woman's heart? He is selfish, monstrously selfish—"

"He's proud, Rhawnie," his mother corrected me.

"Well, so am I proud! If he thinks I'm going to go chasing after him after all this time—! I won't do it. I won't go to him. I am going to stay here and marry Steven and have a hundred babies and I never want to see him again! Never!" I cried and cried, and nothing Elise could do could comfort me.

Later that day I told Steven that I had made up my mind: I would become his wife. He kissed me on the cheek and said, "That's wonderful, Rhawnie. Mother will be so pleased."

I said coolly, "I would have expected you to be a little happier about it."

He laughed and said, "But I am happy! I'm delirious! Can't you tell? You're just feeling a little touchy today because of—"

"I am not feeling touchy," I informed him tartly. "And I don't want to talk about your brother, do you understand? I don't love him, I love you. He is undeserving of love. Please see what you can do about the divorce. I think we should get married as soon as possible."

"You're sure?" he said softly.

"Of course I'm sure!"

He grinned boyishly. "I would have expected you to be a little happier about it."

"What? Oh." I felt ashamed of myself. "Forgive me, Steven. I am happy. It's a good feeling, knowing you have done the right thing, made the right decision. Kiss me please. I'll be fine."

His kiss was very sweet, if a shade brotherly. "You're beautiful again," he said softly. "A pleasure to look upon."

"You really think so?" I pinched my forearm. "You see, flesh! I'm even getting a little fat."

I tried to be cheerful for Steven's sake, but most of the time I wandered around the chateau like a grieving spirit. I sat down at the piano in the drawing room one day and morosely picked out the melody to "Two Brothers." It didn't make me feel any better.

"Would you like me to play something for you, Rhawnie?" Elise McClelland came in, smiling brightly. "I haven't heard you sing in ages."

"I don't want to sing," I said quickly. "My throat is sore. I can't." Really my heart was too heavy, but I didn't tell her that.

"You don't sound very cheerful," she observed acutely. "Do you want to talk about it?"

"I am cheerful enough," I said. "And there's nothing to talk about."

Thereupon I burst into tears and ran out of the room.

We celebrated Christmas at the Chateau Lesconflair. Seth did not come home.

The senior McClellands and Steven were talking about going back to America soon. Steven missed his children badly. Garth consented to let Sean enroll in the Sorbonne for the spring term, but he warned his son that this was his last chance. If they threw him out of the Sorbonne he would have to come home and work as a field hand at Highlands.

Then one morning soon after the New Year Steven came into the drawing room. I can't remember what I was doing there, probably moping.

"Well, this ought to cheer you up, Rhawnie," he said. "You'll be a free woman soon and we can marry. Finally! And after the wedding—I thought something small and quiet, right here at the chateau—we'll set sail for home."

I looked up. "I don't understand. What are you talking about?"

He showed me a scroll of paper. "Your divorce, Rhawnie. Apparently Seth has filed himself. All you have to do is—"

"What's that? Divorce! Where? Show me!"

He unfurled the rolled document and spread it out on a table. I peered at it.

"This doesn't mean anything to me!" I said, frustrated. "It's all in French!"

"Of course it is. We're in France, remember?"

"But what does it mean?" I asked. "Tell me, Steven!"

"It means that our own petition has gotten bogged down or lost in a shuffle of papers on some bureaucrat's desk, and Seth has beat us to it. He filed for divorce on his own, and he must have a very good lawyer, because—"

"You mean—you mean *he* wants to divorce *me*!" I said angrily. "I don't believe it! Where, where does it say that!"

Steven pointed out the appropriate passage, it was a meaningless jumble of letters to me.

"But he has no right to do this!" I said, stamping my foot. "I'm the one who's divorcing him, remember? Of all the arrogant, selfish things to do."

"All you have to do is sign," Steven said. "Down here, under his signature."

"Sign!" I squawked. "I will sign nothing, do you hear me! He thinks he can get rid of me so easily—! Well, he's wrong! I'm going to take this stupid paper to Paris," I rolled it up and brandished it under Steven's nose like a club, "and I'm going to tell him what he can do with his divorce! He had no right to do this! He's such a pig-headed moron that he couldn't even stick around long enough for me to be well, he had to jump on his horse and ride away because he had some idiotic idea that—"

"That you loved me, not him," Steven said softly.

I stopped my tirade immediately and my hand flew to my mouth. "Oh, Steven. Oh, Steven!" I threw my arms around his neck and he held me. "What am I saying? I don't want to hurt you, Steven, but you know how it is with us, with Seth and me. We're Gypsies, both of us. We're not happy unless we're travelling and fighting and cheating someone. Can you see that? We belong together, we always have. Since we first met in Russia and the old Gypsy Ursula predicted that my life would be his life. He is my fate, my destiny! And I am his. And I've been so cruel to you, to tell you that I wanted to marry you and now to—"

"That's all right," he said with an odd little laugh. "I didn't believe you anyway. None of us did. So," he held me away from him, "you want to go to Paris? Get your hat and coat. If we start now we can be there by early evening." He smiled tenderly. "I'll miss you, Rhawnie. But I'm not sorry I met you and fell in love with you. I wouldn't have missed it for anything."

"Oh, Steven!" I threw my arms around his neck again and hugged him tightly. Then I ran upstairs to put on a travelling suit that Elise's Parisian dressmaker had made for me and to throw the few things I owned into a valise. Divorce me, will he? I thought angrily. That's what he thinks.

Elise came in. "Oh, Rhawnie, Steven told me. I'm so glad!"

"What do you mean you're glad? That your stupid son wants to divorce me?"

"That you want to stop him," she grinned. "I knew it would end this way. Don't worry about Steven, darling: he'll be all right. He has his children and his career and he'll find a wife someday. But Seth has nothing, only his wits and his anger. He needs you, Rhawnie. Be good to him."

"I will try," I said. "But first I'm going to break his head."

The ride to Paris seemed interminable. I sat on the edge of my seat the whole way, clutching the divorce paper in my hand. Steven attempted to converse, but I wasn't in the mood. What if, I thought, what if he's found someone else? And that's why he wanted to rush this thing through! I don't care! I'll break her head, too. I don't care if she's the Queen of France!

We arrived at the house on the Rue de Montmorency

after nine o'clock that night. At first the house looked deserted. But when I pounded the knocker, that model of a woman's hand in brass, Jules opened the door. At once his face became wreathed with smiles.

"Ah, Madame!" he cried happily. Ah, so he knew we were married then. "Madame, it is so good to see you! What a happy occasion! It has been a long time!"

"Yes, Jules," I said, "a very long time!" I hugged him tightly.

"Good evening, Monsieur," Jules said to Steven, who came in behind me. "I will tell Monsieur Garrett that you are here."

"Don't tell him, Jules," I said. "We'll see him ourselves. Where is he?"

Jules said that Seth was in his study, then Steven put his hand on my arm and said, "I'll let you go in alone, Rhawnie. I don't really want to watch the carnage."

"You're not coming?" I asked surprised. "But you will wait—"

He shook his head. "You don't need me now. Just—don't be too hard on him, Rhawnie. I think he did it for you, because he wanted you to be happy."

He kissed me softly, nodded to Jules, and went out. He gave an order to the coachmen and they drove off.

I let out my breath in a sigh and straightened my shoulders. I gripped the divorce paper securely and said, "Well, Jules, into the lion's den, eh? How is he tonight? Black or white or grey?"

"Dark grey, Madame," said Jules seriously. "Verging on black."

"Ah, that's bad," I grunted. "Listen, Jules, give me ten minutes, then bring in some champagne." He nodded understandingly. "Divorce me, will he?" I muttered to myself. "I'll stuff this thing down his throat!"

Seth was sitting in a wing chair in front of the fire with a glass of brandy in one hand and a smouldering cigar in the other. He looked like he had just come in from riding. His boots were dusty and so were his tan breeches. His dark brown coat was rumpled and his white shirt was open at the throat. He didn't look up when I came in.

"So," I said, "this is how I find you after you betray me, enjoying yourself, swilling your brandy and smoking your stupid cigars!" I advanced on him and he lifted his head. I could tell from his surly expression and the watery look in his eyes that he had been drinking a lot. "You send your filthy lawyers to do your dirty work for you and then you come home and drink yourself to death because you know you're the same coward you always were and that you don't have the spine you were born with or the decency to come and tell me face to face that you don't want to be married to me anymore!"

I stood in front of him and held the scroll under his nose. He glared up at me.

"First you have the audacity to leave me at your parents' house without so much as a goodbye or an I-wish-you-well, and then you send me this this piece of nonsense! You are as big a moron as ever, Seth McClelland! To think you can get rid of me by sending me a—a paper! You think a piece of writing can end what we had? You think a piece of writing will erase your memory from my mind? This thing means nothing to me! I refuse to accept it! Writing? Bah. You don't get rid of an old horse by handing it a piece of writing! You don't cut off a diseased limb by writing it a letter! You don't tell someone you don't love them anymore by sending them a page full of drivel that they can't even read! Do you know what I think of this divorce of yours?"

I waved the scroll over his head and then pitched it into the fire.

"That's what I think of it! And don't you dare try and

send me another because it will end up in the same place. Divorce me, will you! I'd just like to see you try!"

He grabbed my wrist and pulled me onto his lap. His arms went around me and he kissed me, hard and long. The brandy spilled on the carpet and he eased off for a second to flick his cigar into the fire. Then he kissed me again and again, until I was limp. I sighed and slid down a little so that I could rest my cheek on his shoulder.

"And that's what I think of you, Gypsy," he murmured. "Welcome home."

"Nice to be here. Kiss me again." His mouth moved over mine. "Oh, that's nice. What a silly boy you are, Seth. I let you go off on your own for a little, and you start doing crazy things. You can't be trusted."

"I thought you wanted Steve," he said.

"Steven is much too good for a dirty little Gypsy like me," I told him. "You are the man for me. Always and forever."

Jules came in bearing the champagne and a couple of glasses. I told him to bring over a low table and we would help ourselves.

"Whose house is this?" Seth asked when Jules had gone.

"It is my house," I said, popping the cork on the champagne and pouring. "And Jules is my butler and this is my champagne and you just spilled your brandy on my carpet. You will have to learn to be more careful." I gave him a glass and we touched rims. "Ah, thirsty work, getting your husband back," I said when I had drained my champagne. "Harder even than getting him in the first place." I squirmed around on his lap and refilled our glasses. "I tell you, when I saw your signature at the bottom of that paper, I wanted to—"

Seth laughed. "Steven shouldn't do too much of this sort of thing. He'll end up in jail." He sipped. "My brother, a forger!"

"What are you talking about?" I said. "I saw your name as clear as anything. It was the only thing I could read."

"But I didn't put it there, precious. I'm not the schemer. Steve is. And I detect my mother's fine hand in this, too. We're both victims of a conspiracy."

I stared at him blankly for a moment, then I threw back my head and laughed heartily. "Ah, so this brother of yours has a little Gypsy in him after all!"

"Maybe you should change your mind again," Seth suggested.

"No, I have chosen the right brother this time. But you'd better not try to confuse me. I am very easily confused still." We watched the fire for a few minutes. "How do you like that Steven!" I said in an amazed voice. "He tricked me! Because he knew I loved you and that I wouldn't come to you any other way."

"You wouldn't?"

"No. I was very angry with you. I'm still angry with you, but I've decided to let you make it up to me. After we finish this champagne."

He kissed my neck and started to take the pins out of my hair. The fire cracked. I felt happy and dreamy, and I thought about what a fine man Steven was and how good he had been to me.

"Seth, can I talk to you? It's very important."

"Of course, Rhawnie."

"We are going to be real married people now. Forever and ever, until we die. I will never lie to you, ever again. But I don't want an old lie to come between us." I put my head on his chest he stroked my hair. "I want to tell you that when I told you that I didn't sleep with Steven, that was a lie. We did, at the chateau when we were escaping." Seth didn't say anything. I looked up anxiously. "But that's all, I swear it, just that once! We couldn't help it. And—and it wasn't even very good. You are much, much better! Oh, now you're angry with me," I wailed, lowering

627

my head again. "I never should have said anything!"

"You thought you were dying and you lied anyway," he said in a voice laden with reproach.

"But for a good reason!" I assured him quickly. "Because it's not good for brothers to hate, and I thought you would hate him more if you knew. But now that we are really married again you might wonder about it from time to time, and you would doubt me. It's better to tell the truth now, and get it over with."

"Is that how you regard truth, Gypsy? As something unpleasant and distasteful?" I heard a little laugh under his words and I looked up quickly.

"You're not angry with me? You forgive me?"

He sighed. "Little idiot. Put away your truths and your lies for the time being. There's only one truth that interests me. You're here and you love me." He kissed me. "But no more lies, understand?"

"No, no," I said eagerly. "No more lies! I have learned my lesson!"

"And no more stealing. How many more angry Barons and Sons of Dan are roaming the earth right now, looking for you?"

"None, I swear it! No more stealing and no more lying. I promise! May the fire jump out and consume me if I'm wrong!"

He laughed and put his two hands on the sides of my face. "You're as crazy as ever. As beautiful and crazy as ever. I love you very much."

"And I love you," I said softly, "and I'll never let you out of my sight again. And if you die first, I will die, too, because I wouldn't trust you not to get into trouble—"

"Hush. Bad luck to talk of death," he said. "I see the champagne is gone, and the fire is dying. Come on, Gypsy, it's time for old married people like us to be in bed."

We stood for a few moments in front of the fire with our

arms around each other, together, in our house.

"I feel very excited," I said. "About us. We're really going to have fun now, aren't we, Gypsy?"

"Yes, Gypsy," he said laughing, "we really are."

I was eager to have our Adam with us, and Seth sent for Adam and Anna and David Thatcher. I sang in the great houses of Europe for the next six years and Seth was my business manager. He liked the job because he had plenty of time to gamble and we both liked the travelling. We had a wonderful time and we made a lot of money from *gorgio* audiences who wanted to hear the Golden Gypsy sing, but I was very happy when I got pregnant and had to stop to give birth to Eva.

Adam is a real little Gypsy. He has a gift with horses, and he loves cards and dice and poker chips. Seth and I still gamble because we like it too much to stop and I suppose we have influenced him. Some people think the way we are raising our children is a disgrace. I tell them that I was an accomplished thief when I was Adam's age, and if he can deal off the bottom of the deck when he's seven or eight, what's the harm? I turned out all right, and so will he.

Garth and Elise are back at Highlands and we'll take their grandchildren to see them soon, on our way to San Francisco. Seth says he thinks we should stay in one place for a while and have another baby. Sean never finished school, but he didn't go home, either. He's travelling and having adventures somewhere. I wonder if he'll go to Russia?

Steven is Governor of Louisiana now! He says he won't run for national office because he is unsympathetic to the causes that the voters of the South consider important. He hasn't married and I wish he would, because I would feel better.

Seth and I had to travel a long way to find love, only to find that love had travelled with us. Now love will stay with us for the rest of our journey.

And that's no lie.

There are a lot more
where this one came from!

ORDER your FREE catalog of ACE paper-backs here. We have hundreds of inexpensive books where this one came from priced from 75¢ to $2.50. Now you can read all the books you have always wanted to at tremendous savings. Order your *free* catalog of ACE paperbacks now.

ACE BOOKS ● Box 576, Times Square Station ● New York, N.Y. 10036

Don't Miss these Ace Romance Bestsellers!

_____ #75157 **SAVAGE SURRENDER** $1.95
The million-copy bestseller by Natasha Peters,
author of Dangerous Obsession.

_____ #29802 **GOLD MOUNTAIN** $1.95

_____ #88965 **WILD VALLEY** $1.95
Two vivid and exciting novels by
Phoenix Island author, Charlotte Paul.

_____ #80040 **TENDER TORMENT** $1.95
A sweeping romantic saga in the
Dangerous Obsession tradition.

Available wherever paperbacks are sold or use this coupon.

The Novels of

Dorothy Eden

$1.75 each

07931	**Bride by Candlelight**
07977	**Bridge of Fear**
*08184	**The Brooding Lake**
*09257	**Cat's Prey**
*12354	**Crow Hollow**
*13884	**The Daughters of Ardmore Hall**
*14184	**The Deadly Travelers**
*14187	**Death Is A Red Rose**
*22543	**Face Of An Angel**
*47404	**The Laughing Ghost**
*48479	**Listen To Danger**
*57804	**The Night of the Letter**
*67854	**The Pretty Ones**
*76073	**Shadow of a Witch**
*76972	**Sleep in the Woods**
*77125	**The Sleeping Bride**
*86598	**Voice of the Dolls**
*88533	**Whistle for the Crows**
$94393	**Yellow Is For Fear and Other Stories**

5H

The MS READ-a-thon needs young readers!

Boys and girls between 6 and 14 can join the MS READ-a-thon and help find a cure for Multiple Sclerosis by reading books. And they get two rewards — the enjoyment of reading, and the great feeling that comes from helping others.

Parents and educators: For complete information call your local MS chapter, or call toll-free (800) 243-6000. Or mail the coupon below.

Kids can help, too!